CHRONICLES OF ARAX
BOOK 3

THE BATTLE OF YATIN

BEN SANFORD

STENOX PUBLISHING
Clarksburg, MD

First originally published by Page Publishing 2022

Cover art by Karl Moline

ISBN 979-8-9886249-4-3 (pbk)
ISBN 979-8-9886249-5-0 (digital)

Printed in the United States of America

He soared through the firmament, the magantor's white wings coursing the clear sky as he descried the dark forms scurrying below. Terin drew his sword, a dull glow emanating along its blade as the warbird swept down upon their prey, its beak silent and silver eyes focused.

Torry Cavalry harried the gargoyle band, cutting down stragglers along the periphery, catching the creatures on open ground. Terin's magantor swept over the grassy fields, the force of its wings bending the golden reeds of the dying grassy as he passed. The great avian outstretched its talons, snatching a gargoyle from the ground, its claws piercing the creature's back and breast, crushing its lungs as it lifted before releasing the gargoyle through its ascent. Terin looked back as the gargoyle dropped like a stone, its broken body impacting the soil amidst its fellows as other magantor riders repeated the process all around him. Flashes of laser alit the sky off his left, where Kato's magantor circled the enemy, dispatching them at will. The Torry Cavalry herded the gargoyles closer, whilst the magantors plucked them from their clustered ranks. It was an effective tactic of destroying small bands of gargoyles in quick order. This was the third such group Terin helped them destroy since he left Corell. Terin's magantor circled back, sweeping below, snatching another gargoyle in its talons.

"Kai-ggh!" the creature squealed, its war cry dying in its throat, the warbird soaring high into the air before releasing its broken prey.

The skirmish ended in moments, eighty-six gargoyle corpses littering the field. Since Morac's defeat at Corell, his surviving minions suffered dearly. Countless gargoyle bands such as this were hunted down and destroyed piecemeal by Torry Cavalry. Most of the surviving gargoyles fled east, making their way to Notsu, where Morac ordered his legions to concentrate and reconstitute, but his forces were scattered and strung out over countless leagues.

Terin sheathed his sword, his avian circling the battlefield as he stroked the bird's feathered neck, the gesture soothing the magantor as it soared gracefully through the crisp morning air. The magantor was a gift from the Jenaii, a warbird bred in the royal stables of El-Orva and presented to Terin by King El Anthar. The magantor was named Wind Racer, for it coursed the heavens with effortless grace and speed. Its feathered coat was white like fresh fallen snow, with bright silver eyes that bespoke a deep intelligence, unnerving foes with their piercing gaze. Its talons were black with silver tips that were as sharp as swords. Wind Racer was larger by half than the magantor that bore him from Fera and intimidating to behold, though the bird took to him as if he was born to it. It was a wondrous gift, and he recalled El Anthar's words to him the night of Cronus and Leanna's wedding, when the Jenaii king presented the magantor to him upon the battlements of the inner keep.

"A Champion of the Torry Realm requires a worthy mount. Accept this token of friendship between our peoples, Terin, son of Jonas, keeper of the Sword of the Moon, child of prophecy, and bane of darkness. I have raised Wind Racer from a hatchling, feeding him from my own hand. He is the mightiest of my warbirds and shall bear you in the battles to come."

Kato's magantor drew up beside him, the Earther seated behind its driver, freeing Kato to use his pistol whilst the other maneuvered. Controlling a magantor was a difficult skill to master, though Lorken took to it well enough. Unfortunately, Kato was given only the barest instruction and could do little more than steer the beast in the general direction that he wanted. Kato pointed to a place on the ground below, where a number of cavalry were gathering for their postbattle review. Terin acknowledged, following Kato's mount to the place indicated. Several of the other magantors followed in kind, while others scouted farther afield for stragglers they might have missed or another group altogether. They were many leagues south of Corell, clearing the southern approaches of the palace of gargoyles. They started southwest, working their way ever eastward. Other Torry

Cavalry and magantors swept the regions north and east of Corell, finding numerous clusters of gargoyles and Naybins.

*****

Dresila peered through the lens of the optic, the image of the soldier's broken spine displayed in rich detail. She adjusted the device as Kato had shown her, which detailed the proper sequence to repair the damaged tissue.

"Carefully roll him onto his stomach," she ordered her sister matrons assisting her.

"Will it work?" the soldier asked warily as they eased him into position upon the narrow cot. He spent days abed since the battle, his broken back rendering everything below his chest useless since his fall from the inner battlements. He relived that fateful moment over and over again in his mind, as the gargoyle crashed into his legs, the force of its weight knocking him from the battlements onto the causeway of the inner palace. He spent the past days stewing in his soiled bed, wondering what hope had he without his legs. He needed help for the simplest of things, like relieving himself or shifting himself to a more comfortable position. Often such help was not readily available as the matrons' wards were all overflowing with too few matrons to attend the basic necessities of every wounded soldier. But then he heard rumors of the Earther and his strange magic that restored sundered flesh, wondering if it could restore him.

"It hasn't failed yet, soldier, and I see no reason for you to be first. Now shush while I continue!" Dresila admonished, setting the device upon his back, above the damaged tissue. She followed Kato's instructions, the device emitting its mysterious humming sound, bathing the soldier's flesh with golden light. She watched the spinal cord reattach through the lens, the connective tissue and nerves regenerating around it. Within moments, the process was complete.

"I...I feel my legs!" the soldier cried happily, trying to gain his feet before another matron put a hand to his shoulder, advising against it. Too many days abed required him to ease his transition.

They continued on, leaving the soldier to his own devices, tending the soldier on the next cot, suffering a broken and infected leg. And so they continued throughout the day and night, stopping only to recharge Kato's wondrous gift through its solar regenerator.

*****

"What you suggest would leave us helpless if Morac renews his attack!" Corry argued.

General Bode stood opposite her, overlooking the map unfurled across the table, his eyes trained on their southern kingdom. They gathered in the king's private sanctum in the bowels of the upper keep, the princess; Commanders Nevias and Dar Valen; King El Anthar; Ministers Antillius, Veda, and Monsh; Master Torg Vantel, and himself. Bode hastened his return to Corell, leaving the 3rd Army to his subordinates far to the east. They pursued Morac's surviving legions as far as he dared without straining his own lines of communication. Morac was in no position to renew his assault until spring. His legions were decimated. The Benotrist 8th Legion lost over half its strength, with the gargoyle legions suffering far worse. His own Army suffered in kind. He doubted he could field more than twelve telnics fit for duty. With the 5th Army destroyed, the fate of Torry North fell to Fonis's 2nd Army and his own battered 3rd. As desperate as their situation was, it was the happenings in Yatin that concerned him most. If Yatin fell, and from what he learned, that possibility seemed very likely, then Torry South would be exposed. The fact that Prince Lorn led the 4th Army to Yatin's defense meant that his fate was now tied to that crumbling empire. That left Torry South with only the 1st Army to defend it. The Torry Realms needed what he could not supply—men. The survival of Prince Lorn and the Torry 4th Army was paramount. They might not be able to drive the gargoyles from Yatin, but they could check their advance. Lorn needed aid, and he had no men to spare with the distance that separated them, but Bode thought to aid them in *other* ways.

"Send Terin to Prince Lorn," Bode said again, knowing the Sword of the Moon was the only feasible aid they could render.

"Lorn has not asked for aid," Corry said evenly. "Besides, Terin has not completed his induction into the Torry Elite."

Terin was expected to return to Corell by day's end to partake in his marking ceremony, where he and Cronus would be formally inducted into the King's Elite. Her claim that he hadn't completed his training sounded weak and desperate. Squid Antillius observed the exchange, sympathetic to Bode's counsel. The general hastened his return to Corell to address this dire situation, knowing the gravity of their strategic position.

"There is wisdom in the general's counsel, Highness," Squid interceded.

"*Wisdom?*" Corry asked sharply.

"Victory is not without risk. Despite our victories, Tyro still wields far greater power than we. To overcome his advantages, we must take calculated risks in order to make gains," Squid advised.

"Terin's place is here, at Corell. I will *not* send the realm's greatest asset on a fool's quest. The Yatins will have to fend for themselves. We cannot protect every realm that Tyro threatens, while our own stands upon such perilous ground!" she retorted.

"If Yatin falls, Lorn falls with it. Then Torry South will follow. Send Terin to Lorn, and send Kato with him," Bode said emphatically, for if Torry South fell, it would undo all they accomplished in the north.

"Kato also?" she asked darkly. She had grown fond of the Earther in the brief time they shared after the siege. Though she strongly disliked Raven, she found Kato respectful of her position and sensitive to the needs of the realm.

Bode nodded, affirming his suggestion, the look of the others seeming to agree with him.

"Perhaps I should send Master Vantel, Cronus, and Commander Valen as well!" She tired of the exchange. They were all anxious to save her brother, but where was Lorn when the realm needed him most? Once again, he shirked his duty to Corell, marshalling a Torry Army to Yatin's defense while the fate of Torry North hung in the balance. If not for General Bode, Terin, and their Jenaii allies, Corell would have fallen.

"You may retain my 1st Battlegroup for Corell's defense, Princess. I have reconstituted their telnics, filling the vacant ranks of the 2nd Battlegroup with soldiers from the 1st, but it still numbers ten telnics. It should suffice if Morac makes a hasty return. If he waits to call upon reinforcements from the north, the process will delay him until spring," King El Anthar offered. With the Naybins threatening their border, the Jenaii needed to depart Corell in the coming days.

"Your Battlegroup is most welcome, Your Majesty," Chief Minister Monsh bowed, offering the gratitude of the Torry Realms.

"We are forgetting an inconvenient fact that Kato's loyalties are not mine to command," Corry said.

"True, but he seems agreeable to help in whatever way we have asked, Highness," Squid pointed out.

Corry gave Antillius a withering look, wondering if he was deliberately testing her patience. "What is the opinion of the rest of the council?" she asked, her gaze sweeping the faces gathered about the room.

"There is wisdom in the general's counsel," Dar Valen relented. "We must help the prince. I fear our position when Morac returns if our southern flank is compromised. Perhaps I can dispatch—"

"Your magantors are needed here, Commander. They are our eyes upon the enemy and our shield against a gargoyle host passing over the Plate," Bode said.

Corry was relieved that Bode didn't wish to strip away all of Corell's defenses.

"I must confess that I am wary of sending Terin away south. We are helpless against Morac and Dethine's fell blades. Shall Elos remain with the Jenaii Battlegroup to counter this threat, Your Majesty?" Commander Nevias asked the Jenaii king.

"Elos has other tasks that I require of him," El Anthar stated bluntly.

"Then I would caution against sending Caleph away," Lutius Veda warned.

Corry could see Bode's frustration, his measured breath and white knuckles as he pressed his hands to the table, standing over the map, his eyes fixated on their southern realm. There was yet one voice unheard from, one that she respected above all the others.

"Torg, I would have your counsel?" she regarded the Master of Arms standing across from her, his steel-gray eyes scanning the map studiously.

"The boy is as ready as I can make him. No matter your decision, this will be a close-run affair. The battle in Yatin is likely joined, and no force of arms you send will arrive before it is decided. An individual, however, might reach Lorn in time to aid his cause, and the only individuals that might alter the battle are Terin and the Earther," Torg stated the facts, masking any apprehension of sending his grandson in battle yet again.

Corry sighed, resigned to the bitter reality of what she must do. "Very well," she said icily. "Terin will go, and Kato with him if he so chooses."

"A difficult decision, Highness, but a necessary one," Squid acknowledged.

"Difficult but not final, Antillius. My decision is not without condition. As acting regent of the realm until my brother chooses to return and claim his throne, I will order Terin to return to Corell at the first sign of spring, before Morac will most likely continue his campaign," she said firmly.

"A fair and wise compromise, Highness," Bode conceded.

"Highness, we have other matters for your purview," Eli Monsh said.

"Proceed, Chief Minister," she ordered, growing weary of it all, the affairs of the realm weighing upon her, annoyed by the mundane details that required her attention while also dealing with larger matters that would decide if they all lived or died.

"The city-state of Sawyer is without a minister since Sais Gallo's recent demise," Eli Monsh began, referencing the sudden death of their ambassador under mysterious circumstances. The city rested at the western end of Lake Monata, straddling the vital trade artery connecting the Torry Realms, the Macon Empire, and the Jenaii Kingdom. The death of their ambassador blinded the Torries to the recent political machinations within Sawyer, especially the maneuverings of the Macon Empire.

"An obvious Macon plot. King Mortus is ever the opportunist. We should have expected this," Lutius Veda seethed. As minister of trade, he warned the king repeatedly of the Macon's ambitions upon Sawyer.

"And with our armies otherwise occupied, he will likely take advantage," Squid added.

"And if so, we are in no position to stop him," Corry said.

"Perhaps or perhaps not. Either way, we must know what is transpiring there," Nevias said.

"I can leave on the morrow, Highness. My recent task in Central City is concluded, and my journey to Bansoch to assume the ambassadorship can hold until the situation in Sawyer is resolved," Squid offered.

Corry regarded the others for objections, finding none. "Very well, Antillius. You have my leave to go, but I suggest you travel under another guise. We are at war, and I think it unwise to announce your loyalties so brazenly," she advised.

"Perhaps a merchant?" Chief Minister Monsh opined.

"Or a chronicler?" Dar Valen offered.

"A minstrel," Torg quietly advised. "Galen can accompany you, providing a credible companion for your false mask."

"A minstrel," Squid agreed. "And my escort?"

"Someone who is familiar to you both and the region," Minister Veda said. "Perhaps Cronus Kenti. A worthy task for his first mission as a Royal Elite."

Corry meant to object, but a chorus of agreements amongst her council forced her to acquiesce. Cronus had just wed, and she desired them to share more time as husband and wife, but such was war and the foul choices it forced upon them. Of course, any such guise would be questioned if they traveled by magantor, but time was of the essence, and a risk they would have to take.

*****

He coursed the heavens, his gray white wings full with the wind. Gazing skyward, he beseeched the great Yah to reveal himself, to allow mortal eyes to behold his majesty. Alas, he was unworthy to be granted such purview, for even the champion of the Jenaii was as any other in the eyes of the Most High. Though Elos could soar high into the firmament, he could never attain the airy heights of Yah's domain as the deity watched over the affairs of his creation from the upmost heavens and beyond.

Elos swept over the surrounding lands despoiled by war and ravishment. Thousands lay dead across the hellish landscape, stretching far beyond the palace walls, their bodies rotting in the late autumn sun. Some were heaped into great piles, where many fell in proximity. The Nayborians slaughtered before Corell's north wall, and the Gargoyle 6th Legion to the west were so decimated, their soldiers slain in great numbers in close space. Thousands more piled at the base of the outer walls, slain at the battlements' edge or by the withering archer fire short of the wall. They were set afire, their pyres still burning days after being set, the smell of burning flesh permeating the fetid air. Elos passed over the outer battlements, circling Corell's highest citadels before setting down upon an outcropping of the inner keep.

Alen received him upon the platform, awaiting his return. The Jenaii champion called upon the former Menotrist slave to meet him upon the airy heights, beyond the ears of others. Elos outstretched his legs, his wings folding gracefully as he set down. Alen regarded the Jenaii warrior with unspoken awe, bowing reverently as Elos landed.

"Alen," Elos regarded him evenly, his silver eyes appraising the former slave for some unknown purpose.

"Champion Elos," Alen bowed again, uncertain of Elos's proper appellation.

"I am Elos, Alen. You needn't acknowledge my title of champion of my realm. I am a servant to my people."

"Elos," Alen corrected.

"And you are Alen, a palace messenger of Menotrist origin," Elos affirmed.

"Yes," Alen bowed ashamedly of his past. Despite his current place and service, a part of him would always be a slave, his eyes betraying this awful truth.

"You speak yes, but I sense great shame in you," Elos observed.

"I...I am lowborn, and you are..." Alen struggled to speak, averting Elos's piercing gaze.

"And I was born with wings to attain the heavens," Elos finished Alen's thought.

"Yes," Alen confessed. "Flight is a wondrous ability."

"It is a gift," Elos corrected him. "A gift bestowed upon my people as Yah's faithful, to better serve his will. But it is you, Alen, as a human, who receives Yah's true blessing."

Alen was taken aback, never hearing of men being blessed. He was born a Menotrist slave, berated by his betters and put upon. "What blessing?"

"Freedom."

"I was born a human and a slave. Freedom was not my birthright," Alen made a face, Elos's words making little sense.

"You speak of status and appellations ordained by men and gargoyles of the mortal realm. Your true gift is beyond their terrestrial limitations. The freedom I speak of is your own heart." He touched a hand to Alen's chest. "And of your own mind." He moved his hand to Alen's head. "You are given free will to follow his divine path or your own. Your choices define you, Alen, not the misfortune of your birth. All men have a choice, even slaves."

Alen understood little of Elos's strange revelation, and the Jenaii warrior could see the doubt clouding his eyes.

"You have a choice, Alen, to continue serving as a palace messenger or accept a far greater purpose. All men have choices. Some are small, while others are grand. The recent events in your life now afford you an opportunity. I ask you this, Alen, do you wish to heed a higher purpose?"

"I wish to serve in whatever way to defeat Tyro."

"And if I offer you a far greater role to achieve that end?"

"Then I shall do as you bid."

*****

She rested her head upon his chest as they lie abed, closing her eyes as he ran his fingers through her hair. The dim candlelight shone weakly off the stone walls of their chamber, Cronus's eyes following the thin shadows across the ceiling, his thoughts elsewhere. He savored these moments with his beloved, sharing as much time as duty allowed. Leanna was equally occupied with the wounded, helping the matrons with Kato's equipment, having spent so long upon the *Stenox*. It was a strange paradox that of all the humans of Arax, it was Leanna that understood the Earthers technology the most. She idly ran her fingers over his chest, caressing the skin above his heart, where the sigil of the Elite would mark his flesh this night.

"Here," she said, touching the place where the brand would burn him, cringing at the thought of his suffering.

"Tonight," he affirmed, thinking of what Minister Antillius had told him earlier rather than the marking ceremony. He dreaded leaving her again, though duty called him to Sawyer. It was to be a simple journey there and back, but such plans were oft waylaid by the fortunes of war. Things were fluid, plans changing with events beyond their control.

Leanna sighed, bemoaning their fleeting time. Her heart mourned his leaving her once again, called away to a far-off land, far from her. She couldn't help but think of Rego, when he marched off to fight marauding gargoyles, only to be caught up in war and carried away in its tumult. Once gain he was to journey on a brief errand and return, but doubt clouded her spirit.

"When last we parted, you vowed to return and claim me as your wife, a vow you fulfilled. You must promise again to return to me," she said, running her fingers north to his face, her blue eyes finding his green staring back at her as she rested her chin on his chest.

"I promise." He smiled, losing himself in those sea-blue depths.

*****

Lush farmland stretched to the horizon as they coursed overhead, continuing northward until the citadels of Corell broke the horizon, the light of the waning sun alighting its western face. Lush farmlands transitioned to blackened fields as they drew near, with broken chimneys and bleached bones visible amid the charred ruins. From afar, the palace stood resplendent, its white walls and towering citadels presiding over a jade sea of forests and fields, but the closer they drew, the more visible the scars of battle marred its majesty. Large swaths were cut away from the Zaronan forest to the west, where Morac's legions cut timber for their towers and siege works. The fields about the castle were despoiled by battle and the enemy's encampments, the grass worn into dirt. Heavy rain the day before reduced much of the battlefield to mud. Thousands of soldiers dotted the tortured fields, still gathering the dead and clearing debris. The grounds before the main gate were littered with thousands of ballistae stone munitions of various sizes. They were carefully gathered and returned to the palace to be used in the next siege, should that occur. The dead were a grislier matter. Many were gathered in piles and set ablaze, only for their fires to wane before they were charred. Many would have to be relit several times or stacked with wood to fuel the flames, the recent rains only compounding the problem. The most pressing issue was the main gate, which Morac damaged beyond repair. Its metal was cut away in large shards twisting from its frame. Each of the gates along the north tunnel suffered in kind, destroyed by the fell power of Morac and Dethine's swords. Commander Nevias marshaled a small Army of smiths and engineers to repair the damage, but the task would take all winter, if at all.

Terin guided Wind Racer to the south-facing magantor platform jutting from the inner palace, the warbird setting down upon its stone lip, its black talons scraping the white stone. Kato's mount circled the battlements before setting down on the west facing stable.

*****

Terin and Cronus waited in the outer corridor of the throne room, clad in pleated kilts with their chests bare. Terin released a nervous breath, the cool air raising pimples upon his naked chest. There was little spare time since his arrival, where he landed, bathed, and was ushered forth in rapid succession. Cronus was the first familiar face he encountered, greeting him here, similarly attired as they waited for the ceremony to commence.

"How was your journey?" Cronus asked, torchlight playing off his bare chest.

"We slew a few hundred, but there are thousands roaming free," Terin reflected, thinking of their poor farmers and common folk facing the gargoyles scattered across their land. Fortunately, most were retreating whence they came, but enough devolved into raiding parties to cause undue mischief elsewhere.

"And we only evacuated those who dwelt thirty leagues to either side of the east-west road between Corell and Notsu." Cronus shook his head, thinking of those who remained just beyond that imaginary line, blissfully going about their lives. They were now in the path of any gargoyles straying off course.

"Our cavalry harried any group that wandered far from the road during the invasion and continue to do so during the retreat. We have dominion over the sky as well, something we lacked at the outset," Terin assured him. It was the bands of gargoyles that broke west or south that concerned him most as they might slip through their patrols that were strongest near Corell. Once they reached thirty leagues, there was little to stop them but individual farmers and smaller holdfasts. Commanders Tevlin and Valen prioritized the larger bands of gargoyles, but groups numbering less than twenty were ignored for other priorities.

"It seems we have as many problems to address in victory as Morac has with defeat," Cronus reflected.

"Then I am thankful for them," Terin said, not daring to dwell on the consequences if they had lost.

"It is time," Torg's rough voice drew their attention, stepping into the corridor, calling them hither with an open hand toward the doors of the throne room.

Terin took a deep breath, following Cronus into the cavernous chamber. They stepped briskly across the room, torchlight flickering off the white mirrored stone floor. He could see twenty-nine members of the Torry Elite gathered before the throne, awaiting them in a broken semicircle, flanking the throne and facing them. He noticed his father among them, standing nearest the dais, regarding him with obvious pride. Corry presided over the exclusive assemblage, sitting on her father's throne, her blue eyes following him intently since they entered. A heated brazier rested below the dais, between the broken halves of the semicircle of warriors. He could see the light of its heat glowing above its iron rim, with two branding irons embedded deep in its embers. Torg led them forth, skirting the brazier and ordering them to kneel, facing the throne. There they knelt, with chests bared and their hands resting on their thighs as Torg stood before them. Besides the present ranking member of the royal family, only members of the Torry Elite were allowed to attend a marking ceremony, the formal initiation of their select group.

"Cronus Kenti, commander of unit, do you disavow all former titles, loyalties, and positions to accept your place among your brothers?" Torg asked sternly.

"I so disavow!" Cronus affirmed.

"Do you accept the title of King's Elite?"

"I humbly accept the appellation of a King's Elite to the Torry Realms, to safeguard the House of Lore and defend the realm to my dying breath. This I so avow."

"As commander of the Torry Elite, master of arms of Corell, and protector of the king, I declare you, Cronus Kenti, a King's Elite!" Torg declared as Zane Velle, the next ranking Elite present, handed Torg one of the branding irons, its heated end glowing brightly, smoke pouring off its tip.

Cronus braced himself as Torg pressed the brand to his left breast, wincing painfully as it marked his flesh. Torg removed the iron, leaving the sigil of the Torry Elite burned into his chest, two crossed swords. Cronus struggled stifling his scream, his labored breath robbing him of his voice. Another Elite stepped forth, rubbing salve into the burn, as Torg returned the iron to the brazier, before helping Cronus to his feet.

"Highness, I present Cronus Kenti to the Torry Elite!" Torg stepped aside, granting Corry a clear view of their newest member.

"Step forth and be received by your brothers, King's Elite Kenti." Corry waved an open hand to his fellow Elite standing to either side of the throne.

Their fellow Elite gathered near, each clasping forearms with Cronus, welcoming him into their brotherhood. Corry found their camaraderie endearing, envying their fellowship. She couldn't help but wonder had she been born of the Sisterhood, if she might similarly share such a bond with her fellow warriors? She regarded Terin where he knelt, patiently awaiting his turn, imagining the anticipation was killing him. His was to be an even more special initiation as the first champion of the realm, with a unique marking worn by no other. After several moments, the others grew quiet, allowing Torg to proceed, Cronus taking his place among the others.

"Terin Caleph!" Torg began, his strong voice sounding across the still chamber. "Do you disavow all former titles, loyalties, and positions to accept your place among your brothers?"

"I so disavow," he affirmed.

"Do you accept the title of champion of the realm?"

"I humbly accept the appellation of champion of the Torry Realms, to safeguard the House of Lore, and defend the realm to my dying breath. This I so avow!"

Torg regarded him proudly before stepping aside, allowing the princess to address him.

"Accepting the appellation of champion, you shall hold no authority of command or title. You are sworn to protect the throne and the realm, influencing others only through your individual acts and deeds. As champion, you stand outside the purview of all other posts within the realm. You are commanded by the throne and your own will, to fulfill your oath as you feel led. Do you so avow?" Corry asked.

"I so avow, Highness!" Terin bowed his head.

"As sitting regent of the Torry Kingdoms, I name you champion of the realm!" she declared, regarding Torg to proceed.

"As commander of the Torry Elite and master of arms of the realm, I mark you champion of the realm!" Torg declared, as Zane Velle proffered the second brand. Torg carefully aligned the heated metal before pressing it into Terin's chest, the brand sizzling as it touched his flesh.

Terin winced, fighting the pregnant screams trying to burst from his throat, not wishing to show weakness before his fellows, and especially Corry, who regarded him with sympathetic blue eyes, his anguish paining her heart. Fight as he may, he could not stay the tears squeezing from his eyes. Another Elite rubbed salve over the wound, the brand marking him as champion, two crossed swords with a third rising between them, piercing the blades where they met, with separate marks depicting the sword's glow. 'Twas a brand commissioned long ago and never used until now.

Terin caught his breath despite the pain's lingering intensity that continued to fester. He couldn't imagine covering the wound with a full tunic, wishing for nothing more than to bathe in cold water. Torg helped him to his feet as the princess called for him to receive his brothers' welcome. He heard little of what she said, the pain overwhelming his senses, as one after another greeted him. He recalled little of the whirlwind of welcomes until his eyes found his father's staring back.

"Well met, Terin," Jonas regarded him proudly.

*****

"You leave on the morrow," she said with her back to him, staring forlornly to the west, starlight shining clearly in the moonless sky. She stood upon a stone outcropping atop the inner keep, with her arms crossed as he stepped near.

"You sound displeased," Terin said, stopping at her side, setting his hands upon the rampart.

"I saw my father off to the east, and he perished. I now send you to the west, into the unknown," she said, unable to look at him.

"I will return," he assured her, touching a hand to her shoulder.

She turned sharply, her blue eyes finding his. "Will you?" she challenged, not believing it.

"I will," he said, his eyes softening, lifting her hair behind her ear. "*I promise.*"

"You promise?" She laughed bitterly. "War guarantees nothing but suffering and loss, Terin. Who are you to challenge its omnipotence?"

"Who am I? I am the one who loves you," he said fiercely.

She regarded him for a time, her eyes searching his, finding the kindred spirit they shared. She noted the thick cloak drawn over his naked shoulders, and the fresh brand marking his chest, a sticky salve oozing over the wound. She winced, reliving the moment the metal touched his chest. The branding of Elite warriors was a brutal practice that made little sense to her. Most kingdoms used brands to mark slaves, which were always upon their upper left thigh. A brand upon the chest was the mark of a warrior, an honored ritual traced back to the founding of the Middle Kingdom. Other realms practiced it as well, each creating a distinct sigil for their Elites. Surprisingly, her brother and father shared the mark of the Torry Elite, having suffered the tutelage of Torg Vantel. Her father once explained that he could not ask his Elite to suffer such without doing so himself, and now Terin was similarly branded. She touched her fingers above the mark, running them around the brand, along the healthy flesh, outlining the wound.

"How badly does this hurt?" she asked, her eyes on his chest.

"It is nothing." He shrugged, but she could feel him tense as her fingers drew closer to the brand.

"Haven't you been warned not to lie to royalty?" she admonished.

"It hurts," he confessed, smiling sheepishly.

"I know. Perhaps tomorrow you might chance covering it with cloth. I do not wish you continuing to bare your chest for all to see and catching the eye of any fair maid," she warned, touching a finger to his nose.

"You overestimate my charm." He shrugged.

She shook her head at his misplaced humility. Did he not know how handsome he was? Illana Ornovis and Enora Fonis each spoke of his...attributes. Of course, what did she expect as he was raised a farmer's son, living a simple existence. He would always see himself as such, even though he was the champion of the realm and the grandson of Torg Vantel. Other than the House of Lore, no family in Torry North was as highly placed as House Vantel. The blood of kings and Tarelia flowed in their veins.

"You will seek out my brother, win his campaign, and return to me without getting yourself killed. Do you understand me?" she growled, squeezing his face between her fingers.

"I promise," his voice squeaked through his compressed cheeks.

"Promises are vain reassurances. Do what I ask and return, and stay not a day longer than necessary."

"Yes, Highness," he squeaked, trying to smile through her iron grip.

"Good," she released his face. "Now kiss me."

The morning found Jonas standing outside his son's chamber, resigned to bid him farewell once again. He released a weary sigh and stepped within, finding the boy filling his pack with spare clothing, tose powder, a pair of daggers, bowstring, cook pan and utensils, and numerous other items he would need for his journey.

"Father." Terin's face brightened as he entered the room.

"Son." Jonas smiled easily, placing a firm hand on his shoulder. "I see you are packing for your next journey," he said, observing the items spread out on his cot.

"When last we parted, I left on a different journey," Terin recalled the last time he saw home before leaving for Rego.

"Then we were at peace, but now you are going off to war, with every enemy spear trained upon you." Jonas sighed, picking up one of the daggers, examining it.

"We've been at war for so long now that I have stopped worrying over it." Terin shrugged.

"When you become a father one day, son, you shall know my grief. There is nothing ordinary about war, especially this one. We are at the end of an age, for good or ill, and our actions will be weighed and measured by posterity."

"Posterity, history, destiny, I grow weary of it all. Everyone looks to me as some prophetic hero come to save them. If they only knew how lost I feel," he confessed tiredly, stuffing the items in his pack.

"I sympathize, but they are not wrong to look to you for deliverance. It is your destiny."

"My destiny? What makes you so certain, Father? What divine providence has ordained us with such power? I don't know why I can invoke such power in this sword of yours, but I believe it's nothing more than happenstance." Terin shook his head.

"Happenstance? Dumb luck? Coincidence? Do you truly believe that?" he asked, reproaching his son.

Terin stood there silently, unsure of his answer.

"You were born to this destiny, son. It falls to you to heed its call. No one else can do what you are called to do. *No one.*"

"What makes you so certain, Father? You claim our gift was given us by your mother's kin. Either explain their significance or forgive my disbelief. Who are they?" Terin asked, tired of the subterfuge regarding his lineage.

"She was born to an ancient house, one far older than any known throughout the realms of men, a house entrusted to a great purpose," Jonas began.

"Entrusted by whom?" Terin challenged.

"By Yah."

"Yah?" Terin made a face. Prince Lorn spoke at length of the ancient deity, extolling his divinity, guidance, and omnipotence. The Jenaii also worshipped the deity, claiming the god had stricken their ancient temple with a falling star, calling them to deliver its remains to the Tarelians, who forged the Swords of Light from the strange material. Squid also counted among Yah's faithful, though he was less vocal of his faith than Lorn, or the less-passionate Jenaii who simply stated their belief in Yah as mere acknowledgment of fact rather than religious adherence. Now it seemed his father counted among Yah's adherents, though strangely never professed such faith in all their years together.

"Our ancestor was the first disciple of Yah upon Arax. It fell upon him to draw the people out of their darkness, into Yah's greater glory. He succeeded for a time, but the hearts of men rejected his teaching and betrayed his realm. He fell in battle with many of the faithful, his death condemning Arax to her darkest age."

"Kal?" Terin whispered, as no other but the ancient king fit his father's description.

"Aye, Kal the blessed, Kal the merciful, Kal the conqueror, Kal the devout, Kal the—"

"Kal the dead," Terin added the more pertinent appellation. What his father spoke of was the obvious ramblings of a madman. People oft fancied that they were truly the lost offspring of one royal line or another, looking to be accepted into their true family. It was the stuff of fairy tales and the daydreams of young children.

"Mind your tongue, Terin!" Jonas admonished, his purple eyes ablaze. Terin had never seen his father so displeased with him.

"Sorry, Father." He lowered his eyes ashamedly before looking again at Jonas. "Kal's line died with him, so the legend claims. Upon his death, his Queen Celenia cast herself into the sea when word reached her of Kal's fall. There was no mention of offspring. Is this the lineage you claim we sprang from?" Terin challenged, not believing it.

Jonas was also taken aback by Terin's tone. The boy would not back down, demanding the truth that Jonas had kept from him for so long. "Not all of King Kal's legend is true, Terin. Whether his queen cast herself into the sea or not, I do not know, but they did have a child, and that child was ushered to safety, hidden from men that would have seen him dead."

"And how do you know this?"

"Because it is in our blood."

"Our blood?" Terin asked skeptically. King Anthar spoke of their blood with a strange reverence. Was this why? Did he know?

"Terin, let me start at the beginning. I meant to tell you this eventually, but your hasty departure forces me to do so now." Jonas sighed, motioning Terin to sit upon the bed to hear the lengthy tale.

"In Kal, Yah foresaw his hopes for mankind, a man whose heart much reflected his own. Yah raised him up, calling upon Kal to assume the mantel of his glory, bringing forth a golden age of peace, where all men were granted the liberty to exercise their free will. Only then would Yah know his true followers from his false children. And so it was in those ancient days that Kal unified much of the land under his dominion, granting all men the freedom to worship as they will, affording all men equality before the throne, whether wealthy or poor, noble or peasant. He set forth Yah's will in his sacred code, divine laws to regulate the realm of men, laws guaranteeing the rights of free worship, limiting the power of kings, nobles, and chieftains. Such laws were predictably unpopular with said nobles and chieftains and rejected by those whose religious fervor could not abide coexistence with any other. Most, however, simply did not believe in Yah and disdained his adherents."

"If most commoners and nobles held either disdain or apathy toward Yah, why did they follow Kal to begin with?" Terin asked, wondering how Kal was able to forge so great a realm in the first place.

"The fear of another malevolent entity aided their unity," Jonas answered.

"Gargoyles," Terin guessed.

"Yes, that foul species that has plagued mankind since we first stepped upon Arax. Before Kal's ascension, the gargoyles plagued the land, threatening to engulf the world in their festering darkness. It was during Arax's darkest time that Yah bestowed his divine gift upon his favored acolyte, instilling in the gargoyles great fear in his presence. With such power over the creatures, Kal could turn any defeat into certain victory, his mere presence driving the creatures to madness. And so it was, as his victories grew, men flocked to his banner, discarding their differences to fight their common foe. With countless victories, men named him king, his realm stretching across the face of Arax, reducing the remnant of the gargoyle race to their last redoubts along the Mote and Plate Mountains. He chose Celenia as his queen, her beauty only exceeded by her intelligence. King Kal and Queen Celenia presided over the Golden Age of Man, an age of peace where men were unshackled to achieve their higher purpose, to live for more than mere existence. 'Twas an age of abundance, where the populace kept the greater part of their own bounty. Gone were the days where nobles and potentates garnished the labor of their lesser, starving the people for their own greed. His codes ushered forth an age of science, knowledge, and discovery unparalleled in our history. Alas, this vision of lasting progress and abundance was betrayed by those who served their own senseless greed, forsaking their king for their individual positions, which crumbled beneath their feet after his death."

"What happened?" Terin asked, his father's explanation sounding more like rhetoric than history.

"Kal was given two great tasks. One was to advance Yah's vision for Arax, the other was the elimination of the gargoyle curse. Though he greatly reduced the gargoyles' numbers, driving their remnant into the recesses of the Mote and Plate Mountains, he had not eliminated them completely. By the third decade of his reign, he marshaled his armies to complete the task. At the apex of his power and campaign, he was betrayed, set upon by many of his vassals who opposed his reforms. When word of his fall reached Queen Celenia, she was rumored to have thrown herself into the sea, as retold by those who witnessed her tragic end. Those faithless vassals who betrayed King Kal later sacked the capital city, robbing its treasures and slaying those who kept faith. And so Arax fell into a dark age, as all that Kal achieved was left in ruin. Without his unique gift and Yah's guidance, the gargoyle curse returned tenfold, spreading across the land like a foul malignancy, eventually destroying those that betrayed their king. Such was the judgement of Yah," Jonas explained sadly.

"If Kal kept faith with Yah, why did the god not spare him? What god punishes his most trusted servant? It certainly does not urge others to take up Kal's mantle," Terin asked.

"Yah did not strike down Kal, nor did he pass judgement upon him. Kal was faithful and true, but no man, not even the great king, is without blemish. Despite Kal's detriments, Yah kept faith with his most devout servant. Kal was ready to usher forth Yah's will to the world, but Arax was not ready to receive it. So Kal was removed to punish mankind for their rejection of Yah."

"But he died all the same. That doesn't sound like justice," Terin said.

"Yah's blessing did not fail the fallen king, son. Yah protected the one thing that Kal valued above his own life and realm…his son."

"Kal had no child," Terin said. "The legends say the queen was barren," he remarked. as Queen Celenia and King Kal failed to conceive after nearly three decades of marriage.

"Yes, she was believed barren, until Yah blessed her in her fifth decade, granting them the child they so long desired, a child whose birth was kept secret as Kal marched off to war. Once Kal fell, his most loyal guardians spirited his queen and child away, leaving others to spread false tales of her demise. With a small band of followers, each great warriors, scholars, or craftsmen, she journeyed into exile, dwelling where men would not find them. There they remained, shielded by Yah and undiscovered by the realms of men until my grandfather chanced upon them."

"Your grandfather?" Terin made a face, his father's strange tale growing more complicated the more he tried to explain it.

"My father's father," Jonas explained.

Terin recalled the gargoyles' unnatural fear of them was a gift of his grandmother's line, then who was his grandfather?

"My mother's kin dwelt in the Kalinian Vale, as her people came to call it, though outsiders referred to it as the Vale of Odom. They dwelt in Kalinian for centuries, each generation passing on their gift to the next. By the time of my mother's birth, everyone that dwelt in the vale was related by blood, each a direct descendent of King Kal himself through his son, Kalin. Each instilled great fear in the gargoyles that dwelt in all the lands around them. The gargoyles came to believe the valley of Odom to be haunted and, after a time, never ventured there again. The gargoyle presence surrounding them, however, shielded the Kalinians from the realms of men. And so they dwelt there through the centuries, sheltered in obscurity, rarely venturing forth into the outer world."

"What drove them to venture from the safety of their vale?"

"There were times when the small populace of the vale produced certain…imbalances between the genders. Sometimes there were too few or many men or women, encouraging the unpaired to find companionship elsewhere, bringing them into their fold. Such occurrences were rare, however, as most held no desire to step even briefly from their home. Others, however, ventured forth for a far greater purpose," Jonas's voice trailed cryptically.

"Greater purpose?" Terin asked.

"To recover the Swords of Light that were carelessly lost by the unworthy. 'Tis another skill gifted our bloodline by Yah. We are drawn to the swords, able to find them when need or desire drives us, even if buried or hidden away. The Swords of Light were intended for our hands. The Tarelian smiths forged them from the materials given them by the Jenaii, who brought them across the great sea to our shores. The Tarelians wisely gifted their creations to men of stout hearts, who used their power to forge kingdoms to contest the gargoyles' advance upon the realms of men. The Northern Kingdom, established by Clorvis Cal, cleared the gargoyles from the northwest coast beyond the tributaries of the Reguh, driving them into the Cress, Mote, and Plate Mountains. The Middle Kingdom cleared the lands south of the Plate, expelling the gargoyles from the Lone Hills and along the Nila. The Western Kingdom eventually forced the gargoyles from the Cress Mountains before their eventual demise. The Eastern Kingdom drove the gargoyles from the Tur Valley and Lake Veneba. Their kingdoms, for a time, seemed destined to expunge the gargoyles from Arax, but alas, the hearts of men betrayed them. Though their flesh was willing to accomplish this task, their hearts were less stout. The kingdoms founded by the Tarelians were inspired by Kal's ancient realm but had forgotten the divinity that guided his benevolent reign."

"Yah," Terin echoed.

"Yah." Jonas sighed. "Men had all but forgotten the god of Kal, recalling fondly his just rule but forgetting the inspiration that guided his rule. And so it came to pass when the Tarelian Realms converged upon the gargoyles' last redoubts that the fates betrayed them. The prince of the Northern Kingdom was slain by Menotrist tribes, drawing his father from the fray. The Middle Kingdom was assailed by Yatin, causing them to abandon their campaign along the Plate. The Jenaii withdrew to combat a Naybin invasion, leaving the Eastern Kingdom alone to finish the task that they were unsuited. Within two centuries, all the swords held by the three kingdoms were lost or stolen and their kingdoms falling to ruin with them, save for the Middle Kingdom, whose King Vantor II repented for his arrogance and received the prophecy of the one who would return the Sword of the Moon to the realm."

"So your mother's kin sought out the lost swords?" Terin asked.

"Sought and found them, most of those that were lost, anyway," Jonas affirmed. "The first we found along the Vorun Gap, where

King Telfin III fell, dooming the Western Kingdom without his fabled sword. Soon we gathered two other Swords of the Stars, before stealing the greatest of the Swords of Light, the Sword of the Sun."

"Your kin stole the Golden Sword?" Terin's eyebrows rose in surprise. "Why? By doing so, they doomed the Northern Kingdom."

"The Northern Kingdom was already doomed. Their once great kings were driven to madness, forsaking their mandate to counter the gargoyle threat. Instead, their evil kings abandoned their fellow men to the gargoyles' mercies. They even forsook their sister realm, the Eastern Kingdom, ignoring their pleas for help as they were overrun. And so our kin set out and retrieved the Golden Sword of the Sun, spiriting it away to the Kalinian Vale."

"They had the Sword of the Sun?" Terin asked incredulously. "I thought Tyro found it. How came he to possess it if your mother's kin had it in their vale?"

Jonas snorted at the false beliefs that permeated their faulty history. Even the chronicles of the Middle Kingdom were filled with countless untruths. Some misbeliefs were unimportant, like the chronicles crediting Clorvis Cal of the Northern Kingdom for having constructed Fera and Nisin Castles, where in truth, Nisin was constructed by order of the eastern king that bore his name. Much of the greater falsehoods surrounded the flawed men who first wielded the Swords of Light. The men of ancient Tarelia were keepers of knowledge for untold centuries and thought themselves the only survivors of Kal's ancient kingdom. They had no way of knowing that Kal's heir survived, and his descendants dwelt in the shadows of the Mote Mountains in the far north.

"Tyro did not find the sword. It was given him," Jonas corrected him, admitting a cruel truth that plagued Jonas for decades.

"Given him?" Terin was aghast. "By whom?"

The small chamber grew suddenly still, cold pimples arising across his bare limbs, as his father looked away, his purple eyes staring toward the far wall but seeing nothing.

"I gifted him the blade," Jonas confessed.

Terin paled, his world crashing around him. His father gifted Tyro the very weapon he used to forge his empire, an empire that threatened their existence, that slew countless thousands of their people, and slew their king.

"Why?" was all Terin could utter, his heart pounding in his ears.

This was the part Jonas dreaded most of all, finally revealing the dark truth he kept hidden from all, save his dearest Valera. "It is our birthright and duty as the blood of Kal to contest the gargoyle curse. The Swords of Light were a gift from Yah, intended for our hands, to aid us in this quest. The swords we recovered were hidden away in the vale, save for one of the lesser Swords of the Stars, which my uncle Terik wielded as chief ranger. It fell to him as the eldest son of or house to protect the vale from outsiders threatening our small populace. By the time of my birth, our people were few in number, far reduced from low birth rates and disease that afflicted us in the previous century. Despite our weakening position, our power and repute kept the gargoyles at bay. Then something changed. The gargoyles surrounding our vale for thousands of years were driven off by a Menotrist overlord named Agar. His uncovering of our vale led many to believe that the time to fulfill our destiny had come to pass and that the Menotrists were instruments of Yah to aid us in our quest to destroy the gargoyles."

"They weren't, were they," Terin said.

"Sadly, no. The enemy of my enemy must be a friend, or so my uncle foolishly believed. Upon finding our people in the Vale of Odom, or Kalinian as we refer it, Agar was dismayed to discover our unique effect upon his gargoyle foe. My uncle Terik invited Agar into our vale, offering his sword arm to the Menotrist campaign against the gargoyles. My grandfather was equally naive when offering my mother's hand to the overlord's eldest son and heir, Aleric."

"Your mother's hand? Where was your father at this time?" Terin asked.

"I was not yet born, Terin."

Terin's head was swimming, trying to follow all his father was saying, wondering how Tyro came into this tale, and surprised to learn, by Jonas's tone, that the Menotrists played a nefarious role in this strange yarn.

"Agar accepted my grandfather's proposal, inviting my mother into his home as a ward and my uncle Terik as a sworn sword in his gargoyle campaign. Terik quickly gained renown, using one of the Swords of the Stars and smiting gargoyles in great numbers, driving them from the Mote Mountains. It should have been a happier time, but my uncle and mother soon learned that their Menotrist hosts were no servants of Yah. The Menotrists were a wicked and vile people who mistreated their Benotrist subjects most cruelly."

This revelation took Terin aback. He had come to loathe the Benotrists for their barbarity and oft pitied the Menotrists who suffered their tyranny. How soon they had forgotten that it was the Menotrists who first enslaved the Benotrists, subjugating them for centuries.

"Agar's eldest son, Aleric, grew envious of Terik, resenting the praise he garnered from his father's vassals. Aleric coveted Terik's sword and, in an act of betrayal, murdered him while falsely claiming he was slain in battle, thus claiming the Sword of Light for his own. My mother, who was Aleric's betrothed, argued in her grief that the sword needed to be returned to her people. Aleric refused and struck her, causing her to flee. Unbeknownst to Aleric, his younger half brother, Taleron, had fallen madly in love with my mother and spirited her away. Aleric searched in vain for them, cursing his brother for stealing his promised bride. Taleron wed my mother, and they dwelt in secret, where I was born."

"Taleron was your father?" Terin asked, finally learning the name of his paternal grandsire.

"Yes, and your grandfather. He was Agar's son by his second wife, a Benotrist peasant girl who won his affection. Taleron's Benotrist bloodline brought him into constant conflict with his full-blooded Menotrist half brother, Aleric. Taleron was a skilled swordsman and warrior, far superior to his elder brother. Taleron oft pleaded to his father on behalf his mother's kin to lessen their harsh treatment. His father ignored his pleas, increasing the suffering of his Benotrist serfs. After Taleron absconded with my mother, his father punished his mother's kin for his crime."

"So Grandfather Taleron was both Menotrist and Benotrist?"

"Yes, though he will never acknowledge his Menotrist blood." Jonas sighed.

"*Will* never? Does he yet live?"

"He lives."

"Where does he live?" Terin's heart was racing, discovering that his grandfather still lived.

"North."

"North? In the northern provinces of the realm, or north as in the Benotrist Empire?" Terin's heart pounded, wary of the answer.

"The Benotrist Empire."

Terin opened his mouth as if to speak, but words escaped him as Jonas continued.

"My father and mother dwelt far beyond my grandfather Agar's reach for several years, until they learned of his passing. Agar fell in battle, slain by a gargoyle war party somewhere between the Mote and Plate Mountains. My father claimed that it was Aleric who slew their father, but he was likely blinded by hatred for his elder brother. It was then, at my mother's urging, that we returned to the Kalinian Vale, seeking shelter with her kin. My father agreed, though his motives were elsewhere. She revealed to him her family's history, their unique gifts and their sacred duty to expunge the gargoyles from Arax. Most importantly, he learned of the other Swords of Light hidden in the Kalinian Vale, swords that could balance the scales against his brother. Upon reaching the vale, he urged my maternal grandfather, Cal, to take up arms against the Menotrists, extolling the virtues of his cause and listing the crimes the Menotrists inflicted upon their people. My grandfather Cal told him that the swords were intended to use against the gargoyles, not foolish, misguided Menotrists. He assured my father that the sword Aleric wielded would betray him in time, and they would simply retrieve it when it did so. He said only the blood of Kal were intended to use the swords and did not fear Aleric's threat.

"My grandfather's answer enraged my father, who warned him of the Menotrists' danger to everyone in the Vale. My father soon learned that a true Kalinian was drawn to the swords and urged me to find them for him. I was but a child, but I loved my father deeply and wished to please him. One night, once everyone else had fallen asleep, I retrieved one of the swords from the recesses of a deep cavern, where my mother's kin had hidden it. Once I set my mind to finding it, it called to me like a beacon lit upon the shore, guiding a ship to port on the darkest night. I woke my father and gifted him the wondrous blade. I remember so clearly that night as if it were yesterday. My father's eyes drew wide with wonder upon seeing the weapon. I remember him hugging me fiercely and gifting me the necklace that he carved, the very charm I gifted to you, with my mother and grandmother's visages carved into the bosa stones that adorn it. My father ordered me to protect my mother as he left in the dead of night, telling me to not speak a word until he was gone. I asked him why he was leaving, and he told me it was to protect us from his brother, who he intended to slay. He promised to return in a fortnight, but I never saw him again."

"What happened?" Terin asked, wondering what befell him but recalling that his father acknowledged that his grandfather was still alive. He was curious where Tyro entered this story.

"Of what transpired after he left, I can only piece together, with vital details lacking. We learned that my father attacked his brother's holdfast, slaying a number of his brother's warriors and freeing a gargoyle Aleric had captured and intended to execute. The gargoyle happened to be a powerful chieftain, who pledged himself to my father's cause."

Terin grew suddenly pale. He knew this tale, finally realizing who Taleron truly was. "*Tyro*," he gasped, his heart pounding so fiercely that it might burst from his chest.

"Do not speak that name, son. To me, he will always be Taleron, not the monster that spawned that wretched empire."

"Yet you are the heir to that empire," Terin said, wishing this were a nightmare that he could wake from. No wonder his father never spoke of his kin or history. When he learned that he was Torg's grandson, he was surprised but proud, but this…

"I am heir to my mother's legacy, Terin, as are you!" Jonas said indignantly. "My father believes me dead, and so shall it be. He forsook me the day he bonded with our mortal foe. No friend of gargoyles can share a bond with the House of Kal."

"Why didn't Ty—Taleron return for you?"

"My uncle Aleric returned first, with hundreds of soldiers and brandishing my uncle Terik's sword. He barely survived my father's assault, his lesser sword blocking the Golden Sword, though losing several fingers in the exchange before fleeing. Unfortunately, he quickly realized where my father found the Golden Sword and gathered what men he could and assailed the Kalinian Vale to exact vengeance and retrieve whatever swords that remained. My mother and I kept hidden in the upper vale once my father departed, as she debated whether to leave or not. By such happenstance, we were spared her family's fate as Aleric swept into the vale, slaying everyone. Only my mother and I survived to tell this tale. With my father and uncle on opposing sides of a growing war, we had no choice but to flee. We made our way south, traversing the dangerous lands frequented by gargoyles, wild tribes, and slavers. The gargoyles kept at a distance, however, finding our presence unsettling whenever we crossed paths. We eventually came to dwell in Torry North, the last of the kingdoms established by the Tarelian order, other than the Sisterhood. By this time, I had become quite skilled with a sword and bow, learning much from my father and mother's kin before they were slain."

Terin continued to listen, hanging on his father's every word.

"We came to dwell in the province of Tavera, which rests in the shadow of the Plate Mountains, a region oft beset by roving bands of gargoyles. The local proctor offered a fair bounty for gargoyle heads. I quickly demonstrated my unique skill in vanquishing them in great numbers. Such small bands of gargoyles were helpless against my Kalinian blood that stripped away their courage and rage. While I collected gargoyle bounties, my mother tended the wounded and ill people of the province, using the healing skills taught by her people, which were far superior to that of the local matron's guild. Our fame spread throughout the region and came to the attention of Lord Teverin, who ruled the region. He invited us into his service, where I first met Squid and became fast friends. By now, rumors had already spread of a revolution in the north, where a Benotrist rebel wielding a magical sword had aligned with gargoyles. It was then the extent of my folly was revealed. My mother died of a broken heart upon hearing of my father's deeds, leaving me alone as the last of Kal's line."

Terin's heart broke for his father, finally realizing the grief he had borne all these years. "Did you try to reconcile with him, try to turn him from his dark path?"

"Do you believe I could have convinced him to forsake his new *friends*? Or to turn away from his vengeful path? His hatred for the Menotrists could never be assuaged," Jonas said sadly.

"But he probably believes you died at their hands, further fueling his rage. Wouldn't knowing you live temper his anger?"

"And what might he have done if he knew I lived? He wouldn't turn on his gargoyle friends as I would demand. No, he would have expected me to forsake my duty to my mother's blood and make common cause with creatures I am blood sworn to oppose. I was the last Kalinian, and it was my duty to oppose the gargoyles. Our sacred vale no longer protected me, and I swore to aid the one realm I knew to be true in opposing the gargoyles."

"The Torry Realm," Terin affirmed.

"The Torry Realm." Jonas sighed. "I followed Lord Teverin into battle as we joined Prince Lore during the sadden wars, eventually driving them from the Plate Mountains. It was during those years that I befriended Lore and found the Sword of the Moon. When word reached us that my father slew my uncle Aleric, I knew he must have taken my uncle's sword as well and that the Torry Realms would need a powerful sword to match them. My mother's kin had searched for the Sword of the Moon after it was lost by King Vanlar so long ago, but Yah clouded their vision in seeing it. Its location was revealed to me during the war in a vision as clear as the sun on a cloudless sky.

"When I took hold of the ancient blade, I knew Yah had shielded it from our vision throughout the centuries so that it would not fall into my father's hands. It was preserved to contest his might when he dared cross into Torry North. Only the blood of Kal wielding the Sword of the Moon can stand against the Golden Sword in Morac's possession, your sword and your blood," Jonas affirmed, placing a hand to Terin's heart.

"If your god protected the Sword of the Moon from Ty—Taleron, why did he not protect the Sword of the Sun as well? Would our cause not be so desperate if we held the stronger blade?" Terin asked.

"I do not question his will or reason, I simply obey. We were born for a purpose, and we are the last of Kal's line, and it matters not which blade you wield, for Yah's blessing will guide your hand."

"If we are meant to wield the swords, then why did you offer it to King Lore when you confessed your love for Mother?" Terin asked, figuring his father's answer would be as ambiguous as his last.

Jonas sighed tiredly, his shoulders sagging with shame. "I betrayed my king, Terin. My mind tried to refute what my heart so desperately wanted. We cannot control who we love, Terin. Your mother won my heart, consuming my waking thoughts, tormenting my dreams. It is an awful fate to love the one woman you can never have. I cared not for my destiny or the threat from my father at that time. I could think of nothing but your mother, my dearest Valera. What choice had I but confess such to my king and offer him the weapon he would need in the wars to come. Who but Yah could have spoken to Lore's heart and stayed his vengeance? Who but Yah could grant him the wisdom to show me mercy and gift me my heart's desire? And here you sit today, the product of the union of Kal, Benotrists, Menotrists, and House Vantel. You, and you alone, hold the promise and threat of all those bloodlines."

At the mention of the Benotrists and Menotrists, Terin was suddenly struck by his father's paternal heritage. Tyro was the son of a Benotrist mother and Menotrist father, making Terin a child of both warring factions. He thought of the cruelties each had inflicted upon the other, and now he stood between them. His father's mother was of Kalinian descent, gifting him her blood, a gift from Yah to his ancient kin. Terin's own mother was a daughter of House Vantel, the keepers of the ancient Tarelian holdfast that served the Torry Throne. Terin wondered who he truly was. Was he a Torry son, of the blood of Torg Vantel? Was he the grandson of Cordela, the descendent of King Kal? Or was he the grandson of Tyro, heir to his dark legacy?

Jonas saw the conflict in Terin's countenance, his son's troubled thoughts playing cruelly on his weary face.

"Who am I?" Terin sighed tiredly.

"You are *my* son," Jonas said proudly, placing his hand on Terin's shoulder.

"Am I?" He lifted his blue eyes to Jonas's purple, noticing for the first time the tint of gold speckled within his father's iris, matching the hue of Tyro's cruel eyes. "Or am I the grandson of Torg, the heir of Kal, or the heir or…Taleron?"

"You are all of those, but you are the blood of Kal before any other," Jonas affirmed.

"And how would Taleron see his grandson facing him in battle?" Terin asked curiously.

"He can never know. My mother oft spoke of his obsession with the Kalinian bloodline once she revealed her heritage. He believed siring me granted legitimacy to his cause. Perhaps that was why he waited so long to remarry and sire another heir, finally giving us up for dead. If he knew we lived, he would tear the world asunder to reclaim what he thought was rightfully his. And what more could he hope for than to pass on his empire to his son, who is a descendent of King Kal?"

His other heir! Terin thought in alarm. "Tosha," he thought aloud.

"Tosha." Jonas smiled. "The half sister I haven't met, but you have. What is she like?" Jonas asked, though Terin shared much of this tale already, suddenly recalling his father's interest in Tyro's daughter whenever she entered the tale.

"She's…different." He sighed, searching for words best to describe her. He again told of his interactions with her, recalling Tyro's obsession with her siring a male heir. He wondered if Tosha knew who he was, how would she receive him? It was then a sudden chill passed over him as he recalled the conversation he shared with her when they sailed into Tinsay, when she noticed his necklace, thinking the visage in the center looked familiar. She admired the craftsmanship, comparing it to her father's. Such irony was not lost on Terin. He then recalled when he lost it during his escape from Fera, suddenly wondering if Tyro came to possess it. And if he did, would he remember it? He voiced his fears to his father.

Jonas froze, the realization washing over him that his father might know that he lived. "You said you lost it. You never spoke of how," Jonas's words sounding more accusatory than intended.

"Morac tore it from my throat after our duel. I know not if he discarded it, kept it, or lost it soon after. Would your father remember it after all these years?"

"He would never forget it, and you mentioned earlier that Tosha thought it familiar, and you revealed that I carved one of the faces adorning it. If it somehow came into my father's possession, he would…" Jonas's words trailed as he contemplated the repercussions.

"He would be enraged. He would see our acts as betrayal. I have seen into his eyes, Father, and the man you once knew is no longer there. He is cruel and twisted, forsaking the last vestiges of his humanity. He lives for his empire above all else, placing his legacy upon its prosperity. I've seen those that suffered under harsh rule. Cronus is haunted even now by what he endured in his dungeon. What will he do if he discovers who I am?"

"He would hunt you to the ends of the world," Jonas admitted, closing his eyes.

"And what will my friends think of me once they learn I am Tyro's spawn?" Terin put his face in his hands.

"They will hate that part of you and *love* the rest, son. I hold the greater taint, for half of my blood I draw from him, whilst you but a fourth."

Terin doubted others would see it that way. What would Corry think once she discovered he was the grandson of the man who slew her father?

"Guard your feelings, son. I wished not to burden you with these harsh truths, especially now when you are to again depart, but you needed to hear them from my own lips. Some may judge you harshly for the blood you share with my father, but this is a burden you must bear for my sin. It was I that placed the Sword of the Sun in my father's hand, condemning all of northern Arax to his dark rule. I have atoned for this sin by placing the Sword of the Moon in my son's hand to counter my foolishness. To you falls this sacred duty. Though you are the heir of Kal, and Taleron, and the grandson of Torg Vantel, you were not born to rule or claim kingship of this world. You were born to destroy the gargoyles."

"And what of Kal's other mandate, to usher forth a world in Yah's image?"

"That is the duty of another, one more suited to such a task of statecraft," Jonas said, as if he already knew to whom that task would fall.

*****

Terin stood upon the lip of the magantor platform, staring blankly to the horizon, his mind a maelstrom of conflicting emotions and unanswered questions. His father's lengthy tale was too convoluted to grasp in one sitting, and even now questions came to mind that he hadn't time to conjure during Jonas's full telling. He meant to ask his father what became of the other Swords of Light harbored in the Vale of Kalin or the one his great uncle Aleric wielded before falling to Tyro? Tyro could just as easily have three more Swords of Light at his disposal, not counting the one in Dethine's possession. He also meant to ask of their surname. From where did the name Caleph derive? It certainly wasn't passed down through his paternal grandfather or great-grandfather, for Tyro would have recognized it upon their meet. Was it Kalinian? If so, Tyro would have recognized it as well. It certainly isn't of Torry origin, for no other bore that name as far as he could tell. Did Jonas create the name himself, deriving it from Kal in some way?

Terin shifted suddenly as a giant black beak nudged his shoulder, nearly knocking him from his feet. He turned, his blue eyes meeting Wind Racer's bright silver, the magantor greeting him as if purposely drawing him from his troubled thoughts.

"I see you are ready, my friend." He laughed, touching a hand to the bird's neck, stroking its white feathers. A tilt of its head acknowledged Terin's words as if the warbird understood his human tongue.

"A beautiful creature, a worthy mount for a great warrior," Corry's familiar voice called out as she drew near.

"Highness," he greeted her, taking a knee as she approached, his eyes fixed to the hem of her azure gown, swirling about her sandaled feet. A soft hand caressed his cheek, drawing his gaze to hers as she stared deeply into his eyes. She wondered when she had come to loathe seeing him bend his knee to her? All she knew was that the more she loved him, the more it pained her. She took solace that such protocols would be set aside once they wed. Her brother might have a say in the matter, but as acting regent, she could simply declare the betrothal and bypass Lorn altogether. Lorn would grant her this boon regardless, so she would wait. Besides, marriages were usually arranged by the matriarch of the family, a role she filled for their house since her mother's passing, though royal marriages were an exception.

"Rise," she commanded as he gained his feet. Her guards remained farther back within the stable, gifting them a brief period alone before the others arrived.

"You came to see me off?" he asked, a wane smile passing his lips.

"Is it not within my purview to see to the readiness of my charges?" she challenged, lifting an admonishing brow.

"I yield." He smiled, lifting his open hands in surrender.

"Very wise, good sir. Remember that while the enemy flees in terror before you, yet you tremble before *me*." She poked his chest.

"You have me there." He shrugged, confessing that truth. He was hopelessly smitten, beguiled by her beauty, but most of all her strength and intellect. She had a way of seeing through any facade, stripping men bare, revealing their thoughts. Even now she noticed his dour mood that he tried concealing with an easy smile, plagued by all that his father revealed. He should be humbled yet proud of his Kalinian heritage, but his thoughts were on his other lineage. He was Tyro's grandson, that dark truth consuming him. All he had done up to that moment, all that he sacrificed in the defense of Corell and Torry North, could never cleanse the stain of his birth. When Corry learned the truth, would she still look at him as she does now? How could she? He was Tyro's spawn.

"What troubles you?" she asked, seeing through his false smile.

He paused, wary of the thin ice upon which he stood. He could not divulge one part of what his father said without her inquiring further, quickly unraveling his entire story. The whole tale was interconnected, and he only heard it himself that morn. "I spoke with my father earlier." He sighed, his blue eyes betraying him.

"Whatever you spoke of seems to have grieved you. What was it concerning?" she asked, touching a hand to his cheek.

"I…" He turned away, letting her hand fall, staring off in the distance. How could he answer without the whole awful truth spilling out before he was to depart? "Corry…" He turned his eyes back to hers. "I can't tell you, not now. Please, let me tell you when I return, when I am ready," he pleaded, the hurt in his eyes rending her heart.

Whatever Jonas told him had broken his spirit. She never saw him like this, for it was so unlike his nature. She wanted nothing more than to take him in her arms and kiss away his sorrows. She again touched his face, losing herself in his sea blue eyes. "I love you," she said, her voice but a whisper, before drowning in the swirling wind of those airy heights.

"And I you, remember that when I tell you what troubles me."

"There is nothing you can ever say to quell our love," she reassured, caressing his cheek.

"No matter what may come, never doubt my love or my loyalty. To you and your family I am pledged, and so shall serve until my dying breath. Your house owns my loyalty, and you my heart, you and no other," he affirmed.

His strange affirmation took her aback, piquing her curiosity on what his father had revealed.

Terin noticed her apprehension with his odd behavior and resolved to forsake his doubts and self-pity. Taking a deep breath, he straightened his back, regarding her proudly. He vowed then and there to venture to Yatin and aid Prince Lorn to his upmost, resolving to turn back the gargoyle invasion and return Lorn to Torry North, where he would sit the throne and claim his kingship. Terin did not know Yah, the god of his Kalinian ancestors, but if he quieted his heart, he could almost feel an omnipotent pull guiding his spirit. Was this strange pull the ancient deity steering his path? Were the inclinations always guiding his character actually Yah directing his choices? He reflected on the solace he felt whenever he followed this path and the inner conflict when he did not. He thought it was the sword that guided his hand, and it was to an extent, but might it not be more than that? Was not the sword a divine gift from Yah to the mortal realms? Was it not intended for the same purpose as the House of Kal? His father's words rang true when he quieted his mind to listen. Only then could he hear Yah whisper to his heart, revealing his true purpose. The line of Kal ended with his father and himself, and they were not meant to rule or establish kingdoms as the heirs of Kal. Nor were they the heirs of Tyro and his dark realm. They were born to one purpose, to protect the realms of men from the gargoyles. No one ever need know his heritage, for he would never claim it. He would simply do his duty, destroy the gargoyles, and return to the woman he loved.

"Take heart, Corry. I will shield your brother from whatever harm may come his way and return to Corell, and to you."

"I know you will return to me, for if not, I will haunt you for all eternity, in this life and any that follow. Am I understood, Terin Caleph?"

"Yes, Highness." He smiled, taking her in his arms. There upon the airy heights of Corell, they kissed, desperate yet gentle and all-consuming.

*****

Kato paused at the stable entryway, observing Terin and the princess for a time, before leading his mount onto the open platform. He had grown accustomed to the great warbird, its gentle nature suited to one unfamiliar to riding such wondrous beasts. Commander Valen picked out the bird specifically for Kato, for its unusual acceptance of new riders, contrasting the surly nature of its brethren. He put the beast to good use after the siege was lifted, hunting down retreating gargoyles across the surrounding lands, often letting a trained rider take the reins, freeing him to shoot with more accuracy.

Lucas followed Kato, leading his magantor onto the platform. Torg assigned the Torry Elite to accompany them on this journey, adding the fiercest member of the Torry Elite to Terin's sword and Kato's gun. Together they would make a very small but very deadly contingent that Lorn would make good use of.

"Highness, Terin," Kato greeted, stepping near.

"I loathe to see you go but am glad that you shall be at Terin's side," Corry said, touching a hand to Kato's check.

"I will see him safely to your brother and safely back." Kato's easy smile assuaged her heart.

"You are a man of his word, Kato. You bring honor to your name," she said before shifting her gaze to Lucas, who stood farther back.

"Princess." Lucas bowed, his mop of brown hair swirling in the wind. He was of a height to Terin, thick necked with light brown eyes and a heavily muscled frame.

"Master Vantel speaks well of you, Lucas. I am comforted that you shall accompany them on this perilous journey." Corry left unsaid that she asked Torg for his finest warrior to aid Terin, and he named Lucas.

"It is my duty and privilege," Lucas affirmed, his baritone voice and thick neck matching his rugged stature. It was as if he were a younger Torg. He was by far the toughest Elite Terin had engaged in hand-to-hand combat, besting him repeatedly in the training pit, though Terin managed his share of wins, few they may be.

Cronus, Galen, Leanna, and Squid soon joined them, each bidding their farewells before taking flight. Cronus embraced his wife, hugging her fiercely before climbing into the saddle, his great avian shifting, its talons scrapping the floor of the platform. Cronus regarded her with pained green eyes, loathing their parting once again.

Squid spoke briefly with Terin, drawing him away from the others before gaining the mount he shared with Galen. Within moments they were off, soaring through the heavens, journeying southwest before disappearing over the horizon.

Kato and Lucas followed, taking to the sky as Terin climbed into the saddle, his eyes catching Corry's, the sun playing cruelly upon her moistened cheeks, betraying her tears. Wind Racer strutted along the platform, his massive wings outstretched, bounding off the stone lip, briefly slipping from sight before gaining lift, soaring over the battlements and beyond.

Corry and Leanna stood silently, watching as the men they loved took flight, following their retreating forms across the morning sky, disappearing into the lonesome horizon.

CHAPTER
3

Tenin Harbor

Ben Thorton sat astride a spirited brown ocran, his large hands resting upon the pommel, his blue eyes surveying the endless columns of captives shuffling along the wharves. He regarded the pitiful dregs with cold indifference, observing the sullen faces and shattered spirits of the Yatin prisoners, slavers herding them to the waiting ships. They were a collage of captive warriors and citizens, the former still clad in the purple tunics of the harbor garrison. Nearly every able-bodied male under the age of forty was collected after the harbor's surrender, as per the agreement of submission that spared the city total destruction. 'Twas common Benotrist practice to enslave entire populations of resisting cities. Commander Torab's 2nd Gargoyle Legion laid siege to Tenin Harbor for four moons, as Admiral Mulsen crushed the Yatin 1st and 2nd Fleets at Cull's Arc just north along the coast, the victory completing the city's encirclement by land and sea. Torab struggled mightily restraining his gargoyle legion as the siege progressed but was pressed by his Benotrist allies to capture the city intact, its large population a valuable commodity if taken alive. The most profitable slave trading came from seizing a port city, where the slaves were taken close to shore and quickly transported to market rather than collecting them from sources inland, where disease and arduous transport thinned the stock. Standard Benotrist practice was to first gather young males, removing them from captured cities before continuing with less aggressive elements of the population. Soon, the slavers would cull a sizable percentage from the women and children of Tenin, slowly reducing the native population to the elderly and select women and female children, leaving the city open for eventual Benotrist migration.

"Our work here appears done," Nels Draken said, sitting astride a green mare, beside him. They ventured here from Telfer, to oversee the siege of the Yatin port and investigate the dangerously independent Admiral Mulsen, who instigated the Yatin invasion long before the emperor desired, forging the orders of the gargoyle general, in order to hasten the attack. Thorton's arrival at the siege proved fortuitus to the Benotrist-gargoyle forces as he systematically leveled several redoubts guarding the city, his powerful rifle blasting large holes in the thick stone. Eventually, the garrison submitted, dooming much of its populace to ignominious slavery. They retained the harbor magistrate and bureaucracy to oversee the port's occupation, but even these vestiges of Yatin influence would eventually be swept away.

"We're not done just yet," Thorton snorted, his narrow gaze sweeping the expanse of the Grand Horn, where sails of the Benotrist 5th and 7th Fleets dotted its surface. Tenin Harbor was constructed upon the western tip of a peninsula, jutting prominently into the Tenin Bay, with the Tenia River running along its southern edge. The Grand Horn ran along the city's northern edge, a small gulf that cut into the peninsula, separating the land mass in the center of the bay from those to either flank. From above, the land appeared as three fingers converging upon the bay, with Tenin Harbor resting at the tip of the center finger. The outer fingers ended farther west of the center, enveloping the entrance of the bay. The Yatins built smaller redoubts upon each of the outer fingers, guarding the mouth of the bay. The southern finger ran along the southern bank of the Tenia River, ending at Caras Point, where a large watchtower presided, with a sturdy curtain wall surrounding it. The northern finger, which was separated from Tenin Peninsula by the Grand Horn, ended at North Point, where a far larger fortress guarded the northern mouth of the bay, with a series of turrets and curtain walls with massive bulwarks lining its upper battlements. Thorton could see the standard of the 2nd Gargoyle Legion, two black clashing fists upon a field of white, blowing above the highest tower of North Point, across the Grand

Horn. The 2ⁿᵈ Legion stormed both Caras and North Point by force, putting their populace to the sword. The garrison of Tenin could hear the screams of their countrymen echoing over the waves of the Grand Horn and the waters of the lower Tenia. The gargoyles brought the survivors to the upper battlements of either fortress and along the shores opposite the city, mutilating their victims with cruel creativity, the barbarity unnerving the garrison, hastening its capitulation.

Thorton shook his head at the atrocities these primitive people committed against each other. A softer head and weak heart would shrivel at the sight, applying modern sensibilities to the conditions these people lived, insisting to interject on behalf of the downtrodden. He knew that lasting peace would only come about when one realm violently overthrew all others, bringing Arax under one rule. Then, and only then, could mercy and rule of law be slowly implemented. Civilization was oft a painful and cruel progression, before leading to a better world. Thorton fully expected Space Fleet to find them at some point, and Arax would be better served if it was ruled by one voice in such negotiations. Any division would be exploited by Earth's powerful bureaucracies, which were accountable to no one but mindless bean counters in Brussels. He explained all this to Tyro, regaling the despot with tales of his home world. He imagined the surprise the Earth directorate would experience when they discovered this world teeming with *human* life, the first of its kind outside of Solar System Prime, other than the countless planets that they terraformed.

"What else have we to do? The harbor is pacified," Nels pointed out.

"Matters that are not in your purview, Nels," Ben reiterated, just as he had done for the last eleven days whenever Draken pressed to leave Tenin to join the battle at Mosar. Thorton received word from the emperor to await Regula at Tenin. Tyro's vice regent had just arrived that morn, awaiting him at the City Forum, where Admiral Mulsen and General Torab established a joint command post, with the council of Tenin overseeing the operation of the city.

"Then another night of celebration it is. I shall inform the others," Nels conceded, happy to make the most of their delayed departure. The others would be glad to partake of wine, women, and song for one more night. The men in question were the members of Tyro's Elite accompanying them on this campaign. There were twelve at the outset, but three perished at Telfer.

"No drinking after sundown. I want everyone sober if we leave at sunup," Ben said, spoiling Nels's plan.

"We are leaving then?" he asked, confused with Ben's answer.

"Maybe. Maybe not," Ben Thorton said, observing a rich litter drawing near along the wharves, carried by eight young male slaves in brief livery, with iron collars fastened about their necks. They were slight of build, chosen more for their aesthetic attributes than brawn. Atop the open litter was a richly adorned merchant in long burgundy robes. With various assorted jewelry adorning his neck and arms. His long auburn hair was woven in braids, draping his shoulders in a fashion no male should wear. Thorton noticed another slave walking alongside the litter, fanning his master. Thorton shook his head for it was winter, though a rather warm winter day with the sun bearing down overhead.

"Make way! Make way!" two heavily armed warriors shouted, preceding the merchant's entourage, clearing their path, making their way toward Ben and Nels.

"Hail Thorton," the merchant called out as his litter bearers halted.

"Well, you know my name. What's yours?" Thorton scowled.

"I am Atar Rorn!" The man's face fell, insulted that he was unknown to the Earther.

"Never heard of you," Ben said dryly, unimpressed.

"I am third councilor of Tinsan Province!" he declared indignantly as if to impress upon them his importance.

"Still never heard of you," Thorton said, his patience wearing thin.

"I know of you," Nels said with that practiced smile he oft used to ingratiate himself. "The House of Rorn's reputation extends as far as Tro. You are merchant house, I believe?" Nels asked.

"I participate in the trade of various goods," Atar conceded. "And I know of you, Nels Draken. I recall your recent visit to Tinsay, where one of my stewards received you at the city magistrate. You were on urgent business of the throne," Atar said, regarding his return from Molten Isle, where he encountered Raven after his rescue of the princess.

"What do you want, Rorn? We've more pressing matters to attend," Thorton growled.

"Very well," Atar smoothed the folds of his robes after stepping down from his litter, rising up to his full height, which was two heads shorter than Thorton. "I was informed by General Torab that I cannot claim any slaves taken in the Yatin Campaign until they are shipped to Tinsay."

"General Torab's instructions came from me. No Yatin captives are to be processed for private sale until removed from occupied territory by military authority," Thorton stated.

"I was granted exclusive slaver rights to the Tenin territory by Admiral Mulsen! He guaranteed me as many captives as my ships could carry at a cost of twenty certras per head!" Atar proclaimed.

"This is a war zone, not a marketplace, Rorn. Whatever assurances Mulsen made to you do not override *my* authority!" Thorton said, leaning forward in the saddle, his menacing stare unnerving the merchant.

"But…but I've brought half my merchant fleet with me, fourteen vessels patiently awaiting cargo. If I return empty-handed, I shall suffer grievance financial ruin," Atar pleaded, withering under Thorton's gaze. "The cost of the merchandise will triple once it reaches Tinsay."

"And if I allow you to fill your ships with Yatin cargo, the other Benotrist slavers would protest vehemently at such favoritism. Admiral Mulsen should've thought of that before he made that offer, or did you offer something else in return?" Thorton asked, knowing Mulsen likely used merchant houses like Rorn's to lobby for his war plans at court.

Atar paled, his guilt written clear upon his feminine face. He fumed at the injustice of it all. Promises were made and political capital spent to support this campaign, and now this Earther meant to ruin his endeavors, and there was naught he could do about it.

The Earther was second among Tyro's Elite and could kill him for any infraction, proven or insinuated. But men like Atar were not oft refused, and when they were, their passions overtook reason.

"What gives you authority to make such decrees!" he snapped, realizing he overstepped.

"Do you care to find out?" Ben asked calmly, resting his hand on his holstered pistol.

"My apologies, Emperor's Elite," Atar quickly corrected, backing a step.

"Accepted." Thorton moved his gun hand back to the pommel of his saddle. "My declaration was made for the good of the empire. To grant preferential treatment to one citizen over another corrupts the rule of law that binds the divergent elements of the realm. If I allow you to profit from this campaign over your fellow merchants, they will protest that unfairness to the emperor. Do you wish the emperor to investigate how you won favor with Admiral Mulsen?"

Atar again paled, understanding the cliff he trapped himself upon. Perhaps Thorton's even hand wasn't completely to his detriment. Nothing good would come of the emperor discovering Mulsen's subterfuge, which would implicate him as well, but the cost of this venture was devastating to his margin. "You are very wise," Atar conceded.

"Do not worry yourself, Rorn, for your economic ruin doesn't serve the empire's interest either. You may fill *two* of your ships with Yatin slaves, even taking your pick of the lot. That should more than cover your expenses on this venture."

"You are most gracious," Atar swallowed nervously.

"I think I am, Rorn. I could've arrested you for collusion in compromising an imperial military campaign. I suggest you fill your two ships and leave. I want your fleet gone by sundown."

"Very well." Atar snapped his fingers, signaling his litter bearers forth as he turned to leave.

"And, Rorn," Thorton said as the merchant turned back, his wary gaze regarding him with apprehension. "You will of course withdraw your support for Admiral Mulsen and his subsidiaries. In fact, you will not speak with him ever again."

"Of course." Atar Rorn bowed, climbing into his litter, his slaves carrying him away.

"You have a way with people, Thorton," Nels snickered as Atar's entourage moved off along the wharf. "You remind me of Raven in that regard, though your speech is far more refined."

"Don't ever compare me to Raven." Ben scowled.

"Do you hate him that much?" Nels asked curiously.

"I don't hate Raven. Hate breeds irrational thoughts. When it comes to killing men, cold logic trumps emotion. As far as Raven is concerned, we are divided by the choices we each have made. He made a choice long ago that destroyed any kinship between us. I made a choice to leave his company upon arriving on your world. I made a choice to pledge my gun arm to Tyro. Raven, in turn, made a choice to dishonor Tyro's hospitality on his visit to Fera. Therein lies the chasm between us. Emotions have no place in my heart as far as Raven is concerned."

"Emotions cannot be ignored, only buried where they fester." Nels shrugged.

Thorton gave him a look, before they rode off to the city forum.

*****

General Torab glowered as Admiral Mulsen entered the inner sanctum of the city forum. Torab despised Mulsen's arrogance, bristling at his willingness to take full credit for the capture of Tenin. He was audacious enough to claim General Yonig's victories at Salamin and Telfer for his own. Mulsen was also human, another shortcoming to the eyes of a gargoyle of Torab's prejudice. Torab was also fiercely loyal to his own commander, Yonig, knowing he was responsible for their harvest of victory.

"Hail, Torab!" Mulsen greeted, passing through the archway, entering the chamber where Regula and Torab awaited, with a dark-haired harbor official trailing him. Mulsen swept into their midst with practiced flare, his red cape swirling in his wake, with the sigil of the 5th Fleet, a golden ship sewn boldly in its rich folds. It was another irksome trait of the Benotrist admiral to adorn himself with a cape bearing his fleet's sigil, an adornment his fellow admirals had the good taste not to follow.

"Admiral Mulsen," Regula greeted him formally, standing before a large map table in the chamber's center, his face alit by the lanterns hanging from the domed ceiling.

"What's he doing here?" Torab hissed, pointing a clawed digit at the Yatin official standing behind him, with his head bowed.

"Ah, this is Councilor Hattis of the Tenin council. I have chosen him as my personal attendant during my stay in their fair city. Hattis, my cape!" Mulsen commanded, the fellow untying the article and folding it neatly, setting it aside, hiding his shame with a mask of indifference. This was clearly another demonstration of Mulsen to humiliate the ruling oligarchs of Tenin, making one of their councilors his attendant.

"Send him away!" Regula ordered, a strategy forum no place for a captured foe to listen in on. The fact that Mulsen thought nothing of it demonstrated either his arrogance or incompetence.

"Of course, Lord Regula, that was my intention before we began to discuss delicate matters. Hattis, be a good servant and wait for me at the end of the corridor. There is a comfortable place to kneel on the stone floor there." Mulsen smiled wickedly as the Yatin official bowed and withdrew. Once the fellow stepped without, Mulsen turned back to his gargoyle associates. "Now, my Lord Regula, what brings your eminence to this fair port? I assume it is to appraise the emperor of our victories and to speed the reinforcements needed to quickly conclude this campaign?" Mulsen decided to play offense, pushing back the apprehension gnawing in the back of his mind on Regula's purpose here. As vice regent of the empire, Lord Regula rarely ventured far from Tyro's side.

"You don't lack for arrogance, I'll give you that," Ben Thorton said, stepping from the shadows along the side of the chamber off his right, the large Earther unsettling Mulsen's calm facade.

"Emperor's Elite," Mulsen greeted, visibly shaken by his presence.

"The emperor sent me to oversee your campaign. He is pleased with our military successes, but certain irregularities have come to his attention," Regula stated.

"Irregularities?" Mulsen lifted a dark brow, his narrow face drawing taut.

"It seems General Yonig's orders were altered, causing him to initiate the Yatin invasion a full fortnight before the time of the emperor's choosing. Though Yonig's invasion took the Yatins by surprise, the emperor ordered our legions to wait until the princess was secured from her pirate captors. On this matter, he is most… displeased," Regula said, his studious red eyes regarding the nervous admiral.

"Do I stand accused?" Mulsen asked, indignant at the insinuation.

"Do you?" Thorton asked bluntly. "Why don't you tell us what you did exactly."

Torab glared at Mulsen, his red eyes alit with building fury, the realization of Mulsen's manipulation of Yonig's orders dawning on him. "You initiated the invasion before the emperor commanded? You have betrayed us!" Torab hissed.

Mulsen flinched, backing a step, half expecting Torab to climb over the table and assail him.

"I make no such confession," Mulsen denied the charge, though none believed him. "But if someone had, then they have done the empire a great service. The longer our legions were positioned along the border, the Yatins would likely have detected them, discerning our intent. We would have lost the element of surprise. Look at the end result. We have exceeded all expectations!" he pleaded, turning his desperate gaze to Regula. "The emperor *must* recognize our success and reinforce our efforts."

"Unfortunately, we cannot commit any additional resources to the Yatin Campaign at this time. The emperor has shifted the bulk of our reserves to our eastern campaign. Morac's legions have slain King Lore and the 5th Torry Army upon the plain of Kregmarin. Even as we speak, they are placing siege upon Corell," Regula informed them.

"The Torry king is deadsss?" Torab asked, pleased by the news.

"He is, and the Torry Realms soon with him, which lessens the urgency with the Yatin Campaign. With the Torry Realms conquered, the Yatins will soon follow. Their fall is now inevitable. As such, you will have to make do with the forces currently allotted you," Regula said.

"Without reinforcements, our invasion will lose momentum! Especially if the Torry southern armies intercede. We must finish Yatin quickly before the Torries decide to do so!" Mulsen pleaded.

"Maybe you should've thought of that before initiating the invasion, Admiral. That's why strategic decisions are made at the highest levels, where all theaters of operations are considered. This war is larger than your campaign," Thorton said, taking a seat, planting his feet atop the table.

Mulsen regarded him carefully, the Earther's relaxed state taking him off guard. Was it a ruse to put him at ease before killing him, or was the Earther simply disrespectful of this forum?

"Even if the Torries intercede on the Yatins' behalf, they would compromise their southern flank, where the Macon Empire threatens. Yonig has taken Telfer, and each of you has taken Tenin. You have also destroyed two of three Yatin Fleets at Cull's Arc. You have sufficient forces to complete your conquest, Admiral. Thorton will return to the front and oversee Yonig's attack on the Yatin capital. I shall join you at sea, Admiral. We shall advance to Faust, where the Yatin 3rd Fleet is moored," Regula said.

"Which you would've already accomplished had you not ordered Torab here, to stand down when he planned to storm Tenin at the start of the siege. Instead, you spent four moons waiting for Tenin to surrender. Why is that, Admiral?" Thorton asked, crossing his thick arms over his chest, leaning back in his chair without a care in the world. "It didn't have anything to do with your arrangements with the Tinsay slaver guilds to capture the harbor intact and the people with it, did it?"

And there it was, the hint of Mulsen's personal gain in this campaign. General Torab was on the verge of apoplexy, his red eyes bulging from his skull.

"Now, Admiral, do I need to investigate the ledgers of every Tinsan merchant to find evidence of your profiteering, or can we simply move on with conducting this campaign and forget your conflicting interests? Besides, as far as the admiralty and our people are concerned, you are a great hero. Executing you for suspicion of treason wouldn't serve the empire's interests." Thorton shrugged, his reassurances failing to calm Mulsen's racing heart.

"See to your fleet, Admiral. We sail on my order," Regula dismissed Mulsen.

Thorton's blue eyes followed the humbled admiral out the chamber before gaining his feet to address the gargoyle lord. "Do you need any of my men for your detail?" he asked Regula.

"I have thirty members of the Imperial Elite accompanying me. They shall suffice should Admiral Mulsen have other plans. When shall you depart?" Regula asked.

"We ride out come sunup," Ben said, placing his black Stetson on his head before stepping without, leaving the two gargoyles alone in the chamber.

"The admiral mustsss be punished!" General Torab fumed, finally able to vent his fury.

"I shall deal with our ambitious admiral, General. You, however, are to oversee the transition of this harbor to Benotrist control. For that task, you will not need all of your legion. Dispatch twenty telnics to support General Yonig at Mosar," Regula commanded, dismissing Torab.

*****

"That was quick." Nels Draken smirked, greeting Ben Thorton at the base of the city forum. The former free sword handed Thorton the reins to his mount as several passersby parted, wary of the large Earther.

"We are done here. We leave in the morning, so tell the men to ready their magantors," Ben said, mounting his ocran. The issue with their magantors was their most difficult obstacle since their losses at Telfer. Thorton sent their few surviving warbirds to Tinsay to acquire new magantors, ferrying them to Tenin. This forced Thorton and the others to reach Tenin by ocran, greatly slowing their pace. Then they spent the better part of the past twenty days bonding with their new mounts.

"I already sent them to the magantor pens to see it done."

"Good work," Ben said, easing his ocran onto the street.

"There is something I need to show before we leave." Draken smiled.

"Make it quick."

*****

The flames swirled above the basin torches, alighting the vast chamber in flickering light. The shifting flames revealed the girl's figure as she moved across the floor, her long white gown clinging desperately to her achingly feminine figure, its skirts dropping freely below her hips, flowing as she danced. Her dark eyes swept the gathering crowd surrounding the center floor, where she performed, the sheen of her black hair reflecting the shifting light. She paused, stopping suddenly in the center of the floor, capturing every eye awaiting her next movement with anticipation. The slightest smile curved the corners of her lips as she began to sing, her sweetly feminine voice carrying in the still air.

"What do you think?" Nels asked, standing in the shadows of the chamber. He knew the girl was beautiful and graceful but was curious if her voice was enough to stir his comrade's cold heart. Thorton exhibited little interest in romantic pursuits, leading some to wonder if he was so inclined, but Nels knew he mourned a lost love that he refused to speak of, a girl whose voice stirred in him great passion. He learned that Ben blamed Raven for her loss, that tragedy explaining his animosity toward his old friend.

Ben Thorton regarded the girl as she again moved across the floor, her silken voice rising and falling as she glided, her achingly feminine form stirring memories long buried.

"I asked what you thought?" Nels asked again.

"Ask how much she costs," he said, his eyes narrowed, following her across the floor.

"Cost?" Nels made a face. "She is not a slave. Her father is the proprietor of this theater. She sings because it pleases her, not because she is bound to."

"Is she Yatin?"

"Well…yes, I believe so," Nels sounded uncertain.

"Then she is subject to my governing authority. Bring her over here!" he ordered.

"Verry well." Nels sighed, pushing through the crowd, before stepping onto the center floor, causing a chorus of protests from the crowd. Two guards in light mail over brown tunics stepped forth to intercede but yielded upon seeing the sigil of Tyro's Elite emblazoned upon the chest of Nels's mail, a sword and whip dividing a sun and moon. The crowd quickly grew quiet. Most were Benotrist sailors and merchants, gathering in the establishment for wine and entertainment, but even those in a drunken stupor were able to recognize their Emperor's Elite.

The girl stopped her performance, backing a step as Nels strode forth, his black cloak swirling in his wake. Her eyes drew desperately wide beholding his stern countenance.

"Have I offended?" she asked, with as much steel in her voice as she could muster.

A stick-thin silver-haired man hurried forth, stepping between them. "What is this concerning, sir?" the man asked in a panicked voice.

"Does she belong to you?" Nels asked.

"Belong? She is my daughter," he explained, taken aback by the question.

"Emperor's Elite Thorton demands your audience, come!" Nels stepped aside, waving an open hand to where Thorton stood along the side wall.

The man swallowed past the lump growing in his throat before taking a step.

"Her too." Nels pointed at the girl.

The man froze, fear creeping further along his spine, wondering for what purpose they required his daughter.

"Father, it is no trouble." The girl touched a hand to his arm before advancing toward Thorton, steeling her nerves, her head held high. Her courage quickly waned nearing the towering Earther, the crowd parting as they passed. She stopped before him, craning her neck to meet his piercing gaze.

Thorton examined her at length, his eyes following the contours of her face. She possessed high cheekbones and expressive large dark-gray eyes that bespoke a deeper intelligence, staring back at him through her thick lashes. Her light olive skin was without blemish and shone as the torchlight played off her flush cheeks. He noted the swell of her bosom lifting the top of her bodice. She was breathtaking, her beauty matching the sound of her voice. Her singing reminded him of another woman, of memories long buried, of a voice that still haunted his dreams.

"How old are you, girl?" he asked.

"This is my nineteenth winter," she said.

"Has my daughter offended you, sir? Has she broken one of the new laws that we are unaware? There are so many that if so, I deeply apologize," her father nervously explained.

"Name your price?" Thorton asked, his blue eyes fixed to the girl's gray.

"Price? I do not understand," the fellow stammered.

"Your daughter. Name her price!" he repeated.

"But…she is free. Admiral Mulsen granted the artisan guilds protection to preserve the culture of our fair city, where my theater and house so serve."

"I know what Mulsen promised, but his words hold little worth to the new governor the emperor is sending to oversee this city. You are chattel unless granted protection by an authority far higher than our good admiral. Now name your price, and I will guarantee your house protection."

"But she is free," he again pleaded.

"I can claim her as contraband, as well as yourself, your family, and all those you employ," Ben threatened.

"What you ask, I cannot give," her father bravely said, tears squeezing from his eyes.

"I'll go with you!" the girl cried. "But spare my family."

"No, Ella!" her father implored.

Thorton regarded her, impressed with her willingness to sacrifice herself to save her family. He expected much less from a woman but reminded himself that she had little choice, for either way her fate was sealed. She had more to gain by appearing noble, yet she was intelligent enough to recognize it as such.

"A wise choice, girl. I will inform General Torab that your family is under imperial protection and will be removed to Tinsay Harbor. Bring her!" he told Nels, jerking a thumb toward the girl before turning to leave.

"Tinsay?" the man said, wondering why they would be uprooted if they were under imperial protection.

Thorton turned back, suddenly doubting the man's intelligence, hoping his daughter didn't inherit his stupidity. "Do you truly believe any of your people are safe in this fallen city?"

"I…" He meant to speak, but the words wouldn't come.

"I'll arrange safe passage for you and your kin. Don't worry about your daughter. She'll be safer with me than with you."

Gregok

"*Blue sixty-two! Blue sixty-two!*" Lorken shouted, peeking above the head of his center, his eyes following the safety cheating close to the line, leaving Orlom in single coverage along the right seam. A sea of simian faces circled the field, cheering from the viewing stands to his left and jeering along the ones to his right. Raven's eyes met his across the deadly space between them, with a line of gorilla warriors separating them, clad in matching leather shirts and trousers, with thick polished helms in opposing black and silver.

"*Set! Hike!*" Lorken took the snap from center, rolling to his right as the apes forming his offensive line yielded to Argos's push up the middle. Lorken released the ball as Argos's hands grasped empty air, his fingertips grazing Lorken's left arm as he slipped free. The crowd to his left cheered, the ball dropping into Orlom's grasp at midfield, before the cornerback tackled the young gorilla.

"First down!" a referee declared, clad in green. The gorilla official held his fist clenched into his chest, indicating a completed pass, before extending an arm toward the far end zone, indicating a first down.

General Matuzak looked on from his viewing box, amid the near stands along midfield, a wide grin stretching the breadth of his broad face, enjoying the game his nation had come to love and embrace. Football might've originated on Earth, but the apes considered the game their own after the Earthers introduced the sport to their ape allies after the conclusion of the Ape Revolution. The apes took such a liking to the game that leagues quickly formed throughout the empire.

"Ah! Another mighty feat by your groom, lass," the ape general's voice boomed at Jenna, sitting nervously beside him, her small hands folded in her lap, twisting the folds of her emerald gown between her fingers. She took little solace in her royal treatment as she sat the position of honor beside Matuzak. Few humans were liked, let alone regarded so highly. Only the Earthers held the apes' trust, and as Lorken's bride, Jenna was received by all with kinship. Despite such kind treatment, she could think of nothing but the peril her husband was in, playing this barbaric sport. Lorken was driven into the ground countless times throughout the contest, forcing her to cover her eyes until he emerged from the pile of bodies lying atop him. He and Raven were asked to partake in the game upon their arrival at Gregok, each placed upon opposing teams, representing the Manglar and Volmar tribes. From afar, she could see Raven gathering his teammates in a circle, appearing quite animated, though she couldn't make out the words.

"Blast it, Krink! Can't you cover Orlom for three seconds?" Argos berated the lanky cornerback, visibly upset with his teammate.

"That was more than three seconds, Arg. Lorken escaped the pocket again. Even I can't cover Orlom by myself longer than that!" Krink shot back, catching his breath, resting his furry hands on his knees.

"Listen, fellas, we have the lead, and time is running out." Raven looked over to the timekeeper along the sidelines, who controlled the sand pouring through the glass. It was a primitive but uniform means of pacing the game. He wondered if Brokov could manufacture some timepieces for the apes to better regulate the games. He shook the thought from his mind, knowing Brokov would only berate him for suggesting it for such a childish use.

"Goril, stay back and help Krink with Orlom," Raven told the free safety, who ventured too close to the line on the previous play. "Gullar, cheat close to the line *before* the snap, then roll back to cover the deep middle. The ball is going to your guy Tormack," Raven warned the right corner.

"How do you know?" several chorused the same question.

"Lorken always follows up that last play with this one, if the secondary lines up the way I told you. Arg! Just flush him from the pocket."

*****

Lorken stepped up to the line, surveying the field before taking the snap. The free safety remained back, cheating closer to Orlom's side. The strong safety drifted closer to the line before pulling back to the deep middle.

"*Blue alpha seven!*" he called the audible. "*Set! Hike! Hike!*" Lorken took the snap as Argos crashed the right A gap, tossing the center and guard aside, as Lorken rolled left, escaping the rush, spying his receiver running down the left seam. He caught sight of Raven sweeping around the left tackle, blocking his escape. He paused briefly to set his feet and throw over Raven's outstretched hands, when a massive weight struck his back, Argos driving him into the ground, while stripping the ball from his grasp. Lorken grunted, buried under Argos's massive bulk, reaching in vain for the loose football, before Raven dove upon it. A chorus of boos echoed along the near side crowd, voicing their displeasure. Thunderous cheers sounded along the opposite side as Raven's fumble recovery secured the victory for the Manglar Tribe. Horns sounded as Raven came to his feet, marking the end of the game.

"Ughhh," Lorken moaned as Argos climbed off him, before lifting him to his feet. He stood on wobbly legs, his breaths coming slow and labored, while thousands of gorillas poured onto the field from the victors' side.

"You all right?" Raven asked as dozens of gorillas gathered near, slapping him on the back, obvious members of the Manglar Tribe celebrating their triumph.

"I should've known," he wheezed, shaking his head for not realizing that Raven read the play.

"Yeah, you should've known when we beat you every day in practice back in the academy whenever you ran those plays together,"

Raven recalled the glory of their youth when he was the starting middle linebacker and Lorken the quarterback.

"Nice hit, big guy," Lorken said as Argos stood at his side, his massive arms crossed over his chest, ignoring the growing crowd surrounding him, lauding his great play.

"It felt good," Argos grunted, basking in the glory of his triumph.

"My back would disagree with you." Lorken groaned, running his hand over his aching spine.

The sea of excited faces quickly parted, making way for General Matuzak, his wide boots imprinting the soil as he strode forth. Even among his fellow apes, his immense size stood out, rivaled only by Argos's massive frame. Matuzak's black fur matched his linen shirt and loose trousers. A broad sword rode his left hip, resting in a silver scabbard, affixed to a thick belt stretched around his muscled girth. He stood eye level with Raven, with wide-set brown eyes and flaring nostrils. His incisors protruded prominently below his dark purple lips. His brisk pace left his guards trailing behind, with Jenna struggling to keep up, holding the skirt of her gown as she walked.

"Well done, my boys!" Matuzak's booming voice thundered as he drew near, setting a heavy furry hand to Raven and Lorken's shoulders, Argos standing opposite him. "The Manglars will celebrate this victory for some time. I wish my gorillas could test their skills against other realms, but our Araxan brothers take no interest in it."

"That is a sign of their weakness, General. The Earthers are the only humans brave enough to step on a playing field with us!" Argos growled proudly, slapping Lorken on the back, the blow nearly knocking him from his feet.

"More like the only ones stupid enough." Lorken shook his head.

"Bah! You've brains enough to woo this lovely lass, my boy," the general regarded Jenna with a toothy grin.

"You got me there." Lorken shrugged, smiling proudly at his beautiful wife.

"Just use your brain a little more the next time you take the field, and you might win," Matuzak said.

"Brains won't help him any, General," Raven said. "It's like I always say, defense wins championships."

"According to the manuals you left us, that phrase goes back five hundred years." Matuzak called out Raven for not only stating the obvious but claiming credit for the age-old idiom.

"You don't say. Well, who knew." Raven shrugged.

"Yeah, who knew?" Lorken rolled his eyes.

"Bah! Caught you in another fib!" Matuzak ruffled Raven's short hair as if he were a boy. Raven would've walloped anyone else for such a gesture but simply shrugged, allowing Matuzak such liberty. He respected the general deeply, more so than anyone he ever met, save for his father, whom the general reminded him of in so many ways. Raven received the gesture with pride, like a strong man, who even in his prime was like a boy in his father's presence.

"Come, my friends. Food and celebration await us in the palace. We have much to discuss, and I shall reveal why I sent Argos across Arax to fetch you," Matuzak said, waving them off the field.

*****

Cheer, cheer for old Gregok.
Wake up the echoes, cheering his name.
Send a volley cheer on high.
Shake down the thunder from the sky...

Raven and Lorken shook their heads as hundreds of gorillas filled the great hall of the palace, singing a bastardized version of the Notre Dame fight song, their voices sounding off the green walls in drunken revery. The evening found them seated at the high table with Jenna, as honored guests of General Matuzak. They marveled at the spectacle as hundreds of apes sang their own version of the song, replacing the tittle with the name of their revered capital fortress. Of all the species and peoples of Arax, the apes were the most imitative, finding foreign ideals, music, or inventions and claiming them as their own. Whereas most Araxans looked upon the Earthers with wary suspicion, the apes found them rather fascinating. When they first arrived upon Arax, the Earthers quickly embroiled themselves into the politics of the Ape Coast, where most of the ports of call were occupied by vassals of the Casian Federation, the merchant empire that controlled most of the sea-lanes of southeastern Arax. The Casians employed large standing armies of mercenary apes and humans to protect their interests, while the ape mainland was hopelessly divided between the twenty-seven separate tribes of the Ape Federation and the six mountain tribes in the southeast that hadn't joined the federation. Though some apes attempted to unite the tribes and cast the invaders from their shores, all failed until Matuzak. The boisterous, charismatic warlord was befriended by the Earther Raven and his comrades during an altercation with a Casian overlord. The incident quickly degenerated into a full-scale war.

The Earthers gifted Matuzak chronicles of their own history as a means to promote understanding between them. The general, ever imitative as his species is wont to be, found inspiration in George Washington and the colonial revolution against the British Crown, comparing the Casian occupation of the Ape Coast to British rule in the colonies. The mercenary Matuzak quickly shifted his focus in fighting the Casians to defending *all* ape tribes, not just those allied to him. With the Earthers' help, the Ape Revolution spread across the land, driving the Casians from their coast and crushing those that remained. The apes allied to the Casians either joined the revolution or were destroyed. Thus was born the Ape Empire, though the appellation did not match the political reality of their loose tribal coalition. The term *empire* was more of a means to unify the thirty-three tribes, creating a symbol to coalesce. Many thought to raise up General Matuzak as a figurehead, in which to unify the tribes, anointing him the first emperor of the ape nation, but he flatly refused. He was adamant that no ape should be raised so far above any other. He looked to the Earthers' revolution for inspiration, denouncing royalty and kingship as blights upon the free spirit of intelligent beings. No, he remained as general of the ape tribes until a true government could be formed.

Matuzak wanted to build a legacy that lasted beyond flawed hereditary lines. The Earthers' history was replete with the failings of such dynasties, one falling after another, until they learned the benefits of meritocracy, where leaders were chosen for their competence for a finite period, their authority granted by the consent of the governed. And so it was for this purpose that Matuzak asked for the Earthers' help, not for their martial prowess or force of arms, but for their knowledge of representative government.

Matuzak called the chieftains of the thirty-three tribes to gather at Gregok to set forth his proposal of establishing a republic. The chieftains were ignorant of the gathering's purpose, enjoying the festivities where they brought their football teams to compete against their fellow tribes, drinking and eating with great merriment. This boisterous feast was the pinnacle of the celebration before Matuzak would gather them again in the great hall on the morrow to present his proposal. He expected resistance from the diverse interests of the many tribes. The smaller tribes would insist on equal representation of each tribe, while the larger tribes would argue power to be distributed by population. Some were concerned with their local interests and how such a union would affect them.

"Another cup!" Chief Gargos of the Manglar Tribe declared, rising to his feet, raising his tankard into the air. He was nearly of a size to Matuzak, with the usual broad face of a gorilla, dark flaring nostrils and black fur. He was clad in brown linen shirt and trousers, with a broad sword riding his left hip and an ax his right. "To our Earther friends! For restoring my faith in their species!" The ape chieftain declared, his voice booming throughout the cavernous hall, his fellow apes chorusing their agreement.

"The Earthers!" they chanted, hundreds of deep gorilla voices sounding off the walls.

The chamber itself was square built, each wall forty meters in length, with massive arches rising from its sides, meeting in the center of the ceiling. The arches matched the forest-green hue of the palace walls, presiding over the dark-brown stone floor. Lanterns hanging from the ceiling bathed the upper portion of the chamber in an emerald glow. Basin torches along the periphery further illuminated the great hall, as serving lasses in brief livery hurried to and fro, shuttling plates of steamed food and cool ale. The ape lasses were slight of build, with narrow chins, white fur, and small flaring nostrils. Araxan apes were unique in that each gender possessed their own distinct coloring. Unlike Araxan humans, where each gender was similar in size, Araxan male apes were far larger than the females.

Raven slowly gained his feet, every muscle aching from the game earlier, standing behind the high table, overlooking the scores of long tables spread across the main floor, where sat hundreds of gorillas. The gorillas were enjoying the auspicious feast, raising their empty tankards when they needed refilling and devouring numerous courses throughout the meal. Raven let out a loud belch, drawing the attention from his simian host, several hooting in applause.

"To our friends!" Raven hoisted his tankard, the ale spilling from its lip as he did so. "Of all the intelligent beings of Arax, you are the most like us. Like us, you treasure freedom. You choose your leaders for their strength and replace them if they are weak. No ape kneels to any other ape, just as we kneel to no one. We are *brothers*, bonded in battle, and we Earthers salute you!" he declared, downing his tankard, swallowing every drop, the crowd roaring in approval as he continued.

"Lorken and I were latecomers to your football tournament, and because of the injuries to starting players, the Manglar and Volmar Tribes accepted us as their replacements. Perhaps one day our home world will discover our whereabouts and make contact with your people. When that day comes, I expect every professional league will recruit your players for their teams, especially your linemen. And here's to the greatest defensive tackle I've ever played with...*to Argos!* Here's to you, big guy!" Raven declared, as a young ape lass refilled his drink, before he downed another.

"*Argos! Argos!*" the hall erupted, cheering Matuzak's champion. Argos rose from his place at Matuzak's side, snorting proudly, basking in their adoration, as Raven continued.

"To each of you gathered here, I make this promise. If the Casian League tries to retake lands belonging to you, we will personally sail into Teris, Coven, Milito, and Port West and level each city to rubble!"

The apes roared in thunderous approval. And so it went throughout the feast as one chieftain after another raised his cup, proclaiming their unity and fondness for their brothers. Matuzak smiled inwardly, the festivities going as he hoped, to remind the chieftains that what drew all apes together was more important than what drew them apart.

*****

The late evening found him atop the battlements, staring out at the Harderan Forest disappearing into the western horizon and the weathered peaks of the Ape Hills silhouetted against the starlit sky beyond them. Gregok was smaller than the massive fortress of Fera, but its green stone outer walls still rose nearly one hundred feet, connected by eight turrets lining its outer battlements. Eight smaller turrets along the inner battlements mirrored their larger counterparts, rising thirty feet above the outer walls. Towering citadels rose above the central keep, with a collage of observation and magantor platforms spread throughout.

Raven marveled at the engineering of these vast superstructures, wondering how they were constructed with only ancient technology. He asked Matuzak this, and the general claimed the fortress was built with the aid of Tarelian engineers, who built all the great castles of Arax. They were built to check the advance of the gargoyles that plagued the land in those dark days. Gargoyle invasions often broke upon the airy heights of the great palaces, their wings taxed attaining the battlements. The success of the castles allowed the ancient realms to expel the gargoyles from their lands, eventually confining them to the Plate Mountains. Gargoyles had long been expunged from the Ape Hills, and Gregok's walls had never been tested since. With the gargoyle threat removed, the palace was abandoned through much of the apes' history, their tribal society having little use for it. It served mainly as a gathering place whenever the chieftains of the tribes needed to meet. After their revolution, Matuzak ordered the ancient holdfast restored to its former glory, garrisoned by a force drawn from each tribe as a symbol of national unity. It was a miracle that the apes demonstrated such unity when they rarely agreed on the simplest of things. It was testament to Matuzak's leadership and charisma. Only he was able to pull off this newfound ape brotherhood, drawing them together where no else could. Matuzak had a way of enforcing his will upon others through his persona rather than brute force, making everyone feel as if they were part of a grand purpose. He was similar to Raven's father in that regard.

Raven shook his head, finding it odd that of all the people on Arax, it was the apes that were most similar to him. While Cronus was the one Araxan he considered his best friend, it was the ape nation that he would go to war to protect.

"I thought I'd find you up here moping about like a lost lanzer. You aren't yourself lately for some reason, despite your colorful speech earlier. What ails you, lad?" Matuzak's deep voice drawing him from his melancholy. He looked over his shoulder as the large gorilla strode across the turret, before stopping at his side and placing his black leathery hands upon the rampart.

"Just getting some fresh air."

"*Buraq!*" Matuzak belched, pounding a fist to his chest. "Aye, things are a little gassy down there. It's to be expected with hundreds of gorillas gathered in one place without the open air to clear the stench." Matuzak grinned.

"You ain't so bad, General. You should smell what it's like with my brothers, father, and grandfathers gathered around a campfire. Whew." Raven winced at the memory.

"Hah! You Earther humans are more like us than Araxan humans. They are a prissy lot. Most would blanch at such things." Matuzak laughed.

"Oh, there's plenty of pansy waist humans back on Earth. Hell, we can't even fight a war without some pencil-necked ninny telling us who we can't kill."

"Ah, so I've read in your historical chronicle. I'll remember that when I call for a formation of a new government. No ninnies in charge of any department."

"Something like that." Raven laughed.

"So what's on your mind, son? You came up here for more than fresh air."

"Ah, just worried about the kid. He's somewhere out there, supposedly making his way back to us." Raven waved an open hand toward the northwest where the endless forest and Ape Hills bled into the horizon.

"I've ordered every border post to send out patrols to look for him. Kato seems a clever lad. I'm sure he is en route. He's probably found a buxom lass and is enjoying her embrace while we sit here worried about him."

Raven wished it were true but knew Kato was too honorable for his own good. He was either still with Cronus or dead. There were rumors circling of the Torry king camped at the crossroads with a large host. Others claimed the Torry king had continued on, marching north to face a Benotrist force marching on Bacel, but the last reports were days old. Unless the Torry king marched with a hundred thousand men, he was probably marching to his death. Tyro was marshalling a vast host in the east and would send all he had against the crossroads. Raven could already guess where Kato was, somewhere fighting beside their Torry friends. Cronus was probably marching with his king as well, the fool. Raven cursed himself for letting them go. He should've tied them down and sailed off. That was the only way to save them from themselves.

"You can't fix stupid," he recalled that age-old Earth phrase that his instructors at the academy muttered whenever he did something rash. If Cronus or Kato got their fool selves captured, he wouldn't be able to sneak into Fera to get them out a second time. All he could do was threaten to blast the fortress to bits, and that would require more firepower than a pistol or rifle. Hell, he'd need Brokov to construct a mobile laser cannon to do the job. Of course, he doubted Cronus would let himself be taken captive again after his last visit to Tyro's house of horrors. He'd die first. Well, it was all water under the bridge anyway as their fates were out of his hand.

Raven's other thoughts were of Tosha, thinking of her constantly and the baby she carried—his baby. The longer they were apart, the more irritable he became. Why was it that the one woman who drove him insane was the one he loved? Sometimes he just wanted to strangle her and kiss her at the same time. She tortured his dreams, preventing him from a peaceful night's sleep since they parted.

"What's her name?" Matuzak asked, drawing him from his thoughts. "Her name?"

"Your princess, Tyro's whelp. What is her name again?"

"Tosha." He sighed tiredly.

"She must be quite a lass to make you so confounded." Matuzak laughed.

"Oh, she's quite a lass, all right. She has all the tenderness of a starving grizzly."

"Then she's just your type. The creator's hand is in this pairing, I surmise," the general reflected. The apes oft spoke of the creator, the omnipotent being that supposedly created Arax and placed their simian ancestors upon these sacred lands. Ironically, the god of the apes was of a human visage, as they claimed he created mankind in his own image. Raven never commented on their religion or beliefs. He thought it silly, but it did him no harm, and he respected their beliefs. People can believe what they want for all he cared. All that mattered to him was that they were his friends.

"Tyro's daughter and you." Matuzak snorted, trying to picture it.

"Yep, but I try not to think about who her father is." Raven scrubbed his face with his hand. "I can't wait to meet her mom. I'm sure she's a real sweetheart too."

"Is that your next journey, the Sisterhood?"

"Aye. I promised her I'd be there."

"Be there? For what?"

"For the baby." Raven gave him a look, trusting Matuzak with the information.

"Then why are you here? You should be with her," the general scolded him.

"She's fine for now. Besides, I made a promise to an old friend, and I'm here to help him with whatever it is he needs done." Raven slapped Matuzak on the shoulder.

"I didn't know you were so fond of me." Matuzak gave a toothy grin.

"Other than Cronus and a few others who are all likely to die, your people are the only friends we have. This is the only place we are welcomed. Tyro has a bounty on our heads so high every man hunter this side of Fera is hunting us down. The Naybins are Tyro's ally, so scratch them from the list of safe havens. We just pissed off two of the ruling families of Tro, so we won't be welcome back there anytime soon. The Casians probably hate us more than anyone. The pirate factions of Varabis will want our heads once they find out we handed Monsson over to Tyro. We've made enemies out of enough Macon merchants to add that to places we're not welcome. The Sisterhood will put a price on my head once Tosha imagines my next misdeed. Considering all that, you can see why we value the few friends we have, General."

"Then stay," Matuzak offered. "Make our land your home. You have always been welcomed here, and not by me alone, but all the chieftains, which is no small feat. I know you have refused other kings' offers to join their Elite, and I would not ask that of you. But I would offer you a safe haven, a shelter from the storms sweeping over Arax. When you again sail off to distant lands, you may leave your families in our keeping. What I am offering you and your crew is citizenship in a new Ape Republic. What say you, Raven?"

"A republic?" he asked, curiously.

"A republic," Matuzak affirmed, placing his black leathery hand on his shoulder. "Tomorrow, the chieftains of each tribe shall gather in the great hall, where I shall propose a new central government. My people are wary of such power vested in one authority, yet we must be united, to face the threat brewing from afar."

"Tyro." Raven shrugged, naming the one threat to them all.

"Aye, though there are others."

"So what do you propose? If your people only trust tribal authority, how can you get them to agree to something else? Those traditions run pretty deep." Raven understood tribal attachments as his own father still held such affinity for his Inupiat customs. Of course, Raven thought it easier to simply say Eskimo but never to his father's face without a punch in the arm.

"Tribal loyalties must be honored and upheld. This is paramount in any negotiation. And yet we must be unified to protect our people from again falling prey as we did when the Casians used our division to steal our lands. How to balance these conflicting interests is what confounds me. That is why I asked you to come."

"That is why? What can we do?"

"I have looked far for an answer to this problem and may have found it in the tome you gifted me when you were here last, the chronicle of your world's history. We are not of Earth, this I know, but there are parities. I am reminded of your land, America. At their founding, they were presented with similar conflicting interests, though their divisions were between varying states of unequal size rather than our tribal entities. For my proposal to work, we must strike a balance between tribal authority and a central government. The term, I believe, is what your founders called *dual federalism*, where a state and a federal government held separate authority over the same geographical area. So we must establish the same, dividing authority between the tribes and our republic. We must also strike a balance in the power of the republic, giving equal consideration to tribe size and the individual tribes themselves. Those of greater size will demand greater representation, while the smaller will demand each tribe be given equal voice."

Matuzak's revelation sent Raven's poor brain spinning, using terminology a primitive warlord had no business using. Raven had to remind himself that despite appearances, Matuzak was no mere primitive but an insightful and wise leader who understood that individual liberty could not flourish without a government that was both limited in its power and yet strong enough to safeguard its citizenry. Such a notion was lost on Matuzak's foreign contemporaries, as the realms of men were ruled by monarchies.

"I sent Argos across Arax to fetch you for this grand exercise."

"What do you want us to do?"

"I don't need your gun hand or martial skills, my boy. I have need of your knowledge. I need your aid in constructing a constitution, one that balances all the conflicting interests of the tribes. I'll have need of your archives to help in this endeavor. You, Raven, shall help in building this world anew, and for your help, you and the others will be richly rewarded."

"Your money is no good with us, General. We don't take money from friends. Besides, you're one of the few friends we have left, and if you need our help, you have it."

"If not coin, then citizenship!" Matuzak insisted.

Raven thought on it for no more than a second. "All right. I'll ask the others for their vote. I would be honored to call your land my home."

There, upon the battlements of Gregok, Raven joined the Ape Republic.

*****

The following morn found the chieftains of the thirty-three tribes gathered in the upper hall, each sitting on a massive throne along the periphery of the chamber, facing each other in a circle. The thrones were austere, forged in iron with wide-set legs to bear the chieftains, girth. Each throne was spaced equal distance apart, symbolizing the equality of each tribe. Flanking each throne stood the champion of each tribe and tribal elder.

Raven and Lorken stood off to the side, observing the heated debates between the vying factions. The smaller tribes predictably argued that all tribes carry the same voice in any formal union. The larger tribes debated the opposite, basing representation on population. The six tribes of the southwest, who did not join the revolution against the Casian League, were wary of committing to any union at all and were weary of the other tribes' disdain for their inaction. Matuzak waited for the debate to run its course, standing beside his Earth friends before finally stepping forth to address the chieftains, stepping in the center of the chamber.

"We have gathered here in this ancient hall to decide the fate of our tentative union. Our new empire is no empire at all, merely a loose joining of our collective strength. A true empire exercises authority over its subjects, and no gorilla in this hall would ever support such a notion, nor would I propose one. But if we are to safeguard our sovereignty and independence from those who would take it from us, we must forge a strong central union!" Matuzak declared.

"In time, such a government would supplant tribal authority and rule over us!" Hukor of the Narsus Tribe argued.

"Such is the danger in any political post or regency, but we can safeguard against such tyranny. Any central government must have checks and balances…" Matuzak paused, realizing most had never heard such terms. He rephrased. "It must be set up so that there are separate parts of government that keep one another in subjugation to each other, preventing them from overstepping the boundaries of their own authority, preventing any group or individual from gaining dictatorial power. To help us build such a union, I sent for our Earth friends." Matuzak nodded to Raven and Lorken, who shrugged and waved at everyone.

The apes did not trust humans, their species causing them nothing but problems, save for the Tarelians. But the chieftains of the thirty-three tribes saw the Earthers as friends of the ape nations, welcoming them into this sacred council.

Matuzak continued, explaining the separation of federal and tribal jurisdiction, laying out the principles of dual federalism, where the authorities of each entity worked within the same geographic territory. He spoke of the need for a strong central government, which would regulate commerce with foreign powers, establish a national Army, and act as one voice for their collective defense. The powers given to the national government would be limited to those agreed upon by their collective will and transcribed in specific detail before this council. All other governing authority would fall to the individual tribes themselves.

"But how shall the tribes be represented?" asked Nagovok, chief of the Armos tribe. "Shall a tribe small in number like mine be given equal voice?"

"That would be unfair to my tribe. We are three times your number!" Growled Hutoq of the Hutor Tribe.

"And what weight should we honor you, Hutoq? Your faithless tribe failed to heed our call in the Casian War!" Chief Gargos of the Manglar Tribe snorted, deriding the Hutors and the other five tribes that did not join their revolt.

"If you want us to join your union, then we demand our fair due!" Hutoq countered.

"The chopping block is your traitor's due, Hutoq!" Hukok of the Narsos Tribe chided.

Hutoq arose from his throne, stepping menacingly toward the center of the floor at the affront to his honor. The Hutor Tribe's distance from the conflict and proxy war with the neighboring Traxar Tribe convinced their elders to ignore the pleas of their fellow tribes during the Casian War.

"Still your temper, Hutoq, chief of the Hutor," Matuzak said calmly, soothing the chief's rage as he stepped between them.

Hutoq grudgingly backed a step, his respect for the general staying his anger.

"We must respect each tribe among this council, whether they be large or small, or joined in our revolt or not. We must agree that despite these differences, we each now hold equal voice in this council before we can proceed to discuss the issues that divide us. Is it agreed?" Matuzak asked, stepping back to the center of the floor, his brown eyes sweeping the stern faces of the chieftains.

"Aye!" they each chorused.

"Very well," he continued. "As for the question of representation, the smaller tribes naturally desire an equal voice for each tribe, while the larger seek power based on their greater populace."

A murmur of agreement passed among them.

"Then we must compromise. Our Earth friends shared a similar problem long ago in one of their realms," Matuzak explained. He continued at length, expounding the tale of the first Constitutional Convention and retelling the issues dividing them and laying out his proposal for a bicameral legislative body, with an upper house granting equal weight to each tribe and a lower chamber weighted by population.

The convention continued for days, the chieftains finally agreeing on the bicameral legislative compromise proposed by Matuzak. The upper assembly of the legislature was named the Quam, with one Quam representative elected from each tribe. The lower assembly was named the Onom, its representation based on tribe size. It was in the Onom where all laws would originate, before passing to the Quam. The Onom and Quam represented the legislative branch of the new government. The most debated issue was the establishment of a chief executive, to oversee command of the national Army, sign bills into law, and oversee appointments to the national tribunals and ministers of state, each requiring approval by the Quam.

The chieftains were wary granting such authority to one individual without restraints upon his power. It was agreed to name the chief executive by the Earth moniker *president*. He would serve one term and be prohibited from partaking in any government function ever again. The president would be elected by electoral weighting, granting each tribe a total vote based upon combined numbers of their membership in the Quam and Onom.

A judicial branch was also established to interpret any laws passed by the legislature and signed by the president. The high tribunal consisted of seven elders agreed upon by the tribal elders of the thirty-three tribes and given to the president, who selected from the list to advance in the Quam for approval. Each high tribune would serve twenty years. A decision by the high tribunal could be overturned by three-fourths vote in both the Quam and Odom, whereas a president veto could be overturned by two-thirds of each legislative body.

The chieftains were concerned by the power of any unified government infringing upon the sovereignty of the tribes; therefore tribal authority held dominion in their respective territories, save for the needs of the nation's collective defense and establishment of a universal currency. National taxation could only apply to trade that crossed tribal and international boundaries.

Raven marveled at the parallels between this convention and the one that birthed the United States. "To begin the world anew," Matuzak quoted an ancient American statesman, as they were introducing a revolutionary concept of governance into this world of monarchies and tyrants. He thought of the irony that of all the species on this planet, it was the apes that embraced their ideas, establishing the only republic in this savage world.

*****

Ten days hence

Raven walked along the cobblestone pathway that ambled through the palace foregrounds. The morning sun hung above the eastern sky, shining brightly off the emerald walls of the ancient fortress.

The lush Harderan forest stretched endlessly to the west, with open fields carpeting the palace's north and eastern approaches. Towering porian and paccel trees encroached upon the southern and western walls, an obvious hindrance to the palace's defense should a siege ever again arise. Of course, Gregok had not seen battle for centuries, suffering periods of abandonment and neglect. Such was expected since Gregok was constructed to counter the gargoyle presence in the Ape Hills, from which they were expunged long ago. Now the ancient fortress was undergoing a rebirth as a symbol of national unity of the ape tribes.

The convention continued at a painstaking pace, the Chieftains hashing out the most mundane details of their constitution. It seemed the various territorial disputes between nearly all the tribes needed to be agreed upon before ratification. Some squabbles were easily resolved, like the possession of contested wells that separated the Volmar and Corgak Tribes, where each tribe agreed to the communal sharing of the wells and to assuage previous slights by exchanging a dozen brides between them, wedding highborn lasses to warriors of the other tribe. Other disputes were far more difficult, like the control of the Testo River that flowed between Nargos and Carvos territory. Far more difficult was the partition of the coastal territories that were taken during the Casian War. Many of the lands once belonged to one tribe but were recovered by another. All these disputes needed reconciliation before ratification could commence.

The apes were fearsome warriors, but they argued like fisher wives bartering over the most mundane details. The morning session once again devolved into an argument concerning a three-year-old dispute over the fraudulent sale of a lame ocran. Raven took that moment to step outside, making his way into the wood line beyond the western wall, where Argos and Lorken were target shooting. Scores of militia encampments surrounded the castle, with countless warriors sparring with swords or engaged in feats of strength or wrestling. Many waved as Raven passed, urging him to join in. He and Argos spent many a night visiting with each of the different campsites, engaging in various activities. Many were impressed as Raven won most of the bouts, which was unheard of with Araxan humans, defeating the champions of nearly half the tribes, garnering him respect among his simian host.

"Raven!" one gorilla shouted, thumping his chest.

"Garm!" Raven grunted, thumping his chest in turn, greeting the Manglar warrior as he passed.

"Raven!" another cried out, running up alongside the big Earther.

"Orlom," Raven greeted Lorken's teammate from the big game. The gorilla was lanky, standing nearly seventy inches, with a youthful grin and expressive large eyes.

"Arg and Lorken are just ahead. Can I go with you?" Orlom asked excitedly as the open campgrounds gave way to the forest edge. Orlom's feet nearly bounced as he walked, elated to see the Earthers' weapons in action. He wore the thick-soled moccasins of an ape warrior, loose linen trousers and shirt, and a battle-ax strapped across his back.

"It's not much fun just watching. Do you want to learn to shoot?" Raven asked.

"Yes!" Orlom hooted excitedly, bouncing from foot to foot, not believing Raven would offer such a boon.

"Settle down, little buddy, it's not that big a deal. Come on." He waved him along, continuing through the tree line. The sparsely placed trees grew thicker as they went along, thick underbrush giving way to the open forest floor, with towering porian and lupecs blocking the sun. They could hear Lorken and Argos's distinct voices up ahead and the flash of laser through the trees.

"Agghh! Blast it!" Argos growled his displeasure, another blast going awry. Raven found them facing a low embankment with thick stones propped up along its base.

"Ha! Ha!" Grigg hooted, mocking Argos's poor aim. The young ape did so safely atop a tree limb some paces behind them.

Argos took a menacing step toward the young gorilla after holstering his pistol. "Come down here!" He growled loud enough to wake the dead.

"You could shoot me down, but you'd miss," Grigg taunted, as Lorken tried to calm Argos's temper.

"I can always shoot the limb you're sitting on, Grigg," Raven warned.

"Raven!" Grigg smiled, ignoring Raven's warning. He quickly slid down the tree, his bare feet striking the soil before standing erect.

"You best apologize to Arg before he removes one of your arms, kid," Raven ruffled his head.

"Sorry, Arg…" Grigg said before Argos brought his fist down atop the young ape's head, driving him to his rump.

Orlom hooted excitedly at Grigg's misfortune before Argos slapped him upside the head, knocking him in the dirt.

"Why don't you youngins quit lying about, and we'll show you how to shoot," Raven said.

"Harumph!" Argos snorted, walking back to his shooting point, while Grigg and Orlom came groggily to their feet.

"All right, Argos, let's try that again," Lorken said as the large gorilla stepped back to the line. "Remember to *squeeze* the trigger with a smooth, even pull. Don't jerk it."

Argos's right hand hovered over his holstered pistol, his dark eyes fixed upon a tree stump halfway up the embankment. Lorken told him to aim for a discolored notch near the trunk's center. Argos drew, extending the weapon as he fired, the blast passing over the stump.

"*Aghh!*" he roared in frustration.

"Easy, Arg." Lorken winced, Argos's roar piercing his skull. It amazed him how Argos seemed to shoot fairly well in combat yet struggled in practice. Most people suffered a degradation in accuracy under duress. An expert marksman could expect as much as a 30 to 40 percent drop. Of course, most of Argos's shots in combat were close range. Lorken had him repeat the process again and again, forcing him to focus on his front sight and trigger control, until he grouped his shots before increasing his speed. Raven stood off to their right, instructing Orlom and Grigg on the basics. Each would stop and hoot excitedly with every shot that came anywhere near their target.

"Easy with that, Grigg!" Raven scolded his young friend, who celebrated by aiming the weapon in the air, taking it from his hand.

"Uh! *Uh!*" Grigg grinned, pointing out the rotting log they were using as a target, where the last shot struck the edge of the moss-covered husk.

"That's not a good shot, kid. You missed the target by a yard. That means a man with a sword would be close enough to bury it into your gut. This is a dangerous weapon. Keep the barrel pointed in a safe direction, and only shoot what you mean to destroy. Now let's do this again, real…*slow.*"

And so they continued throughout the morn and afternoon, instructing the three apes in basic marksmanship and gun handling. Grigg and Orlom required extensive training in safety. Lorken thought they were lucky not to be killed by their carelessness. He could hear Raven barking at them throughout the exercise, wrestling the pistol from their hands whenever they aimed anywhere other than the target. Whenever one of them hit anywhere near the target, they would instantly lose muzzle awareness and began taunting the other while hooting excitedly. The two young apes aged Raven several years in as many hours. When they were finally done, Orlom and Grigg sped off to the castle with Argos storming after them, shaking his large head in disgust with his performance. His shooting was fair at the start, but whenever Lorken instructed him, he grew agitated, and his aim worsened. Once Lorken stepped way, Argos settled down and started practicing proper trigger squeeze. Lorken looked over to Raven, who looked haggard.

"Well?" Lorken asked, crossing his arms with that "I told you so" look on his face.

Raven's hopes to recruit new crewmates looked rather bleak. They needed crewmates that they could trust not only in character but competence. Orlom and Grigg were greatly lacking in the latter.

"I need a drink."

CHAPTER 5

Notsu

Morac's procession passed through the gates of Notsu under a cold and clear sky, kneeling crowds greeting him along the avenues in obeisance, their heads bowed to receive their lord. The Benotrists marched in good order with polished armor and disciplined ranks, as if returning from a glorious triumph. Morac ordered slouches beaten so as not to mar the impression of his infallibility to the good citizens of Notsu. The disaster at Corell was not so easily hid from those who knew what to look for. There was more than one smirking face in the crowd, but Morac only saw the one belonging to a dark-haired youth kneeling along the street off his left. Morac ordered the boy brought to him, staring down at the frightened youth from his mount, with Kriton riding up beside him.

"Does our return amuse you?" Morac softly hissed.

"No…no, my lord." The boy trembled, his pale eyes fixed to the ground, where the ocran's hooves shifted on the street's stone surface.

"A lying son of Notsu!" the Benotrist guard behind the boy grunted, forcing him to his knees.

"Perhaps." Morac shrugged.

"Give his worthless carcass to me!" Kriton snarled. "I shall feast on his insolent heart." The boy cringed, feeling Kriton's feral eyes upon his neck.

"No," Morac dismissed Kriton's suggestion with a wave of his hand. "A dead slave serves no purpose. Death merely releases the slave from its duties." Morac chose his words carefully, instructing the youth on the new social order of Notsu and his place in it.

"What do you want done with him?" Kriton snarled impatiently. He was not a lickspittle or lackey to be awed by Morac's creativity.

"The crowd seems overly somber, especially upon the day of their lord's joyous return. Stand up, boy," he ordered with a voice far too kind.

"That's it, stand up," Morac urged, the boy gaining his feet, his eyes trained on the ground. "No, that won't do. Look to your people," he said, directing him to lift his eyes, staring nervously to those gathered around them.

"Now…*smile*," Morac ordered, spreading his hands as if they had the power to spread the boy's lips.

Morac shook his head at the youth's false grin. "Tsk, tsk, that will never do. You cannot lift the people's spirits with such an effort. How can those further away see how happy you are?" Morac asked.

The boy stretched the corners of his mouth to their utmost, hoping to appease the new lord of the city, his pained smile obvious to those daring to look at him.

"Those further back still cannot see your happiness. Perhaps you need help expressing your joy. Widen his smile," Morac ordered. The guards held the boy down, cutting his lip corners open, his screams echoing through the still air. Morac felt the fear coursing the crowd, the cruel act having its desired effect.

"Onward!" Morac ordered, now in the right mood to meet with the ruling council of Notsu.

*****

Morac stood before the ruling council of Notsu, whose members sat stiffly upon the stone benches circling the center platform. Their long robes draped their skeletal forms like fine raiment decorating a corpse. These once proud men sat joyless upon their seats of false power, like puppets on a string. They ruled Notsu in name only, their posts little more than advisors to the Benotrist ruling governor, Daylas, the twenty-first ranked member of Tyro's Elite. He was a ruthless administrator, lacking even the barest of charm. They knew Morac's return was anything but glorious, for his Army was going into winter quarters so far from Corell. His mere presence meant that Torry banners still blew above the White Castle, for what good it did any of them here.

"I have returned from Corell in great triumph!" Morac addressed the council, pacing slowly around the stone circle, his dark eyes regarding their gaunt faces. They knew his words false, but none would voice their doubts.

Kriton stood near Morac, his arms crossed over his chest, his terrible crimson eyes staring at one council member after another, fixing each in turn with his terrible gaze. It was a cold reminder of the price of defiance. All knew that Kriton was third among Tyro's Elite and keeper of the dungeon of Fera. His reputation far exceeded Daylas's, who oversaw the cruel torture of many of their citizens suspected of subversion.

"I have bled the Torry ranks, removing any ability for them to attempt an offensive ever again in our lifetime. Thousands of their dead liter the ramparts of Corell and its surrounding lands. They can do naught but stand idle upon its blackened walls, awaiting my return come spring. The months of winter will torment their minds as they hold up in their castle tomb, awaiting their inglorious end. They are without hope. They spent precious blood they could not afford to stave off their inevitable demise, a mere delaying tactic as my legions rest and reorganize here at Notsu, with more legions coming south to reinforce my Army. Come spring, I will renew my assault upon Corell, ending the Torry Realm. You will hold a festival, celebrating our triumph. Let the people of my city know of their lord's fell deeds."

"Of…of course, Lord Morac." Minister Niotic bowed his head. *Festival?* he thought bitterly. There was hardly enough to eat at it was. Now they would waste precious stores to convince the people of Morac's infallibility.

"Excellent. Governor Daylas is familiar with each of your families. I expect *every* member of your households to be present so I might greet my esteemed subjects."

Minister Niotic understood his true intent, their children's fate resting on their perceived obedience. Even fidelity was no shield if one of their daughters caught Morac's eye. They were well aware of his collection, with two highborn women from Notsu taken during his previous stay.

"As I will use Notsu for my winter quarters, I will require you to provision my soldiers," Morac said, swallowing the wince from his pained injured leg. The wound he received at Kregmarin had yet to fully heal. He was losing patience as it robbed him of his mobility, causing him to sit out most of the battle at Corell, while that fool Terin roamed the battlements uncontested.

"Lord Morac, we…" Minister Blevin spoke before thinking better of it.

"You have something to say, Minister?" Morac asked.

"My lord, we…our food stores are much depleted. With winter upon us, we are facing starvation. We cannot hope to feed your vast host with what resources we have left. Shall we be reprovisioned by the empire?"

"And why are your stores so depleted?" Morac asked.

"The war interrupted the harvest of our tributaries, my lord. The Torry 5th Army drew much from our stores during the Kregmarin Campaign, and your legions took another portion soon after." Blevin did not point out that Morac nearly emptied Notsu's food stores upon seizing the city, for angering the Benotrist warrior served little purpose, as their survival depended upon his mood.

"Perhaps your provisions would be fully stocked had you not emptied them upon learning of King Lore's death at Kregmarin and sending them west. You think me blind? I know full well of your subterfuge, giving me false smiles while plotting my demise. Many of you sitting here sent most of your wealth and kin to Torry North long before I first reached your city. Even if my spies did not tell me of this, I could see it from the scant number of your family members that remain in this city. I was willing to overlook this as we are at war, but the poor performance of your troops at Corell leaves you no room to fail me. You *will* feed and house my troops. If you cannot, remember there are other things my soldiers can eat," he reminded them, appraising the meat on their bones.

*****

"Wine, master?" the slave girl offered Morac, the calnesian folds of her brief black gown shimmering in the sunlight bathing the chamber. She knelt at his feet, offering the goblet in her outstretched hands, her eyes trained to the floor.

Morac leaned forward in his cushioned chair, running his fingers along the silver collar gracing her delicate neck. "Ah, Velesa." He smiled, taking the goblet, undressing her with his eyes. Velesa was one of the seven slave girls still in his keeping. Two perished at Corell, the unfortunate victims of a Jenaii fire munition exploding in their midst. Three from his harem managed to escape when the Torry Cavalry swept into their camp seven days before. After that incident, he kept them chained and in coffle throughout the march.

"Rub my feet!" he ordered, pressing his boot to her breast.

"Yes, master," Velesa said, carefully removing his sandaled boots before taking his left foot in hand, feeling his lecherous eyes staring down at her.

"When the emperor first ordered the raiding of caravans, I never imagined the treasures our raiders would return with. You were a pleasant surprise," he gloated.

"I am happy that it pleases you, master." She seethed in impotent rage, unable to vent her true fury. She was taken long before Kregmarin. Velesa was the youngest daughter of a Bacel wine merchant. Her father had vast holdings throughout western Arax, including iron mines west of Gotto and vineyards along the upper Flen. It was during a journey to the vineyard estates when her caravan was beset by hundreds of vile raiders. Most everyone was slaughtered, save for her and four other girls. They were taken north, where Morac's legions were camped west of Lake Veneba. Morac took great interest in adding highborn girls to his collection. Since she was a maiden, he affixed a golden collar to her throat, signifying her purity. Once he spoiled her virtue, it was replaced with silver. Like all his golden collars, he saved her ravishment for a *special* occasion. She shuddered at the memory as he celebrated the destruction of her city by taking her maidenhood that night. Even now, she did not know if her family survived the destruction. If they fled before the siege, they might still be alive, but if they remained, then they were certainly dead.

"Do you miss your golden collar, girl?" he mocked.

"I serve at your pleasure, master." She eased his left foot down before starting with his right.

"It was a glorious night when I exchanged your gold for silver. Of all my collars, you are the most fetching."

"Your words are most kind, master." She bowed, wanting to vomit having said it.

"If you are a good girl, perhaps I shall reward you tonight with a visit. Would that please you, slave?" He raised his left foot, lifting her chin with his toe.

"You honor me, master," she answered, staring into his soulless eyes.

"Then make yourself ready, Velesa," he commanded, as she scrambled from her knees, hurrying out of the spacious chamber. Morac snickered as she stepped without, stretching his sore left leg as he lounged lazily.

"Out of my way, girl!" Kriton's distinct voice echoed in the outer corridor, causing Morac to spill his wine as it touched his lips. The gargoyle clearly dismissed protocol, barging into his chamber without preamble. He was followed by Daylas, the acting governor of Notsu. Much to Morac's annoyance, both Kriton and Daylas were both ranking members of Tyro's Elite, and his post as commander of the expeditionary forces counted for naught in their presence. Only his standing as first of the Imperial Elite garnered him their respect.

"I assume you have sufficient reason for barging into my chambers, unannounced?" Morac asked dryly, taking a sip from his goblet.

"There's news!" Kriton snarled, stepping to his side, leaving Daylas to address them.

Daylas regarded him with pale-green eyes that seemed as lifeless as a corpse, with a nondescript face that matched. He wore a simple black tunic with the sigil of the Imperial Elite sewn upon its front.

"Your news won't announce itself, Daylas," Morac chided.

"We lost a caravan."

"What do you mean 'we lost it'?" Morac asked.

"Forty leagues north, our scouts found evidence of its demise. It was en route to here with provisions for our legions."

"Who is responsible?" Morac asked darkly, trying to calm his temper. They were in a precarious position with their supply chains overextended. Moving goods over rough, barren terrain was beyond problematic. By now, he expected to have conquered Corell, living off the largesse of the Torry heartland.

"Could be Torry Cavalry or barbarians out for plunder, but we've seen no signs of ocran hoofprints. Jenaii raiders are the likeliest culprits," Daylas said.

"Jenaii! This far north and east?" Morac asked.

"If it was just one caravan, I would question it, but this is the second in ten days," Daylas said.

"The second? Why did you not speak of it earlier?" Morac sprang to his feet.

"We are at war. Should I appraise you of every situation that arises? Most of these happenings are local in nature, but with two supply caravans missing, it raises suspicion. That is why I am telling you now, Lord Morac," Daylas added the appellation.

"When it concerns the lifeline of the legions, then *yes*, I expect to be informed immediately."

"If that is your wish, then let me remind you of what I said at outset of this campaign. We cannot sustain the legions south of the Kregmarin Plain without either seizing Corell or securing Tro. It is far easier moving provisions by ship, and the roads linking Tro to Notsu are quite hospitable, unlike the deadly and barren trek north. There is a reason why armies rarely invaded these lands from the north." Daylas shook his head internally at Morac's lack of basic understanding of geography and logistics. The emperor rarely made mistakes, but he questioned the wisdom of appointing Morac to lead this expeditionary force.

"I cannot spare more troops attacking Tro. I'll need every soldier come spring to take Corell," Morac countered.

"I said securing the route to Tro, not attacking the city itself. You only need access to the port to unload provisions. Such things can be negotiated," Daylas reasoned.

"Then why haven't you already done so? I left you in command of Notsu. It is within your purview to make such arrangements."

"I have been negotiating with Tro's trade minister, but there have been…complications."

"Complications?"

"Yes. It seems our Troan friends demand a significant fee for each ship we unload in their port."

"How significant?"

"Eight thousand certras."

"Eight thousand?" Morac growled.

"Yes. Eight thousand. All in advance."

"You didn't agree to that extortion, did you?"

"Not without your approval. The negotiations are ongoing. In fact, I will be speaking with their trade minister again today."

"He's here?"

"Yes. He arrived a fortnight past. His terms were more generous *before* our setback at Corell."

"Fetch him. I'll speak with him myself."

*****

Morac received the Troan trade minister in the city forum dressed in full military regalia, his bloodred cape draping the dark armor adorning his shoulders. Generals Vlesnivolk, Felinaius, and Tuvukk stood rigidly to his left, with Kriton and Daylas his right. Morac's eyes followed the trade minister entering the chamber accompanied by a diminutive aid. The two men wore matching scarlet tunics that fell to their ankles, with broad sashes tied about their waists.

"Lord Morac receives you within this esteemed sanctum," Daylas greeted the Troan minister.

"We are honored to be received," the minister's aide replied, bowing his head deeply. "Minister Denin Regs," he introduced, waving an open hand toward his master.

"Lord Morac, I am honored to meet the victor of Kregmarin and the bane of Bacel. Your fell deeds are spoken of with awe throughout our city," Denin said with practiced courtesy.

"Is that so?" Morac said doubtfully, Denin noticing the menace flickering briefly in his eyes.

"Indeed, the ruling families of Tro respect great achievements. The crossroads have not fallen to invasion in centuries. You did so by crossing the deadliest lands in all of Arax. The Kregmarin is difficult to traverse with a caravan ladened with provisions, let alone six legions. Feeding such a host is as nearly as difficult as the conquest itself," Denin said, his flattery only reminding Morac of his precarious position.

"Yes, and provisioning my legions is why you are here, Minister Regs."

"Of course, and I assume Governor Daylas has relayed our generous terms," Denin said, his smile dying with Kriton's scowl, forcing him back a step.

"He has. And I assume your *generous* offer was a jest. Eight thousand certras to unload our own provisions from our own ships is a grave insult to our emperor. Allowing Tro its autonomy should be reward enough," Morac cut to the point.

"If we are speaking bluntly, my lord, your legions have met with a setback at Corell. With the Jenaii now reinforcing Torry North, your conquest is in grave doubt. Your legions, though much reduced, are positioned here. I see you have no intention of withdrawing them north to the safety of the Benotrist border. If you remain, you cannot supply them along the tenuous routes over the Kregmarin Plain. Oh, many caravans will traverse that deadly ground, but not enough to feed your legions. The prime driver in all economic exchanges is supply and need. You are in need of our port. Only there can you unload and transport enough provisions to feed your Army. As the representative of Tro, I am authorized to arrange such an agreement. I place the price at eight thousand per ship as recompense in the event you actually *lose* this war, my lord. Those funds will aid Tro in purchasing free swords to guard against Torry retribution," Denin presented the cold facts.

"And what prevents me from taking your city outright? I can easily add lord of Tro to my growing list of titles."

"And you would add Tro to your growing list of adversaries. A grave escalation, considering your position, my lord," Denin said.

"It would be a mere inconvenience for me but total destruction for you," Morac warned.

"Perhaps, or perhaps not. Tro is not without…friends." Denin smiled knowingly.

"The Casian League is too far away to aid you against me," Morac pointed out.

"Our common cause with greater Casia resides upon trade, and trade alone. Our allies are actually *far* closer to home."

"And which allies are these?" Daylas asked guardedly.

"The Ape Republic," the Troan minister declared, his eyes sweeping their faces, gauging their response, taking wicked pleasure in their stricken looks. An attack upon Tro would bring the might of the ape Army down upon Morac's beleaguered legions, placing a deadly threat to his back.

"I will convey your terms to the emperor, for sums so vast require his approval," Morac said evenly, tempering his rage, before dismissing the Troans. The others filed out, leaving Morac alone with Kriton, the gargoyle hissing his displeasure.

"We should gut them now and send their heads to Tro!" Kriton snarled.

"There is a time and place for brutality, and a time and place for planning," Morac said, his heavy breath belying his words. His mind drifted, dreams of conquest and revenge consuming him. Since Corell, he was haunted, driven to the brink of madness by his failure, his imagination correcting his mistakes in his waking thoughts. Through the misty haze of his delusions, he saw the rotting flesh of Torry soldiers choking the air, gargoyles feeding on their foul remains. Jenaii warriors raced across the sky, flames devouring their wings, leaving trails of smoke in their wake. The walls of Corell were soaked in blood, her proud gates open to his advance. Tro lie in ruins, her ships sunk, her wharves aflame, and the heads of their ruling families adorning pikes at the city gates. He saw himself upon the throne of the dead Torry king, the Torry Crown resting upon his brow. The lands of the south prostrated before him, bowing to his inevitable dominion.

"What will you tell the emperor?" Kriton drew him from his delusion.

"The truth. Our Troan friends will find him less tolerant than I."

*****

Corell

Princess Corry sat in council, receiving the reports from her ministers, exhausted by the myriad of problems plaguing the realm. Thankfully the pettiest disputes were set aside for now, allowing her to address issues of extreme priority. The main gate was of utmost concern. She ordered a small Army of smiths and engineers from Central City to oversee the project. They had until spring to prepare for the next siege. Food was another issue. All the lands east of Corell were devastated, their crops either partially harvested or plundered altogether. Minister Thunn performed admirably coordinating the harvest throughout the realm, the excess bounty from the west helping to ease shortfalls in the east. Minister Veda would coordinate agreements with the border kingdoms of Teso and Zulon, along the Nila between the Torry Realms, purchasing their excess yields on his way south, before assuming the ambassadorship at Bansoch. Despite these plans, the realm would still have to severely ration their provisions to make it through the winter. Then there was the issue of the dead and wounded. Commander Nevias oversaw the cleanup of Corell, putting the Benotrist prisoners to use clearing the bodies littering the fields surrounding the palace. The wounded were another matter. Kato's wondrous device healed most of the wounded, but there were still enough with missing limbs and vicious stab wounds to fill the matrons' ward. Unfortunately, Kato took his device with him, foreseeing the greater need in Yatin. There were more mundane matters, like the fletching of arrows to restock what they used and the reorganization of the garrison with the losses suffered.

Another concern was the sudden departure of Elos and another telnic of Jenaii warriors of the 1st Battlegroup. A full telnic left after the battle for parts unknown, unknown to her anyway. Elos was supposedly joining that contingent for purposes he was not at liberty to say. He also took Alen with him, which was suspicious. She wondered what task he was suited to make him so important. General Bode speculated it was a raiding party somewhere north and east, to harry Morac's lines of communication.

Yes, Corry was exhausted with all of it but took solace in the fact that it kept her busy, busy enough to not think constantly of Terin.

There was that name again, always foremost in her thoughts. She wondered where he was at that moment. Probably camped somewhere along the Nila, sharing stories with Kato and Lucas. In his absence, she found herself in Torg and Jonas's company more than not, finding solace in their presence, for each were kin to him, feeling closer to Terin when they were near. Of course, Torg's duties kept him busy through most of the day, training the newest members of the Royal Elite. Jonus often assisted him, Corry enjoying seeing them work together, putting their past differences aside. She knew it was their mutual concern for the *boy*, as they were apt to call him. She always loved Torg, enjoying his grandfatherly charm and protectiveness. With her father gone, Torg was her rock, leaning on him when it all seemed too much. Though Jonas was different, more reserved than his gruff father-in-law, she found him equally endearing. She spent the previous nights upon the battlements listening to his stories. She loved hearing of Terin's childhood, of the mischievous things he would do, which were unsurprisingly few. There was a sadness to Jonas though, an unspoken anguish he would not speak of, though she read it so clearly in his eyes. She wondered at its meaning. She wondered if its source was the same that caused Terin such grief before he departed. Wherever Terin was, he was always on her mind.

I'm a lovesick fool, she thought miserably, hating feeling so weak.

"Highness!" Jonas's voice drew her from her melancholy.

He stood in the doorway, the eyes of her council drawn curiously to his interruption. Ever since his miraculous appearance during the battle, he was a constant source of gossip and curiosity. The father of Terin was a mystery everyone wanted to solve.

"Jonas, is there news?" she asked. Jonas wouldn't interrupt unless there was need to.

"Of a sort. When you are finished here, there are people of interest for you to meet," Jonas said.

"I believe we've said all there is to say for now. Gentlemen, if you would excuse me," Corry said, following Jonas out of the chamber.

*****

"Our cavalry picked them up halfway to Notsu," Jonas explained as they made their way through the corridor.

"Just the three of them?" she asked.

"There are others still captive." Jonas shook his head disgustedly.

"And you believe they are who they claim and not spies of Morac?"

"I believe them, but then again, I am not good at discerning deception." Jonas shrugged.

"Neither is Terin. He can't lie without it showing upon his face." Corry laughed, unable to get the boy off her mind.

"No, he can't." He smiled, before pausing at the chamber's entrance, allowing her to enter first.

Corry found the three women awaiting her, dressed in ankle-length gowns, kneeling, with hoods concealing much of their heads and their hands folded demurely before them. Considering what they endured, she sympathized, but covering themselves would not do in her presence. Four guards stood post around the women, still wary of their motives.

"There is little need to veil yourselves here. Remove them," Corry ordered, the women doing so reluctantly.

"Highness," the one in the center said, her amethyst eyes trained on the floor, auburn tresses framing a delicate face. Corry thought her strikingly beautiful.

"You may stand," Corry said, the women appearing as they claimed, escaped captives suffering Morac's presence for far too long.

"They have been thoroughly searched, Highness," one of the guards pointed out.

"Very good. King's Elite Caleph tells me you were captives to Morac. This is so?" Corry asked.

"Yes, Highness," the one in the center again spoke for the others.

"And your name?" Corry asked.

"I am Keya Niotan, of House Niotan, Highness."

"Of Notsu, I am familiar of your house, Lady Niotan. And your companions?"

"Mia Fladev of Corpi, and Geneve Jordana of Bacel," Keya introduced the others, each bobbing a curtsy in greeting.

"You were taken captive by Morac and served as…" Corry paused, knowing this was a delicate subject, considering what they had suffered.

"Slaves. We were his slaves, Highness," the one called Mia stated bitterly. The woman looked nearer her fourth decade than her third, with rich black hair framing sharp cheekbones and wary brown eyes.

"I see." Corry sighed, easily guessing the manner in which they served.

"No, Your Highness, one cannot see what we suffered. Any slave of Morac suffers humiliation that one cannot imagine," Mia said, her companions lowering their eyes, unable to speak as openly as she.

"Then speak of it as you can," Corry said, asking the guards to step without, leaving only Jonas in the chamber with her.

"Some of us were taken in caravan raids, handed over to Morac if we were *fortunate*," Mia said, recalling those who suffered far worse by the raiders who took them. "I was taken long before the battle at Kregmarin, taken by raiders northeast of Bacel. Geneve was taken shortly after in a caravan southeast of Bacel. Keya was taken after the fall of Notsu, catching the eye of Lord Morac after his triumphant entrance into the city."

"Lord of bones and carrion," Corry spat.

"A fitting description, Highness." Mia sighed.

"I had the displeasure of his company for only a few moments. I can ill imagine suffering him any longer," Corry said.

"I remember that day, Highness. He returned to his pavilion enraged, swearing to see you suffer his collar, forgoing one of gold for one of silver," Mia said.

"Pardon?" Corry asked sternly, knowing there was a dark meaning in Mia's words.

Mia pursed her lips, the words coming harder than she could bear. "Morac placed slave collars on each of us in his keeping. He favored only highborn women, taking pleasure in bringing us low. Our first collar was gold, a symbol of our purity. Once he took our maidenhood, he would replace the gold for silver, usually on special occasions, especially victories. He took mine after Kregmarin."

Corry felt like vomiting, learning how Mia suffered after the death of her father.

"Eventually there were just two golden collars left, Hena and Keya," Mia said, sharing a look with Keya.

"He planned to exchange my collar upon taking Corell but instead offered Hena and I to the Naybin commanders if they could breach the gate, planning to celebrate his victory with…" Keya paused before Corry finished for her.

"With me. He boasted of it while presenting my father's head at our parlay," Corry said, speaking of it more freely in these women's presence.

"Yes." Keya sighed.

"It matters not. He will *never* touch me. I will see him dead or castrated before this war is finished. I will not stand in fear of him. Instead, he will remain in fear of me. Now, is there anything else I should know concerning that worm?" Corry asked, her tone as flat and direct as she could manage.

"He hasn't slept a complete night since the battle. The sleep he does get is fitful and tormented." Mia smiled wickedly.

"His leg is still not fully healed, though he hides it well in front of his men," Geneve finally spoke.

"His leg? What happened to it?" Corry asked, sharing a look with Jonas.

"He suffered a terrible wound at Kregmarin, preventing him from standing for almost a fortnight and walking very slowly several days later," Geneve said.

"Did my father inflict this wound?" Corry asked, wondering if he at least inflicted some measure of suffering upon his killer.

"No, though the king left a severe bruise to his head, causing him agony for days from the jarring blow. The king and his ocran also killed Morac's mount, before dying themselves. Morac called out your father before his Army, challenging him to face him sword upon sword. Your father did so, fighting bravely and inspiring his men. Morac can claim no victory over him, with odds so much to his favor, Highness," Mia said, for she was the only one of the three that was there.

Corry's heart raced, tears fighting to burst free with sorrow and pride. Her father took up Morac's challenge knowing he had no hope against his Golden Sword. To do so in the face of certain death was the mark of true courage.

"Whoever struck the blow to Morac's leg did our cause great service," Jonas acknowledged, the wound keeping Morac out of the Battle at Corell for much of its duration.

"He was engaged with a man he knew, killing the man when another stuck his leg from behind," Mia recalled Morac's injury and the invectives he shouted, cursing the man.

"A man he knew?" Corry asked.

"Yes, a Yatin that he claimed to have met at Fera. The man escaped the palace with a number of other outlaws," Mia explained.

"Yeltor?" Corry's voice rose an octave.

"Yes, that is the name. Yeltor distracted Morac, sacrificing his life for his companion to strike the blow," Mia now recalled.

"His companion?" Corry wondered who that could've been. Perhaps it was Arsenc, but they would never know.

"Yes, but Morac made little mention of him, simply cursing the man. Unfortunately, the blow did not kill him," Mia said with disgust.

"Many brave men fell that day," Jonas sadly reflected, blaming himself for all their misfortune. If only he hadn't placed that sword in his father's hand, none of this would've come to pass. If only his kin ventured from the Kalinian Vale long ago, with the four Swords of Light in their possession, each in the hand of a warrior with the blood of Kal coursing their veins. Why did they wait? That was a question he would ask himself over and over until the day he died.

"Now that you are free, what do you plan to do?" Corry asked, looking at each of the women, receiving an assortment of looks.

"My family dwells in Corpi. I hope to return to them, Highness," Mia said, though the journey would be perilous with Morac's legions between them and her home city on the northeast coast. Mia could ill imagine the reception she would receive. Her maidenhood was gone, greatly damaging her marital prospects. She only hoped her family would receive her kindly.

"You may stay until the way is safe for you to return," Corry offered.

"You are most kind, Highness." Mia bowed.

"I do not know if any of my kin left Bacel before it was destroyed, Highness," Geneve sadly stated her sorry state. All she knew was destroyed, leaving her alone, poor, and soiled.

"Many from Bacel and Notsu have taken refuge at Besos. Perhaps you and Keya can see if any you know are there. If not, we can arrange a place for you in Torry North," Corry said.

"Thank you, Highness," they both said, bobbing a curtsy.

Corry and Jonas stepped without, making their way back to the throne room, where she would hold court that day.

"If we needed any more evidence of Morac's depravity." Jonas sighed.

"He will pay, Jonas. He will rue the day he was born," Corry said matter-of-factly, her calm voice belying the raging tempest within.

"Kal, oh king of ancient times…"

Galen sang, his fingers deftly plucking his mandolin, his voice drifting above their cook fire in the crisp evening air. They set camp in the sparse wilder lands bordering the northeast shore of Lake Monata. Cronus sat before the crackling fire, tending its embers, as Squid stepped briefly away.

Stepping away from the flames, Squid could see the outline of the Arian Hills, silhouetted along the western horizon and the dark expanse of Lake Monata stretching endlessly south. A million stars dotted the heavens above as he gazed skyward, its ancient mystery holding his imagination. He could almost hear the stars echo their ancient melody, a symphony of Yah's glory. Who but the creator could order the cosmos with such wonder? He thought of his parting words with Terin, speaking of Yah's will guiding Terin's path, telling the boy to trust in Yah when all hope seems lost.

"Humble your heart to him," Squid had said. *"Only then can you hear his counsel."*

He wondered if Terin thought him mad for such an utterance, but the boy simply regarded him respectfully in understanding. He seemed troubled by the conversation he had with Jonas but soldiered on with the task set before him. Now Terin was somewhere out there north and west, probably sitting before a cook fire of his own, with Kato and Lucas for company. Squid gazed farther skyward, his eyes seeking Yah's wisdom in that endless expanse.

"Yah, you are my god," Squid whispered in the evening breeze, his words dying in the wind. "My faith is true but my vision dim. I am oft blind to your will, as I now feel. I have sent Terin to aid your servant. May your hand protect him. He is the only son of my dearest friend, and I fear I send him once again into grave danger, but I am not allowed the privilege of placing his life above the needs of the realm. We stand upon the knife's edge. Grant me the vision to see your will and the wisdom to heed it. I have come to know you, Oh Yah, yet I am a poor witness to your glory. Forgive me this fault," Squid finished his prayer and returned to the others as Galen finished the last verse.

"A fine choice, minstrel," Squid commented, stepping nigh.

"The Golden Age of Man," Cronus said, shifting the coals of the fire, though his eyes were far away.

"'Tis my most requested ballad," Galen said with a musical voice. Cronus recalled the eve of the final assault upon Corell, when Galen played that very tune for the men. Whenever the hearts of men grew laden with worry for their current troubles, they looked to the past, recalling happier times with nostalgia.

"A fine age, perhaps, but not the Golden Age of Man, Cronus," Squid said, sitting upon his bedroll beside the Torry warrior. "I once thought as you but found I was mistaken. To believe the best of times happened more than two millennia before our birth is a mockery of all that King Kal fought for. King Kal's reign was but a brief visit to that place where our future lies. The Golden Age of Man is the future we strive to bring to fruition. It shall only come to pass once our faith in Yah's providence has been restored."

"You speak of this god of yours as if you know him, Squid. Long ago, men worshipped many gods, and now they worship none. What sets him apart from the fallen deities whose divinity died with their acolytes?" Cronus challenged. He had witnessed too much cruelty in his time to believe any god of goodwill had a hand in it. Only a god who took pleasure in suffering would allow such evil to flourish, and he wanted nothing to do with such a being.

"He is as he is. He is god. Other gods of ancient times were illusions, fabricated by the minds of the misled."

"If Yah was the only true god, then why did he fail King Kal?" Cronus pressed.

Squid expected that question, and he always feared it. He wasn't comfortable with the explanation that he offered in refute, yet how could he claim ignorance when others sought truth through his answer.

"Yah did not fail King Kal. Kal was loyal to Yah, but though he was ready to receive his blessing, Arax was not. The legends claim that King Kal's death was a reflection of Yah's own suffering. Prophetic scholars argue on this meaning, but always remember that what misfortune is visited upon Yah's servants transpire for reasons beyond our understanding, reasons oft not visible until the whole story is revealed."

"What proof have you that your god exists? And if he does, why does he allow such evil to thrive unchecked in this world?" Cronus challenged.

An easy smile touched Squid's lips as he placed a hand to Cronus's shoulder. "You are seeking answers with your mind, yet to find Yah, you must use your heart. If your heart feels laden and cold, he is not there. As for allowing evil to run unchecked in our world, how can that be true when it is checked by good men, like the one who sits beside me."

Cronus regarded him briefly, before looking back into the flames, thinking upon the old man's words. It was all too strange, this business with an ancient god and his mindless ramblings. Despite this, he knew Squid was a man of reason and a trusted minister to the throne. Would such a man place such trust in a false god? Perhaps Squid could find reason and logic in things he could not see or touch, but Cronus could not.

*****

Cronus narrowed his eyes to the pressing wind, their magantors sweeping over the coastline, the vast expanse of Lake Monata stretching off his left and the rolling Arian Hills to his right. Squid held close behind him, the Torry minister's eyes following the beautiful grayish-blue surface of the massive lake. Galen pressed close beside them, the minstrel gaining confidence with each passing day in the saddle. Cronus thought him too confident for his own good. It took years for riders to master a warbird, and Cronus had little experience, and Galen none. They could do little more than steer the beasts in the direction they desired and take off and set down with great difficulty. In a different time, Squid would be escorted by expert riders, but they were needed where the enemy was, not here, where they likely were not.

Despite their limited abilities, Galen seemed oblivious to these limitations, growing bolder, especially with Squid sharing Cronus's mount this morn instead of his own. Galen breathed in the crisp air, exhaling with exhilaration. No ballad he sung or royal visited could compare to the wonder of flight, to soar through the firmament as if he held dominion of the lands below. Even the waters of Monata shrank before these airy heights. The thrill of it all coursed his veins, driving him to push the bounds of his meager skills. He leaned forward, pressing a hand to the back of the bird's neck, the subtle command signaling the avian into a dive.

"*Packawww!*"

The magantor's scream echoed through its descent, its eyes narrowed as if bearing down upon unseen prey. Galen raised his left fist victoriously as the bird broke out of the dive, sweeping above Lake Monata, where its waves crashed upon the barren shore. He soared northward over the rocky slopes of the Arian Hills, following the contours of the jagged landscape. The magantor responded perfectly to his novice commands as he reveled in the ease of it all. He shifted the reins, turning the magantor back to the shoreline, but his mount did not respond. Panic took him as the bird continued apace, flying ever northward, leaving him unbeknownst of the absence of his comrades.

*****

"Where the blast is he?" Cronus growled his displeasure, his eyes searching the sky for his friend.

"I think we should land, Cronus. It is best we stay in one place and wait for his search to find us, lest we seek one another in an endless circle!" Squid shouted through the wind, pointing to a small flat area above the rocky shore just ahead.

Cronus heard little of what Squid said through the wind but understood the gesture, easing their mount into a gentle descent.

They waited in place for countless hours, their silhouettes visible for countless leagues, standing atop the rock-strewn shoreline.

"I told him to follow our lead, not to deviate from our simple course, fearing that such a thing as this might happen!" Cronus growled.

"Do not trouble yourself further, Cronus, for it is beyond our feeble hands now. We must continue our journey," Squid said.

"And leave him?"

"He has already left us. How long should we continue to search? A day? Ten days? Twenty? We have spent precious time already. We dare not tarry any longer. He knows where we are going. He may have already guessed our course and is already ahead of us. Let us trust his safety and ours to Yah's providence and continue our journey."

"Very well, Squid, but consigning Galen's fate to your god's hands does not expunge our guilt for abandoning him."

*****

One day hence

The late autumn wind pressed the left side of their faces, rolling across the surface of Lake Monata. Squid sat behind Cronus in the saddle, his eyes scanning the shoreline below, following it to the horizon. The shoreline continued in a bland unison, an endless stretch of gentle waves lapping a rocky shore, with the jagged Arian Hills running leagues northward. 'Twas a barren, inhospitable land, ill-suited to human settlement, save for one secluded inlet resting somewhere up ahead.

"Squaw! Squaw!" a flock of lumar sounded, coursing the skies off their left. Squid gazed south, following the birds' flight through the crisp air, sunlight playing off their silver scooped beaks.

"Squid!" Cronus's voice drew his eyes back to the horizon, where the shoreline arced severely inward, and the hills pushed farther inland, surrounding a flat, barren landscape with numerous broken towers circling a small inlet. Crumbling ruins were spread out around the decrepit citadels, ghostly echoes of a long dead city. The surrounding fields were a collage of blotted grass and twisted underbrush, with a small stream meandering the ancient ruins.

"Tarelia," Squid whispered, naming the ancient dwelling of the remnants of King Kal's lost realm and the forebears of the Middle Kingdom. Despite a lifetime of service to the Torry Crown and countless travels on behalf his king, Squid's eyes had never beheld the fabled ruins until now. He could make out the remains of a curtain wall in places. Squid imagined the holdfast in its ancient glory, a beacon of light in a dark world. The largest of its citadels, the Tower of Celenia, was supposedly thrice the height of its sisters, towering above Tarelia, its highest peak visible from leagues south across the lake, and north across the Arian Hills. Any vestiges of the fabled citadel were nowhere to be seen, just a myriad of broken towers spread amongst the ruin. Dull gray walls, overgrown with vines, were all that remained of ancient Tarelia. He could ill imagine the holdfast in its full glory, as the legend of Tarelia grew larger than these pitiful stones. Was this truly all that was left of that once great civilization? The chronicles claim it fell in a single night, overwhelmed by marauding Maltin barbarians. He thought of the knowledge that was lost in its destruction. The great library was fabled to harbor countless tomes of ancient history, scientific theories, and the secrets of Tarelian smith craft. The Maltins burned it all, preserving nothing for posterity. So total was its destruction that no living thing was spared. Every edifice was toppled, and the ground sown with salt so nothing would grow there ever again for hundreds of years.

They circled Tarelia twice over, looking for any sign of life before setting down beside the Nargos, the small river that emptied into Tarelian Cove. They watered their mount and briefly surveyed the ruins, seeking any sign that Galen passed this way. Squid was torn between the urgency of their mission and his own curiosity to explore the ruins, gleaning anything useful from this long dead city. According to legend, the Tarelians were driven out of their first settlements along the Nila, their numbers too few to contest the strength of the Vayon Tribes that swept over much of Arax at that time. The

Tarelians eventually found refuge in this secluded cove, shielded by the Arian Hills and the expanse of Lake Monata. They were great fishermen, living off the bounty of the vibrant Monata. A strong Navy protected their shores throughout the early centuries of their founding. Eventually their naval strength waned as timber for new ships needed to be imported from afar, and without their Navy, they were helpless against the Maltin barbarians that assailed their hold-fast across the open waters of Lake Monata in 527, sacking the city. Tarelia's death was a dagger to the unity of the great kingdoms that were established by the Tarelian Order. Soon after its storied fall, the Swords of Light were lost one by one, dooming the kingdoms of which they were gifted, until only the Middle Kingdom remained. Squid could not help but wonder if Tarelia endured, might the kingdoms she established endured as well? Alas, it was not to be, for the realms of men fail because men are oft consumed by their base inclinations. Now all that remained of Tarelia were these broken ruins resting upon the shores of Monata like empty tombs.

They tarried in Tarelia briefly before again taking to the skies, continuing west.

One day hence

They swept over the shoreline, guiding their magantor throughout the morn before the city of Sawyer broke the horizon. The vast merchant capital straddled the both banks of the Monata River, where Lake Monata fed that deep waterway. Massive stone edifices rose above the city's center, their marble columns rising the height of ten men, lining the face of each structure. The river bisected the city, with a well-built curtain wall of gray stone arcing its circumference. The walls extended along the lake shore, rising the height of three men, with archer towers liberally spaced along its length. The walls followed to the river's edge before continuing upstream to a massive stone bridge straddling the Monata River. Even the bridge was heavily fortified with ramparts fixed along its eastern length. A second bridge was built farther west, where the city walls extended along the riverbank, connecting to its western face, with ramparts facing threats from that direction downstream. Each bridge was built near half a mile within the city, meaning any ship or flotilla attempting to assail the bridges in order to breach the city would fall under heavy ballistae fire from each riverbank throughout that distance.

The Kal-Ro was the central avenue that circled the city, connecting each district and passing over both the east and west bridges, as they were simply named. The Kal-Ro also connected to the two land-facing gates of the city, one upon the north half of the city and the other upon the south. The walls along the land-facing surface were of a height of six men and more thickly built than the river- and lake-facing walls. Clusters of modest stone structures surrounded the large edifices in the city's center, running along the river's edge, while smaller stone-built dwellings stretched to the city's limits.

From afar they could see the Delran Forest gracing the north-western horizon and the open fields that circled the city for countless leagues. As they drew nearer, however, they could see the fields nearest the city, blackened and scorched, with campfires dotting the landscape north and south of the city. Several galleys were listing in the river just downstream of the city walls, their twisted wrecks caught along the shallows of either embankment. Most disturbing of all, they could make out long trenches circling the city, with thousands of soldiers camped behind them. Sawyer was under siege.

"Cronus!" Squid called out in alarm, several magantors drawing near, their riders hurrying them apace, each with two riders, a driver and an archer. The birds were southern bred, with golden-brown feathers and light-gray beaks.

"Macons!" Cronus cursed, descrying the warrior's purple tunics peeking beneath their gold mail. The sigil of a pale magantor on a field of violet was emblazoned upon their chests, designating them members of the Royal Macon Magantor Cavalry. Cronus fought the panic threatening to overtake him, rising up from his stomach, with cold pimples coursing his flesh, akin to the sensation that arises when standing near a high ledge. These men were skilled magantor riders, trained since childhood to master the massive warbirds, whilst he could do little more than basic turns. The city walls were far afield, with a league of open water between them. Soaring nearly five hundred feet above the grayish blue surface, a fall from this height meant certain death.

"We bear no sigil, and yet they attack!" Squid observed, his voice shouting in the wind.

It was an obvious siege tactic to intercept any possible messengers entering or leaving a surrounded city. He could discern the Macon's grim faces as they drew closer, their archers rising in their saddles with arrows notched.

"Hold on!" Cronus grunted.

"Wh—" Squid gasped, their magantor dipping suddenly, dropping from the sky at a severe angle as Cronus slipped beneath their foe, Macon arrows falling on empty air. Squid's stomach went to his throat as the lake's surface grew ominously close, the wind contorting his face, his hair trailing him like a silver flame.

"Packaww!" The magantor scream sliced the crisp air before leveling its descent, its golden wings nearly kissing the surface, speeding toward the city ahead.

Squid craned his neck as an arrow grazed their magantor's left wing, his eyes drawing wide with the enemy magantors fast approaching. He fumbled with their pack that was tied off behind them, working loose Cronus's bow and arrows. The bird shifted suddenly, nearly throwing him from the saddle as Cronus turned hard to the right, another magantor dropping into the space they just occupied, its talons grasping empty air. Squid managed to notch an arrow, twisting awkwardly in the saddle, his eyes fixed to the Macon mount pressing close. The bird was almost upon them, its dark eyes narrowed menacingly. Squid drew taut on the bow, the enemy mount suddenly dipping, bringing its riders clearly in his view, their own archer firing an arrow, as Squid did likewise. Squid winced, an arrow striking his left shoulder, his own shaft speeding harmlessly awry. He lowered the bow, pain coursing his arm, struggling to notch another.

Cronus turned sharply left, the sudden movement causing Squid to drop the arrow. His eyes stared desperately as the Macon archer rose again in his saddle, ready to shoot again.

"Packaww! Packaww!" Magantor screams rang out behind him. Squid stole a quick glance to their front, where two warbirds came swiftly upon them, but tan in color, their riders bearing the sigil of Sayer's garrison, a silver ship upon a field of black. The Sawyer warbirds passed swiftly overhead before sweeping down upon their pursuers, their magantors' talons plucking the Macon riders from their saddles.

Cronus took advantage of the respite, speeding toward the city walls where the mouth of the river met the lake, Squid watching the Macon warbirds flying off with empty saddles. Squid lowered the bow, his eyes growing weary as he scanned behind them, his blurry vision barely making out the winged shapes of their Sawyeran rescuers chasing off another Macon magantor. The Sawyeran mounts broke off soon after, trailing them back to the city as three Macon magantors closed from the north.

Cronus guided his mount above the choppy waves, passing between the walls of the city lining either bank of the river as he entered the city. Archers lining the battlements along each riverbank, held their aim as the magantor passed. He could see men at arms lining the length of the bridge ahead, clad in the orange tunics and gray mail of the Sawyer garrison. He lifted an open right hand, signaling that he bore no weapon or intended no harm as he passed over the bulwarks atop the bridge, before angling northward, setting down upon an open space amid a city square. Scores of soldiers filed into the streets, forming ranks around them, with spears leveled. Cronus eased his sword from his scabbard, tossing it to the street while lifting both hands, Squid's body pressing against his back before slipping off the saddle. Cronus caught hold of him, noticing the arrows embedded in the minister's shoulder and back. Cronus held Squid's still form, feeling the blood ooze through his fingers before calling for aid.

*****

"Ugg!" Squid's world stopped spinning, his eyes opening to a panorama of light and blurred forms. It took an eternal moment before his vision cleared. He found himself abed in a spacious, richly furnished chamber, with Cronus's familiar face greeting him, sitting at his bedside.

"I thought we lost you." Cronus smiled, leaning forward, resting his elbows on his knees.

It took a moment for him to gain his bearings, recalling where he was, when another voice called out to him.

"I told the matrons you were difficult to kill, old friend," Minister Sounor of the Sawyer Council said, standing at the foot of his bed with his arms tucked within the opposite sleeves of his long tunic.

"Sou…Sounor, what ails your city?" Squid asked, his parched voice cracking with ill use and dehydration.

"We are assailed," Sounor said sadly. "For a fortnight the Macons have laid siege. They first appeared to our north, before a second force approached from the south, sealing our land routes from the city, while a flotilla sailed upstream, attempting to breach the city."

Squid recalled the sunken wrecks along the riverbanks to the west, proof that the attempt failed.

"We received no word," Squid explained after taking a drink of water that Cronus held to his lips.

"We sent out two magantors but fear they were overtaken by the enemy," Sounor added, his amethyst eyes regarding Squid.

"A fortnight," Squid repeated, doing the math in his head, though his tired mind wouldn't cooperate. "That would coincide with…"

"With your own travails, yes. King's Elite Kenti has told us of the siege upon Corell and your deliverance. It appears the Macon Empire believes the Torry Realms are likely too far off, or otherwise occupied to contest his claim upon our city. We stand upon the precipice." Sounor sighed.

"Mortus is ever the opportunist," Squid recalled the sentiment of his fellow Torry ministers when they last held council with King Lore, their opinion of King Mortus of Macon proving itself true.

"So it seems," Sounor snorted derisively.

"How fares the city?" Squid inquired.

"We hold for now. Our garrison numbers forty-eight hundred strong, as well as another two telnics of citizen volunteers outfitted with makeshift swords and armor. We have fifty cavalry, but they will be difficult to feed as the siege continues. We dispatched our other cavalry before the siege, their whereabouts unknown, though we ordered them north. Six magantors is all that remain of our once proud contingent, though we have bled the Macons with our losses. With the river blocked downstream, we can only receive supply from across the lake, but the Macons continue to harass our ships by air. Several of our merchant vessels have been set ablaze."

"How long can you hold?" Cronus asked.

"If the Macons plan to starve us, we can endure for a time, perhaps several fortnights, but if they assail the city…" Sounor scratched his chin, trying to make a studious guess. "We will fall. We count nearly fifteen telnics bearing the sigil of the 2nd Macon Army, a red sword upon a field of gold, surrounding our walls."

"They will have to breach the walls," Cronus thought aloud, thankful they didn't face gargoyles who could pass easily over Sawyers walls.

"And breach them they shall if they are willing to suffer the cost. Our only hope is your kingdom," Sounor lamented, knowing that that hope grew ominously dim with the Torry northern armies holding Corell and Rego and little else. Their true hope rested in Torry South, though Prince Lorn had marched into Yatin with half their strength. But alas, what hope had the Torries of breaking the siege when the Macons outnumbered their remaining Army two to one, not counting the fifteen telnics of the 2nd Macon Army camped outside their walls.

"I must get word to Prince Lorn," Squid said determinedly, though he lay hopelessly abed.

"Rest easy, my friend. We shall discuss this again when you wake." Sounor smiled as he and Cronus stepped without, allowing the matrons to again tend his wounds.

*****

"There is another matter that I did not wish to burden Antillius with in his weakened state," Minister Sounor confided in Cronus once they stepped into the outer atrium of the estate, where they brought

Squid. It was the home of Sorlen Kusse, whose estate was nearest where Squid and Cronus set down.

"What matter?" Cronus asked, masking the weariness permeating his body head to toe.

"A stranger came upon our city yester morn by magantor, passing over the siege lines from the north. He was the first magantor rider to breach the Macon siege, passing almost unseen by the enemy until his mount cleared our north wall. What was unusual was his odd attire and absurd tale. It was apparent how poor his riding skills were, and yet he bypassed the Macon patrols easily enough that we thought him a spy. But he spun a strange tale of the breaking of the siege of Corell and that he was sent to our city in the company of yourself and Antillius but was separated along—"

"Galen?" Cronus's eyebrows rose in surprise and relief.

"Yes, that is the name he calls himself. We thought him a spy or buffoon, but strangely his tale is true." Sounor shook his head.

"Where is he?"

"In the city dungeon. Come, let us fetch him."

*****

They found Galen in a fair state, locked in a small clean cell in the bowels of the dungeon. A small cot and wash bucket were the only furnishings afforded him, though most cells had little more than straw thrown down upon a cold floor in absolute darkness. Galen's cell was bathed in torchlight from the outer corridor, granting him some visual bearing. The city magistrate provided Galen the better accommodations until they could discern who he truly was, in the off chance he actually was a Torry emissary, and not a Macon spy.

"Back away!" his jailer ordered, unlocking the cell door, its heavy iron hinge creaking under its weight.

The guard ordered him hither, and he gladly stepped into the light of the corridor, hoping to again state his case, when his eyes found Cronus standing beside a Sawyer minister.

"Cronus!" Galen smiled elatedly, tempering the urge to embrace his friend and kiss him for his deliverance.

"It is good to see you alive. I hope you learned your lesson for flying off like a fool," Cronus regarded his miserable state. The minstrel's tunic was ragged and his long hair unkempt.

"Yes, those creatures are quite cunning, lolling one to think they mastered them before flying off of their own volition. 'Tis a lessen I shan't forget, old friend."

"I am sure you won't." Cronus smiled.

"Now, we only need to clear the misunderstanding with the city officials and attain my release."

"You are free to accompany Torry Elite Kenti, Minstrel. We apologize for confining you thusly, but these are dangerous times," Minister Sounor explained, standing beside Cronus.

"Apology accepted, Minister." Galen bowed, sweeping an arm from his chest with exaggerated deference. "The people of Sawyer are renowned for their civility, manners, and proper breeding. Let us consign this incident to an unfortunate misunderstanding. Perhaps if your people could provide fresh raiment and a hearty meal, I would be most appreciative," Galen said, as Cronus rolled his eyes. Galen's flowery words grew tiresome when he first uttered them. Thankfully, Cronus learned to tune him out during their long trek from Axenville.

*****

Cronus left Squid in Galen's company, once the minstrel was treated to a bath and fed. The matrons feared Squid had lost too much blood, but the fact he still lived gave them hope. Fortunately, the arrow seemed to miss his vitals, embedding his left shoulder and left hip, the latter protruding through his thigh. He required rest, with Galen and Cronus taking turns sitting his bedside, giving him food or water whenever he woke. The matrons moved on to attend the numerous wounded from the skirmishes the garrison and Macons had engaged.

The late evening found Cronus along the lake-facing walls of Sawyer, standing atop a battlement upon the north side of the city. The city walls stretched some distance north along the shore before arcing west and south, where it met the north bank of the Monata River downstream. The southern half of the city mirrored the north, its walls running along the lakeshore to the south, before arcing west and then north to the south bank of the Monata River. From the riverbanks, the walls continued back upstream to the edge of the west bridge, while the lake-facing walls ran inward to the east bridge. The city was further reinforced with deep entrenchments running outside its walls, several meters deep, with aqueous soil that proved difficult to traverse, its suction swallowing feet and sometimes men whole, making them easy prey for archers manning the watchtowers spaced along the walls.

Cronus drew his thick cloak about his shoulders, the brisk lake wind sweeping over the city wall. From his vantage point, he surveyed the mouth of the Monata River, where it met the lake's edge. The city retained a small Navy, which controlled access to the lake, protecting Sawyer's merchant fleet that continued to operate across the lake. It was this vital lifeline that continued to supply the beleaguered city-state. With no significant naval presence upon the lake to contest the Sawyeran Fleet, the Macons relied on their magantors to harry their shipping. The giant avian managed to sink a few merchant vessels but suffered the loss of a magantor that they could ill afford. The giant warbirds were a scarce commodity, and the air arm of the Macon Army was already stretched thin, suffering the loss of two more crews when Cronus and Squid attained the city, stricken by the skilled flyers of Sawyer.

The standard atop the city forum caught his eye, the silver ship upon a field of black rippling proudly in the breeze above its airy summit, defying the vast Army assembled before its ancient walls.

"Cordon the shipwright first raised that banner above our walls during the Maltin invasions thirteen hundred years ago. It has graced our forum ever since," a brown-haired man said, wearing the orange tunic and gray mail of a garrison soldier. Cronus noted the magantor insignia emblazoned upon his mail. He was of a stout build, standing a head shorter than Cronus, with taut facial features and the purple eyes that were common among the natives of Sawyer. The man looked familiar, but he couldn't recall the face.

"You seem familiar," Cronus said as he drew near along the walkway that ran along the inside of the wall. Only a few soldiers manned each section of the ramparts, but a single command would summon the others resting in the billets below.

"I am Arlis, captain of the city's magantor squadron," he declared, extending his hand as they clasped forearms.

"I am—"

"Cronus Kenti, commander of unit, hero of Tuft's Mountain, and now of the Torry Elite. Your legend precedes you, King's Elite Kenti," Arlis stated with obvious admiration.

"I am humbled by your flattery but am just a simple soldier. Only my titles have changed. You seem to know a great deal about me."

"The name Cronus Kenti is well-known in our fair city. Your heroic sacrifice at Tuft's Mountain earned you great renown when Minister Sounor relayed the tale after returning from the council of Corell. You were thought captive or slain, yet now it is told that you escaped the *Black Castle* and crossed the breadth of Arax to reunite with your lady love, the fair Leanna." Arlis grinned, repeating the tale as he heard it.

"I was rescued. I didn't escape," Cronus corrected, knowing no man could escape from Fera on his own. He then recognized why Arlis looked familiar, though he had only seen him in brief passing. "You were the rider that—"

"That slew your pursuers, just yonder," Arlis said, pointing out toward the lake, just beyond the mouth of the river, where his magantor swept over Cronus's, plucking the Macon crew from their saddle.

"Then it was you who saved me?"

Arlis nodded affirm.

"Then I am in your debt. I could not have attained the city without you and your comrades. My magantor skills are feeble at best. To do what you did proves your mastery."

"Our city has a mere six magantors left in our stable. Each of us must be proficient riders if we are to contest the enemy's greater number. I have trained since my fourth year. We are not boastful by nature, but I would choose our riders over any other six in all the realms," Arlis declared proudly.

"I would not disagree. You and your men are heroes to me." Cronus touched a hand to Arlis' shoulder.

"A hero to a hero." Arlis grinned. "So be it. Come, Cronus, let me show you my fair city."

Cronus gladly accepted, but asked first to survey their defenses to better understand their plight. They walked the length of the north wall, surveying the Macon siege lines that mirrored the city's defenses. The Macons held position some three hundred yards beyond the moat, sharpened stakes jutting toward the city from their trenches. The sound of spades striking soil echoed in the late day air. He made out the Macon standards blowing above their encampments, just beyond their trenches, a flaming red sword on a field of gold. He saw thousands of soldiers clad in purple tunics and gray mail moving about along their palisades, strengthening their defenses. Large trebuchets were moved into position across from the north gate of the city, straddling either side of the stone roadway that ran from the gate to the Delran Forest to the northwest. The Macons continued to gather ballistae munitions, as growing mounds of twenty and thirty-pound stones could be seen beside the trebuchets. They were certain to commence a bombardment at any time, most likely upon the north gate itself. A large pavilion, with gold and red stripes, stood out amid the Macon encampment, likely the command tent of the Macon general. A standard blew above the pavilion, bearing the sigil with a red flaming sword upon a field of gold.

"The sigil upon their crests, what is it?" Cronus asked, pointing out the standard above the pavilion, much larger than the rest.

"It is the sigil of the 2nd Macon Army. We have counted twelve to fifteen telnics in their contingent along the northern perimeter and another five telnics south of the river bearing the standard of the 1st Macon Army, a green sword on a field of gold," Arlis explained.

"Twenty thousand," Cronus thought aloud, calculating the city's odds against such a force. An attacking force required a three-to-one advantage to storm a fixed position. The Macons clearly intended to accomplish that goal, knowing the city garrison numbered five telnics, plus what conscripts the ruling council could assemble.

"More than enough to complete the task," Arlis added, guessing Cronus' thoughts. "They have made three sorties in the past nine days, testing our defenses. The last was the assault upriver with a dozen galleys, trying to breach the fortifications near the west bridge."

"I saw the wrecks along the riverbanks downstream."

"Aye. One is ours, a heavy Trioar that took four Macon galleys with it. We recovered half its crew, but the rest were burned, drowned, or taken captive. The Macons lost another three galleys attempting to breach the city, their vessels caught between our walls lining the riverbanks. I doubt they'll attempt another such folly."

"A heavy cost just to probe your defenses," Cronus said.

"A foolish decision, likely to gauge our resolve and readiness. The walls of Sawyer have not been tested in centuries. Perhaps they thought we had grown soft and our walls decrepit."

"And now they know better," Cronus stated flatly. If he learned anything about the siege of Corell, it was to never give up.

"We are both soldiers, Cronus. What help can we hope to receive from your realm? Our people believe a Torry relief Army will sweep down from the north and crush the Macons against our walls, but I know the state of your armies and doubt any help will come before our city falls," Arlis sadly surmised.

"There are too few of us left to guard the north. Our 5th Army was slain to a man upon Kregmarin with our king. The 3rd Army is half of what it was and now checks Morac's legions at Notsu. Our 2nd Army is somewhere between Central City and Rego. Torry North has nothing left to give. Your only hope is Torry South, and our prince has taken half of their strength north into Yatin," Cronus summarized their dire position. The damnable Macon king knew when to strike, when Sawyer was most vulnerable with no friends to save her.

"You state what I already surmised. Only Yah can deliver us now," Arlis sadly conceded, his weary gaze turning to the north, where the Macons busied themselves strengthening their encirclement.

Cronus felt utterly helpless, staring at the man, knowing his people were doomed and knowing of no logical way to save them. He could offer nothing more than false reassurances, which any good soldier could see as lies. Arlis's mention of Yah indicated the spread of Squid's strange religion in these lands.

"My wife and children dwell not far from here, two streets south of where we stand. I overcame my fear of flying a magantor long ago, learning to disregard death. But now…now that I have her and my two daughters, I fear what my death would mean to them. Even worse is what a Macon conquest would consign them to. Fear has become my master, where once I was its. I thought to send them away, perhaps by ship to Torry lands across the lake, but ships are no longer safe."

"As grim as Macon rule is, a Benotrist conquest of Torry North is far worse if they took sanctuary there. Our fates are intertwined, Arlis. Your only hope is to endure as long as you can. Never give in, never give up, even if the siege lasts through the winter. The longer you hold the Macons at bay, the more options we have of breaking the siege," Cronus assured him.

"I know the truth of your words, Cronus, but my mind is consumed with my family's safety. Our food stores grow thin. Our shipping will struggle to bring in enough food to make up the difference. It's simple math. The Macons can starve us out or press a full-scale assault and topple us."

"Perhaps, but not yet. Blood still courses your veins, and a sword still rides your hip. If they attack, then we shall bleed them upon your walls, and that alone shall buy us time."

"Time for what?"

"Time to find another way."

*****

The Macon encampment
Command pavilion

Bram Vecious, general of the Macon 2nd Army, surveyed the map unfurled across the table, with the city of Sawyer and its surrounding lands displayed in detail. His lips curled distastefully, weighing the consequences of their success or failure, wondering which was worse. He felt the cold gaze of Orton Lorvius staring at him from across the table, the king's chief minister's gray eyes questioning his misgivings.

"You doubt the success of this plan?" Lorvius questioned. As King Mortus's chief minister, Orton Lorvius joined the campaign to oversee the throne's interests in advancing their aims. General Vecious's opposition to the Sawyer Campaign was known only to those within the king's upper council.

"I told you, Chief Minister, that these hurried assaults gain us little, throwing men away for negligible result," Bram Vecious snorted.

"Perhaps if your attacks were more enthusiastically embraced, General, the outcome would improve," the chief minister countered, wary of the prickly general's sentiments.

"My enthusiasm holds no weight in the success of this attack, only your meddling!"

"Caution, General, for I represent King Mortus's interests in this endeavor. To question me is to question his eminence," he warned.

"My king commanded me to take that city!" He jabbed his finger through the open flaps of his pavilion, where the north wall of Sawyer rested in the distance. "It is my responsibility to do so without wasting the precious lives of our king's soldiers, soldiers that we shall need if this entire campaign ignites a greater war."

"A greater war with whom, General?" Orton's smug smile stretched the length of his narrow face.

"The Torries will not sit idle whilst we threaten their ancient ally."

"The Torries?" Orton laughed. "They are in no position to contest a siege, let alone our dominion of Sawyer. And they will do well to mind their own interests."

"Their northern armies are occupied, but their southern realm retains enough strength to contest this move," Bram countered.

"Nay. Their foolish prince has marched half their strength into Yatin, selling Torry lives to preserve their Yatin foes. He would have been wise to let Tyro bleed himself killing the Yatins and then deal with the winner."

"Ah, a clever game to play, watching our enemies fight one another, while we pluck the jewel of Monata." Bram tapped the map where Sawyer rested in its center. The independent city-state was long desired by the Macon kings for centuries but was protected by its alliances with the Torry Realms and the Jenaii. Now those realms were embroiled in a desperate war with Tyro, tying their hands from intervening on Sawyer's behalf.

"Yes, a clever game indeed." Orton smiled, for it was his counsel that supported this move, reminding his king that the opportunity to attain Sawyer might never be as easy.

Bram, however, thought otherwise. He did not favor a war upon Sawyer that might distress the Torry Realms whilst the greater Benotrist threat loomed ominously in the north. He trusted little in his king's tentative alliance with the Naybin Empire, who themselves were aligned with Tyro. Any pact with gargoyles was a betrayal of mankind, and Bram wondered how his king could not see it. He was relieved when word reached them two days before that the siege of Corell was broken, though the chief minister did not share his sentiment. Could Orton not see that the Torries were barely hanging on, while they threatened their southern flank? Could Orton not see that Tyro would not stop with Torry North but continue his advance upon their realm after? What gain was there in attaining Sawyer once Tyro united all the lands north of them under his iron rule? He counseled his king on this very point before commencing this campaign, only to be overruled. The king wanted Sawyer and, with it, control of the western half of Lake Monata, and have it he will, the greater consequences be damned. Bram, however, favored a slow, methodical approach, starving the city into submission and sparing as many men as he could. He knew it likely that if things turned sour in Torry North, the Macon Empire might have to come to their aid, just as the Torries came to Yatin's. King Mortus, however, was just as likely to attack Torry South as Tyro advanced, expanding his empire and hoping Tyro allowed him to keep it. Bram knew the only deterrent to future Benotrist aggression was a strong Macon Empire, and that required minimal casualties in this campaign. Orton, however, demanded another assault upon the city, forcing him to throw men against their walls. Only an all-out assault, coordinated with appropriate siege engines and ballistae, would breach the city, and it took time to construct them, but the chief minister dismissed this advice, insisting they assail the city upon their arrival. And so Bram watched helplessly as he sent his men to their death in several futile attempts to take the city, with the chief minister blaming him for their failure, claiming he did not give the attacks his full support. And here he was, forced to send more men to certain death, to appease the likes of Orton Lorvius.

"Perhaps, Chief Minister, you would spare a glance at this map." Bram unfurled another map across the table, depicting the entire Macon Realm and its neighboring lands. "Here I sit north of Sawyer with the entirety of the Macon 2nd Army, fifteen thousand men." He ran his finger in an arc along the bank of the Monata River, skirting the north side of Sawyer, stopping at the lake's edge. "I have deployed three of my telnics far to the north, guarding the passes to Torry North in the event General Fonis sweeps down upon us."

"Highly unlikely." Orton sneered, knowing such a move would leave Rego and Central City open to attack.

"Perhaps, but consider," Bram continued, running his finger along the southern approaches of Sawyer, where five telnics of General Noivi's 1st Macon Army cut Sawyer's land route south. "With five telnics of Noivi's Army here, that leaves him only five telnics in Fleace." He tapped his finger over their capital, countless leagues to their west.

"Your point, General?"

"Our greatest threat lies here, with only General Ciyon's 3rd Army between our capital and our western border." His finger running the length of their border with Torry South.

"Any Torry feint upon our western border will not save Sawyer and will only justify our invasion of Torry North. I doubt our Torry friends are so blind to their strategic vulnerabilities. If the Torry presence in Torry South troubles you, General, I suggest you end this siege quickly and reposition your Army to counter that threat."

"The king has tasked me with taking Sawyer, and I shall do so, Chief Minister. I suggest you confine your attention to matters of state."

"The acquisition of Sawyer *is* a matter of state, General. You should concern yourself with its completion and perhaps investigate how your magantor patrols allowed a Torry warbird to slip through your blockade."

"No siege has ever sealed a city by air, and two of my crews paid with their lives to intercept that magantor," Bram's voice concealed his festering rage. He warned his riders not to venture near the city, fearing they might be slain by the city's reputed magantor squadron. Unfortunately, the heat of battle made them lose sight of their location. They were able to recover the magantors, but trained crews were harder to come by. He had known the slain riders since they were boys, when they were recruited into the Royal Magantor Service. Like any of the soldiers he had sent to their death, Bram felt their loss deeply. It was that bond that soldiers understood and statesmen such as Orton could not.

"The Torry warbird must not be allowed to leave," Orton commanded. His agent inside the city had poisoned the former Torry ambassador, and Orton was wary of any Torry emissaries meddling in this campaign. He desired the city taken as soon as possible, preferably before the Torries knew that it was under siege. They would be less likely to intercede if the city had already fallen.

"I will do my best containing the city, Chief Minister, but overseeing the coming assault takes precedence. And as far as the Torries are concerned, they likely already know what we have done, since merchant ships and Jenaii galleys come and go as they please."

The Jenaii, Orton mused. The Jenaii originally reinforced Sawyer with a squadron of warships, but they were drawn off by the campaign in the east, leaving only their merchant vessels to contend with, though troublesome in their own right. He needed this campaign concluded before they thought to return.

"Very well, General, but you must take this city as soon as possible."

*****

Thump!

The stone ballistae arced over the battlefield, striking the upper battlements of the north wall, stone fragments chipping away where it struck. The morning greeted the defenders with a half dozen Macon trebuchets moved forward of their lines throughout the night, their crews loading thirty-pound projectiles as they cranked them into firing position.

The Sawyer garrison returned the favor, their own trebuchets raining fire ballistae, several striking near the Macon crews, setting grass afire, the gelatinous material burning long after the blades of grass were cinders. The Macons kept pace throughout the morning, firing without respite, striking the walls to either side of the main gate, whilst the Sawyerans returning fire found purchase on a Macon trebuchet, its timbers igniting on contact. The Macons moved two more siege engines into position, with hundreds of stone munitions.

Gaive Dolom, commander of the city garrison, surveyed the damage along the adjoining walls at midday, finding the city's thick ramparts broken in several places but structurally sound. He stood upon the battlements above the north gate, observing the Macon crews in the distance loading their munitions as another fire ballistae struck true, splashing into their midst, setting several ablaze. He watched joylessly as their screams rent the air, the stricken crews scurrying about with flames licking their limbs. Another ballistae struck a trebuchet off his right, setting it ablaze. The other Macon crews responded in kind, a stone munition striking the wall below him, just above the gate. Commander Dolom stood impassive, unflinching as another stone struck below his battlement to little effect. He noted movement in the distance, amidst the Macon encampment, hundreds of soldiers marching in unison, their purple tunics and gray mail a stark contrast to the green foregrounds carpeting the lands north of the city.

"Commander, look yonder!" the soldier standing to his left cried out, pointing excitedly beyond the Macon host.

"I see it," Gaive said somberly as the Macon's drew forth a great ram, drawn by teams of moglo beasts. It was forged of heavy timbers with iron plated along its beams to protect it from fire. The ram swung freely between four massive posts, each the height of two men. The iron spike affixed to its front was cast in the visage of a versk, the vicious carnivore that plagued the sea-lanes of the Araxan coast, its rows of jagged teeth and distinct dorsal fins instilling terror in seafarers for ages.

Gaive disregarded the ram's threat as they held no means of crossing the moat without placing long planks across that deadly space, where he could riddle them with fire and arrows.

"*The river!*" The shouts rippled along the walls, echoing through the ranks.

*****

Cronus followed the sounds of battle through the narrow streets that ran nearest the walls. He left Squid again in Galen's care while venturing into the city, when the battle suddenly shifted to the west, with the Macons attempting to breach the walls where the river split the city. He caught sight of archers lining the battlements above once he cleared the last street, the walls rising imperiously ahead, with wide stone steps built along their base every two hundred paces. Men in orange tunics hurried to and fro, scurrying up the wide steps. Flashes of sunlight reflected off clashing blades farther west along the upper battlements, indicating the enemy had attained the walls nearer the river's edge.

"The river!" men shouted, drawing his gaze farther south and west, where a myriad of structures blocked his view. He cursed under his breath, making his way south through streets no wider than a wagon's width, hurrying apace, passing alleyways even narrower, and avoiding them when he could, rightly thinking they were good place to die if the battle spilled into the streets. He ran into heavy foot traffic coming in the opposite direction, fleeing the carnage ahead. A wealthy woman hurried past, holding the hems of her billowing skirts, her eyes wild with fright, followed by her servants carrying their mistress's treasures. Small double-floored dwellings lined either side of the avenue, the upper floors extending beyond their ground levels, jutting into the street. If he were any taller, he'd surely bump his head into the overhanging upper floors. Up ahead, he saw the intersecting streets widen significantly, with scenes of men passing quickly in each direction. He turned the corner, nearly knocking a woman over who was traveling in the opposite direction, holding a child in her arms. He grasped her arms, steadying her balance before continuing on. The adjoining avenue ended at the river's edge, where the wall jutted within the city proper, running along the north bank of the Monata, before ending at the bridge somewhere to his left. The section of wall running along the riverbank was half the height of the outer wall. He saw archers on the river wall above, firing rapidly over the battlements at targets in the river, indicating that the Macons managed to squeeze a ship upstream into the city.

"Agghh!" men cried out from the base of the wall, their disjointed voices mixed with clanging steel. A flax of garrison soldiers rushed past him, with levelled spears and raised shields.

Cronus held back as the soldiers pushed on toward the end of the avenue, where it met the river wall, joining the battle as men in purple tunics spilled into the street from the west.

"Macons," Cronus grunted as enemy troops flooded into the street, meeting their Sawyeran foes, a clash of purple and orange trading blows.

Cronus threw off his cloak, drawing his sword and stepping forth, his dark-gray tunic and nondescript mail giving no indication of his loyalties. As the Torry Kingdom was still neutral in the conflict, his attire would not implicate his realm, freeing him to intercede. Fortunately, neither side noticed him until his sword found purchase in a Macon soldier's gut, protruding out his back before Cronus planted a foot in the man's chest, jerking the blade free. He snatched the dying soldier's shield, holding it aloft, blocking another Macon's thrust. He stepped to his right, the blade sliding off his shield, positioning his foe between himself and the first soldier he cut down, who lay dying on the street. He drove his shield into the Macon soldier, catching him off guard, driving him back a step, stumbling over his fallen comrade. Cronus immediately drove his blade into the soldier's inner thigh, above the greaves that ran north of his knee, twisting the sword free, the savage cut severing his artery. Cronus spun about, his eyes scanning for any pressing threats before catching sight of another Macon slashing at a Sawyeran soldier lying upon his back, desperately blocking the hasty blows with his shield. Cronus raced behind the Macon, driving his sword through his ribs, before twisting the man to the ground, his body writhing upon his blade. Cronus withdrew his sword, stealing a glance behind him, checking for threats, before helping the Sawyeran to his feet.

"My thanks," the soldier panted, gaining his feet, the battle raging around them. There was little order in the building chaos, both lines breaking apart on contact, their shield walls giving way individual melees.

"Come!" Cronus commanded, weaving his way through the maelstrom toward the wall, spying Macons advancing along the ramparts above from the west, indicating that the turret overlooking the river at the city's edge had fallen. They raced up the nearest stairs, joining the defenders who desperately held the wall above against the Macons pressing from the west. Clearing the last step, he could see over the battlements, affording him view of the river below and the wall running along the opposite bank. The west bridge was upstream to his left, and the massive turrets guarding the city entrance were downstream to his right, where the river and outer walls joined. In the waters below, he beheld a hellish vision, with Macon vessels crowding the river. Several listed severely, drifting back downstream, fires sweeping their decks. Others rowed against the current, driving upstream under withering fire from either bank. Men were pinioned to the desks, arrows feathering their bodies. Fire ballistae struck the rigging of another galley, flames splashing amidship, men jumping from the decks, flames licking their flesh. Several galleys clogged the entrance to the city, their hulls ripped open by traps set below the waterline, short of the city. The current slowly pushed these wrecks downstream or slammed them against the banks. Other ships set ashore nearer the turret guarding the north bank, smoke billowing over said turret, its surface caked in flames, victim to Macon catapults. The Macons used the diversion to set men ashore along the river wall near the flames, setting ladders along the rocky embankment to scale the wall. Over a hundred bodies were piled at the base of the river wall, victims to either spearmen manning the battlements or archers along the adjoining bulwarks, but those forces were now pushed back, with Macons overtaking the battlements.

Macons were now pouring over the battlements along a wide stretch of the river wall, just upstream of the turret, hindered only by the archer fire from the opposite bank. The Sawyeran soldiers upon the outer wall were blocked by the flames engulfing the turret connecting the two walls.

Cronus winced as a sheet of flame erupted below the west bridge, warming his face. There, below the bridge, a Macon galley blew apart, caking the west side of the bridge in the gelatinous material that was set ablaze. It was a fire ship, intended to damage the bridge, but the sturdy structure stood unmoved, though scores of men manning its battlements were set ablaze, their wretched screams haunting the smoke-filled air.

The sound of clanging steel drew Cronus to the task at hand, as he worked his way west along the causeway built into the wall. The Sawyerans strangely overlooked his presence, their attention fixed to the enemy pressing their front. The causeway was wide enough for four men to stand abreast with interlocked shields and spears thrusting between.

"Agghh!" a Sawyeran cried out just ahead, pushed from the lip of the causeway to the street below, a Macon spear piercing his gut. The defenders were strangely thin along this section of the wall, which drew Cronus to add his sword where it was needed. Only few remained holding their ground upon the causeway, stabbing at the Macons with spear thrusts between their shields. The Macons responded in kind, keeping their shields up, driving the defenders back across the battlements. Another Sawyeran stumbled, a Macon spear finding purchase in his thigh, ripping a vicious gash, blood pooling the gray stone of the causeway. With no parapet lining the interior of the causeway, men could fall easily off its stone lip to the street below. The wounded soldier's comrades tried to buy him time to withdraw, slamming their shields into the Macons' steel wall, to no avail, their weakened front exposing another to spear thrusts into his arm. That soldier dropped his spear, withdrawing as the line gave way, Macons knocking two others from the causeway, their bodies striking the unforgiving street below, the fall killing one and breaking the other's back.

Cronus paused upon a small turret, short of the contested portion of the wall, where a small catapult was placed, its crew hurling fire ballistae upon the ships below. Cronus directed them to the enemy sweeping across the causeway.

"Fire upon our own walls?" the crew commander asked dismissively.

"Yes, or lose this turret, your lives, and the wall itself!" Cronus shouted.

The man conceded, his pained look obvious from afar. Cronus acknowledged him before gathering his comrades and a few others that attached themselves to his cause, drawn by his decisive nature and sensing that he knew what he was doing, following him onto the causeway with the Macons drawing near, cutting down the Sawyerans in their path.

"Form shields!" Cronus commanded, interlocking his shield with his fellows just as the catapult crews followed with a ballistae barrage, flaming projectiles passing over their heads. One of the ballistae struck the bulwark behind the Macon fore ranks, flames splashing in their midst, while others fell harmlessly awry.

"Forward!" Cronus commanded, filling in beside the few Sawyerans still afoot, with the Macon front ranks shifting with the fire munitions dropping in their midst. They continued forth, shields smashing into shields, Cronus jabbing his sword between the seams, his blade striking the flat of a Macon shield, before slipping through the gap, striking something soft. The Macon across from him cried out, his sword slipping from his weakened grip, a large gash torn from his elbow. Cronus drove forth, smashing the man with his shield, as another Macon off his left staggered with a sword piercing his stomach. Fire munitions continued to arc overhead, cutting the Macons' only avenue of retreat. The Sawyerans lumbered forth, more men racing along the causeway to attack the enemy.

The sounds of battle grew louder below as two units of the city garrison flooded into the streets, overwhelming the Macon troops holding there.

The Macons blocking their path lowered their spears and swords in surrender, as Cronus's gaze drifted to the outer walls, where the Macons poured over the battlements, the chaos along the massive turret guarding the river allowing the Macons to advance upon the wall, cross the moat, erect ladders, and scale the ramparts, though suffering horrendously, the dead gathering below the wall. It was for naught as the defenders rushed fresh troops to drive the attackers off the outer wall, feathering them with arrows throughout their retreat across the muddy moat.

Baroom!

Horns sounded retreat, ending the Macon attack from all points along the walls. Those gathered along the riverbanks under the shadow of the city's walls, struggled returning to their ships, retreating under withering arrow fire, archers upon the battlements taking aim as they clustered together, trying to board their ships. Many found the ships they arrived on sunk, sinking, or run aground, their hulls ripped open on the rocky riverbanks. Many stripped their armor, diving into the river to swim for freedom, the cold water constricting their lungs with arrows dropping all around them.

"Who are you?" the soldier who first followed him into battle finally asked, the others gathering up their prisoners.

"Cronus, and you?" Cronus asked, catching his breath, regarding the exhausted soldier's haggard face and bloodstained mail.

"I am Corba. Cronus is not a common name. You are not of Sawyer."

"Nay. I am not, but I am a friend of your city, Corba." Cronus grasped the man's shoulder, not wishing it known that a Torry Elite had partaken in the battle. Such news would quickly spread, complicating his realm's ability to mediate a peaceful resolution to the conflict, though he doubted war could be prevented between Macon and Torry.

*****

Two days hence

"Hundreds dead or wounded, much of our walls scorched, and the west bridge damaged," commander Gaive reported to the ruling council.

"And the Macon losses?" Councilor Saleron, the elder states-man asked, sitting at the lower stone bench of the city forum that circled the center platform where Gaive stood. Like most forums of Arax, it consisted of a center circled platform with rows of benches circling it, each row set higher than the one to its front. The greater statesmen always sat the lowest levels, as positions of honor. Today, the chamber was nearly empty, with only the sitting members of the council, several commanders of rank, and Squid and Cronus attend-ing on behalf of the Torry Realms.

The garrison spent two days counting their dead and clearing debris from the battlements. The dead were gathered and burned where they could be recovered. Scores still littered the battlefield and the riverbanks. Corpses continued to surface after two days in the river bottom, their bloated bodies drifting downstream or caught among the wreckage along the river.

"We've gathered 163 Macon dead along the outer battlements, and another 207 from the Monata and the river walls. We counted nearly 200 more beyond the outer walls and in the river that we have yet to recover. We collected 200 prisoners and spotted count-less numbers of enemy wounded that managed to flee," Commander Gaive detailed the Macon casualties.

"Such waste," Minister Sounor thought aloud, lamenting the loss of so much human life.

Cronus agreed with Sounor's sentiments, cursing the Macons for waging war upon their human brothers when the greater gargoyle threat loomed in the north.

"Such is the way of men, failing to heed our better nature. How oft has our history been marred by petty ambitions, whilst the gar-goyle threat grew unchecked? If only once, had the realms of men united to expunge their true foe, then we would not be where we now stand," Squid said, his firm voice belying his weakened state. He sat uneasy upon the stone bench, blood oozing through his ban-dages, staining his robes. He was unfit to sit in council but insisted on attending, his health and comfort be damned. When Sounor informed him that the council was to meet, he bestirred himself to join them.

"It is pointless to resist. We should ask for terms. All we are doing is delaying the inevitable," Councilor Guyan Torval conceded, throwing his hands up in defeat.

"And trust our lives to Mortus's mercy?" Councilor Jardone Soldar countered.

"What mercy will he have if we force him to storm our city?" Guyan asked.

"Our city has stood free since our founding fourteen centuries ago. We have endured countless sieges, plagues, and natural calamities, and I would not see us submit so weakly. I care not to see my name ascribed to such cowardice. I would rather see my home burned and bloodline extinguished than for posterity to ascribe my name to our surrender. Perhaps we shall not long endure this Macon siege, perhaps our allies shall not deliver us before the hammer falls, but I would see us rise up with a thunderous voice, contesting our doom! Let Mortus taste our swords and know our fury!" Councilor Saleron declared, the elder man's voice reverberating through the chamber.

"Kings and realms rise and fall, but our bloodlines must endure. What glory is gained from our destruction? Look no further than Tarelia, whose ruins haunt the shores of Monata to this day. I would not see us suffer such an end," Guyan countered.

"To end by sword, flame, or chains matters little when all is done. Such talk serves no end but our ruin. We should look to our deliverance, focusing our energies to that end. I was at Corell during the great council, where King Lore called on all good men to hold faith, to stand together against the vast might arrayed against us. He put action to his words, leading a Torry Army against Tyro's might in the defense of Notsu and Bacel, at the cost of his life. Can we offer any less in the defense of our own city? If we do not resist to our last breath, affording time for our allies to aid our cause, then we will have proven ourselves unworthy of their deliverance," Minister Sounor said, his declaration shaming the weak willed and emboldening the stalwart.

They debated far into the night, weighing their options to resist the Macon siege, repeatedly asking Squid about the disposition of the nearest Torry forces and which were likely to intervene on their behalf. It was Cronus that explained that only Prince Lorn could come to their aid, with the Torry 1ˢᵗ Army the only significant force that was presently not engaged. The council questioned the use of an Army that was located on the far end of the Macon Empire. It would take two moons for such an Army to march north of the Macon Empire in order to reach the beleaguered city.

"What choice have you?" Cronus challenged. "The world is not as we would have it. If your only hope lies in Torry South, then that is where it lies."

"And how shall your prince learn of our plight? He is far away, campaigning in Yatin, if our reports are to be believed," Guyan asked.

"I shall tell him!" Cronus stood, stepping forth into the stone circle, facing each member of the council.

The council regarded him with the deepest respect, not for his title and storied deeds, but for his actions defending the river wall and rallying their soldiers. It was more than a gesture and truly symbolized the unity of their two peoples.

"It is madness! It would take countless days to sail across Monata and find your way…"

"I'll not be sailing far, Councilor Guyan. I shall go as I came, upon my magantor."

*****

Three days hence

Squid insisted on seeing them off, accompanying Galen and Cronus to their ship, where their magantors were tethered. They would sail out of port come sundown, heading east for twenty leagues, before taking to the skies. The Macons were carefully watching the heavens, waiting to pounce upon any magantor leaving the city, but ships leaving at night were difficult to interdict. Squid hobbled along, his wooden cane scrapping the stone lip of the wharf, flanked by his two young companions. Their journey had drawn him close to both of them, the sort of kinship that arduous travels oft invoke. It reminded him of his travels with Jonas in their youth, remembering fondly the adventures they shared. The minstrel was a bit pompous and often too willing to ingratiate himself, but he was loyal to his friends and the Torry Realm. It was Cronus, however, that Squid was most fond of. He could see why Terin took such a liking to the man. He reminded him so much of Jonas that he caught himself more than once calling him that. He thought of the time when Captain Raven threatened to destroy Tyro's Navy as well as their own if Cronus was harmed after his capture. When he learned of Raven's plan to exchange Princess Tosha for Cronus, he thought only of the political repercussions. Now he understood Raven's motive, Cronus Kenti was a good man, and he was grateful that he survived Tyro's dungeon. And here Cronus was again, embarking upon another dangerous adventure for sake of the realm.

"Fair you well, my friends. Once you set ashore, make haste, for time is fleeting, and Sawyer's fate will be decided by the slightest of measures," Squid advised.

"We won't be waiting to set ashore before taking flight, Squid. We will find Prince Lorn. You just have to keep stiffening the council's spine in case they start to waffle," Cronus said.

"Very well," Squid smiled, touching a hand to each of their shoulders, seeing them off. They ascended the gangplank as the crew lifted anchor. The ship pushed away from the wharf, lowering oars, making its way upstream before disappearing through the mouth of the river, passing from sight. Squid said a silent prayer for his friends. He waited awhile, staring east up the river where their ship disappeared into the night. There was much for Antillius to do, including finding out what happened to his predecessor, Sais Gallo, whose strange death drew him here to begin with.

CHAPTER

7

Terin stared into the crackling flames, his thoughts consumed with what his father revealed, the words twisting his innards like iron barbs. Part of him took solace in his connection to Kal, awestruck that he was descendent of the ancient king. By itself, the revelation would swell his laden heart and explain many of his unique gifts. Alas, it all felt like ash in his mouth, the pride of Kal's blood tainted by Tyro's betrayal. All his fond memories of his father were tainted as well. Every time he closed his eyes, trying to conjure his father's kind face, the image transformed to Tyro's cruel visage sitting his throne. He vividly recalled Tyro's face upon the throne when he first met the dark lord, remembering sensing something familiar in Tyro's carriage but dismissing it out of hand. Only now did he scold himself for disregarding his first instincts, which were proving sagacious.

Could Corry ever forgive my taint? he thought bitterly. His grandfather killed her father he suddenly realized. Tyro did not wield the blade but placed the sword in Morac's hand. The image of King Lore's head adorning that gruesome pike played again in his mind. He put his head in his hands, knowing she would never forgive him. How could she when he couldn't forgive himself.

"You all right?" Kato's calming voice asked, the Earther taking a seat beside the fire. They set camp upon a hillside overlooking the Nila, its easy current meandering the valley below, the sound of its lapping waves echoing dully in the dark, with the clear starry sky painting the firmament above. They were somewhere between the Minor Kingdoms of Teso and Zulon, setting their magantors down in a sparsely populated region where thick forest crested the northern slopes of a rock-strewn ridge with unforgiving southern slopes overlooking the Nila below. In peaceful times, they would have visited the greater holdfasts of these lesser realms, each a friend of the Torry Kingdom. They were currently pressed for time and traveled with speed and stealth, forgoing hospitality and protocols for campfires in the wilds.

"I am well, just weary," he lied, lifting his head, returning Kato's easy smile.

"You've been unusually quiet the entire journey. If I were to guess, I'd say you miss your princess." Kato nudged his shoulder.

"Perhaps." Terin smiled, using the assumption to mask the true source of his misery.

"Then we better win this fight in Yatin so you can return to her," Kato reassured him, trying his best to cheer his young friend, mimicking Raven's characteristic unfounded optimism. Arrogance, not optimism, he reminded himself. Raven falsely boasted their ability to destroy Tyro all by themselves. *Two hundred thousand apiece,* he said, as if it were a simple matter.

"Where is Lucas?" Terin craned his neck, not seeing their comrade nearby.

"He's down below, fetching water." Kato jerked a thumb toward the Nila below.

"Fetching water or washing the bruises you gave him?" Terin grinned. Lucas and Kato were constantly grappling, sharing techniques each had learned over the years. Lucas was the fiercest hand fighter in the Torry Elite, Terin suffering in countless bouts against him. Only after numerous beatings could Terin begin to hold his own. Lucas would often take it easy on his fellow Elite until Torg reprimanded him for doing so.

"*Sparing their pride won't spare their life,*" Torg would growl, forcing Lucas to beat his comrades until they improved.

"*Collect skills or collect bruises,*" Torg oft repeated during their sessions.

Lucas was a force of nature, taking larger men from their feet with blinding swiftness. It was surprising to see Kato best him more than not, twisting Lucas in ways no other ever had. Though Kato was the smallest of the Earthers, he exhibited greater quickness and dexterity than his fellow Earthers, with a martial knowledge that rivaled or exceeded Torg Vantel. To Torg's credit, he was not threatened by Kato's skill but embraced his knowledge, gleaning whatever the Earther could teach. Lucas eagerly embraced Kato's tutelage, adding his various killing and disabling blows to his repertoire. They dragged Terin into their bouts, improving his martial skills in ways he didn't think possible. In close, unarmed combat against multiple foes, Kato emphasized swift killing blows, attacking the eyes, heart, and throat, any of which was the quickest method in removing an opponent from the melee. Such strikes were often difficult to land unless in close quarters. If unarmed against larger groups, he emphasized stunning blows to gain separation to flee. If unable to escape, Kato advised remaining in the periphery and delivering crippling blows, usually targeting the knee joint. Kato was exceptional with his feet, as well as his hands, executing a dizzying array of moves.

"I have as many bruises from Lucas, as he has from me," Kato moaned, removing his jacket, soothing his right shoulder.

"And I have more than each of you combined." Terin rubbed his neck where the muscle on his left side was strained.

"You gave as good as you got," Kato reminded him. "And in a short time, you'll be beyond my feeble skills." Kato was impressed with Terin's rapid improvement. The boy was naturally gifted, able to master techniques quicker than anyone he had ever trained with. It was almost unnatural.

Terin laughed. "Kato, you've beaten me every time, sometimes so quickly I can't even blink. You truly think I will surpass you?"

"Yes. To be truly great at anything, Terin, we must set aside our pride and accept instruction. If one weds such humility with natural ability, one will achieve greatness. You have more natural ability than anyone I've ever met, and I come from a world far more populous than Arax."

"Earth," Terin affirmed. "What is it like? I asked Raven, and his description was somewhat…confusing." Though it was difficult to describe something to someone who had no concept of what you were speaking.

Kato shook his head how Terin would change the subject whenever he was complimented, humble to a fault. "Let me guess, he spoke of football, food, and scantily clad women?" Kato rolled his eyes.

"Well, those were the first things he spoke of." Terin shrugged. "But he described buildings that reached the clouds, a large canyon that stretched hundreds of leagues, ships that sail the stars, and countless wonders that I could not comprehend."

"You've seen the holo displays on the *Stenox*," Kato said.

"Yes, but most were reenacted ancient battles. I assume your world has advanced since then?"

"Huh." Kato scratched his head, wondering why he hadn't used the holo program to display Earth in its present state, as well as the countless lunar bases across Solar System Prime and the colonies established on their terra-formed planets. Since a picture's worth a thousand words, it could have spared him countless hours of explanation.

"I can't simply describe Earth, just as you can't describe Arax. You can only explain what you know and where you live. A Jenaii would know little of Enoructa or the Ape Empire, just as a Benotrist would be ignorant of the Macon Empire," Kato explained.

"Don't you and the others speak one language and hail from the same lands?"

"We all speak the common tongue of Earth but are from different countries. I am from an island realm called Japan. I was born in a city called Nagano."

"Naguno?"

"Nagano," Kao corrected.

"Nagano," Terin repeated. "What is Nagano like?"

"The most beautiful place on Earth." Kato sighed. "Of course, it is my home, and we are all biased."

"Yes, Raven said his homeland was the best, a place called Colorido and Wyming."

"Colorado and Wyoming," Kato corrected him. "I've been to both of those places, and they are not as diverse or beautiful as Nagano, I assure you. Yes, they have mountains and rivers, but so does Nagano. We have mountains and streams, beautiful Nanohana flowers that carpet the land in vibrant yellow. We have hot springs and ski slopes, with deep mountain lakes and ancient shrines."

"It sounds beautiful," Terin said, regarding Kato's faraway look. "I feel the same of my home."

"Torry North is a wondrous land. You should be proud to call it home."

"But not as grand as Nagano?" he asked with a grin.

"Of course not," Kato said, biting his smile. "I already explained that Nagano is the most beautiful place in all the universe. And since I've traveled the stars and visited numerous worlds, I am somewhat of an authority on the matter."

"You make a sound argument, and I yield to your greater knowledge," Terin conceded with a mock bow.

"You gain wisdom, child. That is a phrase my grandfather would always say whenever we agreed with him." Kato laughed at the memory.

"What was his name?"

"Hinato Nakamura, my father's father." If he closed his eyes, he could see him now, regaling Kato with ancient stories, his eyebrows knitted together as he expounded.

"His name is different from yours," Terin said, though it wasn't unusual in his own family history. On Arax, some inherited their surname from either their mother, father, or were simply known by their given name. He wondered where his own surname originated.

"Not so," Kato said. "My true name is Kaito Nakamura."

"Then why…"

"Why am I called Kato?"

"Well…yes?" Terin made a face.

"Do you believe Raven's true name is Raven or Lorken's is Lorken? No, they are their squadron call signs. Ben Thorton's was *Torch*, but he preferred his own name, so they obliged him. Brokov and I were fleet officers and use our proper names at all times, until coming into Raven's company on our ill-fated voyage that ended on your planet. *Kaito* was apparently too difficult for Raven to say, so he shortened it to Kato. I've since grown used to it."

"Kaito," Terin tested the name.

"Very good, you pronounce it better than Raven, and he's been mangling my name for years."

"Kaito," he repeated.

"It means *supportive*," he gave Terin the basic interpretation.

"You are aptly named. You have been nothing but helpful to my people, Kaito," Terin again spoke his true name, grateful for his friendship.

"It is my honor, and please, call me Kato. It has been my name since our arrival on this world, and it sort of fits now."

"Kaito, Kato, or whatever name you call yourself, you are a great friend, and it is I who is honored to serve beside you."

"Then we are equally honored. I could not stand aside and allow your people to face the darkness alone. The gargoyles and their allies are savage beasts, willing to waylay your civilization and submit the weakest among you to cruelties I could not allow. I just wish Raven and the others felt as I."

"It is hard to fault them when they have all slain so many of the enemy. We couldn't have saved Cronus without Raven and the others."

"Saving Cronus was simply paying an old debt. What did we really accomplish? What mercy was it to free Cronus, only to have him return to face such odds? We could do more, so much more. The fate of your realm stands upon the precipice, and my friends claim it is not their fight, sitting on their asses in the Ape Empire, while the fate of Arax hangs in the balance." Kato shook his head.

"You are a good man, Kato." Terin placed a hand to his shoulder. "Thank you for standing with us, but do not judge Raven too harshly. He and Lorken risked their lives to free Cronus, and before you think it means naught when we still face such odds, there is a large difference between suffering death in the dungeons of Fera and dying with a sword in your hand. Besides, one Earther is all the help we need."

"Maybe not. Thorton is a better marksman than I. Let's just hope I get to shoot first. That will make up the difference."

"Do you believe he will be waiting for us in Yatin?" Terin asked.

"That's where you last saw him, isn't it?"

"Yes, at Telfer, but that was a long time ago. If he remained in Yatin this entire time, you would think that Mosar would've fallen by now. The Yatins have no one to match him," Terin reasoned.

"True, Ben's whereabouts are a mystery. He could be anywhere as far as we know. Tyro might have recalled him, sending him elsewhere, but he was sent to Yatin for a reason, and from what you said, I doubt he expected to find you at Telfer. As for Yatin resisting his threat, he might've been occupied elsewhere in Yatin before joining Yonig's attack on Mosar. Either way, we'll find out soon enough."

"What caused Thorton to break off from the rest of you?" Terin asked. He recalled Lorken and Ben's brief exchange at Fera but couldn't understand what they were speaking of.

"It's quite sad really, so pointless." Kato sighed, tossing a twig into the fire, his eyes staring into the crackling flames.

"They were friends once, weren't they? Raven and Thorton, I mean."

"Yes. The best of friends. Closer than brothers. Even closer than any of us, or you with Cronus." Kato sighed.

"Then what happened? What could've caused such a falling out?"

"As some men die of a broken heart, so Thorton died so long ago, before I really knew him. Oh, he is still walking about and breathing air, but he is as dead as any corpse."

"I don't understand."

"Raven won't speak of it, and Lorken only sparingly, so my details are a bit faulty, but from what I know, Thorton was madly in love with his wife, a beautiful girl named Jenny. She was also Raven's sister. They even had a child, a boy, I believe."

"They truly were brothers," Terin said.

"In a way, yes. They were the best of friends, even before Thorton met Jenny, but Jenny's love only strengthened the bond between them. Anyway, Jenny was a Space Fleet pilot, the same as Raven, Thorton, Lorken, and Zem. There was a fierce battle with our old nemesis, the Aurelians, and Jenny died. Thorton blames Raven for her death, but I don't know all the details. Brokov and I only knew all of this in passing. It wasn't until we were assigned together on our ill-fated voyage that we came to know them as we do now."

"That is why he hates Raven?" Terin asked sadly.

"He doesn't hate Raven. Hate would be a sign of life, and as I said, Thorton is dead."

"Huh?" Terin made a face.

"The opposite of love is not hate, Terin. Love and hate are two sides of one coin. The opposite of love is apathy. Thorton doesn't care anymore, at least in matters of the heart. He is broken in a way we can never mend. And yet he has found a new purpose with Tyro, for reasons I cannot explain. Which in turn forces me to counter his threat, balancing the scales in your war."

"Whatever happened to the child?" Terin asked curiously.

"I don't know, but I believe he lives with Raven's kin."

"Such madness." Terin sighed. If only the fates were kinder. Had Jenny lived, Thorton would likely still be with his friends. Perhaps Terin and Ben would be friends as well, if he was still a member of their crew.

"Such is love and war, Terin. Such things rarely make any sense, just madness and folly."

They sat in silence for a time, until Lucas returned with a net full of fish and a childlike grin painting his face.

"Look what I found." Lucas hoisted his catch into the air, stepping into the light. Despite his reputation for his rugged physical prowess within the Elite, he was a jovial soul.

"We already ate," Terin said, counting at least five large Pestos in the net, thrashing about.

"Don't look a gift horse in the mouth," Kato said, though neither of the other two understood what a horse was, or the phrase, but they caught the meaning. They helped Lucas clean and cook the fish, partaking a second meal before checking on their magantors and retiring to bed, their journey only beginning.

*****

Yatin, southeast of Tenin

Ella gathered the kindling in her arms, hurrying back to where they set camp. She found her "master" sitting on his saddle pack, stretching his stiff legs as the others busied themselves with various tasks. The two gargoyles in their party were off scouting farther ahead. The warrior with one eye was attending their magantor mounts, while the others went down to the stream, meandering along the base of the hill, where they were camped. Their camp was set within a copse of trees, with a clear view of the open land to their east.

Ben Thorton followed the girl with his blue eyes as she arranged the kindling amidst a circle of gathered stones before hurrying off again. He barely spoke a word to her since Tenin, making him wonder why he took her. Reason would suggest leaving her behind to her fate, but when he heard her sing, he couldn't. Ella's voice reminded him too much of *her*. She wasn't his lost love, far from it, but she touched that last vestige of his old self that lingered painfully. It was a part he had tried to expunge, but Ella's voice rekindled those dying embers.

Ella gathered another armful of kindling, picking over dead branches carpeting the floor of the copse, the long skirt of her woolen gown swirling at her ankles. Her master ordered her to wear the modest garment, obviously to not tempt his companions' lecherous stares. Strangely, her master had not touched her in any way, keeping her at a distance, except when eating or sleeping, where he kept a watchful eye on her. She should be frightened for being snatched from her home, but she was not. She heard the others refer to her new master as Ben, or Thorton, or both names together. He was a stern, somber man whom others followed. By his odd clothing and strange weapons, she could tell he was an Earther. Tales of the strange visitors from that far-off land reached Tenin, the stories detailing their fearsome appearance and powerful weapons. If the Earthers were in league with Tyro, then her people were doomed. She quickly returned to their camp, arranging the kindling onto her previous haul, feeling Thorton's eyes upon her as she worked.

"Go fill these," Thorton said, tossing their water satchels at her feet.

She barely acknowledged him, stepping away without saying a word. She wondered at times when he would rape or beat her, but looking into his haunted eyes dispelled that fear. For reasons she could not explain, she knew he would not hurt her. She sensed a part of him drawn to her, with another part pushing her away. He hadn't declared her a slave, placing no brand or collar upon her. Was he waiting for a time to do so properly? Or had he brought her along for his simple amusement? And why did she not fear him? She scolded herself for seeing him as less the monster than he was. He stole her from her home, like a bully or a thief. He deserved her hatred, but for some unseen reason, she did not hate him or loathe him. She simply sighed as she walked down the slope to the stream below. Several of Thorton's comrades were loitering near the water's edge, each regarding her comely features before averting their gaze. She belonged to Thorton, and not one of them would contest his claim. She ignored their gaze, filling the satchels as she waded into the water, lifting her skirts with her free hand. No sooner had she filled the first satchel when the second slipped from her grasp. She cursed her misfortune, rushing after the pouch bobbing atop the swift current, water splashing her gown.

A hand snatched the lost satchel from the water before it slipped hopelessly away.

"My lady," Nels Draken greeted, gifting her the lost item with a mock bow.

"Thank you," she curtsied, the humble act further dampening her skirt.

"You are most welcome. I couldn't have our guest distraught over a lost satchel," he said, his charm reaching his eyes.

"Guest? That is a far kinder appellation than a slave expects," she said coolly.

"Perhaps, or perhaps not. I don't believe our Earther friend has decided on your disposition," Nels said, guiding her up the riverbank.

"Whatever his intent, I am clearly not free to choose my own path. My life rests in his mercy, and I doubt he has any."

"He has already granted mercy to you and your kin, Ella," Nels reassured her.

"How so? He stole me from my home and exiled my family to Tinsay."

"And you think it unkind? Everyone that dwells in Tenin are subject to the laws of conquest. Few, if any, will escape the slavers' net. Your family was moved to safety in Tinsay. Where else could they dwell with such assurance? They are now under Thorton's Imperial Protection. And no matter your fate at his hands, it could not be worse than what awaited you had you remained at Tenin."

"Tell me true, good sir, why me? Why did Ben Thorton choose me over any other?"

"You sing beautifully, fair Ella" was all Nels said before stepping away.

"My voice." She shook her head, wondering if it was a curse or blessing. Nels Draken was right in one regard. Whatever her fate, it was far better now than what it would've been. She quickly filled the second satchel, making her way back up the slope when the screech of magantors coursed overhead, heralding the return of the two gargoyles. They set down amidst their camp, bringing news of a slaver caravan drawing near, just beyond the horizon.

*****

Thorton preferred his contingent to camp alone, but the slaver caravan's arrival so late in the day forced him to accept their request for a joint encampment. They set their cook fires along the slope of the hill, just above the stream. They escorted hundreds of Yatin captives, locked in slave coffles into their midst. The poor wretches were joined by the neck, chains linking their collars, with their hands bound behind them. They were separated into several groups along the hillside, each containing men and women, though the latter outnumbered the former three to one.

Ella busied herself preparing her master's meal and that of his men, serving each a plate of food. She offered Thorton the first portion, but he directed her to the others first, starting with a Benotrist warrior named Doulon, ranking lowest among the present Elite. She then served each in ascending order, leaving Thorton last. When she approached him, he ordered her to fetch plates for each of them.

"Sit." He pointed to a blanket he unrolled beside him.

"Why did you not eat before your men? You are their leader," she asked, forking a portion into her mouth, wondering if she overstepped.

"Commanders eat after their men," he answered, removing his Stetson and setting it aside before eating.

"Highborn, kings, and generals always eat before their lessers, at least in Yatin this is so," she said.

"Not where I come from. Others can choose for themselves, but under my command, soldiers come before commanders. If you ask soldiers to lay down their lives for your cause, then you should be willing to put their needs and comfort above your own. That, girl, is leadership 101."

"Leadership 101?" She made a face, taken aback by his odd speech. At least he was talking, allowing her to gauge his character and intent.

"It's a phrase meaning the first lesson in a course of instruction. When it comes to leadership, never ask a soldier to do something you're not willing to do yourself. You see that gargoyle over yonder?" Thorton lifted his chin in Zelo's direction, who sat upon his bedroll, wiping down his sword, with an empty plate sitting beside him.

"Yes." Ella shivered whenever she looked at the fearsome creature.

"His name is Zelo. We have guarded each other's backs for some time now."

Ella averted her gaze as Zelo lifted his dull red eyes to hers. He was unusually calm for one of his kind, but she could imagine those dull red orbs bursting into a savage crimson.

Thorton pointed out each of his comrades, detailing their province of origin, rank within the Elite, and some personal attributes that set them apart. She was surprised to learn that four of them were not Benotrist or gargoyle but foreign free swords, recruited into Tyro's Elite. Though Thorton was dangerous, she felt strangely safe in his presence. The Benotrists and gargoyles were brutal in their conquests, demonstrating their cruelty in imaginative ways. She recalled their vicious treatment of her people, images of tortured souls and dismembered corpses still fresh in her mind. She noticed that he took no pleasure in others' suffering, which made him better than his contemporaries by far, but he was still a brute. She cried herself to sleep the first night of her captivity, longing for her family. She fully expected Thorton to defile her that first night and every night thereafter, but he hadn't touched her in any way. His comrades did not as much as look at her, let alone address her. Only Nels Draken spoke to her, other than her master.

Master, she thought curiously. Was he her master, or something else? It was difficult to guess since he rarely spoke until now. His dark-blue brooding eyes stared through her guarded veils, as if her mind were laid bare. She sensed no anger in him, only a barren soul haunted by a painful memory. Nels claimed it was her voice that drove him to claim her. She wondered if that was connected to his suffering in some way? Why was she even trying to understand him? He stole her from her home.

When she gathered their dinnerware to wash them in the stream below, she passed a slave coffle set near the water's edge, wary of drawing their attention. She noticed several slave women freed from their bonds to spoon food into the captives' mouths. She kept a fair distance upstream of the coffle, washing the wares in the closing dark. She wept at the sight of the poor wretches locked in the coffle. They sat upon the damp grass, their ragged clothing soiled and torn from abuse. Crude collars were fixed about their necks, with their hands bound behind them in thick manacles. They were filthy and smelled of urine and waste, even upwind. The slavers were farther back, gathered around cook fires, drinking wine and sharing stories of their *adventures* in this war-torn land. They boasted of slaughter and enslavement meted out upon the Yatin subrace, their boisterous laughter echoing loudly in the early evening air.

Ella noticed a female captive shuffling closer to a male captive, each fastened at the end of their respective coffles. Even in the closing dark, she recognized the spark of affection between them. The woman reached as far as she could, her leg touching his. She wondered their relationship, guessing them husband and wife or betrothed. They were too intimate to be blood related. Ella couldn't make out their features in the dim light, the woman's face hidden beneath disheveled brown hair.

"Agghh!" the woman screamed, a slaver's lash striking her thigh.

"Yena!" the male captive cried out her name, the drunken slaver stepping between them.

"I told you that you are no longer his, girl!" The slaver coiled his whip before unlocking her from the coffle, half dragging her by the hair to his bedroll.

The male captive struggled futilely against his bonds, helpless to stop him.

"Tehles!" she screamed her husband's name, as the drunken slaver took liberty, kissing her neck.

"Help me, Tehles!" the slaver taunted, mimicking her voice. "Help you? Who will help him?" he asked darkly, firelight reflecting off his dark eyes. He called out two of his companions to fetch Tehles, while forcing the woman to her knees.

"Yena, I am sorry!" Tehles cried out as the slaver's companions unlocked him from the coffle, throwing him to the ground before the woman.

"I grow weary of your calling out his name, girl. Beat him!" the slaver snarled.

His companions kicked the bound Yatin, striking every part of his flesh as he couldn't stay the blows with his hands bound. His screams eventually dulled to whimpered moans, blood pooling the ground beneath him.

"Remember this lesson, girl!" The slaver pushed her head to the grass, uncoiling his whip.

Crack!

"One for you, the rest for him!"

She cried out, the lash striking her thigh, as he took a step toward Tehles, striking him in turn.

"No!" Yena screamed as more blows fell, tearing Tehles's flesh. Ten, twenty, thirty lashes fell, blood splashing off the end of the whip.

"Mercy!" Ella pleaded, rushing to intercede, throwing herself over Tehles's bloodied body.

"Move, wench!" he spat, his foul breath hanging in the air.

"She doesn't have a collar," one of the other slavers exclaimed.

"I can rectify that once she learns some manners," the slaver glowered, striking her with the whip.

"Agghh!" Ella winced, the lash tearing at her back, but she held firm, protecting the quivering Tehles.

Her defiance only fueled his rage as he struck twice more.

Zip!

Blue laser illuminated the night air, burning a cavernous hole through the slaver's right shoulder, the offending limb dangling at his side by tenuous strands of sundered flesh.

Zip!

A second blast removed the appendage cleanly, the slaver's arm dropping away. The slaver's two nearest comrades stepped forth with drawn swords, only to be cut down by Thorton's laser. Another came at him from the left but tumbled facefirst, Nels Draken's blade taking him in the knee. Zelo cut the throat of another approaching their right, while Neon and the others formed a protective circle around their commander.

Ella squeezed her eyes tightly, not daring to look, the screams of dying men dulling the pain of the welts rising over her back. She held tightly to Tehles's trembling body, the poor slave no longer making a sound other than his labored breath.

"Tehles!" Yena called out, her watery eyes wild with fright, struggling to gain her feet.

"Agghh!" the whipper cried out, smoke pouring off the stump of his right arm, the laser's heat sealing the wound.

Thorton holstered his pistol, closing swiftly upon the miserable wretch, who suddenly turned, sputtering gibberish, which Thorton ignored. The Earther knocked away his good arm before wrapping his fingers around the slaver's throat, hoisting him into the air with one arm.

"You can beat, mutilate, and rape your slaves all you want, but she doesn't belong to you!" he growled, his free hand pointing to Ella.

The slaver's eyes bulged. He meant to protest then plead for his life but couldn't utter a sound, as Thorton's grip tightened, crushing his throat. He thrashed helplessly, beating Thorton with his left arm and legs, to no avail. The Earther squeezed until the slaver turned blue and grew ominously still before tossing his lifeless corpse aside like a loaf of bread.

Ella was staring now, looking up at Thorton's towering form with a strange sense of awe. The other slaves were too frightened or numb, averting their eyes from his terrible face. His voice never rose above a deathly growl, which further unnerved those around her. He spared her a brief glance before sounds of protest from the other slaver captains drew him away. She watched him disappear in the darkness before seeing his terrible weapon flash in the darkness. The sound of clashing steel and dying men echoed in the night.

A long time passed. Nels Draken was the first to return, wiping blood from his sword, gifting her a mischievous look. The others soon followed, with Thorton in the lead. He snatched her by the arm, pulling her to her feet, dragging her back to their campsite atop the hill.

"What of Tehles?" she pleaded the poor slave's case, looking back to where he lay still upon the ground. The woman Yena worked her way over to her beloved, her hands still bound behind her, pressing her head to his back.

"Nels," Thorton said, ordering his comrade to see to the captives.

*****

Ella knelt on her bedroll, the light of the cook fire illuminating her naked back as the woman tended her bruises. The woman was freed from the coffle to tend her wounds, cleaning the vicious welts with a damp cloth. The woman appeared to be in her third decade, with matted golden hair and a comely face, the travails of her capture aging her beyond her years. Nels went through each coffle, searching for a healer, finding this woman.

"You are fortunate. The skin is unbroken, but the welts will remain for a few days," the woman assured her.

Ella winced, the pain feeling far worse than she described.

"Thank you, you are very kind." Ella would've smiled if not for the tears she fought to hold.

"Kind? It was you who took the whipping of another. What caused you to do so?"

"I don't know. I just saw the poor woman cry out for her companion. She looked so frightened, and those men…they were beating him to death." Ella shivered at the memory.

"They were animals and deserve what they got. Your friend saw to that."

"My friend?" Ella asked, craning her neck to look at the woman.

"The large man with the strange clothing and weapon. He is quite fearsome."

"The Earther?"

"Whatever an Earther is, then yes, that one."

"He is my master, not my friend," Ella corrected her.

"Your Master? Then why do you not wear his collar?"

"I…I don't know. He hasn't deigned to give me one." She shrugged.

"Hmm, men are protective of their favorite bed slaves," the woman mused aloud.

"He hasn't…he hasn't touched me in that way," Ella said, thankful the night masked her blush.

"Oh." The woman was unsure of what to make of that. Ella was lovely, and why else would a man take her captive?

"What of Tehles, is he well?" Ella asked.

"He has not stirred since last I saw him. Your friend's—your master's men are seeing to him."

She doubted they would spare him a thought since he was a Yatin captive. Did it matter if he lived? One of the other slavers would simply add him and the others to their coffle.

"What will your master do with us?" the woman asked.

"He will not claim you. He is hastening south, so I expect him to give you to one of the other slavers."

"There are no other slavers. Your friend or Master or whatever he is to you slew them all. Him and his comrades."

*****

"Stay out of trouble," were the only words Thorton spoke to her that night, leaving her to wonder her place and his plans for her. The morning light revealed their handiwork. Ella stood dumbstruck, finding corpses strewn across the hillside. She lost count at twenty-three, but there were likely many more.

Did he do this for me? The thought was foremost in her mind.

"Gather up our things," Ben Thorton told her before setting off back down the hillside. She watched as he first checked on Tehles, who still lay unconscious upon the ground. A brief inquiry with the healer and Yena resulted in Thorton drawing his pistol, blasting a hole through Tehles's head.

Ella gasped as Yena screamed, Thorton pushing her to the ground. Thorton then ordered some of the slaves freed and brought to him.

"You can free your people once we're gone. We're heading south, so I suggest you head east. If you want my advice, I'd gather what food you can and make for the Rulon Gap. If not, you can always find another caravan and give yourselves up. You'll probably die either way, but it's none of my concern," Thorton grimly stated, dropping the keys to their comrades' shackles at their feet.

He marched back up the hill, Ella's watery eyes greeting him.

"Tehles?" she asked, wondering why he could be so cruel.

"Don't give me that hurt look, girl. I put him out of his misery. He wouldn't have lasted two days, and do you think his *friends* down there would wait for him to heal? He'd only slow them down, and I doubt any of them will survive the week as it is."

"How can you be so cold?" she finally vented her fury.

"Cold? I just gave them a fighting chance, which is more than they deserve from me."

"They are my people. They are not soldiers, just peasants. What justice is there in your treatment of them?"

"Justice? Your people are as guilty as any other. Yatin armies have invaded and enslaved their neighbors for centuries. Those Benotrist slavers my men slew are the sons of freed slaves who suffered under the Menotrist yoke for generations. Every realm on Arax has killed, raped, and enslaved their neighbors. I can't make any of you love each other. All I can do is help the strongest realm conquer all the rest and then tame the beast. Only then will you have lasting peace. Once that day comes, you will understand why I have done what I have done."

"Enslaving the world is not peace," she said, drying the tears staining her cheeks.

"The first step in ending slavery is to end war, Ella. Once Space Fleet discovers your world, they will demand the end of such barbaric institutions. Tyro knows this, as I have explained to him what *my* people will expect once they discover this world. Your planet must speak with one voice when that day comes. One voice and one realm."

"If slavery is barbaric, then why have you subjugated me thus?"

"Does a collar grace your throat?"

"No," she said warily.

"Then quit your bitching. You're not a slave, just merely under my protection. Of course, if anything happens to me, I'm sure any of my comrades will gladly put one on you." With that, he stepped away, leaving her with that grim possibility.

Eastern foothills of the Plate Mountains

Cold air escaped his lips in wisps of white, with swirling winds sweeping through their encampment. Winter was upon them, its biting chill felt most cruelly in the upper foothills of the plate. Alen stumbled briefly on an upraised root of a large porian, his arms full with kindling, managing to keep his feet. They set camp within the shelter of the towering trees, only their cook fires giving away their position if one could get near enough to spot them. He passed between countless tents of gray and brown carpeting the forest floor, with Jenaii warriors milling about, resting from the previous night's action. They set camp here ten days before, immediately conducting operations as soon as the first tents were erected. Elos's warriors started with the raiding of supply trains passing west of Lake Veneba, easy prey for his swift cohorts, striking and withdrawing, leaving no trace of their presence. These initial raids accomplished two goals, depriving Morac of vital provisions while supplying their own encampments. Elos dispatched his first units to the plate once the siege of Corell was broken, where they set about raiding supply trains closer to Notsu. Elos led this larger contingent deeper north, expanding their raids to targets along the Benotrist border.

Alen felt the curious stares of the Jenaii warriors, unable to gauge their interest by the impassive faces they all seemed to have. He lowered his eyes, avoiding their scrutiny, though all of them treated him decently. Perhaps it was his own self-doubts plaguing his mind. How could one such as him look upon these great warriors with any shred of confidence? He was born a slave, a gently used palace slave at that, with no martial skill to speak of. What was he compared to these great warriors?

"Wait!" a Jenaii warrior called out, freezing him in place.

Alen closed his eyes, expecting a reprimand or abuse by the soldier's tone.

"You dropped this." The silver-eyed warrior picked up a piece of wood that must've slipped, setting it back in his arms before returning to his tent.

"Thank you," Alen whispered, releasing a breath. The warrior was just being kind, but he could never tell what the Jenaii were thinking with their stoic demeanor. With the Earthers, it was easy as they always spoke their mind, constantly setting him at ease with their jovial banter and crude speech. Alen felt wholly inadequate for the role Elos intended for him. The Jenaii champion brought him along to lead a Menotrist revolt from within the Benotrist Empire, a seemingly impossible task considering the oppressive control their masters employed. Most of the slaves in the eastern half of the empire were Venotrist and other sub groups, with the Menotrists concentrated in the west. The latest raids targeted lesser holdfasts just within the Benotrist border, slaying the local proctors and freeing numerous slaves, some of which were brought back to their camp. Elos assigned these recruits to him, expecting him to lead them in the battles to come. They were just field slaves, with no martial skills to speak of, but Elos insisted that Alen was up to the task. He responded by sending them out to gather firewood and attend other simple tasks that their encampment required.

The howl of the easterly gale echoed through the upper branches of the trees above, their boughs bending with the wind, stripping what leaves remained. He was thankful for the fur cloak and trousers Elos gifted him, each a necessity in this harsh environment. Few Araxan men ever wore trousers and never slaves. He found them far more modest and comfortable than the brief garments he was forced to wear as a palace slave. Alen hurried apace, their command pavilion just head, where a number of commanders were gathering. Alen took a deep breath, dropping the kindling near their cook fire before approaching the guards, who waved him in.

"It won't take Morac long to discern our activities, Champion Elos," a commander of unit pointed out, staring at the map unfurled across the table the others gathered around.

Elos noticed Alen enter, calling him forth to stand with the others. Elos insisted that he participate in the commanders' briefings. Eventually he would oversee them, unbeknownst to him.

"Eventually. Our raids will not escape his attention when the dire strait of his tenuous supply trains becomes more apparent," Elos said, his eyes scanning the north end of the map, where the southern approaches of Nisin were depicted in rich detail. Therein lay his true objective, the Benotrist heartland in the east. The land was ripe for rebellion, Tyro's brutality making the meekest of men bitter for revenge. With so many soldiers campaigning south or already dead at Corell, Tuft's Mountain, and Yatin, there was never a better time for rebellion. He expected Morac to call upon even more reserves when he renewed his campaign come spring, further depleting the soldiers needed to quell uprisings.

"There is rich farmland in this region," another commander of unit pointed out, indicating a deep valley thirty leagues northwest of their encampment.

"With the harvest in, their granaries will be full," another reasoned.

"Unless Morac stripped it bare on his march south," another said.

"We will target it to be certain. If full, the food will allow us to expand our recruitment," Elos said, before calling on Alen. "How goes your command, Alen?"

Alen paused, feeling every eye upon him. "I…I set them to gathering wood. I will show them how to set snares like Commander of Flax El Hatu showed me," he said.

"Very good. Commander El Sero will provide them instruction in using a pike. From there we can progress to spears and swords." Elos was careful to not judge him harshly, cognizant of the former slave's fragile confidence, something he needed to rectify.

The unit commanders continued with their reports and outlining the proceeding days' objectives before Elos dismissed them, following Alen to where his recruits were gathered.

"You must earn their respect if you are to lead them," Elos said as they left the command pavilion.

"They know I was a palace slave. They will never look to me as a leader." He sighed as they walked.

"You spent a lifetime in Tyro's presence. You know the workings of the empire, if only in obscure observance. These men we brought for you are all fighters by nature, lacking only experience and skill, which will come with time. Sometimes one must take respect if one lacks time to earn it," Elos advised. They brought back two dozen men from their raids, choosing those with spirited natures and a commitment to fight. It was not surprising to Elos how many refused to take up arms, resigned to their life of servitude. Once a man's self-worth was stripped away, he was easy to control. In time this might change, but time was a luxury they did not possess. He needed fighters, leaving the rest behind to their fate.

"How can I take respect?" Alen wondered, uncertainty in his voice.

"Remember the first technique I showed you?"

"Y-yes," Alen recalled the brutal tactic.

"Which of your men is the strongest?"

"Galbo, I believe," Alen said, Galbo being of a height with Elos with sinewy arms and a sour demeanor.

"Here's what you will do."

*****

Alen gathered the men together, the lot of them still wary of taking orders from a *palace slave*, but with Elos beside him, they hurried to obey. They were mostly field slaves, with two of them merchant chattel that were taken from a caravan. Most were outfitted with fur trousers or kilts, with thick cloaks to survive the cold of the camp's elevation. It never escaped Alen's attention that every one of them was larger and stronger than him. He stood nervously at Elos's side while calling Galbo forth, the ornery field slave suppressing a sneer, reluctantly obeying the command. Galbo rose up to his full height before him to emphasize his advantage. Alen swallowed nervously, feeling Elos's silver eyes upon him, forcing him to forsake his fear. He struck Galbo in the throat without warning, catching him off guard, before circling quickly behind him striking the back of his knee, the former field slave's face planting in the ground.

"Supremely done, Alen," Elos commented dryly, as Alen helped the stricken Galbo to a sitting position, the poor man wheezing, struggling to breathe with the others looking on with slackened jaws.

Elos and Alen went on to instruct them on more effective and lethal strikes and crippling blows that were better suited for combat. Elos forced Alen to take the lead more than not, extolling his experiences in the fighting arena of Fera and his escape. The men needn't know what role he played in the arena battle where Raven simply tossed him atop the square block to toss down the weapons the others used to win the battle. The simple fact was that he *did* survive the arena, and he *did* escape Fera.

"With most armor, the throat is not a viable target area. Nor is it advised when an opponent is prepared. The knee, however, is the key target in armed and unarmed combat. A quick thrust can collapse the joint. These strikes can remove your opponent from the battle," Alen parroted what Elos had beaten into his brain.

And so it went through the following days, with Alen and the Jenaii instructing their new charges in basic forms of combat. Elos told Alen to focus on using pikes at first, as the sword required more skill, and as the rebellion spread, pikes were more readily available. Either weapon required men to work in unison, and that would take time as well. Elos also was short on time, his presence required elsewhere before spring arrived.

Siege of Mosar

General Yonig surveyed the Yatin capital from his pavilion, his dull red eyes sweeping the expanse of the city's north wall that stretched in a large arc around the northern half of the city. He spied the upper battlements of the Yatin Royal Palace peeking above the city's walls, a towering structure that rested in the city's center, along the southern bank of the Muva River that bisected the city. A rapacious glow passed his eyes, visions of his victorious triumph playing merrily before him. He envisioned his glorious entrance into that fabled hall, his heavy boots marching over the jeweled floors of Yangu's palace before sitting the throne, overseeing the Yatin emperor and his court prostrated in supplication before him. He conquered numerous cities since the outset of the campaign, claiming lordship many times over, but lordship of Mosar would be his crowning achievement.

He shook the image from his mind, lest the vision consume him, distracting Yonig from the task at hand. His pavilion stood seven hundred yards from the city's north wall, while his forward most pickets waited three hundred yards forward.

The Yatin capital stretched along the slow, winding Muva, which bisected the city, with two massive curtain walls that circled its perimeter, one upon the northern half of the city and the other the south. Both walls started at the river's edge upstream, arcing around the city, before ending again at the river's edge downstream. The north wall had become brittle with time, its once proud towers, each the height of seven men, broken in places, their gray battlements cracking with ill use. The great south wall was all that remained of the city's once impressive defense, well-built and maintained during the previous centuries due to the greater Torry threat to their south. While the southern wall was the height of nine men, with well-maintained battlements and catapult platforms, the north wall was oft ignored, fallen to disrepair, the very wall that Mosar now needed to defend against Yonig's vast gargoyle host.

The gargoyle general could see sunlight playing off the helms and shields of the Yatin soldiers manning the battlements along the north wall, their heads peeking above the parapets or around the broken ramparts above. Yonig noted the sorry state of the Yatin defense and was tempted to immediately unleash his legions upon Mosar. The walls were not of a height to prevent his gargoyles from flying easily above. He could order the attack this day and seize the capital by the next morn, putting the garrison to the sword, but such was folly. He would lose most of his soldiers in such a gamble, soldiers he needed to secure these lands after victory was established. No, he would proceed as he had thus far through the Yatin heartland, with a deliberate and measured pace. He instilled discipline in his gargoyle soldiers, taming their savage frenzy, often brutally. They despised his treatment, but the results spared them wasteful slaughter that their mindless frenzy incurred. His attack upon Telfer bled his legions thirty-two telnics, but that was against a stalwart fortification designed to break a gargoyle assault, and he incurred almost equal loss upon the enemy at Telfer and Salamin Valley. His legions suffered only ten more telnics of casualties with their advance through the Yatin heartland by exercising discipline and restraint while decimating cities in systematic annihilation. Larger cities were surrounded or set ablaze, whilst unwalled villages were overrun in night raids, killing the enemy as they slept. His legions spent several moons advancing through central Yatin, stripping the land bare as they passed, slaying all in their path, save for those taken by Benotrist slavers shadowing their advance. They burned what could be burned and smashed the rest to rubble. They ate off the land, consuming crops, grass, and trees, leaving much of the Yatin countryside an endless trek of charred grounds and twisted ruins. The fall rains that followed transformed the landscape into a desolate muddy waste.

Yonig took stock of his situation. He left ten telnics of the 1st Gargoyle Legion at Telfer. To garrison the fortress whilst the remnants of the 1st and 3rd Gargoyle Legions joined him at Mosar. Twelve telnics of the 1st Legion and thirty-six of the 3rd Legion was what remained, leaving him few troops to squander on a hasty attack with little planning. He would use his forces judiciously. General Torab had dispatched an additional twenty-three telnics of the 2nd Gargoyle Legion after his conquest of Tenin. It would take time for them to reach Mosar, and he lacked the power to fully envelope the city without them. He deployed the thirty-six telnics of the 3rd Legion in a wide arc, mirroring the length of the north wall, taking up position along a broken line of toppled structures and open fields. Like most ancient cities, Mosar grew beyond its original walls, with dwellings sprouting farther afield of the city. The Yatins wisely razed many of the structures nearest the city walls, denying the gargoyles nearby staging areas and shelter. Yonig's legions now stood upon the broken rubble, using much of the material to reinforce their siege works, a series of trenches spanning the length of their perimeter, facing the north wall. The banners of the 3rd Gargoyle Legion, a black mace upon a field of red, blown above the palisades, jutting from the siege works. He kept the remnant of the 1st Legion to his rear, holding them in reserve, but sending two of their remaining telnics across the river to harry the southern approaches of Mosar.

Yonig would hold position until the reinforcements of the 2nd Legion arrived. His spies reported that Mosar was held by the twenty-five telnics of General Yoria's 1st Yatin Army and ten telnics of the city garrison, commanded by Commander Yakue, along with Commander Cornyanna's eight hundred cavalry. Yonig was also keenly aware of the Yatin 2nd Army mustering along the eastern border, numbering twenty-five telnics, commanded by General Yitia. The Yatin 3rd Army, under General Jutol, was last reported marching north toward Mosar from the southern border. He needed to bring Mosar to heel before either the 2nd or 3rd Armies converged on the capital. He brought over one hundred catapults and trebuchets from Tinsay, his soldiers moving them into position while gathering stone munitions to hurl into the crumbling walls. Yonig outfitted thirty of his telnics in breastplates, greaves, and helms, the armor preventing them from taking flight but better protecting them once he ordered them forth. He would wait for Torab's reinforcements before commencing the attack, but if any Yatin relief appeared imminent, he would attack. His Benotrist magantors kept constant watch upon the eastern and southern approaches but were hindered by a large stretch of swamps running north from the Torry Border.

*****

Thick foliage pressed the edge of the path as the Torry columns exited the Yagan marshes, before following the road into the Cuslom Forest. The weary soldiers trudged along, enduring a light morning rain and brutal fog that lingered into midday. Their outlook brightened stepping onto the hard soil of the forest road, leaving the damnable marshes behind them.

The unseasonably warm day allowed him to forgo his cloak, storing it in his saddle pack as he led his ocran out of the swamp. His sea-blue eyes scanned the area up ahead, staring through the narrow slits of his silver helm. The narrow pathway sharply expanded, transitioning into a broad dirt roadway, the width of three wagons. The Yagan Marshes were a twisted menagerie of thick topac trees, with their willowy vines winding around their smooth trunks and impassable bogs where a man could slip from sight, sucked into the ground in an instant. The Torry 4th Army spent countless days traversing this dangerous ground since crossing the border. The sight of towering paccel trees up ahead, with their thick trunks, lightened the weary soldiers' hearts. The early winter had stripped their branches bare, coating the forest floor with their broad, dead leaves. The forest floor was still alive with thick underbrush, limiting their view beyond either side of the road.

"Will you ride now, Highness?" Jentra snorted beside him, the grizzled warrior constantly chiding his prince to spare his feet, looking more like a haggard foot soldier leading his mount by the reins. He reminded his future king that he should not be seen disheveled and spent, lest the soldiers doubt his ability to lead. Lorn scoffed at such pretense, insisting to endure with the men, to know their suffering. Besides, a long march was good for his legs.

"If only to scout ahead," Lorn conceded, climbing into the saddle. They were a quarter of the way from the front of the column, the Army strung out for miles along the narrow causeway that wound through the Yagan Marshes and the Cuslom Forest. Oftentimes, the trail narrowed where only two men could pass side by side, the column closing and expanding with the width of the road. Scouting to their flank was even more treacherous. The swamplands were rife with venomous serpents and roctors, the carnivorous reptiles that grew the length of two men, with rows of jagged teeth. Lorn recalled the haunting cries of men being dragged off the trail, caught in the jowls of the vicious beasts. Unfortunately, serpents, reptiles, and deadly bogs were only a few of the dangers making the Yagan Marshes such an impassable barrier, a barrier that was rarely breached and oft protected Torry South and the Yatin Empire from each other. The border of each realm passed through that deadly ground and was manned by small outposts painstakingly erected in the center of the inhospitable terrain. It was this obstacle that delayed Lorn from coming quickly to Mosar's aid. He sent emissaries ahead to Mosar when the Army first set out from Cagan, to negotiate their passage through Yatin territory. It took precious time before word reached the border outposts, granting them safe passage. Fortunately, Emperor Yangu acquiesced to their offer, though the distrust between their peoples was a constant barrier. They were met at the border by two Yatin Elite and a commander of telnic from the 3rd Yatin Army, emissaries of Emperor Yangu. They were to join with the 3rd Yatin Army some leagues north before moving on to Mosar, but the reports he received of late cast doubt on the readiness of the Yatin Army. The gargoyle invasion had taken the Yatin Empire by complete surprise, which impacted their musters. Lorn's spies reported the grim news that none of the surviving Yatin Armies were fully mustered, some marshalling only half their full levies.

"Agghh!" a man cried out, drawing Lorn's gaze up ahead, a dark form knocking a commander of unit from the saddle. Scores of winged forms swept down from atop the trees, their pointed ears arcing back, fangs curving menacingly through their descent.

"Gargoyles!" men shouted in alarm, struggling to lift their shields in time, the creatures dropping into their midst, swinging their curved swords. The cries of wounded men rent the air, gargoyle blades cutting vicious gashes along their necks, backs, and shoulders.

Lorn drew his sword, urging his mount forward into the fray, with Jentra following, struggling to keep pace with his zealous prince. The blood drained from Jentra's face as a creature swooped down from above, gliding over the trail with its outstretched wings extended, leveling off, angling directly for them.

"Kai-Shorum!" the creature screamed, shouting its war cry while drawing near, its crimson eyes alit with a fiery blaze. Jentra could see into its open mouth, its forked tongue extending beyond its glistening fangs, rippling like a red serpent slithering in the air.

Lorn drove his mount forth, his left hand tight on the reins, with his right upon the hilt of his sword. The creature meant to knock him from the saddle, its sword slowly arcing forward as it drew near. Lorn crouched below his ocran's head, holding his sword straight up in front of him, forcing the creature to angle lower, its fiery gaze fixed to Lorn's chest, where he intended to strike. The gargoyle angled ever lower, furious as Lorn crouched farther below his ocran's head as the beast dipped its neck, its horns jutting straight ahead but below the creature. The gargoyle's eyes blazed eyeing Lorn's blade, bringing its own sword to parry the blade, before knocking him from the saddle.

Lorn pulled hard upon the reins, rearing the ocran into the air. The creature released a curdling scream, its body impaled on the ocran's horns. It thrashed violently, swinging its scimitar wildly over the ocran's head, futilely trying to strike Lorn, its efforts doing naught but ripping its own guts on the horns.

Jentra rode past Lorn, driving his sword into the creature's back, before Lorn's ocran lowered its head, driving its foreleg into the creature, pushing it off its horns, the blow skewering the gargoyle, its innards spilling onto the ground.

They continued on with gargoyles dropping into their midst, assailing the column up ahead. The soldiers gathered their wits, interlocking shields overhead, driving their spears between the seams. Lorn spied two ocran running past with empty saddles, their riders' likely victims somewhere ahead. They cut into the tree line, maneuvering along the column, racing ahead, ducking their heads below low-hanging boughs.

"I am too old for this," Jentra cursed, with branches cutting his thighs and arms, another snagging his cloak, almost ripping him from the saddle.

"Nonsense. You're the fittest man I know, Jentra," Lorn replied.

"Bah!" Jentra snorted, wondering how Lorn heard him in all this chaos. He ducked his head, another branch jutting inconveniently in their path, wondering where their fellow Elite were. They were just behind them before all this business started, but even they would struggle keeping pace with Lorn's ardor.

Lorn swept back onto the trail, where several gargoyles were clustered, their backs to the forest while swinging their scimitars, two dead Torries at their feet, while holding others at bay. Lorn burst from the tree line, striking them from behind, lopping a gargoyle head while charging into their midst, his ocran knocking another to the ground. Jentra broke left, his sword catching another creature across its left wing, tearing a vicious gash along the appendage. A few soldiers broke from the column, taking advantage of the gargoyles' disorder, cutting them down in detail, as others joined the fray after gaining their wits. Several surviving gargoyles fled, forsaking the battle as they were hopelessly outnumbered.

"You take great risks, Highness." Jentra scowled, drawing his mount up alongside him, their fellow Elite filing in around them, their lathered mounts winded from following Lorn's path through the forest. The scene grew less chaotic as commanders slowly gained order amidst the column, hindered by their limited line of sight in each direction, obscured by the bend of the forest road. The cries of wounded men echoed dully amidst the sea of a thousand voices and the rattle of steel. Jentra caught sight of a few winged forms bounding through the trees in the distance, making their escape.

"War is fraught with risk, old friend."

"Aye, but not needless ones. Your life is too important now," Jentra stated, now that word of his father's defeat at Kregmarin reached the Army two days before, his fate unknown. Some urged the prince to forsake this campaign and return to Corell to claim the throne and command its defense, but Lorn refused. Such an act would be too late to affect happenings in the north, while abandoning Yatin would cost them Torry South. Lorn trusted Corell's defense to Yah's will and the wise rule of his sister. Jentra argued that the realm needed its king, and he could not claim the title by law until he first sat the throne.

"What good is a king to a fallen realm?" Lorn had refuted. Yah revealed his will to Lorn, guiding his intervention on Yatin's behalf.

"I've trained in swordplay since I was a child. If I cannot hold my ground in battle, then I should not be king," Lorn said, dismounting once he saw a wounded soldier lying on the trail, unmoving with blood pooling beneath him.

"Send word up and down the column. I want the dead cleared, the wounded tended, and the Army to resume march immediately!" Lorn commanded.

"We don't know the state of the Army. The enemy might—"

"This was a raid, nothing more," Lorn said, throwing a glance to a gargoyle carcass nearby. "There was no strength in it. They concentrated their attack on those mounted, hoping to slay commanders of rank and harry our advance. We must push on. We must reach Mosar before they assail the city. The war depends on it." Lorn removed his helm, kneeling beside the stricken soldier. He felt his labored breath before easing him to his back. Lorn sighed dejectedly as he beheld the large pool of blood that spread out after turning him over. He'd seen enough battle to know that no one could survive such loss and live. A large gash ran the breadth of his abdomen, just below his mail, and another across his inner left thigh and a vicious bite mark on the side of his neck. The man was unresponsive, blood continuing to drain from his wounds. Lorn drew his dagger, opening his leg further to quicken his passing. 'Twas another decision to weigh his conscience, but he couldn't delay the Army for men that were sure to die anyway, while there were living men that depended upon their speed. At that moment, Lorn thought of his father, wondering his fate. Did he suffer terribly before his fall? Was he captive? Which fate was worse? Did he escape with a portion of his men, or did he receive a quick and noble end? The message he received only mentioned the defeat at Kregmarin and Morac's invasion of Torry North. He again steeled his heart, shutting such thoughts from creeping into his mind. He placed his trust in Yah's divine will and placed the fate of Corell in Corry's capable hands. She was wise and cunning, far wiser than he, and had good counsel from Torg Vantel and the king's ministers. He shook such thoughts from his mind, refocusing on the task before him.

Lorn placed his fingers to the dead soldier's eyes, closing them before gaining his feet as the column reformed to resume march. By late day they would have details on the final tally, thirty-four dead, thirteen of which were commanders of unit or above, thirty-six wounded, and a dozen missing. Gargoyle losses were nearly equal. By morning of the following day, they would be clear of the forest, with open farmland and flat ground stretching to the horizon and the banners of the 3rd Yatin Army greeting them north of the forest, a black sword on a field of green, the sigil lifting in the winter breeze.

C H A P T E R

10

Siege of Mosar stage two

Thump!

The aged battlement crumbled, fissures spreading from the place of impact in festering tendrils.

Thump!

Another stone ballistae struck below the first, crumbling a massive section of Mosar's north wall, leaving a jagged scar in the ancient bulwark. The north wall of Mosar was crumbling before the heavy blows of Yonig's catapults and trebuchets, dozens of breaches opening along its length. Yonig surveyed the damage with reserved satisfaction, eying the broken ramparts and uneven battlements rendered impassable by the relentless barrage. The morning sun broke upon the city through a small break in the stormy sky. He nodded to his subordinates to commence the assault. His original plan to await his reinforcements was waylaid by two discoveries from his spies and magantor patrols. His spies indicated that the Yatin 1st Army and the city garrison numbered far less than their full muster, the invasion catching them unprepared and unable to consolidate their forces before he reached the city. Some reports claimed the Yatin 1st Army mustered only sixteen of their twenty-five telnics and the garrison only six of their ten, making their forces far weaker than he expected. His magantor patrols spied a large contingent marching north to relieve the city but were still many leagues south. Danger and opportunity forced his hand as he ordered his legions forth to claim the city before the enemy armies could join. He ordered two telnics across the Muva upstream nearly a full moon ago to harry any enemy forces marching north. He had yet to hear of their success or failure, but his scouts reported that they entered the Cuslom Forest some time ago before passing from sight. He preferred to wait for his own reinforcements and striking the city in force but lacked the luxury of time. The time for holding his ground had run out, forcing his hand.

Haroom!

Horns sounded, signaling his telnics forth. Carka birds circled lazily overhead, anticipating their coming feast, the birds braving the stormy sky and distant thunder for the promised carrion. The defenders upon the broken walls steeled themselves as the gargoyle host marshaled forth afoot in ordered ranks, their chest armor, helms, and shields contrasting their leathery black flesh and narrow red eyes. These were not the gargoyles of legend, screaming maddened war cries as they flew into battle. These were the disciplined scions of Yonig, drilled in the tactics of their human counterparts. They marched over the expanse of scorched earth and rubble that stretched beyond the wall, littered with the remains of men and gargoyles from previous skirmishes, as catapults hurled stone and fire ballistae overhead, striking the battlements ahead. The Yatins returned fire in kind, their ballistae finding purchase in the gargoyle formations. The wretched screams of burning gargoyles drowned in the din of battle as a familiar war cry echoed above.

"Kai-shorum!"

Gargoyles shouted, flying above their armored brothers, as a telnic of the lightly armed creatures took flight. Yonig unleashed the eight telnics of his air assault, one wave at a time, sending the lightly armed warriors to harry the defenders atop the battlements, while his heavy ground assault closed upon the wall. Arrows spewing from the battlements thinned the approaching wave, targeting those in the air over their heavier protected counterparts afoot. Some shafts bounced harmlessly off the round helms of the gargoyles in flight, others penetrating the creatures wherever they struck. Scores of gargoyles tumbled from the sky, some striking their comrades below, their weight snapping the necks or backs of those struck, whilst others embedded in the scorched ground. Flames and arrows rose to meet the first wave attaining the battlements, Yatin spears and swords greeting them as they set down. Others lingered briefly in the air before dropping suddenly onto places of their choosing. Many clung to the stone canopies covering the watchtowers, holding there until their full strength was restored, the slanted rooftops exposing them to Yatin archers below. Others sought out weak points along the wall, though with nearly five thousand Yatins atop the battlements, such points were difficult to find. More concentrated their strength upon single points along the battlements, sweeping down upon Yatin soldiers with terrible ferocity. Yatin defenders jabbed at the creatures between interlocked shields, the familiar tactic proving difficult as the gargoyles descended from above, front, and behind simultaneously. Yatins stabbed hundreds of gargoyles, driving them from the battlements, blood issuing from their wounds, whilst others were felled in kind, gargoyles dropping into their midst, necks and limbs breaking under their weight. Most of the Yatins had never seen a gargoyle before the siege, let alone facing them in battle. Despite the gargoyles' reputed nature, the green soldiers were unprepared for their maddened frenzy.

The creatures crowded over the shield walls, slashing madly with their scimitars or swinging maces with jagged spikes. They continued on with spear tips piercing their breasts or with swords driven through their middle, clawing at the Yatins' eyes, their jaws snapping, biting whatever they could. The defenders finally drove off the first wave, half the gargoyles dead or dying before the second wave was open them. The second wave feigned toward the wall before passing over, bypassing the defenders crowding the battlements, setting down on rooftops of the dwellings beyond. Yatin bowmen followed them with their eyes, releasing shafts in the passing swarm. Scores fell from the sky, tumbling with mortal wounds or gliding through their descent, arrows feathering their limbs. The Yatin bowmen continued firing at the gargoyles gathering upon the rooftops behind them, but too few found purchase before the third wave was upon them.

*****

General Yoria, commander of the Yatin 1st Army, observed the battle from the battlements of the northeast fortress resting several blocks south of the wall. It was one of six such redoubts throughout the city, three to each side of the river, placed equal distance from the emperor's palace resting at Mosar's center along the south bank of the Muva. Each fortress was the height of ten men, with a single turret to each corner of its battlements and a single tower rising from its center, with a purple minaret spiraling above.

Yoria directed the defense of the city from this position, reinforcing the city garrison that held the walls of Mosar. Yoria's own men were positioned along the adjoining avenues, preparing to intervene wherever needed. Off to his left, he spied the sigil of Mosar's garrison lifting in the breeze above the north gate, a purple tower upon a field of white. Commander Yakue, the garrison commander, stood below his standard, his black cape billowing in the wind, overseeing the defense of the wall. The battle was hours old, the gargoyles pressing their attack along the wall, wave after wave setting down upon the ramparts or passing overhead, setting down on rooftops between the redoubt and the wall. He could see the foul creatures stalking along the rooftops before jumping onto those standing below, catching them unawares. Yoria ordered all his archers to higher ground to clear the gargoyles from the rooftops. A great sheet of flame burst atop a watchtower off his right, men jumping from the battlements, flames licking their flailing limbs, as a fire ballistae struck their own munitions.

"Send two units to reinforce the wall!" Yoria commanded, pointing toward the ruined tower northeast of their position, his aide relaying the order to the corresponding commanders below. He could make out the top of the wall where the garrison troops clung desperately to the battlements, their numbers thinned significantly. Men stumbled along the ramparts, stabbing desperately at gargoyles sweeping down from above or crawling over the walls. Others retreated into smaller groups, taking cover within makeshift shield walls, their pockets shrinking, gargoyles swarming all around them. Yoria continued to feed reinforcements wherever the defense appeared thin, but as the day drew on, the breaks were growing too numerous to fill. The greater threat was the more heavily armed gargoyle telnics drawing near the walls afoot, their disciplined ranks and interlocked shields affording them greater protection than their lightly clad brethren. The armored columns broke off toward several breaches in the crumbling walls, Yatin bowmen taking up position to either side of the broken battlements. Nearly half the Yatin catapults along the north wall were destroyed or overrun. Gargoyle catapults advanced behind their ranks, raining fire upon the battlements above. Yatin fire munitions spewed from the walls throughout the morn, striking the serried gargoyle ranks below to great effect, their steady stream reduced to sporadic strikes as the battle progressed. The breaches in the wall were wide and low enough for the heavy gargoyle infantry to climb over the broken rubble. Yatin infantry filled the gaps, driving their spears through the openings. It was a steady slog, men and gargoyles contesting every nook and crevice. The gargoyles piled the dead at other places along the wall, using the macabre mounds to ease their climb. Successive waves of gargoyles still passed overhead, setting down beyond the wall, attacking the defenders from behind.

General Yoria ordered more men forward to counter this tactic, the entire wall descending in chaos, men and gargoyles hopelessly intermingled. Men struck down gargoyles to their front, while other creatures struck from behind. Gargoyles swept down from above, their scimitars glancing off helms or finding home in necks or shoulders. Others simply landed on their foes, crushing them under their weight before being struck down in kind.

Thud!

The sound echoed over the din as the giant ram struck the north gate. Yatin archers targeted the crews as they drew back a second time.

Thud!

The heavy timbers held as Yatin arrows riddled the gargoyle crew, thinning their ranks, others hurrying to replace the fallen. Archers atop the north gate stood under a thick canopy, blunting the gargoyle attacks from above. Gargoyles bypassed this obstacle, setting down upon the area behind the main gate in great numbers, hoping to open the gates from within. General Yoria deployed three units to counter this, anticipating such a move. Those precious units were quickly driven back as hundreds of gargoyles descended into their midst.

"The gate has fallen!" The cries went out as Yoria shifted his steely gaze to his left, gargoyles pouring through the open gate, their shield walls driving the scattered defenders back into the city proper. He was prepared to order more men to fill the breach when the standards of Commander Yakue were torn down from atop the battlements, gargoyles swarming over the wall. From this distance, he could not discern the fate of the garrison commander, only the panic spreading through the ranks along the wall, a sprinkling of men forsaking their posts cascading into a full retreat.

*****

The Yatins struggled restoring order to their broken ranks as men ran south through crowded streets. The lighter-clad gargoyles took to the rooftops, racing ahead of the gathered mobs before dropping into their midst, slashing with their scimitars. The retreating soldiers mingled with civilians that hadn't evacuated prior to the battle, further hindering their efforts. With his lighter-clad gargoyles racing ahead, General Yonig ordered his heavy infantry through the avenues afoot, grinding those in their path with their interlocked shields and straight swords thrusting between their seams.

Yonig stood upon the north wall, the standard of his 1ˢᵗ Legion, a red claw upon a field of black, gracing the broken battlements. His dull crimson eyes swept the expanse of the city, following the chaos spanning the entirety of the northern half of Mosar. His telnics swarmed through the emptying streets, driving the defenders back through the city toward the three bridges spanning the Muva, the only avenues of retreat left to their panicked ranks. He ordered several lightly clad telnics ahead toward the center bridge, where they were repulsed. The Yatins wisely strengthened the vital causeways, with bulwarks and platforms lining the bridges' sides and ends. Hundreds of gargoyle corpses littered the waters of the Muva or were strewn upon the banks of the river, proving the futility of such a hasty assault. Yonig eyed the three fortresses along the northern half of the city. His first assault upon these sturdy redoubts were bloodied failures, leaving scores of dead gargoyles clustered below their towering ramparts. He ordered his troops to bypass these bulwarks for now, isolating their garrisons while pushing south to the river. He needed to slay as many Yatins as he could whilst they were in disarray, seizing the city before they could be relieved.

Despite the discipline Yonig instilled into his legions, even he could not completely stay their bloodlust, oft derailing his greater objectives. Countless units were distracted by easy plunder, breaking off from the attack to batter down doors, slaughtering civilians hiding therein. Even citizens brandishing clubs and makeshift weapons inflicted needless casualties upon his thinning ranks. He knew men would fight fiercely to guard their loved ones, even if their cause was futile. Yonig cursed the wasted opportunity. Had all his forces converged upon the bridges, he might've trapped most of the Yatin Army north of the river, killing them at his leisure.

*****

He ran apace, his sandaled boots slapping the stone surface of the east bridge, an arrow whizzing past his ear, striking a fellow up ahead in the shoulder. He passed between the towering bulwarks guarding the north end of the bridge, where Yatin archers overlooked the chaos below, their steady fire picking off gargoyles that strayed near. General Yoria grunted, his labored breath slowing his retreat before stepping off to the side of the bridge, his aides and personal guards forming a protective perimeter around him.

"Up there." He pointed tiredly at the towers rising from the center of the bridge.

"General, we need to get you to the other side of the river!" one aide exclaimed.

"Our retreat stops here. We hold them at the bridges or lose the city entirely."

Within moments they attained the battements of the watchtowers straddling the width of the east bridge. Two open massive gates were centered below it, allowing soldiers and civilians to pass through as they emptied out of the northern half of Mosar. It took the better part of the waning day to relay the order to his subordinates, commanding them to hold the center and west bridges. He lost count of the casualties his Army suffered, but no telnics seemed stronger than 60 percent as they funneled across the east bridge. He surmised similar results with those passing over the center and west bridges. Thousands of Mosar's garrison troops filtered through in small groups of fifty or less. He ordered them to gather and reform along the southern bank of the Muva. Many were missing helms, shields, and even swords, but there were plenty replacements among the fallen.

Flames spread across northern Mosar, wooden dwellings igniting like straw in a firestorm. With no one left to douse the flames, the fires festered into a dire conflagration. The wind picked up, pushing the flames from one dwelling to the next. Thickening smoke issuing from their scorched remains polluted the air in darkening billows. The foul wind pressed the smokey air southward across the Muva, furthering the Yatins' misery. Men and gargoyles fought throughout the night as the battered Yatin Army escaped across the bridges. Yonig's gargoyles drove toward the center bridge in two giant pincers, trapping thousands north of the Muva, where their ranks were winnowed by flame and sword. Others continued to escape over the east and west bridges, until those avenues were closed by the middle of the night. Some stripped their armor, chancing the river, the cold water claiming as many lives as drowning.

By the break of dawn, the Yatin's weary Army waited along the Muva's south bank, staring with sunken eyes and laden hearts across the river, where fires continued burning throughout the north half of the capital. The gargoyles lined much of the north bank of the river, staring back at them with glowing red eyes. The foul creatures stood statue still along the wharves of the riverbank in disciplined ranks, their stout formations making any counterattack futile. The northeast redoubt had also fallen, its garrison slaughtered to a man, while the north center and north west fortresses still bore the standard of the Yatin 1ˢᵗ Army, a rearing purple ocran upon a field of gold.

As the second day progressed, the gargoyles strengthened their hold upon the north half of the city, eradicating the last pockets of resistance, save for the two remaining redoubts. By midday, the north center redoubt fell, hundreds of gargoyle corpses littering its battlements attesting to its stout defense.

By nightfall, gargoyle trebuchets were brought into the city, hurling missiles across the Muva, as the Yatins stripped the south wall of its catapults to respond in kind. Yonig slipped three telnics across the river upstream, sending them to cut the road south of Mosar, picking the most brutal of his troops for the task, each lightly clad and mobile, ordering them to loot, hit, and flee if confronted in order to regroup and return when the enemy forsook the chase. The lands south of the city were a mix of rolling hills, farmlands, and forests. Yatin cavalry drove the creatures off during the day, but they returned at night, slaughtering any Yatins clustered in small groups outside the city walls south of the city. The wretched creatures celebrated their victories, feasting on their victims as the sun rose to a clear sky on the third day, when the singing of volu birds echoing in the crisp air grew ominously silent. Several of the gargoyles gazed curiously south as a column of cavalry paraded north over a distant hillside, bearing the sigil of the 4th Torry Army, a silver sword upon a field of black. Beside this standard was another, bearing a gold crown upon a field of white, the sigil of the House of Lore.

The Torry prince had arrived.

*****

"Highness, I strongly advise against this!" General Avliam, commander of the 4th Torry Cavalry, cautioned.

"I appreciate your counsel, General, but it is I that shall treat with the Yatin emperor," Lorn affirmed, donning his silver helm, his mount shifting once he relaxed its reins.

The Torry 4th Cavalry held position beyond ballistae range of Mosar's southern walls, its gray ramparts silhouetted against the clear sky. The Torry riders swept over the adjoining hillsides, converging upon Mosar from three separate directions, slaughtering gargoyle raiders throughout their approach. Each rider kept the severed heads of their kills, the hideous trophies dangling from their saddles. They departed Cagan with five hundred riders and two hundred axillaries from their reserve, Prince Lorn bringing most of Torry South's Cavalry to bear, leaving Regent Ornovis one hundred axillary riders to defend Cagan.

The Torry 4th Army continued to draw near, their twenty telnics strung out for leagues, trudging through the endless farmlands and forests stretching to the horizon. The Yatin 3rd Army marched beside them, their commander, General Jutol, mustering eleven of his Army's fifteen telnics before setting out from his post along the southern border, an improvement upon the seven telnics that were assembled when he received Prince Lorn crossing into Yatin. It was still a far cry from his full complement, a problem shared with the Yatin 1st and 2nd Armies as well.

"I shall remain with my command, Highness," General Jutol said, riding alongside Prince Lorn as the emperor's emissaries awaited up ahead to escort Lorn into the city.

"Very well, General. Coordinate with General Korath on the placement of his troops. I will see to the state of the capital," Lorn said. General Korath commanded the Torry 4th Army and was still several leagues to their rear, bringing his Army north.

Lorn drew away, his dozen Royal Elite following their liege as Jentra rode beside him. The imperial emissaries waited some two hundred paces ahead, along the cobblestone road leading to the south gate of Mosar. They sat astride snow-colored ocran, wearing rich amethyst robes with gold capes that bespoke their regal post.

"I like this not," Jentra whispered his discontent, thinking it folly to trust the Yatins with their lives. For all they knew, the Yatins might have already capitulated and offered up Lorn's head to negotiate better terms. The prince dismissed such fears, reassuring his faithful comrade that Yah's hand was guiding their path and to trust in that.

"You should stay with the command, Jentra. I trust you to oversee the Army in my absence over any other," Lorn said.

"General Korath can see to his troops. My place is guarding your back, since you fail to see the threats that so obviously surround you, My Prince." Jentra shook his head, stressed by Lorn's stubborn disregard for his own safety. With the king dead, the realm could ill afford its prince to perish as well. The latest news from Torry North was most dire, with Morac surrounding Corell with a vast host. If the princess was slain or taken, then House Lore fell to Lorn alone. The Yatins were longtime enemies of the Torry Realm, and only their desperation drove them to open their city to the Torry Army, but things could change swiftly in these perilous times. With Lorn entering the city with only a handful of guards, he was placing himself, and the Torry Realm, at the Yatin emperor's mercy. Emperor Yangu was a reputed tyrant, with little love for his Torry neighbors, and Lorn would be wise to not trust him.

"Take heart, Jentra. I know the doubts that cloud your heart and plague your thoughts, doubts of my placing blind trust in an omnipotence that you cannot see. I cannot ask you to take such leaps of faith based solely upon my word. But I have relayed his will to you time and again, and it has never proven false. When Terin came upon us in the wilds, relaying the ill tidings in Yatin, it was Yah's hand that guided him to us, revealing his will so clearly on what he asked of us. It is by his will that we departed for Cagan to rally our forces to come to the Yatins' aid, and I am bound to obey Yah in all things, for in him do I trust above all else. If he asks that we come to Mosar's defense, then I trust him to protect me entering the Yatin capital."

"But Yangu cannot be trusted," Jentra countered.

"True, but *Yah* can."

*****

They rode through the gates of the city, their silver mail and azure tunics standing out amidst the sea of purple and gray of the city garrison. The emissaries led their small column through the wide avenue that ran from the south gate to Mosar's central district, where the minarets of the emperor's palace towered in the distance. The street was Mosar's widest causeway, with stone edifices lining either side, marble columns supporting their heavy stone roofs. Fitted white stones lined the surface of the avenue, resting atop a mortar epoxy and layers of gravel and crushed stone. The street was slightly higher upon its center, allowing rainwater to drain to either side. Soldiers posted along the street observed the new arrivals with a mix of curiosity, apprehension, and relief. Their war-weary faces and soiled raiment belied their sorry state. Some stood with bandages wound around their limbs, blood oozing through. Countless others waited out of sight. Dwellings across the southern half of the city overflowed with wounded soldiers and civilians. Hundreds of citizens gathered along the avenue to see the Torry prince, their eyes alit with renewed hope, setting aside their distrust of the Torry Realm in the face of the gargoyle threat waiting across the river.

Jentra kept his wits, scanning the crowd for threats, but only finding dispirited and shattered faces staring back at him, looking for deliverance. He noticed every caste in the gathering crowds, master and slave, rich and poor, male and female, patrician and peasant, all watching as they passed. The crowd was an endless sea of broken spirits and sullen faces. Many of the people wore threadbare garments torn and bloodstained. One child held tightly to a woman's skirt, most likely his mother. The woman was young, barely into her third decade, with ginger hair framing what was once a comely face but now bearing vicious claw marks across her cheeks and forehead. Her left arm ended at the elbow, with bandages wound over the stump. He would later learn that she was a refugee from north Mosar, fleeing her home when the gargoyles swept into the city, one of thousands of survivors now sheltering south of the river. He spotted another man hobbling with a makeshift crutch, dragging a useless left leg that was twisted in an unnatural angle. Others bore the scars of a losing fight, their faces swollen with missing eyes or teeth. These were the fortunate ones, Jentra reminded himself, imagining the fate of those who did not escape the gargoyles' wrath. The state of its people marred the ancient beauty of the stately avenue on which they trod. He again marveled at the structures lining the causeway, each representing many years of labor of master craftsmen. The city magistrate rested off their left, with pillars lining its western face, rising the height of three men, and large steps built into its base, descending to the street. The city forum rested off their right, its pillars spiraling higher than the magistrate's with statues lining its rooftop, cast in the visage of sea nymphs with their heads arced back and their arms thrust toward the heavens, presenting their breasts seductively. Jentra thought the statues more appropriate for a brothel than a place of governance, but they reflected the Yatins' lustful culture.

If Lorn found such displays distasteful, his countenance revealed it not. He was of a singular focus, the expulsion of the gargoyles from this land.

"The locals do not appear friendly," the Elite riding upon his other flank opined.

"They don't appear unfriendly either, Vage. They are simply survivors." Lorn regarded the populace with pity, most being homeless refugees, suffering the loss of limb or loved ones.

"They should be grateful for our aid," Vage Delis snorted. He was of an age with Lorn and served among the Torry prince's personal guard since his appointment in the Royal Elite. For two years he followed Lorn from one adventure to another, traveling the breadth of the realms and beyond. Like his fellow Elite, it was not lost on him their prince's sacrifice coming to the Yatins' aid. They traveled half the length of Arax, marching through foul swamps and battling gargoyle raiders to reach the city, whilst their own kingdom was beset by Morac's legions. They should at least be afforded gratitude and courtesy.

"They are grateful, but their minds are too disordered to acknowledge it," Lorn said. "Keep your wits, Vage. We are not here for their gratitude or friendship. We are here for a purpose."

"Aye," Vage conceded.

The crowds grew in size as they continued on, people spilling out from their shelters as word spread. The emperor's palace rested at the end of the causeway, the impressive structure overlooking the Muva, which ran along its north face. A curtain wall ran the length of its perimeter, the height of six men, with jagged gray battlements jutting prominently above. The inner palace towered above the outer walls, its dark bulwarks the color of pure obsidian. It rose the height of ten men, with its amethyst citadel spiraling into the heavens, the sigil of the Royal House of Yatin gracing its minaret, a rearing golden ocran upon a field of black. Soldiers in purple tunics and gold capes with bright gold mail lined the ramparts above and manned the massive gate centered on the east face of the curtain wall. The immediate area surrounding the palace was open space for several hundred paces up and downstream, where thousands of Yatin soldiers lined the open expanse, facing the gargoyle host gathered upon the opposite bank. Despite this low vantage point, Lorn could make out the dark ranks massing along the north bank of the Muva. Smoke still drifted above the northern half of Mosar, the dark vapors twisting above the ruins like tortured spirits. The center bridge rested up ahead, with men and gargoyles facing each other from opposite ends of the causeway.

"Prince Lorn, I present the royal palace!" one of the Yatin emissaries declared before leading them through the main gate.

*****

"Prince Lorn II, son of Lore!" The court crier heralded his entrance into the throne room, which he entered alone. The chamber was half the size of Corell's throne room but richly adorned with purple stone arches running the length of the chamber like the ribs of a great beast, with gold-plated columns running the length of either wall, supporting the structure. Large lanterns hung from the ceiling, their fiery glow reflecting off the dark mirrored stone floor with jewels embedded throughout its surface. The throne itself rested upon a raised dais at the end of the chamber, cast in wrought iron and covered in gold. Large tapestries hung behind the throne, bearing the sigil of the Yatin Royal House, a golden rearing ocran upon a field of black. A dozen Imperial Elite flanked either side of the dais, with bright gold cuirasses over purple tunics, with matching greaves and helms. They stood statue still, following Lorn with their eyes. Upon the throne sat the Yatin emperor.

Yangu III, emperor of the Yatin Empire, sat his throne, his countenance twisted painfully, masking his contempt as he received the Torry prince. High cheekbones and narrow features framed his pretentious face, with long brown hair draping beneath a golden crown with sapphires, amethysts, and rubies embedding its rim in ornate splendor. He wore black robes over a silver tunic that draped to his ankles. Several members of the Yatin court stood off to the side of the throne, adorned in the robes of courtesans and ministers and one clad in the garb of a soldier with four braided cords adorning his shoulder, marking him a commander of Army.

Lorn stopped short of the dais and knelt, paying homage as protocol required of visiting royalty. The chamber remained eerily quiet as Emperor Yangu did not quickly grant Lorn leave to rise.

"Rise!" Yangu finally commanded, his cold voice echoing in the still chamber.

"Emperor Yangu!" Lorn greeted with authority, projecting the strength his title demanded. He could feel Yangu's pale blue eyes taking his measure, looking for any defect or misstep. The Yatin emperor was a reputed tyrant and libertine, with countless wives and concubines. He was prone to fits of anger, demonstrating great cruelty at court. The emperor likely viewed Lorn's arrival with suspicion. Yangu looked frail and weathered, silver tainting his brown hair, and his face gaunt as if starved. Did he still mourn his eldest son's fate? Or was he sick with worry over the state of his realm? His robes draped his emaciated form like linen drawn over bones.

"What draws your eye to my realm, Prince Lorn, whilst the fate of your own stands upon the precipice? Corell is beset by a mighty host, and yet you lead a Torry Army into *my* realm while it is needed elsewhere?" Yangu asked.

Lorn noticed the Yatin general standing off to the side, stiffen, obviously displeased with his emperor's tact. The difference between Lorn and Yangu could not be starker, with the Torry prince clad in silver mail helm and greaves over an azure tunic, his armor stained in blood and marred from battle. Yangu was clad in the trappings of court, with ornate raiment and his jeweled crown upon his head.

"I received word of my father's fate once we already entered your realm, Emperor Yangu. Forsaking attainable goals only to intercede once the battle for Corell was already decided would be foolish. I must trust the fate of Torry North to my sister and generals, while the battle for Yatin is joined."

"What do you gain by aiding our cause? Would it not profit your realm to allow your enemies to devour one another and only intercede to finish the winner? We are age-old enemies, Prince Lorn. Surely your counselors have educated their future king on our bitter history? Am I to trust your naivety on such matters or trust my own doubts of your sincerity? Is it not more likely that you have come at this opportune moment to present yourself as the savior of my people, garnering their loyalty to depose their rightful liege?"

General Yoria winced, aghast that his emperor would asperse the Torry prince, offending a potential ally with the enemy storming the gates. He left thousands of his men dead or dying on the other side of the river. The Mosar garrison was devastated, with barely one in three of their full musters still manning the battlements. They needed the Torry troops if they held any notion of defeating Yonig's legions. Without them, defeat was certain. He expected the Torry prince to depart, taking his Army with him, leaving Yatin to its doom.

"Any wise ruler would question the motive of an age-old enemy offering friendship during a time of great duress. I came upon one of my countrymen, a boy really, who fought beside your soldiers at Telfer. He relayed the tale of your nation's plight, regaling the horrors visited upon your people by our common foe. It was then that I traveled to our southern realm, rallying our forces to your cause. Despite your suspicions on our motivations, my people can ill afford for Yatin to fall under Tyro's dominion, a knife to Cagan's throat. The threat to Torry South must be lifted before I again march to the defense of Torry North." Lorn wanted to explain Yah's vision of Yatin's demise if he failed to intercede, but reserved any mention of the deity until he was certain of Yangu's reception. He was caught off guard by the Yatin emperor's sudden resistance to their alliance. Did not Minister Yotora agree at the council of Corell with Prince Lorn's plan to bring the Torry 4th Army here? Did he not plead for Torry intervention? Lorn would later learn Yangu imprisoned Minister Yotora upon his return from Corell, his inquisitors torturing the emissary to determine if he was a Torry spy for agreeing to allow a Torry Army into their realm. Yangu was only swayed to reason by the collective urging of his ministers and generals for the need of the Torry alliance. He eventually relented, releasing Minister Yotora and granting the Torry Army permission to cross into Yatin.

Yangu's eyes narrowed severely as if struggling to keep his true thoughts from reaching his lips.

"The Torry 4th Army awaits beyond your southern gates. We came posthaste from Cagan to aid you in your time of need. With your leave, Emperor Yangu, we will enter your city and prepare a counterattack to retake the northern half of Mosar," Lorn further explained, laying out their desired course.

"You present yourself before my throne without guard or escort, delivering yourself into my hands. The Yatin and Torry realms have long been enemies. Our strong southern walls were built to protect Mosar from Torry aggression. Am I to trust that the future Torry king has marched hundreds of leagues only to help his *enemy*? Think you my eyes are blind to the affairs in the east? Your father has fallen at Kregmarin. To claim kingship of the Torry Realms, you need only to return to Corell and sit upon its vacant throne. Yet you delay your birthright to come here," Yangu vented his true thoughts, unable to curb his tongue.

General Yoria lowered his head, dejected by the emperor's harsh words. Only a fool would insult an ally at such a time, repeating his paranoia over Prince Lorn's motive. The Torry prince would surely turn and leave, taking his Army and Yoria's hope with him.

The emperor's guards stirred as Lorn drew his sword. Their alarm eased when Lorn raised an open right palm whilst placing his sword upon the floor before the dais, before backing a step. The court gasped. The surrender of a royal blade was a willing forfeiture of life or command. His act was unprecedented. He was their apparent savior, the head of the rescuing Torry Army. For what purpose would he submit?

"I have come for your sake and mine, for your people and mine, for humankind and those aligned with us. The threat before us is greater than my life or yours, greater than either of our royal lines, greater than the Torry Crown or the Yatin throne. Tyro must be stopped. To rush to the defense of Corell would be folly. I entrust its safety to our northern armies. Nor shall I return to claim my throne while Yonig's blade looms over Torry South's neck. The safety of the realm takes precedence. I have come to aid you in battle against our common foe, not to usurp your reign. If you believe my words false, then take up my sword and strike me down. I've instructed my Army to follow your direction if I am killed in any way. No vengeance shall be exacted from my death," Lorn declared.

Yangu's face contorted painfully, wondering what to make of Lorn's gesture. He would like nothing more than to accept the offer and strike the prince down, but no monarch would sacrifice himself in such manner without recourse. There must be some hidden motive in Lorn's bold act, portending great power that Yangu could not ascertain. Only a powerful man would offer himself up in such a way, and that gave him pause.

"Pick up your sword, son of Lore. No harm shall befall you by my hand. General Yoria shall treat with you on the placement of your troops and the assault you wish to plan," Yangu dismissed him.

*****

General Yoria escorted Prince Lorn to the uppermost citadel of the palace, overlooking the city from the open platform circling the tower mid distance from the battlements below and the minarets above. Yoria rested the flat of his hand upon the parapet circling the platform, pointing out the disposition of forces spread throughout the city. The palace's location in the center of Mosar afforded them an optimal view of the river, where most of the forces were concentrated.

"The gargoyles hold all the city north of the river, as we hold the south." Yoria pointed out the gargoyles lining the wharves and the avenue running the length of the riverbank. They could make out a dozen trebuchets along the water's edge, hurling fire and stone munitions across the river, but only the smallest munition could reach all the way across the watery expanse. Thousands of Yatins faced them from the south bank of the Muva, holding position along the base of the palace and along the wharves that stretched between the bridges. Yoria repositioned twenty trebuchets from the south wall to the river, countering Yonig's fire. Hundreds of corpses littered the Muva, their stench reaching even the highest battlements. Fires still burned unchecked throughout north Mosar, especially in the poorer districts, where the small dwellings were constructed with wood and straw.

Lorn's eyes swept the length of the Muva, searching for any apparent weakness along the enemy front. The gargoyles concentrated their heavy infantry near the three bridges, leaving their lightly clad troops along the waterfront between them. It made sense as the lighter troops could always fly over the river, posing a threat to the entire length of the Muva, forcing the Yatins to guard every space along the front.

Lorn scanned farther afield, examining the burnt-out dwelling stretched two leagues north and east of the city, while a forest straddled either side of the Muva downstream and a large section of northwest of the city. He examined the possibilities there before turning his gaze back to the city, finding the standards of the 1st and 3rd Gargoyle Legions lifting in the breeze above the north wall, where Yonig's command post was likely positioned. The gargoyle general probably stood there now, overlooking the battlefield as he did.

"What is your count on the enemy?" Lorn asked.

"I have few hard numbers," Yoria conceded.

"Your best guess?"

"We counted thirty-two to thirty-eight telnics in the 3rd Legion and another ten to fifteen in the 1st before they assailed the city. I will guess their combined losses nearing twelve to eighteen telnics," Yoria surmised.

"We slew another two telnics on our way north," Lorn added. That would put Yonig's current strength anywhere between twenty-two and forty-one telnics. Splitting the difference gave him a number nearer thirty telnics. Thirty telnics was a far cry from the one hundred combined telnics that both legions began their campaign with, plus the other fifty telnics of the 2nd Legion, last reported in Tenin. Yonig likely garrisoned Telfer with several thousand troops, suffering heavy casualties in that siege and the trek through central Yatin. That meant that what they were facing was what remained of the 1st and 3rd Legions. That still left whatever the 2nd Legion might send from Tenin, plus any other reinforcements Tyro decided to add. His first priority was clearing the sky of enemy magantors in order to mask his movements. His warbirds were already undertaking that task, having slain seven Benotrist magantors in as many days. His second priority was provisions. His men brought enough food for two fortnights but would require massive resupply as the Yatins' own stores were rapidly depleted. He ordered Grand Admiral Kilan and the 1st and 3rd Torry Fleets to advance to Faust, the vital port city resting at the mouth of the Muva, to resupply the Army and protect the Yatin port from the Benotrist Navy. The Benotrist Navy savaged the Yatins at Tenin, destroying the 1st and 2nd Yatin Fleets. A few surviving galleys escaped southward, joining the 3rd Yatin Fleet at Faust but were hopelessly outnumbered once the Benotrist Navy continued southward.

General Yoria's guarded posture belied his unease. It seemed he wished to speak honestly with Lorn but held back out of his reserved nature or for his loyalty to his emperor. Lorn gave a cursory scan behind them, confirming that they were alone on the platform.

"Something troubles you, General?" Lorn asked quietly.

Yoria's brown eyes flashed briefly, taken aback by the prince's inquiry. Though just a dusting of silver tainted his rusty mane, the general looked aged beyond his forty-one years, despite his crisp tunic and polished gold armor.

"My emperor has become afflicted with madness since word of his son's desecration reached the court. He has been prone to melancholy and fits of rage, but his mind ever served the benefit of the realm. I know you only by reputation, Prince Lorn, and I place great trust in speaking so openly to a foreign potentate, but time is fleeting, and my people stand upon the brink." Yoria's voice broke with desperation.

"You are very brave for speaking thusly of your liege, though I see where some would question your loyalty," Lorn said.

"My loyalty is ever to my emperor but also my people. I fear his madness may never lift, and I dare not think of the consequences if this is so. I hold this city with only fourteen telnics, twelve of the Yatin 1st Army, and two of the city garrison, with eight hundred cavalry. I cannot hide the truth of the emperor's state from our only savior. Without your Army, we will be undone, and the emperor can only see you as his enemy."

"His mistrust is founded in our history. He is wise to do so. Only time and actions of consequence can mend old wounds, General. I came to save your people and drive Tyro's minions from your land. Once accomplished, I shall return whence I came. Only then will your emperor's trust in my word be ensured."

"Even if all comes to pass as you intend, he shall see deception in every kind gesture. I say this, Prince Lorn, to warn you of his fragile mind. For the sake of my people and your own, I ask that you proceed very carefully. Even an act that you think is trivial can be interpreted differently in the emperor's eyes."

"I hear your counsel, General, but I was aware of your emperor's disposition before I set out on this campaign."

"And you came nonetheless?" Yoria asked curiously.

"My trust is not easily earned, General, and I certainly do not trust the fragile mind of Yangu, but I trust in Yah. It was his counsel that sent me here and his will that I serve."

Yah? Yoria grimaced, recalling where he heard that name, until drawing it from the crevices of his mind. Was that not the deity once worshipped in the Zoran Province, before it was outlawed by Yargu II hundreds of years ago? Yatin emperors ever since connected the religion to the old Western Kingdom overthrown by their ancestors and thus a threat to Yatin rule. Many who dwelt in the Zoran Province were descendants of the old Western Kingdom and rose in revolt several times in the past three hundred years. If the Torry prince followed this ancient god, then Zoran might follow him over their own emperor. His spirit sank with this revelation.

Were all royals touched by madness? he wondered. Had he just confided in a madman his deepest concerns?

"Have faith, General, for I am not *touched*. I did not speak of Yah for you to be easily converted. I am simply speaking the truth. The god of Kal has spoken to me, and I follow his will and his alone. I know your emperor's distaste for the worshippers of Yah, but I will not forsake him to assuage your trepidation. The road before us is fraught with toil and suffering, but we will save your people. Yah has revealed this truth to me. If we fail, you will know him to be false," Lorn challenged.

Yoria opened his mouth, but no words were forthcoming. What could he say?

"Now let us retake your city." Lorn placed a hand to Yoria's shoulder.

*****

The Torry 4th Army passed through the south gates of Mosar the following morn, sunlight reflecting off their silver helms and gray mail, their standard, a silver sword upon a field of black, was placed upon the battlements of the east bridge, where they relieved the Yatins holding the vital causeway. In the proceeding days, the Torries would take up position upon the center bridge, shifting the Yatin 1st Army to the west bridge, where Yoria could consolidate his battered cohorts.

*****

Three days hence

General Yonig cursed his timidity for not taking Mosar when the opportunity presented itself, stopping at the river, whilst the Yatins reconstituted their disordered telnics. They held him at bay until the Torry 4th Army arrived, strengthening their tenuous defense. Now they were of a number to his own, firmly entrenched along the river. He could do naught but wait for his reinforcements, which were days away. Yonig sucked the slather building along his fangs, his dark crimson eyes sweeping the length of the river, standing upon the highest battlements of the north center redoubt. The structure rested some distance south of the north gate. Hundreds of his gargoyles perished taking the small fortress, but it provided an excellent command post from which to direct his legions. Mosar was an ancient and massive city, divided in almost equal parts by the slow-flowing Muva, with three large bridges spaced evenly across the river's expanse. Three roadways ran north-south, across the bridges, to six separate city gates, three along the north wall and three the south. Yonig's command post overlooked the center road running from the north gate across the center bridge, before angling slightly west after the river, before heading south, ending at the south gate. This center causeway was wide enough for a dozen wagons to pass over it side by side. The causeway passed by his redoubt, as well as the imperial palace that rose imperiously in the city's center, just beyond the river. There were five other small fortresses besides the one he claimed for his own, each the height of ten men with towering ramparts and catapults lining their battlements. Each of the six redoubts were positioned in a circle within the city, each aligned with one of the three bridges, one tower to the north and south of each bridge.

Yonig placed three hundred gargoyles in each of the three redoubts in his possession, garrisoning every key position within the city. The bulk of his heavy infantry held position at the north ends of the three bridges, the only avenues of advance the Yatins and Torries could use to assail him. If the fools dare test his strength, he would gladly oblige them. The bridges were well built, with fortified platforms overlooking each end and a large bulwark straddling their center, where ramparts overlooked those passing beneath. The Yatins held the middle bulwarks of each bridge, crowding their battlements with archers and infantry. Yonig again cursed himself for not at least seizing these middle bulwarks when the opportunity presented. Most disconcerting was the loss of so many magantors in recent days. He began the siege with eleven magantor scouts. Now he had only three. He could now only send them out together in force, concentrating their patrols to his east where the Yatin 2nd Army was likeliest to appear.

"General! Looksss!" an aide hissed, pointing out activity along the east bridge, where hundreds of soldiers marched across under the standard of the 4th Torry Army.

Horns echoed across the river, signaling attack.

*****

"Shield formation!" Torry commanders ordered, their columns passing under the central bulwarks guarding the bridge, emerging from the north end of the passageways that ran beneath the battlements. Their rectangular shields covered their formation like the armor shell of a tacidern as they neared the north end of the bridge.

Gargoyle ballistae spewed from the north bank of the Muva, some passing harmlessly overhead, others striking true, stones caving holes in their formations, while fire munitions spread flames amidst the crowded ranks. The insistent fire slowed their advance, forcing them to close ranks before continuing their march upon the north end of the bridge, where gargoyles awaited them behind palisades of overturned wagons and piled corpses and timber. The gargoyles guarding the bridges were similarly equipped with interlocked shields, with sturdy helms, greaves, and mail. The Torries had to break formation to negotiate the palisades blocking their path, exposing themselves to archer fire and gargoyle spears. Men climbed over the cluttered debris, arrows piercing their stomachs or thighs, where no armor protected them, the wounded and dying adding to the obstacles hindrance.

Haroom!

Horns sounded again along the length of the river, Torry soldiers advancing upon the center bridge, the sigil of the House of Lore raised upon their standards, a golden crown upon a field of white, their column led by Prince Lorn. He marched to the fore as they closed upon the enemy holding the north end of the bridge.

Haroom!

Yonig cursed the foul horns as the third blast sounded, signaling the Yatin 1st Army across the west bridge. He only took solace in his heavy infantry guarding each bridge, the enemy's numbers counting for naught on those narrow causeways. Each of his commanders upon the bridges positioned their telnics a quarter distance across the bridges, slowing any attacks before they could breach the north end of the bridge. It would be a slow, painful, and bloody slog, bleeding each Army in equal measure. Flame, stones, and arrows passed over the combatants, the clash of steel ringing out over the din. He could see men and gargoyles drop from the bridges, caked in flames or tossed over to clear the way for the living.

Yonig regarded his position carefully, the entirety of his 3rd Legion spread throughout the city, though concentrated at the river and key chokepoints, numbering twenty-eight telnics in all. His 1st Legion, numbering a scant ten telnics, waited north of the city, safeguarding the western and eastern approaches and the trebuchets that he hadn't brought into the city. As Yonig considered bringing the

1ˢᵗ Legion into the Mosar to blunt the Yatin/Torry attack, another sound echoed west of the city.

Yonig's gaze shifted to where the forest met the open fields northwest of Mosar. There, in the distance, a mighty tumult echoed over the din.

"*Ka!*" he cursed, hundreds of cavalry bursting from the trees, sweeping over the battlefield. A closer view would discern the standards of the 4ᵗʰ Torry Cavalry, a silver lance piercing a black shield upon a field of white, and the standard of the 2ⁿᵈ Yatin Cavalry, a charging blue ocran on a field of orange.

The gargoyle 1ˢᵗ Legion was ill prepared to face such a force, their telnics spread uselessly along their perimeter, mirroring the north wall, with several thousand farther afield guarding the approaches. For the Yatin and Torry Cavalry coming upon them so sudden spoke poorly of the troops guarding the west. They were likely already dead. Such a possibility was confirmed once the massive wall of infantry emerged behind the cavalry, the Yatin 3ʳᵈ Army commanded by General Jutol.

The Torry and Yatin Cavalry swept over the battlefield, smashing the gargoyles' center, disordering the legion's ability to form ranks before continuing on to the east, cutting down gargoyles like a sickle cutting grain. Gargoyles broke ranks, retreating to the city walls.

"Packaww!" Torry magantors screeched overhead.

Yonig looked up as the great avian swooped down from the heavens, jumping aside as a fire munition struck the battlement of his redoubt. Yonig gained his feet, smoke and flame obscuring his sight as he coughed, struggling to make sense of the chaos. A dozen of his aides and guards were dead or burning, victims of the foul warbird. He caught sight of a dozen magantors dropping their fire munitions amidst his troops guarding the bridges. One magantor tumbling into the river near the west bridge, a large pike piercing its breast. Another was set upon by a flax of gargoyles that managed to gain enough elevation to assail it. They stabbed repeatedly, slaying the beast and its rider before crashing into a storehouse along the north riverbank.

"Order retreat!" Yonig hissed, forsaking the city to save his legions and concentrate on the one enemy within his grasp, Jutol's 3ʳᵈ Army.

C H A P T E R

11

Siege of Mosar stage three

Thump!

The arrow bounced off his shield that he held overhead, racing along the avenue, his guardians struggling to keep pace. Coming upon a gargoyle standing in the middle of the thoroughfare, Lorn lowered his left arm, driving the flat of the shield into the creature's chest. The sound of the gargoyle's scimitar scrapping his shield pained his ears, the emphatic blow knocking the creature from its feet. Lorn passed on as Jentra drove his sword into the gargoyle's gut, twisting the blade, dragging it along the width of its torso before continuing on.

Jentra cursed Lorn for not even slowing down while he cleaned his kills. Keeping Lorn alive was difficult enough without the prince placing himself in the fore ranks, pursuing the enemy through the streets of north Mosar. He stole a cursory glance, spotting scores of gargoyle archers upon the rooftops up ahead, losing their volleys into the Torry ranks flooding the street. Once they broke from the bridge, Lorn ordered them up the central avenue that ran from the middle bridge to the north gate of Mosar. The street was the largest causeway in the city, with stone edifices lining either side, each liberally spaced with gaps large enough to place unit-sized formations between them.

"Reform!" Lorn shouted with the fore ranks growing haphazard, individuals drawing too far afield. The gargoyles were in full retreat, but a number turned back upon their pursuers, swarming targets of opportunity. The Torry columns advanced, finding more of their fellow Torries dead upon the street, dismembered and half eaten, a warning not to break off from their ranks.

Jentra drew up alongside his prince, interlocking shields, his fellow Elite forming up bedside them. Hundreds of Torry soldiers closed ranks, pausing their advance to dress their lines. Dozens of gargoyles lingered upon the avenue, observing their human foes as their brethren drew farther away.

"Packaww!"

A Torry warbird passed overhead, its gray-white wings silhouetted against the clear sky, passing northward before depositing a fire munition farther north. Gargoyle screams rent the air, the munition exploding amidst their retreating host.

"Forward!" Lorn commanded, wasting little time driving the enemy before them.

*****

Yonig reached the north gate of Mosar, directing his troops as they neared the wall, sending his heavier armed levies through the gate and the lightly clad troops to the top of the wall, reducing the traffic flow through the narrow chokepoint. The telnics he sent from the city joined with the tattered remnants of the 1st Legion, managing to slow the Yatin 3rd Army's advance, though Jutol's Army pushed them back toward the walls in an ever-shrinking pocket. With every passing moment, more gargoyles exited the city, joining the battle north of the wall. Armored troops held the front, whilst their lightly armed comrades sprang from the top of the wall, dropping onto the Yatin ranks. Yonig kept enough troops upon the wall to stay the Torry and Yatin advance from the south, while committing the rest of his telnics to the Yatin 3rd Army, whose formations began to waver.

*****

General Jutol sat astride a dusty gray mare, the ocran shifting nervously with the sound of battle as he surveyed his lines. His telnics were aligned before him, forming a loose arc around the north wall, with the 4th Torry Cavalry covering his right flank and the Yatin 2nd Cavalry his left. He planned to press the gargoyles back to the walls of Mosar, whilst the Torry 4th Army and Yatin 1st Army advanced northward through the city, squeezing the enemy between them, but Yonig managed to quickly bring thousands of troops to bear, forsaking Mosar and throwing all he had against him. With every passing moment, more gargoyles issued from the gates or sprang from the battlements. He could see thousands more massing along the broken bulwarks of the north wall, like insects crawling from a nest. His own troops seized Yonig's trebuchets that remained outside the city, using the siege engines to lob ballistae into the gargoyle host.

"Kai-Shorum!" gargoyles screamed, dropping into the Yatins' midst, slashing with their scimitars as men lifted their shields, stabbing desperately with their short swords. Hundreds of gargoyles lay dead amidst their serried ranks, each slaying nearly as many Yatins in the exchange. Hundreds more sprang from the battlements, sweeping over the Yatin ranks like dark waves lapping ashore.

Jutol's ability to hold his ground depended upon the 4th Torry Army and 1st Yatin Army seizing the north wall from the other side, but he had no means of knowing their progress, the wall blocking his line of sight. The battle was hours long, his battered Army suffering 25 percent casualties with enemy attacks intensifying. The cavalry guarding his flanks fared well enough, using their mobility to scatter any gargoyles gathering there. The center, however, suffered great duress. He observed weary soldiers hoisting their shields overhead, struggling to parry creatures dropping all around them. Arrows arced overhead, disappearing in the encroaching mass.

"Sound retreat!" Jutol relented, his aides relaying the command. Withdrawing in the face of the enemy was a difficult maneuver, which he drilled his men relentlessly whenever training allowed during previous musters, but they hadn't practiced the tactic in the recent season.

Men in the forward ranks thrust their spears between their shields while backing a step, their progress dependent upon those behind them moving first, negotiating the dead and wounded littering their path. It was a painfully cumbersome process, with cavernous breaks in the ranks opening with devastating result. Gargoyles poured into the fissures, striking down Yatin infantry from their exposed flanks. The gargoyles fared just as poorly whenever their lighter armed troops met the Yatin shield walls, hundreds of their dead piling wherever the lines met.

*****

Jentra ducked, a fire munition passing just overhead, striking a structure off his right, flames caking its stone surface. He lost sight of Lorn amidst the wall of infantry stretching endlessly along the avenue. He followed the sounds of clashing steel to his left, where gargoyles spilled out from the adjoining street, meeting the Torries with a shield wall of their own. He cursed, wondering when the gargoyles adopted human tactics. At least their armor prevented them from taking flight, but it made them far harder to kill. The gargoyle incursion numbered fewer than two units but brought the Torry advance to a halt, forcing them to close ranks around them. Those farther north continued on alone, their fellows caught up in the action behind them. The gargoyles' pocket slowly shrank, Torry infantry cutting them down but costing them precious time. It seemed every step since they left the bridge was beset with obstacles. The gargoyles set traps throughout their lines of march, collapsing building in places, their fallen debris blocking key points throughout north Mosar. Fires were alit, with one spreading across the causeway, forcing them to navigate the flames. Fire and stone ballistae rained from the fortress up ahead, until Torry magantors silenced the catapults positioned there. Gargoyle archers sprang up upon the rooftops all along their route, firing into their midst before slipping away, only to reappear elsewhere. The damnable creatures fought an effective delaying action, striking them from one flank while fleeing another. Lightly armored gargoyles sprang upon them from above, while heavy armored columns struck head on, each action confounding their pace. Jentra could only guess that the Torries and Yatins advancing along their flanks were experiencing similar resistance. Jentra skirted the melee off his left, working his way forward before catching sight of several blue tunics in the sea of white and gray. A few of Lorn's Elite were with Jentra, following their captain as he fought his way to their prince's side.

"Highness!" Jentra caught his breath, reaching Lorn's side as the Torry prince paused, holding position a block south of the massive redoubt that served as Yonig's command post. Flames drifted above its battlements, where Torry magantors pelted its rooftop. The main gate at the base of the structure was loosely reconfigured, the gargoyles repairing it after smashing it themselves when they swept through the city. Their makeshift repairs would fare poorly against a Torry ram, which Lorn ordered forth.

"Jentra, how fare you this fine day?" Lorn asked, his easy mirth stiffening the spines of those nearest them. If their leaders seamed nonplussed by the violence raging around them, men were apt to mimic their indifference. If there was one positive trait that stood out among Lorn's many attributes, it was his cool indifference in the face of great tumult.

"I'm still alive," Jentra snorted, wondering how much longer any of them could make that claim.

"Let us keep it that way. That's my royal decree." Lorn smiled, watching the soldiers up ahead break down the gate of the redoubt before charging into the fortress.

"Highness, wait!" Jentra called out as his prince led the way, racing up the crowded avenue, Torry soldiers pouring into the fortress. Jentra took solace in the scores of men preceding them through the broken gates, trusting Lorn's safety to those who were likely to clear the enemy from his path. The first ones through did not think to bring torches, with gargoyles waiting for them in darkened corridors and dim chambers. The clash of steel sounded in the dark, men as likely to fall upon one another as the enemy. It took time to sort out the madness before advancing farther into the fortress. Jentra passed under the broken porticus that was rent asunder like torn parchment. Beyond the broken gate was a vast chamber with adjoining hallways and stairways breaking off in several directions. Bodies were strewn across the floor, the cries of the wounded drowning in the din of battle. He followed Lorn up a stairwell off their left, a dozen soldiers preceding them up the narrow passage.

"Kai!" Gargoyles screamed, charging down the stairs, their scimitars clashing against raised shields. Men buckled under their weight, tumbling backward, gargoyles thrashing atop them, their eyes glowing in the dim light. Several tumbled, tripping those farther below, bodies crashing into one another. Soldiers hacked away at whatever flesh the creatures offered. One gargoyle raised its sword before Lorn took it at the wrist, blood issuing from it stump. The gargoyle shrieked, standing atop a pile of stunned men as Lorn kept his feet a step below their cluster. The gargoyle shifted, Lorn's follow strike meeting empty air, falling upon a Torry soldier laying beneath him, pressing upon the man's shield that separated them. The man's eyes drew wide as the gargoyle's head reached over his shield, jowls snapping, the man's arms pinned beneath as the fangs grew ominously near.

Jentra lunged forward, driving his sword into the creature's neck, his arm outstretched over the men piled between them. Lorn shifted around the mound of flesh, his sandaled boots stepping on bodies cluttering the stairs. Some voiced their displeasure at being stepped upon, but Lorn ignored their pleas, moving past the mess as another gargoyle raced down the stairs to meet them. Lorn's shield met the creature's sword, his own blade thrusting quickly into the creature's side, jabbing repeatedly. Jentra came up beside him, stabbing the creature's left wing, driving it into the opposite wall. Lorn slipped around him, rushing up the stairs as others gained their feet to follow.

They slew several others before reaching the summit, sunlight shining through the portal above. They passed through the opening, stepping onto the battlements, few gargoyles remaining atop the fortress, its battlements littered with burning catapults and dozens of corpses strewn across the stone walkway. Men flooded the platform from opposite corners of the fortress, slaying the few gargoyles refusing to take flight. Jentra watched as several gargoyles climbed over the ramparts, their wings spreading, springing into the air. Archers managed to drop two of them before the others fled to the safety of the north wall, which remained in Yonig's hands.

Lorn stepped toward the rampart, sweat stinging his eyes as he stared out across the city. The view was breathtaking, the northern half of Mosar spread out before him in terrible splendor. He could see men and gargoyles battling atop the redoubt to his west, winged forms circling above its contested battlements. The sounds of battle echoed through the streets nearer the north wall, where the gargoyles still held position along its entirety. He could make out their winged silhouettes atop the wall, firing arrows into the streets below. The standards of the 4th Torry Army flew above the redoubt to the east as his troops pressed on to the north wall. Lorn could see the Yatin 3rd Army beyond the wall, withdrawing northward, the enemy host issuing from the city driving them back.

"Highness?" Jentra asked, wondering Lorn's thoughts. He could see Lorn working things out in his mind.

"Signal the telnic commanders to move to the wall with all haste. Yonig is abandoning the city to destroy Jutol. We cannot delay."

*****

The Yatin 1st Army and the Torry 4th Army pressed on toward the wall throughout the day, slowed by Yonig's actions, until they drew within the shadow of the north wall. Gargoyle archers held the battlements and watchtowers above, firing into the humans gathering below. Others operated the catapults along the larger platforms, hurling ballistae farther afield. Unfortunately for Yonig, the north wall of Mosar was built to hold against an attack without, not within, leaving the Yatin and Torry infantry numerous openings. Soldiers poured over the base of the wall, racing up the open stairways running along the inside of the wall. Some stairwells were closed within the workings of the watchtowers, men struggling to navigate their narrow confines. Gargoyles set traps throughout, men stepping onto collapsing stairways, with jagged spikes placed below. Others tripped ropes, triggering vats of oil and flames spreading in their midst.

Lorn forsook his forward command at the captured redoubt, leading the assault upon the main north gate. He passed under the archway of the city entrance, the ruined gates twisting off their hinges like tortured spirits. His blade struck a fleeing gargoyle along its left wing, the blow collapsing the creature to the ground before driving his blade into its back. Men passed around him, chasing the enemy beyond the city walls.

"Form up beyond the wall!" Lorn commanded, others relaying the order. Yonig's vast host waited beyond, driving Jutol's beleaguered Army farther northward. Lorn strode forth beyond the gate, directing men into position as a gargoyle sprang from the battlements behind them, its curved fangs arcing menacingly, its bright crimson eyes fixed upon the Torry prince.

Jentra stepped before his prince, raised shield meeting the creature's attack, its scimitar scrapping the flat steel. Jentra kept his feet, twisting his arm, the gargoyle's weight sliding off his shield. Two other Elite closed upon them, driving their swords into the creature's back, pinning it to the ground, while Lorn hacked its neck, the gargoyle's screams piercing their skulls as it thrashed violently.

"Keeping you alive is killing me!" Jentra panted, regarding Lorn as he shook his head.

"We must press on. The enemy means to destroy Jutol's Army!" Lorn affirmed, returning his gaze northward.

"My Prince!" a commander of Telnic shouted off their right, flashes of blue light illuminating the northern horizon.

*****

General Jutol reformed his men for the third time during their withdraw, redressing his lines with Yonig's growing host pressing his front. The Torry and Yatin Cavalry slowed the enemy advance long enough for him to do so, paying a heavy toll in the exchange. The Tartaro Forest rested half a league to his rear, and they might find shelter therein if they could reach it. The Torry 4th Cavalry again retreated to his right flank and the Yatin 2nd Cavalry to his left, as his battered Army received the enemy. The heavy armored gargoyle telnics were still far off, but the lighter-clad gargoyles were constantly on their heels, harrying their forward ranks with maddened fury.

"Archers!" The command went out as hundreds of arrows issued from the rear, striking the gargoyles attempting to fly over the fore ranks.

"Drat!" Jutol cursed at the archers' ineffectiveness. He lost too many bowmen, the few remaining struggling to concentrate their fire. They couldn't stem the tide with more gargoyles pressing their center, devastating his ranks. Scouts reported Yatin and Torry soldiers emerging from the north wall, forming ranks and advancing on Yonig's rear.

Jutol sighed with relief, preparing to give the order to advance, when his eyes suddenly drew slack.

Zip!

Blue laser erupted from the Yatin general's skull, his corpse slipping from the saddle in a quiet thud.

Ben Thorton shifted his aim farther left, finding a Yatin unit commander dressing his lines, his blast striking the fellow in the back. The laser continued cutting a path through several soldiers aligned to his front. Thorton shifted his aim to the rear echelons of the Yatin 3rd Army, firing off several hurried blasts into the gathered host, each laser passing through multiple targets before stopping. He shifted position to the other side of a thick porian, his men taking shelter in the tree line around him with acres of open ground separating them from the battle to their south.

"They're crumbling," Nels Draken said, observing Yatin troops breaking in panic. He stood off Thorton's left shoulder, within the shadow of the Tataro Forest.

Ben Thorton snorted, ignoring Nel's obvious assessment, firing off several more blasts, the panic his weapon induced killing more Yatins than the laser.

*****

"Withdraw!" Prince Lorn commanded, the fate of Jutol's 3rd Army becoming apparent, the flashes of laser fire preceding the complete collapse of the Yatin front. Nightfall was drawing close as the battle continued. Laser flashed along the flanks of the doomed Yatin Army, striking the cavalry operating there.

"Withdraw!" Jentra relayed the order, the Torry 4th Army and Yatin 1st repositioning within the city and along the north wall of Mosar.

The Torry and Yatin Cavalry returned from battle as the sun set in the western sky, passing through the broken gates of the north wall, most bearing two riders and some, three. Both contingents suffered 25 percent casualties, many falling under Thorton's withering fire. Commander Avliam sought out Prince Lorn, the battered sigil upon his breastplate dented and marred. He found Lorn still outside the walls, waiting for the last of their men to pass within the city.

"Highness!" Commander Avliam hailed.

"Commander," Lorn regarded the weary cavalryman, whose black cape was torn away, helm battered, and breastplate dented. The man looked to have aged ten years in a day.

"The enemy is reforming to our north. They have decimated Jutol's Army. The damnable Earther slew the general before unleashing his fury upon the packed Yatin ranks, spreading panic. The Army broke, and the gargoyles swarmed in. He then took aim upon our cavalry. I ordered my men to snatch whatever survivors we could, doubling up and returning here in all haste."

"It is the best you could do under those conditions, Commander. See to your men and move your cavalry to the south side of the city. Your mounts will do us little good for the foreseeable future. Coordinate with the Yatin Cavalry and scout the southern approaches of the city in case our gargoyle *friend* slipped another force to our rear."

The commander saluted, pressing a fist to his breast, before riding on through the gate.

"Packaww!" a lone magantor screeched overhead, passing south over the city walls. Lorn ordered all his avian away from the enemy and Thorton's deadly fire. Gazing northward, he could make out the enemy pickets in the distance. The coming night would reveal the state of Yonig's legions, whether they were strong enough to counterattack or battered enough to need to regroup. With that, Lorn turned, following his last men through the gate.

*****

Zip!

The next morning opened with laser fire striking a sentry atop the wall, overlooking the north center gate. Soldiers along the wall quickly took cover as another sentry tumbled from the battlements near the gate. Torry and Yatin soldiers crouched below the parapets, Thorton targeting anyone stealing a glance over the wall. The gargoyles erected a makeshift barricade mirroring the length of the north wall, much of which was built around their former siege works. They would strengthen their position throughout the day, with palisades jutting from the siege works and trenches deepened. The sound of spades echoed through the still morning air, with the quiet flash of laser fire striking any defender presenting themselves.

*****

"How many?" Lorn asked, his eyes scanning the length of the map rolled across the table. General Yoria and General Korath joined Lorn within the bowels of the northwest redoubt, with dozens of subordinate commanders gathered about, each reporting their losses and disposition.

"Several dozen between the northeast and northwest gates," General Korath estimated the casualties lost to Thorton's weapon. "These do not include how many he targeted further within the city."

"I can count five that I know of on the battlements above," General Yoria snorted, bemoaning the damnable Earther's deadly aim.

"We don't dare look over the ramparts without him knocking us from the wall," a Yatin commander of telnic growled.

"The gargoyles could assail the wall, and we'd be none the wiser until they were upon us," Jentra added.

"Then why haven't they?" General Korath asked the obvious question that was on all their minds.

"They are weak as well. How many thousands did we slay driving them from the city?" Calbo Reis, commander of the 5th Torry Telnic, asked.

"Commander Valen?" Lorn looked to his magantor commander, whose warbirds had the best view of the battle until Thorton's weapon drove them off. Denton Valen was the younger brother of General Dar Valen, who commanded all magantor forces in the Torry Realms.

"Yonig's combined force at the battle's end looked no more than fifteen telnics, perhaps twenty if stragglers and reserves he placed elsewhere are thrown in, My Prince," Denton said.

"That means we outnumber him now," another Torry commander cheerfully opined, the others not sharing his misplaced merriment.

"At what cost? Jutol's Army is gone, and we lost thousands retaking the city," a Yatin commander stated dejectedly.

"Not all of Jutol's men. Over three thousand have returned. I sent them to the south wall to reorganize," General Yoria said. "Of my own Army, we've counted two thousand casualties retaking the city."

"Four thousand," Korath added, listing the dead, wounded, and missing from the Torry 4th Army. A sizable number of the wounded would return to duty, but Jutol numbers were staggering.

"Yonig won't sit there indefinitely. Even gargoyles have to eat," another commander stated.

"They'll eat the dead, and there's no shortage in that regard," Jentra reminded them.

"He doesn't have to assail us. He'll just wait for the Earther to riddle our ranks and then simply march over our bones," Korath snorted.

"Thorton's intervention was not unforeseen. We have been bloodied, just as we have bloodied Yonig. He will not renew his assault without reinforcements. Our scouts spotted a large contingent of the 2nd Legion moving south from Tenin some days ago. He will wait for them before renewing his assault. We have time to prepare them a proper reception. I want a minimal force along the north wall, just large enough to appear that we'll contest it. Pick those who are swift of foot. They will withdraw at the outset. Keep a second rank behind the nearest dwellings of the wall, with specific avenues of retreat. Set traps everywhere else. I want a layered defense, our troops reinforcing each row of dwellings, strengthening the further south the enemy penetrates. I mean to bleed Yonig's legions for every step. I'll trade him the north half of Mosar for ten thousand gargoyles," Lorn declared, sweeping the austere assemblage, his eyes meeting those of every man present.

*****

"You don't approve?" Lorn asked once the commanders cleared the room, leaving him and Jentra alone, staring at the map of the city.

"It's risky, but I don't know what choice we have. The Earther's weapon limits our options. Men don't respond well with planned withdraws. Once a soldier gets it in his head that it is planned to run away, he will do so when it is convenient for him and not for his commander. You will need to drill them relentlessly on this maneuver."

"I've ordered Korath to spread the word and will advise Yoria to do likewise."

"Will you treat with the Yatin emperor before we proceed?" Jentra asked derisively, unable to mask his true opinion of the Yatin regent.

"Not until our men are repositioned and our chain of command fully reestablished."

"He'll blame you for the loss of his 3rd Army," Jentra reminded him.

"He is suspicious by nature. It is not unexpected."

"I don't trust him. At least with the gargoyles I know what to expect and what to do about it."

"We share the same foe, and he will see reason."

"Your faith in the Yatin emperor will be our undoing."

"I hold no faith in men, Jentra, only Yah, and Yah led me here."

"Yes, he led you here, and all of us with you, with enemies all around us and allies who are as likely to kill us as the enemy."

"Do you wish reassignment? I could have you return to Corell and aid my sister," Lorn said with sincerity. Jentra oft chided him on his reckless adherence to his god, but the grizzled soldier wouldn't leave his side even if he was ordered.

"Mind your tongue, Lorn. You'll not be rid of me that easily. Besides, by the time I attained Corell, the battle would be over. Let us hope you still have a kingdom to return to when this campaign ends."

"Yah would not have sent me here if Corell had fallen."

"You are certain?" Jentra snorted.

"I am." Lorn smiled, placing a hand to his friend's shoulder.

*****

He sat his throne, his emaciated bones suffering its unforgiving steel, his mind tortured with falsehoods, whispered by imaginary counselors.

"*The Torry prince has come to steal your throne,*" one phantom warned.

"*The Torries are in league with the gargoyles,*" another cautioned.

"*Jutol was betrayed,*" the first argued again.

"*Trust not in Lorn's promises.*"

He began to repeat the mad ramblings, muttering them loud enough for the guards nearest him to overhear.

"My Emperor?" one guard asked, thinking Yangu was addressing him.

The emperor's eyes drew suddenly wide, as if struck by freezing water. He gazed warily over the throne room, wondering where his make-believe advisors had gone.

"Summon Minister Shatero!" Yangu ordered.

The emperor waited impatiently, the moments passing like cooled lava, as if the laws of time and space conspired against him, until his faithful servant appeared.

"Minister of Inquiry Shatero!" the crier heralded.

Minster Shatero glided across the throne room, his robes swirling about his ankles, his arms tucked within the rich crimson sleeves of the garment. He was a nondescript man with a shaven head and dull yellow humorless eyes. A natural observer would struggle to find anything of note in his appearance other than his shiny dome and voluminous robes that swept the floor as he passed. The emperor bid him rise before he could fully prostate himself before the throne.

"How may I serve you, My Emperor?" the minister of inquiry asked, his voice as bland as his expressionless face.

"Guards, leave us!" Yangu clapped his hands, his guards withdrawing from the chamber as he descended the dais.

"You called for me, My Emperor?" Shatero whispered.

"Yes, my old friend." Yangu ran his hands along Shatero's blood-speckled sleeves, the garment's hue masking the stains of his victims' blood. As minister of inquiry, Shatero was charged with rooting out conspirators, spies, and the disloyal. Shatero's own spy network reached every part of the empire and beyond, though his failure to detect the gargoyle legions gathering at the border damaged his reputation in his emperor's eyes. Of course, the suddenness of the gargoyles' movement to the border prior to the invasion afforded little opportunity for his spies to detect and report before Yonig crossed into Yatin. Shatero redeemed this blunder by uncovering dozens of *plots* against the empire through forced confessions. The emperor did not question his inquisitor's dubious techniques, just his results. Once a man was brought to Shatero's dungeon, he would eventually confess his treason. The cries of his victims echoed through the lowest levels of the palace, a constant reminder to any who thought to betray their emperor or voice their misgivings on matters of state.

"Enemies surround us," Yangu whispered, ever cognizant that someone might overhear from the shadows. "Traitors infest our ranks, while Torries and gargoyles vie for dominion of my realm. My generals betrayed me at Telfer and Tenin, and now Jutol's 3rd Army has been destroyed. The Torry prince claims ignorance in the matter, but I know he planned this. His Army occupies *my* city, while my own men die in the thousands. I would know his true intent."

"I shall find the answers you seek, My Emperor." Shatero bowed. Plucking one or two of Lorn's closest confidants would be easy to achieve amidst the chaos. It would just require appropriate care and timing.

*****

Three days hence

He struggled finding targets along the wall. Thorton rested behind the newly reinforced trench, his rifle trained on a helm peeking above a parapet along the battlements of the northwest redoubt, resting some distance behind the wall.

Zip!

The blast took the unsuspecting Yatin sentry through the skull. He lost count on how many Torries and Yatins he slew along the walls, putting the number somewhere near a thousand. They responded by keeping out of sight, leaving the north wall nearly undefended. Seeking out human targets was producing ever-diminishing returns, so Thorton shifted to the wall itself, blasting chunks from its base. The gargoyle trebuchet crews stared slack-jawed as the Earther toppled section after section of the wall that their munitions could not achieve with thousands of stones.

"General Yonig requests your presence," Nels said, standing beside him in the siege trench, gargoyles crowding to either side of them.

"I'm busy," Thorton snorted.

"He wishes to coordinate the attack, and we can hardly do so without you."

"What attack?" Thorton squeezed the trigger, blue laser streaming over the battlefield, striking the upper battlements of the nearest turret. Stone fragments spewed from the tumult, raining over the adjoining causeway.

"The attack upon the city." Nels pointed toward the crumbling wall in the distance as if the answer was obvious.

Thorton lowered his rifle, giving Nels that quiet, disgusted look the former free sword had come to know so well.

*****

Yonig's pavilion, five hundred meters behind the siege lines

She felt his dull crimson eyes upon her as she set the table, ever wary of his intent. Gargoyles were notoriously wicked and cruel once aroused but unpredictable in moments of levity. She feared for her life when Thorton ordered her to attend to the gargoyle general whilst he was off slaying her people. The gargoyle general spoke little other than grunted commands. She was wise enough to know that her life rested on Thorton's threat to kill anyone that harmed her, even the general. She spent her first two days stitching the seams on the pavilion walls that were torn when it was overrun during the gargoyles' flight from the city. Fortunately for Yonig, the Torries had little time to plunder its amenities.

"The Emperor's Elite," Yonig's aide de camp announced as Thorton, Draken, and Zelo entered therein.

Ella turned at the mention of her benefactor, bobbing a nervous curtsy while smoothing the folds of her dress. She found it strange to be thankful for his company, but having spent the past days surrounded only by gargoyles made her rethink her opinion of Ben Thorton. She caught his eye examining her if ever so briefly, inspecting her for bruises or signs of abuse. Once he was satisfied with her treatment, he advanced to the center of the pavilion, where Yonig regarded them with guarded apprehension. Ella could sense the general stiffen when treating with the Emperor's Elite, especially Thorton. His usual calm was barely contained, the fiery embers straining to be released in his eyes.

"What's this I hear about an attack?" Thorton cut to the point. Their reinforcements from the 2nd Legion were some days off, and the enemy was contained. If anything, he thought he should cross the river upstream with a small host and blast away at the south wall until the 2nd Legion arrived. By then they could simply surround Mosar and starve them out.

"Read this," Yonig hissed disgustedly, handing him a scrolled parchment.

Nels and Zelo looked over his shoulder, each reading the grim news.

"When did this come in?" Ben asked, handing it to Nels.

"This morn."

"It's long on dramatics and short on details. The message speaks only of Morac's defeat at Corell and of his retreat to Notsu. There is nothing of casualties or disposition of forces. The only mention of the enemy is that a Torry and Jenaii host drove them from the field," Thorton said.

"We must crush the Torry prince *now* before they reinforce him!" Yonig's eyes flashed briefly. Word of Morac's defeat reached the defenders as well, raising the spirits of the Torry soldiers.

"You would throw your remaining troops at Mosar? You'd be fighting street to street all over again, but this time against a foe who is your equal. It won't be like last time when the Yatins fled from the fight. A full Torry Army now reinforces them. They've all but abandoned the north wall because they *want* you to take the bait. It will be a meat grinder. You'll lose half your troops before you reach the river," Thorton warned.

"And how long should we wait before the Torries send a second Army or the Yatins gather another host from their eastern border?" Yonig hissed.

"Then I'll slaughter them in the open. Don't throw away a sure, slow victory for a hasty defeat," Thorton warned.

"Do you mean to overrule me?" Yonig's chest puffed indignantly.

"I can, but I won't. It's your Army and your plan. You've done well so far. The victories at Salamin Valley, Telfer, and Tenin are yours, not Mulsen's," Thorton reassured the general, reminding him that he was sent here to chastise the traitorous Admiral Mulsen, who ordered the invasion without the emperor's consent. Despite this, Yonig's legions performed far beyond all expectations, but due to Mulsen's subterfuge, no reinforcements were forthcoming. Yonig needed to conquer Yatin with the forces he had. The original allotment of three legions for the invasion did not take into account for Torry intervention. If not for Thorton's intervention, Yonig would have likely been slaughtered between Jutol's 3rd Army and the Torry and Yatin Armies from Mosar or have any hope in winning this campaign.

"The emperor should execute the fool!" Yonig's eyes blazed at the mention of Mulsen.

"He will be dealt with, but not by you or I, General."

"Very well. You would counsel against my attack but not forbid it. Explain!" Yonig said curiously, the fire in his eyes abating.

"Since no further reinforcements will be committed to this campaign, you must conserve your strength. An attack on Mosar will cost you thousands, if not all your troops. You have led your legions to many victories, with your expulsion from Mosar the only setback. Even that defeat ended in the destruction of the Yatin 3rd Army. But I caution you, General. The history of my world is replete with great generals who won countless victories, growing drunk with success, pushing their luck before suffering fatal defeats. I believe attacking

Mosar head-on will be a fatal mistake," Thorton explained, recalling Napoleon, Robert Lee, and Yamamoto, to name a few.

"You stated my greatest weakness in this campaign, that no reinforcements will be sent to secure our victories. I must end this campaign now, for the enemy does not suffer this same weakness. Every day they grow stronger. We must strike now. If we kill the Torry prince, then we gain far more than Yatin. We will end this war."

Thorton removed his hat, scratching his head, pondering Yonig's dilemma. Victory and defeat stood equally upon the edge. He regarded Yonig, looking for any weakness in the general. He didn't like the gargoyle, and Yonig didn't like him, but they respected each other. Yonig proved himself a brilliant commander, and Thorton demonstrated his deadly power.

"All right, General, what's your plan?"

*****

The next morn

Sunrise broke upon the battlefield with columns of gargoyles in dull armor drawing near the north wall, without arrows or ballistae contesting their advance, the broken ramparts greeting them with eerie silence. Ben Thorton scanned a broad length of the north wall through the scope of his rifle, finding few targets of interest. He held his fire, saving the laser's energy for the day ahead. If things went poorly, he'd have little time to recharge his rifle.

Behind the trench line, the standard of the 2nd Gargoyle Legion lifted in the morning breeze, two black clashing fists upon a field of white, their telnics arrayed for battle despite a forced march throughout the night to join the siege. Their twenty-three telnics doubled Yonig's force. The newcomers gazed hungerly upon the Yatin capital, having marched hundreds of leagues from Tenin. They yearned to be released upon the city, but their commanders kept them in check, with whips or sword points when necessary.

The armored gargoyle columns of the 1st and 3rd Legions broke off toward different breaks in the wall as they drew near. Thorton watched as they disappeared within the broken wall. Yonig stood two hundred meters to Thorton's east, observing the attack from the siege lines facing the northeast gate. He began the siege with twenty telnics of armored gargoyles between the 1st and 3rd Legions and forty-eight telnics in total. He was reduced to twenty-four telnics between the two legions, only seven of them armored. The twenty-three telnics of the 2nd Legion brought his new total to forty-seven. He didn't have a good count on the Yatin and Torry forces within the city but knew it was far less than his reports indicated at the outset of the siege. Those scant numbers were further narrowed by the first assault upon Mosar, the Yatin and Torry counterattack, and Thorton's murderous fire. Yonig's assessment was not far off with the strength of the Yatin 1st Army at eight telnics and the Mosar garrison at three. The Torry 4th Army was the greater problem at seventeen telnics.

"Send the order!" Yonig commanded his aide.

*****

The few soldiers holding position at the base of the north wall melted away as the gargoyle columns drew near, withdrawing farther into the city. The gargoyles advanced under a pall of silence, breaching the wall and holding position along its base. Torry and Yatin pickets observed the gargoyles reassembling below the shadow of the wall, with interlocked shields and spears leveled. They formed in small cohorts of one to three units in size but refused to advance.

*****

"What now?" General Korath asked warily. Most of his men waited just south of the north wall, gathered in unit-sized elements. They nervously awaited the gargoyle advance, yet the creatures kept in disciplined ranks along the wall. Both armies waited impatiently, the tension festering.

"Hold for now," Lorn answered. They stood upon a low rooftop some distance south of the northeast gate but below Thorton's line of sight.

"The men grow restless, My Prince."

"Let them come to us, General."

"Once the battle begins, we shall have no means to direct our front, only our reserves," Korath lamented.

"No battle is ever clean, and command and control will be nearly impossible in these conditions. If it's any consolation, Yonig will suffer equally in this regard, if not more so," Lorn said. Defending the city should give them a greater advantage, but Thorton's weapon forced them to use unconventional means.

Harroom!

Horns sounded in the distance, drawing their attention southward. Jentra sent mounted scouts across the river to find the source of the commotion. Lorn repositioned their reserves farther south before the riders returned bearing the grim news.

"Gargoyles are attacking the south wall!"

*****

The entirety of the Mosar garrison manned the southern wall but numbered only three telnics, led by Telnic Commander Yakaron, the ranking commander to survive the initial assault upon the city. The Yatin 2nd Cavalry and Torry 4th Cavalry supported them, but their effectiveness was hindered once the enemy took flight. Most of the garrison's archers were deployed across the river, awaiting the attack from the north. Lookouts along the south wall sounded the alarm as thousands of gargoyles emerged along the horizon, elements of the 1st and 3rd Legions who crossed the river upstream under the dark of night before sweeping around to the south.

Torry and Yatin Cavalry spewed from the southern gates of the city, breaking off east and west to strike the enemy from the flanks, while the garrison troops held the battlements.

"Kai-Shorum!" Gargoyles screamed, running apace before bounding into the air, gaining lift, closing upon the city. The well-built south wall was far sturdier than the north, constructed to counter an expected Torry invasion during the previous centuries. Despite its towering battlements and broad turrets, it was not high enough to stop a gargoyle attack. The few archers that remained held their aim until the creatures drew dangerously close, their scant numbers making every shot crucial. Thirty arrows struck true as the creatures neared, dropping them just short of the wall. The garrison troops awaited them upon the battlements, staring helplessly as the gargoyles passed overhead and into the city. Hundreds of gargoyles soared over the wall, setting down upon rooftops farther north. The following waves swept down upon the battlements, some knocking soldiers off the wall with the force of their descent. Yatin soldiers thrust spear tips upward, impaling scores of gargoyles before they set down in their midst.

Hundreds of gargoyles flocked to the upper battlements of the three redoubts just north of the southeast, south center, and southwest gate. The small fortresses were lightly manned with barely fifty soldiers guarding each rooftop. Gargoyle war cries rent the air, men countering with their own battle cries.

Commander Yakaron blocked a gargoyle scimitar, the creature's blade glancing off his shield as he drove his short sword into its stomach, innards spilling upon the causeway of the battlements. He turned as another gargoyle swept down from his right, its scimitar arcing dangerously close before meeting the upraised shield of a Yatin commander of flax guarding his flank. The soldier to his left stumbled backward, his spear impaling a gargoyle as the creature pressed on, driving him from the lip of the walkway, carrying them both over the precipice. He stared briefly northward, where the center avenue of the city passed under the south gate below him, running north through Mosar. His heart sank as he beheld the grim vision. Gargoyles swarmed the center redoubt just to his north, like insects buzzing a hive. Men stood upon the battlements of the small fortress, fighting desperately as their ranks thinned. Further north, citizens fled along the avenue with gargoyles sweeping down from the rooftops, their scimitars cutting them as they passed. He ordered all reserves to the south wall, but even that would not stem the tide. Hundreds of gargoyles passed unhindered overhead, with more approaching the battlements.

*****

Jentra cursed Lorn's obstinance as the prince ordered him across the river, leading half their reserve telnics to aid the south wall. They needed every man to hold the north, but Lorn couldn't leave the Yatin populace to the gargoyles' mercy. As foul as that choice was, the several thousand gargoyles passing over the south wall paled to the tens of thousands waiting to swarm the north. So Jentra grumbled, cursed, and faithfully led three telnics of Torry soldiers across the center bridge,

"Keep in close ranks!" he bellowed. It was instinctive for men to break off and engage the enemy wherever they found them. It took discipline to keep men in line when the cries of women and children rent the air, urging them to swiftly act. Even his iron stomach twisted at the ghastly sights unfolding before them. Gargoyles crouched over their human victims along the avenue, sinking their fangs into living flesh. One creature withdrew its bloodstained face from a screaming woman's breast, lifting its crimson eyes to Jentra across that deadly space. The ghastly visage kindled his anger, urging him to break formation and drive his sword into the wretched creature. He swallowed his pride and doused his ire, keeping his head upon the task at hand.

"Column to the left!" he ordered five units to break east along the adjoining avenue. "Column right!" Another five broke west.

"Forward!" he commanded his remaining twenty units, which advanced along the center avenue running through the heart of Mosar, slaying scores of gargoyles along their path. Gargoyles ran along the rooftops, springing into the air, sweeping down from above. Soldiers lifted their shields overhead, greeting the creatures with spears. A few would land a lucky blow, but most were skewered, their bodies thrashing violently, spear shafts and swords piercing their flesh. The soldiers interlocked shields overhead, supporting the creatures' weight until they were sure of their kill, before turning their shields, dropping the creatures to their feet, stabbing them again for good measure. They moved methodically along the avenue, their disciplined ranks clearing a path with minimal casualties.

Arrows arced overhead, where archers now took position upon the rooftops, targeting the gargoyles spread throughout the city. The creatures made the skilled bowmen a priority, closing on them wherever they stood.

"Fools!" Jentra cursed the Yatins for not surrounding their precious archers with infantry, since range weapons were the most effective in reaching the gargoyles crowding the rooftops.

Smoke billowed from buildings farther south, drifting into the sky in tortured spirals. He could see people jumping from burning dwellings. From a distance their bodies appeared as little more than droppings, insignificant if one chose to put such tragedy from their mind, but each dropping was a human life snuffed out or crippled. Gargoyles sprang from rooftop to rooftop across the avenue in the distance, like a swarm of insects spreading over ripened crops.

*****

The north wall

The gargoyle 2nd Legion moved forth, attaining the battlements of the north wall, whilst the armored telnics of the 1st and 3rd Legions advanced into the city.

Haroom!

Horns sounded, signaling the 2nd Legion's continued advance.

"*Kai-Shorum!*" they shouted, springing from the north wall, flying above their heavy infantry below.

Torry and Yatin soldiers met the gargoyle advance in small unit-sized elements dispersed throughout the northern half of Mosar. The battle quickly devolved into a hundred small skirmishes, with walls of shields colliding and lightly clad gargoyles springing upon the humans from above.

Lorn left command of their reserves to General Korath, leading a small contingent into the fray. He ran north, along a narrow causeway, his Elite keeping pace before turning sharply west through a narrow alley. A gargoyle archer standing upon a rooftop above loosed a shaft, Lorn shifting his shield overhead, the arrow bouncing harmlessly off its steel. He continued on, his men following on his heels. The gargoyle released another shaft, the arrow bouncing off a soldier's breastplate. The creature stumbled, an arrow piercing its back. Lorn burst onto the adjoining street, making a cursory glance to his left before breaking right, his men filling in to either side. They found themselves just behind a small cohort of armored gargoyles, catching them unaware with their backs to them, advancing down the street.

Lorn closed immediately upon the center of the gargoyle line, jabbing his sword into the back of a gargoyle's neck where the armor did not cover.

"Agghh!" the creature's gurgled scream died in its throat, alerting only those nearest him. Seven more dropped in unison, the Torry Elite striking along the breadth of their formation. The Torries cut down the next row and part of the third before the fore ranks were aware. A line of Torry infantry filed into the street ahead, trapping the creatures between them. A gargoyle archer tumbled from the rooftop above, arrows feathering its torso. Torry archers emerged along the rooftops to either side, taking aim at the lightly clad gargoyles of the 2nd Legion crowding the rooftops farther north or coursing overhead, exposing their undersides.

Lorn's bold maneuver succeeded, decimating the small gargoyle cohort. He reformed his men behind the Torry lines after finishing the last of the gargoyles between them. 'Twas but one of a hundred small engagements that were taking place throughout the city. Success in one held meaning only to those engaged close-by. Torry and Yatin units engaged armored gargoyle cohorts through the streets of north Mosar, whilst lightly armed gargoyles roamed freely above. Torry and Yatin archers fired from open windows and rooftops before slipping away, only to emerge elsewhere to strike again. Other gargoyles gathered atop dwellings overlooking troops formed up in the streets below, descending en masse amidst the enemy.

Trebuchets positioned south of the wall fired into the crowded ramparts, balls of fire splashing amidst the gargoyles gathered there.

General Korath dispatched another telnic of reserves west along the north bank of the Muva, countering a gargoyle column threatening their left flank.

What flank? he cursed to himself, unable to determine where most of his men were from the low rooftop he occupied, just northwest of the center bridge. The view offered an advantageous view west and east along the avenue snaking along the river and a third of the way north along the central causeway to the north wall. He shared the makeshift position with a unit of infantry standing shoulder to shoulder with shields interlocked, surrounding a dozen archers targeting any gargoyles drawing near. The upper battlements of the north center redoubt peeked above his line of sight, winged silhouettes circling above its highest bulwarks, some falling clumsily from the sky, obviously stricken by arrows that he couldn't make out at this distance. Smoke drifted above the city to his direct west, flames licking the upper levels of dwellings nearest the wall where it met the river downstream. Screams rent the air in each direction, melding in a ghastly chorus of pain, anger, and battle. Small battles spilled out at different points long the causeway that ran along the riverbank, Korath's reserve telnics beating back the creatures wherever they emerged. From this vantage point, he could see the lighter-clad gargoyles concentrating in several different parts of the city, gathering along rooftops to set upon units in the streets below.

Balls of flame splashed into the gargoyles' midst wherever they gathered, diluting their massed formations. Korath nodded approvingly at their trebuchet crews' efficiency. Most were Yatin, with a few Torry catapults sprinkled in. They wisely ordered them withdrawn from the north wall for this very purpose.

"Any word from Prince Lorn?" Korath asked his aids who gathered near.

"The last report placed him somewhere north and east, General, but that was some time ago."

He could be dead for all we know, Korath growled inwardly. What hope had their kingdom if Lore's heir fell in battle? None, it seemed, their hopes resting on a knife's edge.

"General!" a soldier cried out before flashes of blue light struck from above.

Zip! Zip! Zip! Zip!

Laser fire bathed the soldiers gathered upon the flat rooftop, several blasts tearing large chunks from the structure beneath their feet. The sound of cracking timbers and dying men melded with the smell of burning flesh. A dozen soldiers lay upon the roof, cavernous holes burned through their torsos, heads, or limbs. Korath stumbled as the world shook, his eyes following the blue lights to a magantor circling overhead.

"Thorton!" he spat, before falling through the fissure.

*****

He swept through the air, circling over the dying city, spitting death and ruin upon his enemies below.

Zip! Zip!

Laser splashed into a Torry formation gathered along the center avenue, north of the middle bridge, scattering their ranks as a gargoyle host drew near.

Zip! Zip!

Two hurried blasts struck near the Yatin Cavalry, harrying the gargoyles beyond the south wall, the laser sending dozens of mounts in disarray, several throwing their riders.

Zip! Zip!

Laser struck a turret along the wall near the southwest gate, where the Yatin defenders just drove off a gargoyle assault.

Thorton's magantor circled the imperial palace, his fellow Elite guarding his flanks, their own warbirds soaring just off his wingtips. Gargoyles were driven off the upper battlements of the imperial palace, which rested near the middle bridge, just south of the river. The imperial standard lifted in the breeze, a gold rearing ocran upon a field of black, flying proudly above the highest ramparts where palace guards in purple livery cheered after slaughtering the gargoyles assailing their bulwarks. Thorton's warbird descended, circling the palace beyond archer range, training his rifle upon the crowded battlements.

Zip! Zip! Zip! Zip!

Thorton bathed the upper palace in laser fire, his deadly weapon cutting down defenders like dry grass. The screams of wounded men echoed over the din, smoke pouring off seared flesh.

Zip! Zip! Zip!

The royal guards crumbled under the murderous fire, Thorton's merciless volley decimating their ranks.

"Kai-Shorum!" Gargoyle war cries echoed over the city, cheering their new champion as Thorton's laser decimated Yatin and Torry strongholds at will. Hundreds of gargoyles renewed their assault upon the imperial palace. Others swept over the south wall, driving the defenders from the battlements. Even the success the Torry and Yatin Cavalry assailing the gargoyles south of the city was certain to reverse when Thorton fixed his aim upon them. Battle raged throughout the northern half of Mosar, Yatin, Torry, and gargoyle soldiers intermingled in hundreds of small engagements.

Alas! The city was doomed, the deadly pall drawing over their haggard spirits like a noose methodically choking hope and victory. Thorton lifted his rifle, finding a Yatin commander of significant rank standing along the avenue, north of the west bridge, the fellow's head fixed within his sights.

Zip!

"Packaww!" Thorton's magantor screeched, laser piercing its left wing.

Zip!

Laser flashed overhead, Thorton's warbird dropping suddenly, missing the follow shot, its right wing working frantically through its rapid descent.

Kato shifted his aim, his rifle resting against the trunk of a porian within a small copse of trees southeast of the city, as Thorton's crippled mount dropped from sight.

Siege of Mosar stage four

Laser struck the magantor full in the breast, its narrow beam passing through. The warbird dropped like a heavy stone, its Benotrist rider thrown clear, his body striking the east face of the palace wall. Yatin and Torry soldiers alike looked to the heavens with renewed hope. Kato's laser swept the air, forcing Thorton's fellow Elite from the sky.

Zip!

A blast took Zelo's mount through the neck as he fled the city, the magantor struck dead as he passed over the north wall. Zelo sprang from its back, extending his wings, gliding to safety.

Nels Draken forced his magantor lower, skimming the rooftops north of the Muva, keeping below Kato's line of sight.

Zip!

Another magantor screeched above and to his right, laser piercing its center. A follow blast took Garvo, the Benotrist Elite, through the back.

Torry archers took aim below, an arrow nipping Draken's magantor's right wing, dislodging several feathers as he passed.

Zip!

Kato brought down another magantor passing northwest of the city bearing two riders, one falling from the saddle, the other gliding its stricken mount to the grounds beyond the wall.

*****

Thorton cursed as his magantor dropped, the stricken bird taxing its good wing through its descent. The north bank of the Muva grew larger in his vision, the surface coming swiftly upon him. Yatin soldiers stood upon the river road below, receiving him with leveled spears and raised shields. A few hurried blasts scattered them before his mount set down in their midst, landing roughly on the fitted stone causeway. Thorton jumped clear, rolling several times before gaining his feet, blasting several Yatins standing near. He slung his rifle over his back, drawing his pistol before making his way north through the dangerous streets.

*****

Kato shifted aim to the southeast redoubt, its rugged bulwarks peaking above the south wall, gargoyles swarming its battlements, forcing the defenders into the fortress interior.

Zip! Zip! Zip! Zip!

Laser fire tore into their crowded ranks, slaying several and scattering dozens. He scanned the skyline of Mosar through the rifle's scope, stopping at the upper battlements of the imperial palace. The royal standard lifted in the breeze, torn, ragged, and obscured by a cloud of smoke. A small cohort of palace guards held the northeast corner of the palace roof in an ever-shrinking pocket, hundreds of gargoyles swarming the battlements. Kato paused, his finger easing off the trigger as a white blur appeared in his periphery, a large magantor passing over the south wall crossing his line of sight.

"Good hunting, Terin." He smiled, lowering his rifle.

*****

He coursed through the crisp air, driven by a maddened fury, his will and desire bound to his master as if they were of one mind. Wind Racer soared through the firmament like a passing apparition, his great white wings outstretched and silver eyes fixed keenly ahead.

Terin closed his eyes, suppressing the pull of his father's sword ever briefly to gain his bearing, before losing himself to its awesome power. Lucas drew up alongside him, his own magantor strangely obedient to Wind Racer's course, as if the two warbirds were mentally linked. Terin took one last breath before the plunge, opening his eyes as Wind Racer circled the uppermost battlements of the imperial palace, before setting down amidst the gargoyles gathered there. Wind Racer cleared a path, gargoyles scattering before him, Terin leaping from his back, the Sword of the Moon flashing brightly in his hand.

Split! Thrust! Split!

Terin moved instantly upon the nearest gargoyles, cutting them down in quick order.

Split! Split!

He cut through upraised blades, tearing into exposed flesh, the gargoyles nearest him frozen in place, transfixed by his father's sword. Or was it his father's blood? Even aware of his devastating effect on the gargoyles, he could not see it when lost in the thick of battle. Those farther off stared in wonder as the gargoyles nearest him stood statue still, allowing him to cut them down like infant saplings, while those just farther afield fled his presence, taking flight from the palace and leaving the battle altogether, their bloodlust transformed into frightened desperation.

Lucas set down upon the palace roof, dismounting as fast as he could manage, trying to find Terin amidst the chaos. A gargoyle rushed forth as his feet touched the platform, its red eyes dull and wild. Lucas took its head before realizing the creature was unarmed. Another followed, its wide-eyed stare looking beyond him, as if he wasn't there. Lucas ran his blade along its throat, the creature not even altering course to dodge the blow, oblivious to his presence. He swung his blade overhead, severing the outstretched wing of a gargoyle passing above. He cut down two more before catching sight of Terin's sword flashing amidst the fray, scores of corpses littering the battlements between them. He rushed to reach his side, dodging flying limbs and splashing blood issuing from Terin's blade. Terin moved apace, cutting down whatever gargoyles lingered dumbly upon the palace roof, leaving little for Lucas to do but finish his kills. Lucas thought he was more likely to die breaking his neck tripping on a corpse than falling to a gargoyle blade.

Terin's eyes came into focus as the last gargoyle dropped dead at his feet, its body rent nearly in half, its blood dripping from Terin's blade. He turned about, staring off in each direction at the surrounding city. Smoke drifted above the vast structures along the riverfront, men and gargoyles battling in the streets.

"Who are you?" a palace guard asked warily, standing a safe distance away as Lucas came to his side. A dozen other palace guards filed in around their comrade, each staring dumbstruck at their benefactors.

Lucas acknowledged the fellows, noting their battle-worn armor and bloodstained garments and the rearing golden ocran upon a field of black emblazoned upon their chests.

"We are of the Torry Elite, sent by Her Highness Princess Corry to aid our crown prince and defend your realm," Lucas declared, stepping forth to address them.

"Our gratitude, but where has your comrade gone?" the guard asked, his eyes drifting over Lucas's shoulder.

Lucas made a face, turning about as Wind Racer again set down behind them, Terin already in the saddle and taking off before Lucas took a second step.

*****

Zip! Zip! Zip! Zip!

Laser swept away scores of gargoyles still concentrated south of the city, Torry Cavalry hunting the stragglers. Kato shifted aim to smaller clusters gathering along the open fields south of the city, upon the battlements of the south wall or the higher structures beyond.

Zip!

Laser struck a gargoyle midflight, passing between two rooftops in the distance, its wings collapsing with its sudden descent.

*****

"Close ranks!" Jentra shouted over the din, gargoyles swarming their front, flanks, and sweeping down from above. They held position on the center causeway, mid-distance between the middle bridge and the south gate, massive stone structures lining the wide avenue to either side. The spacing between soldiers shifted constantly as they advanced, contracting and expanding as they moved apace. Too close hindered their mobility, while too far created gaps in their line.

"Close ranks!" Others echoed his command through the formation stretched out some distance behind him.

Jentra stood two ranks back, holding his shield overhead, interlocked with those around him. He sagged under the weight of a gargoyle dropping upon them, its claws scraping along the polished steel, paining their ears. He thrust his blade between the seams until finding resistance, before jabbing again, the creature's cries drowning among thousands of other screams, its thrashing causing their arms to strain, bearing its weight. Eventually they would tilt their shields, dropping the creature in their midst. It was a dangerous maneuver, allowing a potential threat to get close. Even wounded, a gargoyle could rip a man's throat out in a blink of an eye.

"Tilt!" he commanded, the creature sliding off their shields, the nearest soldiers thrusting their swords into its thrashing body. They immediately returned their shields overhead, more gargoyles setting down upon them. Another was dropped off his left, soldiers stabbing repeatedly but unable to lift their shields before another climbed through the opening, lunging through the gap overhead, its jowls snapping while squeezing through. The nearest soldier lowered his shield between the creature and himself, claws scraping its surface.

"Agghh!" the creature screamed, a Torry blade twisting through its back.

More gargoyles followed through the gap, other breaks forming as soldiers tried closing it. Their shield wall started to collapse, fissures spreading throughout the formation with gargoyles dropping into their midst. A gargoyle head rolled to Jentra's feet, while a soldier off his right writhed on the ground, a gargoyle biting into his face. The formation began to break apart, engaging the gargoyles in a thousand separate battles.

Jentra crouched, bracing himself with a creature sweeping down from above, its pointy ears arced back as if pressed by the wind, slather gathering along its fangs. Feral eyes glowed like embers, fixed to Jentra with insatiable bloodlust. Two others followed close behind, their full wings narrowing as they dived, glowing eyes fixed hungrily to Jentra.

"Come and take me!" Jentra growled, his eyes peeking above his shield and sword gripped tightly in his right hand.

"Kai-Shorum!" they screamed, hundreds filling the sky, their guttural chants raising the hairs on Jentra's neck as they drew nigh. Thousands raced afoot upon the flanks of the beleaguered column, testing Torry discipline with maddened bloodlust, but lightly clad gargoyles afoot were not nearly as dangerous as those dropping from above. Jentra's heart pounded as they drew closer, hundreds of glowing eyes testing his courage, their winged forms blotting the sun.

Whoosh!

A sudden white blur swept overhead, large black talons with silver tips snatching the two lead gargoyles from the air.

"Packaww!" Wind Racer sounded, crushing the gargoyles in his powerful talons, catching another in its beak, before passing on.

Jentra's eyes narrowed, not believing his sight as the magantor sped through the crowded sky, its rider raising up in the saddle, wielding a silver sword, striking out at gargoyles as he passed. He lost sight of his savior, the magantor disappearing into the gargoyle mass, the rider's sword issuing a luminous azure glow, which shone through the gargoyle host.

The Sword of the Moon danced in his hand, finding gargoyle flesh as he passed underneath. Severed wings, limbs, and heads flew off his blade as he soared through the firmament.

The gargoyle host broke, scattering as Terin passed through their midst, flying off to whichever direction took them from his fell blade. The gargoyles afoot below froze in place, transfixed by his sudden appearance. The Torries exploited their sudden pause, breaking from their close ranks, cutting down gargoyles where they stood along the length of the avenue. Jentra followed his men into battle, as Terin sped northward.

*****

Lorn thrust his blade into the gargoyle's back, kicking the creature's carcass off his blade before blocking another turning to meet him. His men filed in alongside him as they fell upon another small cohort from behind, the creatures not expecting an attack from the north end of the street while pushing toward the river. It was one of hundreds of small engagements taking place throughout the north half of the city. The defenders dispersed their troops in unit-sized elements to avoid wholesale annihilation to Thorton's weapon. Of course, such a desperate tactic removed the defensive advantages of the city but prevented their total destruction. It denied Thorton a strategic victory against their concentrated forces and placed the fate of the battle in the outcome of these small and scattered engagements, which neither side could effectively manage. The battle degenerated into roving mobs often stumbling into one another. Most of the Torry units kept in close ranks, breaking formation only to strike down vulnerable enemies, before quickly withdrawing to their shield walls, even if it meant allowing a number of gargoyles to slip away.

"Bleed the enemy! Preserve your strength!" was the order given, the survival of the Army a higher priority to that of the city.

Lorn acted independent of the Torry host, leading his small band in and out of Torry strongholds, seeking targets of opportunity.

Lorn brought his shield across his face, blocking another slashing blow, the Torry Elite to his right slaying the offender. The skirmish ended, the remaining gargoyles fleeing, a dozen of their comrades littering the street.

Lorn lowered his bloodstained shield, catching his breath, his men forming a protective circle, scanning each direction as Lorn decided their next path. Their hit-and-run tactics required them to stay on the move, preventing the enemy to fix their location, yet Lorn paused, his gaze drawn to an adjoining alleyway crossing the street just to their south, where he intended to go. He could feel Yah's presence, warning him against this plan. His men shifted uneasily with this pause, knowing the danger lurking behind every dwelling, street, and rooftop. The sounds of battle echoed near and far, a disjointed symphony of chaos, battle, and death. The street was littered with the bodies of men and gargoyles. Abandoned dwellings lined either side, smoke issuing from some, choking the air with noxious fumes, limiting their view. The stone structures that wouldn't burn were cracked, with large fragments missing along their rooftops, spilling into the street. Men were as likely to die from falling debris than enemy arrows. Spirals of smoke twisted into the clear blue sky, the din of battle contrasting the empty street.

Lorn lifted his shield as a dozen winged forms emerged along the rooftops of the alleyway he intended to traverse.

"Archers!" one of his men called out as the forms took shape of gargoyles with arrows notched. The Torries quickly closed ranks, interlocking their shields once the first arrows flew, the shafts bouncing off their thick steel. They carefully withdrew up the street, keeping a tight formation, the gargoyles firing at will, with other archers springing up along the rooftops northward, shadowing their retreat, firing intermittently. Others took flight, crossing over the street to the opposite rooftops.

"Agghh!" a gargoyle shouted as a dizzying array of blue light struck it in midflight. It tumbled, impacting the street, as laser fire swept the rooftops. Streams of blue light sped through the air like meteors shooting across a midnight sky.

Lorn's gaze followed the source of the laser, losing sight beyond the horizon, to somewhere in the south of the river.

"Highness!" one of his men called out, the laser shifting farther overhead, striking targets somewhere to their north, likely the redoubts and north wall, where the gargoyles rested in the shooter's line of sight.

Whoever was shooting was clearly an ally, and *that* changed everything.

"Come!" Lorn ordered, moving south to find General Korath and reconstitute the Torry 4th Army, retaking the offensive.

*****

Zip!

The blast brained a gargoyle midflight, its corpse dropping from sight, Kato shifting aim to his next target. He stood upon a turret of the south wall, resting his rifle upon the stone parapet, scanning the north half of Mosar.

Zip!

His next blast struck the crowded bulwarks of the northeast redoubt, gargoyles scattering with his laser passing through their midst.

Zip! Zip! Zip!

Laser spewed over the serried ramparts, slaying a dozen, scattering the rest, the survivors springing from the fortress roof, gliding to the street below.

Kato lifted his eyes above the scope, taking cursory stock of his immediate surroundings. Yatin soldiers flooded the turret and its adjoining walkways, buoyed by his and Terin's sudden arrival. Gargoyle corpses littered the turret, their foul blood pooling across the gray stone. The gargoyles were in full retreat, fleeing the southern half of Mosar, as Yatin and Torry soldiers cleared the streets below. Certain of his surroundings, Kato went back to work.

Zip!

His next shot took a gargoyle in the chest atop the north wall.

Zip!

His follow shot struck below the broken battlements near the north gate, spewing stone fragments where it struck. A second blast crumbled a good portion of the wall above, where a score of gargoyles lost their footing, the walkway giving way beneath them. A few were caught up in the debris, but most spread their wings, gliding to safety.

Zip! Zip! Zip!

He continued along the north wall, picking off targets silhouetted upon the battlements. He shifted aim to several crowding the rooftops farther south, dispersing them with deadly fire. A white gray blur passed in his periphery, as Wind Racer swept across the river, circling the west bridge, before setting down upon the redoubt overlooking the north end of the bridge, with Yatins and gargoyles crowding its turrets and walkways.

"Unbelievable." Kato shook his head at Terin's courage and stupidity.

*****

Wind Racer set down in the center of the turret, gargoyles scattering as Terin leaped from the saddle, his blade flashing brightly.

Split! Thrust!

He cut down the nearest gargoyle, the creature staggering as he pierced its breast, kicking it off his blade as it fell backward. Terin spun around his wounded foe, driving to the north end of the turret, gargoyles climbing over its ramparts, taking flight and scattering to the winds.

Split!

He caught another at the ankle, the severed limb falling away as the gargoyle sprang free, blood issuing from its stump as it spread its wings.

Split!

He caught another along its left wing, shredding the appendage halfway from wingtip to back, the creature stumbling from the parapet, falling to the riverbank below, its right wing working desperately to ease its descent.

Terin sighed in frustration, the remaining gargoyles escaping his blade, abandoning the bridge to their Yatin foe. He stopped at the turret's edge, overlooking the northern half of Mosar. He saw thousands of gargoyles fleeing the city, bounding rooftop to rooftop, making their way to the north wall. Thousands more lingered, swarming Torry and Yatin positions along the length and breadth of the city. Laser flashed off his right, sweeping away pockets of gargoyles wherever they appeared in Kato's line of sight.

Zip!

Laser streamed southward toward the bridge turret, as Terin brought the flat of his sword across his body, the beam of blue light angling off its surface, striking the riverbank upstream.

Zip! Zip!

Two more laser blasts followed, Terin's sword again blocking their path, sending them awry. Terin swatted them away, an other-worldly calm steadying his nerve as he fixed their source to his direct front, mid-distance to the north wall, where Ben Thorton stood alone in the center of a deserted street.

*****

"Shit!" Thorton snorted, lowering the rifle from his shoulder, assessing his weapon's poor results. Tyro wanted Terin alive, and he targeted his limbs, but the boy's damnable sword blocked the blasts just as it did at Telfer. Once was a lucky coincidence, but several times meant something more, something *much* more. This impossible display meant one thing, that taking Terin alive was near impossible, and taking him at all was probably impossible as well, at least in open combat.

A warring faction of Yatins and gargoyles spilled out in the street from an adjoining avenue, several blocks to his south, some distance between Terin and himself.

Zip! Zip! Zip!

Ben's laser tore into the Yatin soldiers, thinning their ranks and renewing hope in the gargoyles' eyes, the creatures setting upon the stunned humans.

Zip!

Laser fire streamed overhead, striking the upper portion of the structure off Thorton's left, blasting chunks of stone into the street below. Thorton raced to the opposite side of the street, debris showering in his wake.

*****

"*Agghh!*" the young Torry soldier cried out upon his back, a gargoyle biting into his stomach, the creature feasting on his crippled foe lying in the middle of the street, hundreds clashing around them in desperate battle. The creature's senses rang in alarm, retracting its fangs from his victim's bowels, blood caking its face, lifting its head as Lorn's blade took it across the back of the neck, nearly hewing it free.

Lorn's men swept into the serried street, striking down gargoyles already engaged in battle, his contingent gathering in strength as they advanced, picking up stragglers and Torry units they came upon. His plan to disperse the Army to avoid Thorton's weapon now hindered his ability to take advantage of the changing battlefield.

"My Prince!" a commander of telnic hailed, making his way from the opposite end of the street.

"Commander Tulos," Lorn greeted, catching his breath, men passing in either direction, driving off the remaining gargoyles. "How fares your men?"

"I've reconstituted eight units. We cleared all the streets here to the river. The 3rd Telnic is just to our east and the 8th to our west," Tulos reported hurriedly, sweat building beneath his bloodstained helm.

"Where's General Korath?" Lorn asked.

"Gravely injured, I am afraid to report. Commander Farro has assumed command. He is just to our west, north of the middle bridge."

"I'll make my way there. Add these men to yours and continue your advance," Lorn ordered, leaving the forces he gathered to Tulos's care, save for his Elite, who kept close to his side, guarding their prince throughout the battle.

"It is not safe!" Tulos objected. "The enemy can reappear anywhere in our wake and in unpredictable numbers. Take more men with you, I beg of you, Highness!"

"It's not safe anywhere, Commander. The winds of battle now blow in our favor, and I trust my safety to Yah." Lorn slapped Tulos's shoulder, moving on as laser fire passed overhead, striking gargoyle positions to their north. Whichever Earther joined their cause now balanced the scales to their favor, sending the gargoyles in retreat.

*****

They followed their prince to the north bank of the Muva before turning sharply right, skirting the riverfront, making their way to the middle bridge. A few gargoyle stragglers popped up in places, attacking them out of fear than any coordinated effort. Smoke billowed above the city, fires spreading unchecked on both sides of the Muva. A caliginous plume of poisonous vapor drifted over the river, obscuring the skyline to the south. Hundreds of corpses littered either shoreline, the current washing their dismembered bodies upon the riverbanks. Hundreds more drifted downstream, bobbing along the slow current like dead fish riding the surface. A Yatin galley listed severely along the south bank, flames covering its upper deck and masts. The sounds of clashing steel and dying men echoed morbidly in the fetid air.

Torry soldiers along the riverbank greeted them with hearty cheers, hope blossoming in their battle-weary eyes. Lorn directed them northward along whatever street was near, where most of their vast host was already engaged. Lorn caught sight of hundreds of gargoyles fleeing south Mosar, swarming across the middle bridge, their tired wings unable to carry them across the river. Torry infantry pressed from the south, driving them onto the bridge, where other soldiers held position along the north end of that vital artery.

"Prince Lorn!" one of his men shouted, his eyes drawn where a single warrior stood alone upon the center of the bridge, forward of the men holding the north end. The gargoyles swarming over the south end of the bridge suddenly paused, bewitched by an other-worldly power, as the warrior lunged forth, dazzling azure light emitting from his blade.

The Torries watching the scene unfold stood dumbstruck by the spectacle.

Split! Thrust!

Terin cut down the nearest foe, the creature's right arm flying off the end of his blade, his follow thrust piercing its breast. He smoothly retracted his blade, advancing on another, who stood frozen in place, its red eyes dim with fright.

Thrust!

He cut down the creature, moving apace from one side of the bridge to the other, gargoyle flesh spitting off his blade. Those farther back fled south or sprang from the bridge, their tired wings only able to glide to the river's surface. Few could swim, the others thrashing desperately to stay afloat while bobbing downstream.

"Who is that?" more than one voice asked, as Lorn looked on.

His Elite remembered well the young scribe they accompanied so long ago to the House of Antillius before venturing south. They recalled the ethereal light of his magical sword as he held it aloft in Squid's home, while the king's minister spoke of its mystery. They received word of the victory at Corell and the grand tales of his fell deeds, but now they could see his handiwork for themselves. No flowery telling could match the wonder of their own eyes.

"To the bridge!" Lorn commanded, men flinching with a large white blur passing overhead.

Wind Racer set down upon the middle bridge, Terin climbing upon his back, taking to the sky as Torry soldiers swept forth. Lorn raced along the river, his Elite following his hurried pace to reach the men gathered at the bridge, and Terin, but that hope quickly dimmed as the Torry champion sped off, his magantor flying straight north, its beautiful white wings passing beyond their line of sight.

*****

Thorton grunted, catching his breath after racing north through the city, each street contested with men and gargoyles battling throughout. Debris and corpses littered his path, slowing his pace as much as the Yatin or Torry soldiers requiring his attention. He kept to street level, using his pistol at close range, figuring whichever of his former Earth friends was targeting him wouldn't see his laser fire from their higher position. He stopped short of the north wall, taking refuge in one of the few structures still intact, a sturdy built barracks of some sort, making his way to its debris-cluttered rooftop. He nestled himself amidst a pile of stone rubble gathered at its southeast corner, lying prone, scanning afield through his rifle's scope.

Bursts of laser fire flashed across the city, striking targets throughout the northern half of Mosar. Thorton followed their source to a massive turret along the south wall, zooming in with the scope's optic and finding Kato's familiar face on the other end.

Ben sighed in resignation, not wishing to kill his former friend, but Kato had struck him first. No, the blast struck his mount but could've just as easily slain him had its fall been more pronounced. He resigned himself to the task at hand, fixing Kato's right arm in his sights. He needn't kill him, but the blast would cripple him all the same.

Zip!

Kato shifted aim as Thorton squeezed the trigger, the blast grazing his jacket sleeve. Kato dropped immediately below the parapet, panting heavily at his close call.

Zip!

Another blast followed, passing overhead where his head was a moment before. Kato crawled twenty paces to his west before stealing a glance over the battlement.

Nothing. Wherever Thorton took the shot from was beyond his line of sight, and without using his rifle scope, he wouldn't find him without Thorton sending another blast his way.

*****

Thorton scanned the length of the battlement where Kato ducked, sweeping his scope left then right for any sign of him. He was tempted to blast several holes along the south wall, forcing Kato to show himself, but a follow blast would give away his position. Ben snorted as multiple juicy targets emerged throughout his line of sight. A column of Yatin infantry marched up the avenue in his direction, a dozen Torry soldiers took up position along a rooftop to his southeast, and the upper ramparts of the Imperial Palace loomed invitingly in the distance, its battlements teeming with soldiers. None of these mattered though, not until he found Kato.

Kato was his primary concern until a large white magantor passed his line of sight, speeding northward over the center of the city, a familiar rider visible through his scope. The emperor wanted the boy alive and unharmed, but that might not be possible considering his impressive abilities. *Why would Terin venture into the heart of the gargoyle Army?* gnawed at the back of Ben's mind, but he didn't have time to contemplate the reason as he squeezed the trigger, taking his shot.

Zip!

Terin outstretched his blade, deflecting the blast targeting Wind Racer's breast, the laser angling sharply west, striking the riverbank some distance beyond the city walls.

Zip! Zip!

Laser fire swept the rooftop where Thorton took the shot, but he had already moved, knowing his blast exposed his position. He slipped away, descending the shaking structure to reposition elsewhere, cursing Terin's sword and Kato's aim.

*****

Wind Racer coursed over Mosar, his powerful wings pounding the air like thunderclaps, bearing Terin onward into the fray. Gargoyles and men scurried in the streets below, sunlight playing off their helms like a thousand flickering stars. Terin's heart hammered in his chest, spinning his sword after deflecting Thorton's blast. He lost sight of Thorton somewhere to his west, struggling against the pull of his sword to find and finish him before he caused further harm, but the blade called him elsewhere.

Are you the blade's master or its slave? Corry once asked him, and times like this he began to wonder.

"No!" He shook the doubt from his mind, renewing his trust in his father's sword and blood, surrendering his will to its otherworldly power.

Trust in me, Terin, for your blood and sword are instruments of my will, Yah's voice echoed so clearly in his ear.

Pimples rose across his flesh, the deity's words echoing above the din in a thunderous whisper that only he could hear. A serene calmness overtook him, as Wind Racer rose high into the air before descending upon the north wall, his eyes drawn to the gargoyles crowding its battlements, surrounding a gargoyle commander standing in their midst, issuing commands with authority.

*****

Yonig retreated to the north wall, ordering his troops to reinforce his last line of defense, while sending others south to stiffen the resolve of his breaking ranks. He kept five heavily armed telnics at the wall in reserve, only releasing them if all else was lost. He could clearly see the disaster afflicting his Army, half his troops fighting on with savage fury, the other half fleeing in terror, bewitched by the enemy's foul sorcery. Yonig's blade was stained with the blood of his own troops. He cut down several to stiffen the spines of their faithless brethren, but even this did little to turn the frightened cowards. From his position atop the battlements east of the north gate, he scanned the length of the wall to either direction, seeing thousands of gargoyles swarming over the bulwarks, fleeing across the fields north of the city. His more stalwart troops turned a few back into the city, but the rest were hopeless, their fiery eyes stricken with terror. He wondered what brought about this transformation? What could strip such creatures of their wits and nerve? He suddenly recalled a similar thing at Telfer.

"Packaww!"

His aides froze, staring skyward, as his own eye slits followed their beguiled gaze.

Loose arrows! The command died in his throat, unable to make an utterance as his archers stood statue still, transfixed by the looming dread. There, sweeping down from the heavens, came Wind Racer, bearing Terin into the heart of Yonig's strength. Five thousand gargoyles surrounded Yonig's position, aligned forward of the north wall, the entirety of his precious reserves, kept back from the battle until utmost need arose. It was these soldiers that implemented his orders most effectively, the hammer of his legions, yet all their might counted for naught as they beheld their doom. Five thousand spears lowered as Terin passed into their midst, Wind Racer sweeping over the north wall, his great talons clearing a path for Terin to leap upon the stone walkway.

Split! Split!

A commander of telnic was cloven in half, Terin spinning clear, the blade shattering the creature's shield, cutting it shoulder to opposite hip. A second creature stood still, a dumb expression transfixing its face, before he chopped it down, its torso slipping from its waist. Bright azure light burst from Terin's blade, illuminating his countenance with a terrible resolve.

Split! Thrust! Thrust!

He glided across the broken battlement, cutting a path through Yonig's guards, who received his judgement without protest, his feet moving across the uneven walkways littered with debris and corpses.

Yonig stood in place, his feet frozen to the stone beneath them, no longer his to command. His bloodstained cape lifted in the breeze, trailing his helm like a bright flame, his sword lifting feebly in his right claw. Terin cut his way toward Yonig, giving himself to the sword's will. It was all but a dream, only fragments remembered when all was said and done. Even those vague tendrils of consciousness quickly waned once the power of the sword exhausted itself and him with it. He remembered little if anything when giving himself to its full power, yet this one act would dwell forever in his memory. Full understanding returned to his sea-blue eyes as he beheld the gargoyle general. Five braided cords upon either shoulder denoted Yonig's supreme rank, his polished mail and bloodred cape standing out amidst his soldiers. Yonig's lips stretched weakly above his cruel fangs, unable to muster anything but strained indifference to contest Terin's threat.

Split!

Yonig's head lifted freely from his neck, spinning slowly, his dying eyes regarding Terin briefly before drawing dim.

There, atop the north wall of Mosar, Terin cut the heart from the gargoyle legions, throwing down their feared general with final authority before moving on.

Like narrow fissures spreading through rock, the gargoyle host began to break before cracking altogether. Frightened stares transitioned into frenzied flight, thousands swarming through, over, and around the broken wall, fleeing north across the battle-scarred fields.

*****

Nels Draken raced through the winding streets and narrow alleyways, making his way north and east, Zelo close on his heels. They lost sight of their comrades long ago, setting their stricken mounts down north of the Muva. He was nearly slain by gargoyles before they recognized the sigil of Tyro's Elite emblazoned on his chest and cloak. They intermixed with a small band of creatures fleeing the battle. Nels lost count of how many of his fellow Elite were slain by the Earther's fire, wondering which of Raven's crew joined the Torry cause. Between the Earther's weapon and Terin's blade, the battle was lost, and no action on his part would change its course.

An arrow whizzed past his shoulder, striking a gargoyle up ahead in the back, the creature howling in anguish as it staggered on. Nels hoisted his shield behind his head without stopping to see where the arrow came from. They continued apace, turning sharply left at the end of the alleyway, more arrows falling in their wake. The north wall loomed just ahead, gargoyles swarming along its base and summit, climbing over one another to escape.

"There!" Zelo hissed, his clawed digit pointing to a break in the wall to their east, with few gargoyles congested there. They wasted little time passing through the wall, the sounds of battle drawing nearer in the streets behind them. Once clear, they were met with the chaotic sight of thousands of gargoyles streaming across the trodden fields. Smoke drifted above the city behind them, pushed overhead upon a southerly breeze. Nels gazed farther north, where their Army disappeared into the southern edge of the distant forest. It was there where they prestaged ocran and provisions in case the battle went poorly. Thorton ordered it done even when victory appeared certain.

Always have a fallback, Thorton told them repeatedly, his words proving prescient.

Two of their fellow Elite remained with the provisions, as well as Thorton's slave girl, Ella, and those Elite's magantor mounts. Nels wondered if they were still there or if they had run off. If they left, Thorton would skin them alive if he ever caught them.

*****

"Sire." Commander Farro saluted his prince with a fist to his chest as Lorn stepped onto the north wall through a broken stairwell. Stepping carefully around a cavernous break in the walkway between them, Lorn made his way toward a large stretch of battlement that remained intact nearer the north gate. The adjoining walkways were cleared of gargoyle dead, their corpses thrown over the side, gathered in great heaps below. Torry and Yatin soldiers flooded the streets south of the wall. The sounds of battle still echoed throughout the city, the remaining gargoyles being cleared street by street, house to house, a costly, tedious task that further bloodied their ranks.

Lorn's tired eyes swept the fields north of Mosar. They were a battle-scarred, desolate ruin, dividing Mosar from the forest in the distance. Hundreds of gargoyle corpses littered the landscape, way-laid by Torry and Yatin Cavalry sweeping back and forth before the city walls, slaying any stragglers that lingered. Others simply bled out, earlier wounds finishing them after they passed the wall. A large part of the gargoyle host escaped, repositioning north of the city, at the edge of the tree line in the distance.

Lorn removed his helm, the cool air soothing his heated brow. Blood and sweat stained his face and tunic, his once resplendent armor dented and marred. The waning sun hung low in the western sky, putting a merciful end to this bloody day.

"Where's the Earther?" Lorn asked warily, expecting laser blasts to spew into their ranks at any moment.

"Which one?"

"Thorton."

"Somewhere north, Highness." Farro lifted his chin in that direction. "We still see his weapon flash from time to time, probably keeping their skittish ranks from breaking, especially with their general dead." Farro regarded Yonig's head adorning a pike protruding above the north gate.

Lorn paid the grisly trophy its due reverence. Word spread like wildfire through the city of Terin's fell deeds. His actions at the bridge and the imperial palace were the stuff of legend, but his bold flight to the north wall into the might of Yonig's host, where he struck down the gargoyle general, was impossible. The men spoke of him with awe. Even the most grizzled warriors were dumbstruck by his brave acts. Once Terin struck down Yonig, the enemy completely broke, their last holdouts fleeing the battle witless and panicked.

"I saw it with my own eyes, and I still cannot fathom it." Farro shook his head, having stood upon the center bridge when Terin swept over the north wall. He was able to observe the entire scene from the bridge's high battlements.

"There is a reason he was named champion of the realm," Lorn said with a tired smile.

"Champion?" Farro gave him a look, his brown hair lifting in the breeze. "It's unnatural. Nothing can explain his power. He swept over the city like a cleansing wind, driving the gargoyles off wherever he passed. Even the Earther's blasts bounced off his blade. He flew into the center of their host and slew Yonig, without the thousands of gargoyles surrounding him raising a blade. Once he struck him down, the others broke, scattering to the wind. Like I said, it's unnatural."

"Where is he now?" Lorn asked, frustrated at missing Terin at every turn.

"Somewhere in the city, helping root out the gargoyles that remain."

"Others can attend to that. Send him to treat with his prince!" one of Lorn's Elite declared, standing near.

"There's little point in that," Farro explained. "My men have tried, but the boy has a glazed look about him, as if possessed. Nothing will deter him from hunting the enemy. Like I said…*unnatural.*"

"He is a child of prophecy, Commander, and prophecies are never natural. Garlis," Lorn summoned his ranking Elite forth.

"My Prince," Garlis acknowledged, stepping forward of his fellow Elite crowding the battlements behind them.

"Take two flax with you and find Terin. Bring him to me. We'll reestablish a command post at the north center redoubt, just south of here," Lorn ordered.

"Aye." Garlis bowed and withdrew.

"Reinforce the wall, but keep most of your troops south. We aren't moving any further with night closing in, and Thorton can target any position along the wall if he chooses. Let's not give him any easy pickings," Lorn said.

"It will be done, My Prince," Commander Farro said before recalling their cavalry.

*****

Torchlight played off the gray stone as they gathered in the great hall of the north center redoubt, the shifting flames illuminating the scorched walls. The battered fortress changed hands numerous times throughout the siege, men and gargoyles contesting every step throughout the fortress each time it was contested. Most of the dead were cleared away, but many still remained. Half-eaten human corpses bore testament to the gargoyles' cruel nature, the macabre scene never failing to empty one's stomach of the human survivors. Even Jentra was tested by the ghastly sights that seemed to have no end.

Jentra stood at Lorn's side as the Yatin and Torry Commanders gathered in the barren hall. Enough debris was cleared away to make room for a table with a map of the city unfurled across it. His tired muscles and old bones ached, a humbling reminder that war was a game for younger men, yet here he stood in defiance of his age.

I'm still younger than Master Vantel, he reminded himself, chastising his foolishness. If a man of Torg's years could best men a third his age, then what right had Jentra to voice complaint? Besides, a dozen gargoyles fell to his blade this day, proof that he wasn't ready to be put to pasture. He recalled the hundreds of young men that died this day under his command, their collective faces flashing before his eyes whenever he gave them thought. Most fell in the narrow confines south of the river, set upon from above whilst traversing alleyways and winding streets. The wretched creatures set fires throughout the city, proving deadly to poorer residential districts crowded with the Yatin populace in wooden ramshackles. Few had any means to fend for themselves as Emperor Yangu denied them arms, fearing revolt as much as the gargoyle invasion.

Fool, thought Jentra sourly. What was the fate of realms when the survival of humanity rested in the balance? Lorn understood this, understood the true threat before them. He did not hasten to Corell to claim his crown when the battle he needed to wage was right here. Jentra didn't understand this before, counseling against it, but he wasn't too proud to admit he was wrong. The gargoyles were the enemy wherever they could be found. For good or ill, the Yatin Empire was no longer a threat to the Torry Realms. It was a broken, devastated land, but enough of it still stood to be a shield against Tyro.

"General Yoria," Lorn began, addressing the Yatin commander standing across the table.

"I have two thousand men manning the wall from the river's edge to just beyond the northwest gate," Yoria said, running his finger along the map of the city in a wide arc, following the outline of the wall. "I have placed four telnics just south of the wall as you suggested, Prince Lorn. They can easily fill any gaps should they arise, if the enemy counterattacks this night. My remaining troops are securing the west bridge and tending our wounded, of which I have no count." Yoria sighed wearily.

"Farro?" Lorn asked his acting general of 4th Army.

"We hold the wall from this place between the northwest and north center gates, eastward to the river's edge upstream, with three telnics," Farro said, running his finger in an arc along the wall, starting where Yoria left off, continuing to the river's east end. "Five more telnics are in reserve, with the rest spread throughout the city. Our casualties are over five thousand, perhaps as high as seven thousand," Farro grimly stated.

"What of General Korath?" Jentra asked.

Farro shook his head, having received word before this meet of his demise.

"Take a knee," Lorn commanded him as Farro shared a wary look around the chamber, the others nodding in approval. He circled the table, stopping near his prince and knelt.

"My Prince." He bowed his head in supplication.

"Commander Farro, do you accept the command of 4th Army?" Lorn asked with firm authority.

"I so avow, My Prince."

"Avow!"

"I pledge my life to the defense of the Torry Realms. I pledge my fealty and fidelity to the House of Lore. I vow to command the 4th Army as an instrument to those aims and no other. I avow to place the preservation of the throne, the realm, and the 4th Army above my own life. I so avow!" Farro declared with equal authority.

"I bestow upon you command of 4th Army. Rise, *General* Farro!" Lorn offered his hand, helping the general to his feet. In times of peace, the commission of a general was conducted in the throne room of Corell with great pomp and ceremony. Lorn regretted not offering his newest general his due regard, but such was war. If they survived this conflict, he made note of all those due such honors, and the list was already a lengthy one.

"General Avliam," Lorn ordered his cavalry commander to report.

The grizzled general's long mane was matted, taking the shape of his battered helm, which rode his brow for most of the past three days. His silver mail was dulled and broken in places. His white tunic was stained with blood, dirt, and grime, his green eyes hopelessly bloodshot. Jentra thought the man might fall dead at any moment, by the looks of him. Of course, the same might be said of any of them. Few, if any, had more than a brief nap these previous days.

"The enemy has been cleared from the southern approaches of Mosar," he began, running a finger in a large arc beyond the southern walls of the city. "Our scouts report no sightings to our direct east along the north bank of the Muva. General Cornyana reports similar findings to our west. The enemy is now concentrated to our direct north, within the confines of the forest."

"Their strength?" Jentra asked.

"Uncertain, but I surmise at least ten thousand," Avliam said somberly.

"That many?" General Farro winced. He would be lucky to field as many with the casualties his Army suffered.

"It is far less than what they started with," General Yoria snorted. Yonig entered the Yatin Campaign with three full legions. With several telnics garrisoned at Telfer and Tenin, the bulk of his legions was brought to Mosar. Their reduction meant they could not advance on Mosar again without another legion of reinforcements, which seemed unlikely considering Morac's invasion of Torry North. Even Tyro's Empire had its limits.

"Their numbers are not the threat, Thorton is. Until we neutralize him, we cannot advance," Jentra growled.

"Yah has provided for our every need, Jentra. Put faith in that." Lorn touched a hand to his friend's shoulder.

Jentra couldn't miss the unease of the commanders gathered therein at the mention of Yah. Two of his fellow Elite visibly stiffened, though he noticed most nod in agreement. Lorn was adamant throughout the campaign that he was led more by his faith in Yah than military sense. He couldn't dismiss Lorn's preparedness, however, as he coordinated the logistics of the campaign with astute professionalism and drilled the men relentlessly with the scant time allotted them. Despite this, Jentra couldn't make sense of marching into hostile Yatin lands to aid their old foe. Was it not wiser to let the gargoyles and Yatins bleed each other? He advised as much, but Lorn wisely didn't heed his poor counsel. But Lorn couldn't have known that they would arrive before the city had fallen or the timely arrival of Terin and Kato to counter Thorton's threat. Of course, Lorn would claim all was foreseen by Yah, which further reinforced his belief. Jentra couldn't bring himself to believe in Lorn's god, not yet anyway. He simply summed up this whole campaign as dumb luck, as any number of things could've brought their ruin, but here they stood in defiance of all reasonable odds.

"I assume you are referring to our benefactors, whoever they are," General Yoria said, visibly uneasy with Lorn's proselytizing, which only fed Emperor Yangu's paranoia. The Yatin emperor's fragile mind saw plots in every direction, fed by his delusions. He knew as well as anyone that their new alliance could easily shatter with the slightest misunderstanding.

"Yes, where are our new friends?" General Avliam asked. "The Earther spared my command countless casualties."

"The Earther is at the river, tending the wounded," General Farro said. Yatin and Torry casualties were gathered along the open space of the city wharves, their numbers too great for any edifice to hold while they decided their fate.

"Tending the wounded? Is he a healer?" Yoria asked.

"A wizard, more likely. Rumors are spreading that he possesses magical powers to mend sundered flesh and restore eyes and limbs," a Torry commander of telnic spoke aloud.

"It is not magic," a strong voice echoed from the doorway as a stout built Torry Elite stepped forth, his silver helm resting in his left hand, its once resplendent sheen marred and dented. His mop of brown hair clinging to sweat-stained scalp. Unlike his brethren, his brown eyes showed only weariness of battle, not the dire lack of sleep that afflicted the others.

"Lucas?" Lorn was taken aback, questioning his tired eyes. He last saw Lucas at Corell, nearly a year ago. His sudden appearance meant he arrived with Terin and Kato.

"Highness." Lucas stepped near, starting to kneel before Lorn waved off such formality.

"By your presence, I surmise you arrived in Terin's company?" Lorn asked.

"I have, My Prince. Myself, Terin, and Kato the Earther departed Corell at the behest of her Highness Princess Corry to aid you in this campaign," he explained, revealing Kato's identity to those who didn't know which Earther rallied to their cause.

"How goes the war in the north? We just received tidings of the victory at Corell, but it was scant on detail," Lorn asked, the missive he received merely stating that the castle was relieved by a combined host of General Bode and the Jenaii.

"It's a lengthy tale, My Prince," Lucas warned, feeling every eye in the large chamber upon him.

"Perhaps an abbreviated version for now and a more detailed account later on." Lorn smiled.

And so Lucas began, starting when the king marched east to Notsu and ending with the victory at Corell. He made the story as brief as he could, emphasizing Terin's role in the entire affair, telling how he threw back the enemy time and again, driven by the awesome power of his father's sword. His strange effect on the gargoyles, his ability to strip them of their courage and wits, seemed beyond the power of the sword itself, portending something else altogether. He also explained Kato's role in the breaking of the siege of Corell and the timely arrival of the Jenaii. The joyous news was tempered by the massive casualties suffered by the Torry Realm. The 5th Army was destroyed to a man, and the 3rd was nearly cut in half. Bode would hardly be able to hold Corell with the forces remaining him. As Lorn ran the grim numbers through his head, the others asked Lucas more details of Terin's fell deeds. All of them witnessed Terin flying to the north wall and slaying Yonig, driving off his host. No sword itself could manifest such power.

"Where is Terin now?" Lorn asked the question on all their minds. He sent Garlis to fetch him some time ago and hadn't received word of his success.

Lucas paused, knowing the answer would not sound the way he intended.

"Speak, Lucas!" Jentra ordered sternly.

Lucas winced at Jentra's harsh tone. As Elite prime, Jentra was feared and respected among their brotherhood. "He is resting, Highness," Lucas confessed.

"Resting?" Jentra snorted. "His prince has summoned him! Go fetch the boy and bring him here!"

"Jentra." Lorn raised his left hand, calming his zealous protector. "I believe there is more to this than Lucas has stated."

"Aye, Highness." Lucas sighed, grateful for Lorn's understanding.

"Take me to him. Farro, you know my wishes. Coordinate them with General Yoria," Lorn addressed his general, he and Jentra following Lucas from the chamber.

*****

Terin flinched, a sudden tremor running the length of the left side of his body. It was enough to stir him from his slumber. Torchlight on the near wall illuminated the small chamber. He found himself abed with three pairs of eyes upon him, one sitting upon a chair at his bedside and the others standing near the door beyond the foot of the bed.

"Lucas." Terin winced, making out his friend's face staring back at him from the door, beside another familiar face that he couldn't quickly place until he recognized it as Jentra. His eyes shifted to the one sitting his bedside, surprised to see Lorn's sea-blue eyes staring back. He shifted suddenly, trying to rise before Lorn put a hand to his chest, keeping him abed.

"Rest easy, Terin," the prince commanded. Lucas explained the exhaustive effect the sword exacted on his body. They sat his bedside for several hours, waiting for him to stir. Others visited throughout the night, except Kato, who wouldn't leave the wounded, tending them with his magical *healing wand*, as the soldiers called it.

The last thing Terin recalled was clearing a dwelling of gargoyles with Lucas at his side. Anything thereafter was lost to him.

"How long have I…" his voice trailed weakly.

"You've been asleep most of the night. It is nearly sunrise," Lorn said.

"You've been by my bedside all night?" Terin asked guiltily.

"For the better part. We've taken turns waiting for you to wake." Lorn left out that they each slept on the floor for much of the night. Such was a soldier's life, getting sleep wherever and whenever they could but never truly resting.

"The battle?" Terin asked, but the very fact that he was in their presence portended well for the Torry cause.

"We've retaken the city." Lorn smiled wanly. "Aside from that, we are still locked in a stalemate with the enemy camped within sight of the north wall, and Thorton's weapon preventing us from marshalling to meet them. Thanks to you, we have bled them enough to confine them to a defensive posture."

"We're not in much shape to go on the offensive ourselves," Jentra snorted.

"Not today, old friend, but a few days of rest and healing will do wonders in that regard," Lorn reminded them.

"Kato?" Terin asked of his friend. He hadn't seen him since they approached the city during the battle before splitting off, Kato setting down south of the city, as Terin and Lucas flew on to Mosar.

"He is tending the wounded," Lucas assured him, standing at Jentra's side.

"Oh, good." Terin smiled, grateful that his friend brought his wondrous healing tools with him. The matrons at Corell made good use of them after the siege. They were sorry to see him leave for Yatin as there were countless wounded still to treat, but he knew Lorn would have greater need of it. The most critical of the wounded at Corell were already treated or expired before they left. Kato instructed the matrons on the principles of triage, prioritizing order of care. The healing instruments could only work at a certain speed, making some wounds impossible to treat before the patient expired. Regenerating destroyed tissue was also time-consuming, preventing them from restoring many severed limbs until after everyone else was treated first. Most wounds to major arteries were fatal, the patient bleeding out long before they could be treated with Kato's instruments, unless he was nearby at the time.

"Yes, *very* good. Another blessing from Yah," Lorn agreed.

Jentra wanted to say it was more good luck, but he could only use that argument so many times before proving Lorn's point.

"Yah." Terin's eyes had a faraway look, recalling what his father revealed to him before leaving Corell and the stain of his dark heritage. He looked away, not able to meet the prince's eyes, knowing his grandfather was responsible for all their woes, especially King Lore's death at Kregmarin.

"Terin?" Lorn drew him from his melancholy.

Terin couldn't bear to speak of what truly troubled him. How would it be received? The Torry prince wrongly heralded his deeds, thanking him for their deliverance. In truth, his kin were responsible for all their woes, at least part of his kin. Yes, he was the blood of Kal and Torg but also Tyro, and one taint can spoil the whole. He found the prince's clear blue eyes both calming and unnerving, as if he could see into his soul. It should be unsettling, yet he found Lorn's presence comforting.

"My apologies, Highness. I am out of sorts. A condition that I find myself more often as of late."

"Lucas told of the draining effect the sword has on you during battle. This happened several times at Corell, did it not?"

"Yes, the longer the battle, the more lasting the effect. But I am growing resistant," Terin said.

"He was abed for two days after the final assault on Corell, sire," Lucas added, refuting Terin's downplaying of the sword's effect on him.

"These magical swords don't seem to affect anyone else who has wielded them," Jentra said. Of course, how often had they witnessed anyone wielding them?

"Is not the answer obvious, my friend?" Lorn gave Jentra a knowing look.

"Nothing is obvious to me right now. I haven't slept longer than a short nap for days," Jentra snorted.

"The swords were forged for their true bearers, a people born to wield their awesome power."

Terin's heart raced with the prince's words, wondering how he knew.

"What people?" Jentra made a face, Lorn once again speaking in riddles.

"A people that are no more, save for the boy who rests before you and the father who sired him," Lorn's voice was but a whisper yet carried through the chamber like a thunderclap.

Terin meant to speak, but the words wouldn't form, the expression on his face betraying him.

"I know, Terin. There is nothing about you that Yah has not revealed."

"Nothing?" Terin's eyes drew wide.

"Nothing. I know of you and your father's kin, both his mighty sire and his mother's rich bloodline. A heritage that none but your parents know. The stain of your paternal grandfather is washed clean by your paternal grandmother's blood and your mother's Torry lineage," Lorn said.

Terin's heart pounded in his chest, his darkest shame laid bare.

"His father is not native Torry?" Jentra asked, trying to make sense of Lorn's revelation.

"No, he is something *far* more." Lorn's reassuring smile setting Terin's heart at ease.

"Something more? What in the blazes does that mean?" Jentra snorted.

"It is not my place to say, nor would it be safe to speak of it aloud. There is more that even Terin is unaware, deep truths that Yah will reveal to his chosen, when he is able to bear them." Lorn knew that if word spread of Terin's true heritage that Tyro would be consumed with his capture, an obsession that would cause Terin's death or torment, even if his grandfather intended differently, for the blood of Kal could not abide the taint of Tyro.

"So we trust our lives and the fate of the realm to a boy without Torry blood?" Jentra's eyes narrowed severely.

"You cannot speak so without dishonoring his mother's kin, Jentra," Lorn said, amused by his friend's ignorance, and his expected reaction to his next revelation.

"And she is Torry?" Jentra forgot that part of Lorn's ramblings.

"Very much so, my friend. You would know her through her family name…Vantel," he said, giving Terin a knowing smile.

"Master Torg?" Jentra's scowl softened.

"Is her father," Lorn said.

Jentra stiffened, straightening his spine at the mention of his beloved commander and mentor. Jentra's ranking within the Elite was second only to Torg Vantel. If the boy was Torg's grandson, then it didn't matter his father's kin. Jentra didn't care if Tyro was related to the boy as long as Torg was his grandfather.

"I expect much of any man with Torg's blood coursing his veins, but you seem up to the task," Jentra regarded him.

"That's as much praise as Jentra has ever given." Lucas snickered, the older warrior giving him his famous scowl.

"Don't you have other tasks to attend?" Jentra snorted.

"The princess commanded that I watch over Terin and guard his flank. A nigh impossible task once he draws his sword and charges blindly in one direction and then another." Lucas shrugged innocently in his defense.

"You have followed her command with utmost zeal, Lucas, but you'll do him no good without proper rest. Get some sleep. Terin will still be here once you do," Lorn commanded.

"As you command, sire." Lucas bowed.

"And, Lucas?" Lorn said before he stepped without.

"Yes, sire."

"Speak not of Terin's lineage with anyone else."

"I never would, sire, though many at Corell already know he is the grandson of Master Vantel and the son of Jonas Caleph," Lucas said, though neither he nor Jentra knew who Jonas truly was, other than a warrior who served in the Elite long ago.

"You should rest as well, Jentra. I can watch over Terin," Lorn added as Lucas stepped without.

"I'm not here to watch over the Torry champion. I am charged with watching over you. And that is a task nearly as impossible as the task your sister asked of poor Lucas," Jentra reminded him. "At least Terin has the excuse of the sword for his reckless behavior."

"I stand guilty of your charge." Lorn lifted his hands in mock surrender. Jentra followed him faithfully for years, often against any soldier's good judgement.

"All right, I'll take my rest and leave you in his company. You two should get along quite well, considering your mutual suicidal inclinations." Jentra shook his head, following Lucas out the door.

Lorn's tired laugh indicated that Jentra's harsh words were merely playful banter. The fact the grizzled Elite spoke so freely with the future king was endearing. Despite his religious zealotry, Lorn lacked the arrogance of a high-born prince. 'Twas a trait he observed when they first met in the wilderness so long ago, after his flight from Telfer. Or was it genuine kindness that he mistook for a lack of arrogance? Terin decided it was kindness that guided Lorn, a kindness that permeated the Royal House of Lore, a kindness that guided father, son, and daughter.

"You and Jentra remind me of your father and Torg." Terin grinned.

"You mean we are doomed to become two cantankerous old men one day?"

"Well, your father wasn't cantankerous." Terin shrugged.

"Just Torg then?" Lorn smiled, having a little fun with Terin's grandfather's reputation.

"Well, he is not softhearted, not on the outside, anyway." Terin smiled.

"You mean to say that Torg is soft on the inside?" Lorn lifted an amused brow.

"A little perhaps, when no one is looking," Terin conceded.

"More than a little, Terin, especially when it comes to his grandson." Lorn knew Torg's gruff manner was more show than substance, though he would never call him on that.

"True, though I thought he hated me at first."

"Why is that?"

"Because he disliked my father. I thought he was a suitor for my mother's hand, until he told me the truth."

"A suitor for your mother's hand?" Lorn laughed, trying to picture it in his head.

"In all fairness, I never considered the possibility that he was my grandfather." Terin shrugged sheepishly.

"Aye, and a great one he is." Lorn patted his shoulder.

"He is great, and the finest warrior I've ever known," Terin added.

"You are mistaken. Your father is greater, though you'd have little reason to know that."

"My father?"

"Jonas, son of Taleron, the blood of Kal," Lorn whispered.

"And how do you know of this, Highness? My father only spoke of it before I departed Corell and swore none knew beside himself and my mother."

"How do I know? I thought I already explained. *Yah* speaks to me, revealing his will and plan for mankind. It has been my driving force since I was a headstrong youth, spoiled and arrogant, until he gifted me a dark vision." Lorn's voice trailed, his blue eyes growing vacant as if lost in the past.

"Vision?"

"A future. A terrible future, unless I yielded my selfish will to his divine authority, placing my faith in him and him alone. Not since the age of Kal has Yah spoken directly to a mortal man. Not since your ancient kin has Yah revealed his will so clearly to a mortal man," Lorn said, though men had had visons at times, like his ancient kin, King Vantor who received the prophecy of the man who would find the lost sword of the Middle Kingdom.

"And Yah revealed to you my lineage?"

"When I first beheld our terrible future, I trembled with fear, beseeching Yah to remove the vision from my mind, but he refused. *See and remember, son of Lore,* he spoke to me."

"What was the vision?" Terin asked, though fearing to truly know.

"Gargoyles sweeping over the land, my family slain, our people slain, Corell in ruin. Their caliginous tide swept over all the lands, Yatin, the Jenaii, the Casian League, Macon and Nayboria, and the ape tribes. All were swept away like leaves to the wind. I wondered the purpose of the vision. What power did I have to contest such a future? What role could I play to counter Tyro's dominion?"

Terin thought to speak but couldn't put words to thoughts.

"How could I change the course of history when the tide was already cresting? *You are not alone, son of Lore*, Yah reassured me, lifting my spirit. 'Twas then he revealed my *brothers*, brothers not of blood, but of spirit, who would stand by my side to contest Tyro's dominion. You, Terin, are one of my true brothers, sent by Yah in our time of greatest need. Your birth was foretold long ago, long before King Vantor II of the Middle Kingdom revealed the prophecy of the one to find the lost Sword of the Moon. Your birth was foretold long before the rise and fall of ancient Tarelia. Your birth was revealed to Kal himself, before he fell in battle, a divine vision from Yah to his most faithful servant. You are his only descendent, his line dying or living through you and you alone. It is through you that his divine gift endures, the power to strip gargoyles of their courage and sense. Against you, they cannot stand. It is Kal's blood that enables you to call upon such power, Kal's blood that ordains you a child of prophecy. It is Kal's blood that calls out to the Swords of Light, drawing you to them, their own power symbiotic to your own. In my hand, your sword can cut through any object and would guide my hand to preserve my life. In your hand, it is so much more, enhancing your power to drive off gargoyles tenfold. The swords were forged for the descendants of Kal. They were forged for you."

"The smiths of Tarelia were unaware that Kal's descendants lived when they forged the swords, Highness," Terin pointed out.

"They did not know that the blood of Kal dwelt within the Kalinian Vale, but Yah knew. It was Yah that bestowed the divine gift to the Jenaii, who in turn gifted it to the Tarelian Council. And it was the Tarelian smiths who used the gift to forge the Swords of Light."

"But they didn't forge the swords for the blood of Kal. They gifted them to Tarelian warlords to counter the gargoyle invasion of Arax."

"True, but they were ignorant of Kal's descendants, otherwise they would have gifted the swords to their rightful owners."

"Then why didn't Yah reveal the Kalinian Vale to the Tarelians? With their blood and the Tarelian armies behind them, they could've swept the gargoyles from the face of Arax. Why would Yah allow this carnage to continue through the centuries?" Terin asked, questioning their god's wisdom.

"For the same reason he allowed Kal to fall in battle and his kingdom with him. Arax was not worthy to receive his mercy."

"Then what hope have we now? What is the point of trying if Yah deems us unworthy? We cannot win without him."

"Yah would not spare Arax for the sake of one faithful servant, with a populace that rejected him. Nor would he spare Arax the gargoyle curse unless they acknowledged his divinity. The realms established by the Tarelian Order were always followers of Kal but not always of Kal's god. Those first warlords given the Swords of Light were marginal believers in Yah, the kingdoms they established flourishing by this trace of loyalty. Their descendants quickly forgotten those shallow roots of worship, their realms falling into ruin as they followed their own inclinations. Without Yah's guidance and blessing, their realms fell one after another, betrayed by human failing, avarice, madness, and cruelty. Only the Middle Kingdom endured, realizing their folly only after losing the Sword of the Moon. Only then did Yah spare them for this appointed time, as an instrument of his true servants."

"True servants?"

"You and I, Terin. We are charged to implement his vision for our broken world."

"So was Kal, and Yah forsook him," Terin argued.

"Yah does not forsake his faithful servants."

"Kal died, Highness. Yah did not spare him when he punished the rest."

"No man lives forever, Terin, not in this mortal realm. But Yah gifted Kal that which he treasured most…his son. A child that would continue his line until was born one to fulfill his quest…You."

"I may have his blood, but I am no king. Men cheer my name for the enemies I've slain. I am only a soldier, nothing more. Kal was a great warrior and a wise king. That is too great a burden for any man. Besides, I may be Kal's heir, but *you* are my king."

"Terin Caleph." Lorn shook his head, awed by the young man's humility. "You do not covet power or glory, and that is why you are Kal's true heir. Yah understands that the burden on Kal was too great for any one man. That is why he has split the burden. To you falls the role of champion, the physical manifestation of Kal's ancient might. You are the bane of the gargoyle species. That is your role. To me falls the burden of implementing Yah's law upon Arax, a law that will earn me the ire and hatred of the ruling aristocracy that betrayed Kal in those ancient days."

"And why will they not betray you as they did him?"

"Because, Terin, the people in Kal's day did not believe in Yah, but our people will. Even now our faith is taking root across the Torry Realms. The threat of Tyro has only hastened their conversion like fire to dry grass, spreading until the land is consumed in its conflagration. The time of Yah is at hand. A time for the heir of Kal to lead our people into battle."

"The heir of Kal or the heir of Tyro?" He sighed.

"The sin of the father does not fall on the soul of the son, or grandson." Lorn stood, reaching out his hand, helping Terin to his feet, before handing him his belt wound around his sword and scabbard.

Terin wrapped the belt about his waist and knelt, presenting the sword to his prince.

"I pledge my life, my sword, my sacred honor to the rightful heir of the Torry Realms, Lorn II, son of Lore. I forsake any claim to Tyro's Empire and Kal's ancient realm. I so avow before Almighty Yah and my rightful king," Terin pledged.

"Arise, Terin. I do not accept your vow. It is not your place to disavow your rightful claims. Perhaps in the end, should we reign victorious, we can revisit which rights we intend to claim, reject, or pass to another. Today, you are the champion of the realm. I can think of no greater title or one more worthy to bear it. Now come, we have much to attend to. The battle is ended, but the siege endures."

C·H·A·P·T·E·R

13

Siege of Mosar stage five

"Any sign of him?" Nels grumbled beside him, under the shade of a thick porian.

Thorton stood behind the tree, his rifle resting along the side of its trunk. Scanning the length of the north wall in the distance, he made out a few targets of interest standing post along its broken ramparts but none worth revealing his position. The late-morning sun shone brightly over the scorched earth separating the forest from the city walls, an expansive trek of trodden foliage, muddy trenches, and burned fields. Thousands of men, ocran, and gargoyle corpses were strewn across the bloody fields, ripening in the cool morning air. In another day, their bloated corpses would start to smell, adding further to the noxious fumes hanging in the air for endless days. The smell of decay and death was a constant reminder of their own fragile mortality. To Thorton, it was but one of countless miseries of battle, to be regarded with as little interest as any other. He couldn't ignore its effect on his comrades, however. Only four of their fellow Elite survived the carnage beside Draken and himself. They, like their gargoyle legions, came into this battle drunk on victory. The battle of Mosar sobered them to the harsh reality of war. They took half the city, nearly taking the whole before being driven off once the Torries arrived, adding their strength to the wavering Yatins. Thorton's arrival tipped the scales, allowing Yonig's legions to retake the northern half of Mosar. Alas, their victory turned to ash as Kato and the Torry champion arrived to again tip the scales to the Yatin cause. Their bitter retreat last eve from the city nearly scattered their remaining cohorts. Thorton stiffened their resolve, rallying them north of the city and appointing Yonig's replacement to reorganize their battered telnics.

Draken was dismayed as the gargoyles, who once loathed and feared Thorton, suddenly looked to him for guidance. Several lingered nearby, awaiting his orders, which they would deliver to General Kaskos, the 3rd Telnic Commander of 1st Legion, that Thorton promoted to general. He was the only commander of rank that stood out in Thorton's eyes, able to rally his wavering troops throughout the retreat. Even now, he busied himself reconstituting their disordered mob into an Army, a task made difficult as they huddled within the forest.

"Any report on our magantors?" Thorton asked, scanning the length of the wall, magnifying the image in his scope to better identify the differing insignia of the soldiers positioned there.

"They're dead or gone, save one. Most of our ocran as well. I managed to commandeer a few ocran from the slavers," Nels said. All their mounts they previously kept here were scattered to the winds during the chaos. The Elite Thorton assigned to protect them managed to keep hold of the one warbird, three ocran, and Ella.

"The slavers are probably the ones who took ours anyway," Ben snorted. The slavers in question were a dubious lot, many foreign-born opportunists trailing the Army. Most of the more reputable Benotrist slavers were still en route from Tenin.

"Most likely, but difficult to prove. I didn't find any of our mounts in their caravan. Of course, we don't need proof, and they likely sent them off once taking them. They are a crafty lot," Nels said.

"Keep an eye on them. Anything suspicious and I want them dead, every last one."

"Little point in that. They are leaving," Nels said.

"Leaving, huh. Well. good riddance."

"You don't like slavers much, do you, Ben?"

"Not particularly. They are somewhere at the bottom of humanity with lawyers, bureaucrats, and politicians."

"Lawyers?" Nels made a face.

"The second lowest form of man" was all Ben would elaborate.

"What's the first?"

"Bureaucrats."

"You are a strange man, Ben." Nels laughed.

"If things go as I predict, you'll know what I'm talking about. In the meantime, it looks like we have a long ride home without our magantors." Ben growled, lowering his rifle.

"We're leaving?" Nels asked.

"Eventually," Ben stated the obvious, leaning his rifle against the tree while lifting his Stetson, allowing the winter air to cool his brow.

"The emperor will not be pleased. Yonig—"

"Yonig's dead, Nels, and most of his troops with him."

"You are the ranking Elite, Ben. If you think we should retreat, I will relay the order."

"Don't get ahead of yourself, Nels. We aren't leaving until we have to. The enemy has reinforced the city, preventing us from attacking with the troops we have. General Casket—"

"Kaskos," Nels corrected him.

"Cascute," Ben continued, still mangling the pronunciation, "has about ten full telnics. The enemy has double that, maybe more. Rule of thumb requires a three-to-one advantage for an attacking force to take a defensive position. That means we cannot attack."

"Then what are we to do? We cannot stay here indefinitely."

"Not indefinitely, but there are other ways to win a war, Nels."

"Without seizing their capital?"

"What good is a capital if you can't keep it?" Ben shrugged as if the entire situation was of little concern.

Nels stood there with a blank look on his face.

"Look, there are advantages and disadvantages in both human and gargoyle armies."

Nels thought on that for a moment. Humans were more disciplined and could be redirected in battle, withdrawing or advancing upon command. Human armies suffered fewer casualties due to their discipline. Gargoyles could march day and night, far outpacing their human counterparts as they literally ate off the land as they went.

Human armies required extensive logistical support to advance over land. Then it dawned on him. "*Food.*"

"Very good, Nels. How would you go about exploiting that?"

"Well…we could send a raiding party at night to burn their granaries."

"Their granaries are well fortified, and along the south bank of the Muva, in the center of the city. The granaries, however, were not built to feed that many troops for more than a few fortnights. They need to resupply Mosar from an outside source," Ben explained, getting Draken to work it out for himself.

"The river," Nels finally concluded.

"The river," Ben agreed. The Muva was easily navigable with a gentle current. The westerly winds drove sails easily upstream. With the Torry Navy now reinforcing Faust, the Yatins could safely send reinforcements and supplies upstream. Thorton didn't have to take the city. He could simply hold position and send out raiding parties downstream to cut Mosar's lifeline.

"So we hold here while we harry their shipments?" Nels asked.

"Yep. Unless you have a better suggestion."

"What of Kato? He could lead their armies out of the city, his gun matching your own."

"Have we seen him all morning?" Ben asked.

"No," Nels conceded.

"That's because he is hiding. He knows, as well as I do, that if we stick our necks out, the other might shoot it off. First shot wins. And what that means is neither of us is going to move on the other. So here we sit, like the western front, 1916."

"The western front?" Nels made a face, scolding himself for asking. All the Earthers would often make references from their home world that made little sense to anyone else. It made even less sense when they tried to explain it. Raven was even worse than Thorton, rambling on about utter nonsense, always quoting some ancient philosopher named Yogi, or Yugi Bera. "*Let's pair up in threes,*" he once said before they went on a mission when they were in the employ of the Troan Council. He recalled another time while they made port, and Raven talked the crew out of going to the finest tavern, claiming, *"No one goes there anymore, it's too crowded,"* using another quote from his favorite philosopher.

"The western front was a theater of operation during the First World War on my world, where the advance of firearms rendered offensive operations futile," Thorton answered, not bothering to choose words that Nels could understand.

"An interesting tale," Nels lied.

"You didn't understand anything I said, did you?" Ben made a face.

"Not a word."

"Then why didn't you say so?"

"Well, you seem quite confident of your plans. I didn't want to discourage you."

"General Patton once said, *'If everyone is thinking alike, then no one is thinking.'* I don't ask you things so you can agree with me, Nels. I want you to think for yourself."

"Thinking for ourselves is paramount when working for one's self. We are now employed as Imperial Elite, sacrificing freedom for generous compensation."

"You think I would ever sacrifice my freedom for a few coins?"

"Perhaps I misspoke," Nels quickly retreated.

"I chose to work *with* Tyro, not for him, for the betterment of your world. My loyalty still rests with Earth. One day, Space Fleet will discover Arax and treat with your people, *all* of your people, Nels. Even these Yatins that our gargoyle friends seem to hate beyond reason. Tyro will eventually conquer all of Arax, and the Yatins, Torries, Macons, Troans, all of the people will be his subjects and his responsibility. This torture, cruelty, and genocide will have to cease. My people will not abide it when they arrive."

"If your fellow Earthers will not suffer our harsh behavior, then why are you helping our cause and not the Torries? Their compassion and sense of honor are well noted and more in line with your own."

"The Torries do not care to conquer Arax. Only Tyro holds to such a goal, and only a united Arax can maintain their sovereignty when dealing with the bureaucrats my people will likely send them." Thorton growled. He could not explain the intricacies of the Earth

Bureaucratic Corp. and their inane ability to muck up the simplest task. Once word spread throughout Space Fleet that they discovered an Earth-like world, populate with human life-forms, the entire consortium would rush to Arax to investigate for themselves. Even if the Earth Political Corp. respected the sovereignty of Araxan Kingdoms, the Galactic Corporations would be quick to exploit Arax's divisions, establishing mineral and trade agreements with the separate kingdoms, replacing their rulers with their own puppets. The discovery of a livable, nonterraformed world, capable of supporting human life, would shake the Earth Consortium to its core. Even if the politicians and bureaucrats were able to keep the corporations out of Araxan affairs, Arax would still be overwhelmed with tourists, hell-bent on meeting the *new* humans. Ben knew the best outcome for both Arax and Earth was if Arax was represented by one sole authority, who spoke for *all* the people and claimed dominion of the entire planet. A divided Arax would only prolong its full integration into the Earth consortium. Only full integration would give the Araxans power to control the inevitable flow of Earther immigration. Of course, to achieve the unification of Arax required the brutal tactics of Tyro's minions. He explained all this to the Emperor, warning him what would likely come to pass once Earth Space Fleet discovered his world.

"You are a strange man, Thorton." Nels shook his head. "You have aligned with Tyro for our collective benefit, at least in your own opinion. You speak of things none of us understand but speak of it with such conviction that I believe you."

"Good, now that you realize that I know what I'm talking about, go fetch Cusscuss, and I'll tell him our plans."

Kaskos, Nels thought to correct him but decided against it. He started to wonder if the Earther was mispronouncing the general's name on purpose.

"Send Ella to me while you're at it."

"As you command." Nels smiled, stepping away.

The girl was never far off, attending their makeshift campsite set farther within the tree line. She gathered her skirt in hand, making her way to her temperamental master before dropping into a deep curtsy.

"Save your knees, girl, I don't need your fake curtesy," Ben snorted, his eyes running the length of her comely form. Her once lovely dress was soiled and bloodstained as she treated the wounded and tumbled in the dirt countless times during the chaos of the retreat. She spent most of the siege attending Yonig, while Ben was elsewhere, fearing for her life in the gargoyle camp. The creatures never abused her throughout the campaign, fear of her master restraining them, though their behavior changed drastically this past day, from quiet loathing to deep reverence. They knew she was Thorton's lady, and their behavior toward her changed with their behavior toward him. He was no longer the emperor's feared lieutenant but their savior.

"You called for me?" she asked, exhaustion evident in her weary voice.

"Sing me a song," he commanded, taking up his rifle, again surveying the walls of Mosar in the distance. She expected such for it was the one demand he made of her since taking her captive. Whenever he asked her to sing, he would become disturbingly silent, tending other tasks as an excuse to look away as she sang. It was as if he was beguiled by her melodious voice. *"Music stills the savage heart,"* her father once told her. Until Thorton stole her away, she never understood the meaning of his words.

> She gazed to the sea
> To seek her lost love
> She sang to the sea
> To summon him home…

Her voice echoed softly, her song carrying upon the air as he stared through the lens of his scope. He remained strangely quiet while she continued, as if he was somewhere else, in a different place, in a different time. She once dared ask him what he was thinking whenever she sang, why he grew strangely quiet. He would not answer, a vacant look passing his sad eyes. She wondered why he asked her to sing if it brought him such pain. He was an impossible man to understand, demonstrating acts of violence and compassion without consistency. She never knew what to expect of him except that he was never cruel, at least not to her.

*****

"Careful," Kato said, standing over the matron's shoulder as she stared through the optic. She struggled to block the sound of the Muva lapping the riverbank behind her or the moans of wounded men laid out along the wharves all around her. She ignored the glare of the morning sun upon her face, focusing on the damaged tissue displayed so vividly in the Earther's strange device.

"He keeps moving," Matron Ilesa complained as the wounded soldier moved, shifting the optic.

"It's all right, it will come back, look." Kato touched a reassuring hand to her shoulder as the image returned.

Ilesa released a relieved sigh. The young woman was clearly nervous learning to use the strange device but honored that the Earther thought her worthy to do so. As an apprentice, she examined dozens of corpses, learning to identify the various organs of the human body. The Matrons' Guild taught the various functions of many of the organs, but the purpose of others was a mystery. The Earther, however, explained their purpose in enough detail for her to understand, as they moved from patient to patient. The device was no larger than her fist, resting upon the soldier's abdomen, pressed upon his naked skin. A large puncture wound rested below the device, blood clotting beneath a bandage pressed over it.

"You see the tear there?" he pointed out.

"Yes, along the lining of the stomach," she said.

"Very good. Run your finger along that line...there," he indicated as she touched the optic, running her finger where the soldier's stomach tear was represented.

"Now, *initiate*," he said, pointing out the corner of the optic where the order would be executed.

She smiled gleefully as the wound sealed, restoring the damaged tissue.

"Well done, Ilesa. Now I'm going to remove the dressing from the puncture wound. Remember what we did before?"

"Yes," she recalled, having repeated the process a dozen times already.

"Here goes," he said, his easy, calm voice setting her at ease as he removed the bandage.

She quickly slid the device back over the wound, pleasantly surprised that little blood issued forth. The image of the open wound and the damaged tissue below it quickly appeared on the view screen, with the recommended treatment alit in bright red upon the green field. She touched the initiate portion of the screen as the wound swiftly mended, the tissue regenerating to its original form.

"Well done, I think you have the hang of it." Kato patted her slender shoulder as she sighed in relief.

"Agghh…I…thank you," the soldier gasped, catching his breath as he lay upon the stone wharf, his back and neck aching from resting so long on the unforgiving surface. The top of his tunic was ripped open, exposing his torso, where the matrons set him upon the wharf during the night, gathering most of the wounded in the open expanse upon the north bank of the Muva. Across the river, hundreds more were similarly gathered along the riverbank and the palace grounds. At first, soldiers with mortal wounds were disregarded for those that could be tended by conventional means, but Kato quickly corrected that thinking, demonstrating the power of his *miracle* device. No sooner had the city been secured, then he hurried to aid the wounded. The arch matron was at first taken aback by the strange Earther, who swept into their midst, ordering her charges about as if he were Prince Lorn himself. It didn't take long for her and her sister matrons to witness the fruits of his labor, healing soldiers one after the other. They quickly started gathering the mortally wounded, seeing the way they could be saved. The arch matron quickly agreed, adjusting their triage accordingly, placing those with mortal wounds ahead of the others. The wounded were constantly being moved into position along the riverfront, carried upon stretchers by their fellow soldiers. Several thousand were stretched out in a continuous line, many dying before Kato could reach them.

Two young girls gathered about the healed soldier, offering him water as he moved to a sitting position, the fellow staring at Kato in disbelief.

"Can you continue on your own?" Kato asked Ilesa.

"I believe I can," she said, hiding any doubts with an air of confidence.

Kato gained his feet, stepping back as she moved to the next soldier, a Yatin commander of flax, with his ruined left eye dislodged from its socket. 'Twas the third such injury they treated and a good test of her skill. The poor soldier was beyond agony as two of his comrades held him in place while Ilesa worked to cleanse the wound and regenerate the eye. Within moments the soldier was restored, his pain washed away by Kato's *magical* device.

Kato stretched his sore muscles, forgetting the last time he stood up. He'd been up all night and through the morn treating one casualty after another. He looked west along the riverfront, where hundreds more awaited treatment. The device's power would need to be recharged before they finished. Looking east, his heart sank, with hundreds more still lining up along the wharves that he just cleared. He counted dozens of civilians among the new arrivals, some severely wounded or burned. They should've been given priority with those he was now treating, but warriors took precedence. If only he had another *Regenerator*, but such was war and the privations of being stranded on this alien world with scant resources. Hundreds of soldiers loitered along the wharves, staring at Kato with a mix of awe and curiosity. At times, commanders would order them to other duties, but their numbers swelled with those he healed joining their ranks.

A sudden murmur swept through the disordered ranks, men parting as a small entourage emerged between two stone warehouses to his direct east, men taking a knee as a dozen men in distinct silver armor over blue tunics stepped into the clear, led by a black-haired warrior with strikingly handsome features that radiated authority. Kato met the man the night before, though their exchange was brief, the fellow explaining that Thorton fled the city, repositioning with his host, north of Mosar. That was when Kato broke off to treat the wounded. If Ben Thorton was outside the city walls, he saw no need to present him an easy target by manning the battlements. His mere presence in the Torry ranks prevented Ben from renewing his assault on the city—as long as he wasn't killed by Ben first, that is.

"Arise!" Jentra ordered men to their feet as Lorn made his way toward Kato, with Terin and Lucas by his side.

"Again we meet, Kato of Earth." Lorn extended his hand, clasping forearms with Kato, as Matron Ilesa paused, regarding her prince with a polite bow.

"Please, Mistress Ilesa, continue," Lorn softly ordered, not wishing to delay her in her task.

"You look better than I last saw you." Kato smiled, eyeing Terin.

"I thought I was past the effect of the sword." Terin shrugged.

"You fought even longer yesterday than the final assault at Corell. All men have their limits, Terin, even you," Kato said.

"He is growing resistant to its effect," Lucas spoke in Terin's defense.

"True, but his body still suffers the strain, and that requires time to heal," Lorn said. "Gentlemen, I would like a word with Kato in private."

Terin and Lucas thrust their fists to their chest and backed a step, as Lorn led Kato to the water's edge, standing upon the lip of the wharf.

"I regret the brevity of our exchange last eve, Kato. I was unable to fully express my deep gratitude for your aid in battle and for…" Lorn spread his open right hand, sweeping the length of the riverfront between the middle bridge to their west and the eastern bridge to their east. "Well, for all this." Lorn nearly wept with joy at the miracles Kato's wondrous tool undertook for all the wounded soldiers. Lorn stood there beside the Earther, his dark mane lifting in the late morning breeze, his battered helm resting in his left hand.

"It is my honor to serve the Torry Realm and her future king, Prince Lorn." Kato bowed his head respectfully.

"No, it is my honor, Kato." Lorn shifted his sea-blue eyes to Kato's brown, regarding him intensely, as if to discover the Earther's deep mystery. "Your comrades did not come with you," he stated, as if he already knew.

"They believe they already did enough. I disagreed." Kato shrugged, ashamed that Raven and the others weren't at his side.

"They have done the Torry Realm a great service, Kato. Do not disparage their deeds because they have not met your commitment. They did rescue my sister and Commander Kenti, neither a small achievement. Raven and Lorken also reduced several thousand of Tyro's minions, if the rumors are to be believed."

"Probably hundreds, but who really knows. We are capable of much more, and they just don't see it," Kato lamented.

"They are good men, Kato. Sometimes such men need time to see the truth as others do."

"That's what Rav often said about Thorton when he went off on his own. He was certain that he would eventually come back to us. How wrong he was." Kato shook his head.

"Tell me of your friend?" Lorn asked curiously.

"Thorton?"

"Yes, Thorton. Why does he serve Tyro?"

"I wish Raven were here, he could explain it better than I." Kato scratched his head, trying to put his thoughts to words.

"They were friends," Lorn said, knowing that much.

"The closest of friends. More like brothers. If not by blood, then certainly by marriage," Kato explained.

"Marriage?"

"Ben wed Raven's sister."

"If they share such a bond, what drove them asunder?"

"She died."

Lorn thought to ask what drove them apart, but Kato interjected.

"She died, and Ben blamed Raven. This happened just before we came to your world. Before Ben set out on his own, he could barely look at Raven without thinking of her. It was intolerable. So we set him ashore, and he left. It was only much later when we learned he joined with Tyro. Why he did it, I can only guess." Kato looked away, pained by the memory.

"A broken heart." Lorn sighed regretfully. There was no recourse to such an ailment, no recompense to mend its fissures, save for one. Only Yah could grant Thorton peace and return him to his fold.

"A broken heart," Kato lamented.

"And for this, he would kill his brother?" Lorn asked.

"I don't know. They exchanged blasts at Fera, and he and I fired upon one another here, but we didn't strike each other. Was that by accident, or did neither of us really want to? It's all so needless."

"He must have joined with Tyro for a reason."

"Well, it wasn't for gold or glory. He cares nothing for either of them," Kato said.

"Then what does he care for?"

"With Thorton, who knows? Raven often said that Ben was the smartest pilot he knew, the ablest with a pistol too, besides Raven, of course. He could've risen high in the ranks but cared little for promotion. The tactics that won Raven great renown in the battle of Ganymede were designed by Thorton, and he gave all the credit for their success to Raven. He was happy to do so, for all he cared about was her, and now she is gone."

"So that is it," Lorn surmised.

"That is what?" Kato made a face.

"His lady's death created a terrible void in his soul, a void his friends' love could not hope to fill. He could only fill it with a sense of purpose, an idea greater than himself. A purpose..." A faraway look crossed Lorn's tired face.

"Tyro's a coldblooded killer. What *greater* purpose does helping him serve?" Kato asked doubtfully.

"A coldblooded killer." Lorn sighed. "That description matches Thorton as much as Tyro. Tyro was not always the man we now know, Kato. Few men are born so vicious, though the human heart is naturally wicked. Most become as vicious as Tyro while suffering life's cruelties without reason to guide their better natures."

"There is no reason to butcher innocents, enact genocide, or enslave thousands. Whatever happened to turn Tyro's heart merely magnified the darkness that was already there."

"Darkness dwells in all of us, Kato, even you and I. Perhaps it is stronger in others, and their hearts are bound to the light by the merest of cords. Once those tenuous cords are severed, they lose themselves in a dark sea."

"You sound more philosopher than crown prince." Kato smiled.

"Truth is not a philosophy, my friend. I merely look to understand my enemies. Only in doing so can we overcome them."

"I try not to understand what I know I must kill." Kato sighed. "It makes it easier."

"It is a heavy burden when the one you must kill is one you once called friend."

"Yes. It's most…unfortunate." Kato shook his head.

"Might I ask why?"

"Why?"

"Why you have joined our cause? Why pain yourself over killing your friend on our behalf? We are strangers to you, just as Tyro."

"You are not strangers to me, Highness. I know Cronus, Leanna, and Terin, just as I knew Arsenc. They are among the few friends we have in this world. I couldn't leave them to Tyro's mercy. And with Ben helping Tyro, I…I couldn't stand aside and let him tip the balance."

"You could have, but you chose not to, and for that I am forever in your debt." Lorn placed a hand to his shoulder.

"No, I serve mankind, the same as you. And by the look of things around here, we all owe you a far greater debt." Kato's tired eyes swept the opposite bank, where countless bodies lined the shoreline and half-sunken vessels jutted above the surface of the Muva, their hulls ripped open, exposing their skeletal remains. Fires still burned unchecked throughout the southern half of Mosar, smoke billowing in tortured spirals into the sky. Blackened rooftops and crumbling structures dotted the riverfront.

"Very well then, Kato of Earth. We can agree that our debts are paid in full."

"Kato, just call me Kato."

"Kato," Lorn affirmed, clasping hands with him. "I was told by Lucas that my sister named you *friend* of the Torry Realm. 'Tis an honor rarely bestowed, and not gifted in my lifetime. I would offer more for your aid, if you would have it. I know you are far from home, and no one from Arax could ever comprehend how far across the heavens your home truly lies. There rests the awful truth, that you might never return to your home. You may be stranded on our world like a castaway spit up from the sea upon a desert isle, trapped by an endless expanse of ocean. We can never supplant your loved ones or native land, but you are welcome to make our realm your home. I would be most honored to call you my countryman. A place among the Royal Elite awaits if you choose to claim it."

Kato knew what the weight such a prestigious honor meant. Any member of the King's High Elite carried the authority of the Crown, outranking the generals and ministers of the realm in matters of war. Highborn lords and regents would offer their daughters in marriage to win the favor of the King's High Elite. It was a chance for him to establish a new and prosperous life on this strange world. Kato thought to reject it, for he did not come to their aid seeking wealth or glory, only honor. Yet here was the future king of the Torry Realms offering an outsider the highest honor he could bestow upon him. Would it not be dishonorable to refuse such a gift? Besides, had he not cast his lot in with the Torries already?

"Your words and trust honor me, Prince Lorn. I could not accept your generous gift without explaining my first oaths to my native country and my home world, oaths that I swore myself to their defense, pledging my loyalty to them above all others. Any vow I make to you would prove false should my people ever find us."

"And if they never do? You could die of old age upon our distant shores before your people discover you."

"I have come to accept that possibility." Kato steeled his heart to never seeing his family ever again.

"I am grieved for your loss. I mourn my father, whilst you have lost your entire world."

"My grandfather once said that our lives are judged by a few moments. A man might live a righteous and pious existence but succumb to terrible temptation for one moment, a moment that spoils all his labor. Conversely, another man might live a life of greed and self-indulgence and, for one glorious moment, risk his own life for another. Such a man would be remembered for his one good act."

"Men make such judgements, but Yah considers the whole," Lorn reminded him.

"Yes, your god." Kato smiled, not certain of the prince's primitive beliefs. "Your god may judge the whole, but men judge that *one* pivotal moment or moments. I truly miss my grandfather, but his wisdom and words carry on in my heart and memory." Kato touched a hand to his chest and then his head. "Whether I see him ever again or not, I can honor his memory by seizing that one pivotal moment by which I will be forever judged. Our coming to your world is that moment. I cannot believe it happened by mere chance. Our arrival corresponds with the pinnacle war of your world's survival. I cannot stand aside and observe history when I am charged to participate. I have sworn my loyalty to Japan and the Earth confederation after that. If you can accept my loyalties to each of them above the Torry throne, then I will accept your generous gift."

"I can accept your divided loyalties, Kato."

"Then I am your man, My King." Kato smiled, taking a knee.

Lorn's breath caught in his throat, taken aback by Kato's acceptance, before placing a hand to his head. "Arise, Kato of the King's High Elite. I so name you," Lorn declared, his voice loud enough for Jentra, Terin, and the others to bear witness.

*****

Ilesa and Kato worked feverishly throughout the day, moving from patient to patient as quickly as the regenerator could work. Her red dress concealed much of the blood staining her garment. Her brown hair was disheveled, clinging to the sweat of her face. She knew she looked an awful mess but strangely never felt better in her life, using the power of Kato's miraculous gift to heal these brave and suffering men. She would weep silent tears for those they were too late to save, many succumbing to their injuries even as they started treatment.

There was a Yatin boy, a recent conscript no older than fourteen years, who died just as they reached him. He lay upon the wharf, calling out to a mother who wasn't there, a vacant look passing his eyes, his spirit lifting just as they were about to treat him. She gently closed his eyes, pressing a kiss to his forehead before moving dutifully on, her heart breaking at the sight.

"It's all right," Kato would whisper, his gentle voice soothing her tortured mind, granting her the strength to continue on. Her heart would race every time he looked at her with those soulful brown eyes that turned beautifully upward at the corners. He was the most exotic man she had ever seen, beautiful and kind.

They had to pause several times, the device needing to *recharge*, as Kato explained it, using the light of the sun to restore it. The process was not terribly long, but even a brief delay would cost the lives of men in desperate need. Kato took advantage of this delay to move wounded men up and down the line, prioritizing those with the least amount of time to spare.

"Please, sir, please help my friend," a piteous voice cried out as Kato moved among the wounded. There, upon the unforgiving stone, sat a Torry soldier, his right foot bent in an unnatural angle, cradling his friend in his arms. The friend was ghostly pale, his lips tortured with pain, trying desperately to hold his guts in place, his innards spilling out between his fingers.

Kato knelt beside them, touching a hand to the man's forehead. He was a boy, really, looking no older than eighteen years, his desperate green eyes drifting in and out of consciousness, staring back at Kato with that haunted look of a dying man. His skin was deathly cool, shock taking hold of him.

"Stay with us," Kato said, touching the boy's face, forcing his eyes to stay open. He needed time for the regenerator to charge, time this young soldier didn't have.

"Can you help him?" his comrade asked desperately, holding tight to his friend, his own blue eyes searching Kato's brown.

"I can if he can hang on for a few moments," Kato assured him as Ilesa hurried to his side after he called out to her.

"It's almost ready," she said, looking at the charge indicator that he earlier showed her.

There were others equally desperate to be next treated, but none more so, and none that could be easily moved to him.

"What's your friend's name?" Kato asked, encouraging him to talk to occupy his mind. The soldier's foot looked awfully painful, but he ignored the agony to hold his friend.

"Jaris. He is my neighbor and friend, my best friend," the soldier said, tightening his grip on Jaris's shoulders.

"Where are you from?" Ilesa asked, setting the regenerator beside them.

"We live near a small village, west of Tuk, Matron," he said, respectful of her position.

"That is a beautiful region. My family is from Vilacia, just south of there," Ilesa said, sharing a careful look with Kato.

"Jaris has to live, my lady," the soldier pleaded. "He is betrothed to my sister. They are to wed upon our return. Theirs is the perfect love, pure and true. I couldn't bear her grief should he die." Tears ran down his cheeks.

"Let's see what we can do," Kato reassured him, letting out a relieved sigh as the regenerator was ready. He quickly set it upon Jaris's naked chest after tearing his tunic. No sooner had it started to mend the damaged tissue, Jaris expired.

"I'm so very sorry" was all he could manage to say.

*****

Kato and Ilesa worked throughout the day and into the night, until the regenerator ran out of power, leaving many wounded to wait until morning. Most of the life-threatening injuries were already treated, leaving wounded extremities for last.

"You have to rest," Ilesa said as they shut down for the night, with hundreds of wounded men looking on, desperately waiting their turn. Many of those who were healed moved amongst their brothers, bringing them food and things to cover them from the cool night air.

"Might as well sleep here." He sat down near his pack, using it for a pillow.

"So much death." She sighed, sitting down beside him. He just sat there for an eternal moment, looking across the river, hundreds of torches reflecting off its surface. It looked so peaceful, contrasting the carnage concealed by the night.

"Yes, so much death. So much loss and heartache," he said. Behind him stood a flax of warriors handpicked by Prince Lorn to guard him. He needn't ask their purpose as they stood vigil over him throughout the day as they tended the wounded. It was strange to be named to the King's High Elite, only to then be assigned men to guard him, but such was the importance of his work. Despite all the good he had done, it was the failures that stuck with him.

"You are troubled," Ilesa said, not missing the solemn look passing his face.

"I keep thinking about the two boys today, the ones who lived near you."

"Yes, it was very sad," she said, recalling the boy dying in his friend's arms.

"It reminded me of a story my grandfather once told me, a song, really."

"A song?"

"Yes, my grandfather loved music, all kinds of music, music from every land on Earth, whether it was contemporary or ancient. There was one that was very sad, a Scottish ballad about two soldiers taken prisoner far from home. One was to be freed, and the other executed. Their people believed if you died in a foreign land, your spirit journeyed home by way of the low road, the road of the afterlife, while the living returned home via the high road, the road of the mortal realm. The song is sung from the point of view of the condemned man, telling his friend he will return home before him by way of the low road."

"How sad," she said.

"Very sad. The dying man tells of his lost love, that he shall never meet again in life, and she is forced to wait until old age takes her to join his spirit in the hereafter."

"Just like the boy who died in his friend's arms today." She now understood why it struck a memory.

"Yes, a man dying in a foreign land, forced to take the low road back home."

"Such a sad song." She sighed.

"Sad, but beautiful," he said, looking deeply into her light purple eyes.

"Then sing it. Sing it for me." She smiled softly.

"I don't know if I remember the words, and many that I do are difficult to interpret."

"Then do your best, and let me judge its worth."

"Very well.

> By yon bonnie banks
> And by yon bonnie braes
> Where the sun shines bright on Loch Lomond
> Where me and my true love were ever wont to gae
> On the bonnie, bonnie banks of Loch Lomond
> O ye'll take the high road and I'll take the low road
> And I'll be in Scotland before you
> But me and my true love will never meet again
> On the bonnie, bonnie banks of Loch Lomond…
> Loch Lomond.

Before he finished the last verse, she was crying, the song touching that part of her heart that she so desperately tried to shield. There was a story behind every dying soldier, if one had time to know them. Every loss was felt more so if you knew them. So many had died in this war that she couldn't function if she contemplated the impact each loss meant for their loved ones. This song, this ancient ballad, perfectly tore down her defenses, laying bare the sense of loss.

"I didn't mean to make you cry," he apologized, touching a gentle hand to her shoulder.

She smiled, regarding him with tear-blurred eyes. "You are a good man, Kato. In all my life, I have known many a good man, but none as you."

It was there upon the bank of the Muva that she fell in love with Kato of Earth.

*****

Two days hence

White sails graced the western horizon, a purple anchor upon a field of white, adorning the lead vessel, sigil of the 3rd Yatin Fleet. The lone warship led three battered merchant vessels to Mosar's aid, bearing provisions for the starving city. Men lining the battlements near the river cheered heartily at the beautiful sight, until the condition of the ships dampened their zeal. The forecastle of the first merchant vessel was blackened, its upper rigging hastily pieced together. The center mast of the second galley was a severed stump, the fore and aft masts bearing its burden. A line of gargoyle skulls were stuck on pikes, running the portside of each vessel, a grim warning to any of the creatures that thought to again attack them. The mismatched rigging and masts of the lead warship indicated that it too suffered significant damage. This small flotilla was all that remained of the original thirteen merchant and three warships sent from Faust, the small fleet suffering repeated gargoyle attacks downstream.

*****

Terin walked nervously at Lorn's side, sunlight playing off his silver helm and cuirass as they crossed the middle bridge, stepping onto the center avenue of Mosar. The people crowded the sides of the street, cheering their names as they passed.

"Caleph! Caleph!" they shouted.

"Prince Lorn!" others cheered.

Terin winced with their adulation, wondering if they would curse his name if they discovered his true heritage.

"They would honor you, regardless, son of Kal," Lorn whispered in his ear, as if hearing his thoughts.

"It is unsettling when you do that, sire," Terin whispered back.

"When I speak the truth?"

"No, when you know what I'm thinking."

"'Tis no magic or divine insight to guess what you're thinking, Terin. It's written plainly on your face. You possess many commendable attributes, but cunning is not one of them."

"I know I am not good at hiding my emotions," Terin conceded, tugging at the collar of his tunic. The new material was stiff and uncomfortable, as he rarely wore it, having stuffed it deep in his saddle pack. With the fighting quiet these past few days, he spent most of his time guarding Prince Lorn. Such duty required a proper presentation. As Jentra reminded him, *"If a guard looks as fierce as he is, it will likely deter an attack,"* and so Terin spent his evenings polishing his armor and helm and keeping his attire in good order.

"I don't like this any more than you," Lorn noted his discomfort, his own attire once matching Terin's in stiffness. It took a while to break in new garments. Their soldiers needed to see Prince Lorn in all his glory as their regent. A leader must look the part as much as he acts it. It was an inconvenient truth of leadership and monarchy. Pomp and ceremony were vital in instilling confidence in the governed. Terin's appearance was equally important as the Torry champion and guardian of the prince. Though he was similarly clad as his fellow Elite, with much of his head covered by his helm, the people recognized him from afar. The awestruck looks of dismay and wonder at the battle's conclusion transformed into hearty cheers wherever he went. Word spread throughout Mosar of his fell deeds, followed by the gossip such things always produced. Some claimed he was the ancient warrior Monartin, reborn, a mythical champion of the 1st Yatin emperor. Others believed he was a secret prince and younger brother of Lorn, hidden from greater Arax until now. Some thought he might be a wizard, using magic to ignite the Sword of the Moon. His close friendship with Kato only fueled this particular rumor. Many, however, took him for what he claimed to be, a Torry warrior serving his prince.

"Prince Lorn!" a woman cried out from the crowd, a Yatin garrison soldier holding her back. "You have saved us," she cried, tears running down her cheeks. Terin felt pity for the woman. She looked well into her fourth decade, with matted brown hair framing sad gray eyes that bespoke terrible loss. She probably lost a husband or son in the siege, one of countless thousands to suffer in this battle, or one of tens of thousands to suffer in this war.

Lorn regarded the poor woman with a polite nod as they passed, continuing along the wide avenue. Towering pillars of the city forum rested up ahead on their left, the statues of sea nymphs lining its rooftop, catching Terin's eye with their wanton looks. They passed along the eastern face of the imperial palace, which rested just southwest of the middle bridge, overlooking the Muva. Palace guards met them at the main gate of the castle, centered along the east wall, their distinct gold capes setting them apart from the city garrison. Terin craned his neck, his gaze following the height of the curtain wall circling the palace, his angle at the base of the wall blocking the towering inner battlements and the amethyst citadels from view. Terin hadn't visited the royal palace since the battle when he drove the gargoyles from the palace roof before passing on. He wasn't nervous then but was wary meeting the Yatin emperor now.

The palace guards struck fists to chests, bowing their heads as Lorn approached, the gates swiftly opening and Lorn and his Elite passing within.

*****

"Prince Lorn II, son of Lore!" the court crier heralded as they entered the throne room. Terin's gaze followed the purple stone arches running the length of the chamber and the gold-plated columns supporting the structure to either side. The lanterns descending from the ceiling illuminated the great hall, reflecting off the jeweled floor. Only four of them entered the chamber with Prince Lorn, the rest remaining in the outer corridor. Terin kept to Lorn's side, with Jentra and the others a step behind. He could feel the cold eyes of the Yatin emperor upon him as they drew near the dais, where he sat his iron throne. He appraised Terin with pale blue eyes, peering from his gaunt face. The man looked like a skull with skin stretched over it, his angled cheekbones and protruding chin jutting prominently. Terin averted his gaze, focusing on the rich tapestry hanging behind the throne, a golden ocran rearing into the air upon a field of black. He counted nearly twenty royal guards standing behind the throne and to either side, wearing bright-gold cuirasses over purple tunics, with matching greaves and helms. Dozens of imperial ministers and court officials were also in attendance, gathered behind the throne.

Lorn knelt at the base of the dais, Terin and the others following in kind, before Yangu bid them rise.

"So the Torry prince finally sees fit to grant me an audience," Yangu greeted him coldly.

Terin was taken aback by the emperor's rudeness. Did not Lorn just save his city? Should he not be grateful? The man's mental state was clearly unstable. Terin again averted his eyes, turning them again to the tapestry rather than risk Yangu's ire.

"My apologies, Emperor Yangu. Matters of the Army have delayed our meet," Lorn politely explained, though Yangu's distrust was evident in his sickly pale eyes.

"Affairs of *your* Army, I presume. Such matters did not prevent General Yoria from visiting with his emperor when requested," Yangu challenged.

Terin felt rage with the Yatin Emperor's audacity. Who was he to order Prince Lorn about as if he were his subject or lackey? Did his realm's survival not depend on Lorn's generosity and sacrifice? Then he remembered Yeltor's treatment at the hands of this man. Yeltor risked his life time and again to rescue Yangu's firstborn son, only to fail against impossible odds. Yangu rewarded his bravery with banishment. Such was the gratitude of Yangu. Here was Lorn, receiving similar treatment, but Lorn was no soldier or vassal beholden to Yangu but the future Torry king. Terin could feel Jentra's anger behind him, his impatient breath heating his neck.

"General Yoria is a fine general," Lorn stated evenly, treading carefully with each word. Yangu was a prickly sort who took offense easily and was suspicious of the most innocent of acts.

"The enemy still lingers beyond our gates. Why haven't we driven them off?" Yangu challenged.

"The enemy holds position within the forest to our north, and the Earther Thorton still lives. Any assault over open ground would cost us dearly," Lorn explained.

"We have an Earther as well. I say pit them against each other, while we finish the gargoyles." Yangu leaned forward on his throne, his bone-thin fingers clutching its iron arms.

"The Earthers are not fools, Emperor Yangu. Neither dares show himself without risking the other shooting him from afar."

"Cowards!" Yangu roared, spittle spraying from his lips.

"Wisdom and courage are often mistaken for one another," Lorn said dryly.

"The gargoyles must be driven off!" Yangu insisted.

"I would advise against it until we are reinforced. We hold Mosar with more than twice the gargoyles' numbers. We have slain Yonig, and their forces dare not test us directly again. Winter is upon us, and we can starve them before they do the same to us."

"We are starving now," Yangu's voice lowered dangerously.

"The Torry Navy has reinforced Faust. Supplies are now flowing—"

"Flowing?" Yangu growled. "Three of nine ships survived the last journey from Faust, beset by those foul creatures! Three measly ships!"

"Three ships with enough provisions to supply Mosar and our armies for a fortnight, and more ships are underway," Lorn reasoned.

"And your men will get their fill first, I assume." Yangu sneered.

"Soldiers eat first, whether they are Yatin or Torry. But there is enough for the good citizens of Mosar as well."

"Unless your promised ships fail to appear. Do you take me for a fool, Prince Lorn? I know what you are doing. You feed my troops and my people with food from your Torry-flagged merchant ships, stealing their loyalty. Then you spread your religion, proselytizing your false god!"

"Yah does not claim dominion of mortal realms, Emperor Yangu, only the souls of men. Yah is no threat to your sovereignty. As far as proselytizing, I have not done so with your people. I have merely stated my faith in Yah, leaving others to decide for themselves."

"Sedition!" Yangu screamed.

"Sedition?" Lorn raised a skeptical brow. Faith in Yah did not preach insurrection.

"You think me blind? Your god is the same deity worshipped in the Zoran Provinces, a foul nest of traitors plotting to restore the old Western Kingdom, the same kingdom established by ancient Tarelia, *your kin!* With one hand, you would gain my people's loyalty by giving them food, and with the other, you would rally them to your god!"

"Any of us can find enemies in friends if we choose to see what is not there. We have come in friendship, to find common cause with you and your people, Emperor Yangu. We have shed blood fighting by your side. The bonds forged in battle are the most unbreakable of all," Lorn again appealed to reason, sensing the emperor on the verge of apoplexy.

"Friendship? You think I don't know who stands beside you?" He pointed a bony finger to Terin, refusing to look at him.

Terin's heart pounded, wondering if Yangu discovered his heritage.

"Terin is champion of the Torry Realm, so named by my father, King Lore," Lorn stated calmly, unmoved by Yangu's declaration.

"Champion of the realm? Nay. He is a Tarelian! Only a Tarelian could wield such power!" Yangu shouted. "Curious, is it not, that he miraculously appeared at the outset of the gargoyle invasion, arriving at Telfer with my faithless Elite Yeltor before abandoning the castle and returning to Corell to report our demise. Now you are here as our savior. Am I to be grateful for your aid in a war that *you* started?"

Jentra snorted, struggling to restrain himself with the emperor's aspersions. They should gather the Army and march back to Cagan, leaving Yangu to Tyro's mercy. But Lorn seemed unaffected by Yangu's accusations and derisions.

"Oh, yes, I know the cause of this war." Yangu's eyes glazed maddingly, his voice rising with the accusation as if he uncovered a grand conspiracy. "You meddled in the Wid River Valley. You sought to expand your power into lands claimed by Tyro, forcing war upon us all over your greed."

And there it was, Yangu's paranoia displayed in all its madness. He masterfully pieced together several loosely connected facts, weaving a grandiose conspiracy. Every new fact was twisted to further prove his delusion.

Lorn released a heavy sigh, knowing this moment would come to pass, as Yah had revealed to him. He felt Jentra and the others stiffen behind him, Yangu's guards putting their hands upon their sword hilts. They were hopelessly outnumbered five to thirty, the emperor's guards inching forward, awaiting Yangu's command.

Torchlight played off the madness in Yangu's eyes, a stupid grin stretching the width of his bony face. At the snap of his fingers, his guards would slay the Torry prince, ending the *Torry conspiracy* in one swift stroke. The order hung expectantly upon his lips, straining to be uttered, when his gaze shifted unexpectantly to Terin.

The power of his sword flowed through Terin's body, lighting his countenance in an otherworldly light. Yangu's jaw slackened as he beheld the power radiating from Terin's face. The madness in Yangu's eyes fell away as he stared dumbstruck.

"I..." Words failed the Yatin emperor, his face contorting painfully as if possessed, his eyes going out of focus. His posture softened as he quietly sat back on his throne, his eyes shifting to Lorn as if just noticing him.

"Welcome, Prince Lorn." Yangu smiled, as if greeting an old friend.

"Emperor Yangu," Lorn greeted in kind.

"The city is secured, I am told. Provisions are presently adequate. What is the state of the enemy?" Yangu asked as if his previous rant never transpired. The imperial guards stood down, sharing relieved looks among themselves. Jentra made a face, wondering if Yangu changed his tact or was stricken mad. Terin stood dumbstruck, wondering what just happened.

Lorn was not surprised at all. He continued on, discussing the disposition of the gargoyle forces north of the city and their raids upon their shipping along the lower Muva. Yangu discussed tactics and the disposition of their forces as well as civil affairs of the city pertaining to them. Yangu was visibly pleased with Kato's assistance with the wounded and planned a grand celebration for all the city once the enemy was finally driven off. Once they finished, Lorn regarded Yangu respectfully and stepped without, his confused escort following him out of the throne room.

Terin didn't say a word until they were outside, making their way across the middle bridge.

"What ails the Yatin emperor?" Terin asked quietly enough for no one else to hear, walking close to Lorn's right.

"He is mad, or touched, as Jentra would say." Lorn gave Jentra a grin, the older soldier walking at his left.

"A mite more than touched." Jentra snorted. "He is dangerous."

"True." Lorn shrugged in agreement. "But dangerous or not, we still must deal with him until we can push back the enemy and return home."

"Yes, end this campaign so we can start the next one," Jentra stated the grim truth.

"I don't understand what happened back there," Terin said

"The emperor's sudden change in demeanor?" Lorn asked.

"Well...yes. I thought he might kill us, and all of a sudden he speaks as if he was a different person."

"Oh, he did mean to kill us," Lorn said, matter-of-factly.

"Then why didn't he?"

"Because of you, Terin."

"Me?"

"Yes, you. The blood of Kal is a powerful force to behold when properly applied," Lorn explained.

"But I didn't do anything."

Jentra snorted at that statement.

"You believe that?" Lorn lifted a curious brow as they reached the middle of the bridge, their hair lifting in the breeze.

"I...I don't know."

"You glowed like the blasted sun," Jentra said.

"Glowed?"

"Yes. The power of Kal rose up in you, cleansing Yangu's troubled mind...for a time."

"For a time?"

"Yes, for only Yangu can permanently change his heart. Your bit of magic was a temporary fix. It afforded us time to step away before the madness returned. Once it does, he will vent his fury upon whomever is near, creating conspiracies on the unfortunate wretch who suffers his gaze," Lorn explained.

"Then we are doomed unless we can soon drive Thorton off." Terin sighed.

"Have faith, Terin. Yah has not led us here to be undone by Yangu's fragile mind. We hold the stronger position, and Thorton can do little but harry our supply routes."

"We hold the stronger position, but we have a city to feed, while his troops can eat the trees if they must," Jentra said bluntly.

"Perhaps," Lorn paused, stepping toward the side of bridge, setting his hands upon the low stone parapet that ran the length of the causeway. From this height, they could see beyond the west bridge for some distance downstream, where the Muva lazily wound its way around a bend in the river, before disappearing into the forest. "We have safeguarded Mosar from the current gargoyle threat. The city's fate now rests yonder, to the sea." Lorn waved an open hand westward.

"Faust," Jentra affirmed, naming the Yatin port strategically positioned at the mouth of the Muva.

"Faust," Lorn said, as the Torry Elite fanned out around him, guarding their crown prince, while listening to his explanation. "We can resupply the city by sea via the Muva. The gargoyle raids on our convoys along the river will grow weaker as we thin their ranks. The fate of Mosar rests upon our ability to hold Faust. The Benotrist Navy will force the issue. If they seize Faust, the game is up, and Mosar will starve."

"That is why you sent Grand Admiral Klan to reinforce the Yatin Fleet," Jentra said. Lorn sent the Torry grand admiral before departing Cagan, leading the 1st and 3rd Torry Fleets to Faust, adding their strength to the Yatin 3rd Fleet.

"Where he will face the might of Tyro's armada and the cunning Admiral Mulsen. The Benotrist admiral is a brilliant strategist, as his victory at Tenin proves. He destroyed the 1st and 2nd Yatin Fleets with little cost of his own," Lorn explained.

"A lot of good we can do him here. We've got our own troubles," Jentra snorted, looking northward where Thorton sat hiding somewhere in the forest with ten thousand gargoyles.

"The Army cannot help them, but Admiral Kilan doesn't need our Army. But we can afford to lend him certain…assets." Lorn regarded Terin with a knowing look.

"You wish me to aid our fleet?" Terin asked.

"It is a risk I believe is necessary."

It wasn't lost on Terin that Lorn used the same strategy as General Bode when he advised Corry to aid the crown prince by sending Terin and Kato in place of an Army. Armies were difficult to move and might not reach the battle until too late. Wind Racer could reach Faust within a day or two, and Terin's sword could give the Torry Fleet a decisive advantage.

"I know you must feel as a game piece, being moved across the board." Lorn placed a hand to his shoulder.

"No, I am honored by your faith in me, Highness. I will go wherever you need me. Will Kato go with me? I think you need him to keep Thorton in check."

"I agree. Kato is needed here, but you will not be going alone. I think it only fair if you lend me your friend that I lend you mine," Lorn regarded Jentra.

The older warrior thought to protest, questioning the wisdom of forsaking his duty to guard Lorn for guarding Terin but kept that thought to himself. "When do we leave?" Jentra shook his head.

"Tomorrow morn."

*****

"What is your name?" Kato asked the young girl, squatting before her, his elbows resting on his knees.

"Aila, my lord," her voice squeaked as she backed a step, clutching her left arm to her chest, a bandage wrapped around the stump of her hand. She was obviously frightened of him, as any child her age should be of the mysterious stranger. She looked no older than five years, with dirty blond hair and expressive large blue eyes that drew fearfully large looking shyly away, hiding a vicious burn that covered her left cheek.

"Aila, that is a pretty name." Kato smiled, trying to set her at ease. The matrons claimed she was found wandering the streets alone when a Torry patrol found her and brought her to them. Hundreds of wounded still awaited treatment, many with severed limbs that required time to regenerate or lesser injuries that could wait as Kato worked on those more pressing. They managed to clear thousands of wounded from the wharves, where they were placed, too numerous for any one structure to hold. With the remaining wounded numbering a few hundred, they were housed in the storehouses along the north bank of the Muva, between the middle and east bridges. The wounded were scattered across the open stone floors of the massive structures, with little more than loose straw for a bed. Matrons hurried back and forth, tending their charges, cleansing wounds. They recruited several dozen washer women to shuttle food and water to the wounded men and civilians, while others hauled away waste buckets, struggling to contain the awful stench permeating the stale air. The large doors facing the river were kept open to clear the air, though those within suffered the biting cold for the fresh air.

Kato passed the operation of his regenerator to the matrons, freeing him for other duties, though he returned from time to time to check on them in case problems arose.

Ilesa oversaw the operation of the device, becoming quite adept with it. She reminded them that it could only work so fast and required sunlight to recharge its solar cells, so they used its power judiciously. With the most pressing patients already healed, they worked their way through the rest, selecting those whose wounds could become problematic, especially gangrenous. Kato found little Aila standing amidst a crowd of wounded men, each suffering similar injuries of missing limbs or hands.

"May I see your hand, Aila?" he asked kindly, the girl tentatively offering it. Kato smiled again, trying to set her at ease, tenderly removing the bandage wrapped around the stump of her wrist.

"Agghh!" she whimpered, the bandage pulling on the dried blood connecting her tissue to the cloth.

"Well, that's not so bad," Kato lied, examining the decay starting to take hold along the wound. Unfortunately, the matrons were overwhelmed with the number of wounded to properly treat everyone. They ran out of poultice dressings a long time ago. This wound would not have been so poorly treated in peaceful times, but there was no reason to ignore it now.

"Would you like to come with me, Aila?" Kato offered, his words failing to move her.

She stood there, shaking her head, tears running down her cheeks.

"I'll make it better, I promise," he pleaded with expressive eyes to match her own.

She reached out as he lifted her into his arms, carrying her to the front of the warehouse where Ilesa finished treating an injured Yatin's broken leg. The dozen soldiers guarding the matron backed away as Kato stepped near, each regarding the Earther with deep reverence. He was called the *Great Wizard* by the men, appreciating his wondrous instruments of healing and death, a champion to match Thorton just as Terin matched Morac.

"She is next, Ilesa," Kato said, setting Aila upon the table where the healed Yatin climbed down from testing his leg.

"Thank you, Mistress Ilesa, Master Kato," he cried happily, stepping away.

The young matron thought to voice her objection, pointing out that soldiers came before civilians, but knew better than to question Kato.

"Let me see the child," Ilesa said, carefully lifting her arm, examining the vicious wound. She stifled a gasp, seeing the decay already festering before giving Aila a false smile to reassure her. Whoever tended her wound did a poor job. She doubted it was one of her sister matrons, for the wound wasn't even cauterized.

Kato picked up the regenerator, setting it over Aila's wrist, as Ilesa placed the arm on the table. Kato stared through the optic, the outline of the girl's missing hand taking shape in luminous red on a green field. As soon as the image completed, he pressed the initiate light.

"Be still, child," Ilesa commanded, holding the arm in place, as Aila cried, trying to pull away.

"It tickles!" Aila squealed, a beady feeling coursing her growing flesh. She stared saucer-eyed as the hand slowly regrew, the decay disappearing with the new tissue expanding from her wrist. Aila gasped as the *magic* restored her hand, lifting it before her eyes, working her new fingers.

"Well? How do they work?" Kato asked.

"My fingers!" she said, wiggling them excitedly.

"That answers that question." He laughed. "Now lie down, Aila." She gave him a guarded look before complying.

"Now, let's see what we can do about this," Kato said, placing the device over her burnt cheek.

*****

"That was kind of you," Ilesa said, wrapping her cloak tightly about her shoulders. She found him standing alone along the wharf, staring out across the river, lost in thought. She recalled the rumors surrounding the Earthers, imagining them differently, cruel and ominous. How wrong she was, she scolded herself, at least as far as Kato was concerned. He was charming and gentle, caring as much for the poorest of the people as he did his comrades. He was intelligent as he was powerful, taking precious time teaching her more about her craft than anyone on her world could ever know. She never heard tell of a male healer, as men lacked the *nurturing* touch and empathy of the fairer sex.

"Healing a child isn't kind, it's just basic decency." Kato shrugged as she stepped beside him.

"Basic decency *is* kindness, Kato. You are a strange man." She laughed, shaking her head.

"Strange looking, maybe." He smiled, touching a finger to the corner of his eye. The Araxans found his appearance bewildering, especially the upturned corners of his eyes. All the Earthers were different and unique to the Araxans, whether it was Lorken's darker skin, Brokov's light skin, or his strange eyes. Or their larger stature, especially Raven's. He knew he was an oddity to these people, who strangely resembled the Middle Eastern humans of Earth, though smaller, beardless, and olive skin with varying shades. Even that was not an accurate comparison. Araxans seemed delicate and exotic, almost breathtakingly beautiful in a way, a different race of humans altogether.

"Different looking, perhaps, but still quite handsome." She blushed, the words escaping her lips. She didn't mean to say that but found herself out of sorts whenever he was near.

"Now *you* are being kind, my lady." He winked, putting her at ease. He was always putting her at ease; she reminded herself.

"Honesty is not kindness," she said, wondering why she was still talking, digging her hole deeper. She still recalled the moment they shared along the riverbank several nights before.

"Handsome, huh." He smiled, calling out her forwardness. "That reminds me of something my grandfather once said."

"He called you handsome?" She made a face.

"No, not that. He said he could prove there was a god."

"A god?"

"Yes. He could prove it because only a divine power could give beautiful women low self-esteem so they would settle for us." He grinned.

"Are you claiming all men are beasts?"

"Pretty much, yes. We are completely unworthy of your beauty, but we appreciate it all the same."

"Are you mocking me?" She lifted a flirtatious brow.

"I just called you beautiful. Does that sound like mocking?"

"Beautiful?" she asked, liking the sound of his voice describing her so.

"Very beautiful. And kind."

"I don't feel very kind, Kato. I would not have healed that poor girl before all of our soldiers were healed first, as protocol demands. It rends my heart the decisions I must make, deciding who lives and dies by cold logic." She lowered her eyes, overwhelmed by fatigue, these past several days taking their toll.

"Making hard decisions is not cruel or cold. Your decisions are made for the greater good, and only a kind heart can be trusted to make those decisions, a kind and strong heart." He touched a hand to her shoulder.

And so they talked for a time. He told her of his adventures in Space Fleet and of their coming to Arax, explaining it in a way she could comprehend. She spoke in kind of her home and kin. Her family were landed gentry with a vast estate in Vilacia, near Tuk. That much he already knew from their previous talks. As the daughter of a wealthy house, she was expected to marry upon serving her apprenticeship as a healer. Her mother would likely find a suitable match, and she caught herself dreaming of her own preferences, of a man from a far-off world named Kaito Nakamura.

*****

Kato's voice rang out in the night air, a small crowd gathering around as he sang a rendition of Bobby Vee's "Take Good Care of My Baby." They were drawn by his lively tune, the strange melody piquing their interest as passersby stopped to listen along the riverfront. Others built a bonfire from the broken timbers of a sunken galley, warming themselves as they took a brief respite from their troubles.

"Do you have another song?" a Torry soldier called out as Kato finished the last verse.

"Well, let me think," Kato said, taking a seat on a short, overturned barrel, staring into the crackling flames of the bonfire as a hundred pairs of eyes looked expectantly at him, before deciding on "Dream" by the Everly Brothers.

Kato sang, the romantic melody much softer than the previous tune. He noted the effect it had on those gathered around the fire, each staring quietly into the flames, swaying with the music, each lost in thought. He saw Torry soldiers, Yatin soldiers, Yatin merchant sailors, citizens, and matron healers in the sea of faces. He knew music was a balm to laden hearts but underestimated its effect on these weary souls. He followed that with "Dyamako Bushi," the song of the mountains, an ancient ballad from his homeland, the one his mother would sing to him as a baby, rocking him to sleep. He caught Ilesa's moist eyes staring back at him from across the fire before waving her over.

"That was lovely." She gifted him a smile as he stood, offering her his seat. She thought to refuse his kindness, but he gently touched her shoulders, forcing her to accept.

"Where I am from, Ilesa, it is customary for gentlemen to offer their seats to ladies. You wouldn't want me to break with tradition, would you?"

"If you insist." She smiled, wondering how he stripped away her defenses, turning her protest into eager acceptance. He gave her an infectious smile, beginning another song called "Daydream Believer," an ancient ballad originally sung by a group of bards strangely called the Monkees.

He reached out his head, pulling her back to her feet, singing as they danced, holding her closer than appropriate, but she didn't protest. Her heart quickened, staring up into his dark-brown eyes that twinkled with life. The Earthers were a strange lot, she surmised, bold and mischievous. Her mother would be aghast with the liberties he was taking, but to her it felt natural. He was a foreigner, an alien actually, and yet he fit her perfectly, as if she had known him her whole life.

Once Kato finished, a Yatin soldier started to sing an ancient ballad known throughout Arax as the "Weary Soldier." His began low, barely above a whisper, only rising with his growing courage, as others joined in, the familiar melody reminding them of home.

> I long for home
> Please grant me peace
> Let me rest beside the river
> Let me sleep upon the shore
> When I fight no more battles
> When I fight no more wars
> I'll return to my home
> Kiss my lady love
> Hold my baby boy
> Then I shall fight never more
> And forsake these awful wars
> To dwell in the valley
> Where lies my home.

Kato listened as they sang, marveling at the touching moment. Here they were, Yatin and Torry alike, each longing for home and loved ones, bound together through blood, sacrifice, and friendship. He would sing with them if he knew the words. He felt Ilesa's right hand interwoven with his left, squeezing softly, liking the feel of her touch. The lyrics lacked the rhyme and prose of a poet's ballad, probably of a peasant origin, but its words touched a nerve with the laymen and women gathered round.

Terin made his way along the wharves, following Lorn and Jentra, who were just up ahead, drawn toward the growing crowd and festive music. They arrived at the conclusion of Kato's song and the beginning of the crowd's rendition of the "Weary Soldier." He was surprised to hear Lorn and Jentra joining in, standing in the back of the crowd, unnoticed until they were spotted by those nearby. A hush followed, running through the crowd as soldiers began to take a knee.

"Arise!" Lorn commanded, spreading his hands in an upward manner, calling them to their feet. "I enjoy a good song as much as you. Please, continue," he said, standing apart as the crowd gave way.

Jentra remained steadfast at his side, wary of an assassin's knife striking out from the dark, where any number of threats could lie in wait. Terin was the opposite, feeling quite at ease, lost in the melodies as the crowd continued in song. A few Torry soldiers who had kin in neighboring Teso recited a ballad from that small kingdom. This was followed by several Yatin songs, most of which were drinking ditties. One, however, stood out, an ancient ode to fallen Tarelia. The singer was a lad, no older than Terin. He wondered why the boy would know such a ballad, considering the Yatin Empire displaced the old Western Kingdom established by the Tarelian Order.

> Telfa, Oh Telfa
> Our mighty King
> Who vanquished the gargoyles
> From this sacred land…

The boy continued.

Terin was taken aback, forgetting the Tarelian influence that once ruled this land.

"Who was King Telfa?" He overheard Jentra ask.

"He was the general sent by the Tarelian Order to vanquish the gargoyles from this land. He established the Western Kingdom and wielded one of the lesser Swords of Light," Lorn explained.

"Oh." Jentra spoke no more of it, knowing the lad was singing his own death song if one of Yangu's spies overheard him praising the fallen Tarelian Realm that the Yatin invasion displaced.

Terin stared numbly into the flames, thinking of Corry and his promise to return. Did Lorn know of the dire state of Torry North? He couldn't be absent if Morac returned. Only his sword could match the Benotrist lord's. *One more battle,* he reminded himself. One more battle and he could return home, to Corell, to…her. If he closed his eyes, he could see her visage staring back at him, her bright-blue eyes smiling as they found his. He now understood what Cronus felt when he promised to return to Leanna, only to be dragged farther away. He felt as if a noose was tightening about his throat, pulling him to the west, to the sea, and farther from her arms.

"Terin," Kato called out, drawing him from his melancholy.

"Kato," he greeted his comrade as the Earther stepped near, exchanging pleasantries with Lorn and Jentra, while Ilesa bobbed a curtsy before the prince, standing at his side.

"Lady Ilesa," Lorn regarded her before clasping Kato's arm. "I approve your choice of companions."

"My time with her has been quite educational," he said, causing Ilesa to blush. Lorn smiled, recognizing her interest in the brave Earther.

"Lady Ilesa, walk with me." Lorn offered her his arm, leaving Terin time to bid his friend farewell.

"I wish you were coming with me," Terin said.

"So do I. I promised the princess that I would look after you, but I can't leave Thorton outside these walls unchecked," Kato lamented.

"You bear the greater burden. I should be staying to look after you."

"I can handle Thorton. You just keep the sea-lanes open or we'll all starve." Kato slapped his shoulder.

"Thank you, Kato, for everything."

"It is my pleasure, Terin. You just keep safe, or your princess will have my head, and Lorn's as well."

*****

"Are you certain?" Lorn asked.

Ilesa nodded, regarding her crown prince with fierce determination as they stood apart from the others.

"And he feels the same?" he asked, looking at Kato standing among the others, lost in conversation.

"Very much so. My mother is not here to approve, but as regent, you can bless our union. I am certain they would approve my wedding to a member of your High Elite."

"You would hasten such a thing?"

"Time is fleeting, My Prince, and never more so in war. I would know such happiness in the time we are given, for no one can know where these troubled winds may take us."

"Very well, my lady." He placed his hand upon her head, granting his blessing.

They returned to the others, where Lorn had Kato confirm his feelings for the Lady Ilesa. Jentra and Terin looked on in dismay as their friend professed his love for one of their own.

*****

It was a simple ceremony, with the King's Elite and the Guild of Matrons gathered around them as they knelt upon the wharf on the north bank of the Muva, with Lorn addressing their small assemblage.

"The Lady Ilesa and Kato of the King's High Elite deserve a far grander ceremony than this, a ceremony as worthy of any other, heralded throughout the Torry Realms with praise unending. Alas, it is not to be, we precious few standing in substitute for their deserved assemblage. Ilesa, the fair and lovely, I hold you in great esteem, a blessed healer and worthy mate for our brave Kato. And, Kato, friend of the Torry Realms, member of our High Elite, and savior of so many, I extend the hand of friendship and kinship." Lorn smiled, taking Kato's hand and placing it in Ilesa's.

"May your union be blessed!" Lorn declared, drawing them to their feet, where Kato took his bride into his arms.

*****

They stole away before dawn, heading south, their magantors' wings kissing the treetops before breaking west, staying beyond Thorton's line of sight. Jentra kept his magantor on Wind Racer's wingtip, the winter air contorting his face as the rising sun warmed his back. They cut northward after a time, finding the Muva, following it to the sea.

CHAPTER

14

Siege of Mosar stage six
Two days hence

The late morning found Kato upon the upper battlements of the north center redoubt, scanning the distant tree line through his rifle's scope. Cool air escaped his lips in smokey vapors as he made out the familiar winged forms gathered amidst the foliage. If only he knew Thorton's location, he could risk blasting the damnable creatures wherever he found them, but he couldn't risk exposing his location. He expected to find Ben somewhere in his scope doing the same thing, looking for him along the walls of Mosar.

"First shot wins," he whispered to himself, his scope sweeping slowly east to west. Kato donned a Torry helm and cloak to help mask his features, but Ben was certain to see his rifle he held in his hands. This was the second time he dared look for Thorton since the battle, the first being the previous day when he scanned for just a brief period. With Terin gone for two days now, he questioned the wisdom of risking his life this way. If Thorton killed him, there would be no one here to oppose him, all their effort gone for naught. He had to be careful, very careful.

"Two more minutes and I call it a day," Kato whispered, his scope stopping suddenly at a familiar shape poking out behind a tree trunk. He zoomed in, making out the details of a laser rifle, following the length of the barrel, where the black sleeve of a Space Fleet jacket was visible, the rest of Thorton's body concealed behind the tree. It was him, all right, the jacket clearly Earth made.

Zip!

Kato's blast struck Thorton's right elbow, burning a large hole through the joint.

Zip!

His follow blast struck the upper trigger mechanism of Thorton's rifle before it lowered with his ruined arm. Kato held his aim as Thorton's body slid to the ground, clutching his elbow to his chest. Oddly, the rifle never left Ben's hand, as if it was glued in place. He scanned to both sides of the tree trunk, waiting for Ben to emerge from either side. He couldn't bring himself to kill him, and with a ruined elbow, he might not have to. He could make out Ben's left shoulder peeking out from the opposite side, his back resting against the trunk of the tree. He could just send a blast through the tree if he upped the setting on his rifle but thought to give Ben a chance. Kato had him trapped, and he knew it.

"Come on, Ben, give it—"

Zip!

Thorton's blast took Kato's right hand at the wrist as it gripped his rifle. Kato slipped behind the bulwark, his hand dangling from his arm by the barest tendrils of flesh, the sound of his rifle clanging of the stone floor, ringing in his ear.

*****

"Stay down, Kato," Thorton growled, training his pistol scope on the place where Kato slipped below the battlement.

"Agghh!" the Yatin prisoner whimpered off his left, clutching his shattered elbow, his watery eyes staring at Thorton with contempt as he sat on the ground, his back leaning against the tree.

"Clever trick." Neon grinned, standing farther back in the tree line. Thorton waited several days for Kato to take the bait, forcing the Yatin captive to don his jacket, tying his arms to the rifle but away from the trigger.

"It took long enough," Thorton snorted, keeping his scope on the upper battlements of the redoubt, ignoring the pained sounds of the crippled Yatin. He spent untold hours waiting patiently for Kato to fall for his ruse, wondering if he wasted his time, until Kato struck his decoy.

"Ah! But your patience is rewarded," Neon said, stepping near to the Yatin prisoner, certain that he wasn't in Kato's sight before running his dagger across the prisoner's throat. He cut the binding fastening the fellow's arms to Thorton's rifle, tossing the weapon to Thorton, who holstered his pistol and inspected the rifle for damage. Kato blasted a hole clean through the upper trigger assembly, rendering the weapon useless. If he was back on the *Stenox*, he could repair it, but not here in the wilderness.

"Fetch my jacket," Thorton said, drawing his pistol to resume scanning.

*****

Ilesa's heart went to her throat when they brought him through the door, carrying him upon a litter with him holding his nearly severed right hand with his left. She rushed to his side, the blood draining from her face while examining the vicious wound.

"Can you help him?" Prince Lorn asked, standing at his opposite side as she looked up into the prince's desperate eyes.

"Set him there." She directed them to an open space on the storehouse floor.

"It's all right, Ilesa, just do as I showed you." Kato forced a smile, trying to set her at ease.

She quickly fetched the device, hoping it had enough energy to do the job, after she just finished restoring a soldier's severed foot. Regrowing limbs was taxing for the regenerator, the lengthy process taking significant time and power. That was why Kato always treated amputees last unless a major artery was involved. She fumbled the device, her nervous fingers afflicted with worry.

"Relax, you've done this hundreds of times now," Kato assured her, ignoring the throbbing pain running north of his wrist.

"Hundreds of times on others, but not on you. Now be quiet," she scolded, holding the device over his hand before activating it.

"Wow, that does itch," he said as his hand regrew.

"My gratitude, Lady Ilesa," Lorn praised, as she released a pregnant sigh.

"Thank you, My Prince," she said before giving Kato a hard stare.

"You look angry." He smiled, wiggling his fingers.

"Your *friend* did that?" she asked.

"He could've killed me, so I guess I should be thankful."

"So he crippled you instead."

"In all fairness, I thought I crippled him first, but it was likely a decoy. I should have known Ben might pull that one, it's the oldest trick in the book."

"Oldest trick in the book? You have a tome dedicated to such things?" Lorn asked curiously.

"One of his Earth expressions, most assuredly," Ilesa said, giving her husband a disapproving glare.

"It means he was clever, and I wasn't." Kato shook his head, gaining his feet while working his hand. "Looks as good as new, Doc." He winked at her.

"Another Earth idiom?" Lorn asked, Ilesa's nod affirming it so.

*****

Two days hence

The magantor patrol approached the city from the south, kissing the treetops to avoid Thorton's line of sight. They returned from a long patrol, heralding good tidings. The Yatin 2nd Army had arrived at last, marching from the eastern border, General Yitia marshaling twenty-one telnics, four shy of their full muster. They were still three days' march from Mosar. The news spread like wildfire through the ranks, lifting their spirits, but displeasing Lorn, who hoped to keep it secret lest the enemy discover their approaching doom and slip the noose. If Thorton was the leader he believed him to be, he probably already knew. Kato had yet to chance the wall again, waiting for others to fix Thorton's location before engaging his old friend.

Most distressing to Lorn was Emperor Yangu's growing anger with General Yitia, whose Army was finally arriving. Yangu blamed their late arrival on the general's obvious treason, delaying his Army in hopes that the gargoyles destroyed the Yatin emperor so as to name himself emperor of the realm. A wise man would point out that the 2nd Army's levies were dispersed along the eastern border in remote locations at the outset of the invasion. Mustering them required time, a fact no one dared mention to the fragile mind of the crazed emperor. Fortunately for Yitia, his Army was still a few days off, affording Lorn time to divert Yangu's attention to other matters. These tactics only distracted Yangu for a time before his thoughts returned to Yitia. New concerns swirled around the *treason* of Yitia's subordinates, as many of his levies were drawn from eastern provinces with known loyalties to the old Western Kingdom. Yangu thought to send his next eldest son, Prince Yaglar, to assume command of the 2nd Army. Yaglar was a boy of ten and as unsuited for command as Prince Yanku was at Salamin Valley. General Yoria and Prince Lorn convinced Yangu to change his mind on this tactic, pointing out the danger of sending the young prince beyond Mosar, where the enemy could fall upon him as they did his brother.

"One lost prince was a terrible blow to your realm, Emperor Yangu, a second would be devastating to the people," Lorn sagely advised, catering to Yangu's vanity.

*****

Two days hence

The morning found the enemy gone, the gargoyles having withdrawn during the night.

Once the patrols returned with news of Thorton's withdraw, Lorn called for a council of war in the imperial palace. Nearly a dozen commanders of rank gathered in the council chambers, including Yakaron, the new commander of the Mosar garrison, his predecessor having fallen at the outset of the siege; General Yoria, commander of the 1st Yatin Army; General Farro of the 4th Torry Army; and General

Cornyana of the 2nd Yatin Cavalry, who stood beside General Avliam of the 4th Torry Cavalry. Kato and Lucas attended as well, standing behind Prince Lorn, who stood across the map table from the Yatin emperor. Kato observed several court ministers gathered behind their emperor, including one dressed in voluminous crimson robes and dull yellow eyes that seemed to stare right through him.

"The enemy has fled," General Yoria declared, opening the council.

"North, I hope, whence they came," Yangu spat.

"We believe so but need verification. I sent magantor patrols east and west along the river. They returned shortly before this council, reporting nothing for thirty leagues in either direction," Lorn said, sweeping his fingers along the length of the Muva, as depicted on the map.

"What of the area north of us? Did you not think to send them there?" Yangu mocked.

"General Avliam?" Lorn called upon his cavalry commander.

"I have patrols covering areas here, here, and there." He pointed out a large swath of territory extending north of Mosar. "Two patrols reported contact somewhere in this vicinity, as well as heavy sign leading in that direction." He pointed out a position twenty leagues northwest.

"Then they are not attempting to engage Yitia's Army," Yoria voiced his relief that the enemy was truly withdrawing.

"Send word to Yitia to make for Mosar with all haste. I want the capital reinforced," Yangu commanded.

Lorn knew if General Yitia reached Mosar that Yangu would likely have him slain. "Emperor Yangu," Lorn said respectfully, before advising against such a move. "The enemy is on the run and presents no threat to the capital. We have an opportunity, a very narrow one, to pursue them before they reach the safety of Telfer or Tenin, joining their strength to either garrison."

"You would have me further bleed my armies?" Yangu questioned suspiciously.

"To the contrary, Emperor Yangu. If we can destroy the remnant of Yonig's main Army, it will ensure the sovereignty of your empire," Lorn advised.

"And if Tyro sends another legion, my armies would be caught far from their supply chains and spread thin, allowing Tyro and his damnable Earther to destroy them in detail."

"There are risks in every decision," Lorn agreed.

"Risks I shall not take, Prince Lorn. It is *my empire* in the balance, not your precious Torry Realms."

"All of our lives are at stake, Emperor Yangu, and none more so than my men and I!" Lorn thundered, his harsh tone taking Yangu and the gathered commanders by surprise. The time for niceties had run their worth, and Lorn would not further suffer Yangu's aspersions.

"Do not play me false, boy! You are here to steal my realm, using the pretense of your god to proselytize and turn my people against me!" Yangu spat.

"We have traveled far, leaving behind our kin and home to aid your dying realm, receiving naught from you but ungratefulness and suspicion. *No more!*" Lorn thundered. "It is I who fights for your city and people in the foremost ranks, whilst you sit safely in your palace. My men have shed blood defending your lands, Yangu. Would you have done the same for us? Every man here knows the answer. How do you reward these favors? With treachery!"

Lorn's rebuke split the chamber in half, Yatins gathering to one side, and Torries the other.

"I know who stands behind you, Emperor Yangu," Lorn called out Minister Shatero, whose dull yellow eyes flared with surprise.

"You dare—" Yangu protested before Lorn cut him off.

"You dare, Yangu. Did you not order your minister of inquiry to take a hostage from among my circle to extract confessions of betrayal from their lips? Any fool would know such witness under pain of torture is likely false."

Yangu's eyes drew wide with alarm, wondering how Lorn learned of that, sharing a look of betrayal with Minister Shatero.

"You are mistaken, Prince Lorn, I have taken none of your men captive," Shatero refuted.

"Because you failed, and not for lack of trying. Do you care to state that this is not so?" Lorn challenged.

Shatero closed his lips, unable to utter a falsehood to Lorn's face, beguiled by the prince's strange power.

"I thought not." Lorn shifted his attention fully to Yangu, who seemed to shrink before him. General Yoria closed his eyes in shame. He knew Yangu's mind was fragile, but this plot went beyond madness. The Torry-Yatin alliance was on the brink of collapse. Only Yangu could embrace defeat with victory finally within their grasp.

"How…" Yangu started to ask, his addled brain unable to finish the question.

"How did I know of your betrayal? Yah revealed it to me."

"Yah?" Yangu's eyes drew even larger.

"Yah, whom you deny and mock, and holds dominion of our mortal realms. Yah the creator, Yah the redeemer, Yah who in his benevolent mercy called me to lead our Army here, to save your people."

"Your god is not my god," Yangu whispered weakly.

"My god is God, whether you acknowledge him or not. I have not called you out before this council to slay you or break our alliance. I have held my tongue since our first meet, knowing this day would come. You have many sins to answer for, Emperor Yangu, but I am not your judge. That responsibility falls to Yah."

Yah, the false god of the Tarelian Kingdoms, Yangu thought bitterly.

"Not the Tarelian Kingdoms," Lorn spoke aloud Yangu's thoughts.

Yangu's jaw dropped, awestruck by Lorn's power.

"Had the Tarelian Realms truly followed Yah, they would not have fallen to ruin. They were faithful to Kal's Kingdom, but not to the god that raised Kal up, not with their hearts anyway. The old Western Kingdom that your ancient kin displaced did not worship Yah, and they fell. You can avoid their mistake, Yangu. The choice lies before you. You can embrace Yah, preserve your empire, and receive his blessing, or you can reject him and suffer his judgement."

"Are you threatening me?" Yangu mustered the strength to answer back.

"No harm will befall you by my hand or any Torry. Yah will pass judgement, and he alone will deliver it. As for me and my men, we march north!" Lorn declared, striking his fist upon the map.

The commanders gathered about the table stared at where he struck, eyeing the port city of Maeii, which rested forty leagues south of Tenin along the Yatin Coast.

"Maeii?" General Farro lifted a curious brow.

"Maeii," Lorn affirmed, tapping his fore digit upon the map where the port city rested. "I've already sent a magantor to Faust, ordering Grand Admiral Kilan to surround the port after defeating the Benotrist Armada sailing south from Tenin. We will complete the envelopment by land, along this line of march." Lorn ran his finger from Mosar, northwest to Maeii.

"You can't hope to catch the gargoyles along that route. They will simply head due north, Prince Lorn," General Farro pointed out the obvious flaw. "The gargoyles can outpace us, and we will be limited by our lines of supply."

"They could head north, but I don't believe they will. Yonig's legions cut a wide swath through central Yatin, scorching and devouring the land as they went. There is little left there to feed their Army on the way back. The lands to our northwest are yet untouched. They will follow this route, breaking north somewhere short of Maeii. Our cavalry can race ahead, harassing and herding them south and west, until we can catch them. Every man will pack twenty days of hardtack, and we will eat as we march. The fleet will resupply us once we reach Maeii."

If we reach Maeii? Yoria thought somberly. The Army could suffer any number of problems en route, and there was no certainty of victory at sea. The Benotrists had a very large armada. Their armies might reach Maeii only to find a Benotrist Fleet waiting for them. In that event, Tyro could just as easily commit another legion to the campaign and slip them behind them. He shivered at the thought of their armies far from resupply, caught at Maeii between the Benotrist Fleet and a gargoyle legion. The gargoyles wouldn't even have to fight them. They could simply let them starve and walk over their bones after.

"You will order General Yitia to move north immediately," Lorn looked Yangu in the eye.

"He is a traitor. I do not trust him," Yangu insisted.

"He is no traitor, but even if he was, would it not be wiser to keep him far from the capital and between you and the gargoyles?" Lorn logically pointed out.

Yangu bowed his head, resigned to cooperate. Lorn knew well that Yangu might have been tempted to betray them once they marched north, but his little display here removed any such notion from Yangu's mind.

"So what are we waiting for? We're wasting daylight," Kato said, making his way to the door.

*****

"I don't know if I can manage it without you," Ilesa said, wishing her words could influence him to stay with her.

"You sell yourself short, my love. You are far better than I. I've seen you handle it with a care I could never match. You have the healer's touch. I trust you with the regenerator more than myself."

"I hate being separated from you. You are too important to scout in the advance parties. You should remain with the main host." *You should remain with me* was what she truly meant.

"I can save more lives killing gargoyles. Do not fret, Ilesa. I will join you at Maeii." Kato smiled, losing himself in her light-purple eyes.

"Maeii is far away, and the way is perilous."

"All will be fine. We shall go north. We shall meet in Maeii and take the high road back."

The high road. She smiled, recalling the story he told her that night when she first realized that she loved him.

"Forgive me my fears, Kato. I am remiss to worry you so. I…I have treasured these nights we have shared, treasured my time with you." A pleasant shudder coursed her flesh, recalling the intimacy they enjoyed. The love they shared was beyond imagining, all-consuming, and pure. How could a single act be considered both disgusting and beautiful based solely on the intent of the actors involved? The answer was as clear as the sun above. Intimacy was symbiotic with love. Without love, it was only lust, fleeting and cold.

"Don't apologize for your fears, my love. They are merely our brains advising us to be cautious. The way is dangerous, but nothing in this life is without risk. Our lives are brief, mere snippets of time in the greater expanse of the universe. They are precious only to us and those who know us. Don't hold tight to what we might lose but to what we have shared. Those moments, those beautiful precious moments are eternal. They live on long after our days have come to end." He hooked a fold of her black hair behind her ear, taking her in his arms, kissing her gently. They remained in each other's embrace for an eternal moment before he mounted his ocran and rode off through the north gate of the city.

Terin stood upon the prow of the *Torry Wind* as the warship cut the cresting waves. The morning sun slipped through the gray sky, lighting the right side of his face, the lapping waves echoing dully in his ears. The Yatin coastline rested several leagues off starboard, its gray jagged cliffs silhouetted against the rising sun. Terin wrapped his cloak about his shoulders to fight the biting air, staring longingly at the endless expanse, the wine-dark sea running beyond the horizon to his northwest. They departed Faust two days past, driving north for Maeii, hoping to cut Thorton's escape. Dozens of Torry galleys preceded their vessel, the vanguard of a vast armada seeking battle with the Benotrist Fleet somewhere to their north. When Terin and Jentra first reached Faust, the Yatin 3rd and Torry 1st Fleets had already engaged the Benotrist 5th Fleet in three skirmishes, several leagues north of the Yatin port. Nearly a dozen warships were lost to each side, neither fleet able to gain traction against the other. The small battles were a tactical victory for the Torry-Yatin alliance, preventing the Benotrists from seizing Faust and cutting the vital supply route to Mosar. By the time Terin reached Faust, the alliance fleet was reinforced by the arrival of Admiral Nylo and the Torry 4th Fleet, along with two massive warships, the magantor carriers *Elohim* and *Bandor*. With these reinforcements, and the services of the Torry champion at his disposal, Grand Admiral Kilan proceeded north to give battle to the Benotrist Fleet, before advancing to Maeii. The grand admiral kept the 3rd Torry Fleet in reserve, transferring several of its galleys to the 1st Fleet to replace their losses and assigning the fleet to secure the supply routes to Mosar, leaving him the Torry 1st and 4th, along with the Yatin 3rd Fleets to give battle.

Thoughts of a coming battle were furthest from Terin's mind as he stared forlornly in the distance, losing himself in the endless sea. His memories swirled around the one person that consumed his waking thoughts. He cared not for his duty or destiny, cursing their encumbrance for drawing him farther astray, farther from her arms. He fondly recalled the last time he traveled these waters, sailing north to Tinsay aboard the *Stenox* to rescue Cronus. He was so enamored with the wonders of the ocean at that time, nearly overlooking the wonders of that ship. He sorely missed the speed of Raven's vessel, cursing the slow-moving war galley he found himself upon. He wished nothing more than to engage the enemy, seize Maeii, and be done with the Yatin Campaign so he might return to Corell, to home, to her. The more he thought on it, the slower the ship seemed to move. The first day out of Faust, there was no wind, forcing the fleet to row its way along the coast while following the current where they could. The weather soon changed, the darkening sky gifting them favorable southerly winds. For now. Of course, favorable winds could just as easily turn sour, and sailors held no greater fear than being caught at sea during a storm.

"Brooding again, I see," Jentra said, resting his forearms on the bulwark beside him.

"Just thinking." Terin sighed, not wishing to reveal what was truly on his mind, or who.

"You are as moody as Prince Lorn. I can't count the times I've seen him staring at nothing."

"My apology, Jentra. I guess I haven't been a good companion," he regarded the older warrior.

"No need to apologize. I'm not one for idle chatter anyways."

"You sound like Torg." Terin smiled.

"So you've said."

"I didn't mean to offend," Terin quickly withdrew his remark.

"It's no offense to be compared to your grandsire, Terin. There is no warrior I respect more than Master Vantel. Here, have a look," Jentra said, drawing his sword, offering its jeweled hilt to Terin.

He lifted the weapon from Jentra's outstretched arms, his eyes drawn to its cloudy blade. The blade was murky white and black, the two colors ever shifting along its length, with tints of silver appearing and disappearing as he turned the sword. The cross guard was black steel, arcing toward the tip of the sword, protecting the wielder's hands, with sapphires and emeralds embedded along its reverse side.

"It's beautiful," Terin gasped, wondering if its properties were akin to his father's sword.

"A masterpiece, forged by a master craftsman unequaled since the smiths of Tarelia forged your wondrous blade," Jentra said with pride.

"If I didn't know, I would have believed it be a Sword of Light. Where did you find it?"

"It was given me by the man who forged it, a gift for my service to the realm and my being named Elite Prime and protector of the crown prince," Jentra said proudly. The designation of Elite Prime was second only to Torg within the Elite.

"Whoever it was, was a master indeed."

"True, there is no one finer than he."

"Who was he?"

"Your grandsire, Torg Vantel," he said, thinking Terin would've figured that by now.

"Torg." Terin shook his head, marveling at his grandfather's work, recalling the blades he forged for Miles Standarn.

"Aye, he personally forges swords for every member of the King's Elite, taking great pride in their quality, making each sword specific to its master, striking a perfect balance of strength and weight."

"I didn't know." Terin wondered if Torg would forge one for him.

"I am surprised you didn't. The war has likely delayed him in finishing your blade."

"He might not do so for me, considering…"

"Considering no blade he forged could match the one you bear?"

"Yes." Terin shrugged sadly. He would like nothing more from Torg than a sword crafted by his own hands. It would be a part of Torg that Terin could take with him and perhaps pass on to his own children one day as he told them stories of their famous great-grandsire.

"Every member of the Elite receives a blade crafted by Master Vantel, and you will be no different. He will not overlook you because of the wondrous weapon you wield. Every member of the Torry Elite takes great pride, not only in the blade Torg forges for them, but the fact that their commander, the second-ranking man in the realm, does so personally."

"I doubt Torg will have time considering his present duties." Terin sighed.

"Only a fool would doubt Torg Vantel, and you don't look a fool to me, boy."

"Oh, I am a fool, Jentra. At least I feel so." He shrugged.

"You're a humble lad, I'll give you that. Anyone else who possessed your ancestry and that blade would be a right smug twit. I've seen plenty of highborn lads whose arrogance exceeded their ability. I expected not to like you," Jentra recalled that night in the wilder lands when Terin came to their camp after fleeing the siege of Telfer.

"That is fair considering the tale I spun upon our first meet." Terin smiled at the memory.

"Aye, an unbelievable yarn, but a true one it now appears," Jentra snorted, regarding his flight from Fera and the battle at Telfer, lamenting the bad tidings that followed.

"I didn't know you felt so strongly about me then."

"Just my distrusting nature, which I blame our prince for."

"Lorn? He seems quite trusting."

"Aye, too trusting. As his guardian, it falls to me to exercise an equal measure of restraint and distrust with those we encounter, else he'd get himself killed," Jentra growled.

"And now he sent you away with me," Terin said, understanding what troubled Jentra's mind.

"Aye, to protect you as I did him, but it's truly a waste. Lorn's decisions were rash but strategic in nature and well-thought-out, affording me time to adjust and intercede as best I could. Your rash decisions are immediate and on a tactical level, where I can do little to aid you. I spoke with Lucas before we departed Mosar. He was to guard your back in battle, as per Princess Corry's order. How could he do so when you fly off on your magantor at the slightest whim whilst Lucas was afoot and without warning of any kind. I'll have to do my best to keep you alive, an even harder task than I had with our reckless prince. At least with him my old bones could keep pace. So keep me in mind when the battle starts and you speed off toward the enemy."

"Cronus scolded me many times for losing him in battle." He smiled.

"He sounds sensible, I like him already," Jentra grunted.

"I know you would like him. He is much like you, a great warrior and a true friend."

"What he did at Tuft's Mountain speaks to the man's courage, and what you did to free him speaks to yours."

"No, all I did was go along. Raven and Lorken are the ones that freed him."

"How many of Tyro's soldiers died by your sword during your escape?"

"I…I don't know." He shrugged.

"Hmm…Too many to count. That is more than merely *going along*. You put yourself in danger for a friend. I respect that."

"From you, that means a lot," Terin said gratefully.

"Praise should never be freely given. It should be earned. Anything less taints its worth."

"You sound like Torg again." Terin laughed.

"Cantankerous and old, that sounds like me," he confessed.

"You are not old, Jentra, you just like to say you are."

"Now you sound like Lorn."

"Then I am honored." Terin gave a mock bow before giving him back his sword. "I could never replace Lorn, but you can take Torg's place when he passes."

"Me? Replace Torg?" He nearly burst in laughter at such an absurdity. "Only the House of Vantel holds the post of master of arms and commander of the Torry Elite," Jentra reminded him.

Terin was taken aback, forgetting that Torg spoke of their family's unique place in the Torry Realm. There was something amiss about his explanation that slipped his mind at the time. Torg's post was supposed to go to his son once he came of age and sired an heir, whereby Torg would resign and pass on his knowledge to his grandson, as his own son took up his post. Torg's son had two grown sons already, and yet Torg remained at Corell, serving the Crown as he had done for decades. He asked Jentra of it, the older warrior thinking on it for a time until his face broke in understanding.

"That's it," Jentra said.

"That's what?"

"I once overheard one of the lads asking Torg when his son would take his place, seeing that Torgus had long since come of age and sired two sons of his own. He said that his grandson would take his place and that he would retain his post until that day. I always thought he meant one of Torgus's sons, but the grandson he meant was…you."

"No." Terin shook his head. "I know nothing of forging weapons or his strategic brilliance. It might have been true if I was named his apprentice at an early age, but none of my instruction—"

"You are his heir, not of House Vantel, but his post as commander of the Elite."

*****

Three days hence

He scanned the horizon, spying dozens of tiny forms in the distance, breaking the horizon along the surface of the sea. Terin pushed Wind Racer further, the cool air pressing upon his face as he moved north for a closer look. The great avian swept well below the darkening sky, his wings kissing the white caps of the choppy surf. Terin barely held on, following Wind Racer's lead, the bird strangely knowing his intent. Two magantor riders from the *Bandor* accompanied him, one to each flank, their riders deftly maneuvering their mounts in the shifting winds. Terin marveled as they moved as one, rider and mount, the fruit of twenty years in the saddle. He wondered if they thought him false, after hearing his exploits at Fera and Corell. Without the madness of the blade guiding him, he looked completely out of sorts in a magantor saddle, though Wind Racer went far proving otherwise.

They pushed on, driving hard until the distant forms took shape, empty mast poles rising above massive hulls, with two rows of oars jutting from their sides. Terin urged Wind Racer skyward, soaring well above the lead vessel, the ships' crew firing arrows from their upper decks, their shafts falling pitifully short. They circled the lead vessel, their magantors' wings shifting in the uneven wind, observing the sigil of the Benotrist 5th Fleet lifting above the forward mast, a golden ship upon a field of red. Craning his neck left and right, Terin spotted the enemy fleet stretched to the horizon. A quick guess put the armada over one hundred vessels, perhaps more. A broader search would likely find more beyond the horizon, but they wouldn't risk venturing any farther, circling the lead vessel before speeding south, returning to their fleet.

*****

Regula stood upon the deck of his flagship *Pang*, his dull red eyes staring intently over the unforgiving sea. He assumed overall command of the Benotrist Armada, the 5th and 2nd Fleets to his front and the 7th trailing. Regula contemplated his dilemma having been sent to Yatin by the emperor to dispose of the insolent Admiral Mulsen, who initiated the Yatin Campaign of his own accord, defying Tyro. Such an affront required Mulsen's death. This was not a simple matter. He could not outright execute Mulsen. To do so at this critical juncture would undermine the campaign. He received the ill tidings from Mosar of Yonig's fall, further complicating his choices. If victory was already assured, he could not execute Mulsen without sowing discontent in the Navy, which was why he needed the admiral to die in battle. Unfortunately, the advent of the Torry Fleet made victory anything but assured. He already positioned Mulsen to the front of their battle line. He would use the charismatic admiral as an anvil, meeting the enemy host, head-on, with the eighty-four warships of the 5th Fleet, the once massive fleet reduced from its pre-invasion strength of one hundred and twenty. Admiral Kruson's 2nd Fleet would follow in support with twenty-seven vessels, leaving the fifty ships of Admiral Onab 7th Fleet in reserve with fifty galleys,

307

along with the magantor carriers *Morbus, Croon,* and *Temurs.* The three massive warships were instrumental in smashing the 1st and 2nd Yatin Fleets at Tenin.

Regula knew the Yatin 3rd Fleet was somewhere to his south. His magantor scouts spotted their purple sails full with the wind, driving north to meet him, the same fleet Mulsen's 5th Fleet engaged at Faust. There were mixed reports of the Torry 1st Fleet reinforcing the Yatins at Faust, with scant information pertaining to their strength and disposition. The Torry 1st Fleet was commanded by Grand Admiral Kilan, and Regula doubted Kilan would have come alone. For all he knew, there could well be two or three Torry Fleets sailing north with the Yatins. He was not a naval tactician, but he understood military strategy and the principles that applied to both land and sea. The Torry-Yatin Armada wouldn't be sailing blindly into battle. Torry magantors repeatedly tracked their position, reporting their strength to Kilan. Knowing this, the Torry grand admiral would not be rushing into battle unless he had forces to match. There was power behind the Torry Fleet. He had seen enough Torry magantor patrols to suspect at least one magantor carrier in the Torry Fleet, perhaps more. If there was one unfortunate truth, it was that the Torries were better magantor riders than the Benotrists. The Torries mastered magantors for centuries, while the Benotrists just decades. In fact, only the junior ranks were filled with Benotrists. After Tyro's ascension to power, he recruited scores of magantor riders from many eastern freeholds to train and build the Benotrist Magantor Corp, offering rank and privilege to each one. The recruits quickly assembled a mighty magantor corps and convinced their former freeholds to join the Benotrist Empire, fueling much of Tyro's early expansion. Even now, the majority of the upper magantor command was filled with the former freeholders, including General Naruv, who surprisingly fought beside Tyro throughout the revolution. Some say it was his influence that convinced Tyro to recruit the freeholders to begin with. It was Naruv who held overall command of the Benotrist Magantor Corps and served high in the emperor's council. Regula grudgingly acknowledged that without Naruv's help, the empire could never have built their magantor carriers, let alone man them.

"My lord?" Captain Velo, captain of the *Pang*, asked, awaiting Regula's command.

"Give the order to Mulsen to advance on the enemy, with Kruson to support him."

"And Admiral Onab?" Captain Velo craned his neck, staring over his shoulder, where Onab's 7th Fleet trailed them.

"Inform him to follow us," Regula said, bright crimson flashing briefly in his eyes.

"And where shall we lead him, Lord Regula?"

"Mulsen is the anvil. We shall be the hammer."

*****

Grand Admiral Kilan stood upon the foredeck of the *Vigilance*, his flagship and the pride of the 1st Fleet. The massive warship had a double hull, its main deck 48 feet beam, and 268 long, boasting an array of large crossbows and trebuchets along her upper and main decks. Four rows of oars jutted prominently from each side, one more than the next largest ship in the Torry Navy. An iron ram jutted prominently from the bow, its head cast in the visage of a magantor, its silver beak cresting the waves.

Kilan stared briefly to the upper masts, their blue sails furled despite the favorable winds, his oarsmen merely holding position, awaiting the enemy fleet. Staring east, the ancient ruins of Carapis circled an inlet cove, broken white columns jutting skyward like skeletal remains. It was once a bustling colony of the old Soch Empire, a key stopover along their trading routes, until the ground shook the city to pieces, casting down its building, rendering the port useless. The cove and its surrounding waters were now littered with jagged rock formations just below the surface, ripping apart the hull of any ship daring to draw near. A series of quakes followed in the proceeding centuries, further demolishing the once proud city. No one dwelt there now, the city and its surrounding area a desolate, barren wasteland. Sailors believed the region haunted, sharing tales of phantom voices issuing from its ancient ruins, carrying on the wind as their ships passed the shore. Kilan traversed these waters many times upon merchant ships in his youth but never heard a sound as the old mariners described. Others claimed to have seen ghostly apparitions floating above the shoreline, beckoning them hither. He never saw that either, consigning such things as superstitious nonsense. What wasn't false were the physical dangers the region presented to ships that passed near the shore, risking their hulls opening on jagged rocks that lay just below the water. Even now he could see two half-sunken merchant galleys, rotting near the shore, their wrecks likely caught upon the rocks below the surface. One was there since he was a lad; the other was newer, its state of decay placing its demise five to eight years in the past.

Kilan gazed westward, eying the islands of Donah Carapis, some five miles off shore, each nearly as desolate as the ruins of Carapis. Most of the islands were little more than piles of rocks scattered over several leagues. Two, however, were quite large, simply named the north and south isles. Each was nearly two miles long and a half mile abreast at their widest. Each ran northeast to southwest, with the north isle resting slightly farther east of the south isle, with a deep channel running between the two isles. 'Twas there where Kilan positioned Admiral Nylo and the 4th Torry Fleet, with its thirty-eight warships, the rocky summit of the north isle shielding them from view of the approaching Benotrist Armada until they drew danger-ously close.

Kilan set his weathered hands upon the bulwark, releasing a heavy sigh, the late afternoon sun obscured by the darkening sky. Much rested on the day's outcome, the fate of the Yatin Campaign and perhaps Torry South itself, their fates in the balance by the bat-tle's outcome. The Torry 1st Fleet, with fifty-eight warships, waited just south of the isles of Donah Carapis, with the Yatin 3rd Fleet, with its thirty-two warships aligned to their east. The magantor carriers *Elohim* and *Bandor* remained well behind the armada, their precious warbirds essential to his plans for victory.

"You couldn't have picked a more morbid place for a battle, Admiral," Jentra's gruff voice echoed, stepping to his side. "What's the name of this dreadful place?" he asked, lifting his chin toward the shore.

"The fabled city of Carapis," Kilan answered as if Jentra should've known.

"Carapis? I thought the city was larger than that pile of rocks."

"It was grand enough in its day, but these ruins are sixteen centuries old. They say all glory is fleeting, as are the graveyards of dead civilizations. The ruins you see now are a poor reflection of the grand city that once stood there. Look yonder to the north isle off our portside bow. Do you see the gray heights upon its center?" Kilan asked him.

"Looks like more rocks."

"Yes, but those rocks were once the watchtowers of Donah. The beacons lit upon their uppermost battlements could be seen for many leagues, guiding ships to and from the isle, where the Sisterhood now rule. Those ancient towers helped ancient mariners reach the home isle of the Soch Empire, resting north and west from that point. The towers once stood the height of twenty men, if the legends are to be believed."

"Donah?"

"They were named after the first sea lord of Soch, whose corsairs founded their empire, eventually gaining dominion of much of northwestern Arax. Their empire stretched from Faust to Tinsay and as far inland as Laycrom."

"And the Isle of the Sisterhood, so the legends go," Jentra recalled.

"The isle was their capital, the home of their ruling class," Kilan added.

"And their greatest weakness," Jentra recalled the legend of General Melida, who invaded the isle and slew the Soch king Vagar at the port now known as Bansoch, establishing the federation of the Sisterhood.

"Yes, the Soch kings were betrayed by their arrogance, allowing the exclusively female slave population on the isle to grow out of proportion and control. Some believe it was as high as one hundred to one. When Melida's small Army landed upon those shores, she easily fomented rebellion and overthrew the Soch. Once their king was slain, the remaining strongholds of the Soch quickly capitulated."

"Why? They still controlled much of the interior as well as ports along the coastline."

"Their position in the interior was fragile, as were their remaining holdfasts along the coast. Tenin and Faust had already fallen to the old Western Kingdom. Their remaining coastal position was long and thin, and with enemies at their back and front, their unity fell apart."

"Their empire doesn't seem very impressive if it fell so easily."

"They believed their home isle secure, thinking women could never rise from their chains. Their home isle was also their most fertile land. Without it, they were doomed."

"The Gorga Valley was fertile enough. And if not, they could've retaken Tenin. The Tenia Valley—" Jentra tried pointing out.

"The Tenia is not fertile, and the Gorga is only navigable up to the convergence of the Andler. The Muva is fertile and navigable, but the Soch only had a tentative hold of Faust for a brief period. By the time of Melida, they had lost hold of all lands south of here, as well as Tenin, and mighty Carapis was long shaken to ruin." Kilan waved an open hand toward the jagged coastline.

"Bad luck, then." Jentra shook his head.

"Bad geography and poor choices," Kilan continued. "One, you might overcome, but the two together will doom even the strongest of realms."

"Aye, the Sisterhood has likely endured since then due to their rich lands and isolation, while Torry North is surrounded by hostile realms."

"True, but Torry North possesses the most valuable lands in all of Arax."

"How so?" Jentra made a face.

"The Stlen and Pelen river valleys contain the most arable farmlands in the world, and both rivers, along with the Nila, are navigable."

"You can move armies on roads as well as rivers, and we have hundreds of roads traversing Torry North," Jentra pointed out.

"Armies, yes, but for merchants moving goods, the cost of overland transport is many times the cost of sea transport. When you factor in the costs of maintaining roadways, the cost grows even higher."

"Perhaps you are biased, being a sailor since you could walk," Jentra said.

"Wars are won on land, but wealth is won on the sea."

"But right now, it is the war that counts," Jentra pointed out, gazing off starboard at the war galleys cresting the waves, counting nearly a dozen trioars in the 1st Fleet, their offset oar structure striking a balance of power and speed. The rest of the fleet consisted of smaller but swifter bioar, whose double decks of oars were offset by their sleeker hulls. The ships of the fleet ranged anywhere from 150 to 220 feet in length, and twenty-seven to forty-one beam, the only exceptions being the massive *Vigilance* and the magantor carriers trailing the fleet. Most of the vessels had an upper inner deck overlooking a lower deck circling the ships. Giant crossbows and catapults lined the decks, the larger trioars possessing larger arsenals, with the lighter bioars boasting longer rams upon their prows.

Farther off starboard, the purple crests of the Yatin 3rd Fleet lifted in the breeze. The Yatin Fleet consisted of bioar vessels, with a dozen single-oar deck ships. All their heavy galleys were sunk at the battle of Cull's Arc, north of Tenin, leaving the thirty-two galleys of Admiral Horician's 3rd Fleet the only remaining ships in the Yatin Navy.

"Is the boy ready?" Grand Admiral Kilan asked, catching sight of Terin standing upon the deck of the *Torry Wind*, some two hundred meters off their portside bow, his snow-white magantor perched upon the deck beside him. Terin and Jentra spent the journey moving from ship to ship, familiarizing themselves with the ships of the fleet, though finishing each tour upon either the *Torry Wind* or the *Vigilance*.

"The boy is never ready but somehow manages to win the day. He shall be there when and where you need him most. Just don't include him in any of your plans. The sword will guide him where he is needed."

"That is inconvenient," Kilan snorted. A great tactician allocated his resources accordingly. Terin was a game piece that moved freely across the field of play. To an admiral like Kilan, that was maddening.

"Inconvenient, perhaps, but effective. I've seen him in battle at Mosar, and what he did to the gargoyles…" Jentra lacked the words to describe what he saw.

"We're not fighting gargoyles this day but men of flesh and blood. I doubt they'll scare as easily," Kilan said dismissively.

"It's a fair argument, Grand Admiral, but once you see Terin in battle, you'll understand."

"They say he is the grandson of Torg Vantel."

"Aye, that he is."

"I'll place my trust in that."

"You have your doubts. I did also."

"Only a fool wouldn't. Our future king orders our fleets north against unknown strength, and this boy is sent to balance the scales? It reeks of desperation or…madness."

"That *boy* slew Yonig. He flew his magantor into the middle of the enemy host and struck him down. The craziest thing I ever witnessed. He performed similar fell deeds at Telfer, Corell, and Fera, if the witnesses can be believed, and I believe them."

"So be it," Kilan relented.

Harroom!

Horns sounded from the lead ships, calling crews to arms. Within moments the horizon came alive with crests bearing the sigil of the Benotrist 5th Fleet, a golden ship upon a field of red. They pressed against the wind, furled masts offset by oars cutting the waves. Kilan counted at least twenty sioar (single row of oars) vessels spread out in a skirmish line along the enemy front, with the heavier bioar and trioars trailing in their wake. The Benotrist Fleet would soon pass the mouth of the channel between the isles of Donah Carapis, spotting the 4th Torry Fleet waiting therein.

"Give the signal!" Kilan ordered.

A sea of blue masts unfurled across the Torry 1st Fleet, full with the wind, drums echoing in the bowels of the ships, the oarsmen adding their strength to speed the vessels north.

The purple sails of the Yatin 3rd Fleet unfurled thereafter, joining the Torry charge. Braziers blazed upon the decks of both fleets, their crews preparing to hurl fire ballistae upon their foes. Between the isles of Donah Carapis, Admiral Nylo ordered the 4th Torry Fleet forth, their gray sails unfurled, speeding northeast for the Benotrist right flank.

The Yatins deployed their dozen smaller sioar galleys forward in a single skirmish line, mirroring the Benotrists, joined by eight bioar galleys of the Torry 1st Fleet. The smaller vessels shifted with the surf, their crews struggling with the mounting waves. Fire ballista arced from the upper inner decks as the lines of ship drew in range. One Benotrist munition struck true, striking the forward mast of a Yatin sioar, flames consuming its purple sails. Most ballista flew harmlessly awry, the wind carrying Yatin and Torry munitions over their targets and forcing Benotrist munitions into the sea short of their mark. Within moments, the lines of ships were too close to miss, fire ballista erupting across the decks of a dozen ships. A Torry bioar met a Benotrist sioar head-on, both rams glancing off each other, oars snapping as they passed port to port. The larger Torry vessel spewed heavier fire as they passed, fires engulfing the Sioar's single trebuchet, its crew jumping into the sea, flames licking their flesh. Further east, one Yatin and two Benotrist galleys ran afoul of jagged rocks below the surface, the sea pouring into their broken hulls. Two other Benotrist ships struck a heavier Torry bioar from opposite sides, their rams punching large holes amidships starboard and port, the vessel's lower hold filling with water as the Benotrists reversed oars. Another Torry vessel struck a Benotrist sioar center port, the sound of buckling timbers echoing dully over the pressing wind. The Torry and Yatin ships furled sails upon contact, lest the wind drive them northward into the heart of the Benotrist Fleet trailing two hundred meters behind. The main body of the Benotrist 5th Fleet followed the skirmish line, its sixty-four vessels arrayed in three separate wedge formations, side by side. Each formation had a larger wedge of fifteen to seventeen bioar vessels, with a smaller wedge inside it of five larger trioar galleys.

Admiral Mulsen stood upon the deck of his flagship *Torch,* a massive quadoar (four rows of oars) galley, nearly of a size to Kilan's *Victorious* and the only quadoar in the Benotrist Armada, other than the three magantor carriers. Mulsen overlooked the battle from the upper inner deck, standing behind the bow as the battle unfolded before him. His flagship was the tip of the inner wedge of the center formation. The sound of drums echoed in his ears from the lower hold, setting the oar slaves' pace. The bioar ships forming his outer wedge tightened their gaps as they drew near. His orders were clear to all captains: smash through the skirmish line and converge on the center of the alliance fleet, where Kilan's flagship was likely to be. His lookouts reported the Torry Fleet up ahead, forming into two wedge formations, and the Yatin 3rd Fleet in another wedge, nearer the shore. He spied a Torry bioar off his right, slip beneath the waves. Farther west, a pair of Benotrist sioars listed severely before disappearing amidst the surf. The surviving ships in the skirmish line broke off, each maneuvering to escape the colliding fleets.

"The west!" the lookout shouted from the crow's nest, pointing excitedly as the fleet passed the north isle of Donah.

Mulsen caught sight of the gray sails of the Torry 4th Fleet passing between the isles of Donah, driving northeast toward his right flank. He half expected such a tactic and shifted accordingly, signaling the right wedge of his fleet to engage the Torry 4th Fleet, and ordered Admiral Kruson's 2nd Fleet to fill the gap. The damnable southerly winds allowed the Yatin-Torry Fleet to close upon him with full sails, whilst his ships relied upon oars. Once the battle was joined, however, they would have to furl their sails, negating that advantage. Mulsen knew he needed to avoid the Yatin-Torry rams at the outset due to the speed the wind granted them.

The Torry 4th Fleet and Mulsen's right wedge met first, the Torry ships striking them just east of the Donah Isles. Admiral Nylo kept his sails full mast, driving his ship into the Benotrist wedge, keeping full speed, Benotrist ballista finding easy marks upon his sails. Four Torry masts burst into flames, Benotrist munitions striking true. The Torry crews returned fire, flames splashing against the hulls of the bioars forming the outer wedge. The Torry helmsmen avoided direct contact, skirting Benotrist prows before turning into their flanks. The sound of rams breaking timbers echoed over the din, delivering mortal blows to six of the Benotrist bioars. Two Torry vessels succumbed to flames ravaging their decks. Hundreds of sailors jumped into the cold sea, many disappearing beneath the choppy waves.

Further south, the rest of the Benotrist 5th and 2nd Fleets approached the Yatin-Torry Armada. Mulsen could see the upper masts of the *Vigilance* as his wedge neared the Torry center, knowing Kilan was one of the silhouettes standing upon its upper deck, staring back at him, their two flagships separated by the outer wedges of their respective formations. A Torry bioar struck the lead vessel of his outer wedge, the ram buckling timber along the portside bow. The stricken ship lifted slightly into the air, the Torry ship snapping oars as it pulled away. The Benotrist vessel planted three fire munitions into the Torry bioar, flames splashing upon its lower masts and bow. The Torry vessel responded in kind, fires erupting along the Benotrist galley's upper deck, with seawater flooding its bow, the ship dipping into the ocean. Mulsen cursed as the lead ship foundered, swallowed by the sea.

Dread filled Mulsen's heart as winged forms emerged along the gray southern sky, counting more than thirty magantors drawing nigh. That meant Kilan had at least two carriers trailing his armada. He cursed Regula taking his own carriers with the 7th Fleet to the west, leaving him without any air assets. The Torry warbirds were a mix of brown and gray, obscured by the darkening sky. What miserable weather for a battle at sea, he cursed, before spotting fire munitions dangling from more than two-thirds of the attacking magantors, each with a single rider. The rest carried two men, guarding the single riders from Benotrist magantors, which were not yet present. Mulsen gazed forlornly to the western horizon for his deliverance, finding nothing but empty sky.

Crash!

The sound of breaking timbers echoed off his starboard bow, another bioar along his outer wedge taking a Torry ram amidship. A dozen Torry and Benotrist vessels listed severely between his position and the Isles of Donah. Others bobbing adrift, their hulls ravaged by flames. More carnage lay to his east, ten Benotrist and six Yatin vessels listing or burning, their crews chancing the frigid waves.

"Give the signal to close ranks!" Mulsen commanded his aide. If the Torries wished to ram his ships, he'd be sure to respond in kind. "Concentrate all arrow ballista on the approaching magantors, keep the fire munitions trained on their ships!" he added, his eyes warily fixed to the winged formation drawing nigh.

"Admiral! Look!" his aide shouted excitedly, drawing his attention off the portside bow as a large white magantor drew dangerously near, far ahead of its fellows.

"Fire!" Mulsen commanded his crew, wondering why they let the Torry warbird so close.

A giant shaft sped from the forward ballista, its crew reloading as its spear hurled toward the magantor, the bird's breast fully exposed. Mulsen's intense stare gave way to disbelief, the bird's rider rising up in his saddle, knocking the shaft awry with a swing of his blade, a bright azure glow bursting along its length.

*****

Terin swept through the smoke-filled air, the fires of burning wrecks twisting into the stormy sky. Wind Racer soared over the debris of broken ships and warring galleys, enemy arrows falling short as he passed. Terin fixed his gaze upon the massive quadoar at the center of the Benotrist Armada, its crest blowing fiercely in the breeze, a golden ship upon a field of red, lifting high upon its forward mast. The power of his father's sword drove him toward this vessel, forsaking all else as hundreds of pitched battles raged all around him. He felt the power surging within, urging him to draw his sword, luminous blue light bursting from its silver blade, bathing him with otherworldly power. Wind Racer dove toward the portside bow of the ship, its stunned crew gaining their wits, loosing a shaft upon them. Terin knocked it away, his sword sweeping below Wind Racer's breast after he rose in the saddle and twisted to the side, stretching out at an impossible angle. The bird's eyes blazed with fury at the ballista crew as they hurried their next salvo, the shaft passing through empty air, the massive warbird crossing over the bow, circling the face of the flagship before setting down upon the starboard bow.

Terin sprang from the saddle, his blade catching the nearest crewman at the elbow. He spun around the stricken foe, taking another across the waist. An arrow whizzed past his shoulder as he moved to the end of the bow, cutting down a commander standing there, a single braid adorning the shoulder of his dark leather tunic. Arrows rained overhead, several Benotrist archers taking aim from the inner deck above. Terin spun his blade, knocking arrows away while advancing across the ship.

"Kill him!" Mulsen shouted as Terin advanced, cutting down his men like straw figures.

Terin raced up the wide stairs, running from the bow to the upper deck, two warriors blocking his ascent with raised shields and leveled swords thrusting between their seams. He brought his blade across their shields in a wide arc, splitting the tempered steel like parchment, blood flying off his sword as it cleared, proof that his deep slash cut true, before their cries had time to issue from their throats. He spun to his left, his blade catching one of the soldiers below the knees as his shield fell away. Terin crossed over, engaging the second soldier as the first slid off his legs, his screams rending the air.

"Fire!" Mulsen shrieked in octaves higher than he intended, urging his archers to finish the intruder.

*****

"By the spirits, he's worse than Lorn!" Jentra growled, approaching the bow of Mulsen's flagship, the glow of Terin's blade illuminating the vessel like a lit beacon. Arrows rained down upon the Torry champion, and dozens of swords rushed to challenge him, but every shaft went awry, and every blade proved false as Terin swept over the upper deck. Jentra's magantor dodged an errant spear fired from a nearby ship, the shaft fluttering in the wind. He grumbled a few choice words, lamenting the impossible task given him by his prince of guarding a madman. The boy was clearly touched, flying forward of their fellow magantors into the heart of the enemy. Only magic or dumb luck protected Terin from the volleys of ballistae and arrows sent his way or the swords raised against him. Jentra knew no such luck extended to his own sorry carcass. His only saving grace was that the enemy was otherwise occupied with Terin. He set down before the bow, upon the inner deck amidst dozens of corpses littering the upper deck, a collage of archers, ballista crews, and soldiers. Terin was already approaching the stern of the vessel, dozens of bodies piled between them. Jentra raced along the deck, struggling to avoid the obstacles strewn across his path, bodies, ropes, and pooling blood creating a hazardous path to navigate.

Mulsen withdrew to the stern, running down the stairs at the opposite end of the upper deck, nearly losing his feet as he touched the lower deck. Reaching the stern, he turned back, frantic eyes following Terin's advance, the Torry champion cutting down two more soldiers atop the stairs with effortless grace, his fierce blue eyes finding Mulsen's below.

Mulsen swallowed past the lump in his throat, trying to will his limbs to act, but they betrayed him. He wanted to jump ship but could only stare forlornly as Terin descended the stairs, unworldly light emanating from his sword. Mulsen's hands gripped the rail of the stern, keeping his feet with the rise of the ship.

Thunder rolled across the sky, the wind whipping his face as Terin strode forth. Mulsen drew away, leaning as far back as the rail would allow.

"Please, I…" The words died in his throat.

Slash!

Terin's cut was swift and true, his blade passing through Mulsen's boiled leather mail, taking him below the elbow and across the chest.

There, upon the deck of his flagship, Mulsen met his end. Terin did not know who he had slain, only that he was an admiral by the four braided cords adorning his shoulders and the red cape with the fleet's sigil sewn into its rich folds.

"Terin!" Jentra's voice carried over the wind.

Even without his comrade's warning, he sensed the danger drawing near. He turned as a dozen soldiers rushed onto the deck from the lower hold, issuing from a stair beside the one he descended.

Split! Split! Thrust!

Benotrist blades snapped as he tore into them, his thrust finding purchase in the lead soldier's breast. He yanked his blade free, spinning around his dying foe, catching another at the arm.

Jentra raced down the stairs, cutting into the Benotrist sailors from behind, striking the trailing warrior at the back of the knee, the blow sending his face to the deck. Jentra didn't waste a moment finishing him, taking the next in the back, driving the point of his sword through his gut before twisting it free. The fellow wore only a woolen tunic, aiding the killing blow. Those still standing between Terin and himself turned back, forsaking the battle and their wits to flee. Jentra stepped to his left as they swept past, driving his sword into the gut of the one nearest, bashing his shield into the fellow's helm while twisting his blade free. A blue blur flashed behind his foe. He lowered his shield, finding Terin standing over the enemy dead, a dozen bodies strewn across the aft of the ship. Several escaped his fury, discarding their weapons and jumping into the sea.

"We must go!" Jentra shouted over the wind as rain droplets began to fall. A Benotrist bioar off their portside erupted in flames, Torry magantors sweeping overhead, depositing three fire ballistae across her deck. The aft ballista crew got off a giant arrow, piercing the trailing warbird's belly. The magantor glided briefly before dropping into the sea, its rider struggling to free himself from the saddle amid the mounting waves.

Terin ignored Jentra as if in a trance, racing down the stairway into the bowels of the ship. Jentra cursed the *madness of the blade*, as others called it. The ship was already doomed. All they had to do was tip over the braziers on the upper deck and set it ablaze. He shook his head, following Terin down the stairs. Terin ignored the next deck, racing to the one below. He was greeted by rows of oar slaves with their backs to him, running the length of the ship. The deck was alit by lanterns dangling above the wide aisle running between the oar benches. The deck was high, affording room for all four rows of oars, their benches offset throughout the length of the deck. There was a massive drum to his right but no sign of the drum master. The oar slaves sat staring ahead, wearing naught but loin garments with their legs joined in a chain coffle affixed to the deck. Their backs were scarred from countless beatings, and not one dared to look behind them, having been oft beaten for doing so.

The sound of feet running on the deck above gave Jentra cause to worry, hoping that Terin would hurry with whatever he planned to do.

Terin wasted little time, racing along the aisle between the benches, striking their shackles as he went. Jentra followed, guarding his back, the slaves staring wide-eyed as they passed, some looked down, frozen with fear, whilst others began to stir, realizing what this meant.

"Move if you want to live, or sink with the ship!" Jentra shouted.

"Agghh!" a Benotrist whip master shouted, charging at them from the bow, brandishing a sword in one hand and a whip in the other. The whip struck out, aiming for Terin's leg. The sword blocked its arc, the tip of the lash falling away as he closed on his foe, splitting his blade. The whip master's eyes went out of focus, transfixed by the luminous blue light emanating from the blade. Terin cut him in half, left shoulder to right hip, returning to strike the oars slaves' shackles without breaking stride.

"You'll find swords that way!" Jentra directed those rising from their benches toward the stern, as he and Terin continued to the bow. They fought their way through the next level, attaining the upper decks, greeted by mounting waves and a dozen more crewmen issuing from the lower hold. The Benotrists backed away as they again raced up the stairs to the inner deck, attaining their mounts and springing into the air. The ship floated adrift, her helm spinning freely and her oars still. The sound of crashing ships and clashing steel echoed in each direction. Torry, Yatin, and Benotrist vessels were intermingled, some fighting hand to hand with the battle degenerating into chaos.

*****

Grand Admiral Kilan stood upon the upper deck of the *Vigilance* as the massive warship closed on the Benotrist trioar *Gorg*, its large ram approaching the broadside of the enemy vessel. The maneuver was not without risk, bringing the *Vigilance* within range of the *Gorg's* ballista. Five ballistae splashed against the hull and forward mast, flames erupting near its furled sail. Torry soldiers crowded the bow, holding position with interlocked shields, in case the enemy tried to board her once they struck.

Kilan cursed the rising waves as they drew near. If the ram hit high, the damage would be minimal. He needed to impact at or below the waterline.

"Hold!" a commander of unit shouted over the wind, urging his men to keep their shields interlocked, arrows bouncing off their curved steel, men struggling to keep their feet with the rocking ship. A fire munition struck those gathered closest to the bow, splashing across their shields, flames licking between their seams. The Torry ballista crews returned fire, striking the *Gorg*'s upper deck, fire engulfing several archers.

Smash!

The Torry ram struck the *Gorg* just above the waterline, the weight of *Vigilance* pushing the bow lower with the wave, the ram breaking free, tearing more of the *Gorg* with it.

"Reverse oars!" the Torry captain ordered, trying to back away from the stricken ship.

Kilan held tight to the rail of the upper deck, struggling to keep his feet with the choppy sea. A large spear passed over his left shoulder, drilling a sailor behind him to the deck. He sighed in relief as his flagship drew away, the *Gorg* listing hard to port, its crew abandoning ship.

"Hard to starboard!" the captain ordered the *Vigilance* toward the next ship in line, the Benotrist trioar *Spite,* which was already engaged with the Torry trioar *Makor.* The outer wedges of both fleets had broken apart, the surviving ships engaging their foes at will. Once that transpired, Kilan ordered his inner wedge, with the quadoar *Vigilance,* through the warships to engage Mulsen's inner wedge after Terin dispatched the Benotrist flagship. His magantors further devastated the Benotrist Fleet, setting a dozen vessels hopelessly ablaze and damaging several more. He lost six magantors in the exchange, the others returning to the *Elohim* and *Bandor* to reload. Kilan lost sight of the larger battle, not able to see beyond the warring ships in his vicinity. He caught sight of Terin's glowing sword several hundred yards to his north. The boy set down on another

Benotrist galley, racing along its deck, dispatching the crew like a vengeful spirit, before again taking to the skies.

Off his starboard bow, the Torry trioar *Victorious Wind* drifted east, flames sweeping her upper decks. 'Twas the second trioar he lost so far, but the enemy suffered doubly. To their west, Nylo's 4th Fleet fully cleared the strait of Donah, driving back the right wing of the Benotrist 5th Fleet. To their east, the Yatin Fleet was giving as good as they received, trading ship for ship.

Clap!

Thunder rumbled again across the southern sky, the horizon cast in ominous gray, filling Kilan with a growing dread. Storms were any sailors greatest fear. They were bad enough in port, but to be caught at sea during a storm was a harrowing experience. Kilan sailed through many storms and twice lost his ship, surviving with determination and dumb luck. He had no choice but to press on with the enemy to his north, the rocky coast of Carapis to his east, and the storm to his south.

Where are our magantors? he thought miserably, wishing to finish the enemy fleet before pressing north, the enemy was nearly broken, another Benotrist trioar listing at its bow, and two others burning wrecks. He braced himself as the *Vigilance* rammed the *Spite* at its starboard bow, caving the Benotrist trioar's hull, the *Makor* riddling its upper deck with fire ballistae.

"Reverse oars!" the captain of the *Vigilance* ordered, the ship pulling away with the sea flooding the *Spite's* bow.

"Give the signal, Captain! Wheel right!" Kilan ordered, turning his wedge of ships toward the shoreline, taking the Benotrists engaging the Yatin 3rd Fleet in the rear. They would finish the enemy, unfurl their sails, and outrace the storm northward. That was Kilan's plan until enemy magantors appeared in the western sky.

✳✳✳✳✳

They came from the west, their dark wings blending with the caliginous sky, their large wings shifting with the winds as they passed over the isles of Donah Carapis. They split off as they passed over the south isle, twenty-five magantors angling toward the Torry 4th Fleet and twenty-five toward the Torry 1st Fleet. They were the full complements of the Benotrist carriers *Morbus* and *Croon*, leaving the air contingent of *Temurs* to guard the 7th Fleet as it approached from the west.

The twenty-five warbirds from the *Morbus* swept over the Donah Strait, striking the rear of the Torry 4th Fleet, catching their crews unawares until directly upon them. Fifteen of their magantors carried fire munitions, the others flying guard, looking out for Torry warbirds. They dove, dropping their loads before breaking off, scoring three direct hits on the Torry trioar *Vengeance*, two hits on the bioar *Queen Galena*, two hits on the trioar *Fist*, and single hits on the bioars *Dorun's Fin*, *Fluren*, and *Fost*.

The twenty-five magantors from the *Croon* broke southeast, angling for the Torry carriers *Elohim* and *Bandor*, which trailed the fleet with four bioars in support. With most of the Torry magantors engaged to the north, they were without adequate protection.

"Forward!" the Benotrist unit commander shouted, pointing his sword toward the Torry ships up ahead, his voice faint in the wind.

Crack!

A thunderclap sounded in their ears, startling their magantors. They pressed on, raindrops slapping their faces and the wind whistling in their ears. They counted three Torry magantors circling over the flotilla, their riders shifting into formation upon spotting their approach. A cautious smile touched the Benotrist commander's lips, seeing no sign of other Torry warbirds. They caught the Torry carriers at the perfect moment. Three against twenty-five would be little contest. He directed his ten guard birds forward to clear the way.

The Torry magantors broke off as the Benotrists drew near, trying to circumvent their guards to engage those with fire munitions. Guard magantors bore two riders, one driver, and one archer. The magantors exchanged arrows as they passed, their shafts fluttering uselessly in the wind. The Benotrist commander saw the futility in the engagement, ordering his munition laden birds forth, correctly believing the Torry archers could do little against them. His men shouted in alarm, their voices drowned in the wind. His magantor jerked violently as if stricken, twisting to his right, a white-gray shadow passing underneath, its rider brandishing a glowing azure sword.

*****

Terin passed under the Benotrist commander, gutting his magantor from tail to throat, the bird's innards spilling out as he veered away. He pressed on before circling about to reengage, greeted by the frightened eyes of men and magantors staring back at him with knowing dread. Wind Racer pressed into the strengthening wind and rain, fearless and resolute. He drove on the nearest Benotrist magantor, twisting into a dive as they met. Terin's saddle went sideways as Wind Racer dropped below the enemy bird so as not to entangle his wings with the chain of the fire munition dangling from the Benotrist's saddle. Terin held tight, stretching out his sword as they passed, severing the chain, sending the munition into the sea. Wind Racer straightened his wings, Terin's follow strike clipping the Benotrist magantor's tail, causing it to nearly throw its rider.

Four of the Benotrist magantors broke in panic, fleeing back whence they came. Several took evasive maneuvers, whilst the rest pressed their attack. Wind Racer circled again, closing on his nearest foe. He passed overhead, plucking its rider from the saddle, his black talons piercing the fellow's back and breast before releasing him, his screams lost in the wind.

Jentra looked on in disbelief, pushing his magantor to join the fray, watching as Terin struck down another warbird. The boy was using maneuvers that even the most skilled handlers would never attempt, doing the impossible time and again. Like every member of the King's High Elite, Jentra was a trained magantor rider, but even he could not hope to keep pace with Terin, let alone do what he was demonstrating with such ease.

"Guard the boy?" He growled in the wind. "That's a useless endeavor." He snorted. He had his hands full just trying to stay near him long enough just to say he was there. Jentra wasn't one to believe in Lorn's god, but nothing short of divine providence explained what his eyes were seeing. The boy was blessed, for no mortal could do what he was doing. Terin's warbird plucked another Benotrist from the saddle, dropping the poor wretch in the sea, his limbs flailing like a puppet on a string as he fell.

Fires suddenly erupted on the deck of the *Bandor*, the Benotrists scoring two hits on the Torry magantor carrier. Another scored a hit on the bioar *Order* before a ballista spear took the beast full in the breast, bird and rider dropping in the choppy sea.

Jentra pushed on, maneuvering his mount behind a Benotrist guard magantor, whose archer was staring ahead, looking for targets, not seeing the danger in his wake. Jentra wished he could dip under the bird and gut it like Terin, but a common blade would only glance off its hide, unless he held position long enough to drive his sword into it. The archer finally noticed him as he drew nearer, notching an arrow as he flew overhead. The arrow fluttered in the wind, bouncing off the bird's outstretched talons before they knocked the archer from the saddle and struck the driver in the back. Jentra passed on, leaving the enemy rider slumping in his saddle with a broken right arm and ribs and his archer tumbling to the unforgiving surf below.

"Packaww!" a magantor sounded beside him, Jentra finding a Torry magantor rider off his right wing, the fellow regarding him before seeking out the enemy. Raindrops obscured his vision, the weather worsening by the moment. The battle be damned. If they continued on much longer, both fleets would go to the bottom. Within moments, he began to see more Torry warbirds contesting the skies, obviously returning from battle to their north, only to run into the Benotrist magantors attacking their base ships. Visibility was becoming a problem with rain and wind picking up. He spotted a Torry warbird off his left, flying with an empty saddle. Another below and to his right struggled in the wind, a large spear piercing its left wing, hoping to reach the carrier below. He lost sight of the Benotrists, most breaking off for their own fleet. The glow of Terin's sword chasing an enemy warbird shone brightly to the northwest, away from the flotilla.

"He's the death of me!" Jentra growled, chasing after him, when they should both be setting down to ride out the storm.

*****

Both fleets disengaged as the weather deteriorated, forsaking the battle for calmer waters north of Carapis. The remnants of the Benotrist 2nd and 5th Fleets were intermingled with the Torry-Yatin Armada at times, their crews exchanging ballista fire whenever they drew near in the turbulent sea. The magantor carrier *Elohim* trailed the fleet, its oarsmen fighting the choppy surf as the steady rain turned to a downpour. The *Bandor* trailed even farther, her escort vessels forsaking the carrier, lest they capsize in the mounting waves. Both ships recovered most of their magantors, stowing the birds safely in their holds as they continued on.

"Raise sails!" Grand Admiral Kilan ordered the captain of the *Vigilance.*

"The winds will tear them to shreds in this storm or capsize us," the captain warned.

"The winds have shifted northwest. We must outrace the storm," Kilan answered, holding fiercely to the rail of the upper deck, another wave washing over the prow. Even with the oarsmen working feverishly, the captain could see them drawing dangerously near the shore. They already saw two more ships rip their hulls on the rocky shoals near the shore. Another ship off their portside stern went bow first into a wave and never came up, the whole ship swallowed by the sea.

*****

"We have to set down!" Jentra's voice died in the wind, bringing his magantor alongside his overzealous comrade.

If Terin heard him, he showed it not, his eyes transfixed, drawn to something up ahead that neither could see in this foul weather. They felled three more Benotrist magantors since leaving the flotilla. They pressed on for a time, hoping to assail the Benotrist magantor carriers that must lie somewhere west of the Donah Isles, but forsook such folly as the storm worsened, returning to the fleet. They passed several ships already, leaving Jentra to question why they hadn't set down on any of them. A sudden gust lifted Jentra's bird into the air a dozen meters above Terin, the sudden lift causing him to lose sight of the surface below. He brought his mount back down as the gust passed, his heart reaching his throat.

"I'm a fool following a madman." He growled, stating his miserable position. Jentra would have a few choice words with Master Vantel if he survived this, asking his commander to explain his grandson's behavior. He lost sight of where they were going, the visibility reduced to nothing. He could only see Terin in this rain, simply following the boy, and trusting he knew what he was doing, or trusting that the boy's sword knew what *it* was doing.

Terin swept down through the stormy sky, Jentra shifting course to follow, as a ship took shape below them.

"He isn't really going to do this?" Jentra asked himself, the color draining from his face as the ship grew ominously close, its narrow hull rising and twisting in the tumultuous sea.

Wind Racer outstretched his talons, planting firmly upon the vessel's stern, Terin dismounting in a flourish, his sword flashing brilliant in the driving rain.

Only then could Jentra see that the vessel was a Benotrist warship, a bioar, by the look of its size. With this foul weather, there would be no chance of taking flight again. It was here they would stay throughout the storm or die trying to take it. Or die trying to land on its shifting deck, he reminded himself. Unlike Terin, Jentra wasn't guided by a magic sword. He could only draw on skill and good sense. Since following Terin negated his good sense, he leaned on dumb luck instead. He wasn't trained to land in such foul conditions, so that narrowed which attribute would guide him through. He set down at the edge of the stern, the rocking of the ship smashing the portside railing against his magantor's left leg, the beast throwing him off in pain. Jentra rolled across the deck, his shoulder striking the starboard rail, a giant swell splashing his face. He groaned, struggling to gain his feet on the swaying slippery deck.

Where is he? he wondered, gaining his senses, his eyes blurred by the wind and rain, until a bluish light glowed farther ahead, somewhere amidships.

*****

Terin raced across the upper deck, cutting down crewmen wherever he found them, catching most hopelessly unaware, surprised to find a Torry warrior running at them from out of nowhere, cutting them to pieces.

Split! Split! Thrust! Slash!

He cut down two more sailors manning the center mast, trying to adjust their sails in the driving wind, when he caught them by surprise. He passed on, taking another across the back of the neck, his head flying off his blade and over the side of the ship. Jentra struggled up the stairs to the upper deck, losing his footing on the slippery deck, his knee striking the second step. Grunting a few choice words into the wind, he gained his feet, pulling himself up the stairs a step at a time, one hand on the rail and the other gripping his sword. He reached the top, only to find Terin already on the bow, able to see him by the glow of his sword through the driving rain and waning daylight.

"It might as well be nightfall with this overcast," he grumbled, before questioning the wisdom of landing on the enemy ship and killing their crew when they would need that very crew to maneuver the vessel.

Of course, Jentra thought miserably as Terin disappeared, the glow of his sword lowering out of sight in the distance, knowing he went below deck. Jentra reached amidship, counting fourteen bodies littering the deck from the stern, Terin's obvious handiwork. Where were the rest of the crew? he wondered. Only a fool would stay below deck in this storm, dooming themselves to a watery grave should the vessel founder.

*****

His father's sword stilled his pounding heart as Terin descended the wide stairs to the lower hold. The sway of the ship knocked him against the wall, his armored mail protecting his shoulder. The mail was tied off below the arm so he could lose it if he was tossed overboard. Torchlight shone dimly off the bottom step, in weak tendrils issuing from the lower hold. The sound of the oar drum grew louder with his descent. His feet wanted to set a cautious pace, sending that beady feeling up his legs, but the power of the sword commanded his flesh, pressing him on. He reached the bottom, stepping onto the upper oar deck, a hundred grim faces greeting him.

"Who—" a sailor uttered, brandishing a whip when Terin halved him at the chest, his body dropping in several pieces, his whip hitting the deck with a distinctive thud.

Terin brought his sword to the ready, scanning the dim hold for other threats. The other eyes staring back at him were chained to their benches, displaying a myriad of emotions, wondering Terin's identity and intent. They were slaves chained to their benches until death claimed them, knowing nothing but misery and the lash. They reeked of grime and sweat, even in the chill air. Their sunken eyes and gaunt faces bespoke their sorry state. They wore little more than loin garments and chains. Terin could only guess how long they served on this ship, not imagining anyone surviving such treatment more than a year, perhaps more if they were exceptionally strong. These thoughts raced through his mind as he began to strike their bonds.

"Fight or die!" he shouted, setting them free row by row.

*****

Jentra held tight to the rail of the upper deck, knowing he would never reach Terin before the mad fool was already halfway through the lower hold. He decided to stay put until Terin reemerged somewhere above deck. He tried to make out other ships in the storm, but the rain was too heavy, and daylight already gone. He thought he could make out one of the Donah Isles off portside but couldn't be certain, the foul weather blinding him to anything beyond a short distance around the vessel.

"Agghh!" the sound of fighting grew louder from the lower hold as men spilled out onto the top side deck just below him. He took a step toward the rail of the upper deck before catching sight of Benotrist sailors in their distinct boiled leather mail and tunics, fighting with half-naked men with broken chains dangling from their ankles. The Benotrists swung their scimitars to good effect, killing two for every one of their own, but there seemed no end to the number of freed slaves issuing from the lower hold. Jentra held position, letting them sort this out. He couldn't step into the fray without both sides mistaking him for their enemy.

"Where are you, Terin?" Jentra growled, wondering how long he should wait before going below to find him. Thankfully, that decision was made when Terin emerged at the stern, where their magantors were perched. Terin quickly turned, racing along the starboard side of the outer deck, leading a small Army of freed slaves, each brandishing a weapon or whatever substituted for one.

"He is my friend!" Terin shouted as he passed below Jentra, pointing him out to his *new* friends.

Jentra took that as his cue to join the fray, descending to the outer deck to guard Terin's flank. By then, the upper deck was awash with freed oar slaves overwhelming the Benotrist crew. The last holdouts were pushed to the bow, the freed slaves crowding them along the upper and outer decks. Terin moved to the fore, cutting into their close ranks, the light of his sword glowing brighter in the dying light.

Split! Slash! Split!

His rapid strokes snapped shields and swords with ease, driving the desperate Benotrist sailors back against the rail of the bow. A few climbed over the ship's side, jumping into the choppy sea. Those that remained stood helpless, transfixed by the fell power of his sword, resolved to their fate.

Slash! Slash!

Terin cut into them, desperate to end the battle as the ship drifted aimless amidst the storm. The rocking of the ship knocked half the men from their feet, friend and foe alike, many falling into the legs of those still standing. Terin's left foot slipped on the wet deck, but he kept his feet, bringing his sword down upon a Benotrist that fell at his feet, nearly cutting him in half across the back. Jentra lost his footing with an oarsman rolling into his legs, his face planting on the slippery deck. Another fellow landed on his back as he started to rise, the swaying ship making their footing impossible.

"Man the ship!" Jentra ordered once the bow was cleared of Benotrists. Jentra looked up, catching sight of Terin at the bow, his mail and blue tunic stained with blood. Rain poured off his hair, losing his helm sometime during the battle.

The freed slaves acknowledged the urgency of his command, splitting up to oversee the operation of the vessel. Some pushed to the stern to man the rudder, others to the mast poles, testing the sails' condition. The overcast sky and driving rain hindered their sense of direction. A flash of lightning allowed them to make out the coastline to their east, the ship drawing dangerously near the rocky shoals.

"We'll have to ride out the storm on this ship!" Jentra said as Terin stepped near, the glow of his sword waning with the battle's end.

"Where are we?" Terin shouted over the wind, looking starboard and port, unable to see another vessel nearby.

"I don't know, somewhere along the coast of Carapis. We should push north, perhaps set ashore once we clear Carapis!" Jentra advised, though Terin could only make out a few of his words.

Their new crew already set out to redirect the ship to the northwest, turning from the dangerous coastline. Some were former sailors before being chained to an oar bench.

"*Wave!*" a dozen voices cried out in warning, their shouts dying in the wind as a giant swell struck portside. The ship listed severely to starboard, her hull nearly perpendicular to the surface, seawater washing over the ship.

Jentra held fast to the portside rail, the strength of the wave nearly breaking his grip. The massive wave eased, the ship righting itself, tilting back in place. Jentra wiped the water from his eyes, looking around for his young comrade.

"Terin!" Jentra shouted, panic gripping his heart.

"Terin!" he shouted again, his eyes frantically scanning the deck.

"Ter…" His voice died in his throat, his eyes finding Terin's sword embedded in the deck. Jentra tried to gain his feet but stumbled, his chin hitting the deck as the ship was tossed about. He slid across the deck, catching hold of Terin's sword, ripping it from the deck, before sliding to the starboard rail. Gaining his feet, he stared over the side of the ship.

"Terin!" he shouted, seeing nothing but darkness and rain.

He was gone.

CHAPTER

16

A bright morning sun shone upon the coast, revealing what war and weather had wrought. The shores of Carapis were littered with wreckage and bodies thrown up by the storm. Broke ships jutted from the surf, their hulls ripped open by treacherous rocky shoals. The dorsal fins of versks coursed the waters between Carapis and the Donah Isles, feasting on the corpses caught in the current, with several capsized vessels drifting in their midst. The entire coastline and waters were littered with debris, a collage of broken masts, sails, and corpses drifting upon the surface.

She set ashore north of the ancient ruins, her crew fanning out along the beach, the sun rising above the coastline, paining their eyes.

"Captain!" one of her crewmates shouted, pointing out several men huddled under a makeshift canopy of broken timbers and a torn sail stretched overhead.

"Letesha, Aila," Captain Veneva ordered her lieutenants to quickly surround the canopy, trapping the fellows therein.

"I see you in there!" Veneva declared, stopping several paces short of the makeshift structure, her versk skin boots imprinting the wet sand.

No response.

Veneva nodded to one of Letesha's girls, who approached the canopy from behind, tearing the sail away, fully revealing four trembling sailors huddled in the sand. She could tell that they were Yatin by their tattered yellow cloaks and tunics. The fourth was Torry, a lad no older than fifteen. They were armed with only a knife between them, brandished by one of the Yatins, with a corded braid gracing each shoulder.

"Who are you?" the man challenged, gaining his feet on shaking knees.

"No one to trifle with, boy. Drop your knife and crawl forward!" Veneva commanded. The men were in no state to challenge them. The man holding the knife favored his left leg, a bloody bandage wrapped around his knee. His arms trembled from the cold. It was a miracle any of them made it ashore in these treacherous waters.

The Yatin commander of flax tightened his grip on the knife, his bloodshot eyes darting back and forth from one of the women to another. They were dressed similarly in black, boiled leather mail over wool shirts and fur trousers. Their hair was tightly woven in thick braids, draping beneath gray helms. Their attire was both brutal and austere. Short swords rode their hips, along with shackles and whips, indicating their grim profession. He lost count at twenty, but there were probably more.

"Drop the knife!" Veneva warned one last time, her words having no effect on the Yatin. He knew full well what grim fate awaited him if he acquiesced.

Snap!

The whip wrapped around his throat, its sound whistling in the crisp air, taking the Yatin by surprise. Letesha yanked him forward before he could think to cut her whip, the man stumbling to the sand. Veneva strode forth, driving her sword through his back, twisting the blade several times before tearing it free and chopping his neck for good measure.

"You!" She pointed her bloody sword at the others. "Crawl out of there with your heads low!"

The two Yatins and the Torry quickly obeyed, shuffling weakly through the sand before they were ordered into a prone position. Their hands were swiftly bound behind them with shackles affixed to their feet.

"Take them to the boat. The rest of you fan out! We have work to do, and no time to waste!" Veneva ordered her crew. She looked north along the coast, ever watchful for returning ships. It was strange for neither side to maintain some presence after a battle to collect their survivors, but she hadn't seen any ships the entire morn. They stopped first at the Donah Isles, collecting captives there before searching here. Most were in a sorry state, freezing, hungry, and out of their minds. She saw that look before, the glazed eyes of men who suffered trauma. They were easy prey, lying upon the beach as her crew simply collected them, though some put up a fight. If they were severely injured, she simply put them down. There were enough survivors that Veneva wouldn't waste precious space in her ship's hold for damaged stock.

"*Kill any we don't take*," she warned her crew, not wishing to leave witnesses behind. She regretted not having more than one ship at times like these. She could've made a fortune off these easy catches. Perhaps with this bounty, she could purchase a second ship, eventually building her own fleet.

*****

"This one has promise," a woman's rough voice echoed in his dream. Terin held his breath, another cold wave passing over him, drowning him in the surf. He fought his way to the surface, disoriented by the night sky and dark sea.

Terin, he heard Jentra's voice over and over again, each time a little fainter as the ship sailed away, leaving him alone, hopelessly adrift on the dark sea. He was unable to break free, the dream repeating itself time and again, fighting against the waves and cold. He had no memory of crawling ashore or wrapping himself in a tattered sail that washed up beside him. There he lay, exhausted, unconscious, and spent.

"Is he dead?" another voice asked.

The first woman touched a hand to his neck, finding his faint pulse. "He lives, Aila." She smiled, looking over her shoulder to her comrade, who stood in a wide stance, working her whip in her hands.

"Bind him!"

*****

"We must go back!" Jentra slammed his fist on the table in the grand admiral's cabin. The two men stared daggers at each other across the table, a map of the Yatin coastline spread between them.

"We must reconstitute the fleet, Jentra. We are in no position to send out rescue parties with most of our ships scattered to the winds and the enemy armada still out there somewhere!" Kilan countered.

"Without Terin, we are lost. The prince would expect—"

"The prince expects us to seize Maeii. *That* is our priority!"

"Not at the cost of Terin," Jentra warned.

"What has come over you, Jentra? I thought you were wary of the boy?"

"At first, and with good reason, but I know my own eyes and what they saw. No power on this world can replicate what I watched him do. We cannot spare him."

"I thought you didn't believe in Lorn's god. Should I count you now an apostle?"

"I don't believe in children's tales or such nonsense, but I believe the boy is blessed."

"The boy or the sword?" Kilan's eyes went to the blade now riding Jentra's hip, opposite his own crafted blade.

"You think I can summon such power by merely possessing this blade? No." Jentra shook his head sadly. "Terin was born to wield its full power. In my hand, it is far less."

"Even if this is so, you ask me to send a ship I cannot spare back to Carapis to find a boy that certainly drowned."

"He could've washed ashore."

"Perhaps his corpse, if the versks didn't claim him first, but not alive. Not in that storm or water that cold."

"You don't know that!" Jentra growled.

"I know the sea, Jentra. I've spent five decades with a ship beneath my feet. I know what men are capable of and what they are not. I wouldn't send a single vessel back to Carapis when the enemy could very well still be there in force. I won't risk the lives of many for the life of one."

"You would if that one life can save so many more."

"That's only if he lives, which I doubt. I won't waste the lives of an entire crew for odds that small."

"Then send more ships!"

"I can't spare more ships!" Kilan roared. "Of all three fleets, I've only gathered forty-two vessels. Forty-two!" he emphasized the gravity of the situation. "And one carrier, the *Elohim*." The *Bandor* was still unaccounted for along with so many other ships. They were not all sunk, with many scattered along the coastline or farther out to sea. Over a dozen had returned to the fleet throughout the morn. With the skies clear, Kilan ordered magantors from the *Elohim* to scout the waters north, south, and west for any sign of their ships and direct them toward the fleet, as well as search for the enemy armada.

"As second among the Torry Elite, I hold the authority to order you back to Carapis," Jentra warned.

"Normally that would be true, Jentra, but I obey a higher authority, the orders of Prince Lorn," Kilan reminded him of Lorn's instruction to seize Maeii.

"If the prince was aware of the situation, he would order otherwise."

"Perhaps, or perhaps not, it is not my place to guess his mind."

Jentra nodded quietly and left the cabin, making his way topside. The cool ocean air hit his face as he stepped onto the outer top deck. He shook his head at the tranquil waters with the late day sun playing peacefully off their surface.

Where were these calm waters yesterday? he thought bitterly.

The Yatin coastline rested at the edge of the horizon, a narrow strip of gray and green below the eastern sky. A flock of Soren passed over the bow of the *Vigilance*, continuing west over the lapping waves. The *Torry Wind* rested a hundred yards off starboard, half her upper deck scorched from ballista strikes. Half her catapults were charred ruins, and her forward mast broken, its sails lost in the storm. The *Smith's Anvil* rested farther ahead, half the oars along its portside snapped off from a passing Benotrist trioar. Jentra counted twenty vessels with similar damage, some with tattered sails, scorched decks, missing oars, or suffering heavy casualties. The fleet was in little condition to continue on to Maeii, let alone return to Carapis to rescue anyone. It was a fact he could concede to Kilan, though it pained him so.

Yah, if you are real, your faithful servant has need of you, Jentra said a silent prayer on Terin's behalf.

*****

By dusk, another twenty-three vessels made their way back to the fleet. Returning magantors brought news of the *Bandor* making its way northward to join the fleet. Admiral Kilan was relieved with these tidings after his other patrols spotted a Benotrist Fleet to their west, numbering thirty vessels, including the three enemy carriers *Morbus*, *Croon*, and *Temurs*. He immediately launched his air flotilla, twelve munition and ten guard magantors. His warbirds reached the enemy fleet just as the sun slipped beneath the western sky, scoring four hits on *Temurs* and two on *Croon*. Nearly a third of the attacking force succumbed to enemy warbirds and ballista.

"Light up the decks!" Kilan ordered the braziers fully lit to guide his returning flyers to the *Elohim* in the closing dark.

The next morning the sky was filled with twenty enemy warbirds sweeping over the Torry Fleet, scoring three hits on the bioar *Clorvis*, two hits on the bioar *Fortune*, and three hits on *Elohim*. Only half the enemy magantors returned to their fleet. The crew of the *Elohim* fought the flames, but to no avail. By late morn, the ship was abandoned, its surviving magantors dispersed to other ships in the fleet until the sails of the *Bandor* broke the horizon. The ship suffered numerous munitions strikes and storm damage, with only a single mast remaining to speed the ship, but it survived. The magantors of the *Elohim* were shifted to *Bandor* before Kilan ordered another strike on the enemy fleet.

And so it went for two days, the fleets striking at one another, losing the other's location and finding it again. Kilan was pleased to discover that *Temurs* was sunk after their first strike. By nightfall of the first day, *Croon* joined its sistership at the bottom of the sea. By the end of the second day, both remaining carriers *Bandor* and *Morbus* suffered near-fatal blows, both their decks ravaged by flames. Their respective magantor wings were similarly depleted, leaving the Benotrists with only eight magantors and the Torries twelve. The Benotrists suffered another four ships sunk to Torry magantor strikes and the Torry-Yatin host losing five of their own. By morning of the third day, the Benotrist Fleet withdrew. Six more ships found the Torry-Yatin Fleet, bolstering the armada.

Kilan took little solace in his apparent victory, his own fleet in little better shape than the enemy. If not for the damnable storm, he could've destroyed the 5th and 2nd Benotrist Fleets before turning their combined strength on the Benotrist 7th.

No. He shook his head. The Benotrist magantor strike upon his carriers was only stymied by the storm and Terin's reckless intervention. The battle could've been a complete disaster. Terin slew enough enemy magantors to balance the scales in their favor. Now he was gone. Jentra had taken to the skies several times to battle the enemy magantors with Terin's blade, with mixed results. Oh, it was a fell blade indeed, allowing Jentra to gut several of the warbirds from underneath, where a common blade would not, but the sword did not bestow upon him that extra dimension that it did Terin. Jentra could not drive the enemy host to madness by his mere presence, an ability that Terin demonstrated with ease.

"You asked for me?" Jentra said, stepping to his side upon the upper deck of the *Vigilance.*

"Aye," Kilan uttered, his eyes fixed to the northern horizon. "I have dispatched five ships to Carapis to search for survivors. It appears the enemy has withdrawn. You may go with them, as is your prerogative, but I advise against it."

"And why is that?"

"You and I are alike in many ways, Jentra. Our minds are martially focused. We think in concrete terms, basing our decisions on discernable facts and logic. If you ask me to move a fleet from Cagan to Bansoch, I can calculate the necessary provisions required to get there and back, based on the season of travel, the size of the fleet, and factoring hostile threats along such a route. I know this through experience on the sea and in command. If I asked you to defend a fixed point on a map, you would similarly calculate the expected strength of the enemy and the geographical strengths and weaknesses of said point. Then you would determine how many men and what resources you need to defend that position."

"What does that have to do with me returning to Carapis?"

"The principles I speak of, principles of logic, math, and reason, cannot be relied upon with the sword you now wield. If Terin was born to wield that blade, then it would not have forsaken him unless…unless it was ordained to do so by the higher power that guides it. Our prince would name that power Yah, and we can argue if this is so or assign a myriad of other explanations to its nature."

"Is there a point to all this?" Jentra asked impatiently.

"Whether Terin sacrificed himself to spare the sword, leaving it embedded in the deck of your ship, or if he was merely washed overboard, the fact remains that it came to pass by a power beyond our understanding. Terin performed feats that are impossible, that violate all the rules of logic that I explained. Make a mental list of all his deeds, and then ask how he could have been swept overboard, leaving his sword behind? Only a divine omnipotence could explain it."

"And?" Jentra growled.

Kilan slowly shifted his eyes to him. "The sword was meant to fall to your hand, and you are to deliver it to the prince. Leave Terin to me."

"Lorn would not accept that. He would—"

"Let Lorn decide that. You can do nothing to help Terin that I cannot do in your place. The prince awaits us at Maeii. We are tasked with delivering the sword to him."

Jentra was quiet for a time, staring intently into the admiral's eyes, as if thinking of some retort. "On to Maeii." He sighed, stepping briefly away before turning back. "You should know that there was a Yatin oar slave on the ship Terin liberated before he was swept overboard. The fellow is a fisherman from Maeii, where he was captured at the outset of the campaign and chained to the oar. He can point out the dangerous waters near the port to avoid and give you an acceptable map of the port."

"That would be most helpful."

"Aye. Almost as if Terin chose that ship for that reason," Jentra added, stepping away.

*****

The storm soaked the Bangor Valley, turning the trail into a river of mud. The Torry 4th Army pushed on through driving winds and rain, following the grassy edge of the impassable road. Fourteen thousand men quickly turned these grassy areas to muddy waste as well, further hindering their advance. Many were outfitted with fur trousers and cloaks to curb the winter chill, but they were quickly soaked with rain. Supply wagons fared even worse, their heavy wheels sticking in the aqueous soil. For two days the storm lingered over the vale before passing inland, but the damage was done. The good weather at the outset of the march allowed Lorn to drive his Army sixty leagues north and west, overtaking thousands of gargoyles that fell piecemeal to his 4th Torry Cavalry or herded by the Yatin 2nd Cavalry to be decimated by the Torry 4th Army. Nearly twenty thousand men of the Yatin 2nd Army paralleled his advance several leagues off his right flank. Farther to the Yatins' right were elements of General Avliam's 4th Torry Cavalry, searching for stragglers that broke north from the others. All was going well until the storm turned their advance into a crawl, delaying their assault on Maeii. By the time sun broke the clearing skies, the damage was done.

Lorn meant to curse his stupidity for ordering this march but thought better of it. He could sense Yah's will in undertaking this task and in time would understand his purpose. Such reasoning did not serve him well at present as every delay allowed more gargoyles to slip their grasp. Their methodical slaughtering of gargoyles was reduced to a trickle.

"Prince Lorn!" General Cornyana, commander of the 2nd Yatin Cavalry, hailed, his ocran galloping to meet him from up ahead.

"General," Lorn greeted afoot, leading his ocran by its reins beside a column of infantry.

Cornyana dismounted, leading the mount farther off the trail where they could speak without hindering the Army's march, Lorn's Royal Elite forming a protective circle.

"The way improves ahead, Prince Lorn," Cornyana informed him.

"What of the enemy?"

"They are breaking north, unfortunately. They must have discovered our intent, driving them to Maeii. General Yitia has reported contacts to our north and east. They were small engagements at first, a handful of gargoyles at most, but the latest reports are increasingly larger, unit size and above."

"We haven't seen groups larger than a unit since the outset," Lorn said.

"Yes, it appears Thorton ordered the remains of Yonig's legions to disperse, making their way north on their own."

"But not Maeii." Lorn shook his head.

"Not now, no, but that was their plan originally by their route of march. I believe they are now angling for Tenin or points further north. Do you wish to redirect our armies due north?"

Lorn thought on the matter before shaking his head. "No, General. We must take Maeii. We will be in desperate need of resupply, and our fleet can meet us there."

"Only if they drive off the Benotrist Fleets first."

"They'll be there, General. Yah was very clear on that detail."

"If you insist, Highness." Cornyana bowed politely, not voicing his disbelief in the prince's god. Since Prince Lorn saved his people, Cornyana didn't care what he believed. Personally, he believed in swords and strong arms to wield them, both of which the Torry prince supplied plenty to their cause.

"Highness, with the enemy breaking north into the path of Yitia's Army and Avliam's Cavalry, the way is clear for us to Maeii. Perhaps I should race ahead with my cavalry to scout the approaches to the port. Perhaps even seize it if it is unguarded," Cornyana suggested.

"How many days ride is it?" Lorn asked.

"A day's ride by ocran, and three by foot."

"How many mounts have you?"

"Four hundred thirty-seven by last count," Cornyana said, the number a far cry from the eight hundred he started with before the siege of Mosar.

"Take four hundred and thirty-seven of my men with you. Double up each ocran. They can dismount shy of the port while you scout its defenses," Lorn said.

A cunning smile played across Cornyana's face. "Aye, Highness. A simple tactic to double my force."

"Yes, and if Maeii is lightly held…"
"I will take it."

*****

Two days hence
Sixty leagues northeast of Maeii

Kato rested his hands on the pommel, his spirited ocran shifting slightly beneath him, the beast's unease giving him reason to pause.

"What do you think?" Commander Devron asked, the rest of the cavalry detachment filling in around them as they overlooked the small hamlet below.

Kato gazed across the small valley, counting a dozen thatched huts straddling either side of a small stream. A couple wooden structures dominated the center of the hamlet, Kato wondering their purpose. The surrounding farmlands were in obvious neglect, their owners having likely fled at the outset of the gargoyle invasion. The far ridge was covered in trees, obscuring their line of sight to anything that lay beyond. Kato lifted his rifle from his back, scanning the surrounding landscape through its scope. A muddy path stood out, running from his right, passing through the hamlet, and disappearing in the tree line on the opposite ridge. The trail looked recently used, likely evidence of a gargoyle group passing this way. Not a day had passed since departing Mosar without coming across gargoyles of some sort. General Avliam spread out his cavalry to cover more ground, breaking them into groups of fifty. Kato rode with Commander Devron's group since leaving Mosar, often patrolling farther afield of the other groups, overtaking hundreds of gargoyles while losing only a handful of their own.

"The village looks empty," Kato said, lowering his rifle.

"The scouts say the trail running through the vale is fresh with gargoyle sign, at least thirty," Devron informed him.

"Thirty, huh." Kato sighed. Thirty was larger than any group they came across in days. "Any hoofprints?"

"We found some sign off to our north, a half dozen riders, no more."

They were at the extreme north of the Torry patrols, meaning any ocran farther north were not theirs.

"How old were the hoofprints?"

"A day, perhaps longer."

A day or longer, Kato thought. Ocran prints? He doubted they were Yatin. No Yatin civilians would be retreating north, and all the Yatin Cavalry were far to their south, guiding Prince Lorn to Maeii. *Benotrist then,* Kato surmised. He was wary of any ocran hoofprints since he didn't know if Thorton withdrew by ocran or magantor. If it was Thorton, it would put him miles away by now. It could just as easily be Benotrist slavers that forsook their catches, beating a retreat north.

"Let's move out, we're wasting daylight," he said, kicking his heels, urging his mount into the vale.

Commander Devron rode beside him, his men following. Kato skirted the south side of the village, a third of their column following him, the others splitting off, twelve cutting across the shallow stream, skirting the north side of the village, with Devron leading the rest through the village center.

Zip!

Laser streamed from the tree line on the opposite ridge, striking Kato's mount in the breast, the beast tumbling into the wet grass.

Zip! Zip! Zip!

Laser fire swept all around Kato's fallen mount, striking the Torry riders nearest him. Kato was thrown clear, his left shoulder hitting the damp soil. He struggled catching his breath, the blow knocking the air from his lungs. The sounds of screams and clashing steel echoed from the village, though Kato couldn't get a clear view through the tall grass. Nor could he raise his head without exposing his position. Laser flashed overhead, striking targets farther back. With his rifle slung over his back, he began to crawl.

Commander Devron's ocran swerved between the thatched huts, gargoyles flooding into his path from the makeshift structures.

"Kai-Shorum!" a gargoyle screamed, springing into the air, taking the soldier in front of him from the saddle.

Devron rode past, lopping the head of another gargoyle standing in his path. Laser fire flashed to his south from the wrong direction, making him fear for Kato's life. He swung his sword left and right, hacking away at gargoyles crowding his way, catching one along its shoulder and another across the face. He split a wing on a third, his ocran trampling two more under hoof.

The center Torry column within the hamlet followed Devron through the pathway, cutting down gargoyles at will, the creatures slashing at the passing beasts with their scimitars, dropping several. Others climbed atop the thatched huts, springing down on passing riders. One creature spread its wings, diving upon a passing Torry, the solider thrusting his sword through the creature's gut. The blow couldn't stop the wounded gargoyle from knocking him from the saddle, where he was quickly set upon, several gargoyles chopping his limbs before eating him alive.

"Stay down, Kato," Thorton said to himself, scanning the place where he fell into the high grass.

"Do you see him?" Zelo asked, standing at his side within the tree line. The gargoyle stared in wonder at Thorton's handiwork. Nearly the entire southern column of Torry Cavalry lay dead or dying, their few surviving ocran racing off, riderless. The north column was racing into the village to avoid exposure in the open ground. The center column was mired in battle within the village. Their position provided them a clear view of the entire small vale, with the village below, surrounded by acres of open ground. It was the perfect trap, and Thorton sprung it brilliantly. The Torry Cavalry contingent was now entirely within the small hamlet, where Thorton could easily kill any attempting to retreat. Thorton lured the Torries into the vale by marching a large group of gargoyles through it, leaving obvious tracks that a blind man could see, while he circled back from the north, taking up position on the far ridge, the tree line masking their location.

"He's somewhere in the grass," Thorton said, expanding the magnification on his pistol scope.

"Why didn't you kill him?" Neon asked, his one eye squinting painfully in the bright sunlight. Neon was rightfully nervous of Kato, the damnable Earther having tipped the battle at Mosar to the Torries' favor, ruining all their plans. Now they were in full retreat,

Yonig's once proud legions reduced to a scattered rabble. Of Tyro's Elite that followed Thorton from Fera, only he, Zelo, and Draken remained, and Draken broke off northward days ago to report the events of Mosar to the emperor, taking their only surviving magantor with him. That was a task Neon did not envy the former free sword.

"I won't kill him unless I have to," Thorton said, his voice eerily void of emotion.

"Will he grant us the same consideration?" Neon snorted, not liking Thorton's strange sense of honor.

"Probably not you, Neon," Thorton said dryly.

The one-eyed Benotrist did not care much for that remark. If any other man said such a thing, he'd have drawn steel, but challenging Thorton was a death sentence. The big Earther spoke and did as he pleased, and there wasn't anything anyone could do about it. Besides, he rode with Thorton long enough to grow accustomed to his blunt humor.

Thorton scanned south of the village for another moment before turning his attention to the village itself, where the Torries were slowly gaining advantage. The dwellings blocked much of his view, but there were enough open spaces between them for him to work.

Zip! Zip! Zip!

Laser blasts took one Torry through the chest, dropping him from the saddle in the middle of the village square. The second pierced a soldier's back while engaging a gargoyle, the creature finishing him, sliding its scimitar across his throat. Another blast cut through a Torry and the gargoyle he was dueling, both combatants sinking to their knees in the mud.

Thorton flinched as an intense beam of energy flashed overhead, shielding his eyes.

Crack!

The sound of breaking timber echoed in his ears before the world came crashing down around him.

Kato fired several more blasts, dropping the trees down around Thorton, his large form disappearing in the falling branches. He should've killed him outright, but the same could've been said of Ben. He shot his ocran out from under him instead of killing him. It was the same at Mosar, each exchanging crippling blows but unwilling to kill the other.

Damn you, Ben, Kato cursed his friend's stubbornness for bringing them to this point. No matter, for once again they were even. Kato stood from the tall grass at the edge of the hamlet, turning his attention to the desperate battle therein.

Commander Devron pulled on his reins, circling his mount in the crowded street, slashing another creature before it could finish one of his men sprawled on the ground. The soldier regarded him gratefully, gaining his feet to seek battle elsewhere.

Zip! Zip!

Devron flinched at the flash of laser, but the deadly volley felled the two gargoyles nearest him. He shifted, finding Kato standing in the center of the muddy street behind him, laser rifle in hand, his black trousers caked in mud and jacket soaked.

Zip! Zip!

Kato blasted two more creatures farther down the street at the east end of the village, many gargoyles shrinking away from the dangerous Earther.

"Kai-Sh—" a gargoyle screamed, coming at Kato's left, his quick aim caving its skull, its war cry dying on its lips. Kato shifted aim as the creature flopped in the mud, targeting gargoyles that were standing clear of his Torry allies. The effect was immediate, the remaining gargoyles withdrawing to the two large wooden structures in the village center, one a granary and the other a stable. Both structures were long deserted, their livestock and grain taken either by the former inhabitants or the gargoyle invaders if they passed this way. It was likely the former, as Yonig's legions passed farther east during the invasion. The gargoyles would not have left the dwelling and surrounding fields unburned.

The Torry Cavalry took up position east of the structures as Kato blasted away around any openings where the creatures reared their heads.

"Order retreat!" Kato shouted across the muddy street where Commander Devron took up position afoot, with a shield raised and blade ready, his ocran standing several paces behind.

"It's too far over open ground. If we can clear those buildings, we can take shelter—" Devron tried to explain.

"There is no shelter from Thorton, not here," Kato warned, firing several blasts through the stable, the scream that followed proving one of his blind shots struck true.

Devron paled, realizing the peril they were in. Gathering his wits, he quickly attained his mount, ordering his men to withdraw when a flash of azure light pierced his side, exiting the opposite hip.

"Agghh!" the Torry commander's painful cry echoed hauntingly in the cool air.

Zip! Zip!

More blasts struck the Torry mount nearest him, killing ocran and rider. Kato couldn't see the source of the laser from his vantage point on the south side of the path, the blasts spewing from behind the north side of the stable. Kato fired three hurried blasts through the stable, toward its northwest corner, before backing away, keeping an eye to either side of the structure.

"Kai-Shorum!" Gargoyle war cries sounded, a small host issuing from the stable doors. Kato sent a hurried blast into their midst before spotting movement at the southwest corner of the stable, where stood a Benotrist warrior clad in dark mail and leathers with one eye.

Zip! Zip!

Two laser blasts struck Neon in the gut and breast, sending him to the ground, numerous vitals burned away.

Zip!

A thin blue beam of light passed through the gargoyle mob from the opposite corner of the stable, striking Kato's left shoulder, the blow causing him to stumble, dropping his rifle in the mud. Terrible pain coursed his left side, nearly driving him to his knees.

"I wouldn't do it, Kato!" Ben Thorton warned, emerging from the northeast corner of the stable, pistol drawn. The gargoyles momentarily froze before withdrawing to the stable, Thorton's laser strangely dulling their bloodlust, their furtive glances drifting from Kato to Thorton and back again.

"Ben," Kato winced, looking at Thorton with watery vision, his right hand going instantly to his holstered pistol.

"You go for the gun, I'll cut you down, and it won't be a warning shot or flesh wound this time," Ben warned as Zelo stepped to his left, sword drawn. Torry soldiers stood farther back of Kato, watching as intently as the gargoyles standing dumbstruck in front of the stable, while the two Earthers faced one another from opposite sides of the muddy street.

"Why, Ben? Why did you throw your lot in with these…" Kato regarded the gargoyles standing behind him. "Monsters?"

"That is my business, Kato, and I don't have to explain it to you. I picked a side long before you decided to intervene. Now, I've been extra careful not to kill you when I've had the opportunity, but don't mistake my kindness for weakness."

"And I've spared you, granting you the same mercy. We are Space Fleet officers, Ben, not a tyrant's puppet. What purpose does your aligning with Tyro serve? You know better than this," Kato pleaded, his vision clearing, his hand hovering above his pistol.

"Your side is no better, Kato. Spare me the false pieties of the Torry Realm. They hold slaves and slaughter innocents the same as the Benotrists. Such is expected from their primitive civilizations. Earth was no better during antiquity."

"That doesn't justify genocide." Kato shook his head.

"There will always be genocide until someone eventually wins. By interfering on the Torries' behalf, you are only extending this war, causing more needless death. Tyro can't grant mercy while this war continues."

"Mercy? We've seen Tyro's mercy with those he conquered."

"He's no worse than the Romans, Kato, and like them, he will bring civilization to the barbarians, moving the wheel of progress forward."

"You are mad." Kato sighed.

"Mad? Look around you Kato. This world has not advanced in over two thousand years. Where is the innovation and science? For heaven's sake, they are still using swords, bows, and arrows. They must be united under one absolute ruler, and then I can implement the changes they need to improve *all* their lives."

"And where do the subjugated fit into your vision? Under Tyro's yoke!"

"Slavery will die as it always does, as society advances. Freedom must start somewhere and will eventually spread to everyone. By aiding the Torries, you are sacrificing the long-term good for short-sighted justice."

"Long-term good? Placing free people under Tyro's yoke is unacceptable. What would Jenny say if she were here?"

A dark look passed Ben's eyes, followed by deafening silence. Pimples rose across Kato's arms, standing deathly still as Thorton holstered his pistol, staring daggers at his former friend.

"Don't speak of her," he warned in a voice barely above a whisper.

Kato thought to say something but decided better of it.

"Undo your holster and leave your weapons here. I'll give you safe passage. You can return to the *Stenox* and continue selling your services to the highest bidder for gold you don't need."

"I don't fight for the Torries for gold, Ben."

"No, but Raven sells his services for it. He's no better than a pirate, and here you stand in judgement of me. Enough! Drop your holster and step away."

"I can't." Kato shook his head, his gaze dropping to Ben's right hand, hovering over his holstered pistol.

"You sure you want to do this, Kato? You've already got one hole in your left shoulder. If memory serves me right, I hit your gun arm at Mosar. I was sure of it. Seeing you whole can only mean you built a regenerator since I left the *Stenox*. That means I'll have to make sure of you this time. You can't regenerate the dead. It's not too late to drop your holster and back away."

"I can't." Kato shook his head. He couldn't leave the Torries helpless against Thorton. The odds were already stacked against them.

Ben clenched his jaw, annoyed with Kato's naivety. The air grew so eerily still he could hear his heart beating.

They drew in unison, Thorton pulling the trigger before Kato cleared leather. Kato shifted to his right at the outset, Thorton's laser burning a hole through his chest, his follow shots striking his right shoulder, sending him to his knees. Kato's brown eyes found Thorton's across that deadly space, regarding his old friend briefly before going out of focus, falling face-first to the mud.

"Hold!" Thorton warned the surviving Torries who began to stir after the shock of Kato's demise passed. "Zelo, keep them back!" He growled, pointing to the gargoyles stirring behind them as he stepped across the muddled street.

"Aye," Zelo hissed, leveling his sword at the gargoyles, his feral gaze forcing them to cower.

Ben reached down, grabbing Kato's pistol from his loose grip, easing him onto his back. He slid his hand behind his neck, raising his head as Kato's eyes fluttered, struggling for life, his wheezing growing weaker with each breath.

"You shifted." Ben shook his head. "I would've hit you in the shoulder."

"I…I know." Kato struggled to keep his eyes open.

"Where's your regenerator? I can fix you."

"The pr…prince has it." He closed his eyes.

The words struck Thorton like a blow to the head. "The prince? He's miles away. I can't save you without it!" Ben growled. He meant only to wound him, take his weapons, and send him on his way. It was another mistake he would have to live with, though Kato gave him little choice.

"Give this to Ilesa." He weakly drew a folded parchment from his jacket, his blood staining it. "Tell Raven…"

"Tell Raven what?"

"Tell Raven I…" Kato's voice trailed, his dying eyes drifting out of focus as Ben held him. He knelt there for a time, the others staring numbly as Kato died in his arms, gargoyles and men alike transfixed by the two Earthers' bond. Were they enemies or friends? It made little sense, and to Ben Thorton, that was the damnable misery of it all. Whether they died today, tomorrow, or lived to be old men on this far-off land, the lives they knew on Earth were gone. The only honorable thing left for them was to make this world a better place, a goal he and Kato shared. They only disagreed on to how to best achieve it. He simply chose the side likeliest to win, therefore ending the conflict as quickly as possible before implementing the changes to improve this world. Kato chose to support the realm that best reflected their values. A noble choice, though Ben thought it misguided.

"Farewell," he said numbly, easing Kato's head to the ground, before gaining his feet and picking up Kato's rifle and pistol, handing them to Zelo. He carefully picked up the parchment from Kato's fingers.

"Be still!" Ben warned the gargoyles, who began to stir behind him, staring at the Torries with a glow alit in their crimson eyes.

"What of themsss!" one hissed, raising a finger to the enemy cavalry.

"Leave them to me. Go wait up on the hill," Ben ordered. He needn't warn them to not touch Ella, who awaited him there, each knowing he would kill them if they brought her harm. He waited for them to withdraw before turning his full attention to the Torries, counting fifteen that he could see. None seemed pleased with the turn of events, but none were foolish enough to raise steel yet. Ben nodded to Zelo to back away from Kato's body.

Ben opened the parchment, wondering who Ilesa was, only to discover the horrible truth as he read. "Kato." He shook his head, disgusted by the whole mess.

"You. Come here!" Ben called out a young Torry commander of flax.

The Torry stood unmoved, wary of stepping anywhere near the Earther.

"If I wanted you dead, boy, I'd have already done it. You look like the ranking soldier of the lot, so step forward so we can discuss this without anyone else dying, starting with yourself."

"Very well," the soldier relented.

*****

Ella awaited him where he told her, deep within the tree line, watching over their provisions and spare mounts. She first thought it a test, wondering why he would give her the means to escape, leaving her unguarded. But where would she go? Her only hope would be to reach the Yatin or Torry forces pursuing them. That would place her at the mercy of whichever soldiers found her. Could she trust the honor of men that hadn't seen a woman in a long while? Thorton was a frightening, dangerous man, but he hadn't hurt or soiled her. It was strange really. Most men of his position took young women for carnal pleasure or other nefarious reasons. Some men liked to control others, lording their power over those weaker than they. He did none of these. Oh, he demanded she do her share of the work, fixing their meals and tending their campfires, but it felt no different than the tasks he assigned his soldiers. She could sense animosity between the gargoyles and Benotrists, their peace only held together by their emperor, who was revered by all. Thorton, however, treated his human and gargoyle underlings equally, and the one he called Zelo respected the Earther immensely. The strangest part was that the only demand he had of her was for her to sing. Every evening she would sing by their cook fire, while he stared off in the distance, as if taken by a memory, his mind in a far-off place. The gargoyles and Benotrists were motivated by revenge and cruelty, but he was driven by a different purpose that she could not understand, for he was nothing like them. From what she understood, his fellow Earthers did not share his allegiance to Tyro, and his confrontation with the one he called Kato bothered him deeply, though he wouldn't speak of it.

He told her to remain where she stood, and remain she did, waiting patiently with her thick cloak wrapped about her shoulders. The gargoyles returned first, though only a handful, the fate of the rest she would learn of later. They simply regarded her and passed on, taking position farther within the tree line. Their ignoring her meant Thorton still lived. It seemed an eternity before Thorton and Zelo finally appeared, riding up the hill and through the trees. She caught herself happy to see him well, wondering where such feelings came from. Her sudden elation soured when he looked at her, his face reminding her of pain, loneliness, and death.

She thought to call him master, but he scolded her enough times to not use that appellation, and calling him by name as he asked her seemed wrong at this time. His face was deathly pale, and his eyes void of life, staring ahead as if a thousand leagues away. She knew then that he killed his friend.

*****

"Clear skies. 'Tis a welcome change," Lorn said, riding along the column of infantry. The Army made good time these past two days as the roads dried. The midday sun shone overhead, warming their backs as the howling winds gave way to a mild breeze. The road itself, snaked along the south bank of the Maeii River, which looked little more than a stream. By late spring it would grow to thrice its current size, spilling over its banks upriver. Rolling grassy hills stretched endlessly westward before flattening along the approaches to Maeii.

"I find it agreeable after the storm, sire," Lucas said, riding at his side. The Torry Elite was Lorn's closest companion on the trek north, the two exchanging tales of their adventures. Lorn was most interested in the Battle at Corell, gleaning more details of what transpired there.

"Morac cut through the main gate." Lorn shook his head, wondering why they hadn't foreseen that possibility.

"Unfortunately, sire, as well as all the other gates along the main tunnel."

"I trust my sister is rectifying that situation?"

"It was one of many issues she inquired of during a council of ministers before I departed. As well as maintaining a strong magantor contingent at the palace should Morac renew his assault come spring."

"Considering Morac's clever use of his launch towers, I agree. A strong magantor presence should avoid a repeat of that tactic." He wondered why the builders of the great castles hadn't thought of that obvious flaw. The great castles were built high enough to tax the gargoyles' strength attacking them. By constructing simple launch towers, Morac was able to easily assail Corell. Of course, such flimsy structures were vulnerable to magantor attacks, which the defenders were sorely lacking in the final days of the siege, until Dar Valen arrived to rectify that shortcoming.

Lorn continued asking of the state of Corell's provisions, casualties, and effective strength. He was impressed by his sister's handling of the war in Torry North, displaying a keen understanding of the requirements of the realm. If not for her, he would have no kingdom to one day rule.

"She is an able ruler, sire," Lucas said, affirming Lorn's assessment.

"She always was." Lorn shrugged, not surprised with her performance. "And far wiser than her brother."

"She did have help, sire, where you have done most of this alone."

"Our soldiers did this. I merely pointed the way. Besides, I had the same heroes leading us to victory as she had at Corell." He gave him a knowing look.

"Terin and Kato." Lucas laughed. "They are a matched pair. We couldn't have won without them."

"We all play a part, Lucas. Victory has many fathers."

"And defeat is an orphan," Lucas recalled one of Torg Vantel's many sayings.

"Nay. Defeat has just as many fathers, but they refuse to claim their get."

"Yes, that is true," Lucas conceded.

"You had no small part in these campaigns, Lucas. Terin claims you slew twenty gargoyles at Corell, and I dare venture an equal number at Mosar."

"I don't know if it was that many." Lucas shrugged.

"You didn't count?" Lorn lifted a brow.

"I stopped after ten. Everything after is a blur. There was no shortage of foes at Corell, and killing tired gargoyles atop the battlements is not the same as killing ones on even ground."

"Dead is dead, Lucas. They still fell to your blade."

"Perhaps, but I feel no satisfaction with it. It feels rather…" His voice trailed.

"Empty," Lorn finished his sentence, Lucas nodding in agreement.

"That is why you are a fine warrior, Lucas. You take no glory in killing. It is merely a means to an end. It is merely your duty. Lovers of glory do not live long in war. True warriors understand their mortality and act judiciously and are therefore harder to kill."

"I don't feel hard to kill, sire." He laughed.

"You are still alive," Lorn pointed out the fallacy of that jest.

"Dumb luck," he said, thinking of his fellow Elite that had fallen in battle.

"Master Vantel claims you are the strongest member of the King's Elite and the greatest grappler he has ever instructed."

"I have won more than I lost to everyone I've fought in the wrestling pits, but my sword skills are far less proficient."

"They are not deficient. With our losses at Kregmarin and Corell, there are several openings in the King's High Elite. Perhaps there is a place for you there among your highest-ranking brothers," Lorn offered. Of the one hundred in the Torry Elite, only ten ranked in the *High Elite*. Lorn reflected sadly on how many vacancies he had to fill within his esteemed guard. The losses at Corell were staggering, as well as the twenty-two Elite that fell at Kregmarin with his father.

"I am honored by your faith in me, sire."

"Not just my faith, Lucas. My sister thinks highly of you, and she is a far more discerning judge of character than I. Your magantor skills are excellent, and you managed to guard Terin throughout this campaign, which is no small feat, considering his impulsive nature."

"No, sire. I only guarded him for the briefest of moments before he'd lose me in battle. He survives by good fortune or the divine providence you speak of."

"Fair enough, Lucas, but I still intend to place you among the High Elite," Lorn said as a wounded Torry soldier up ahead caught his eye. He urged his mount onward where the soldier hobbled alongside the column, favoring his left ankle, with two of his comrades under his arms, helping him along.

"Hold!" Lorn called out, the three men stopping in their tracks, craning their necks, startled to be addressed by their crown prince. "None of that." Lorn stopped them from taking a knee. "What ails your friend?" he asked, leaning forward in the saddle.

"He rolled his ankle awhile ago, sire. We couldn't keep him in formation without slowing the whole column. Our commander of flax asked us to escort him," one of the fellows answered.

"Where is your flax now?" Lorn asked.

"Somewhere up ahead, sire," the same soldier said, his eyes growing wary as Prince Lorn dismounted, mud staining his sandaled boots and greaves. His once resplendent armor was dented and dull, the wear of battle taking its toll. His blue tunic was soiled with blood and grime. He looked nothing like a prince of the realm but a battle-hardened warrior. His men respected him because he fought beside them, slept beside them in these miserable conditions, and stood watch at night, taking turns with the men. He ate last during mealtimes, ordering his commanders in kind to eat after the men in their command.

Soldiers come first, he ordered at the outset of the campaign. Word of that order spread like wildfire through the Army after leaving Cagan, lifting the men's spirits.

It was no true surprise when Lorn ordered the injured soldier to mount his ocran, sending his fellows to rejoin their flax.

"Sire, he can take my mount. You should not be afoot," Lucas argued.

"No. I need you to scout ahead. Maeii should not be far off. See if any of our scouts have returned. We need to know the state of things."

"Yes, sire," Lucas relented, pressing his right fist to his heart before riding off.

"What's your name, soldier?" Lorn asked the injured man, leading his ocran alongside the column, receiving strange looks from the men marching beside them.

"Oluss, sire. Oluss Valen."

"Valen? Are you kin to General Dar Valen?"

"I...I don't know, sire. Perhaps he is distantly related."

Lorn asked of his service at Mosar, listening intently as the fellow spoke of the enemy he slew and friends that had fallen.

"When we reach Maeii, I'll have the matrons look at your leg, but if it's a sprain, you'll have to let it heal naturally. They could hasten your recovery with Kato's healing magic, but there will likely be others with greater need. I doubt our Fleets are able to seize the port without significant bloodshed."

"I am grateful, sire, but I should not be on your mount when you have need of it."

"I do have need of it. I need it to carry one of our injured soldiers," Lorn said in good humor.

Some time passed before Lorn spotted Lucas riding back to greet him.

"Maeii is secure, sire. Our scouts have returned. General Cornyana and our armada have taken the port. The banners of the Yatin 3rd and Torry 1st Fleets grace the battlements."

"Where is General Cornyana now?"

"At Maeii. He sent an escort that awaits you at the head of our column."

"Any news of Jentra and Terin?"

"Unknown. The scouts only said that Grand Admiral Kilan is waiting to receive you and for you to come with all haste. There are many wounded as well, and he requests the matrons' services."

"Very well. Take Oluss with you. Order the matrons to the head of the column. I'll gather my escort."

*****

Maeii rested at the mouth of the river of the same name, with a low curtain wall shielding its land-facing side and towers on each bank the height of ten men. Rolling grasslands surrounded the port, their reeds rippling in the wind like the surface of a golden sea.

Prince Lorn's spirited ocran galloped along the narrow road that shadowed the river, his battle-scarred helm drawn low over his face. Beside him rode his sigil bearer, heralding his arrival, a gold crown upon a field of white rippling in the breeze upon his banner. Men atop the battlements cheered his appearance once his crest broke the horizon, leading his great host. The gates of Maeii were flung open as the procession drew near, with Jentra standing at the entrance to receive his prince.

Lorn's mirth at the sight of his friend quickly eased as he beheld his solemn gray eyes staring back at him.

"Maeii is yours, My Prince." Jentra thrust his fist to his heart as Lorn stopped at the gate.

"Jentra, what ails you, old friend? Where is Terin?" he asked warily, craning his neck left and right as if he should miraculously appear.

"It is best to discuss this inside. We have prepared your command post at the city magistrate."

"Lead the way," Lorn replied grimly, his face deathly pale.

*****

The streets of the small port were abuzz with activity, thousands of sailors and soldiers attending a myriad of tasks. The tall masts of the *Bandor* dominated the skyline, with hundreds of workers busying themselves with the ship's repairs. Beside the massive vessel rested the Benotrist quadoar *Torch*, the ship captured when its freed oarsmen found the fleet after the battle, gifting Kilan Admiral Mulsen's flagship and the pride of the Benotrist 5th Fleet. Men hailed Lorn's arrival, Yatin and Torry alike, as he passed, the road skirting the wharves, with warships tied off at the piers. The smell of salty air touched his nose, the endless ocean expanse resting off his right, and tropical frolog trees pressed eastward by the prevailing winds. They stopped at the base of a modest-sized structure, with stone columns lining its west face and a stone stair descending to the street. Lorn dismounted, following Jentra up the stairs with Lucas in tow.

*****

Dim torchlight greeted them as they stepped within the main audience hall, a square-shaped chamber with a stone table in its center, surrounded by open space. Four basin torches rested to each corner, illuminating the outline of the chamber and little else. Grand Admiral Kilan and General Cornyana greeted them at the table, where a familiar sword rested upon its surface, an ominous dull hue barely emitting along its blade—Terin's sword.

"Where is he?" Lorn managed to ask past the lump in his throat.

Jentra relayed the grim tale, the admiral adding the details of the battle itself, finishing with a current disposition of their forces and casualties. Lucas received the news poorly, having to rest his hands upon the table. Lorn kept his grim demeanor, though heard little of what was said, forcing them to repeat the tale a second time.

"And thus we ended here, placing the sword upon this table. Terin sacrificed his own life, preserving this sword for our cause. It is now yours, sire," Jentra finished, waving an open hand to the Sword of the Moon.

"How could it come to this?" Lorn shook his head sadly. Terin's destiny was bound to the realm's. Should he fall, what hope had they against Tyro? Why had Yah's guidance led him here? Without Terin, how could they win? Lorn closed his eyes, focusing to suppress the doubts festering in his heart. If he looked back, he was lost, but how could he not question the steps that led them here? Losing his father was bad enough, but Terin? Yah, long ago, revealed himself to a young Lorn, sharing visions of King Kal and the failings of mankind that doomed his noble reign. The task was too much for any man, including Kal himself. Yah entrusted Kal to vanquish the gargoyle foe and establish order upon Arax in his vision. Any one task was nigh impossible, but both were too much, even for Yah's chosen. In his divine wisdom, the god divided the burden to two men, one his chosen ruler, and the other his chosen champion. To Lorn fell the burden of establishing Yah's authority to a fallen world, to build Arax anew as he intended Kal to do so long ago. He appointed Terin to be his champion, to smite the gargoyles from the face of Arax. Yah's champion was foretold in ancient prophecies forgotten by all save for a precious remnant, adherents of Yah's divine plan. The champion was to be born from the line of Kal. To further strengthen his hand, Yah sent his divine gift to the Jenaii, the ancient star that destroyed their sacred temple, depositing the precious metals among its ruins. Those metals were gifted to ancient Tarelia, forged into the Swords of Light. The swords were intended for the blood of Kal, though the men who forged them never knew that Kal's line endured. And so it came to be that when a son of Kal would emerge from obscurity with a Sword of Light in hand to lead mankind against the gargoyles, he would be joined by a mighty king to glorify Yah to all the nations of Arax. Lorn was that king, and Terin the champion. How could Lorn fulfill their destiny without Yah's champion?

No. He shook his head. *There has to be a way. If Terin is gone, there is still another with Kal's blood, the one who gifted him the sword in the first place, the one who sired him. He could call upon him if Terin was truly gone.*

"Have you searched Carapis since the battle?" Lorn asked.

"I've dispatched five ships to Carapis, with two magantors to quickly relay any findings. The first returned yester morn," Kilan said.

"And?" Lorn asked.

Kilan shook his head.

"Continue your search."

*****

The early evening found Lorn alone upon the wharf, staring out to sea, seeing nothing but starlight reflecting off the clear ocean, indifferent to the biting cold air. He closed his eyes, listening to the lapping waves crashing the shore, reflecting on the heavy cost of attaining this port. Maeii, the name would haunt the annals of Torry history. He lost his right arm for a point on the map. The port was eerily quiet despite the thousands of sailors and soldiers busying themselves throughout the city. Nearly a third of the Torry 4th Army had already passed within its gates, fortifying the garrison. The Yatin 2nd Army should arrive over the next few days. Then what? Winter was already upon them, and the gargoyles left nothing between them and Telfer and Tenin. Central Yatin was laid waste. Whatever came next, retaking Tenin or Telfer were not options. That left them the choice of holding position or withdrawing.

"Was it all for nothing?" he asked himself. "No." He shook his head. If they couldn't advance, neither could the gargoyles. Their intervention denied Tyro the Yatin Empire, at least the southern half. Sometimes you have to accept a half victory as a win when that was the best outcome you could've hoped for. By driving the gargoyles back to the Telfer-Tenin line, they safeguarded Mosar, unless Tyro committed far more to the Yatin Campaign then he could afford.

"You wished to see me, sire?"

Lorn opened his eyes at the sound of Lucas's voice, finding the warrior standing behind him upon the wharf.

"I did. Come hither." Lorn smiled wanly.

"A beautiful night," Lucas said, taking in the sight of the endless sea.

"Peaceful," Lorn said, his eyes following Lucas's gaze, the scenery a pleasant respite from the horrors they had beheld.

"I have never seen the ocean before, save for our brief stay at Cagan before coming here."

"Never?" Lorn made a face.

"I was born near Central City and spent my entire life in Torry North. The closest I came to the sea was Lake Monata, while accompanying Minister Veda to Sawyer two years ago."

"It is a sight all people should see at least once in their lifetime. I've seen it many times during my travels to Cagan."

"That was one thing I was envious of Terin for, his voyage with the Earthers, sailing the ocean. I cannot believe he is gone."

"He…will be missed" was all Lorn could think to say.

"The princess will not be pleased." Lucas shuddered, thinking of her reaction.

"I imagine not. That is why I asked to see you, Lucas."

"How so, sire?" Lucas asked, knowing nothing good ever followed the tone the prince was using.

"I have a task that I entrust to you and no other. It is a grim affair that I would undertake myself if my presence wasn't required here." He handed Lucas a sealed parchment.

"The princess," Lucas guessed the task, receiving the scroll.

"Yes. You are to return to Corell and deliver this to her hand. I have explained Terin's deeds, fall, and my blame for his fate in that scroll. Guard it well." Lorn touched a hand to his shoulder.

"I will leave come sunup."

"Very good." Lorn removed his hand, ashamed for giving this unenviable task to this brave warrior, but he was Terin's friend and traveling companion. There was no one better suited.

She will hate me, Lorn thought miserably. She grew resentful over the years, with many of his duties falling to her in his absence. Since he reached maturity, he spent far more time away from court than in it. She believed he spent his time in selfish or boyish pursuits, shirking his duty as his father's heir. It angered her further that his duties fell to her at their father's behest. How could he explain to her that his absence was necessary for the war to come? She would never have understood the visions that Yah had given him and the tasks he needed to undertake to ensure the Torry Realms were ready for the conflict with Tyro. Few knew the true state of the Torry Southern armies prior to the war, beset with poor leaders and ill-equipped, poorly trained soldiers. Had he not intervened, the 4th Army would've still been mustering at Cagan, and the Yatin Empire would've fallen. If that came to pass, Torry South would have a dagger to its throat and be unable to aid Torry North when Morac returned. They didn't have long to wait for that to happen, perhaps as soon as early spring. He studied the maps of Torry North enough to know the realm was holding together by the thinnest of threads. With the 5th Army gone and the 3rd battered from the battles of Tuft's and Corell, they had little room for error. In fact, they depended on their Jenaii allies to balance the scales, but what if Tyro committed more legions to the campaign?

Lorn needed to withdraw the 4th Army to Cagan, freeing the 1st Army to march to Central City. He would hold a war council on the morrow to confer with his commanders.

*****

Lucas set out the next morning, taking Jentra's magantor, the very one he journeyed from Corell upon before lending it to Jentra at Mosar. Jentra and Grand Admiral Kilan spent the better part of the day urging Prince Lorn to claim Terin's sword for his own, the blade still resting upon the table where it was guarded by the Royal Elite.

"Yah will decide who shall wield it, not I," Lorn insisted.

"And who has your god chosen, sire?" Kilan asked as politely as he could manage, sharing Jentra's doubts of Yah.

"He has not revealed that to me…yet. We can be certain of only one thing, that the man I choose will be worthy to wield it."

"Hopefully the great Yah will make up his mind before we decide our next move," Jentra snorted, leaning against the far wall as Kilan and Lorn stared at one another across the table.

"The decision is already made," Kilan stated the obvious. "We can't stay here. We came this far to drive Tyro back into north Yatin and force a reduction of the enemy. A vast wasteland now separates them from Mosar. Southern Yatin is now secure and acts as a shield for Torry South. The same cannot be said of Torry North. The only help we can give them is the 1st Torry Army, but if it moves from Cagan, we are exposed to any Macon adventurism. The 4th Army must withdraw to Cagan, to free the 1st for Torry North," Kilan explained, agreeing with Lorn's assessment.

"So we came here for nothing," Jentra snorted.

"We came to drive the enemy further north and reduce their strength. We were successful in those objectives," Kilan reminded him.

And we lost Terin in the exchange. Jentra didn't voice that thought.

"Transport will be the most difficult part. Our combined armada numbers seventy-one ships, with two dozen of those unfit for duty. We could fill our holds with our soldiers and still not have enough to transport your host back to Cagan," Kilan assessed the situation. That also included the Yatin ships, which would not leave their own coastal waters unguarded to transport a Torry Army to Cagan.

"Our merchant fleet is still anchored at Faust," Lorn reminded him.

"As was expected until the sea-lanes were cleared. I sent word to them once we reached Maeii," Kilan informed him.

"Good." Lorn sighed, at least one worry he could put to rest. This campaign had too many moving parts for his comfort. Yah did not give him specific instructions, but he felt comfortable with the plans he had made.

"Our Yatin friends won't be keen with our withdrawal," Jentra said.

"I have already spoken with their commanders on the matter. They knew our support was limited to the winter campaign. We have secured Mosar for the foreseeable future. That should hold while we campaign elsewhere," Lorn assured him.

"*Sire!*" a guard said, bursting into the chamber.

"Yes," Lorn answered, knowing they would not be disturbed without good reason.

"You..." The guard couldn't put words to his thoughts.

"Out with it, soldier!" Jentra reprimanded.

"You should come outside, sire." The guard's face grew ominously pale.

Lorn wasted little time doing so, walking quickly out of the room, the others following on his heels. Sunlight struck his face as he stepped without, causing him to pause atop the steps of the port magistrate, lest he lose his footing. He hadn't come all this way to die breaking his neck falling down stairs, unless Yah had a dark sense of humor. He waited briefly for his eyes to adjust before chancing the steps but froze once he could see what awaited below.

A dozen riders stood beside their weary ocran with sullen faces, with a body draping the saddle of the mount nearest him.

"Kato," Lorn whispered, his heart reaching his throat. He quickly descended the stairs, approaching his friend, whose still form hung stiffly over the saddle, his head down and arms dangling freely. Lorn knelt, carefully lifting Kato's head, his lifeless eyes staring back at him.

"How?" he asked sadly.

"Thorton, sire," the rider nearest him answered, a commander of flax who appeared to be their ranking commander.

Lorn closed his eyes, gently lowering Kato's head. The bustling port was eerily still, every soul in the street staring sadly at their fallen hero, the gravity of this loss burrowing into their hearts. First Terin, and now Kato. The gains of their victory were now washed away.

"He fought bravely, sire," the soldier added. "Thorton ordered us to bring him to you so he could be properly buried. Kato gave him this before he died. It is meant for the Lady Ilesa." He handed the bloodstained parchment to Lorn.

"At least he has some semblance of honor," Lorn said, gaining his feet, though Thorton's honor would do little to assuage this loss. "And his weapons?"

"Thorton has them, sire." The commander lowered his head.

Lorn released a measured breath, gazing skyward as the implications struck home. There was no time for sorrows, the war demanding he act without respite. With Kato gone, they had no check on Thorton.

"How far away is General Yitia?" Lorn asked Kilan, who stood upon the steps behind him.

"A day's ride at least," the grand admiral surmised, based on the latest reports on the Yatin general's whereabouts.

"Send word for him to proceed here posthaste. Use ocran. I want all magantor patrols north of here cancelled. Restrict your patrols to the sea and far off the coast.

"Aye, sire," Kilan agreed, knowing the danger Thorton presented to their magantors.

"General Farro?"

"He is just beyond the city gates, bringing the trailing elements of the 4th Army," Kilan said, regarding the Torry commander.

"Have him see to his men and report hither," Lorn ordered, summoning a war council for every commander in the Torry-Yatin alliance to plan their collective withdraw. Even the Yatins would now have to move back from this point. He would oversee the council after seeing to a very unpleasant task.

*****

He found her in a warehouse near the waterfront, where the wounded were gathered, hundreds of sailors spread out across the stone floor. Lorn visited here upon his arrival at Maeii, lending encouragement to the men, assessing their disposition before the matrons arrived. He remembered mentally thanking Kato for his wondrous device that would quickly end the suffering of these brave men. Most of the severely wounded suffered burns from fire ballistae, terribly painful and hopeless to heal without Kato's device. He thought how much they owed the brave Earther. He helped immensely lifting the siege of Corell and saved hundreds, if not thousands of men with his healing device after that terrible battle. Again, at Mosar, he countered Thorton while their armies liberated the city and again healed thousands.

We did nothing to earn his loyalty, but he gave it to us freely, he thought miserably. *What have I done?* Lorn closed his eyes, lamenting his decision to march on Maeii. *What did it gain us other than a few hundred leagues separating the gargoyles from Mosar, at the cost of Terin and Kato.* Was this truly Yah's will, or was Maeii what Lorn *thought* was Yah's will?

No! He shook such doubt from his mind, for to dwell there would make him truly lost. He had to trust Terin's fate to Yah and deal with the matter at hand, and that matter was kneeling in the middle of the floor, treating a wounded sailor.

Ilesa never tired of smiling whenever she healed a wounded person with Kato's regenerator. How could she not smile when joy replaced suffering, and relief replaced pain? She knelt beside the sailor, a man in his third decade with long brown hair that was melted to his scalp. His glazed eyes stared sightless from his burned face, whimpers escaping through his charred lips. His chest and hands were terribly blistered, and she marveled that he endured this long.

Ilesa set the regenerator carefully upon his chest, whispering in his ear not to move. Within moments his flesh started to mend, fresh skin replacing old. His eyes suddenly came alive, vibrant brown irises blinking in wonder as they took in his surroundings. His face quickly followed, handsome nose and lips emerging from their burned ruin.

"Rest for a moment before you stir." She smiled, lifting the device from his chest.

"How?" he asked, staring at her as if she were a goddess.

"A gift from my husband." She smiled, touching a gentle hand to his forehead, shifting his locks from his eyes.

"Bless you, my lady." He wept.

"And you, my brave friend," she said before gaining her feet.

It was then she noticed the prince staring at her from the entrance of the structure, his grim look sending pimples across her flesh. Her breath froze as he started making his way toward her.

"I am so sorry, Ilesa, so very sorry" was all he could manage to say, handing her the bloodstained parchment.

*****

She stood upon the shore, not remembering how far she ran when Lorn said those awful words. She had to get out of there. She ran along the wharf, past the ships tied off along the piers, weaving between the sailors crowding the waterfront until she reached a patch of ground empty of others. Ilesa stopped to catch her breath, her pounding heart nearly leaping from her breast.

The setting sun hung cruelly above the horizon, its fading light matching her own waning spirit. She waited a time before unfolding the parchment, tears dripping on Kato's words.

My dearest Ilesa,

I hoped this letter to never find your hand, but alas, it is not to be. Forgive me for failing you, for failing to return to your arms. I wish I could put words to what my heart is longing to say, but I lack the prose. If you are reading this, then I have fallen and will not see you again in this mortal realm. To me falls the low road which I must use to follow you home, my spirit wandering its path until you join me at life's end, though do not begrudge me if I wish you a long life. Though your heart is breaking, promise me you will live to an old age, savoring all the joys that life brings.

Experience all of these joys for me, for I will be there beside you in spirit. Remember that our lives are mortal, but love is deathless. Whatever has befallen me, I do not regret my choices. My grandfather often said that our spirits are one-half of a puzzle, with jagged lines down the center, where the pieces are joined. We are never whole until we come upon our missing half, the other spirit whose soul aligns perfectly with our own.

My coming to this world was no accident or happenstance. It was ordained by an omnipotence I cannot name, guiding me across the heavens to your arms. You are that missing piece, the other half of me that I didn't even realize I was missing. I only regret that we only had those few nights together, those precious moments that are greater than all my days before. If I have died, then please know I would not trade our times together for continuance of a life without having known you, for how could I live if never knowing my missing half? A poet from my world once said, "It is better to have loved and lost, than to have never loved." Only now do I see the truth in those words, for how can one truly live if they've never loved?

I am grateful that you look upon me fondly, our brief time together concealing my many faults, faults that you would probably overlook with your forgiving nature but are there all the same.

Oh, my sweet Ilesa, I would suffer a thousand deaths to hold you in my arms one last time and feel your lips upon my own.

If I am gone, mourn for me a time, but then move on. You are young and beautiful and deserve the full blessing that life offers. You cannot fill a broken heart with loneliness. You will love again and have children, though I wish I could have given them to you. Do so with my blessing, though I beg of you to choose a man who is as kind and giving as you.

I wish I could say more, my love, to find the words that would lessen this blow, but I cannot. Forgive me this shortcoming, this last failure. Know that I love you, now and forever.

Kato

She lifted her eyes from the letter, staring out across the endless sea with blurry eyes. Above the sounds of sea birds and crashing waves, she could almost hear his gentle voice carrying upon the wind.

You take the high road
And I'll take the low road
And I'll be in Scotland before you
For me and my true love
Will never meet again...

"Kato." She wept, the parchment slipping from her trembling fingers.

*****

Cronus flexed his left hand, the biting cold numbing his fingers, his leather gloves providing little protection. Despite his fur-lined cloak and thick trousers, he felt naked to the pressing wind, soaring through the crisp air, following the outline of the coast below, a jagged line of brownish green and dark blue. They departed Mosar two days past, cutting northwest to the sea before following the coastline to Maeii. They were poorly received at Yangu's court, the emperor delaying their departure with a myriad of nonsensical questions and strange declarations.

"*You were seen leading a vast host through the Yagan swamps. Do you deny it?*" Yangu had asked, sitting his throne, his eyes ablaze.

"*We flew from Cagan, Galen and I, at the behest of Minister Antillius, to treat with Prince Lorn, Emperor Yangu. I command no Army or host of any sort,*" Cronus explained.

"*Tyro is watching us from his enchanted throne, from which he sees all!*" Yangu shouted to no one in particular, as if he didn't hear Cronus's explanation.

"*Where is your Army, General? I ordered you hither before the siege, and you failed me,*" Yangu asked Galen, who sheepishly shrugged his shoulders, at loss for words. Cronus wondered if Galen was ever so afflicted. Yet even the talkative minstrel was struck dumb by the emperor mistaking him for a Yatin general.

Cronus patiently listened to the emperor's ramblings as he spewed a series of disjointed utterances laced with paranoia. The man was clearly touched with madness, as evident by the nervous looks the court ministers and attendants shared with one another. One moment he was cordial and the next berated them with invectives. Eventually they were able to depart with their heads attached, leaving the city posthaste.

Cronus shook the memory from his mind, reminding himself never to return to Mosar. It was now apparent why the Yatin Empire was in such a dire state. Yangu was mad, and no one held authority to check his insanity. This explained Lorn's absence from Corell. He could not allow Yatin to fall so easily to Tyro's legions without dooming Torry South. His intervention seemed to have worked, checking Tyro's advance, saving southern Yatin and securing Torry South's northern border. This should be cause for celebration, another victory for their beleaguered realm, but alas, he had to be the herald of ill tidings, informing his prince of the Macon envelopment of Sawyer.

"Is that it?" Galen pointed ahead, his voice lost in the wind, his mount just off Cronus's left.

Cronus understood his meaning, looking to the northern horizon where a small port city rested upon the coast with dozens of vessels moored along its piers, and a vast host camped around its walls. The sigils of the Torry 1st Fleet came into focus as they drew near. His anxiety eased once his eyes set upon the sigil of the House of Lore raised above a strongly built stone edifice in the center of the port, a gold crown upon a field of white.

*****

"A full withdraw!" Lorn emphasized to the commanders gathered about the table, where Terin's sword rested. Each of the men gathered therein were distracted by its beguiling power, the sword's once vibrant blade reduced to a murky sliver sheen, as if the sword itself was in mourning.

"But we need this port if we ever intend to reclaim Tenin," General Yitia exclaimed, a look of disbelief gracing his continence.

"It is not safe, General," Kilan countered. "We have achieved our objective, driving the enemy beyond Mosar. Much of the land between your capital and here has been laid waste. You would be wise to withdraw your forces along the routes that are untouched, destroying everything in your path."

"Destroying what's left of our heartland? Are you daft?" Yitia growled.

"It will deny those provisions to the enemy. They will come again, General, unless we defeat them in the north. This campaign has achieved its prime objective. The Yatin Empire still stands," Lorn said.

"And had we not come here, the enemy could make use of these lands to stage a counterattack. That is no longer possible without a significant commitment of fresh forces that Tyro can ill afford," Kilan further explained.

"The emperor will not be pleased." Yitia sighed.

Then he can get off his rump and continue the attack himself. Jentra kept that thought to himself. He looked to the day when he needn't constantly guard his tongue, lest he offend their Yatin hosts. Their emperor was a twit. He wondered what good they had truly achieved. Once they departed, Yangu would still be in charge, and he could imagine any number of foolish decisions he might make when left to his own council.

"Sire!" the Elite guarding the outer corridor said upon entering the chamber. Jentra ordered them not to be disturbed except for urgent matters, recalling their last meeting when they heard of Kato's fate.

"Tarlin," Lorn acknowledged the Elite.

"You have visitors, sire."

"Don't dawdle, Tarlin! You don't interrupt a war council with such scant news. Who are these visitors?" Jentra barked.

"A fellow Elite, Cronus Kenti, and a minstrel. They bring word from Minister Antillius."

Every Torry in the chamber knew the name Cronus Kenti, the hero of Tuft's Mountain and named to the Elite by royal decree.

"Send them in," Lorn said.

CHAPTER 17

He soared through the heavens, climbing high into the firmament above jagged mountain peaks, before sweeping into the valley beyond. Wind Racer's squawk echoed through the crisp air, heralding his triumphant return, again carrying him high into the clouds. They passed over other mountain peaks before dropping into another valley in the distance. He ascended and descended again and again, the motion repeating itself, his blue eyes desperately searching the horizon until his heart projected his deepest want. There, in the distance, arose Corell in all its glory, rising above the green Torry heartland in majestic splendor, its white citadels towering above its bulwarks.

She awaited him upon the battlements, her piercing blue eyes finding him in that distant sky, the exquisite details of her beauty growing in focus as he drew near. She called to him, her voice carrying upon the wind, as if ringing in his ear, the sound soothing his heart like a silken caress. She stood upon the highest battlement, stretching her hand out to him as he drew invitingly close, receiving him with heartfelt joy, the warmest smile playing across her face. Terin guided Wind Racer to set down upon the castle, but the magantor continued on, passing over the battlements, indifferent to his will.

"Corry!" Terin meant to scream, his voice dying in his throat as he passed, her smile souring upon her lips, her hands lowering with his betrayal. He tried to lift his hands to her, but they remained at his side. He strained lifting his arm, but it refused to obey as Wind Racer again soared high into the heavens, then down again.

"Easy, lad," an unfamiliar voice echoed, drawing him from the painful vision.

Terin's eyes slowly opened to the surrounding darkness. He blinked several times to no avail, wondering if he was blind. His arms were bound behind him, his fingers touching the three chain links connecting them, granting him little slack. His bare legs rested upon a damp wood floor, which rocked slowly back and forth, the likely source for his dream.

"Wh-where…where am I?" He coughed, the words scratching his parched throat. A rank odor hung heavy in the fetid air, contorting his nose. His cloak, boots, and armor were missing and his blue tunic ragged. His skin pimpled with the cold air touching his flesh. The last thing he remembered was the battle and the deck of the ship giving way, and then…nothing.

"A ship," the masculine voice answered beside him.

"Wh-who are you? My captor?"

"Nay, a fellow captive." The fellow coughed as well. "I am Criose. I was a ballista crew chief on the Torry Trioar *Vengeance*."

Terin was grateful Criose was a fellow Torry, but alarm rang through his weary mind. "Am I blind?"

"No. We're in the hold of a ship," Criose reassured him.

"Whose ship? The Benotrists?"

"It's not our vessel, boy!" another man spat, sitting farther away along the hold.

"The ship holds Benotrist and Torry captives?" Terin made a face. He shivered, feeling the cold ocean through the galley's shell. The stench of the ship's hold reeked of urine and waste. Men were tightly packed in the close, dark space, manacles chaffing their wrists and ankles.

"Aye," Criose affirmed. "Most of these men are Yatin, Torry, and Benotrist sailors who survived the battle and unfortunate to have washed ashore upon the very beach visited by our lady captain."

"Lady captain?" Terin asked.

"Aye. I overheard her shipmates speaking her name, Veneva. Her crew followed the fleet before the battle and set ashore after, where they easily plucked us from the beach."

"A woman is the captain?" Terin asked. It was not unheard of, though rare when men chose a woman to lead them.

"The whole blasted crew are women!" another man growled.

"Where are they taking us?" Terin wondered.

"We can only guess," Criose grunted, shifting his body, his shoulders aching from confinement.

*****

Terin lost sense of time, the darkness of the hold, and the cold seeping through the hull, making every moment an eternal torment. Whether it was one day or ten, he could only guess, until the hatchway above opened, and a stair dropped into their midst, the dim torchlight breaking through, paining their eyes.

"You!" a woman's harsh voice called out to the man sitting nearest the stair. "Stand!" she commanded. Terin could not see her face from where he sat. The man slowly stood, the shackles connecting his feet just long enough for him to move. The man wore a loin garment and a tattered cloak about his shoulders. He could make out his Yatin loyalties by the yellow hue of his cloak. The fellow's bright-green eyes drew wide as a pole with a noose attached to it descended from above, slipping around his neck, where it was drawn tight by whoever held the other end. The pole drew slowly up the stairs, forcing the bound Yatin to follow, his shackles just long enough to negotiate each step. The process repeated continuously until ten of their fellow captives were taken, and the hatch closed. The brief light allowed Terin to take stock of his surroundings. The hold was the length of twelve men resting head to foot, with a low ceiling little higher than his shoulder, with crossbeams that arced lower still. Men were set along the periphery, bound hand and foot. They were all half naked, battered, and filthy, their sullen eyes and broken spirits reflective of his own sorry state. Criose sat beside him. He possessed gray eyes and a matted black mane, with a build similar to his own. He reminded him much of Arsenc, the memory of his lost friend another bitter reminder of what they lost in this war.

After a time, the hatch opened again, and the men returned to the hold. One was dragged, carried by two well-built women in boiled leather mail and fur trousers. Their hair was tightly woven behind their heads in braids. The fellow they dragged was sorely beaten, reddish welts covering his back. They set him against the hull before ordering the other men down. The men were still bound with their hands chained behind them and feet shackled. They said not a word and silently sat with their eyes downcast.

"No talking!" one of the women commanded, her cruel brown eyes sweeping the hold before ordering another ten to their feet and up through the hatch. The process repeated itself until it was their turn to go up deck, one of the women directing Terin up the stairs with the noose about his neck, leading him by the pole affixed to it.

Emerging through the hatch, he was greeted by the sight of rows of men sitting upon benches to either side, their hands chained to oars and feet shackled to the deck. The ceiling was a meter and a half high. The oar slaves wore loose woolen vests over pleated brown kilts, their sullen eyes staring hopelessly forward. They were emaciated and gaunt, their thin muscles straining with their harsh labors. He was led to the far end of the deck, his shackled feet shuffling between the rows of oarsmen. Terin felt lightheaded and starving. He didn't know how long he had been kept in the hold. Where was the Torry Fleet? Why did no one search the shore for survivors?

"Move quicker!" the woman leading him commanded, yanking the pole.

Terin stumbled, his bare knees painfully striking the deck. He winced, giving his captor a disgusted look, which set her off.

"Up!" she ordered, twisting the pole, which tightened the rope around his neck. She was nearly his height, with dark braided hair and a wind-worn face that aged her beyond her twenty years.

He gained his feet with great difficulty, wondering how long he could endure this treatment. He wondered where they were taking them but could guess their intentions. The women were likely slavers. His heart pounded, trepidation coursing his skin like plunging into cold water. Death was a mercy compared to the fate awaiting them. He could only guess their destination, but it was likely some port outside the Benotrist, Torry, and Yatin realms, but where? He needed to free his hands before he could attempt escape and make his way home, but how? Their captors were methodically efficient in their control, and he doubted they'd free his limbs until they made port, and then what? Should he declare who he was and hope they would ransom him back to Prince Lorn? Or might they deliver him to Tyro? Would he not fare better with Tyro than sold into slavery? As much as it sickened him, his paternal grandfather might grant him enough freedom to escape. Of course, Tyro might not believe him and order the Torry champion tortured or slain, but might it be worth the risk? If he revealed his identity, would he not be more valuable as a hostage than a slave? Of course, if they did ransom him to Tyro, the dark lord would likely question his loyalty and lock him away until the war was ended. The more value he held as a hostage, then the more difficult his escape. No, he would keep his identity quiet.

"Up!" his captor ordered, pulling him up a narrow stairs at the end of the deck, before emerging into the open air. He found himself upon the upper deck of a small galley, with an open deck between the fore and aft castles, surrounded by ocean, the midday sun shining off its calm surface. His captor dragged him along the deck, his feet shuffling to keep pace, joining his fellow captives. They walked them around the deck, working their legs for reasons he could only guess. Perhaps it was to prevent stiffness in their muscles or ascertain their health and worth.

"Eyes down!" another woman commanded to a captive farther ahead.

Terin stole careful glances of his surroundings, counting over three dozen crew members clad in similar boiled leather mail and fur trousers, with their hair bound in braids. Though Araxan women were nearly equal in size to Araxan men, they were usually more genteel in nature, lending to their nurturing instincts. These women, however, lacked any such inclinations. They were fierce, strict, and wasted few words. He could sense several overseeing them from atop the aft castle as they were marched around the deck but dared not look up. One fellow was dragged to the side and beaten for doing so, the slavers whipping his back bloody. Terin needed to keep his skin intact if he ever hoped to escape so planned to keep his head down. His heart pounded with thoughts of the life that awaited him if he failed to escape. If he made it to market, he would be reduced to slavery, bound to serve a master or mistress. His pride bristled at such a possibility. He was the Torry champion, the heir of Kal, and the hero of Corell. How could his story end in such indignity?

"*Yah cannot dwell in a proud heart,*" Lorn's words came back to him, shaming his arrogance. Were these other men less than him that he should think this fate unsuited only for him? No one should suffer thusly. His father instilled in him a hatred for slavery, but he never thought on its savagery, as the institution was relegated to criminals and debtors in Torry North, though it still flourished in parts of Torry South. If he survived this ordeal, he swore to Yah that he would fight to end slavery wherever he could.

They suddenly stopped as the prisoners were knelt in a line, with their handlers holding the poles behind them, controlling their every move. A young girl proceeded down the line carrying a bucket, spooning a bland, pasty food into their mouths. Terin never tasted something so foul but devoured it to sate his hunger. Another girl followed with water and a third with a wash bucket and rags to scrub their skin.

"Eyes down!" his handler commanded as the last girl washed his face and limbs before moving on.

Terin waited in place as the captain walked down the line, inspecting each of the chattel, asking their age, skills, and realm of origin. He tensed as she stopped before him, his eyes fixed to her heavy boots. He felt her fingers touch his hair, turning his head side to side before lifting his chin.

"Eyes up," she commanded.

Terin's blue eyes met her stormy gray. She towered over him with black boiled leather mail and fur tunic and trousers, her light-auburn hair bound in thick braids, dangling beneath a steel helm. Her face was wind worn, matching her stern countenance. He struggled reading anything in her posture, her eyes betraying little as she appraised him.

"Your name?" she asked with an even voice.

"Terin," he answered without thinking, cursing his stupidity for not offering a false name.

She touched his shoulder, examining his soiled tunic. The garment was torn from the collar to below his chest.

"You are Torry," she observed, wiping the grime from his garment, fully revealing its blue color.

"Yes," he conceded.

"Only Elite warriors and commanders of rank wear blue, but you are just a boy," she said, tearing his tunic further, exposing his chest. Her eyes narrowed severely, regarding the brand upon his left breast, two crossed swords with a third rising between them, piercing them with three glow marks forming an arc above its tip.

"What mark is this?" she asked curiously. Warriors were marked upon their chests, while slaves were branded upon the thigh, usually the left. She thought the mark was of a Torry Elite at first glance, but it was slightly different, with the third sword.

Terin swallowed, thinking of a lie to placate her but withered under her gaze.

"I…"

"Don't lie to me, boy," she warned with her even tone.

"I am of the Torry Elite." He hoped the half-truth would appease her, but he was a terrible liar, and she could spot falsehoods in men far cleverer than he.

"You!" the captain called out Criose, who knelt beside him.

Criose looked up as she stepped toward him, her fingers gripping his throat.

"You are Torry?" she asked.

"I am," Criose affirmed since there was little point in denying it.

"Do you know this boy?" she asked, twisting his head to Terin.

Criose winced, her nails digging into his neck, his eyes seeing Terin for the first time in clear light. His eyes showed nothing unusual until recognition struck him, the slight widening of his eyes betraying his discovery.

"I don't kn—" he tried to say as she tightened her fingers on his throat.

"Don't lie, slave," she warned darkly, knowing there was more to Terin than what he confessed. She drew her knife, pressing the cold dirk to his throat.

He regarded her with defiant eyes, daring her to kill him and be done with it.

"So be it," she said, the blade breaking his skin.

"Don't! I will tell you!" Terin pleaded. Criose's life wasn't worth delaying the truth since being sold to Tyro was likely no worse than a life of slavery.

She pushed Criose aside before gripping Terin's throat, forcing his head back, looking into his eyes. "Speak!"

"I am Terin Caleph, champion of the Torry Realms, so named by King Lore in the court of Corell," he whispered through her fierce grip.

She regarded him for a time, not easily believing his claim. The boy was too young to be so named. She didn't recall the Torries ever naming a champion but was not very knowledgeable of the workings of that realm. She would doubt his story if not for his eyes that bespoke a naive innocence she had seen little of in her grim work.

"The Torry prince will pay you a hundredfold whatever I might fetch at market. And will pay for all my comrades in kind," Terin chanced, hoping to play upon her greed.

Foolish child, she mused. No slaver would risk ransoming a slave back to its benefactor when payment would come with a bounty on their collective heads. She thought to simply cut his throat and toss him overboard, for the boy might be trouble, but that would waste a potential windfall. She could sell him to his enemy, but she did not trust Tyro. Fortunately for Captain Veneva, she had just the buyer in mind.

"Remove this slave from his group, clean him, and place him in the upper hold!" she commanded.

*****

He dreamed of Corry, visions of his lost love his only respite from this misery. Terin wasn't prone to self-pity but couldn't help to think of the unfairness of it all. He fought at Costelin, Tuft's, Molten Isle, Fera, Telfer, Corell, Mosar, and Carapis, overcoming desperate odds, only to be plucked from that Yatin beach by slavers. He had finally confessed his love to Corry, and she reciprocated, giving life to his deepest desire. He could see her now, facing Morac during their parlay, her fierce aspersions unnerving Tyro's champion. She was so strong that day, far stronger than he, defying her father's killer in the face of such odds. She was strong, intelligent, beautiful, and brave, oh so very brave. She loved him and now thought him dead unless he could escape this wretched hold. He cursed the fetters binding his limbs, bonds that denied him freedom, stealing precious time that he required to return to Corry. How long would she mourn him before another took his place in her heart? How long could love survive a broken heart once she learned of his demise? All they would know is that he fell into the sea. If not for these slavers stealing him from the beach, he would've found his way home to her.

Curse them, he thought bitterly, reproaching his captors.

He lost count of time in his new confinement. He was kept from the others in a small, closed space on the oar deck. It was dark and barely long enough to lie down, with loose straw spread upon the wooden planks. They kept his hands bound behind him, replacing his iron fetters for steel ones, taking no chances once they learned that he was an Elite warrior, not that he could've escaped from iron bonds anyway. It surely meant they were watching him more closely. His shoulders and arms ached painfully from his confinement. He once voiced complaint on the matter, only to be struck with a quirt. The crew were all women as he could see, but he couldn't see much isolated as he now was. He was taken above deck twice a day to be fed and exercised. They stripped away his ragged clothes, replacing them with a knee-length gray woolen tunic. He was thankful for that much at least, for the ship was cold, especially in his small compartment. He still pondered their destination. Would they ransom him to Tyro or Lorn? When he asked, the captain failed to acknowledge him, but the look on her face was less than promising.

He found the crew wholly unnerving. He never encountered women lacking the faintest shred of compassion or feminine grace. They conducted their business with cold efficiency, issuing commands with practiced indifference. Much of that could be attributed to their grim profession. Male slavers were no different, and many times worse in their brutality.

Stand! Kneel! Head up! Eyes down! Eat! Drink! Move! Their orders rarely more than base utterances. The captain's brief interrogation was the only conversation he had with them. The endless hours confined in dark isolation was nearly as torturous as the pain in his joints. He lost track of time, with only his dreams for comfort, but even these betrayed him, his fears turning them to nightmares.

"Yah," he called out to Lorn's god, beseeching him for deliverance but hearing nothing in reply.

"If you care to listen to the pitiful pleas of this wretched man, I confess my pride, my lust, my failings. Lorn said that you cannot dwell in a proud heart, and my pride is now gone. You ask that I believe in you, but how could I not when your gift flows in my blood. To ask forgiveness for our transgressions, we must forgive our transgressors, and I cannot. Release my bonds and place a sword in my hand, and I would kill my captors," Terin said in all honesty, hoping Lorn's god would answer him.

Yah did not answer, and Terin sat in bitter loneliness, forlorn of hope.

*****

They drew him from the hold that evening, scrubbing him raw and dousing him with tose powder to neutralize the odors of the hold. They rinsed his mouth with a foul-tasting liquid, whose purpose he could only guess. He was brought to the captain's cabin, where he was knelt before her bed, his head forced to the floor by his guards, his hands still bound behind him.

"Leave us," the captain ordered, his handlers stepping without as she stood over him.

Terin lifted his head only for her to place her foot on his neck, forcing his face to the floor.

"I haven't given you leave to rise, slave," she said in an eerily calm voice.

She retreated to her bed, taking her seat, her eyes fixed on his kneeling form.

"Lift your head, eyes to me."

He slowly raised up on his sore knees, his eyes adjusting to the dim candlelight that was affixed to the side of the wall. The cabin was small but spacious compared to the hold he'd been kept. A small table was built into the near wall, and a bed ran the length of the far wall, where she sat, staring back at him with predatory gray eyes. He couldn't guess her age, but she appeared older than her true years. Her face was stone, betraying nothing of her intent or character. He swallowed past the lump in his throat, as if staring into a great abyss.

"We drop anchor tomorrow, and the lot of you shall be off-loaded. You have much to learn before then, if you wish to avoid the lash."

"My ransom is worth far more than what I might fetch upon the block," he declared, unable to still his tongue.

"Head to the floor!" she commanded, but he refused, staring back at her with all the courage he could summon. She rose from the bed, lifting the candle from its bracket before gripping his head with her free hand.

"There are alternatives to obedience, shall we explore them?" she asked, spreading his eyelids open with her left hand and drawing the candle near with her right.

His heart pounded emphatically, like a hammer striking steel. He wondered if she would follow through with the threat, but everything he saw in those deadly gray eyes indicated that she would. If he ever hoped to escape, he would need his eyes, and so he relented, the futility of his position giving him little choice. He sighed, lowering his head.

She returned the candle, stepping around him before again sitting on her bed.

"Head up! Eyes to me!"

He obeyed, this time keeping quiet, awaiting her next command.

"Better. You will respond as ordered. Do you understand?"

"Yes," he said disgustedly. He was often humble and unassuming but prideful in a way he never really thought about. Now, she was stripping away his pride, layer by layer, threatening permanent harm if he refused. Death was one thing he might choose over this humiliation, but maiming gave him pause to reconsider.

"*You were born to a purpose,*" he could hear his father say, making death an unacceptable outcome, no matter his wounded pride.

Only he could counter the gargoyle threat, and he had to live to do so.

"Warriors are prideful by nature, and you were the greatest of the Torry Realm, their…champion. Most warriors are difficult to break, yet once I threatened your eyes, you meekly submitted. It seems you are not the warrior that that mark claims," she said, regarding his champion's brand upon his chest. "Or you cling to some false hope of escape," she added, noting the flash in his eyes betraying that truth.

"The arrogance of warriors." She laughed, dismissing his hopes. "Come hither."

He gained his feet, the slack in his manacled feet hindering the effort as he shuffled forth, wary of her intentions.

She regarded him as he stood before her, noting the tension in his stiff posture. She oft took certain liberties with one of her captives before sending them to the block. The boy was easy on the eye, and she humored keeping him for herself, but he was too valuable for her idle pleasure, and she long resisted bringing a male permanently aboard her ship, which would cause strife with her crew. No, she would use him this night and be done with him, using him as she was used by warriors and sold upon the block. But no number of men she took in kind could ever assuage her pain or sate her vengeance. She gained her feet, touching a hand to his face. He stiffened at her touch but dared not draw away. She was not unattractive, but her cruel demeanor was off-putting, and his heart belonged to Corry, and he would not betray her, no matter the cost to their noble cause, destiny be damned. But would he have a choice?

She lowered her hand, wondering why he resisted. No man ever refused this gift, not knowing if they would ever partake of a woman again once they were sold.

"When did you last make love?" she inquired curiously.

He meant to respond but hadn't the words.

"Who was she?" She gripped his throat.

"No one." He coughed, cursing his honesty, his answer taking her aback.

"Never?"

"No." He sighed, angry that she could extract that personal confession from him. He wanted to share that experience with the one he loved, the thought of bedding another making him ill.

She almost laughed, recalling her own stolen innocence, and contemplated plucking his in kind but reconsidered. His innocence was another asset she would leverage in his price with the customer she had in mind. She ordered him back to his hold.

*****

Bansoch

The *Queen's Dagger* dropped anchor along the waterfront, docking near the slaver district, resting on the city's eastern borough. Bansoch was built on the northern shore of the Sova River, where it emptied into the Soch Bay. A tall curtain wall ran the length of the land facing side of the city, and a lesser sea wall ran along the waterfront, just inland from the wharves. A dozen islands dotted the mouth of the Sova, stretching into the bay proper. The queen's palace presided over the Federation capital, its golden minarets spiraling above massive ramparts upon Melida Hill, on Bansoch's western half, the very hill where General Melida slew the last Soch king, Vagar, and was named first queen of the Federation fifteen centuries before.

The ship was greeted by two Bansoch officials dressed in emerald robes with silver stitching along their hems and sleeves, each appearing to be in their fourth decade, their hair bound in cross braids. They caried tablets with chalk to inspect the ship's cargo. Captain Veneva was first to descend the gangplank, greeting the officials before ordering the captives brought ashore for their inspection.

*****

It was late afternoon before Terin was drawn from his hold, his handler affixing the noose about his neck, leading him off the ship. He stole a furtive glance, scanning the waterfront of the city within his line of sight, wondering what port they had docked. The wharves were filled with female sailors wearing boiled leather mail and fur trousers or leather kilts of differing hues. Women soldiers in bright gold cuirasses over silver tunics patrolled the waterfront, their black capes billowing in the balmy air, their hair trailing their golden helms. He shifted his gaze once one caught him staring, hoping she wouldn't challenge his curiosity. He noticed the sigil upon their crests, a cloven black crown upon a field of white. 'Twas the standard of the harbor garrison, the black crown representing the sundered Soch king defeated upon these ancient shores. Terin did not recognize the sigil but correctly guessed where he was—the Sisterhood Federation.

"Eyes down!" Captain Veneva ordered, striking him with a quirt. He hadn't seen her observing him as he descended the gangplank.

"Curiosity is unbecoming," one of the port officials said as he stopped between them for inspection.

"He must be stripped," the other said, regarding the knee-length wool tunic he still wore. All slaves required inspection before entry onto the island, the Federation ever watchful for disease or genetic deformities that could pollute their populace. They rejected only two of Veneva's cargo, a tribute to her discerning eye. Most slavers filled their holds with whatever wretches they came upon, forcing them to sell the unfortunates to mines or slaying them outright. Veneva, however, savored catching warriors and selling her catches at Bansoch, her preferred port of call. The war spreading across the continent provided her ample opportunity to ply her tactics, especially trailing fleets before battle and scooping the survivors. She regretted only having one ship at Maeii, forcing her to leave so many potential catches on the beach. It did, however, allow her to be more discerning, filling her ship's hold with sturdier stock or comely like Terin. She also found several replacement oar slaves for her ship.

"He is too dangerous to unchain," Veneva said.

"Then tear his garment," the official said.

"Very well," Veneva relented, hating to ruin the article, cutting the tunic at the shoulder.

Terin flushed as the garment pooled at his feet, leaving him naked for all to see, feeling hundreds of eyes upon him, though in truth, he was no different than any other poor wretch suffering inspection.

Veneva wisely wrapped a bandage over his left breast, covering his champion's mark, not wishing questions on his origin. Queen Letha favored the Torry Realm and outlawed the import of Torry captives, but Veneva was not averse to such risk. She had numerous customers who gladly partook of such merchandise, customers whose estates and holdings were secluded and beyond the queen's eye.

Terin winced as they touched him, moving him about with their quirts, ordering him to bend, squat, and stand on one foot to assess his health. They inquired about his bandage, as Veneva explained it away as a spear wound, which the officials believed and waved him on. He was dragged forth, passing over the wharf to a holding pen with the other captives, all naked and bound with their hands chained behind them and feet manacled. They would stay in place until they were herded into separate pens throughout the expansive facility.

*****

Two days hence

Terin sat in his small cell, his back against the wall with his head and arms resting over his knees. His wrists were free of their bonds, and he was only restrained by a manacle connecting his left ankle to the floor. Loose straw strewn across the cell kept the cold of the stone floor from seeping into his flesh. He spent the past days being roughly handled, fed a tasteless gruel, and exercised to exhaustion. He was hopelessly spent, affording his mind little energy for anything but sleep. The exercise and food restored much of his luster and strength, just enough to present him at the block in his fullest. These slavers were good at their craft; he reluctantly admitted. They spent the morning working him relentlessly before returning him to his cell. They dressed him in a brief tan tunic without undergarment, cloak, or sandals, his body indecently exposed, as was their intent.

A commotion in the yard drew him from his slumber. He gained his feet, staring through the bars running the length of the far wall, facing the central yard. The yard was some fifty meters wide, with eight sides, and cells lining its periphery. Each pen had three stone walls on their backs and sides, with iron bars lining the front, facing the yard, affording those in the yard a clear view into each cell. Each pen floor rested three feet below the surface, their sunken floors angled slightly to drain runoff.

Staring through the bars of his cell, he saw two dozen new captives paraded into the center of the yard, the slaves in the pen opposite him, staring in kind.

"They're women," Terin said aloud, regarding the captives' gender. They were ushered into the yard, their wrists bound in front of them and their right ankles connected in a coffle chain. They wore uniform knee-length gray tunics, with their hair tied off behind them.

"Aye," Criose affirmed, standing to his left. Terin shared his cell with four others, each native Torries and separated by their chained ankles. The slavers were careful to keep chattel separated to prevent scuffles that might damage them before their sale. Foreign men were notorious for establishing their hegemony within their social groups, and captives were no different. Those likely to end up in the mines or galleys were not worth the effort and were often thrown together.

"I didn't think they took female slaves," Terin said as the captives were ordered to their knees, their handlers striking any that faltered.

"Don't pay them any sympathy, Terin. They won't be slaves for long. They'll serve a seven-year indenture to a mistress before granted freedom and citizenship after another seven years of service. If they choose to serve their indenture in the Army or Navy, they'll gain their freedom in three years and citizenship two years thereafter," Criose explained.

Terin was grateful for Criose's company, having been reunited in their current cell, though able to speak only sparingly whenever the guards were beyond earshot.

"Where did they fetch them?"

"Either foreign markets or coastal raids. By the size of them, they appear handpicked for the Federation Army," Criose said, observing the women's greater size. The Sisterhood continuously strengthened its bloodlines through the centuries, importing women of greater stature. Not one of these captives were shy of sixty-two inches, tall by Araxan standards.

"Eyes up!" a slaver commanded the captive women, standing before them with her quirt in hand. Terin did not recognize the slaver, her steely countenance sweeping the kneeling captives with hard green eyes. The women captives were beyond tears, resigned to their fate after their voyage to these far-off shores. Some thought it a kinder fate than what they might have endured on the continent. Those captured from their homes struggled the most to adjust. More than half the captives were Yatin, purchased from Benotrist captors or seized from one of the coastal ports, where so many took refuge from the gargoyle invasion. Small wars were always a boon to slavers, allowing them to easily fill their holds, but larger wars eventually hindered their profitability with too many captives suppressing the price of their wares and forcing many customers to spend their gold for levies and arms. Fortunately, the Sisterhood was always seeking to bolster its ranks, providing a stable market for all sorts of chattel.

"Spare us your tears!" the slaver continued, pacing back and forth before the kneeling women, her thick boots slapping the fitted stones covering the surface of the central yard. She weas dressed similar to Veneva's crew but for gray leather mail and white fur trousers. "This is no time for tears or fears but a chance to seize the opportunity before you, to rebuild your life in a new image, forsaking the failures that brought you so low. You have a rare privilege that no other slaves in all of Arax are so generously afforded. We bring you here today in full view of these other captives so that you might compare your lot to their sorry state. You were hand selected out of countless others, picked by my crew for your…potential. Potential can be a cruel word, often a reminder of what likely goes unfulfilled, but for now is the only currency you possess. Use it! You have a choice this day. Commanders of the Queen's Garrison will offer each of you a choice, a choice these men that surround you will never again have. You pledge your service to the Army or the Royal Federation Navy, and your term of indenture will be three years. Two more years of leal service grants you citizenship and a permanent home in our land as one of the Sisterhood. Refuse the queen's generosity and you shall serve the full seven years to the mistress that purchases your indenture and another seven beyond that to gain citizenship. The choice, of course, is yours. Choose wisely and you may very well find your-self on these very grounds in five years purchasing slaves of your own to grow your new household," the slaver added for effect, her words gaining purchase in their collective eyes.

"You were right, Criose," Terin said.

"Aye, so spare them no pity, for they will grant you none."

"Perhaps, but their fate is still one of woe. Even if they take up the Federation cause, they still forfeit five years of their lives to rec-ompense what they lost…five precious years." Terin thought on what five years of bondage would cost him. Five years might as well be twenty for what would pass him by, the war, family, friends, Corry. Even if the war was won, she would be lost to him, choosing another whilst thinking him dead. He jerked his ankle, cursing the chain that bound him to this place. He stared through the bars of their cell, his eyes following the slaver march her charges from the yard, likely to cages far more comfortable than their own. Slavers were no more than thieves, stealing lives like a thief steals coins, robbing their victims of what years they had left, consigning them to a cruel fate. What fate awaited him on this wretched island? He recalled travers-ing the narrow sea upon the *Stenox* when they set ashore at Tinsay to rescue Cronus, remembering speaking with Tosha as they sailed into port. Despite her antics, especially her tumultuous interactions with Raven, she was always kind toward him. He never thought about the fate of captives in her native isle.

Aunt Tosha, he thought, shaking his head at his father's revela-tion when he revealed their troubled lineage. Would Tosha believe him if he could tell her of their relation? Could he even gain an audi-ence with her? He doubted that he could, but what choice had he? Would she grant him manumission, setting him free for his actions on Molten Isle? Was Tosha his only hope of liberty? Such thoughts only depressed him further.

"Believe what you like, but I'd rather be a slave to a woman than a man," Sivan said, chained upon Terin's other side. He was a Torry helms-man on the *Victorious Wind,* before being washed overboard at Maeii.

"If you think them any kinder, then you're a fool," Criose snorted, sitting back down.

Terin thought to ask Criose why he believed so when the guards came to fetch him.

*****

He stood in the center of the cold chamber, naked, save for the brief wrap tied above his waist. They washed his mouth, scrubbed his body raw, and sprayed an inviting scent over his chest. His hair was combed into a smooth sheen and his hands manacled to chains affixed to the ceiling, drawn tight enough to force him upon his toes. The secluded chamber was deep within the bowels of the massive facility. Terin was brought here hooded, keeping his face hidden, lest someone recognize the Torry champion by chance. They fastened him in place, removing his hood, his eyes adjusting to the dim light. He cast a wary eye to a glowing brazier along the far wall, heat emitting from its embers. He stiffened, feeling a hand run across his back before a woman stepped before him, her gold-blue eyes examining him head to toe, her impassive countenance filling him with dread. The woman was of height to him, with coal-black hair bound in a tail. She wore a golden cuirass over a black tunic, with steel greaves and vambraces gracing her limbs.

"Bold," the woman said dryly, a sudden blow following her brief utterance.

"Lower your eyes!" Veneva's voice commanded behind him, striking his buttocks with her quirt.

He reluctantly complied, not aware that she was there and wondering how many others stood behind him. His eyes couldn't fail noticing the woman's muscular thighs peeking below the hem of her tunic and the straps of her sandals crossing over her calves. She appeared in her fifth decade, her stern nature masking her exotic beauty. She was a commander of some rank, but he could not guess her station. Whatever the woman offered to pay for him would surely be far less than his ransom would bring. He felt that he was overlooking something and expected the ground to swallow him whole.

The woman peeled away the bandage covering his mark, running her fingers over the unique ridges of the crossed swords with the third piercing them, his champion's brand.

"Do you recognize the symbol?" Veneva asked, coming to the woman's side.

"No, though it is strikingly similar to a Torry Elite, but the boy looks too young to be so named," the woman observed, lifting her hand to his chin, turning his face side to side, the action causing his eyes to again meet hers.

"Lower your eyes, slave. I've granted you no privilege to do otherwise," she reproached.

"He claims to be the Torry champion, so named by King Lore," Veneva said.

"King Lore is dead," the woman answered dryly, continuing her inspection.

Terin didn't bother refuting her. What difference did it matter if she believed him?

"The Torry champion has been a vacant title since its inception, waiting for their *chosen* one to emerge and assume the mantle. Am I to believe you are this fabled warrior, child?" she asked, circling back in front of him, lifting his chin with her slender fingers, drawing his blue eyes to hers.

"Does it matter? Do as you will," Terin said, weary of it all.

"You still have a measure of pride. Perhaps you are a warrior after all." She smiled before her sudden mirth died on her lips. "But pride will not serve you well here, child." She nodded to Veneva, who dealt him three more blows.

"Answer her!" Veneva ordered.

"I claimed no such tittle, though my king so named me before leading our 5th Army to Kregmarin. I began my service fighting at Costelin and Rego before joining Captain Raven on his raid to Molten Isle, aiding his rescue of your crown princess from the pirate Lorn Monsoon. We journeyed on to Fera, returning your crown princess to her father, where I aided Captain Raven in rescuing our friend from the dungeon of Fera, fighting our way through the corridors of that mighty holdfast, before battling Morac upon the battlements of the black castle. I disarmed Tyro's champion and saw him flee my blade before taking to the heavens, where I became separated from my friends, save for a Yatin warrior we rescued during our escape.

"I followed Yeltor to Telfer, battling the gargoyles' assaults upon the purple castle before returning to my native realm. It was there that King Lore bestowed upon me the title of champion as a fulfillment of his ancestor's decree, for I wielded the fabled Sword of the Moon, given me by my father, Jonas Caleph, who found it among the ruins of Pharna. It was ordained long ago that the sword would be found by one that was worthy and belong to his house from that day forth. The king so named me before leading the 5th Army to his doom on the plain of Kregmarin. I remained at Corell, training under the tutelage of my grandfather, Torg Vantel, earning my place among the Torry Elite.

"Corell was soon beset by Morac's legions, and we repulsed countless attacks before the siege was broken by our countrymen and Jenaii allies. It was then I was so marked as champion of the realm before joining Prince Lorn at Mosar, where I slew General Yonig. Our Army defeated the gargoyle legions, driving their remnant from the Yatin capital. I then journeyed to Faust, joining our fleet as they sailed against the Benotrist Armada, battling them off the coast of Carapis. I was thrown overboard during the battle. I awoke to find myself captive in the filthy hold of the vile slaver captain who stands in your company, the lowly thief who stole me from the beach where I washed ashore. *That*, my lady, is the truth, and if you doubt my tale, take me before Princess Tosha, and she will prove I speak true!" Terin declared, meeting the woman's eyes with his own icy glare.

She spoke not a word for several eternal moments, her mind working out all that he said. Veneva pulled back her arm as if to strike him, but the woman lifted an open palm, staying her hand.

"And I thought you too young and pretty to be a warrior, let alone one so famed. Of course, there are other ways to determine if you speak true without bothering our princess," she said, running her fingers through his hair.

If she believed him, then why continue this game? Shouldn't she arrange his ransom and ingratiate herself to the Torry Realm? Or was she considering selling him to Tyro? He could ill imagine meeting his grandsire again, knowing their kinship, only guessing how that meeting would end.

"What became of your sword, child?" the woman asked, smoothing a stray hair from his eye.

"I drove it into the deck of the ship before the sea claimed me, leaving it to my countrymen. The blade would not forsake me unless I willed it so."

"Very noble," she said in a voice that he could not tell was complimentary or mocking.

"But the sword is not enough. My people need me. Return me to them and you shall be rewarded a thousand times the price this slaver will charge you for me," Terin threw caution to the wind, appealing to her greed, if she was so swayed.

"Need you? And why would they need you? They have your blade. What more can you offer than that?" She knew there was more that he was not saying. She was already intrigued by his mysterious ascendence through the Torry ranks, as well as his rich bloodline. Torg Vantel was renowned throughout Arax. The thought of owning his grandson played genially in her thoughts.

"Because…" He paused, thinking better of it.

"Because what?"

"Because I am the blood of Kal," he admitted.

The ladies shared a laugh, until stilled by his determined glare.

"Gargoyles fear my blood. I have slain thousands, sending many more to flight. Return me to my people. Let me save them and in turn save you from Tyro's threat," he pleaded desperately, revealing nearly all in hope of swaying her.

"The blood of Kal?" she asked darkly. "Kal had no heir."

"Believe so or not, but his power flows through me, and my prince has need of it."

She backed a step, taken aback by his outlandish claims. Strangely, she believed him, though good sense should dismiss such foolishness.

"Let me see what I'm buying," she said as Veneva removed his wrap.

Terin blushed, burning with shame as they regarded his nakedness. The woman continued her inspection, examining every inch of his flesh, sharing aloud his flaws and attributes in blunt detail.

The entire ordeal went painfully on as he hung there, helpless and humiliated.

"Very well," she finished. "Remove this mark and we shall discuss price," she said, indicating the champion's mark burned into his chest. His eyes drew wide, wondering how they planned to do that, and why. Why remove proof of his rank among the Torry Elite unless…

His line of thought was broken as Veneva fastened his ankles to the floor, shackling his feet far apart before stepping toward the brazier. His heart pounded as she lifted the iron from the glowing embers, smoke pouring off its flat rectangular brand as she stepped nigh.

"Remain still or I'll have to do this twice," she ordered, pressing the brand to his chest, the mark obscuring the champion's sigil. He fought the scream escaping his throat, eventually succumbing as she removed the iron, steam emitting from his scorched flesh. Veneva rubbed salve upon the burn as they stepped without, leaving him hanging there in the secluded chamber.

*****

"The boy pleases you, Guardian Darna?" Veneva asked, leading her guest into the adjoining chamber, a well-lit sanctum furnished with a small table with blank parchments and quills upon it.

"He shall suffice," Darna said with practiced disinterest.

Veneva smiled, knowing the remark an affirmation. Darna was not one to express overzealousness in negotiations that would drive up the price. Darna was the third guardian of the realm and cousin of the queen. She held command of the garrison of Bansoch. Her rural estate northeast of the city was so vast that it stretched countless leagues north and a quarter distance to Fela to the west. She owned three salt mines, two iron mines and one silver, as well as a small merchant fleet and thousands of slaves, which required her to constantly replenish her stock, especially her mine and galley slaves. Field slaves lived long with good treatment, and the slightest disobedience would send them to the mines or galleys, which kept them docile. Most estate owners favored handsome field slaves, consigning the rest to harsher enslavements, but Darna cared little for the aesthetic qualities of her field slaves, preferring a strong back over a pretty face. Domestic servants, however, were a reflection upon her wealth and status, and she suffered no dullards or eyesores among her household slaves. Her husband would constantly choose the ugliest to serve in the household, but she handled all slave purchases herself. He certainly wouldn't approve of her plans for the boy, but his authority was consigned only to the running of her household, not the grander plans to expand their power.

"And his price?" Veneva asked carefully. A galley or mine slave might fetch fifty certras, a field slave two hundred, and a domestic between two and eight hundred. If the boy spoke true, his ransom was worth a hundred times that, but arranging payment without losing one's head was not worth the risk.

"I asked you to bring me warriors, and if the boy is truthful, you brought an Elite, but…he is Torry." Darna sighed, feigning disappointment.

"You never objected to purchasing my Torry captives before," Veneva challenged. Queen Letha outlawed the import, transfer, and purchase of Torry slaves within the Federation, forcing Captain Veneva to sell them elsewhere or off-load them to buyers willing to risk the queen's wrath. Since all slaves arriving at Bansoch were inspected by officials under Darna's purview, she remained the *only* buyer that Veneva could safely sell her Torry captives.

"Buying slaves that I can hide in a galley or mine is one thing, but for the purposes I intend to use the boy…it is risky."

"Yes, your queen's fondness for the Torry Realm complicates things," Veneva said, wondering why Queen Letha held such an affinity.

Darna knew well that answer but wouldn't share such information with her most trusted lieutenants, let alone a lowborn slaver captain. But even if a part of the boy's tale was true, he would be *perfect* for what she had in mind, far beyond her original plan. "Of course, the boy has certain…attributes that spark my interest."

"Yes, he is quite pretty," Veneva smiled wickedly. "I thought to keep for myself, if it wouldn't disrupt my crew."

"Yes, perhaps my daughter will find him to her liking, but to me that is irrelevant."

"Her preferences have merit, but the boy is also untouched," Veneva decided to increase his price with that last rare tidbit.

"How can one be certain of such?" Darna asked skeptically.

"One can tell if one understands what to look for." She smirked. "Once I discovered that, I thought to keep him that way for your inspection."

"If true, at least the boy has morals."

"Another point in his favor and price."

"Yes, his price. These things are fine attributes, but my primary requirement was for a male of warrior stock. He appears to be a warrior and an Elite, how much so, I shall soon determine. Two thousand certras, all in gold," Darna offered.

"Most generous, Guardian Darna." Veneva bowed. "And what of my other Torry cargo?"

"What of them?" Darna asked.

"I thought to sell them here, if you would be interested," Veneva played the game carefully, the usual haggling of price that Darna took such pleasure in.

"Perhaps I might have use of them."

"There is one that recognized the boy."

"And he verified his story?" Darna asked darkly.

"He did."

"And he knows the boy?"

"Not before they were captured, but when I threatened the slave's life, the boy confessed all to spare the wretch. I am fearful he might spread the tale of Terin's capture by my hand and thought to toss him overboard."

"We can't have that, can we? And killing him would be wasteful. How many Torries have you?"

"More than twenty."

"Very well, I'll take the lot of them. Fifty certras apiece."

"Do you wish them marked before transfer?"

"No, I will see them branded at my estate." Darna dismissed the offer, preferring to place her mark herself.

"As you wish."

"This concludes our business for today. I shall arrange payment and collect them on the morrow after the auction," Darna finished, stepping without.

*****

Terin lost track of time as he hung there, the pain in his arms and the burn in his chest torturing his every moment. It took several days for the pain of his first brand to subside, and now Veneva branded him again, the flat rectangle mark obscuring his sigil.

It was late in the day when Veneva finally returned. She stood before him for a time before addressing him.

"You are fortunate to find your mistress's favor, Terin. If you are a good boy, she may even let you keep these." She touched his groin, a cruel smirk passing her lips.

Whatever happened to this woman to make her so? he thought miserably. She unshackled his hands, drawing his tunic back over him before rebinding them behind his back and freeing his legs. She marched him back to his pen, taking no chances with him. She never once gifted him a chance to test his skills since plucking him from that Yatin beach, and she sure wasn't going to start now. Slavers were careful by nature and exerted complete control of their captives. Once he was sold, that control rested with Darna, and she knew the guardian to be a strict mistress.

*****

The following morn

Thousands gathered upon the auction grounds, an expansive open area before a raised block, some twenty meters square, overlooking a sea of buyers and onlookers. 'Twas a spectacle that became less frequent with the queen seeking to limit its practice, but even she could not end it outright. Like their contemporary realms on the continent, the Sisterhood depended upon slave labor for its mines and galleys, while thousands of indentures worked the larger landed estates. Even the minor merchants and craftswomen throughout the harbor used at least one slave in their household and twice as many female indentures. The realm restricted the number of male chattel, wary of repeating the mistakes of their Soch predecessors, who held one hundred female slaves for every male citizen, sowing the seed of their ruin.

Terin stared out through the bars of the pen, his mind in a dreamlike fog, straddling sleep and consciousness. All the slaves were similarly drugged, their food laced with the strange concoction that morn. 'Twas another means of control the slavers used on their captives, rendering them docile in a dreamlike state as they were brought to the block. The effects would last most of the day, when most would be sold, branded, and shipped to their final destination. Terin and his fellow Torries were moved to a pen at the periphery of the auction grounds, able to witness the disgusting spectacle in the distance. Terin rested his head against the back wall of the pen, his hands again bound painfully behind him. He spent so long in the cursed manacles his shoulders ached constantly, even in his drugged state.

"When will our time come?" a young Torry named Zaran nervously asked, sitting off Terin's left.

"We shan't, boy. We've already been sold," Criose answered him, sitting between Terin and the boy, shaking the fuzz from his vision, struggling to see clearly as another slave was brought to the block. The slave looked no older than Zaran, but from this distance, they couldn't be sure. He was mostly naked, save for a brief kilt wrapped around his waist. The boy staggered across the block, his handlers putting him through his paces as the auctioneer announced the bids.

"Sold!" the auctioneer's voice sounded, pointing out a wealthy merchant amidst the crowd for the winning bid. The boy was dragged from the block, a female indenture taking his place. Unlike her male counterpart, the girl remained mostly clothed, wearing a knee-length tunic, and only ordered to demonstrate basic movements to prove her capable.

"Sold!" the auctioneer declared, a wine merchant from Fela placing the highest bid. And so it went throughout the day, until Terin and the others were drawn from their pen and loaded into a caged wagon, each given a drink of sweet-tasting wine laced with Fleacen powder, which would put them to sleep throughout the journey.

As Terin sat on the hard metal surface of the wagon bed, he struggled to keep his wits before darkness took him, crying out against his hopeless state, but no words escaped him. Wherever they were taking him, it was farther from the sea, from freedom, from ever seeing Corry again. His entire life was a sacrifice, for his realm, his people, his destiny, while denying him the one thing that brought him happiness—her. It struck him, then, that this was how Cronus must have felt, rotting in the dungeon of Fera, thinking his true love was lost to him. But Cronus had friends that knew his whereabouts and possessed the means to free him, whilst Terin was dead to the world. If he was to gain his freedom, he had to find his own way. And with that he fell to darkness.

*****

Queen Letha's palace

Tosha stood upon the terrace, overlooking the city below, the smell of fresh sea air filling her nostrils. She closed her eyes, savoring the familiar pleasures of her native isle. She retired often to the outside or the privacy of her personal chambers, weary of her mother's court. She felt the eyes of palace courtesans, officials, and ruling nobles upon her, judging her obvious condition with no proof of her consort to acknowledge the child. Though wed by the Benotrist ritual that her father's realm adhered, the Sisterhood required a royal consort present before birth to pledge fealty to his future queen and the child they shared. Oaths of fealty were demanded of all but consorts who were kings in their own right, and Raven was no king. He was expected to present himself before the throne and take his place beside her. His absence was an offense to the House of Letha and the realm. Though her mother understood her leanings, the realm would be slow to overlook her yoking herself to a foreigner, as her mother had. A few with longer memories and secret knowledge knew that her grandmother had chosen a foreign consort as well, a fact the queen never revealed to Tosha, hiding Letha's own father's identity from her, lest Tyro learn of it.

"Why have you tempted me, Raven?" She sighed, recalling their first meet upon Molten Isle. She knew even then that she could have no other. What choice had she but to claim him through trickery? Would he have come otherwise? She was the sole heir of two realms, should she not claim what her heart so desperately wanted? What good was such power without taking the one thing that you desired most? And Raven felt the same, even if he was too stubborn and prideful to admit it, she reminded herself to assuage what she put him through. She thought again of their parting on the shores of Veneba, when she told him of their child quickening in her womb, and the concern for the child so clear in his eyes. She loved him all the more at that moment, confirming her greatest hope that he would choose her over his pointless wanderings. What life was there sailing the endless sea when your child dwelt here? If she learned anything about Raven in all the time they shared, it was his loyalty and love for his comrades and family, but she was his family now. Should not his loyalty belong to her above all else? Of course, he would remind her that loyalty was earned, even for her, and recall all her trickery, lies, and subterfuge.

Her eyes opened, drawn to the auction grounds resting southeast of the palace, near the waterfront. It seemed the activities were concluding, crowds emptying into the streets. There was a time she would attend every such event, finding amusement in the spectacle and making a purchase when the urge suited her, but now it filled her with disgust. 'Twas another change Raven manifested in her, forcing her to look at the suffering such a practice caused its victims. Oh, it was usually preferable to death, but its severity should be restricted to criminals, debtors, and evil men, which even Raven would agree as he once consigned that cruel captain to slavery for abusing that child. It finally struck her in Axenville, watching that young girl dragged to the auction block, triggering memories of her own ill treatment by Monsoon, forcing her to put herself in that girl's place. She would never see slavery the same again. If only she could change her father's heart in this matter, but his hatred for his Menotrist kin ran deeper than the ocean, a lifetime of hurts, slights, and savagery kindling the fire within into a raging inferno. He would never forgive the Menotrists for all their sins, aligning himself with gargoyles to destroy his mortal foe. Even that victory could not assuage his pain, continuing his war upon the Venotrists and countless kingdoms along Northern Arax and now with the Yatin and the Torry Realms.

She thought of her last night at Fera, where her father revealed the origin of Terin's necklace and the implications that portended. Was Terin's father Tyro's lost son? It was unthinkable but explained so much. If the last reports from the Torry Realms were true, Terin led the defense of Corell, holding Morac's legions at bay and slaying thousands of her father's minions until the siege was broken. What would her father think when he learned that his plans of conquest were destroyed by his true heir?

"You are brooding again," her mother said, coming to her side, her stormy gray eyes meeting Tosha's gold. Queen Letha sought out her daughter once she concluded court, still dressed in rich silver robes that rippled in the gentle winter breeze, a slender golden crown gracing her thick ebony hair.

"Just needed fresh air." Tosha sighed, returning her gaze to the auction grounds in the distance.

"The throne room can be stifling at times, as well as the people therein."

"I see how they look at me, Mother. They believe I soiled myself, siring a child with a foreign stranger," she said bitterly.

"They are sorely disappointed, that is to be expected. Many hoped you would choose a son from one of our great houses for consort."

"As if I'd choose a pampered weakling from that sorry lot," she sneered. She had seen the sons her mother's vassals brought to court, parading the foppish dandies through the palace as if to catch her eye.

"I once thought as you, seeking strength in a mate rather than choosing to strengthen our bonds to our vassals. Alas, I chose poorly, and it nearly cost me the throne."

Tosha heard this tale numerous times but never from her mother's lips. Letha wed Tyro after his ascension to the throne, only to discover his plans to absorb her realm into his own once their heir was born. She swiftly dissolved their union and foiled a Benotrist landing upon her shores.

"Raven isn't father. He makes no claim upon our throne."

"No, but he is a threat to our social order, which disturbs our more traditional vassals."

Tosha rolled her eyes at the mention of said traditionalists, having often aligned with their political block, hoping to strengthen her bonds with her mother's harshest critics, securing their loyalty. Her wedding Raven spoiled all her machinations. She foolishly thought bringing a man such as Raven to heel would prove her worth in their eyes, but her failure only made her look weak. They would argue that a queen unable to rule her consort was unable to rule the realm. His absence only worsened her position.

"Raven is a threat only to himself," Tosha tiredly confessed.

"Your father would disagree." Letha bit a smile, receiving word of the devastation Raven wrought at Fera with expected mirth.

"Of course that pleases you." Tosha rolled her eyes, not understanding her parents' continued grudge.

"Your father has forsaken humankind, pledging loyalty to gargoyles."

"He aligned with gargoyles before you were wed, Mother. Where was your judgement then?"

"I thought to turn him from his folly but was seduced by his charm, forgetting my responsibility to my throne. My mother had just passed when I first met Tyro, and my father as well. I found solace in his arms, his affection soothing my lonely heart. I thought he would forsake the gargoyles for me, but I was wrong." She sighed.

"Your father died as well? Who was he?" Tosha asked, her mother never speaking of him. Whenever she asked, Letha would turn away, as if pained by his memory. Even Tyro did not know, as Tosha asked him if he knew Letha's father. She thought he was a consort, chosen from their noble houses, but her mother's behavior cast doubt on that theory.

"I vowed to never tell you until you reached maturity, not trusting you to keep this from your father and forcing the few who knew him to remain silent, each taking a vow to remain so. It seems now it is time for you to know the truth."

"The truth?" Tosha asked, taken aback by her cryptic words.

"My father was a king. A mighty king who wed your grandmother Theresa in secret, their union kept secret from their respective realms. It was agreed that if she bore a daughter that she would be heir to the throne of Bansoch, and if male, be given his father's throne."

"And they bore you, meaning grandmother received her heir," Tosha sagely guessed, wondering still who her grandfather was.

"She bore a male heir as well, a man who inherited his father's realm…my brother." Letha sighed sadly.

"Then who was he?" Tosha asked, running the names of the great kings through her head, quickly narrowing the list, until only one truly made sense.

"King Lorm III was my father, and his son, Lore, my brother. Lore was my brother until he was slain by your father's minions," Letha said bitterly, as Tosha recalled her mother's distress over the Torry king's passing.

"King Lore was my uncle, and you thought not to tell me? Why?" Tosha's voice rose an octave with that betrayal. Corry and Lorn were her kin, and she never knew.

"I foolishly thought if your father knew his child had Torry royal blood that it would only hasten him to supplant Lore for your ascension."

"If I had known, I might have turned him from such folly, pleading on behalf my uncle, my blood." Tosha shook her head. It all made sense, the invitation of female royalty to gather upon their shores every six years. It was a return of those with Sisterhood blood in their veins. Corry was the granddaughter of Queen Theresa, and this was as much her homeland as Tosha's. It also meant that the royal houses of Macon and Nayboria had wed their monarchs to the queens of the Sisterhood sometime in the past.

"I believe nothing could have turned him. His pact with the gargoyles taints his reason and compassion. He is beyond redemption."

"Beyond redemption? Castigate my father all you wish, Mother, but are we any different?"

"How so?" Letha regarded her darkly.

"Do we not enslave, punish, and brutalize those that threaten our realm, or subjugate those whose labor we require? Look yonder to the auction grounds for proof of our own cruel treatment of others. Humankind has always enslaved one another. The Benotrists simply sought out nonhuman allies to further their aims when no other humans would help them. Look to our Federation. Were we not founded upon the doctrine of female dominion? Did not Queen Melida lead our foremothers in revolt over the old Soch Empire to establish such an order?"

"She did not," Letha said dryly, refuting another falsehood that clouded her daughter's knowledge of their history.

According to legend, the old Soch kings ruled over the isle, holding hundreds of thousands of female slaves in bondage, believing them easier to control than male slaves. The Soch were inventive and cruel masters who brutalized their chattel, spreading their reign to the continent from as far inland as present-day Laycrom, to as far south as Faust. Their use of male slaves was restricted to the continent, fueling their expansion, but slavery was not their greatest sin. It was their dalliance with gargoyle chieftains, whom they sought to make common cause, that drew the ire of ancient Tarelia. Letha explained this to Tosha, her daughter's rigid posture unyielding, refusing to believe this tale, but Letha continued.

"Melida and Telisa were the daughters of a Tarelian general, trained as warriors by their father as all women of that ancient freehold were. In those days, women and men of Tarelia fought side by side, as they were the last redoubt of King Kal's fallen realm and the keepers of knowledge. It fell to Tarelia to stand against the darkness as the gargoyles spread across Arax, threatening to topple the realms of men. It was the Tarelians who forged the Swords of Light, gifting them to their generals, who used their mysterious power to establish realms to contest the gargoyles. The Northern Kingdom, Middle Kingdom, Eastern Kingdom, and Western Kingdom were so founded, each driving the gargoyles back to their nesting grounds along the Plate Mountains. The old Soch king Vagar undermined their aims, so the Tarelian Council gifted two Swords of Light to Melida and Telisa, to destroy the Soch Empire, using them as a rally cry for the women oppressed by those wretched men. With the Swords of Light, Generals Melida and Telisa led a small host to these shores, gathering a massive Army of freed slaves, toppling the Soch Empire and slaying their King Vagar upon this very hill," Letha said, stretching her arms to the palace grounds surrounding them.

"And enslaving the men of Soch as recompense, establishing the precedence of female dominion that continues to this day," Tosha said, finishing her mother's point.

"No. They slew the men of Soch, every last one. Not one male slave taken by the Sisterhood was of the Soch. Consider Melida's husband, the first consort of the realm."

"Zur Zellion," Tosha named the Tarelian warrior who fought by Melida's side, the fresco painted upon the ceiling in her bedchamber depicting both of them standing upon the shores of Bansoch waging battle.

"Yes, Commander Zellion, who fought bravely at her side, helping her to liberate the female slaves held by the Soch. He helped establish the Federation, the first to bend the knee, acknowledging her as queen. Yes, a man was the first true citizen of our Sisterhood," Letha said.

"Why would a man, a commander, like Zellion submit his men to slavery?" Tosha wondered, always believing the first slaves were Soch captives.

"He didn't, and Melida would not accept that, even to appease her new subjects. The Tarelian men she led in battle wed the leaders of the revolt, forming the first great houses of the Sisterhood, each held in great esteem. Melida did not come to this isle and topple the Soch Empire in order to free its slaves. She came to topple the Soch *because* they supported the gargoyles."

This was new to Tosha, for most women raised in the Sisterhood believed the original purpose of their realm was to establish female dominion and shield their Federation from wickedness of men. What happened to transform their purpose so dramatically?

"The original aim of their revolt was successful, the removal of the Soch threat to the Tarelian Kingdoms on the mainland, but Queen Melida was faced with severe imbalances threatening the tenuous hold she held on her new realm," Letha explained, leading Tosha to correctly guess the obstacle to the Federation's stability.

"No men," she said.

"Yes. With the Soch demise, Queen Melida's people were faced with a difficult choice. Her new subjects were mostly comprised of freed female slaves, with women outnumbering males by large margins. Melida thought to invite men from their fellow Tarelian Kingdoms to dwell in the Federation, but her people were fearful of men reestablishing dominion over them, forcing Melida to implement a code of stratification before importing male chattel."

Tosha knew well the sacred codes, the rules governing the realm, maintaining their social order. Foremost among Queen Melida's edicts was the establishment of maternal inheritance, ordering the lines of succession through the female line. Sons could not inherit lands or titles above daughters. Eventually sons could not inherit unless wed, their wives receiving title before them, and their daughters after. The laws were similar to those on the continent but simply reversed. Sons were soon valued solely on their match to fellow houses to strengthen old alliances, settle disputes, or forge new bonds with other houses of the Federation. It became the wives that led their houses, confining husbands to the managing of the households. Successive generations further strengthened the matriarchal control of the isle realm. Just like the patriarchal realms on the continent, some marriages were more egalitarian, with genuine love between spouses. Many women within the Federation were content to allow their husbands rule their households while occupying themselves with their public role. Others, however, were fearful to surrender any measure of power over to their husbands or consorts, who might use them to subjugate them just as on the continent. It was a mixed bag.

Queen Letha was forced to balance the differing factions vying for the direction of the realm. To one side was the reformers, wishing to move the Sisterhood to a more egalitarian society, where sons were granted equal status to daughters. They hoped that men and women could serve equally in the Army and ruling forum, own land, and practice trade. The traditionalists opposed the *starry-eyed* reformers, believing men would use any measure of freedom to reassert their dominion. Letha naturally aligned with the reformers out of her respect for her father, but with her mother, herself, and now Tosha each wedding foreign men, she could not publicly ally herself with their interests.

"Because of your choice in mate, as well as my own, we are forced to align ourselves with the traditionalists for the near future." Letha sighed.

"You are queen, Mother. Queens must rule as they see best, not bow to the whims of their lessers."

"Queens are not omnipotent. We are bound by the very foundations that placed us upon the throne to begin with. Though I sympathize with our reform-minded sisters, I must deny them for the greater good, and that greater good has nothing to do with the fate of our realm, but the fate of humankind."

"Mother?" she asked, wondering her direction.

"Our forebears were sent to topple the Soch Empire as a means to oppose the gargoyles, for that reason above all others. My duty as queen of this Federation is to oppose gargoyle dominion throughout Arax. As daughters of ancient Tarelia, we are bound to that aim above all others. If I must appease the traditionalists to achieve this end, I will, even if I must consign the men of our isle to brutal subjugation."

"Thus, placing me between you and my father," Tosha lamented.

"You are heir to my throne, Tosha. Your place is by my side, not to follow your father's delusions. There can be no compromise with such evil."

"And if I bear a male heir for father to claim? Would you wage war upon your own grandson?"

"Tyro will never have your child, male or female."

"Mother, I promised," she argued.

"I have permitted you to visit your father through the years, hoping you might soften his heart, turning him from his folly. All that that accomplished is to twist your own thinking to his. Why do you think I have waited until now to tell you that my father was King

Lorm? You have your own rich inheritance and birthright far greater than Tyro's stolen glory."

"Stolen glory? Father is many things, but he earned his place, forging his empire through his own cunning and guile."

"Yes, he built his empire with a stolen sword, using flowery words to convince a naive child to gift him the blade, the very blade his chief lieutenant used to kill my brother."

"A child gifted him the Golden Sword?"

"His son," Letha said, her eyes fixed to the horizon, where the sun shone off the surface of the bay.

"Terin." Tosha's eyes drew wide.

"Terin? The Torry champion?" Letha asked.

"Yes. Father believes his lost son might still live and that Terin can lead him to him."

"And how would Terin know Tyro's son?"

"Because…Terin's father may be his son."

Letha was stunned, the irony of Tyro's ambitions brought low by his own heir was almost too humorous to be true. Terin was also one of those who helped rescue Tosha and Corry at Molten Isle. She started to laugh, unable to mask her mirth. She very much would like to meet this boy, and if her spies were correct, Terin had won the favor of her niece, Corry. The last reports she received placed the boy in Yatin, aiding her nephew in his campaign there.

"You are humored?" Tosha reproached her.

"Mind your tongue, child, I am still your queen. After all the grief your father has given me, I am entitled to take a little pleasure in his misery. He will not have your child for his heir, and his true heir will not have him. Cannot have him." She smiled.

"Cannot have him?" Tosha made a face.

"If Terin is who your father thinks he is, then he can never be his heir, for what does light share with darkness?"

"You are speaking in riddles, Mother."

"Your father once told me about his first wife, his lost love, and the child they shared. There is more to the woman's heritage than he probably told you. Would you care to hear it?"

"If it concerns my brother that I have never seen, then yes," Tosha said.

"We should start with your father's true name…"

*****

Terin awoke to a terrible headache, finding himself locked in a dark, narrow cell with his ankles shackled together, his hands connected in a loose chain and an iron collar affixed to his neck. He tugged at the rough iron band, testing its strength. A small metal ring dangled from the front of the collar for some cruel purpose he could well guess. He was clad in a simple brown kilt, exposing his bare chest. He had no way of knowing where he was or how long he slept. His sleep was restless, the drug they slipped him causing strange dreams, a hellish mantra of twisted memories that never came to pass but felt so real that he mistook them for true ones. Most involved Corry either rejecting his affection or cruelly betraying him for another, the details lost in his dreamlike state. He recalled one vision of Torg driving his sword through his heart upon discovering his kinship to Tyro, and another of his father transitioning into a gargoyle before sinking his fangs into his mother.

Sunlight eventually broke through a small window in the outer corridor, indicating it was morning. His keeper, a stout-built woman in thick leathers, brought him a plate of gruel and cup of water and spoke not a word. More time passed before his keeper returned with two other guards to collect him, attaching a leash to his collar, leading him outside. He burned with humiliation, not understanding how anyone could treat another person that way. Despite the suffering he witnessed in his travels, he was ever mindful to treat others fairly and with respect. It was a value his parents instilled in him since childhood. It wasn't until he left his home in the countryside for the larger world that he saw his first slave, finding the unique institution unsettling. In Torry North, only criminals and debtors suffered in bondage, their duration and labor regulated by the king's law. Everywhere else, it seemed slavery flourished, entrapping innocent men, women, and children to its cruel ministration.

Once outside, he was greeted by rolling hills, surrounding a cluster of buildings, most of which appeared to be pens or various sorts. He saw no sign of his fellow Torries, later learning they were held elsewhere. His heart pounded emphatically as they brought him to a small clearing with a dozen female warriors in polished gold cuirasses over black tunics, surrounding a stone circle some ten meters abreast. He recognized one of the warriors as the woman who inspected him at Bansoch, able to see five braided cords gracing her shoulders, marking her a higher rank than an Army or legion commander. Terin locked eyes with her as she stepped near, his keeper forcing him to his knees as she stopped in front of him.

"I am Darna of House Estaran, 3rd Guardian of the Sisterhood, and…your mistress. When your mistress enters your presence, or you enter hers, you are to kneel and place your head to the ground. Do you understand?" she asked.

"Why are you doing this? My realm will offer y—" he asked foolishly as the guards forced his head to the ground.

"Speak not of your realm or former station. They have no meaning for you now. Accept this and obey," Darna commanded, motioning her guard to raise his head.

"Do you understand?" she asked.

"Yes," Terin glared at her, wanting nothing more than to strangle her.

"You will address me as mistress and lose the defiance I see in your eyes, or I shall burn it out of them," she warned. For the purposes she intended him, he didn't need eyes.

"Say it!" his keeper growled in his ear, twisting his leash in her hand.

"Yes, mistress," he relented, seeing little point in fighting her at this time, from a position of weakness. Part of him wanted to give up and die, forgoing this torment, but he couldn't give up, not yet. He needed to find a way to escape this hell and return to the fight against Tyro.

"Better, but you have much to learn, child. Let us begin!" she declared, stepping away as another slave, a Yatin, was dragged forth to the center of the stone circle, fixing a manacle to his left ankle before freeing his hands. The ankle chain provided enough slack for him to move several yards in each direction.

"You'll need this," one of the guards sneered, dropping a short sword at the Yatin's feet.

"Pick it up!" another ordered as the man stared at it warily before snatching it up.

Terin wondered what they planned to do when the unmistakable sound of a gargoyle's guttural hiss drew his gaze to his left, where two guards dragged the creature into their midst, fastening its left ankle to another manacle in the center of the circle, with enough slack to reach the Yatin slave. Terin noticed that the gargoyle's wings were shorn off, rendering it flightless. The absence of its unique appendages made the creature look rather unimpressive, but its hate-filled eyes and sharp fangs quickly refuted that notion.

Terin's keeper kept him at a distance as the guards dropped another sword at the gargoyle's feet.

"Kill your opponent and you will continue to live!" Darna said, standing off Terin's left with her arms crossed.

Other than the few soldiers and handlers gathered around, there was no grand audience for this spectacle. It made little sense. Darna obviously went through great care collecting her captives, only to have them battle to the death for her sole amusement. Or was there something he was overlooking? His thoughts quickly shifted with the captives giving battle. The gargoyle moved first, rushing toward the human, the rustle of its chain dragging over stone echoing in the chill air.

"Agghh!" the creature hissed, the Yatin's sword meeting its hurried strike. An exchange of blows soon ended as the gargoyle managed to block his opponent's sword while sinking its fangs into the man's neck. Several guards rushed forth, driving the gargoyle back with leveled spears, as the Yatin's body was removed, and another man dragged forth to replace him. The second fellow managed to slay the gargoyle but suffered a terrible gash to his unprotected stomach. They simply slit his throat, ending his suffering before dragging two more combatants forth, a wingless gargoyle and man pairing. The gargoyle finished the man after a brief melee, which seemed to please Darna, allowing her to proceed with her true plan.

Terin winced as he was brought to his feet as the second dead man was dragged away. The gargoyle paced back and forth at the far end of the circle, forced back by the guards' spears, its eyes ablaze for battle until they met Terin being fastened to the shackle opposite him, their vibrant luster shrinking to dull crimson.

"Your sword," the guard said, after freeing his hands, dropping the blade at his feet.

Darna observed curiously as Terin retrieved the sword, glaring daggers at her, ignoring his gargoyle foe.

"Kill the creature or perish, slave. The choice is yours!" Darna said. If the boy died, it would be a waste of the gold she paid for him, but it would answer to his lack of skill, disproving his outlandish claims. But if he prevailed, it would give credence to his tale and the rich possibilities that would portend. Strangely, the gargoyle stood statue still, as if transfixed by the boy. It was most unusual. The gargoyles she purchased were expensive and forbidden by the Crown. Queen Letha detested the creatures and wanted none on the isle. Darna shared her concerns about the possibility of some escaping and building nesting grounds in the island's remote corners, thereby threatening their people. She ordered the wings removed from all her gargoyle captives. The process was quite risky due to their wounds bleeding out if not properly cauterized.

The two combatants just stood there, the gargoyle frozen in place and Terin looking at Darna before turning his attention to his wingless foe. Terin strode across the circle, delivering a forceful thrust the creature weakly met, the blow dislodging the blade from the gargoyle's grip. Terin drove his sword into the creature's gut, kicking him to free the blade.

"Perhaps you are a warrior after all," Darna said. "Let us further examine your skills." With that, the guards drove him back at the point of their spears, while others finished his kill and cleared the carcass. Another wingless gargoyle was brought forth, fixed to the now bloody manacle, thrashing violently throughout the process until its limbs were freed and a sword dropped at its feet. No sooner had it picked up the sword then its fiery eyes fell upon Terin, freezing it in place as Terin closed and finished it.

The warriors surrounding the stone circle looked warily to Darna, who observed the spectacle with masked indifference.

"Proceed!" Darna said as two gargoyles were brought forth to engage Terin. They were slaughtered nearly as fast as the single combatants. Next, they brought three and then four to no greater effect. Darna watched as Terin moved across the stone circle with graceful ease, cutting down his foes as if they were practice dummies.

"Enough!" Darna commanded, having seen enough of Terin's effect on gargoyles.

Terin stepped back as the guards cleared the dead, spinning his sword loosely in his right hand, testing its feel. It felt good holding a sword again, though the cheap iron blade was a far cry from his Silver Sword. He wondered the point of this exercise. Was it a test of his skill? A way to compare the fighting styles of different foreign soldiers? Or was it merely for Darna's sick pleasure? His gaze swept the austere assemblage, noting their growing unease in his presence, uncertain if that was a good thing or not. Selfishly he wanted their respect, but the more guarded they were, the more difficult his escape. He shifted uneasily as they brought forth his next opponent, a Benotrist soldier, as they called out his origin.

If Terin approached a human any differently, it was not apparent to the onlookers as he dispatched the Benotrist after a brief exchange. When they brought out two Benotrists to fight him, Terin paused, wondering the endgame. Did they plan to have him fight until he died? For what purpose? After he dispatched the Benotrists, who seemed afflicted with the same paralysis as the gargoyles, they brought forth a Yatin. He fared slightly better against Terin, able to control his fear, but to do so crippled him in other ways. Terin disarmed the fellow, tapping his sword to the man's throat.

"Dead!" Terin said, backing away, announcing what could have happened if he wished it. The Yatin breathed in relief until Darna interjected.

"Kill him!" she commanded Terin.

"I kill my enemies, mistress, not allies of the Torry Realm at the behest of my captors," Terin said, lowering his sword, gifting her a mock bow.

"Kill him or I'll order him to kill you!" she warned.

Terin brought his blade forcefully down upon the joint of his manacle, a dangerous blow if gone awry. Darna's warriors drew back with shields raised as his manacle fell away, the blow stinging his ankle, though he showed it not.

"I'm free now, Darna. Retract your claim on my person and step aside, so I can take my leave of this place." His eerily calm voice unnerved her soldiers.

"No," she said icily, stepping forward of her guards, stopping a breath away, her gold-speckled blue eyes staring intently into his sea blue.

He tightened the grip on the sword, spinning it in his hand, backing a step.

"What choice have you but to submit?" she said in a voice only he could hear. "Slay me and you die. Run, and I shall find you. Where can you go? You do not know this land or in which direction to flee. You are a collared male on an isle matriarchy. Even free males are forbidden swords and may not travel without escort. I paid two thousand gold for you, Terin. I'll not let you simply walk away. My plans for you will not be wholly unpleasant. We are done here. Drop the sword and kneel. I'll not ask you to kill again," she offered, having learned what she wanted.

Terin stole a glance to the surrounding hillsides, the euphoria of breaking his manacle quickly waning. His hope of ending this nightmare fading as the path to freedom loomed near impossible, but the thought of again submitting to her kindled his defiance.

"I'll not be your slave." He leveled the sword toward her, his pounding heart sounding in his ears.

"As if you have a choice, child." She lifted a dark eyebrow, unmoved by his threat.

He wanted to kill her, to step forth and drive his sword through her cold heart, but something held him back, as if unseen tendrils wove themselves through his mind, binding his will.

If you do this, Tyro will triumph, a voice whispered in his mind.

The sword dropped to the ground, his hand betraying him, as if it that too was now possessed by something beyond his understanding. Was it the blood of Kal that betrayed him, the will of Yah, or some other ethereal force conspiring to force his submission, keeping him alive? He lowered his eyes, refusing to look at the cold smile gracing Darna's lips.

"Bind him!" she ordered, his keepers hurrying uneasily to obey, a healthy fear of him now guiding their steps. They drew his hands behind him, closing tight fitting manacles about his wrists, leading him away.

"Kill the rest," Darna commanded, leaving no captives to spread the tale of what they saw.

C H A P T E R

18

Maeii

Cronus stepped within, his eyes instantly drawn to the sword resting upon the table—Terin's sword.

"Cronus Kenti." A strong voice drew him from the thoughts racing through his brain, thoughts of Terin, since his blade was here without its master. He recognized the face of the man who called out his name, though he only met the man once in passing.

"Sire." Cronus knelt, addressing his crown prince, Galen following in kind.

"Stand," Lorn said, each man taking the other's measure, battle-worn armor and soiled garments making them a matched pair.

Cronus counted five commanders of rank and seven members of the Torry Elite standing along the periphery of the room, one an elder warrior whose grim demeanor set him apart. Cronus was worried that there was no sign of Terin, Lucas, or Kato.

"I was told that Cronus Kenti was in Sawyer, or at least en route in the company of Minister Antillius?" Lorn questioned.

"You were told true, sire. We accompanied Minister Antillius to Sawyer."

"We?" Lorn looked to his comrade, before recalling what Terin and Lucas told him. "Then your friend is Galen the Minstrel, I assume."

"Most assuredly, My Prince." Galen gave a dramatic bow, delighted that his fame preceded him.

"If you know of our mission, then our friends must have told you. Yet I don't see them here, Highness?" Cronus asked, his eyes again drawn to Terin's sword.

Lorn released a tired sigh. These men traveled far, and he regretted having to give them these ill tidings, but waiting only made it worse. And so he told them.

Cronus felt a dagger in his heart as Lorn relayed the awful tale of Terin's loss and Kato's fall. How could this be? No two men were more responsible for their victory at Corell, and now they were gone. Was he a curse to his friends? He thought of his brother Cordi, and then his comrades slain at Tuft's Mountain and the dungeons of Fera. Arsenc at Kregmarin, and now Terin and Kato. The princess would receive this news poorly, and Raven—he could ill imagine what Raven would do. His thoughts began to race from Terin to Kato and back again, weighing the horror of each loss against the other.

"We are lost," Cronus whispered. Only Terin could strip the gargoyles of their courage. He was irreplaceable, driving the enemy from the battlements of Corell time and again, charging headlong into their host, where the brave dare not tread. And Kato, who else but an Earther could counter Thorton?

"We are not lost. We are far from it because of them," Lorn said.

"Forgive me if I feel otherwise, Highness." Cronus hung his head, placing his hands flat upon the table.

"Should the Hero of Tuft's Mountain despair?" Lorn stepped nigh, placing a hand to his shoulder.

Those looking on stiffened at the mention of Tuft's Mountain, knowing the fell deeds done there by Cronus and his brave companions and the suffering he endured after.

"Terin journeyed to Fera, to the heart of the Black Castle, to set me free. How many men would do that?" Cronus said, looking Lorn in the eye.

"Precious few, Cronus Kenti, but I stand before such a man." Lorn didn't give him leave to refute. "We all owe Terin more than we can repay, just as we owe Kato…and you. We mourn our friends but do not serve their memory if we despair. We must go on."

"Grief and despair are not the same, Highness, though I feel an unhealthy share of both. We fight because we have to, for there is no other course, but I despair our chances. I have known Terin for long enough to see his worth. He is unique and possesses a skill we can't replace. You have gained a great victory here in Yatin, but we bring ill tidings, Highness." Cronus hated having to relay such news after the prince told him of Terin and Kato.

"What tidings do you bring, King's Elite Kenti?" Jentra asked, stepping to Lorn's side.

"Cronus, this is Jentra, Elite Prime and my trusted counsel," Lorn introduced them.

"I am honored," Cronus said, offering his arm, which Jentra clasped.

"As am I, Cronus, but to the point, what news have you?"

*****

"Blasted Macon treachery!" Jentra cursed, nearly kicking the table after learning of the siege of Sawyer and the wounds Squid suffered.

"More opportunism than treachery, but dire all the same," Lorn calmly summarized, pacing the room, weighing their options.

"Opportunism? Bah! Cowardice, more like it. He waits for us to be hundreds of leagues away to steal neutral lands. We keep their lands safe from the gargoyles, and they reward us thus!" Jentra snorted.

The others looked equally distraught. Every man at Maeii was beyond exhausted, fighting and marching since departing Cagan, their victory at Mosar now spoiled by the loss of Terin and Kato, and now the Macons pressing their advantage.

"Anger will not serve us, Jentra," Lorn reproached, trying to work out a feasible strategy.

"It might not serve us but still feels good," Jentra growled.

"What can be done?" General Farro asked. "The nearest force we have to Sawyer is Fonis's 2nd Army. We can't move them without exposing Rego and Central City. Once Tyro learned of that, he need only send one legion to take half the realm."

"Besides the fact the Macons deployed enough troops to cover the northern approaches of Sawyer, a thousand men holding the Salucan Gap can hold off twenty times their number," Jentra pointed out.

"And the 1st Army is hundreds of leagues from Sawyer," General Farro said, regarding the 1st Army's position southeast of Cagan.

"We don't have to lift the siege by marching to Sawyer," Lorn reminded them.

"You're not thinking what I think you're thinking?" Jentra made a face, his pounding heart already anticipating what Lorn was about to do.

"Grand Admiral, begin the full withdraw. It may take several trips to ferry our men south, but I'll leave you to coordinate with Generals Farro and Yitia. Everyone will be removed to Faust. Once there, you will continue to move the 4th Army to Cagan," Lorn commanded.

"Yes, sire," the grand admiral agreed. General Yitia acquiesced, his arguments for the Torries to remain rendered impossible with their southern flank threatened.

"How many magantors can you spare, Grand Admiral?" Lorn asked.

"I can spare none, but if your need is dire, then I can weigh it against the threat of the Benotrist Fleet," Kilan reasoned.

"I will need two," Lorn said.

"When do we leave, sire?" Jentra asked.

"Sunrise. We are taking Matron Ilesa with us. That will give her the rest of today to treat the most grievous injuries. The rest will have to wait. Grand Admiral, by the time you reach Cagan, I will be elsewhere. Fare thee well, my friend," Lorn regarded him fondly.

"We shall see it done, sire," Kilan said proudly.

"Cronus, give me your sword." Lorn held out his arms, Cronus setting the blade in his hands, wondering the purpose. Lorn examined the finely crafted blade befitting a great warrior but not of the quality worthy of a Royal Elite. Torg had yet to craft Cronus's blade, an oversight that the master of arms would likely correct when time allowed.

"Highness?" Cronus asked, as Lorn handed the weapon over to Jentra.

"We shall store this with your saddle pack," Lorn said. "Terin sacrificed his life to preserve this blade for our cause. It falls to me to name a worthy master to wield it." He lifted the Sword of the Moon from the table, placing it in Cronus's hand.

"Highness, I am not—" Cronus tried to protest, but Lorn was having none of it.

"Disobedience is unbecoming in a Torry Elite. The sword belongs to the man in whose hands I place it!" Lorn commanded.

Cronus wrapped his hand around the hilt, a sudden jolt pulsing from the ancient metal coursed up his arm. He recalled the night he first held this blade after the Costelin raid, when he escorted Terin back to Rego. Terin let him handle the blade to sate his curiosity. The power the sword invoked that night was but a sliver of what he felt now, as if every particle of his being was charged with an otherworldly power. The blade alit with its luminous azure glow, bathing his countenance with its ethereal light. He wondered if this was what Terin felt every time he wielded it.

"I feel that taking his sword is a betrayal of him," he voiced his troubled thoughts.

"His last act was preserving that sword for our cause, giving his life to do so. Who better to wield it than his dearest friend? He would choose you over any other," Lorn said.

"I will serve as best I can, My Prince, though I will be a mere shadow of Terin's glory."

"I am not asking you to be Terin. I am asking the hero of Tuft's Mountain to do his duty. Now, go rest, both of you. We leave on the morrow."

*****

Carapis

They stood upon the rocky slopes overlooking the beach littered with debris and corpses coughed up by the sea. The stench of decay was mostly gone, with flocks of carka birds feasting on carrion, picking the bones of dead sailors clean. The skeletal remains of sunken wrecks protruded from the surf, where they ran aground in the deadly shallows during the battle. Some ships capsized, their wooden hulls floating like the corpses of dead giants, twisting in the waves.

"Shall we help him, Highness?" Galen asked, observing Cronus working his way along the beach, searching for bodies amidst the broken masts and torn sails that washed ashore.

"I will go. Help the others with the cook fire," Lorn commanded, making his way down the steep slope, leaving the minstrel with their magantors, where Jentra, Ilesa, and their two riders began to set camp.

Cronus rolled over another corpse with his boot, the face decomposed beyond recognition. The back of the sailor's tunic was dark, almost black from the sand and mud. Perhaps the front had a clear patch where he could determine its true color.

"It's not him," Lorn said, standing over his shoulder, the distinct patch of cloth upon the dead man's breast showing a dull yellow.

"Yatin commander of first rank," Cronus noted the single braid adorning the body's shoulder, the equivalent of an Army commander of flax.

"Only a few of the dead washed ashore. Most foundered at sea or drifted to the Donah Isles or beyond. Most are versk food," Lorn said, lowering Cronus's expectations of finding Terin's body.

"I know, but I have to at least try," Cronus said.

"We sent several ships to scour this entire area, looking for any corpse wearing a blue tunic. They searched the Donah Isles and several leagues in each direction along the beach and found nothing."

"How long did they search? Was it thorough or a quick pass over?" Cronus asked, moving to a leg protruding from beneath a torn sail.

"Very thorough. We even searched several leagues inland in case some made it ashore and went looking to forage, but found nothing."

"Did you find anyone alive?"

"A few. Mostly Yatin sailors from the *Mosar's Hammer*, the ship going aground just north of here. Three Benotrist and seven Torry sailors were found throughout the area. They were taken to Maeii."

"You would think more made it ashore," Cronus said, cutting the sail away from the corpse, revealing wormy flesh clad in a brown tunic with an iron band wrapped around the left ankle, the right leg severed below the knee. He drew back from the ghastly sight, the body likely that of a Yatin galley slave.

"Cold water and strong currents make for difficult odds. Jentra said it was dark and stormy when Terin washed overboard. Don't torture yourself, Cronus. There is nothing to be gained looking in vain for his body."

"If I don't find his corpse, he could still be alive," Cronus reasoned, moving to the next body, a tunic stretched over shriveled flesh.

"Looks like he was alive long enough to strip off his leather mail." Lorn squatted over the poor fellow, examining the body closely. He was a Torry sailor by the looks of it, a scabbard riding his left hip, the sword missing. It was surprising how few swords and armor they found washed ashore. Perhaps scavengers picked over the beach before them.

"No matter how many bodies I see, I never get used to it, but you don't seem affected, Highness?" Cronus said, drawing away from the corpse as soon as they identified it.

"Should I be?" Lorn shrugged, indifferent to the body at his feet, before stepping toward Cronus.

"Most men are, even killers who think nothing of taking human life. From what I observed, you take great care in saving everyone you can, and yet you stand here indifferent to the bodies strewn across this beach." Cronus couldn't make sense of it.

"Fair enough, but let me ask you, Cronus, what do you see here?" Lorn waved an open hand to the body they just inspected.

"A dead man."

"And what do you see there, there, and over there?" Lorn pointed out several areas where Cronus already searched.

"More dead men."

"No." Lorn sighed, shaking his head. "Not men, just flesh, flesh in rapid decay. In another week, even the bones will be devoured."

"They are still men," Cronus rightly pointed out, wondering how the prince could be so callous.

"No, they are not men, not anymore."

Cronus gave him a horrified look.

"What you see, Cronus, is the physical elements of men without souls. The soul"—he touched a finger to Cronus's heart—"is the elixir of *life*. Once you die, the soul leaves the body, leaving behind this crude matter we call a corpse. A corpse without a soul is merely flesh. It is nothing but a shell of what once held life, like the skin of a serpent or the shell of a crustacean."

"They are still humans, still men," Cronus said, staring at Lorn as if he were mad.

"Everything that made them human, or men, or alive, is gone. I strive to make this a better world for the living. We honor the dead by honoring what they lived for, not the vessel they journeyed through life with. Terin told me what happened to my father, how Morac desecrated his corpse, parading his head before my sister, believing he desecrated his legacy. The head he displayed to my sister does not reflect who King Lore was or represent his final moments. He died on the Plain of Kregmarin defending his kingdom. What happened to his body afterward is of little meaning."

"I was there when Morac…did that. It had meaning to the princess. He did it to unsettle her but underestimated her strength," Cronus recalled that awful memory.

"Her reaction is understandable. Bodies, though dead, kindle emotions with those who knew them. When we see a body of a close friend or loved one, they remind us of that kinship, similar to seeing a carving or portrait of them. We sometimes bury our dead as a feeble attempt to preserve them in some way, for them to carry on after they are gone."

"Like preserving Kato's body," Cronus said, as Lorn ordered it returned to Cagan, where he would be placed in the royal tomb.

"Yes. I ordered his body preserved to honor his service to the Torry Realms, though that is no longer Kato. The essence that made Kato who he is has passed on."

"Then why honor his corpse?" Cronus asked as they approached more bodies washed up on the beach.

"To honor his memory. We know his deeds, so great that we could not forget. Our children and grandchildren will learn of his greatness, tales of his deeds reaching them from our own lips. But what of future generations? Time is the great erasure. We can remember our greatest acts by immortalizing them with monuments or the written word or both. At least to a degree."

"Memorials only last as long as the realms that construct them."

"Of course, for no works of man are immortal. Only our actions are eternal in the eyes of Yah."

"Yah." Cronus shook his head dismissively as they came upon three more bodies, each wearing the tunics and boiled leather armor of Torry sailors. "Squid spoke often of your god, but tell me, Highness, what kind of god strikes down his servants who have served him well?"

"Being Yah's servant does not shield us from our mortal curse. All men and women will die. What matters is what you do with the time you are given."

"Your father…Kato…Arsenc…Terin…" Each name fell painfully from Cronus's lips, each a precious son or friend of the Torry Realm. Cronus paused, green eyes meeting blue. "They are the greatest of Yah's servants, and he allowed them to be struck down when we needed them most."

"I cannot know Yah's mind. I can only trust my life to him and follow his will," Lorn said.

"How can you know his will?" Cronus didn't believe any of it.

"When I am able to clear my thoughts of all the distractions that conspire to overwhelm me, he helps clarify my vision. It is often not the distractions that lead me astray, but my own prideful heart. Pride is like poison, whispering seductively in your ear all that you wish to hear while leading you to destruction."

"Is not pride essential for a monarch?" Cronus asked. By now they stopped searching, standing in the loose sand, the sounds of the waves crashing ashore, echoing in the air.

"The greater power one holds, the more damage pride can inflict. Pride can close your ears to reason, destroying sound judgement. Yah cannot dwell in a pride-filled heart, Cronus. Only when you expunge such poison will you hear his counsel."

"That still doesn't explain why Yah struck down our friends."

"I honestly don't know." Lorn sighed, his gaze drifting to the sea, losing himself in its endless expanse.

"For some deaths, there are no apparent reasons. We are placed upon this world with free will, to choose whichever path we will. It is not just us who have free will but the natural world itself, a world that can strike us down for no reason at all. Sometimes Yah intervenes to prevent this, to preserve select individuals who serve his plans. Conversely, there are those he strikes down, their death triggering events that serve the greater good," Lorn explained.

"I don't see any greater good in Kato or Terin's death. Kato's death gives Thorton free reign. Terin's death…" Cronus lowered his head, the words catching in his throat.

"Removes our greatest weapon," Lorn finished his thought.

"Yes, which dooms our cause. Ever since I first knew Terin, he had this power to calm my spirit, setting aside my fears, as if all was right in the world. Whenever I fought beside him, I knew we couldn't lose. He wasn't supposed to die," Cronus said sadly.

"Perhaps that is why he was taken from us," Lorn said, keeping his eyes to the sea.

"Explain?" Cronus asked, not following his reason.

"Terin was born to a purpose, Cronus, to be Yah's sword. To smite the gargoyles. Terin is our champion, our friend, our hero. But he is not divine. We mortals tend to worship the doers of miracles, ascribing godhood upon mortal actors. Yah is a righteous god but also a jealous one. It is his power that fuels Terin. Men are not to place any man above Yah. Perhaps Yah took him away to force us to trust in his power fully rather than Terin's."

"Terin was never boastful. He was humble."

"Yes, and Kal was Yah's faithful servant, and yet he allowed him to fall. It is not judgement upon Terin or Kal but upon us."

"Then why punish them?"

"They were not punished, Cronus. They rest now in the immortal realm as Yah's most faithful. It is we who must go on."

"That doesn't make any sense. According to that logic, we can't defeat Tyro unless we submit to Yah's will, but if we become his most faithful servant, he will strike us down."

"No. Kal was removed because his people did not follow Yah's will, so Yah punished them by removing Kal. Perhaps Terin's true purpose was to briefly demonstrate Yah's power, showing our people the way. With him gone, we can still receive Yah's blessing if we all follow his will. Think of our power if an entire realm marches in step to the will of Yah."

"I hear your words, but your voice betrays your doubts, Highness," Cronus said, not missing the uncertainty in his voice.

"I wasn't always as you see me now, Cronus. I was a cruel, petty child, without a trace of humility or kindness," he confessed with a faraway look.

"What changed?"

"I received a vision. A terrible vision, but in hindsight, it was the greatest gift Yah has ever bestowed upon a mortal man."

"What kind of vision?"

"I was shown the fate of our world, our doom, and with it, my suffering. I was shown all the might arrayed against us and what my selfishness would bring about."

"Your selfishness?"

"Yes. Yah revealed the fate of all the realms established by the Tarelian order, one falling to ruin after another, after their thrones passed on to lesser men…faithless men. Eventually, only the Middle Kingdom remained…our kingdom. If we should fall, then Arax would fall with us. Our people were only preserved because a wise king learned of the other kingdoms' folly and awaited the one who would return with a Sword of Light, leading us against the gargoyle foe."

"Jonas," Cronus said.

"Yes, Jonas. But what the vision revealed was that my wickedness would doom us, consigning our people to slavery and death. All of Arax would fall under Tyro's dominion. Yah also revealed the true nature and origin of the enemy."

"The gargoyles?"

"Yes."

"What of them?"

"They are the mortal descendants of the fallen elect, once the devout of Yah."

"Then why are they his enemy now?"

"Their ancestors were immortal and followed one of their own in open rebellion. Yah cast them from his sight. Most were thrown down to another world, to dwell in spirit form to confound the hearts of men, whom they despise. Some were cast here, twisted into the creatures you see now, their eternal lives exchanged for mortal forms, mortal but able to breed in great numbers."

"Why do they hate humankind?"

"Because we are favored by Yah. Of all the peoples of Arax, they are lacking the slightest measure of righteousness, compassion, or love. They strive only for the destruction of humans and humankind, save for those sworn to their cause."

"The Benotrists," Cronus said.

"Yes, the cursed. The longer they serve beside the gargoyles, the further their hearts will wax cold, their cruelties growing in magnitude until there is no possible path to return to the light."

"You can't reason with evil men. You can only kill them."

"Tyro wasn't always evil, Cronus. He was forced to make difficult choices, turning to the gargoyles to help destroy his enemies, enemies who deserved his anger."

"You sound almost sorry for him?"

"I pity him, Cronus. There can be no room in our hearts for hate. We are miserable, wicked creatures, deserving of Yah's wrath, so we must tame our darker inclinations."

"Don't you hate the gargoyles? You speak of the need to destroy them."

"We must destroy them, but I don't hate them."

"Why not?"

"It goes back to the vision I was given. I was shown all the cruel and petty acts I had done, seeing myself for the vicious child that I was and the evil king I would become." Lorn turned his eyes suddenly to Cronus, staring into his eyes with such intensity that Cronus felt his skin pimple. "How can I hate anyone or anything more than myself after seeing my true form? I immediately awoke and dropped to my knees, begging Yah to forgive my wretchedness. I begged him to save my people, to take my life as payment. He didn't kill me, but he took my life all the same. From that night on, I was his. If I die today, I can rest knowing I followed his will. My life is his, and I need only do as he asks."

"And by following him, you are guaranteed victory?" Cronus doubted it.

"Victory is not guaranteed or ensured. Our people might forsake Yah before victory is achieved, just as they did in the days of Kal. When I was shown the full might of the enemy, I despaired, briefly forgetting my faith. Once I shook such doubts from my mind and soldiered on, Yah gifted me a second vision for my loyalty."

"And what did this vision reveal?"

"That I wasn't alone." He gently smiled. "I couldn't carry this burden alone. Yah knew the burden too much for one man, as it was with Kal. He revealed Terin's origin and purpose."

"I know there is more to Terin than he has said."

"There is, and one day I will reveal the mystery that surrounds him, but he was not the only help Yah sent to aid me. There are many, but three stand out above the others. The first is Terin, his powerful blood instilling panic in his foes. The second, however, stands before me." He placed his hand upon Cronus's shoulder.

Cronus made a face, not making sense of Lorn's words.

"I was shown your face and fell deeds. Your first encounter with Terin did not come by happenstance. You and Terin are kindred spirits, both steadfast and loyal. You were meant to be friends. Did you not feel a strange kinship when you first came upon him?"

"Yes," was all Cronus could say, bereft of words, as if Lorn could read his thoughts.

"Yes, like he was a younger brother, much like the one you lost," Lorn said with a timeless look, his words striking the mark.

Cronus looked away, wondering how Lorn could so easily read him.

"So you see, Cronus, Yah did not give me a burden too heavy to lift alone. Terin may be gone, but you are not. It falls to you to wield the Sword of the Moon, to stand beside me against our common foe."

"I will stand beside you, Highness, but I don't believe in Yah," Cronus answered honestly, thinking it all nonsense.

"You are free to believe what you will, but he has plans for you all the same. Come, let us help the others set camp for the night. You will not find Terin's body on this beach."

Cronus shrugged, following Lorn up the rocky slope, when something Lorn said came to mind. "You mentioned seeing the others that would aid you, Highness, saying three stood out from the others. Was Kato the third?"

"No. He was one of the many, but not the third that would play a most significant part."

"Then who is he? Do you know him?"

"I don't know him, but you do." Lorn smiled, saying no more before walking on ahead, leaving Cronus to ponder the cryptic meaning.

*****

They gathered around their cook fire, each sitting quietly with the waves breaking the shore echoing methodically below. Cronus sat deep in thought, staring at the crackling flames as Galen sat beside him. The minstrel was eager to strike a conversation, but knew not to bestir Cronus when he was morose. The others looked even less promising, with Jentra's sour disposition and Ilesa's somber spirit. She was still in mourning for Kato and did not take well to flying, having deposited the contents of her stomach after eating.

Galen found the two other magantor riders even less talkative, both asleep upon their bedrolls. He gained his feet, stepping away to find Prince Lorn, who stood first watch a short distance north.

"Unable to rest?" Lorn asked, standing upon the rocky slope overlooking the ocean, moonlight playing off its surface. Lorn stood with his arms crossed over his chest, his eyes scanning the horizon north along the coast as Galen stepped beside him.

"Sleep has never come easily, Highness. A most inconvenient affliction since childhood, but such a deficiency is not without benefit," Galen said, drawing his cloak about his shoulders with the cool breeze sweeping over the shore.

"A reference to your creativity and imagination," Lorn said, taking one last look to the sea before turning inland to circle their camp, Galen falling in step beside him.

"Very astute, Highness. I have spent many a night conjuring lyrics and ballads until sleep overtook me. I must say, when others spoke of your keen sense of clairvoyance, I thought it an embellishment. Their assessment it quite observant."

"It doesn't require a seer of great wisdom to recognize certain traits that lead to creativity. Most artists have restless minds that are in constant motion. Such obsessions are difficult to douse, even at day's end, leaving you wide awake and staring at the ceiling, or stars above in our case." Lorn pointed a finger skyward, emphasizing his last point.

Galen was impressed. "Very perceptive, My Prince. I sense you are equally afflicted?"

"Sometimes. Whenever I let my troubles master me, rather than the reverse. It is when I look upon the heavens on a clear night sky that I can set my mind to rest. When you gaze upon that endless expanse, stretching beyond our imagining, you begin to understand." He stopped, staring at the starlit sky in all its majesty.

"Understand, Highness?"

"That our troubles shrink before the mysterious vastness of creation. Each of those stars in the sky is a sun as large as our own, with worlds circling them like our own. So vast is creation that any rational man would see his own insignificance before such wonder. When I look upon such a thing, my troubles seem far less significant."

"You believe each of those stars is of a size to our sun?" Galen never considered such a thing. He thought they were celestial objects that alit the night sky. Or perhaps, they were children of the sun and would one day grow to the size of their mighty sire, lighting the night as the sun does the day.

"Philosophers and wise men have always debated the mysteries of the universe. Most are far wiser than I, each offering explanations both thoughtful and brilliant, but that doesn't make them correct, however."

"An interesting summation, Prince Lorn. One equally worthy as any other put forth."

"It is not a theory, Galen, just simple fact. Each of those stars potentially have worlds like ours circling them. On one far away is the Earthers' home world," Lorn casually acknowledged, as if such a revelation was a simple thing. He spoke with such conviction that Galen almost believed him.

"Your god has gifted you this knowledge?" Galen asked, guessing the source of inspiration in his theory.

"Of course. Such things are beyond my understanding. Nearly all of my insight is a gift of providence. We live in extraordinary times, Galen. You, my friend, are privileged to witness the pinnacle events that will shape our world. Who better than a gifted bard to observe these happenings with his own eyes?"

"I am humbled by your generous opinion, Highness. I had not thought on this good fortune. I shall endeavor to produce an epic ballad worthy of your deeds."

"Not my deeds, Minstrel, but all of our deeds, whether they are great or weak, gallant or unbecoming. Let posterity judge our achievement or malfeasance. Simply tell our story in all its pain and glory. You'll have no shortage of songs to sing." He stopped just east of their camp, their magantors standing between their cook fire and them, their silhouettes casting long shadows across the open ground. One of the avian caught Lorn's eye, standing out from the others with its ethereal beauty—Wind Racer.

"Terin's magantor was a wondrous gift from King El Anthar." Lorn sighed.

"A most august gift, befitting the hero of Corell," Galen opined.

"Well spoken. You could pen a storied song on that noble beast, let alone the others, whose deeds are momentous in compare. Perhaps a ballad heralding those lost to history, whose contributions are equally significant. Think of Lady Ilesa. She and her fellow healers labor tirelessly tending our wounded and risk death alongside us. How many of her guild fell with my father at Kregmarin? Ilesa's tale is doubly tragic, losing her true love. How many widows will this war make? Are their sorrows any less than others? How many young maids will not find husbands with so many unwed men falling in battle?"

"It is much to consider," Galen conceded.

"Yes, and you are the bard to tell it. I was told that you have performed for many royal courts. Is this so?"

"Indeed," Galen said proudly.

"Was the Macon Court among them?"

"I was received at Fleace four years past, at the court of King Mortus."

"What did you observe there?"

*****

Four days hence
Cagan Harbor, Soren Palace

They set down upon the palace green, greeted by a unit of regent guards, their spears leveled in alarm until recognizing Prince Lorn.

"Highness," their commander hailed, taking a knee before Lorn waved off such curtesy.

"Commander, please see to my companions, and have the steward provide them the finest accommodations, the Lady Ilesa especially. Escort me and these two gentlemen to Regent Ornovis," Lorn said, regarding Jentra and Cronus. Their weary group was travel worn and filthy and in need of nourishment. Lorn would forgo such niceties until after treating with the military and harbor officials. The hour was growing late, with the sun hanging low upon the horizon, its waning rays reflecting off the surface of the sea. Lorn shared a look with Jentra and Cronus, knowing they had a long night ahead.

*****

"I think we can begin, Highness," Vintor Ornovis said, briefly meeting everyone's gaze before stopping at Lorn. Vintor was second cousin to Lorn and regent of Cagan. He stood of a height to Lorn, with silver overtaking his once dark mane. He was dressed in emerald-hued robes, with silver stitching along the hems and sleeves of his garments. They were joined by Jentra, Cronus, and several commanders of rank, including the garrison commander of Cagan, Telanus Corvis, and Admirals Horikor and Morita. They circled the map table where southeastern Arax was richly displayed. Thankfully, each of the commanders were already at the palace when Lorn arrived, allowing Vintor to quickly summon them to his council chamber. Their resplendent attire stood in stark contrast to the prince and his companions, who looked travel worn and haggard, proving the urgency of what needed to be discussed.

"Cronus," Lorn said, calling upon him to relay his tale.

"Sawyer is under siege by the Macon 1st and 2nd Armies. They have repelled repeated assaults from both sides of the Monata River, as well as flotillas sent upriver. Macon magantor patrols have confined Sawyer's warbirds to the city. All land approaches have been cut, leaving the lake as the only avenue of supplying the city. We were only able to escape by placing our magantors on a ship and slipping away before taking to the skies," Cronus explained.

"We have received no word of this," Regent Ornovis said, before looking to Admiral Horikor, the ranking commander present.

"No news from the sea," Horikor stated, his cool dark eyes studying the Macon coastline on the map.

"General Lewins should still be camped southeast of here," Lorn said, tapping a point on the map mid-distance between Cagan and the Macon Border.

"Slightly east of there, Highness," Telanus Corvis, commander of the Cagan Garrison, corrected, reporting the reposition of the Torry 1st Army.

"Is his muster complete?" Jentra asked. The 1st Army was still short several telnics before the 4th Army departed for Yatin.

"Nearly full. Last report puts them just over nineteen telnics," Corvis affirmed.

"And your garrison, Commander?" Lorn asked.

"Five telnics here at Cagan, another fifteen units at the garrison of Tuk," Corvis answered.

"If you are thinking of relieving Sawyer, Highness, the only feasible path is to send a force up the Nila and set ashore somewhere between Teso and Zulon. Both kingdoms might lend troops to the expedition, and from there, a direct path circumventing the Salucan Gap can be used to attain Sawyer. This operation would take a great deal of time, and Sawyer might well fall before we lift the siege. We would then attack headlong into two Macon Armies. Adding to our troubles, Torry South would be open to invasion," Admiral Horikor explained, the other commanders nodding in agreement, hoping to dispel any notion of starting a war with the Macon Empire.

"I have no intention of marching on Sawyer, Admiral," Lorn said, his words causing collective sighs of relief, his next utterance quickly reversing that.

"I intend to envelop Fleace," Lorn added.

"Highness, that is madness. We are—" Admiral Morita protested vehemently before Jentra cut him off.

"Prince Lorn has spoken, Admiral. The decision is made. We march on Macon!" Jentra's harsh tone settling the debate.

"I will lead the Torry 1st Army to the Gap of Borin." Lorn indicated the point on the map one hundred leagues northwest of Cesa, along the Torry-Macon border. "We shall hold position, while you shall disembark the Cagan Garrison somewhere along this line." Lorn ran his finger along the Macon coastline west of Cesa.

"The garrison, Highness?" Corvis asked in alarm. "We are a post force. We—"

"You are Torry soldiers, Commander. You will go where Prince Lorn wills it!" Jentra growled.

"From there, you will march on Cesa and seize the port in conjunction with the 2nd and 5th Fleets." Lorn regarded Admirals Horikor and Morita, who would oversee the transport of Corvis's troops and engaging the Macon Navy.

"Highness, if we land such a scant force on enemy shores, they will simply sweep us into the sea," Admiral Horikor rightly argued.

"The Macon 1st and 2nd Armies are hundreds of leagues away, besieging Sawyer. The Macon 4th Army is still at Null. That leaves the Macon 3rd Army guarding the Torry border. Our latest information places them somewhere between the gap of Borin and the approaches of Tuk," Lorn said.

"And your presence at Borin should keep them from moving on Corvis's troops when they land," Admiral Morita, commander of 5th Fleet, nodded with approval.

"And should they move against Corvis, the 1st Army will cross over into Macon and take them from behind," Lorn added.

"Even so, Highness, the garrison of Cesa is of equal size to ours. Five thousand men against an equal number holding a defensive position," Admiral Horikor said. He needn't add that Corvis's troops would not likely have siege equipment. Everything would have to be constructed. There were no forests near Cesa to construct new ones either.

"I've been to Cesa three years ago, Admiral. The lay of the land along its western approaches is hilly and uneven. You could hide much of your strength there beyond the walls of the city," Cronus said, his weary eyes staring intently at the map, struck by an idea.

"Hide what strength, King's Elite?" Horikor asked, evidently irritated.

"Not to hide our strength, but our weakness," Lorn surmised Cronus's intent.

"Highness?" Corvis asked, not following what they planned.

"You will deploy with the banners of the 1st Army, Commander. Take the city if the opportunity presents itself. If not, you will lay siege, making the enemy believe the 1st Torry Army is at Cesa," Lorn explained.

"And when the Macon 3rd Army vacates the border, believing we have abandoned it as well, General Lewins will advance into Macon proper." Admiral Morita again nodded in approval.

*****

After a warm bath and change of attire, Cronus joined Lorn and Jentra upon a terrace overlooking the palace grounds, where they were served warm food before retiring for the night. Cronus wanted nothing more than to crawl into bed and sleep for days. He could barely remember when he last slept peacefully.

"Thank you," he acknowledged the servant filling his goblet as he sat the table. She smiled appreciatively at his compliment before circling, serving his comrades.

Lorn smiled inwardly at Cronus's politeness. His father said it was a true measure of a person how they treated those placed below them. That advice served him well through the years, surrounding himself with those who practiced common decency. He could see the weariness in his friends, each struggling to remain awake, which further revealed their character. It reminded him of another thing his father often said: *Fatigue reveals a person's nature, and wine, his thoughts.* He noticed Cronus eating rather slow, his gaze drifting to the mouth of the Nila, the lights of the harbor playing off its still surface. Soren Palace overlooked the harbor proper, its impressive structure towering over the foregrounds that ran to the river's edge.

"Eat well, Cronus. Good food will be a rare delicacy soon as you set sail," Lorn encouraged.

"Sail? Aren't we going with the Army?" Cronus asked, Lorn's comments drawing him from his melancholy.

"I will be with the Army. You and Jentra will be going with Admiral Horikor."

"I'll not leave you again. As Elite Prime, it is my duty to watch over you!" Jentra snorted, staring daggers at his prince.

"I will be well protected, Jentra. I trust each of you to oversee the coastal operations. Commander Corvis seems ill enthused with the entire affair. I expect you to stiffen his resolve. I need our garrison troops to set ashore to force Ciyon's hand," Lorn explained. General Ciyon was the reported commander of the Macon 3rd Army.

Jentra quietly shook his head, knowing when Lorn made up his mind, there was no point in trying to change it.

"You question the wisdom of this, old friend?" Lorn smiled wanly.

"Bah! It's madness. If anyone other than you suggested this perilous strategy, I'd rightly call them mad."

"Is that not what you say with all my plans?"

"Yes," he snorted. "And that is the *only* reason I'm blindly following you into oblivion."

"Fair enough." Lorn grinned, lifting his goblet toward Jentra before partaking.

"What do you know of this Macon general you will be facing, Highness?" Cronus asked.

"Ciyon is young for his rank and a son of a high noble house. By reputation, he is known to be aggressive, unconventional, and vainglorious. He is also rumored to be quite handsome."

"He sounds like trouble," Jentra growled. Aggressive and unconventional were synonymous with dangerously unpredictable.

"You see, Cronus, why I favor Jentra's company?" Lorn smiled, setting his goblet down.

"It's not his charming disposition," Cronus bluntly replied, the remark drawing a laugh from the prince and a mild shrug of agreement from Jentra. The comment reminded Cronus of something Raven would say. It seemed his friend's personality rubbed off on him to some degree.

"As charming as Jentra is…" Lorn lied, "it is his honest appraisal of my actions that anchors me in turbulent water. Brutal honesty is the bane of delusion," Lorn said, regarding his old friend.

"When has my brutal honesty ever swayed your delusions?" Jentra snorted.

"More than you know, old friend." He smiled. He didn't say that his delusions were visions sent by Yah and allowed him little room to maneuver at the strategic level.

Cronus couldn't bring himself to believe in Lorn's god but couldn't help admiring the man. He was a worthy king.

"Highness," a sultry feminine voice called out from the stone archway behind them, where a stunningly beautiful woman walked toward them with two ladies in waiting trailing her.

Lorn immediately stood upon seeing her, recognition evident in the smile breaking upon his face. Cronus and Jentra stood as Lorn stepped to the woman, embracing her before she could curtsy.

"You look beautiful as always, cousin." He kissed her forehead.

"You are too kind," she said as they pulled apart.

"Cousin, you know Jentra." He stepped farther back, allowing his friend a clear view.

"Lady Illana." Jentra nodded politely.

"Jentra, you are as dashing as ever." Illana curtsied.

"Your vision doesn't match your beauty, my lady." Jentra shook his head.

"My vision is excellent, good sir." She gave him a flirtatious wink before looking to Cronus. "And your other handsome friend, cousin?"

"Cronus Kenti, recently named to the King's High Elite and hero of Tuft's Mountain," Lorn said.

"My lady." Cronus bowed, the women greeting him in kind.

"I am Illana Ornovis. Your legend precedes you, Cronus Kenti." Illana stepped forth, extending her arm. The name of Cronus Kenti was held in high esteem in Cagan, though that was not always so, when his friendship with the Earthers brought him into conflict with certain elements within the city council. His actions at Tuft's Mountain changed all of that, and now he was spoken of with revered awe.

"I am honored, Lady Illana," he said, kissing her hand.

"I grieve the loss of your friends, Cronus. I know you were fond of Kato and Terin…" She paused, her eyes growing moist. "Terin spoke well of you."

"It is kind of you to say, my lady. I wasn't aware that you met Terin."

"I saw him briefly when he returned here with Princess Corry and again at Corell after his flight from Fera. He spoke well of you and feared you might not have escaped."

"He was a good friend." Cronus smiled wanly, greatly understating what he meant to him.

"I know." Illana touched a hand to his cheek, her gray eyes staring knowingly into his green. She stepped away before calling her companions forth, introducing them as Lady Giana Fortus and Lady Portencia Galba, each from noble houses of Cagan and Tuk, respectfully. The ladies greeted each of them warmly before escorting Jentra and Cronus to their bedchambers, leaving Illana with Lorn.

"You look lovely, Illana," Lorn again complimented her as his friend passed through the archway.

"Flattery will always earn you a smile, cousin." She winked before leading him to the edge of the terrace, resting a hand on the stone parapet separating them from the palace green below.

"Something troubles you?" Lorn couldn't miss the look that transformed her face from flirtatious to somber.

"Have you sent word to Corry of Terin's fall?"

"I sent Lucas before word reached us of Kato's death."

"Lucas stopped here briefly but did not share this news. He stayed only a day before continuing his journey.

"He was instructed to tell no one except Corry," Lorn explained.

"She will not receive this news well, Lorn. She is fond of him. *Very* fond of him," she said firmly, her eyes staring intently into his. When her father mentioned this news earlier in passing, she received it as a blow to her heart.

"And she will blame me, no doubt." He sighed more from grief than self-pity.

"She has lost everyone close to her except you, and you have rarely been there when she needed you," she said as kindly as she could.

"That makes it all the harder. Everything I have done has been to save our people, and yet I couldn't save my father, Kato, or Terin, as well as countless others. I feel ashamed for sending Lucas to tell her this awful thing, when it is my responsibility, but I have little choice in that. She will begrudge me this slight as well, adding it to my list of sins. She must hate me so." He looked away.

"She doesn't hate you, cousin. She is simply alone and hurting." She could see his countenance begin to crack, the stress of so much responsibility crushing him.

"She has every right to hate me. She has taken the mantle of regent in my absence and faced Morac's legions with no help from me."

"If anyone questions your absence, they now know better and shall hold you blameless. Without your preparedness and intervention, Yatin would have fallen, and Torry South with it."

"I knew what I had to do and trusted Corell's fate to Bode and El Anthar." He didn't say that Yah gifted him foresight to make that difficult choice.

"In time Corry will understand the wisdom of your choice."

"Forgiving me for leaving her alone to face Morac is one thing, but forgiving me for Terin dying on a quest ordered by me is likely beyond her capacity."

"Give her time," Illana said, wishing she could make all the pain and hurt go away.

"Corry's grief will only be repeated five-thousand-fold once the names of the dead are posted. Once word spreads that I have returned from Yatin, the families of our brave soldiers will flock to the palace to see if their loved ones are among the fallen. Our people will not be pleased when they learn I plan to rush off to war in another direction, leaving Torry South defenseless."

"We are at war. Our people know the danger looming ominously over us."

"I have resigned myself to live without their forgiveness for the death of so many of their sons, husbands, and fathers. This war has only just begun, and I fear the price of victory will be greater than our people can bear," Lorn confessed what he longed to freely say. Who else could he confide his doubts than his kin? He could never let his guard down with his men and close companions, lest they lose faith. He was tired, so very tired, only able to move forward by faith alone.

"Our people will bear whatever cost is necessary for they know the alternative," she said, assuaging his guilt.

"They are good people. Only such people could produce the men I've led into battle. If only you could've seen them fighting through the streets of Mosar, advancing under such duress, against all the foul trickery Yonig could throw at them. I've seen boys no older than sixteen years defend their wounded brothers with their limbs hacked off or guts ripped open, caring little for their own suffering. And the wounded…" He trailed off, thinking how grateful he was for Kato's wondrous device. Unfortunately, that reminded him of his widow.

"How fares Ilesa?" he asked.

"She is resting in her chambers." Illana had seen to the comforts of Galen and Ilesa, each retiring before Lorn completed his war council.

"She's barely spoken since Maeii. Her heart is broken." Lorn sighed.

"She looks ill, barely taking her food."

"What do you think ails her?'

"I am not sure but have my suspicions." She gave him a knowing look.

"Oh." He backed a step. If Ilesa was with child, she needed to stay behind.

"What will you do?" she asked.

"I'll speak with her tomorrow. She should remain here at the palace. That is the least I can do for Kato."

"I advised likewise, but she is insisting on going with you."

Lorn looked away, staring westward where the sea disappeared into the night, the darkness mirroring his laden spirit. He could always order her to remain, but something told him not to.

"I will honor her wish, such the fool am I."

*Guardian Darna's estate
Northeast of Bansoch*

Whack!

The blow drove her to the ground of the training yard, the blunt practice sword striking her shoulder. Deva spat blood and sand, gaining her feet, her sword mistress coming at her again, striking her arm.

"Faster, Guardian!" the older woman instructed, granting her pupil no respite.

Deva grunted, receiving the blow in silence for crying out only earned her more blows. She planted her shield arm in the sand, springing to her legs beneath her to gain her feet as her instructor rushed forth. She met the hurried strike with her shield, her counter thrust nearly striking the other woman's hip. A follow strike grazed the woman's thick trousers, missing her thigh by the slightest of margins.

"Umph!" Deva groaned, her shield striking her chin. Her helm came loose, slipping off her head, revealing her short-cropped hair.

"Hold!" Sword Mistress Selenda commanded. She was a stout-built woman approaching her fourth decade, decked out in thick leather trousers, padded blouse, and boiled leather mail matching Deva's training attire. She ordered Deva to don her helm before continuing, prioritizing safety with her charge. Selenda was one of the finest sword mistresses in the Federation and exclusively served House Estaran, personally commanding Guardian Darna's household guard.

Deva replaced the helm, its polished steel covering her skull and face, her hazel eyes staring through its narrow slits. As the eldest daughter of Darna, she was the heir to House Estaran and 4th guardian of the realm. Their ancient house was second only to the queen's, holding the permanent rank of guardian of the Sisterhood, their places of succession following the royal line. Once Princess Tosha bore a daughter, that child would become 3rd guardian, lowering the status of House Estaran in the line of succession. At times, when only one generation of the royal house lived, the head of House Estaran would rise to 2nd guardianship. At other times, they fell as far as the number of living royals pushed them. For this reason, the heirs of House Estaran wed sons of the royal line when they were available, renewing their place in the line of succession. Conversely, House Estaran wed their sons to the throne to strengthen their ties to the royal bloodline. Unfortunately, the last three generations of the royal line wed sons outside the realm. The last son born of the royal line was Prince Lore, heir to the Torry throne, thus unavailable to wed the heir of House Estaran, though Darna's late mother attempted to arrange it nonetheless.

Deva lifted her shield, preparing to receive the next blow as Selenda reengaged, this time catching the sword mistress with a vicious counterstrike, delivering a mortal wound in their mock engagement.

"Very good," Selenda acknowledged. They continued throughout the morn until the sun reached its apex in the clear brisk sky.

"You are demonstrating vast improvement, Guardian Deva. I shall apprise your mother of your progress," Selenda said, removing her helm as they returned to the villa centered on Darna's vast estate.

"Pfft! She'd find fault if I was named champion of the Federation," Deva snorted, if such an appellation even existed.

"Guardian Darna has exceedingly high expectations of her charges and even higher of her heir, Guardian Deva," Selenda said.

Deva knew all too well her mother's expectations. Much of Darna's impatience was rooted in Deva's grandmother's machinations, arranging her parents' nuptials. Deva's father was Gaive Tolus, the only child of Mearna Tolus, a slight-built, soft-spoken man who failed to meet Darna's expectations. It was a political match, wedding the wealth of House Tolus to the martial prowess of House Estaran, forging a power rivaling the queen herself. Such was not lost on Darna's mother when she arranged the match. Further expanding her power, Darna bore five children to Queen Letha's one, allowing her to wed her bloodline to lesser houses to strengthen her position. She began by wedding her eldest child, her son Guilen, to the heir of House Stabos, but the marriage was annulled by Guilen's inability to sire heirs upon his wife, so she claimed, returning the boy to his mother.

Deva strode through the halls of her mother's manse, stripping her soiled leathers and gear as she entered her bedroom, a spacious, richly furnished chamber with large windows and a terrace overlooking the Estaran Vale. A tray of fresh fruit and a pitcher of wine rested on the table near her settee, the servants having brought them whilst she trained. She poured herself a cup before stepping out onto the veranda wearing naught but a long linen sheath, the breeze lifting her short auburn hair.

"What mischief are you up to, Mother?" She narrowed her eyes, swirling her wine in her goblet. Darna had been gone for many days, having sent word ahead that she would be arriving today. Deva could only guess the reasons for her absence with the amount of subterfuge and secrecy with which her mother exercised of late. Nothing good often came from her mother's schemes, nothing good as far as Deva was concerned. She and Darna rarely got along. Perhaps it was Deva's striking resemblance to her father, sharing the color of his hair and eyes, but everything else was her mother's, much to Deva's annoyance.

"Mistress?" a soft male voice called out from the outer hall.

"Enter, Veiya," she ordered without turning around, the slave entering her chamber with a platter of fresh cooked fish and warm bread, placing it upon the table beside her settee. The servant stepped onto the veranda and knelt, greeting his mistress. She kept him there for several moments, her thoughts elsewhere, wondering her mother's schemes before regarding the comely slave, running the fingers of her free hand through his dark hair. 'Twas a shame he was a gelding, the procedure a standard practice for most household slaves to safeguard the integrity of hereditary lines when young heiresses were wed to the sons of political allies. Only the wealthiest houses employed gelded slaves in their households, oft using them for intimate purposes. Her mother kept three such *personal* servants that were exclusive to her, often repeating the age-old phrase *a toy for pleasure, and a husband for breeding.* Considering the disdain her mother had for her father, she assumed the five times they were intimate was in the siring of their five children.

"Return to your duties, my pet. I may have use of you later tonight," she dismissed him.

Finishing her goblet, she returned to her bedchamber to partake her meal, finding her brother sitting on her settee, awaiting her, wearing an ankle-length green tunic and brown robe. He stood of a height shy of her sixty-two inches with his mother's gold-speckled blue eyes and father's long auburn tresses. He fished a swollen grape from her fruit bowl, tossing it in his mouth.

"Move, Guilen." She lightly slapped his hand, reproaching his theft, shooing him from her seat.

"You wound me, Deva." Guilen smirked, stealing another grape as he stood, enjoying the sweet delicacy with their season just ending. It wouldn't be until midsummer for fresh ones to ripen on the vine.

"Incorrigible, no wonder your wife sent you back to us." She rolled her eyes.

"Pfft, she discards husbands like stale bread. Was I her third or fourth? Hmm…" He tapped a slender finger to his lip in false contemplation. "Her fifth, actually. Five husbands, no children, yet it is my fault she could not conceive," he whined.

"It is a husband's duty," she said, forking a slab of fish into her mouth.

"Yes, a husband's duty, but a man cannot seed a barren garden."

"Yet it is still his duty to make it grow."

"Yes, but Mother should have thought of that before binding me to that woman."

"She thought it worth the effort to bind the wealth of House Stabos to our own, but you failed to sow," she taunted dryly.

"Mock me at your peril, sister dear, but expect no such joy with whomever she selects for you. I hear that Counsel Larias has a son your age." He threw that tidbit to gauge her ire.

"He is a dullard," she dismissed the scion of House Larias.

"A handsome Dullard though," Guilen reminded her.

"Stupidity can be passed on to offspring as much as beauty, perhaps more so. No, Mother would not risk the future of our house on inferior stock. Perhaps she might chance it with Thesta, Dorath, or Cojya. They are not to inherit unless I succumb, and that, my dearest brother, will not happen." She tossed a grape in her mouth.

"Intelligence then," he mused, weighing that attribute among the sons of the great houses that he knew but coming up short.

"Intelligence, yes, but Mother cares naught for beauty in our mates," she said sourly, though Darna did not disfavor it either.

"Perhaps you might glean from these what her plans for us are?" he asked, removing two scrolls from the folds of his robe.

"Where did you—"

"From Mother's sanctum," he answered with restrained amusement.

"She will skin you if she discovers your snooping." Deva took the scrolls, unfurling them across her lap.

"Skin me? Her eldest child? Her lovely boy?" He touched a hand to his chest with mock indignation.

"Yes, her precious child." She rolled her eyes, studying the scrolls, careful not to crease the frail parchment and alert their mother of their activity. "This one is a writ of purchase for twenty-two slaves from Bansoch."

"The ones she purchased four days ago?" he asked, wondering what was so special about that.

"Yes, but…" Her eyes kept reading one part over and over, trying to make sense of what she read.

"But what?"

"There is an exchange of two thousand gold to a slaver captain named Veneva for a single item."

"Two thousand for a single slave?" His voice rose an octave.

"Shush! Do you wish to alert the household of our discovery?" she admonished.

He shrugged sheepishly, realizing his overstep.

"Yes, it appears Mother spent an exuberant amount for a slave." She pursed her lips, wondering what drove such a ridiculous price.

"Perhaps she intends to replace Father," he thought aloud.

"She is beyond childbearing years, and no breeding slave would warrant such a price. There must be another purpose." She set that parchment aside before reading the second. "Hmm, this one is interesting," she quipped.

"Do tell, Deva, I can't read your thoughts," he complained. Guilen was irritated by his illiteracy, as males were not allowed to read, write, wield weapons, ride an ocran, or gather together with nonfamily. Young boys were also given little protein, unlike their sisters, creating disparities in height and size. It was a concerted strategy of the Sisterhood to prevent revolt in the male underclass. Freemen were confined to managing the home and could not venture forth without escort. Numerous households opposed these stringent rules, teaching their sons to read, write, and even ride, forming the bulk of the reform political block. Deva's mother fell under the opposite faction, as the leader of the Traditionalists, who fought to maintain the current social order.

"This is an overture from Neta Vasune and Voila Arisone."

"Overture for what?" he asked, for both women were members of the ruling forum and known reformers.

"It appears they are concerned with foreign influence in the royal house."

*****

Darna was greeted by kneeling field slaves and female indentures as she neared her palatial estate. She rode at the head of her small column, sunlight playing off her resplendent golden helm, with blue feathers running along its center from her forehead to the base of her neck. The dark stone road meandered the rolling hills and gentle pastures of her lands for countless leagues in each direction. Long aqueducts stretched to the north, bringing water from the distant hills, their construction dating back a thousand years. A stone fort rested off her left, where hundreds of her soldiers were garrisoned, and dozens of slave billets to her right, where hundreds of field slaves were housed. The field slave quarters were surrounded by a tall stone palisade, with watch towers guarding each corner. Numerous structures surrounded the penned area, including granaries, dining halls, and indentures billets. The main estate rested up ahead, overlooking the Estaran Vale, with a formidable stone wall running the length of its perimeter and a massive gate straddling the road at the base of the hill. Soldiers in matching livery with gold armor over black tunics opened the gate to receive their commander with fists pressed to their breasts.

Darna returned their salute as she passed, her column of soldiers and cage wagons following in her wake.

"Take the boy around back!" Darna commanded her second, a stern-faced commander named Sela Yorin. She was of an age to Darna, with silver tainting her golden tresses and a vicious scar gracing her left cheek.

"I will secure him in the lower keep. What of the others?" Sela asked, regarding his fellow Torry captives. Darna had slain all non-Torries who happened to witness Terin wielding the sword as she tested his skills.

"Ascertain their skills and fitness and assign them accordingly. Single out the one the boy befriended. The boy needs to understand the cost of defiance if he resists, so we will punish his friend for his obstinance."

"It shall be done, Guardian Darna," Sela affirmed.

"Have them bathed, collared, and scented. I shall see to their marking after seeing to my household."

Sela broke off from the column with a dozen warriors and the cage wagons, circling to the rear of the sprawling estate, while Darna continued on, greeted by her family and household servants standing before the marble columns gracing the front of her palatial villa.

Deva stood forward of her family, formally receiving her mother as heir of House Estaran, wearing gold cuirass and greaves over a black tunic.

"Mother." Deva bowed.

"Daughter." Darna appraised her heir, her gold-speckled blue eyes searching for any blemish in Deva's carriage, finding fault with her stature and the softer disposition that she blamed on her husband's genetics, flaws she planned to rectify with their next generation. She continued on, greeting said husband, who was second to receive her.

"Husband," Darna said curtly.

"Guardian." Gaive bowed deeply, greeting his wife with expected reverence. Gaive was short, slightly built with auburn tresses and studious hazel eyes, wearing a gray wool robe over an ankle-length green tunic.

"I am famished. Have the servants serve dinner immediately!" she ordered, shooing him away.

"Of course, Guardian." He again bowed deeply and withdrew.

"Guilen, Dorath, go with your father!" she called out her two sons, who stood among their sisters, Thesta and Cojya. Guilen was eighteen years and Dorath nine, each dressed in matching attire of their father.

"Yes, Mother." Both boys bowed, following their father into the villa.

Darna regarded Thesta and Cojya, the girls matching their mother's thick black hair and deep blue eyes, wearing emerald calnesian blouses and loose linen trousers. Thesta was thirteen years and Cojya ten. Darna snapped her fingers, signaling her aide hither, bearing an object bundled in brown cloth. Darna lifted the cloth, revealing a matched set of double-bladed polished steel swords, with black cross guards and wired hilts.

"For us?" Thesta asked excitedly.

"Of course." Darna smiled, presenting them to her daughters. "They were handcrafted by Bella Duvose, the finest armorer in Bansoch. Look closely and you will see your names etched along the blades."

"Oh, thank you, Mother," Cojya exclaimed.

"You are most welcome, my loves. Now, those are not meant for normal sparring, and be ever mindful of their sharp edge."

"I want to spar right now," Thesta declared.

"Me too," Cojya chorused.

"After we sup. Now put those away and find your way to the dining chamber," Darna ordered before moving on, greeting her chief steward, Itara Vosen, a woman in her sixth decade, who served her house for forty years.

"Guardian." Itara bowed, standing forward of a line of kneeling house slaves and female indentured servants standing farther back.

"Itara, please see to my retinue," she ordered, indicating the near two dozen soldiers and courtesans trailing her.

"Of course, Guardian." Itara clapped her hands, the gesture signaling the servants to attend their varied tasks.

With that, Darna ascended the wide granite steps that ran to the front of her estate, her gold cape billowing in her wake.

*****

"Did anything of note happen during your visit to Bansoch, Mother?" Guilen asked, before sipping his wine.

Darna regarded her eldest child from her place at the head of the table as a slave placed three slabs of roast moglo upon her plate, while another refilled her goblet.

"Is it no wonder the Lady Cora annulled your marriage, child. It is unbecoming for a young man to speak of his own volition," Darna admonished with her calm, deadly voice.

"My apologies, Mother." Guilen took another sip, shrugging off his mother's barb. He had long grown immune to her asperity.

Sitting her left, her husband, Gaive, opened his mouth to say something, but a look from his wife stilled his tongue. She would only tolerate his voice when she deigned to speak to him. Despite her disdain for her husband and disappointment in her eldest son, Guilen, her favorite child was her youngest son, Dorath. The beautiful boy sat her right, partaking his meal with impeccable manners. His long ebony-black hair was combed to a rich sheen, draping beautifully over his slender shoulders. He ate quietly, his expressive large blue eyes paying her a careful glance.

"Anything on your mind, Dorath?" She smiled, affectionately brushing a stray hair behind his ear.

"I am pleased you are home, Mother." He smiled.

"And I am pleased that I was so missed." She lifted his chin with a finger, forcing his beautiful eyes to hers. "How have your harp lessons progressed?"

"I am uncertain. I practice three times every day, but my fingers are very clumsy." He tried to look down, but Darna kept his eyes to hers. He was such a lovely boy that she loathed giving him away one day. Of all her children, that would be one marriage she would arrange with great care, since boys in the Federation were subject to their wife's authority. There were no shortages of matriarchs throughout the realm wishing to bind their houses to Darna's through marriage, and an attractive boy like Dorath would not lack for suitors. His future wife would first have to meet her extreme standards.

"I look forward to hearing you play, my dearest."

"How went your visit to Bansoch, Mother?" Deva repeated her brother's question, staring at Darna from her place at the table's opposite end.

"I believe that was Guilen's question, Deva, and I haven't answered it yet," Darna regarded her heir sternly.

"My apologies, Mother. I only wondered if you met with the queen. It is rumored that she is despondent over news from the mainland," Deva said, referring to the death of King Lore.

"Our queen has better sense than to let her feelings for foreigners present themselves at court. You would be wise to follow her example when you assume your place as matriarch of House Estaran."

I am good at masking my feelings, Mother, especially those concerning you, Deva mused, taking a sip from her goblet.

"Thank you, Mother, for our gifts," Thesta and Cojya chorused.

"You are welcome. I am remiss in not presenting the other gifts I obtained for the rest of you. Guilen and Dorath, I purchased twenty yards of the finest Calnesian cloth. I expect each of you to make good use of it. We shall be hosting several galas over the coming fortnights, and you shall need fetching attire," she said, hoping they would draw the discerning eye of political suitors. Both boys bowed their heads gratefully, though Guilen masked his disdain for such tasks, which were consigned to women on the continent. They were wealthy enough for servants to attend such work, but their mother thought it becoming of them to learn.

"And to you, Gaive, I purchased a new harp, which you shall play for your mother when she visits," Darna said to her husband. She smiled wickedly to herself, recalling when they were first wed, discovering his hatred for the harp. She immediately arranged extensive lessons for him.

"As you wish, Guardian." He bowed his head politely.

"And my gift, Mother?" Deva asked curiously, swirling her wine before taking another sip.

"A very special gift, Daughter. One that you shall come to appreciate far more than any other boon I have ever given you."

"What is it?" Deva asked.

"Patience, Deva."

*****

Terin had no sense of where he was. Since his impressive display, his captors took no chances with him, keeping his hands bound behind him, his legs shackled, and a hood to disorient him. When the wagon finally stopped, they were led within the lower keep of Darna's sprawling estate, built into the hillside on the hill's reverse slope. When they finally lifted his hood, he found himself in a steaming bathing chamber, where they were stripped, scrubbed raw, and bathed. They were clad in slave livery of under garments and a brief white tunic. Their iron collars were replaced with polished steel ones with the name of House Estaran inscribed upon their surface. They would free his limbs at different stages but never freeing both legs and arms together. He looked briefly to Criose but was quickly admonished by a guard with a quirt striking his back, ordering his eyes lowered. They were thrown in a holding cell, where they were drawn out one by one, until only Terin remained. He could hear the faint screams of his comrades echoing through the outer corridors from somewhere in the distance. A long period passed before they came for him, leaving him enough time for his imagination to torture him with whatever they had planned. His legs were freed of their shackles, but his hands remained painfully bound behind him. He leaned his head back against the far wall of the cold cell, staring forlornly at the thick timbers crossing the ceiling above, his thoughts a maelstrom of memories, both fond and terrifying. The horrors of the many battles he partook were revisited cruelly in his mind in extreme detail. He recalled so vividly that fateful day before the gate of Corell, when Morac presented the king's head to Corry. He ached for her sorrow, wishing nothing more than to run the wretched monster through with his sword. His thoughts shifted to the eve of the final assault and their unseen victory, standing upon the outcropping of the inner palace, when he told her that he loved her.

"*Say it again,*" she had said.

And he did.

And they kissed beneath the starlit sky, his heart's desire coming to pass, though he had so little time to savor it. He couldn't imagine that he could overcome so much at Corell and Yatin only to end up here. He struggled to suppress the anger welling up within, trying to lash out at the injustice of it all.

Thousands are enslaved every season, suffering far worse abuse than you, son of Jonas, a voice reminded him, speaking in his head.

Am I not allowed to voice a complaint? he growled back at the unseen source, wondering if it was his conscience, Yah or the beginning of his madness. *Must I always place the fate of mankind and the good of humanity above my own desires? Above my own hopes? My own dreams? I am tired. So very tired. All I want is Corry. To spend what days are left to me with her. She is why I continue on fighting as all my strength fails me. Why should I fight on if I have no future with her?* He closed his eyes, sinking to the floor, his breaking heart drowning his spirit in a hopeless abyss.

If you quiet your—

He refused the voice's counsel. He didn't need quiet or acceptance of fate; he needed to escape, but how?

The voice remained quiet, replacing its words with a blurry image, a narrow beam of bronze that shimmered briefly before fading as he shook the madness from his weary mind.

"It's time!" a distinct feminine voice called out. This voice was the all too real Sela Yorin, Darna's cruel task mistress, who took great pleasure in his misery over the previous days. He would ask where they were going, but she would only refuse him and add a few colorful insults to boot. She ordered two guards into the cell to fetch him.

*****

"Ah, our final *guest*," Darna purred as Terin entered the atrium resting at the back of the estate, with the clear sky shining through its open ceiling. His fellow Torries stood in a coffle off his left, their eyes trained to the floor. As soon as Terin stopped in the center of the chamber, his comrades were ushered without. He followed their retreat with his eyes before Sela struck his shoulder with her leather quirt.

"They are of no concern to you, slave," she admonished.

"Not true, Sela." Darna's false smile stretched painfully across her lips. "His countrymen are very much a concern for our honorable guest. Is this not so, Terin?"

He wasn't sure how to answer or what game she was playing. He chanced a glance, taking stock of his surroundings. Besides his two guards and Sela, only Darna was present, along with a younger woman standing at her side. The younger woman was shorter than Darna, with short-cropped auburn hair and guarded hazel eyes that stared intensely at him. They wore matching gold cuirasses, greaves, and black tunics, with five braided cords adorning each shoulder. They both stood several paces before him, examining him with apparent interest.

"Prepare him," Darna ordered.

They swiftly drew him to his right, placing his left leg into some sort of rack, isolating the limb while tightening several clamps and straps holding it in place. Terin's heart pounded, guessing what would follow next, catching sight of a glowing brazier behind Darna, with several irons heated within its fire.

"Here, this one is unused." Darna removed the iron from the brazier, steam pouring off its glowing end, handing it carefully to Deva.

Deva paused, eying the brand uncertainly. "You wish me to mark him?" She never branded a slave before, her mother insisting on placing every mark herself.

"Of course. I only mark those that belong to me. This one"—she regarded Terin—"is yours."

"Mine?"

"Your gift."

She already had two servants, though they were given her when she was a child, and her mother placed their mark and gelded them, of course. This one, however, was to be spared that alteration, so her mother claimed. He was strikingly handsome in a boyish way, though his eyes seemed much older.

"You are gifting me an uncut male? I didn't think you placed such trust in me, Mother."

"If he was cut, we would have no use for him, at least not what I paid for him."

Two thousand gold! Deva recalled the amount on the writ of sale. *Was it for this boy? Why so much? Who was he to warrant such a price?*

"And how much did he cost?" She tested her mother's honesty.

"Enough to rise my ire if he fails to fulfill the role I intend him, and much of that depends on you."

"And what role is that?"

"Place your mark and we will discuss his role further." Darna backed a step, waving an open hand toward Terin, whose eyes regarded each of them with growing dread.

"Hold him tighter!" Deva ordered the guards, who grasped his shoulders, twisting him away from her as she stepped nigh. She shared a look with Terin, hazel eyes meeting sea blue. There was no pleading or contempt in his long stare, only a sadness that took her aback. She paused before pressing the iron to his upper thigh, holding it briefly in place as he screamed.

Terin tried not to cry out, to not give them the satisfaction of his tears, but pain strips the courage of the bravest of men, and he was no different. The guards rubbed salve into the brand, as Darna stepped nigh.

"See that his hands remain bound. I don't want him touching the mark until it is healed," Darna ordered.

Terin couldn't quell his pounding heart, looking from one tormentor to another. The younger woman at least didn't appear to revel in his misery, but if she was empathetic to his suffering, he couldn't tell. He winced once they freed his leg, the hem of his tunic brushing the edge of his brand. He recalled the agony of his first branding in the throne room of Corell. He endured the pain as that mark was a final rite of his place among the Torry Elite and his title of champion. There was no honor in this suffering, only the indignity of his permanent marking as a slave. Warriors were marked upon the chest and slaves upon the thigh, usually the left. There was no mistaking his station now, even if he escaped, for all would know his lowly state and return him to Darna. If he couldn't escape soon, the war would likely be over, and his destiny wouldn't matter. If Yah directed his course, as Lorn believed, he better reveal it soon, or all would be lost.

"Bring him!" Darna commanded.

$$\text{C H A P T E R}$$

20

Darna's estate

He stirred, slowly waking from the peaceful slumber. He stretched his limbs that were strangely free of their bonds that constrained them for so long. Was this a furtherance of his pleasant dream, or was his ordeal simply a nightmare? He dared not open his eyes, fearing to reveal it all a mirage, conjured by his fondest hopes, but the bed he found himself was far too comfortable to be his imagination.

"You're awake," he heard a familiar voice.

He opened his eyes, finding himself abed in a modest chamber with the woman who branded him sitting his bedside, causing him to flinch. The last he remembered was being dragged from the branding room, fed a foul-tasting gruel, and given water, likely laced with some sort of sleep drug, for he passed out soon after.

"What..." He couldn't form a coherent question.

"What are you doing here? A good question." She stood, fetching a bowl of water from a small table beside his bed. "Drink this," she offered, not unkindly, which further took him aback.

He sat up, startled to find himself naked, save for a loin garment, her eyes fixed to his chest, where the burn obscured his champion's sigil.

"I am Deva," she said as he drank.

"You are the one that marked me," he said warily.

"Yes. It is expected that a mistress marks her property, at least my mother believes so," she said dryly.

"Darna?"

"Yes, though you must address her as Guardian in others' presence."

"But not here?"

"When we are alone, you may speak freely, though be mindful to keep your tone respectful and voice low."

"Alone?" He wondered if there was more to that inference.

"We shall be spending a great deal of time alone, at least today. Tomorrow, however, you shall serve the house steward, laboring in whatever capacity she sees fit. At such times, you must be mindful of your place."

"My place as a slave," he uttered disgustedly. "But why are you treating me so kindly now?"

"My mother purchased you for a greater purpose than a mere house servant."

"I guessed that, but for what?" he asked, knowing his ransom would've brought a far grander price than whatever Darna paid.

"To serve as my consort." If she was embarrassed by this fact, her confident tone didn't show it.

"Your consort?" Terin drew away, not expecting that. "Why me?"

"Why a slave, or why you in particular?"

"Both."

"Free women of the Federation often purchase husbands whenever they fail to find a suitable match with the freemen of the isle. It is not uncommon for them to scour the marketplaces for men of their liking, though the practice is not as popular as it once was. It is rare, though, for highborn to select mates in such a way. Most matches are arranged between houses much like your homeland, though here, the final decision falls to the matriarch of the house instead of the patriarch."

Terin thought to inform her that mothers made such arrangements in Torry North.

"Wed you?" His anger finally drew the courage to speak freely. "Your people steal me from the beach in Yatin, starve, brand and beat me without mercy, and sell me into slavery, and you expect me to wed you?"

"You speak as if the choice is yours." She ignored his insolent tone.

"Where I am from, Deva, we don't purchase wives or husbands."

"Don't you? Does not every household arrange their children's betrothals? Often when they are infants, such matches are arranged. Am I wrong to believe so?" she challenged.

"That's different," he protested, dismissing the lunacy of her argument. Of all the things he expected them to do with him, marriage was not one of them.

"Is it? The only difference in this matter is that your parents had no role in arranging it. Since you are now a slave, it fell to your mistress, who happened to give you to me."

Terin's heart went to his throat. If he wed her, then Corry was lost to him forever. "We are mated then?"

"Not yet, handsome." She smiled. "I will attain my seventeenth year very soon, where I shall attain full citizenship. We shall be wed that very night. Until then, we are to remain chaste."

"How do you know I am chaste?"

"We can't be sure, but Mother believes you are."

He had nothing to say to that, though his blush indicated the truth of it, which she found amusing.

"Why me? Why wed her heir to a foreign captive?" It didn't make sense.

"Marriages are arranged for the benefit of our house, either through strengthening our political position, wealth, or the betterment of our bloodline. My grandmother wed the prince of the realm, Queen Letha's uncle Thesen, an astute political match renewing our bond to the throne. My mother wed the only child of Mearna Tolus, binding her wealth to our house. My mother fears our bloodline is growing soft and sought a warrior to strengthen our martial prowess."

"A warrior? There are many captured warriors crowding the hulls of every slaver ship that weighs anchor in Bansoch. Why me? You could sell me back to my homeland for many times my cost."

"Ah, but you are a special warrior, one my mother is keen to bind to our house, though she has not spoken to your origin, history, or nature. Perhaps you can enlighten me on what makes you so unique?" She sat back down at his bedside.

"She didn't tell you? I told her who I was but didn't think she believed me."

"Then tell me. Who are you?"

"Terin."

"Terin?"

"Terin Caleph, the champion of the Torry Realm. Or at least I was, until your mother had Veneva destroy my warrior's mark." He touched a hand to the tender flesh. The pain of the burn still lingered, though much less than the agony of the fresh brand on his thigh.

"Torry?" She didn't expect that. No wonder the subterfuge, knowing the queen's affinity for the Torry Realm. Should the queen discover they held a Torry warrior as a slave in their household, she would be furious, and yet her mother took the risk regardless.

"Yes, Torry. Minister Antillius oft reminded me of the friendship between our peoples, and yet here I am, your captive. I guess he was mistaken," he said, his voice bitter.

"Is it our sin that you fell into a slaver's hands? You may have been a Torry warrior, but now you are not. You are the legal property of House Estaran," she reminded him.

"As you wish, mistress," he snorted.

"I am not your enemy, Terin. I am actually the only friend you will find in this household. Outside of my presence, you will serve as any other slave in this house until we are wed, and even then, your status will only slightly improve."

"Will I lose this collar then?" He tugged the steel band circling his neck.

"You will be given a new one, a silver collar as befits the status of a bond mate."

"A bond mate?" He made a face.

"Your chattel status will not change, even after we wed, Terin. We don't free slaves in the Federation. You are bound to me until death."

She's insane, he thought miserably, knowing she held his life in her hands, this good treatment dependent upon his obeisance.

"I do not say this to be cruel, just for you to be mindful of your place."

"I am well aware of my *place*." He rested his head back on his pillow.

"I am not so certain. It is a far different status from being a Torry warrior, a…what did you call it? A champion of the realm?"

"The champion. There is only one."

"Truly? And where does a champion fall within the Torry hierarchy? Is it above or below the King's Elite?" she asked curiously, the title of champion holding different connotations in every realm.

"I am both a member of the King's High Elite and his Champion, serving the defense of the realm outside all authority, save the king himself."

"But your king is dead." She thought to catch him in a lie. If he were truly so highly placed, he would know that.

"Slain upon the Kregmarin Plain by Morac. I saw his head placed upon a pike before the gates of Corell, displayed by Morac during a parlay with Princess Corry, to strip her of her courage." His voice trailed with sorrow, recalling the awful sight.

"And you were there?" She lifted a doubtful brow.

"Yes. The princess chose Cronus and I as her escort."

"Cronus?"

"Cronus Kenti, the hero of Tuft's Mountain and my dearest friend."

She was taken aback by his bold claims, his every utterance raising more questions. If the boy was lying, he would be the greatest deceiver she ever beheld. Even a master storyteller couldn't spin this fantastical yarn.

"Was Morac successful in his attempt? Did the princess shrink before such a grotesquerie?"

"He told her to surrender, or he would steal her maidenhood upon her mother's bed with his *trophy* overlooking the act." He tried recalling the exact words.

"And then?"

"She told him if he wanted Corell, to come and take it, declaring that we would fight to our last breath and bleed his legions. She said she would rip open her womb before falling captive to the likes of him," Terin said proudly.

She sensed his admiration for the princess, wondering if he was smitten, but there was time to determine that later.

"If your king is dead, then who do you serve?"

"Prince Lorn will be king. He is a good man, and I am proud to serve him."

"No, you serve me now," she reminded him with a mischievous smile.

"So it seems." He sighed.

"Hmm," she mused. There was so much she meant to ask that it was difficult to decide where to go next. "What of your family? Do they live?"

He thought to claim they were dead to protect them, but she could easily read the falsehood in his eyes. He was not very good at subterfuge or trickery so decided to answer honestly, without revealing more than necessary.

"My mother and father dwell in Torry North."

"Caleph is a unique name. In fact, I have never heard tell of it. Yet you are a warrior highly placed in royal service, a prestigious title without precedent, with a name few, if any have heard of. Is your father a great lord or regent to earn you such an appellation?"

"He is a farmer."

"A farmer? He owns a vast estate like this?"

"No, a small farm that we work ourselves."

"You expect me to believe King Lore elevated the son of a poor farmer to champion of the realm?"

"My father was once a member of the King's High Elite before he wed my mother and departed the king's service. He is more than a mere farmer, Deva," Terin said indignantly. He never had to defend his father's place or honor. He never realized how much he loved him until his memory was besmirched by her comment. Jonas was a great man, the finest man Terin ever knew, and he had come to know many great men. His father and mother sacrificed everything to be together and thus sire him. His mother forsook the Torry throne and his father forsook…No, he wouldn't think it. The Benotrist throne could never belong to the blood of Kal. He never thought of it before, but he suddenly realized that his very existence depended upon two people walking away from two different thrones in order for him to be born. What but love could explain it?

"You love your father," she said, the proof evident in his tone. "And I offended him. I understand, for I love my father and would chastise anyone that offended him." Her father suffered the indignity of a wife that despised him and the slights whispered behind his back. Of course, her father's indignity was not unlike any of the other husbands of the ruling houses. Perhaps such was the fate of loveless arrangements. Deva swore to not treat Terin so. He was easy on the eye, exuding a quiet strength that she found attractive. She hoped he would retain some of that self-worth after enduring the humiliations her mother intended for him.

"Yes, I love my father and mother. I have dined with kings, high ministers and royals from many realms, and there are no two better than those who bore me. They each forsook wealth, privilege, and power to be with one another, without which I would not have been born. Do not belittle those you do not know, Deva. You could never understand their sacrifice."

"I could if you explained it. You are a great mystery, Terin. Draw back the shroud a little further and reveal your true self."

He sighed, realizing he was saying too much but was unable to help himself.

"If we are to be wed, there can be no secrets between us. My mother at first simply sought a warrior for me to wed to sire stronger heirs, but with you she found something more, something worth spending two thousand gold for. What is it that demanded such a price?" Her mother wouldn't risk paying such a price for a Torry slave, even a great warrior. The only Torries she would dare purchase were used in the mines or galleys, far away from the queen's eyes, and those miserable wretches would never warrant more than fifty certras. Once she wed Terin, they couldn't simply hide him away forever. Eventually the queen would know. And if Terin was who he claimed to be, then Queen Letha would demand his repatriation.

He knew he had spoken too much, but he foolishly revealed far more to Darna in hope she would ransom him. All that accomplished was to increase his value for her original purpose. He was also tired and lonely, with only Deva to confide in, though she was his enemy as much as the rest. He would never reveal his kinship to

Tyro, but he already told Darna of his Kalinian blood. If she had any doubts of that, they were expunged when he easily dispatched her gargoyle prisoners. Darna was sure to reveal that information to Deva eventually, so he might as well gain a level of trust with his intended, a trust he could make use of one day.

"Gargoyles fear my blood."

"Pardon?" She drew away, not understanding if she heard him correctly.

"My grandmother's people claimed descendance from an ancient house bestowed with a unique power to strip gargoyles of their courage and wits, destroying them in battle and forcing them to flee in great numbers. It was a gift passed on to all those born of this bloodline."

"If true, then we would have heard tell of this wondrous ability."

"No. They remained hidden from the wider world, keeping to their vale, which was surrounded by gargoyles for thousands of years, the gargoyles learning to avoid their presence, considering their vale cursed. The gargoyles, in turn, shielded their presence from the world of men."

"Where is this vale? If there are more of your kind—"

"The vale is deserted. My father and I are all that remain of its people."

"If your people held such power, then why did they not reveal themselves to the realms of men long ago? They could have seeded the peoples of Arax with your…ability, dooming the gargoyles."

"The realms of men could not be trusted after betraying my grandmother's house so long ago."

"The name of her house?" she asked.

"The House of Kal." He didn't know why he again confessed this secret, telling Darna and now Deva, but he was weary of it all. What difference did it make now anyway?

"The House of Kal? As in Kal the ancient king from whence the council of Tarelia sprang and thus the realms established by their sacred order?" she asked in disbelief.

"Believe as you will, but the truth still remains."

"The truth? Kal sired no heirs unless the legends we have held to are false. I must say, Terin, of all the things I expected from your mouth, that certainly was not it." She laughed.

"It doesn't matter to me if you believe me or not. You asked for the truth, and I have told you. Do with it as you will." He didn't bother fighting with her. What would it gain him to win such an argument? No matter the outcome, he would still suffer their bondage.

"Do with as you will? You claim descendance from Kal the Most High, and I should do with it as I will? Do what? Parade my prized consort across the Federation as Kal's scion, proclaiming my right to rule the world through you? You may believe this gibberish, but no sane person would. But if my mother believes it, then I shall take it as a blessing. One thing Mother never considers in selecting mates for her children is their attractiveness. When she first spoke of wedding me to a warrior, I expected a dull brute with a face to match. Yet here you are, the prettiest male I have ever set eyes upon as her choice for me. If she believes you are Kal's get, then far be it for me to refute such fancy. I will simply suffer my fate of bedding such a lovely creature," she teased.

"Fair enough." He shrugged, shifting uncomfortably with her flirtation. "Fetch another gargoyle from your mother's collection and give me a sword, and you will understand."

"Another gargoyle?" This was the first she heard of it.

"Your mother tested me in some secluded area before bringing me here. She pitted several men against gargoyles before forcing me against them."

"To verify your claim." It made sense, but she was unaware that her mother held any gargoyles captive. It was forbidden by royal decree for any gargoyles to set foot upon their sacred soil. If the queen were to discover that her mother harbored gargoyles, she could pass judgement on House Estaran. Looking into Terin's eyes, she could discern no deception. He truly believed his fanciful tale. Her mother was far more skeptical than she, and if he convinced her of his claim, then…no. It was madness.

"It is forbidden for males to wield swords, Terin. Speak not of it again."

"Then why would your mother desire you wed a warrior if I can't wield a sword? How can I pass on what I know to our children?"

"You shall pass on your blood, Terin. You shall never wield a sword or any other weapon ever again. Nor will you ride an ocran or learn to read and write. All are forbidden."

"I already know how to read and write. Should I forget what I have already learned?"

"You can read?" Once again, he surprised her. So few men or women in all of Arax could read or write, and yet he could. "When did you learn this skill?"

"My mother. She taught me since I was a boy, to prepare me for my apprenticeship as Minister Antillius' scribe." He winced, having revealed information that she needn't know.

"A scribe?" She laughed. She was starting to not be surprised by his outlandish claims. Of course he was a scribe. Next, he would claim to be a friend to the famed Minister Antillius that he mentioned twice now. And why not? He spoke familiarly of the Torry royal family. Perhaps he was on similar terms with El Anthar of the Jenaii or the royal houses of Yatin and Macon.

She asked him to describe how he came to be a scribe and then a warrior, discovering that his father honed his martial prowess throughout his childhood, whilst his mother taught him the scholastic arts. They spent much of the day discussing his family, and his first encounter with Cronus.

"Mistress?" a servant called out from the outer corridor, just as Terin reached the part in his story when they reached Rego.

"Enter!" she commanded, irritated with the interruption.

The servant quickly entered, bearing a large silver tray with food and drink, setting it down upon a small table at the foot of the bed. The slave was diminutive, with long brown hair bound in thick braids, wearing a brief cotton tunic with a steel collar gracing his slender throat.

"Leave us, Veiya!" she dismissed him.

"Of course, mistress," Veiya bowed, casting a jealous glance Terin's way before stepping out.

"He doesn't like me very much," Terin observed warily.

"Domestics are petty creatures. Pay him no mind. Put this on and join me." She tossed him a shimmering silver calnesian tunic. He quickly dressed, feeling her eyes upon him, embarrassed by the brevity of the garment.

"Sit!" She directed him to the chair opposite hers.

He tugged nervously at the hem of his tunic before sitting down, finding her smiling at his discomfort. "Perhaps you have something a little longer? More modest?" he asked.

"You will grow accustomed to it. You look lovely." She lifted her goblet, partaking the sweet wine.

He would never grow accustomed to any of this, he reminded himself. Why had they treated him so poorly before bringing him here? He couldn't make sense of any of it as he ate, forgetting how famished he was. He had been kept in a constant state of hunger for so long he forgot what a wholesome meal tasted like. The meat was a steamed fish of some sort, the vegetables crisp, and the bread warm. He devoured the meal with as much decorum as he could manage. Little did he know what a privilege the meat was, a rare delicacy for free males, let alone slaves. The Sisterhood provided little protein to their sons during formative years, fueling the size differences between the native genders. Imported males were larger by far, requiring a firmer hand in their treatment.

"You must have been famished," she observed, swirling the wine in her goblet, her eyes fixed to his.

"Yes," he said, understating the obvious.

She asked nothing more, simply studying him as he finished eating. His manners were polite, but she could see his lack of cultured experience. He was new to such protocols, as his mannerisms were recently practiced, probably hurried once he was placed as a minister's apprentice. He didn't look like a warrior, much less a king's champion, but he was attractive. *At least his babies will be cute,* she mused delightedly.

"The evening grows late, and I shall take my leave," she said, rising from her chair and circling the table as he gained his feet. "Rest well." She pressed her warm palm to his cheek before stepping without.

Terin stood there for a time, confused by the entire affair, wondering what just happened, when five guards entered his chamber with spears levelled. They spoke not a word, forcing him back where they drew a shackle from beneath his bed, that was affixed to the floor, locking it around his left ankle, followed by close-fitting manacles to his wrists, binding them in front. They put out the lamps and departed. Terin sat down on the bed, resting his head in his hands, plans of escape beyond him.

Quiet your mi—the voice tried to say, before his anger cut it off.

"Go away," he growled. He didn't care to quiet his mind or still his anger. He needed to find a way off this island before he was forced to wed Deva and lose Corry forever, but was too tired to form a coherent thought. He spent another fitful sleep, plagued by the insistent voice that asked him to quiet his mind.

*****

The morning came all too soon. He was roused from his slumber by his guards, who unshackled his ankle and hands, tossing him a coarse brown woolen tunic that was as brief as his finer garment, before ushering him to the house steward.

Itara Vosen awaited her new charge in the kitchens, silver tainting her once auburn hair, with her fists upon her hips as he was thrown to her feet.

"Head to the floor!" she reprimanded.

He scolded himself for letting his guard down, clinging to a false hope that his condition might improve.

"You are to greet every free person and woman upon your knees with your head pressed to the floor. Do you understand?" Itara asked sternly.

"Yes," he said, his voice muffled by his angle to the stone floor.

"Head up when speaking to a free woman!"

Terin decided then and there to make a mental list of every woman on this isle he would one day kill.

"Yes." He sighed, looking up into her cold gray eyes. The woman stood near sixty-two inches, with a mouth that looked as if she swallowed a bee. She wore an ankle-length yellow robe, with green stitching along its hem and collar.

"You will address me as mistress and keep your eyes down when doing so, unless otherwise directed. Am I clear?"

"Yes, mistress." He relented, thinking how easily he could gain his feet and snap her neck. But then what? The guards stood directly behind him. He might disarm one and take their sword, but then what? Once he had a sword, he could easily cut down the others and find his way to the stables, but then what? He didn't know his way around or know which way to flee once he attained a mount, then what? Perhaps he could make his way to the coast before being overtaken by Darna's household guard, but it appeared she had a small Army in her employ. Could he outrun them all? Doubtful, but say he made it to the coast, then what? He would need a ship. No, it was a fanciful dream, but nothing more at this time. He needed information before he could even think of escape, so he would have to suffer this woman's abuse.

"Better, but I can see your proud carriage, and that shall not do for a slave in this household." Itara motioned the guard to affix shackles to his ankles, sixteen inches slack in the linked chains.

"I am told you are a dangerous slave, so you shall require additional limitations until you are properly tamed. Am I understood?"

"Yes, mistress." So much for his freed limbs, just another obstacle to his plan of escape.

"Today you shall work in the scullery. Do you understand what that entails?"

"Maybe." He shrugged, knowing it had something to do with the kitchen.

A blow to his back reminded him to add *mistress* to his response.

"You will become quite familiar with the duties of a scullery over the next two days," she said, turning him over to the head kitchen servant, an older diminutive male slave with an iron collar gracing a stick thin neck, wearing a coarse brown tunic. Like most of the male slaves in the household, he was gelded and displayed overly feminine mannerisms that turned Terin's stomach.

*****

It was nearly sundown when Terin was relieved of his duties and escorted to the bathing chamber. He spent the entire day scrubbing pots, plates, and culinary used by the household and the hundreds of staff and soldiers housed in the surrounding billets. By the time he finished the morning cleaning, it was time for lunch and then dinner. It was grimy, tedious work, and he was struck with a quirt by the head kitchen slave whenever his pace waned. He never learned the man's name, but the term *man* hardly applied. The man, like the other kitchen servants, despised him for some reason, and each apparently held authority to strike him with a quirt whenever they deemed his effort lacking. He was roughly handled, scrubbed and clad in another obscenely brief calnesian gold tunic before they returned him to his chamber. He sighed with relief upon entering, his ankles free of their shackles, thinking of naught but a soft bed after they worked him to exhaustion.

"You are here," Deva greeted him delightedly, sitting at the table with a platter of delicious-smelling food sitting upon it.

He staggered briefly, staring longingly at the inviting delicacies upon the platter. He wanted nothing more than to sit down and eat but paused, wondering if she expected him to kneel in her presence as he was ordered to do throughout the day to every other woman he encountered.

"You must be famished. Come sit," her voice beckoned so soothingly that he almost forgot she was his captor. She came to her feet, her thick robes draping her womanly form, taking his hand and guiding him to his seat.

"Wh-what do I call you here?" He already forgot, his mind hopelessly clouded.

"Deva." She smiled, taking her seat opposite him, before spooning a portion of stew to his mouth.

"Why are you doing this, Deva?" he asked, his voice barely a whisper.

"Doing what, Terin?"

"This." He waved his arms weakly to their surroundings. The bed was turned down, awaiting him. Lanterns were alit in each corner, their slender flames gently lighting the chamber. An inviting fragrance drifted in the air above two incense candles resting on the sill of his window. "You have me worked to death all day, toiling in the kitchens, and then bring me here to…this."

"I worked you to death?" she asked, as if shocked by the assumption. "During the day you serve under the steward's authority, as per Mother's instruction. She has forbidden me from interfering on your behalf. I wish it weren't so. You look so very tired."

He didn't believe her. Her explanation was utter nonsense, but what difference did it really make where he served. The life of a slave was measured in humiliation and drudgery, and he would continue to suffer it until he found a way to escape.

"Tell me more of your adventures? I believe you left off where you and Cronus reached Rego." She took a sip of her wine.

He forgot much of what he told Darna and couldn't remember if he had mentioned the Earthers so decided to omit them until she prodded. He brought up his father's sword and how he gifted it to him and how it aided his bold actions at Costelin and later Tuft's Mountain. She listened with rapt attention to his tale, spellbound by his telling. Unfortunately, when it came to the rescue at Molten Isle, she confronted his obvious omission.

"Did not the Earthers execute the princess's rescue at Molten Isle?" she asked, the manner of Tosha's rescue spread quickly throughout Bansoch soon after.

"Yes, Minister Antillius contracted their services at Central City, and they escorted us to the isle."

"You helped rescue Princess Tosha?" she asked warily.

"Yes and no." He shrugged. "The pirates had split their captives in two locations. I joined Lorken and Miles in rescuing Princesses Corry and Felicia. Raven and the others rescued Princesses Tosha and Deliea."

He rescued the Torry princess. Perhaps he is smitten with her, she thought sourly. It was a fact she would later investigate, but there was a more pressing matter gnawing at her brain.

"You know these Earthers?" She should have been surprised by his acquaintance with the infamous strangers, but nothing at this point was surprising about Terin.

"I know them," he answered reluctantly.

"It is rumored they are vicious brutes. Is this so?"

He looked away, torn by his hope that she might overlook his association with the Earthers and his urge to defend his friends' honor. In all reality, he couldn't downplay his friendship with Raven and the others, their close relationship would soon be known to all once the tales of their journey and escape from Fera spread farther. For all he knew, she already knew this and was merely testing him.

"They are good men, every one of them. Only the evil and ignorant castigate them with such words."

"You are fond of them," she stated, her brows rising with the affirmation.

"They are my friends."

"Friends? I thought you merely knew them. Perhaps there is more you wish to share?" She smiled inwardly, catching his falsehood.

He was too tired to challenge her inquisition. It was an unfair fight from the start. They worked him to death through the day, while she plies him with wine and food, whispering sweet words to balm his tortured soul, prying the truth from his addled mind.

"I know you journeyed to Fera in their company before escaping, making your way home," she said.

He sighed, telling of his adventures at Fera and thereafter, finishing at the council of Corell, when the king decided to march to the crossroads.

"Tell me of Princess Tosha's consort. What sort of man is he?"

"Raven?"

"Yes, that is his name. I have heard strange tales of him. He is their captain?"

"Yes, but the Earthers do not follow our strict hierarchy. Each of his crew are nearly equal in authority. They are truly great friends to each other, and Cronus and I as well."

"But what sort of man is he?"

"Well, he is big." He shrugged.

"Big?"

"Big," he reiterated, lifting his hand a fair distance above his head, before spreading his hands far apart, mimicking the width of Raven's shoulders.

"That is big," she agreed, though thinking it an exaggeration.

"I've seen him toss men aside like dolls, and not tiny house slaves, but warriors in full armor. He is very strong and his weapons even deadlier. He and Lorken slew hundreds during our escape from Fera. He killed hundreds more during his trek across the Benotrist Empire and many more at Tro."

"He is rumored to be a vicious brute, and yet our princess selected him to be her consort. I doubt she has shunned hundreds of marriage offers from every house in the Federation, risking their insult by bedding this Earther, unless there is more to him than I falsely believe. I shall ask you again, and you shall answer honestly, why would she do so? Is he ugly or fair? Vicious or gentle? Of low character or honorable?"

"He is handsome enough if one overlooks his massive size and fierce demeanor, I guess. I never thought of him that way, but my—" He corrected himself. "Tosha was smitten from the start, now that I recall. It was difficult to recognize their attraction through all their fighting."

"Fighting?"

"Yes. They were constantly quarrelling from Molten Isle to Fera, and then from their reunion to Axenville, if what Cronus said of their journey is true." He almost laughed at the memories. Tosha was actually quite kind to the rest of them, venting all her fury upon the one man she was hopelessly drawn.

"He dared argue with his sworn princess?" She was aghast. Such an affront was punishable by death in the Federation. Even a husband wed to a nonroyal would face a whipping post if he argued with his wife.

"The Earthers don't follow our protocols, Deva. They bow to no one. Besides, Tosha started most of their fights."

"As is her prerogative. He has no grounds to refute her. A consort of the realm should know his place."

"And who is going to tell him? He is nearly invincible. And if he isn't, his ship and crew are. He is not like me, Deva. Your people won't find him asleep, washed ashore and helpless. I suggest you grant him a wide berth if he should ever visit your isle."

Tosha's marriage might well doom the queen's house, Deva surmised. Their people would not tolerate Raven's presence unless he submitted to the throne. Tosha was playing a dangerous game, perhaps even more dangerous than whatever Darna was planning. Her mother had yet to confide in her all her machinations. If she truly meant for her to wed Terin, then she meant to move on Queen Letha.

"You asked if he was vicious or gentle and of low character or honorable." Terin drew her from her musings. "Raven is only vicious with his enemies or those he believes are cruel. He is quite friendly to everyone else, especially the laypeople. He has always treated me with friendship that I did little to earn. I was a friend of Cronus's, and that was always good enough for Raven to welcome me into their circle. He is honorable and kind, though he pretends otherwise."

"And you are fond of him. Of course you are friends with the Earthers, and you wielded a Sword of Light, and you flew a magantor, and you claim kinship to Kal, and you were named champion of the Torry Realm. Nothing you claim is surprising to me anymore. I actually believe your outlandish claims, Terin." She could see the spark alight in his eyes, that hopeful look that briefly passed, the look that thought she might free him to return to his world.

Foolish boy, she thought. He would never leave this isle. The sooner he accepted this, the better off he would be. She needed to squelch that hope before it took root.

"You have done all those things as if your life was a song. Bards will sing of your valiant deeds long after we are dust. I must say, Terin, I am pleased to own you. It is not every woman who can claim to have the Torry champion and the heir of Kal as her own slave." She sipped her wine, searching his response through her hooded eyes.

It must be nice to take what you want without guilt or consequence, he thought miserably. Deva and her mother were despicable creatures, but he dare not voice that or his treatment would only worsen. Who could espouse a person's accomplishments and worth and yet gloat of owning them?

"It is growing late, and you have another long day ahead of you, I fear," she said, gaining her feet before touching a hand to his face and stepping without.

Terin quickly stuffed his food in his mouth before the guards appeared, again chaining him to his bed. He spent another fitful night fighting the voice that asked him to quiet his mind when all he felt was rage and weariness.

*****

The next day began as the last, with him toiling in the scullery. 'Twas another day of beatings and drudgery before returning to his chambers, where Deva greeted him with food and wine. She asked him to continue expounding his tale where he left off before the siege of Corell. He of course muted much of his own glory, explaining the battle in detail, though she guessed he omitted his own significance on purpose.

The next day found him in the laundry, mixing lye in wash basins, while other slaves stepped into the water, pounding the cloth with their feet. Some cloth was soaked for several days for more thorough cleaning. Water was in abundance from the vast aqueducts that ran from the foothills in the north, greatly easing the washing duties of the laundry and scullery. Terin spent the afternoon out of doors, hanging the wet clothing and linens upon stringed lines. After the long days in the scullery, he was grateful for the fresh air, though his brief work tunic offered little warmth in the crisp winter air. The estate rested atop an impressive hill, with a curtain wall at its base and surrounded by a sea of green fields and pastures worked by an Army of slaves. It was his first glimpse of the surrounding landscape, save for the limited view from his bedchamber's small window. With the midday sun sitting at its apex yet low in its southern arc, he guessed the aqueducts ran straight north. He spotted well-built stone roads running in each direction, making his best avenue of escape anyone's guess.

"Eyes on your work!" the chief laundress reprimanded, striking his back with her leather quirt. And so it went, for the next three days, with each ending in his chamber in Deva's *cheerful* company. Once she extracted every detail of his journeys, she made him retrace his childhood, providing her much of his history that he didn't think was relevant. Once that was completed, she had him repeat his entire tale, catching any discrepancies and pointing them out, forcing the truth from him.

He spent the next few days scrubbing the privies, the foul work torturing his nostrils. He was surprised to discover the estate's indoor plumbing and privy upon arrival, the technological wonder far ahead of anything found on the continent. It was one of several advancements that Deva espoused to reinforce the superiority of their civilization. Following several days of this unpleasant duty, he moved on to scrubbing floors, his knees suffering their unforgiving surface. Having spent his life on his parent's farm, he wondered why they didn't task him similar labor. He eventually realized that his duties were restricted to the household, performing tasks that women undertook on the continent. Was it a means to further humble him, or a means to confine him within the estate, hidden from sight?

*****

The next morning found him in the central hall, scrubbing its marble-tiled floor, his knees suffering upon its surface, slopping water from a bucket. They kept his feet shackled, the iron bands biting his ankles as he shuffled across the floor. Sunlight broke through the large windows spanning the far wall, casting a blinding glare off the polished stone, paining his eyes. His guards were never far off, standing post along the pillars that supported the roof of the vast chamber. He could see their armored greaves but dared not look farther north, lest his keeper strike him for his curiosity. His normal guards were doubled to four, taking no chances with their charge while he worked in the common area. They were all made aware of the danger he posed, granting him no leave to act upon it. The worst part of working in such a common area was the constant parade of commanders of rank and members of Darna's household traversing the grand hall, from which every part of the manse branched off from. Every time another person of note entered the chamber, his head was forced to the floor in complete obeisance. 'Twas another humiliation for slaves to suffer, and he was treated no different in this regard, despite Darna's lofty expectations for his future. Once he wed Deva, his worth was only to be measured by his ability to sire heirs. He doubted his station would improve much upon that day. He did start to take note of the guards assigned him. Covera was a lanky, auburn-haired soldier who kept watch over him with humorless vigil. Of all the guards, she was the one he was most wary of. Rutesha was three years his elder, with matching blue eyes that were often bored after a short period of duty. If he ever made a move, it would be her sword he would take first. Porcia was younger still and naturally nervous, ever watchful of his slightest move. Velecia was the most outspoken, offering humorous banter that entertained her sister warriors throughout their tedious watch, but she could quickly transition into a guarded stance at the slightest threat. She was not one to be taken lightly. Most annoying of all was his keeper these past three days, Veya Cluse, the steward's vice, a girl of an age to Terin with a shaved head and dressed in cotton trousers and blouse, brandishing a leather quirt. She kept constant vigil standing over him, directing him in every task. She was not unattractive, if she placed any effort in her appearance, but her harsh tongue and fierce countenance were his constant torment.

"Is he the one?" He froze, hearing a young girl's voice behind him.

"He is, My Lady Thesta," Veya answered the girl.

"I want to see him!" a younger girl's voice demanded.

"Of course, Lady Cojya." Veya bowed. "Turn, boy! Head up!" She tapped his back forcefully with her quirt.

He set his rag aside, turning painfully on his knees, surprised to see two young girls, one almost a woman, standing over him dressed in thick trousers and shirts, with boiled leather mail. Their black hair was bound in high buns atop their heads. They had matching blue eyes that stared at him as if he was some strange oddity. Veya had referred to them as Ladies Thesta and Cojya, indicating their high station in the household, perhaps kin of Darna.

"You are Terin?" the elder girl asked, her hands on her hips.

"Yes," he answered, wondering their purpose.

"Mistress!" Veya corrected him with her quirt.

He winced from the blow. It was bad enough to refer to a grown woman as mistress, but to address a child as such was too much.

"I am Terin Caleph, son of Jonas and champion of the Torry Realm," he said proudly, ignoring Veya's correction as she struck him again.

"Don't hit him, Veya. He is cute," the younger girl protested, the command staying the vice steward's hand.

"Mother says you are not to speak of that. Do you understand?" the elder girl, Thesta, asked.

"Your mother?" He lifted a curious brow, expecting another blow for his insolence.

"Darna, the 3rd guardian of the realm!" Thesta declared with an authority beyond her thirteen years. "She is your mistress."

"Oh," he said, surprised that Darna had more children. They were likely as vicious as their mother, as children often mimicked their sires, though his father was nothing like his grandsire. Perhaps he shouldn't judge these girls for their mother's crimes. "I thought Deva owned me?" he challenged Darna's claim.

"You are bound to the heir of House Estaran. Should Deva fail, then you will belong to me," Thesta said proudly.

"And if they both fail, you will fall to me, and I never fail," the younger one named Cojya declared, touching a hand to his cheek.

The child's words twisted in his gut. What sort of bankrupt morals created such children? It was madness, and he had little choice but to suffer it. He shifted his gaze, finding their stare unnerving as they continued examining him.

"Is he tamed?" Thesta asked, uncertain of his obedience.

"Not to my satisfaction, Lady Thesta," Veya snorted.

"Itara agrees with your assessment. Perhaps stricter treatment will correct his behavior," Thesta said, circling him, his shoulders tensing under the child's scrutiny. Terin never thought to kill a child but was quickly changing his mind on that matter.

"Girls, you have lessons to attend," a man's voice called out.

"Yes, Father," they chorused, hurrying off to start their sword lessons as their father drew near.

Terin looked up, meeting the scrutinizing hazel eyes of Gaive Estaran, the patriarch of House Estaran. The man was slightly built and diminutive, wearing an ankle-length yellow tunic and gray robe.

"You must demonstrate proper deference when speaking with my daughters. Deva will be away for several days and expects your training to be complete upon her return. Tomorrow I shall continue your instruction personally. Despite your current station, Guardian Darna plans for you to assume a significant place in our house, a place I believe you are wholly unsuited." Gaive sneered with a superior air.

Terin didn't know how he felt about Deva's sudden absence. He found her presence a cold reminder of what he lost, replacing Corry's sunrise to Deva's dim lamp. Yet the evenings in her company were his only respite from this harsh existence. What awaited him at day's end? A soft bed or a cold cell? He was wise enough to know that his gentle treatment in Deva's presence was their attempt to strengthen his bond to her, for him to associate her with kindness. Now he had to suffer her absence, replacing his time with her with another member of their wretched family.

"Wholly unsuited." Gaive tsked. "You were tasked with cleaning this floor, but your work is shoddy." Gaive kicked over his wash bucket, spilling its contents upon the floor. "Wash it again. All of it! See that he does it properly this time! And administer a proper correction for his current failure!" Gaive commanded, turning away, his robes swirling in his wake.

"I shall see to it, Master Gaive." Veya bowed, before striking Terin's back again.

*****

North of Bansoch harbor
Arch Councilor Dorvena's estate

Deva sat upon the settee in the private atrium of Elesha Dorvena, daughter and heir of Lutesha Dorvena, arch councilor of the Federation Forum, the legislative body of the Sisterhood, answerable only to the queen herself. A staunch traditionalist, Lutesha Dorvena counted among Darna's closest allies, her villa resting just north of the city, some distance from Darna's spacious estate.

Elesha Dorvena was one year Deva's junior, with thick golden tresses framing her sharp countenance and large gray eyes. She sat upon a settee across from her friend as a slave filled her goblet with imported Fleacen wine.

"Where were we?" Elesha purred as the slave stepped without, leaving them to their gossip. "Oh, yes, your brother."

"Guilen?" Deva swirled her wine in her goblet, tucking her left leg underneath her, her gray calnesian trousers caressing her smooth skin.

"No, though he is fetching. The younger one."

"Dorath?" Deva narrowed her eyes, wondering her friend's interest in her sweet little brother.

"Mmm." Elesha swallowed her wine. "Yes, Dorath. He is Mother's choice for my betrothal."

"He is only a child. He hasn't reached his tenth year." Deva thought the idea a bit presumptive. Dorath was her mother's favorite, and even Elesha might be deemed unworthy.

"He will be soon enough. He is quite lovely, if I dare say."

"I guess." Deva shrugged, not really thinking of her brother in that way. In fact, there was only one boy she found herself thinking about these days and why she was here. "What news of the continent have you heard?"

"Oh, rumors?" Elesha perked, ever happy to share her discoveries, though the rumors were merely the reports from her mother's spies and contacts on the continent. Every major house employed some number of informants. Some wealthier houses managed to place contacts within the royal courts of the larger realms. Since Darna kept the knowledge gained from their house's informants to herself, Deva was forced to seek answers elsewhere.

"Yes. What juicy tidbits have you garnered?"

"Where to begin?" Elesha cooed excitedly, her expressive gray eyes wide with delight. "The daughter of the archon of Teris ran away with a ship captain from Port West. Her father demands her return, and the council of Port West has placed a bounty on his head to prevent a schism in the Casian League.”

“Have they been found?”

“Not yet. Some believe they fled to Tro.”

“Hmph. She is foolish to throw her high position away for a ship’s captain.”

“True love is a fickle thing.” Elesha giggled, again sipping her wine.

“True love?” Deva laughed. What was love but an amalgamation of lust, attraction, and reciprocity? If one could manage a wise choice with carnal pleasure, then all the better, but mere pleasure was no substitute for a wise choice for a mate.

“Deva, always the pillar of practicality. You are truly your mother’s heir.”

“No. My mother places no merit in lustful attraction, without which the siring of heirs is made tedious. I believe in balancing the two. Now, what other news have you?”

“Most of the tidings are of the war. So dull. Armies marching here. Battles fought there. So little romance,” she lamented, her eyes drawn to a far-off place. “There are rumors, however, surrounding the Torry princess.”

“Corry?” Deva asked curiously.

“Yes, the former guest of our esteemed queen, before the incident at Molten Isle.”

“What of her?”

“It seems she is the fancy of Lord Morac. He demanded her hand during the siege of Corell, in exchange of sparing the garrison, but she refused him.”

Just as Terin said, she thought wryly.

“He was clearly struck by her beauty, but her heart belonged to another,” Elesha continued.

“Another?” Deva asked darkly.

“Yes, a young warrior who rescued her from Molten Isle and led the defense of the White Castle. They claim he slew thousands during the battle, brandishing a Sword of Light that broke enemy blades and smashed telnics. The gargoyles fled his sight in the thousands. He flew upon a magantor at the beginning of the siege, driving into a host of Benotrist warbirds, slaying a dozen of the great avian before returning to Corell. Others claim he journeyed to Fera to rescue his friend and stole away in the dead of night. Bards sing of his fell deeds from Cagia to Tro, heralding the savoir of the Torry Realms. He was seen sharing a kiss with the Torry princess upon the ramparts of Corell, each professing their love for the other," Elesha swooned wistfully.

"His name?" Deva asked, hiding her rage.

"Terine, Teron, Terian, or something akin. His surname is Caleph. The latest rumors placed him in Yatin, aiding Prince Lorn, where he slew General Yonig at Mosar. Alas, it is believed he fell in battle at sea off the Yatin Coast, after slaying the Benotrist Admiral Mulsen, but no one knows for certain. If so, Princess Corry will be heartbroken."

It's all true, Deva thought sourly. All Terin told her was true except for his affection for the princess. Why else would a slave spurn her advances or wince at her touch? She thought to bend him with kindness, appealing to reason and his good sense to accept the life she was offering. Such tactics were pointless if his heart belonged to another, let alone the Torry princess. No, this would be much harder than she hoped. She suddenly grew bitter. What right had he to deny her? She was his mistress. His life was hers to spare or end. He should be thankful for her affection, yet he pined for another. No, it was unacceptable. She needed to break him, as her mother first advised, but in her own way instead of Darna's primitive means. She needed to break his spirit in a more brutally effective way.

"An interesting tale, Elesha. What other news have you?"

*****

"Again!" Gaive commanded, sitting at the table of the lavish dining chamber, as Terin served him wine. They were alone, save for the two guards standing post at the entry as Terin suffered Gaive's instruction on dining etiquette. He again poured wine into the goblet from Gaive's left before bowing and stepping away.

"Better, but with greater reverence," Gaive added as Terin repeated the task. As the future patriarch of House Estaran, he needed to oversee the running of the household and the duties of each servant therein. He spent the last three days under Gaive's tutelage, learning every facet of running the grand estate. It was information he found useless and mind-numbing. He prayed to Yah to deliver him from this place before he ever had need of it. Despite Darna's plans for him, he was still a slave of their household, a fact Gaive was quick to remind him, if not, then his brief garment and steel collar were certain to do so. With Deva's absence, he was confined each night in a dark cell, a reminder that without her, his very existence was void of pleasure.

Terin was weary of Gaive's condescending tone and pompous airs. Who was he to judge him unsuitable for Deva's hand? It was she that was unsuitable to him. Who was Gaive compared to him?

"Yah can't dwell in a pride swelled heart," Lorn once said, but Terin was proud and angry. Perhaps a child of Yah should humble themselves to hear their god's counsel, but he feared to do so. If he humbled himself in the face of their treatment, he was lost. And what if Yah wanted him to wed Deva? It was unbearable. No, only anger and pride helped him retain his spirit. What else had he than his own sense of self?

"Tonight, you shall serve Guardian Darna and our house at this very table," Gaive said.

Guardian Darna? Terin mentally shook his head at the proper appellation that Gaive always used in referencing his wife. Theirs was a loveless marriage, held together by expectation, duty, and protocol. Gaive feared Darna, and she held no respect for him. How could she when he constantly demonstrated such weakness? And yet he vented all his frustration on Terin, whom he saw as beneath him. Terin only needed one moment alone with Gaive before setting him right, but the patriarch of House Estaran wisely kept the guards near whenever they were together.

"I will do my best," Terin affirmed.

"Master," Gaive corrected his blatant omission, insisting Terin address him properly.

You are more a slave than I'll ever be, fool, he thought sourly. "I will do my best, master," he said evenly.

"You forgot to bow. Repeat it again!"

"I will do my best, master." Terin bowed.

"Better. You are dismissed. Itara will see that you are properly attired to serve at your mistress's table."

*****

The evening again found Terin serving at the dining table, bearing a pitcher of wine as he went from place to place, refilling their empty goblets. He was clad in a shimmering silver tunic, matching the sheen of his collar, whilst a heavy chain linked his ankles, hobbling his mobility. Another slave bore a pitcher of water for the youngest children, Cojya and Dorath. Other slaves hurried to and from the kitchens, bearing platters of food. Each of his fellow servants were strikingly attractive in a feminine way, eunuchs all, and far smaller than he. Theirs was a pitiful fate, consigned to a lifetime of this mean existence. Of course, their fate was likely better than the dregs toiling in the mines or galleys, but at least those slaves would die soon. Not so these pampered captives, who would suffer a long life in their service to House Estaran. He thought that that could just as easily have been his fate, but if they decided to cut that part of him, he might as well break free and kill as many of them as he could since life would no longer be worth living.

He felt Darna's gold-speckled blue eyes upon him as he stood off to the side. He had not seen her since she had him branded, the burn visible beneath the hem of his garment. His eyes were trained directly ahead, but he could sense her predatory gaze through his periphery.

"Wine, slave," Darna softly commanded, ordering him hither and taking his measure.

He shuffled forth, the sound of his chain scraping the floor as he poured from her right. He stiffened as she lifted the hem of his tunic, examining the mark upon his thigh.

"This turned out well," she commented, smoothing the garment back in place before shooing him away. "His manners are greatly improved. Well done, Gaive."

"With much effort, Guardian Darna." Gaive inclined his head, sitting to her left. Terin thought their marriage had all the warmth of a glacier and knew any union he might have with Deva would be just as cold as the years passed. They didn't have years, Terin reminded himself, as Tyro's legions were certain to sweep over Arax without his blood to contest them. Then again, he wasn't the only blood of Kal left to defend the realms of men. His father could fill the breach if need be. If he was willing to fully amend for placing the Golden Sword in Tyro's hand so long ago.

"What are we going to name him, Mother?" Cojya asked, her mischievous blue eyes staring him down from her place at the table.

Name him? Terin thought miserably. Would they take his name from him as well, further stripping his identity until only what he locked away remained?

"Deva will do so once she finds a name she favors. It is an important decision, one that she will have to live with permanently," Darna reminded her youngest daughter.

"Unless she loses her place as your heir, Mother. Then it is I who shall name and claim him," Thesta affirmed, sitting at the opposite end of the table in Deva's place, not sparing a glance with her back to him.

"Do not presume to take your sister's place, Daughter," Gaive warned. He loathed Darna's tact of pitting one daughter against the other to hone their cunning.

"Your father is right, child. You shouldn't assume to replace your sister. It is for me to decide if she fails to measure as my heir."

"Yes, Mother." Thesta bowed before continuing her meal.

"Wine, boy," Guilen called Terin hither from his place nearer Thesta's end of the table. Darna always placed Dorath beside her, her favorite, placing her eldest son near the heir at the table's opposite end.

Terin shuffled forth, filling Guilen's goblet, as Darna was drawn into conversation with Dorath, praising the boy for some small achievement. Guilen kept his hand upon the goblet as Terin poured, watching his mother's eyes fix to his brother before tipping the drink over.

"You fool!" Guilen sprang to his feet while Terin drew away, expecting a blow as every eye drew immediately to them.

"Apologize!" Darna regarded him coolly, reproaching his clumsiness.

What could he say? He didn't do it, or Guilen did so purposely? He mentally shook his head, wondering if this wretched family could get any worse, but apparently every member was an insufferable ass.

"Forgive my clumsiness," he relented.

"My son is a free man of the Federation. You shall address him properly!" Gaive admonished.

Terin's mental list of people to kill was growing longer every day, but vengeance would have to wait. "Forgive my clumsiness, master." He bowed disgustedly.

"I doubt your sincerity, slave. Perhaps I shall oversee your instruction. Father?" Guilen shifted his gaze to his father, beseeching his permission.

"On the morrow if the times suit you, my son," Gaive acquiesced.

"Excellent, I look forward to instilling in this barbarian the expectations of our house." Guilen sneered, dismissing Terin from his presence.

*****

Terin spent a fitful night in a cold cell, suffering the privations of the dismal chamber, awaiting his fate. Again, the voice called to him, asking him to quiet his mind, but he refused. Was it madness, his own imagination, or Yah that spoke to him? If it was the early onset of madness, it did him little good to acknowledge it or he was lost. If it was his imagination, it mattered not either way. If it was Yah speaking to him, he didn't want to hear it. He followed the path that Yah had set for him and was rewarded with chains and slavery.

"If this is how you reward your faithful servants, it's little wonder you have so few followers," he grumbled, staring at the ceiling. A long silence followed as if he expected Yah to answer. "No response?" He shook his head. "I thought I might have earned at least some explanation for all of this." He lifted his chained hands.

Again, nothing.

"Darna foolishly placed a sword in my hand to watch me slay her gargoyle captives, which I did, and was prepared to do the same for her, and what did you do? You burn my hand with the hilt, forcing me to forsake the blade and my freedom with it!" he almost shouted, tears running down his cheeks. "Why? Why, oh divine Yah, would you consign me to this torment? For what purpose am I here? Or is there no purpose? Am I being punished for some failing that I'm unaware? Is this my punishment for sharing Tyro's blood? Have I not atoned for that stain? If not, then free me to continue to atone for Tyro's crimes."

With that, he succumbed, overcome with fatigue, anger, and bitterness until sleep took him, though most of the night was spent by then, and the dawn coming too soon. He was awakened, bathed, clad in a woolen tunic, and presented to Guilen for further instruction in the young master's private chamber.

"Leave us," Guilen dismissed the guards, as Terin knelt, his ankles still shackled.

Terin regarded him warily as Guilen paced the room, stealing a cursory glance to the outer corridor and his veranda, as if searching for something or someone. Once satisfied, he returned to Terin, squatting in front of him, lowering his lips to his ear.

"Nod if you understand, for I dare not speak above a whisper."

Terin nodded, taken aback by the statement.

"I spilt my drink purposely last eve. I knew my mother would allow me to punish you personally, as is her nature. Now to the point of all this. You were once a scribe, is this so?"

"Yes," Terin answered warily.

A smile stretched across Guilen's face, like a malisk eating a tersk. "Good, very good. Could you teach me to read and write?"

Terin made a face, confused by the question, until recalling the laws Deva explained to him about forbidden activities, forgetting they applied to all men, not just slaves. "I...yes, I could, but—"

"It is forbidden, I know. Can you do it?" He meant, would he do it?

"How? Your mother will know."

"Let me worry about Mother. Can you teach me?"

"Yes," he agreed, not willing to throw away a potential ally, but there must be something in his offer for Terin's benefit.

"You do this, and I will help you. Better food, less laborious duties…" he began to offer.

"Help me escape," Terin cut to the heart of it.

"Escape?" Guilen whispered harshly. "Are you touched? Even I cannot escape this place. We are leagues from the sea, surrounded by soldiers and with you in chains," he pointed out.

"Then find a way. My prince will reward you with untold riches. I am a hero to my people. If you save me, my glory would be yours. You might then choose a wife of your own liking."

That last point would stick in Guilen's mind. The thought of wedding another odious wench of his mother's choosing gnawed at his brain. "Let us negotiate that step later. For now, let us agree to a more modest bargain. You begin to teach me to read and write, and I will teach you geography."

"Geography?"

"You can't begin to plan your escape unless you know where to go, can you?" Guilen smiled devilishly.

"Bargain struck." Terin smiled for the first time in a long while.

*****

And so it went for several days that Terin taught Guilen to read, and Guilen taught Terin the lay of the land. They would oft do so in the training yard, where Guilen's younger sisters practiced swordplay under the stern tutelage of Sword Mistress Selenda. They stood off to the side of the girls' training yard, out of sight of others as they took turns drawing maps or letters in the loose sand. Every so often, Guilen would make a scene, shouting invectives and demonstrating his general displeasure with Terin. Terin maintained a constant put-upon look, convincing casual observers of their mutual dislike. As

Guilen explained to Terin, Darna would never allow them together if she knew they were cordial. Guilen would continue his aspersions in his personal chambers, where he loudly ordered Terin about while reading old parchment that his mother thought she'd thrown away. Guilen had obviously planned this out for many years, waiting for someone willing and able to teach him this vital skill. Terin was impressed with how quickly Guilen learned. If Guilen had been taught since childhood, Terin thought he would've rivaled any scribe in the council of Torry ministers. He commented as such, praising his first student as they stood off to the side of the training yard.

"You believe so?" Guilen asked, as he finished spelling out his first complete sentence in the sand, the sound of his sisters' clashing steel echoing in the distance.

"Yes, but I was no master scribe, barely a novice in my brief time in Minister Antillius' service. So receive my praise with that in mind."

"But you were still a minister's scribe. That is more than anything I might attain here. But you were more than a scribe. You were a warrior, an Elite, a champion of the realm, if Deva speaks true."

"It seems so long ago now." He sighed, his eyes far away.

"It may seem so with your days passing painfully long, but in truth, it has been only a brief time. I have endured far longer than you," Guilen reminded him.

"But you are free, Guilen, while I wear these, and this." He lifted his left ankle, shaking the slack in his shackles and tapping his collar.

"Am I any less a slave? I am forbidden to read, ride, bear weapons of any sort, or venture from this estate without a female of my house escorting me. Even my bride will be chosen without my consent."

"As will your sisters," Terin reminded him.

"Perhaps, but Mother will take their desires into consideration. Not so with me."

"Then we best find a way off this island."

"Yes, we should. Now where did I last leave off? Oh yes, the nearest village lies seven leagues southeast along that road." He pointed out the winding pathway passing between two small hills along the horizon. "From there…"

*****

Terin's time with Guilen was vastly restricted once Deva returned, limiting their interaction, though they were able to continue their mutual instruction in some measure. Guilen provided him a general lay of the land, including the nearest ports, fishing villages, and Bansoch, going into further detail explaining the vying factions within the Sisterhood, primarily the traditionalists, led by his mother, and the reformers, led by Neta Vasune and Voila Arisone. Terin asked where Queen Letha fell within this debate, but Guilen couldn't answer, saying the queen was the balance of the two, though he was not privy to the political discussions his mother shared with Deva. His knowledge was limited to whatever he could glean from Deva, and she rarely revealed anything of great use.

Terin split his mornings between Guilen's instruction and the harsh supervision of Itara Vosen, the chief steward. Itara supervised Terin directly, instructing him on all the duties of the household servants, overseeing him demonstrate every single task to her high expectations.

Terin spent his afternoons attending to various household tasks and his evenings serving at Darna's table, under the watchful eyes of the entire household. Darna was pleased with his improved manners and obeisance, lauding Guilen's apparent success. Deva spoke not a word to Terin throughout their meals, sparing him only a casual glance from time to time. After serving dinner and clearing the table, Terin would be summoned to his chamber, where Deva greeted him warmly. She moved on from extracting his storied history to asking more personal questions, finding his likes and dislikes. She discovered what foods he loved and those he abhorred, his favorite color, which was silver, and his love of hunting and fishing. She didn't remind him that such activities were forbidden for him now but listened intently as he extolled their virtues. She shared her likes as well, which he took apparent interest. He was finding himself free of his shackles whenever in her presence in the evenings, giving him a semblance of normalcy while in her company. He suppressed his anger, filling his mind with whatever information he could garner from his captors. If he wanted to escape, he would need knowledge of his surroundings, the position of their soldiers, areas that were commonly patrolled, and the nearest ports. Bansoch was a foolish option, so Terin focused on smaller ports that foreign ships dropped anchor. How to reach said ports while avoiding Darna's soldiers was part of his plan he hadn't worked out just yet. Should he steal an ocran from her stables? Or stow away in a wagon? He first thought he could never kill a woman, but their miserable treatment quashed any qualms he harbored in that regard.

He continued to shun the voice that called out to him to quiet his mind. He decided no deity or providence would deliver him from his chains, only his own actions, and so he became singularly focused. If bowing and humbling himself afforded him greater freedoms, he would give them what they wanted. At times, his mind would lend to fancies of escaping and returning with a great Army to smash the Sisterhood. He smiled at the thought of enslaving Darna and Deva, subjugating them as harshly as they had him.

"Take my hand," Deva said as they walked the grounds of the estate, the late evening air rippling the folds of their garments. Manicured greens and crafted statues covered the expanse of the estate's foregrounds, torchlight dimly illuminating their path as they walked.

"Your attitude is much improved in my absence. Mother praises Guilen for the changes manifested in your behavior," she said.

"I am pleased that you are pleased."

"I *am* pleased. You are more attentive as late and have voiced no complaint of the things I ask of you. It is good to see that you have forsaken your previous life for the one that I offer." Forsaking your princess, she truly meant, hoping to gauge his ire.

"Does it matter? My life before is lost to me. I must accept my fate. I would rather serve as your mate than toil in the fields or mines, so the choice is simple, really."

"Once we wed, you will forsake any other that held your affection for all time," she said, waiting for him to deny any such fancies, though she knew it a lie.

Terin's pause confirmed what she knew. "There is no one."

"Truly?" She lifted a brow. "No girl on that farm you were raised on? No maidens swooning over the Torry champion?"

"No one." He guarded his heart, lest she tear that secret from him as well.

"Very well, even if there was another that claimed your heart, what could she offer that I cannot? Princess Tosha is the sole heir of our queen. Should she sire a boy, then Tyro will claim him as his heir. With the tenuous bond Tosha shares with her mate, she'll not likely sire any more heirs. The throne would then fall to House Estaran. You could very well father the next queen of the Sisterhood. No other woman can offer you a crown."

"If I wanted a throne, I could have already claimed one." He thought aloud, regretting his slip of the tongue.

"Well, this is a tale I've yet heard. Do tell!" she commanded excitedly.

"I have the blood of Kal. I wielded the Sword of the Moon. If I truly wanted the throne, do you think anyone could have stopped me?" he said in a deadly whisper, his tone enforcing the lie. He could hardly tell her that the throne he rejected was Tyro's. Nothing good would come from that. It would only strengthen their greed, claiming Tyro's throne as well. He could picture it now, Darna revealing to his grandfather that she wed him to her heir, promising their first-born son to the dark lord, securing peace between their realms. Tyro could gloat over Terin being his grandson and punished for opposing him, by serving out his days in bondage to Tyro's new ally. Tyro and Darna were very much alike in that regard, seeing their children as a reflection of their power.

"No, I don't doubt that you could. You are honorable to a fault."

*****

"You are far too trusting of him and far too lenient," Darna scolded her the next morn, summoning Deva to her private chambers.

"Where can he go, Mother? We are leagues from the nearest port. He wouldn't make it far alone with a collar affixed to his neck."

494

"I'm not talking about escape, child. He is too dangerous. Far more than you know."

"Dangerous? There may be some truth in his outlandish tale, but he is still a boy. His blood may protect him from gargoyles, but not from us, and he no longer has his magical sword," Deva dismissed her mother's concerns, lifting a tosi from the fruit bowl on her table, taking a bite.

"He is far more dangerous than you know. Kal's blood flows his veins. He is—"

"Kal's blood? Surely you don't believe that fanciful yarn? I believe he is a skilled swordsman and the Torry champion, but he is still only a boy. A boy who is unarmed, alone, and a slave in this house."

Darna's eyes blazed with a cold fury. She rang a bell by her bedside, summoning her steward, Itara Vosen. Their argument began over Deva allowing Terin to walk the grounds without shackles, warning her not to allow such liberty ever again. Deva responded that once they were wed, she would do with Terin whatever she liked.

*****

Itara Vosen escorted Terin to the training yard, where a small Army of Darna's personal guard awaited them. He noticed Darna and Deva standing off to the side, observing him as he was ushered to the center of the training area, his feet dragging his shackles through the loose sand. The shackles looked far sturdier than any he wore before, with heavy links and wide thick bands wrapping snuggly around his ankles. He mentally lost count of the soldiers gathered around him but surmised their number north of forty. Darna's younger daughters stood to her left, and Deva her right, along with most of her female household servants. His eyes stopped at the five slaves kneeling opposite Darna, the only other men he could see other than himself. They wore coarse brown woolen tunics and iron collars, with their hands bound behind them. He recognized Criose among them, his friend regarding him with a knowing look as he knelt in the sand.

"Welcome, Terin," Darna greeted him with a false smile. "You must wonder why we brought you here. There are members of my

495

household that are dismissive of your martial skill. You are here to demonstrate it for them."

He looked down at his shackled feet, wondering if he would be free of their encumbrance and if there was a point in performing well or not.

"Your shackles will remain. Perhaps it is unfair, but such is the burden you must bear. I see that you recognize your former comrades kneeling on the opposite side of the circle." Darna tilted her head to the kneeling slaves facing her, with Terin standing between them and her.

"I'll not fight them," he said defiantly.

"Of course you wouldn't, and I wouldn't ask it of you, proving that even a slave can have honor, especially one such as you. You shall not be fighting these men but will instead fight *for* them."

"For them?" He didn't like her cryptic tone.

"You shall face my sword mistress, Selenda. Should you prevail, your comrades will return to their duties unscathed."

"And should I lose?"

"That would be most unfortunate for them." She sneered.

"Speak clear!" he challenged.

"Mind your tongue, slave, or you'll share their fate!"

"Their fate?"

"Should you lose, then they shall lose their sight, to forever serve in darkness, with you the last thing they shall ever see. It would be unfortunate, for they have served dutifully in my stables, but they can still push a millstone or pull an oar once blinded." Darna spoke in a disturbingly calm voice, as if her words were of little consequence.

Would she truly do this? he thought miserably. He couldn't help notice the panicked look in his friend's eyes.

Darna's sword mistress stepped into the clear, standing several paces before him. She was dressed in thick leather trousers and blouse, beneath boiled leather mail and a steel helm, with her brown eyes staring intently through their narrow slits. She brandished two blunted swords, tossing one to the sand at Terin's feet.

"Pick it up!" Darna commanded, as he stared at the useless blade. She nodded to Selenda to commence.

Selenda lunged forward, as Terin snatched the sword from the sand with unnatural speed, parrying her hurried thrust before striking at the joint on his left manacle. The blade rang in his hand, the manacle remaining affixed, unbent, and unmarred by his emphatic blow.

Darna smirked, having learned the previous lesson well. His shackles were stoutly built, strong enough to bind a moglo or stop a sharpened blade or ax, let alone a blunted sword. Terin stumbled from the failed attempt, barely keeping his feet, the slack in his chain extending no farther than the width of his shoulders. Selenda was upon him instantly, thrusting her blade as he met the blow, managing to perry her thrust. His counterstrike nearly taking her throat, his speed catching her by surprise.

Deva struggled following his sword as it danced in his hands, placing Selenda on the defensive. She backed a step out of his range, collecting herself before reengaging. She closed again, moving to his left, his shackled feet shuffling to match her position, a flurry of strikes and counterstrikes ending with her sword flying through the air, landing several meters away as she scrambled out of his reach, retrieving her sword before he could move two steps. She raced around him, faster than his chained feet could shuffle, before striking from behind. He again managed to block her strike, slipping his blade across his left shoulder as she thrust her foot into his side.

Deva watched attentively as the blow drove him to the ground, Selenda's follow strike missing its mark as he rolled away. Selenda again brought her sword down upon him, his blade meeting her own as he lay sprawled in the sand.

"How…" Deva's question died in her gasp as Terin managed to wrap his shackled feet around Selenda's sword arm, trapping it with his legs before pressing his blade to her throat.

"Yield!" he shouted aloud for all to hear his victory.

Selenda looked to Darna for direction before conceding defeat.

Terin gained his feet as Selenda withdrew, brushing sand from his tunic while keeping a tight grip on his blade. Criose and the others waited with guarded optimism, for Terin's victory should spare them their grim fate.

"Drop the sword and kneel!" Darna commanded, satisfied that his demonstration served its purpose.

"What of my friends?" he asked sternly.

"Do not assume to speak above your station, slave. Do as I bid, or they shall suffer even in your victory!" Darna warned.

Terin slammed the blunted sword in the sand before sinking to his knees.

"Bind his hands!" Darna ordered the guards cautiously approaching him. They fastened his hands, as Darna stepped forth, stopping mid-distance between him and Deva.

"Can you now see the danger he represents?" she asked Deva, her eyes fixed to Terin.

Deva numbly agreed, taken aback by his martial prowess. Selenda was one of the finest sword mistresses in the Federation, and he defeated her with ease whilst chained.

"Do all of you now understand how dangerous he is?" Darna's eyes swept the assemblage.

"Yes, Guardian!" they chorused in unison.

Darna strode toward Terin, her sandaled boots kicking up loose sand as she trod. She shoed his guards away before squatting before him, keeping her voice low enough for only him to hear. "Know this, Terin. Those shackles affixed to your ankles will remain permanently. A close examination will reveal no key hole, for there is none. They are not meant to be removed. I ordered them forged especially for you." She touched a finger to his nose. "I shall inspect them daily for damage should you think to weaken them over time, so put such thoughts from your mind. Here you are, and here you shall remain for all your days."

*****

Three days hence

Darna observed him refilling her goblet, his sullen spirit masking the tempest she felt brewing within. The more measures she undertook to break his spirit, the more she doubted their effect. Each night he served at their table, shuffling from place to place to refill their goblets. She noticed Deva no longer looked upon Terin with playful lust but wary apprehension. It took the demonstration in the training yard for her to see Terin for what he was. Deva could not see past Terin's comely features until then, unable to see the warrior in the boy's pretty face. Darna once thought the same, until seeing Terin easily decimate her gargoyle captives. That moment forever changed how she viewed the boy, convincing her of the truth of his claims. She wasn't certain if he was of Kal's blood, but he was certainly the Torry champion and kin to Torg Vantel, making him heir to a rich bloodline. He was skilled with a blade, far greater than any she had known. Gargoyles were clearly frightened of him, which was uncharacteristic of their kind. These *natural* gifts would pass on to his heirs and therefore to House Estaran through her grandchildren. She originally commissioned the slaver captain Veneva to find her a warrior of good genetic stock for Deva to wed. She never imagined for one such as him. In some ways, he was too good, too important, too dangerous. Should her queen discover him in her possession, she would certainly return him to Prince Lorn, her precious Torry nephew. Of course, once he was wed to Deva, he would be beyond Queen Letha's reach, for even a queen's authority was below a wife's, where the husband was concerned.

"Wine, slave!" their guest, Lutesha Dorvena, commanded, snapping her fingers and pointing to her half-full goblet.

Terin winced at the humiliating appellation, shuffling around the table to reach the demanding guest, who sat Darna's left. He felt the woman's lecherous eyes upon him throughout the evening as he moved from guest to guest and then her hand upon his leg as he reached to fill her goblet, just below the hem of his brief garment.

"Such a lovely boy. Wherever did you find him, Guardian Darna?" Lutesha purred, her hooded eyes following the contours of his face.

"He is a recent purchase," Darna said, revealing as little as possible to the arch councilor. Though Lutesha was a staunch ally and a fellow traditionalist, Darna trusted no one with Terin's origin until he and Deva consummated their union. For all practical appearances, Terin was simply her newest house slave and wine bearer.

"Be still," Lutesha commanded, ordering him to stand still as he attempted to draw away, suffering her touch.

"He is quite lovely," Elesha Dorvena added, sitting across from her mother and beside Dorath, whom her mother wanted to betroth her to.

"A recent purchase and already a wine bearer at your table. He must have served another wealthy house for you to promote him to such a station?" Lutesha asked. Only the most tame and handsome of slaves were chosen as wine bearers, a reflection of their owners' wealth and prestige.

"He is new to the collar." Darna sipped her wine, wishing to move on from the subject. She scolded herself for allowing guests to see him. A boy of his attractiveness always drew the eye of powerful women, especially the arch councilor. Unfortunately, his presence was required for Deva's little game this eve.

"'Tis a pity I didn't discover him upon the block before you." Lutesha smiled, patting his rump, sending him on his way. Most new slaves were purchased at auction in Bansoch, as she correctly guessed his original place of sale.

"He is to wed Deva," Cojya blurted, not noticing her mother's withering gaze with her revelation.

"Wed? To a slave, no less?" Lutesha's gray eyes drew wide.

"Is this true, Deva? Why did you not share this during your visit?" Elesha asked, her gray eyes sparkling with interest from across the table.

Deva sat opposite her mother, visibly uncomfortable with her friend's scrutiny.

"Your manners, child," Lutesha politely admonished her daughter. "Guardian Darna has wisely chosen to strengthen the physical nature of her bloodline after several generations of political matches. Another such pairing would bring diminishing return as House Estaran now stands nearly equal to the Crown. We must never overlook the need to replenish the physical attributes that we so highly value. But I might ask, Guardian Darna, what do you gain by wedding Deva to this comely boy? Your children are already beautiful," she asked, her eyes drifting from Darna to Dorath with obvious interest. Darna's favorite child was only nine years, but Lutesha could see how beautiful the boy would blossom and hoped to bind their two houses with him and Elesha.

"He is more than a pretty boy. He is a great warrior!" Cojya again interjected, causing her mother's gold-speckled blue eyes to painfully narrow. She was certain to punish her daughter in private for her flippant tongue.

"A warrior? Surely not." Lutesha craned her neck, observing Terin standing behind her, his head bowed in shame, feeling her eyes upon him. "He looks more bed slave than soldier."

"His looks are deceiving. His chains attest to the danger he poses, but he will sire strong heirs, else I would have gelded him or sent him to the galleys," Darna said, hoping Lutesha would move on to another topic.

"From where does he hail?" Elesha asked, admiring his hair that matched the golden locks she and her mother shared.

"He was a free sword in the employ of a Yatin admiral. His employers met a cruel end at the battle of Tenin. A slaver captain fished him from the sea, selling him at Bansoch," Darna explained, hiding his true origin.

"War, 'tis men's favorite pastime when left to their own devices," Lutesha tutted. "Which only proves our position in the ruling forum to our reformist sisters who castigate our treatment of our menfolk. They would have us following their softhearted ways into oblivion. The chronicles well note what the women of our isle suffered under the Soch Empire of old. If we allowed men to lift their knees from the dirt, they'd put a sword in our heart."

"Truly, Mother?" Elesha questioned, raising a skeptical brow. "Did Father ever rise up against you when you showed him kindness?"

"Your father was different, child, rest his spirit. But he was of good and proper breeding, like young Dorath, who sits beside you. You haven't seen the likes of men from the continent. They are brutish malcontents at best and murderous villains at worst," Lutesha huffed.

"War is a dreadful thing. Only strength will keep it from our shores, strength of arms, and strength of mind," Darna said.

"Your slave is fortunate. Had he remained in Yatin, he would have been slain or captured, his life forfeit. You now offer him a genteel life, once he is wed, of course," Elesha said.

"If he is wise enough to see it," Darna mused.

"The war is a hopeless cause, so much death and tragedy befalling the realms of Arax," Elesha lamented.

"What is the latest word of the war?" Deva asked with practiced interest, snapping her fingers for Terin to refill her goblet.

"Naught but death and suffering. Thousands of Benotrists, gargoyles, Yatins, and Torries dead or badly wounded. Their loved ones cry out from every corner of Arax. No house goes untouched, from the royal courts to the lowest serf, all suffering in kind. Alas, no house has endured such loss as the Torry Royal House of Lore." Elesha's words piqued Terin's ears.

"Oh, yes, their king fell in battle upon the Kregmarin Plain," Lutesha recalled.

"By Lord Morac's hand, no less," Elesha expounded. "It is said he presented King Lore's head to his daughter during a parlay during the siege of Corell."

"I heard this tale," Deva said, seeing Terin stiffen beside her.

"Yes, that tale spreads like fire on dry grass, but the latest news is far more tragic," Elesha explained with false sadness.

"How so?" Darna asked, her eyes shifting subtly between her guests, Deva, and Terin.

Elesha took a large sip from her goblet, steeling her gaze as she looked into Deva's hazel eyes. "Word reached Princess Corry that her true love was lost at sea, receiving the fell tidings as a sword to her breast. In her apparent grief, she threw herself from the roof of the palace. She is dead. Dead by her own hand from a broken heart."

Smash!

The pitcher slipped from Terin's shaking hands, the sound of it breaking upon the floor echoing loudly off the chamber walls.

*****

502

He sat miserably in a cold cell, his hands hooked over his knees, his mind numb to his bruised back, where Darna ordered him whipped thrice for his clumsiness. Terin cared not, his mind a maelstrom of hopelessness and pain. All was lost to him now.

I killed her, he thought miserably. He failed to escape and return to her before she took her life. She thought him dead, taking her life to end her suffering. Her pain was too much to bear. He understood for now he felt the same.

"Take me, Yah! If you are truly there, then heed my words. Is this what you demand of your followers, to strip them of all they hold dear until they are empty vessels? If that is your price, I want none of it. Let me die." He put his head to his knees and wept.

Time passed slowly that fateful night, sleep escaping his troubled mind.

Quiet your mind, the voice returned with a calm reassurance he no longer fought to ignore or refute.

"Very well," he conceded, emptying his mind, trying to forget all that he lost, his pride, his freedom, his love. He set everything aside, one by one, until his mind was void, his closed eyes staring blankly, fixed to that murky image of blurry shapes dancing amidst inky blackness.

Patience, the voice assuaged his restless inclination, keeping his eyes upon the blurry images until they melded into a narrow sliver of bright light. The light grew in intensity, its murky edges gaining clarity as the vision became his sole focus. He gasped, the intense light abating, the image coming into clear definition.

Terin's head shot straight up, his eyes still closed, the image burning into his consciousness. His heart pounded emphatically with rapture. There before his eyes, the image of the bronze-hued blade danced invitingly before him, a bright golden light bursting along its length.

"Sword of Light." He gasped, awestruck by the vision's revelation. 'Twas the gift of his Kalinian blood, the image revealing the sword as it had with his ancestors before him, calling him to the Tarelian blade like a siren's call transcending time and space. The sword swiftly shrank, its surroundings rising around it like a map growing as if drawn from a single point upon its surface, revealing its place in the full picture.

There it rested on this very estate, under his very nose all this time. It was clearly one of the lesser Swords of Light, its bright sheen dull before the glory of his father's blade, but still wondrous to behold. It held nearly as much power, especially in his fell hand. For the first time since Carapis, Terin found hope.

C H A P T E R

21

Corell

The biting winds swirled about the upper reaches of Corell as she walked the northern battlements, her cape billowing in her wake. Scorch marks stained the white stone along the length of the causeway, scarred reminders of the battles waged there. Sunlight reflected off her polished cuirass and silver helm, the vestiges of her warrior garb and grim reminder of her position now as defender of the realm. She wore leggings beneath her tunic with the colder weather upon them, but her arms were still mostly bare, the bite of the cold raising pimples across her exposed flesh. Her eyes swept the northern horizon, wincing with the tortured remains of the once lush green Torry countryside. The scenic landscape was now a twisted ruin of frozen mud as far as the eye could see. So much was lost during the siege, so much wealth and life. Morac's legions cut a swath through the Torry Realm nearly forty leagues abreast from the crossroads to Corell, leaving the skeletal remains of burned dwellings and ruined crops in their wake. Thousands of refugees were dispersed throughout the realm, further straining their food stores. Her preparations before the siege allowed them to harvest half the crops grown east of Corell, but half was still a half short, and many would starve during winter.

"Highness, you should seek shelter. You'll catch your death in this cold," Commander Nevias cautioned, walking her left.

"The men stand post all day and night in this weather, Commander. I am here only here for a brief time to survey our progress. As acting regent, it is my duty," Corry refuted.

"An acting regent who has performed as well as any king who has ever sat the throne, Highness."

"Your flattery is misplaced, Nevias. At times I feel like a lost child a thousand leagues from home."

"Be it ten thousand leagues and deaf and blind, and I would still trust you to lead us home, Princess. Your father would be proud."

"Our banners still brave Corell's citadels because of Bode, El Anthar, and…" Her voice trailed.

"Terin, aye, a brave lad. He will return soon, Highness, as he promised."

Corry sighed, Terin's absence leaving a cavernous hole in her fragile heart. The last word from Yatin was the breaking of the siege of Mosar. Terin again demonstrated his worth, slaying General Yonig and leading Lorn's Army to victory. Alas, instead of returning to her, he journeyed on to Faust, joining the battle at sea. Corry put Terin from her mind, his absence only causing her pain. She cursed herself for foolishly filling the hole left in her heart from her father's death with Terin. Her eyes were instantly drawn to the outcropping upon the inner keep where they shared that first kiss. Whenever she tried to suppress her thoughts of him, another reminder sprang to mind. It came in many forms, whether it was a place where they shared time together, or words of his fell deeds reaching them from Yatin, or someone recalling a story where Terin performed some selfless or impossible act. They could not escape the impact Terin manifested in their lives.

"Yes, he will soon return," she agreed, hiding her doubts from the aging commander. "How goes our food stores?" She moved on, again putting thoughts of Terin from her mind.

"With current rationing, Corell can feed its garrison for ninety days. Anything longer will require additional supply. Our current sources in Torry North are nearly tapped."

"I have arranged purchase of ten thousand bessels of ottein from Teso and Zulon. I dispatched Minister Veda to Central City to over-see the transfer before he journeys to Bansoch to fill our ambassadorship there," she explained, ordering it done the day Terin and the others departed.

"Ten thousand? Do they have such an amount?" Nevias asked, unaware of this arrangement. Teso and Zulon were the two largest border kingdoms resting between Torry North and South, straddling the lands long the Nila. The House of Lore was connected to both, with Corry's late mother a princess from Zulon, whose mother in turn was a princess of Teso.

"They do. Their yields have increased twofold in recent years due to the security the Torry Realms have provided them," she said. Her family had long labored to stabilize the wilder lands separating the Torry Realms. The Sadden Wars were the culmination in this key aim, shielding the smaller kingdoms from Yatin and barbarian threats. With their lands untouched by the current conflict, these border realms were eager to support their Torry benefactors, selling their excess crop below market rate.

Corry expected Nevias to be miffed by her not sharing this information earlier, but news of incoming provisions would spread through the garrison, hindering their conservation efforts. It was a cold calculation, but she knew men faced with starvation would better husband their resources.

"General Bode is expected by moon's end. He reports most of Torry North clear of gargoyles. Morac has fully withdrawn to Notsu but will certainly renew his assault on Corell come spring," she continued.

"And we will give him the same reception as his last visit," Nevias snorted defiantly.

"Perhaps, but there is much still to do. How goes Master Orvon's work?"

"He has repaired one of the center gates to functional status. The others will take more time. The main gate may be irreparable," Nevias apprised her of the Master Smith's progress. Master Orvon was chief of the blacksmith guild of Central City and oversaw the construction and design of hundreds of steel and iron gates throughout the realm. It was another wise decision on Corry's part to summon him to Corell the very day the siege lifted. Morac's sword tore gaping holes through every gate lining the entrance tunnel. The massive front gate suffered a terrible gash, where Morac and Dethine tore much of it asunder, while several support rods were torn from the outer wall, their broken ends jutting from the breach the Naybin catapults affected. Master Orvon brought a small Army of smiths and stone masons to repair the damage, but the main gate was a total loss.

"See that he is given everything he needs. The main gate must be replaced before spring."

"Of course, Highness," Nevias agreed, having repeatedly provided Master Orvon anything he required.

"How goes the training of your recruits?" she asked, knowing the garrison suffered terrible losses during the siege. She emphasized replenishing their archer losses first before filling out the infantry ranks, but skilled bowmen were more difficult to find and train. Anyone with a basic understanding of archery was pressed into service. Corell needed archers to keep the gargoyles from reaching the outer walls.

"Poorly, I fear say. They are all farmers. Not one in ten have ever wielded a sword or bow."

"I find men are fast learners when their lives depend on it. I expect you to drive that point home." She stopped, fixing Nevias with a knowing look.

"Aye. I shall make it known."

"If they should need further motivation, I can send Torg to oversee their training from time to time." She smiled.

"Aye. They'll find him a mite scarier than the gargoyles." Nevias grinned. He was growing fonder of the princess every day. She possessed a warrior's spirit, a general's mind, and a sailor's humor. She never held command until her father's death and her brother away south. She was always in the shadow of the throne, like a flower unable to bloom 'neath the shade of a tall tree. The tree was now gone, and the small flower blossomed in all its majesty. Nevias had a granddaughter of an age to Corry but could never imagine his dear Ilsa commanding the realm.

"We are still waiting to replenish our oil reserves," she continued to walk the battlements.

"The nearest source is forty leagues southwest," Nevias said, his gaze drifting north of the palace where soldiers worked filling in the siege trenches dug by the Benotrists. The defenders filled the trenches with the enemy dead after the battle, setting them ablaze, the ash alone nearly filling them. There were still batches of holes throughout the length of the siege lines requiring filling. The smell of rotting flesh and burning corpses lingered in the air for thirty days after the battle. Nevias could still smell the noxious odor from memory alone. The princess never voiced complaint of the smell or the sight of so much suffering, enduring it all with stoic resolve. Should anything befall her brother, Nevias would proudly bend the knee, acknowledging Corry as his rightful queen.

"Forty-three leagues," she corrected. "Too close for such delays. The alchemists need time to convert the oil into stable fire munitions. We will need to be fully stocked when Morac returns."

"I'll send scouts to hurry their progress," Nevias agreed. Few knew that the garrison ran dry of fire munitions by the battle's end, their last volleys used on the retreating Benotrists north of the main gate. That information was privy only to himself, General Bode, and the princess. He shuddered to think how close Morac came to taking the palace.

"I want two hundred thousand arrows fletched before the next siege," Corry ordered.

"As you command." Nevias would see it done, even if he had to cut down a forest.

"After suffering such losses, Morac will need time to replenish his battered legions. With Bode's 3rd Army added to our garrison, along with the Jenaii contingent King El Anthar left to aid our cause, Morac will need a far larger Army to assail our walls," she surmised. The Jenaii alone would destroy any launch towers Morac thought to erect, negating that tactic that worked so well in his favor during the siege.

"No two sieges are exactly the same. Both sides learn from their mistakes and adjust accordingly, Highness."

"Folly is the father of wisdom," she quoted that old proverb her father oft repeated.

*****

The afternoon found Corry in the training arena under Torg's tute-lage. Since Terin left, she dedicated her every free moment honing her sword handling. To Torg's credit, he didn't spare her feelings or fuel her pride. He criticized her every flaw until she drilled them from her form. She wondered how much easier it would be if she wielded a Sword of Light, but they possessed only one, and it was far dead-lier in Terin's hand. Yet it was not just his sword handling that made Terin so deadly, it was something more, something she could only sense but never define. His father was similarly gifted. Thinking of his father, she had asked him the source of this strange power, but he wouldn't answer, saying it was Terin's place to tell her. Conveniently for Jonas, he only told Terin just before his departure, forcing her to await his return to reveal this mystery, which she hoped was soon. The battle in Yatin was nearing its end, and there was no reason for him to remain. She thought to send word, reminding Terin and her brother that Terin needed to return *before* spring.

"Umph!" She moaned, Torg's training sword striking her stom-ach, the blow driving her to her knees.

"Again!" he commanded sternly.

She obeyed, putting the pain from her mind. Torg was merci-less, holding nothing back as they battled. He lessened the strikes on impact to avoid undue harm, but the strikes were too numerous, leaving her bruised after every session.

"I'll not train you halfheartedly, Princess," he warned at the start of their first lesson. They agreed that her training should reflect true combat as much as possible. Half measures would only get her killed if she intended to use a sword. Whenever she grew comfortable, he would change tactics, catching her off guard, often with dirty tricks. A spit in the eye, sand in the face, or other nefarious means were used to imprint in her that all was fair when your life was in the balance. He was adamant that when she entered the training arena, she was no princess, royal, or lady fair, only a warrior.

"Better," Torg snorted as she blocked a counter strike that she before failed to match.

Her small victory died quickly, his follow-through knocking her blade from her grasp. Torg was the finest swordsman in the realm and did not spare her his full talent. Combat was a contest of life and death. In the end, all that mattered was victory. She could not match his skill, but that was life, he explained. You still have to overcome unfair contests. Each day she grew stronger, quicker, and more cunning, until one time she was able to best him, touching a dagger to his gut as his blade touched her throat. It was one bout in thousands, but it was a kill nonetheless, though her life would've been forfeit in the exchange. Torg responded with a proud smile, acknowledging her achievement. It was one of her proudest moments.

"Master Vantel, would the princess care to cross swords with me?" Jonas Caleph offered. He stood off to the side, curiously observing their bout.

"If my student desires to test her skills against another, she is welcome to try." Torg backed a step as she acquiesced.

"It is an honor to learn from the two finest swordsmen in the realm, good sir." She smiled, retrieving her sword from where it dropped. She took delight in Jonas's company, accepting him in Terin's place. Since Terin's departure, she found herself mostly in Jonas and Torg's company, each reminding her of Terin in both subtle and obvious ways. She missed him dearly but found solace in his father and grandfather's presence, though the two men could never fill the cavernous void his absence left in her heart.

Jonas treated her with practiced grace, his kills never harsher than gentle taps, but she found him just as difficult to engage as Torg. They were different though, Torg's blunt and brutal efficiency contrasting Jonas's graceful, smooth movements. Engaging one after the other was frustrating but educational, as her bruised arms and rump attested. When he avoided her desperate final thrust, he slipped around her flank, touching his practice sword to her right shoulder.

Corry blew an errant lock of hair from her face, lowering her sword in defeat as the bout ended.

"Your performance is quite improved, Highness." Jonas bowed gracefully.

"You are a poor liar, Jonas Caleph, just as your son." She gifted him a pained smile despite her humiliated and bruised flesh.

"You managed to strike a killing blow on Master Vantel, Princess. That is a feat many of my fellow Elite cannot claim." A handsome smile graced his face, which she found strikingly similar to Terin's.

No wonder the Lady Valera was so taken with him, she mused.

She was taken aback as Torg tapped his training sword to Jonas's, claiming the next bout. Corry backed away, granting the warriors a wide berth. She felt the pimples rise across her flesh in anticipation. The two had not crossed swords since the days of Jonas's youth, before he professed his love for Valera.

Jonas accepted the challenge, taking up a fighting stance as Torg moved several paces, stopping before him, his sword lowered at his side, gray eyes meeting purple. Both men faced each other for an eternal moment, neither making the first move until they finally relented, moving in unison with sudden flurry.

Corry stood spellbound by their clashing swords and swift footwork, their faces betraying little of the battle they waged. Torg drove forcefully, as Jonas moved offline with practiced ease. Torg blocked Jonas's counterstrike, his follow-through missing Jonas's knee. Their pace quickened, Corry struggling to follow their hurried movements, as a growing crowd gathered along the periphery. None of the current Elite remembered Master Vantel so challenged. Only recently had they heard tell of Jonas's legendary prowess, and here they were treated with a rare sight: the two greatest swordsmen of the realm battling before their eyes. There were no cheers or hearty banter favoring one or the other, only respectful silence. Corry could see Terin in both men, the perfect amalgamation of the two warrior bloodlines manifested in the Torry champion. It was thrilling and terrifying to behold, Terin's mighty sire and grandsire, battling in an endless dance, each matching every thrust, swing, and maneuver of the other, as if they were of one mind. She almost forgot their age, their speed and strength matching their younger peers. She was so spellbound by their mock battle that she didn't notice the ever-growing crowd entering the arena or gathering in the view stands.

The two men eventually parted, each unable to fell the other, facing each other with several paces of sand between them, their labored breath and sweat stained garments, the only evidence of their struggle. Jonas raised his sword vertically before his face, saluting Torg with the deepest respect before placing the blade at his feet and stepping without.

Torg saluted in kind, stepping away as the spectators stood dumbstruck by their performance. No one spoke a word as Torg followed Jonas without, the silence hanging in the air long after they left.

*****

The late evening again found her upon Zar Crest, staring out into the endless starlit expanse. Wisps of smokey air escaped her lips as Corry drew her cloak tight, wondering where Terin was and if he was staring at the same sky.

"I shouldn't be surprised to find you here, Highness," Leanna's familiar voice echoed as she stepped to her side at the battlement's edge, her hand clutching her growing womb.

"You should be abed, Leanna," Corry said, touching a gentle hand to her shoulder.

"I shall be abed more than I care to soon enough." She sighed contentedly. She shared her joyous news with Corry as soon as the matrons confirmed her pregnancy, feeling aglow with Cronus's child quickening within. She was ever thankful that a part of him was with her in his absence, unlike their last parting. Had he fallen, they would be forever separated, their lives diverging from that moment, until time and other bonds washed away all that they shared. Their child changed that in so many ways, for if Cronus fell in battle, he would be forever bound to her through their child's blood. It was the one thing that is evenly shared between two people to survive their own passing. She longed for his return, but the child gave her solace and assuaged her lonely heart.

"Cronus will be proud," Corry said, moving her hand to Leanna's cheek.

"He shall. We oft spoke of children, but I doubt he expected it so soon." She beamed.

"It shouldn't be unexpected, unless he is ignorant on how these things can happen," Corry teased playfully.

"He knows, just like every other man." Leanna laughed lightly.

"Not every man. Terin knows nothing of our sex. It took him an eternity to confess his love."

"He was likely frightened out of his wits. You are a princess after all," Leanna reminded her.

"And he is the champion of the realm. He is hardly of peasant stock," Corry said, finding his timidity equally endearing and irritating.

"Yes, but he was not raised as a child of privilege or position, just a simple farmer," Leanna explained.

"What farmer is trained from birth by a master swordsman or taught to read by the daughter of Torg Vantel?" Corry rolled her eyes.

"He didn't know his mother's significance or that his father's martial skill was far beyond other men. He had little to compare it to until he began his apprenticeship."

"He is hardly daft. He should have known he was special," Corry countered.

"Daft? No. Naive? Most assuredly." Leanna smiled, recalling Terin's unassuming nature.

"Yes, perhaps too naive. I intend to have a conversation with Jonas about his son's upbringing. Naivety can only suffice when dealing with honorable men and is wholly unsuited in treating with all others."

"Then it is his good fortune then to have spent all his time in good men's company."

"Cronus and Antillius," Corry acknowledged.

"And Raven."

Corry wrinkled her nose at Leanna's mention of the Earther.

"Raven." Corry shook her head, her memories of the nefarious captain far different than Leanna's.

"Highness, you have shown me nothing but kindness since we first met upon the *Stenox* at Molten Isle. You have allowed me to dwell in your ancestorial home whilst Cronus served in the Elite. You honored each of us by personally placing my hand to his, sealing our union before the eyes of the realm, but you mustn't overlook the worth of a far greater friend to our realm."

"You believe Raven is the greater friend?" Corry raised a skeptical brow.

"Is it not wiser to judge men by their deeds rather than their words? It was the Earthers who rescued you from Molten Isle."

"And they were handsomely rewarded," Corry added.

"They have slain thousands of our enemies."

"For their own benefit, not ours."

"They rescued Cronus when no one else could." Or *would*, she did not add.

"Because he is their friend," Corry said.

"True. They have proven how far they would go to save a friend, and Terin is their friend." Leanna bobbed a curtsy and stepped away. "Fair thee well, Highness," she said, retiring for the night.

Corry lingered a while longer, thinking on what Leanna said. It was true that Raven and the others were fond of Terin, and part of her was jealous that he made friends so easily, where she did not, not true friends anyway. Oh, there were countless flatterers and lickspittles who praised her before the realm, all hoping to gain the favor of the Crown, but 'twas a mummer's show. A royal never truly knew their true friends from false. Perhaps that was why she kept Leanna's company, a merchant's daughter no less, because she saw in her a genuine affection. It was the same with Cronus. He was an honorable, brave man who willingly sacrificed himself for others. He was also beloved by his friends that they risked their lives to free him. Could she garner such loyalty without her title? She wondered if anyone truly loved her.

Terin loves you, you hopeless fool, she scolded herself. She knew that he loved her the moment he set eyes upon her on Molten Isle and every moment they shared thereafter. If he was the only one to truly love her and everyone else loved him, she could live with it. Perhaps her brother's god was real after all, giving Terin so many friends because he needed them along his perilous journey.

At that moment, her eyes found Jonas standing upon the western battlements of the inner keep, staring longingly in the distance. Was he thinking of his son, fighting far off in Yatin, or his beloved Valera, who waited for him at their small home in the Torry heartland? Or were his thoughts elsewhere? He was supposed to return home just after the battle but decided to remain at Corell for a reason he would not say. There was a gentle kindness in his purple eyes that reminded her so much of Terin but also a profound sadness that was absent in his son. His sorrow felt like a broken heart, a personal hurt that she struggled to understand. Did he not wed his true love? Did he not sire a wonderful son? What else could cause this mysterious melancholy in Terin's father? Even from afar she could see his somber face shining in the torchlight atop the palace, resting his weary hands upon the flat of the rampart, staring westward where the endless horizon met the starry sky.

"He's a moody one," Torg's deep gravel voice echoed as he came to her side.

"Torg." She smiled.

"Aye. I thought you might be here. It's always been your favorite place in all the palace since you were knee-high," he recalled.

"And it was you who often brought me up here when my father was otherwise occupied."

"Yes. This was Valera's favorite place as well when she was a wee tot," he recalled all those memories atop the platform, holding his daughter's hand as she gazed with wonder at the surrounding lands.

"It could have been Terin's as well, if he was raised here as he should have been." She imagined a lifetime of growing up beside him.

"No, your father and Jonas had the right of it. Terin needed to be raised far away. Palace life would've ruined him."

"Did it ruin me?" she challenged.

"Of course not. You are a princess of the realm. You are worthy of any privilege this life has given you."

"And Terin is the grandson of Torg Vantel. He too is worthy of such privilege." She wanted to add that he was worthy for her to wed.

"Bah! Being of relation to me is no virtue, Corry. I'm just a cantankerous old man whose glory has long faded." He sighed wearily.

"Oh yes, you are a helpless old man that no member of the King's Elite can best in the training yard." She smiled, slapping his hand. "The finest warriors in the realm quiver fearfully whenever matched with you, Torg Vantel, so spare me this *old man* drivel.

What I saw you and Jonas do today was beyond anything I have seen, save for Terin in battle."

"It was a lie," he snorted.

"A lie? What was a lie?"

"Our duel. Jonas could have beaten me several times but fought to a draw on purpose."

"How do you know?" Her eyes drew wide at the revelation.

"I've handled a sword since I was two years. I know when an adversary is struggling to keep pace or playing me false. Jonas is too good but chose not to defeat me for a purpose I can only surmise."

"To spare your pride? You are Valera's father and Terin's grandfather."

"You think I care a wit for my pride? If he truly respected me, he would have given me his utmost. There is no shame in losing to the finest swordsman I have ever seen."

"You believe he is that good?"

"I know he is. Far greater than I ever was, or ever will be."

"Are you certain? You are the greatest I have ever known. Your name is renowned in every realm of Arax for your prowess."

"Aye, if I were to battle mortal men, I like my chances more than not, but Jonas is no mortal man," he said, his voice almost a whisper.

"What do you mean?" She made a face.

"Your father believed Jonas a child of prophecy, the one to find the lost sword of the Middle Kingdom. The sword passed rightfully to Terin, as the prophecy ordained through the hereditary line of the one who found it. Don't you find it strange that the power Jonas has over gargoyles has passed on to his son? Is it a quirk of nature or something more? How much do we know of Jonas's lineage? Almost nothing. He came to us clouded in mystery. Whatever secret he is harboring is clearly eating at him. I can see it in those gold-speckled purple eyes of his."

"Then who is he?" she asked, more curious of Terin's full origin than Jonas's.

"Who knows." Torg shrugged. "What I do know is that he is beyond normal men. When I sparred with him today, it was as when we last crossed swords in the old days. He knows every move I make before it even comes to my own mind."

"That could just be instinct."

"You've seen Terin in battle. He is the same. He knows where every arrow flies and every blade will strike. And before you claim it is the Sword of the Moon, that same power does not transcend to Elos, Morac, or Dethine, from what I have seen."

"Then what is it?"

"Only he knows." Torg lifted his chin in Jonas's direction before retiring.

*****

The following morn found Corry sitting her father's throne, holding court with the great chamber filled with petitioners. The usual squabbling between differing merchants and landowners filled most of the dockets. Many of the merchants argued over payment of goods lost in transit during the invasion. Usually, she would refer all merchant disputes to Minister Veda, but he was already dispatched to treat with Queen Letha, leaving her to deal with all cases within his purview. She referred all disputes over agriculture to Minister Thunn, but there were countless disagreements between landed gentry that crossed over into the political landscape requiring the Crown to settle.

"Highness, I beseech the Crown to right this wrong. I placed my livestock in Governor Taulus's keeping during the Benotrist incursion in exchange for nine hundred gold certras. He claims the gargoyles slaughtered my livestock, yet his own herds were untouched," Gais Luron, a wealthy landed gentry in the Laris Region, pleaded. The region straddled the demarcation line separating those lands devastated by Morac's legions and those untouched.

"Is this so?" Corry asked as the two men stood below the dais. Governor Taulus's rigid posture belied the volcano about to burst as he held his tongue, waiting for his turn to speak.

"Nine hundred certras? 'Tis a pittance. I secured his livestock on the only grazing lands available, which unfortunately fell in Morac's line of march. I lost three good men trying to move his herds before they were overtaken by gargoyle raiders. What recompense shall I give their kin, Highness?" Taulus argued.

"And I lost two dozen men protecting all the lands of the Laris Region when my house met the muster to arms," Gais countered.

"You will speak only when given leave to do so, good sir. Do so again out of turn, and your case is forfeit," Corry warned.

"My apologies, Highness." Gais quickly bowed his head.

"Governor Taulus. You have an unwed heir and daughter?" she inquired.

"And a second son as well, Highness," Taulus affirmed.

"And you also have an unwed heir and daughter?" she asked Gais.

"Yes, Highness," he answered in kind.

"You also possess the largest land holdings in Laris?" she asked.

"Yes, Highness," Gais affirmed, though nearly all his lands were scorched and ruined.

"And you, Governor Taulus, hold regency of Laris at the behest of the Crown?" she asked, her brow lifting expectantly.

"For five hundred years, Highness," Taulus said proudly.

"Then my decree is thus. Each of your daughters are to wed the other's heir, binding your houses forthwith. Secondly, a third of Governor Taulus's livestock will be given as dowry to Gais's heir. In turn, Gais will gift one quarter of his lands as dowry to Taulus's heir. Each dowry is contingent upon these unions bearing fruit with heirs born to solidify the exchange. As acting regent of the realm, I so order!"

Both meant to argue but wisely acquiesced and dropped their dispute. And so it went throughout the session, with countless petitioners seeking restitution through the Crown. Corry had to navigate the oft treacherous waters and political maneuverings that characterized these disputes. There were at least three claimants upon vacant noble houses, two were victims of Morac's legions, and the third succumbed to a mysterious demise. Others sought restitution from the Crown for the loss of property, which she pointed out that no recompense would be made until war's end. She left out the fact that all the lands Morac ravaged would likely suffer again when his legions returned. With Tyro's champion at Notsu, refitting his battered legions, there was little purpose to remain there unless he intended a swift return.

The assemblage grew suddenly quiet as a flax of royal guards entered the throne room, the crowd parting as they approached the dais, escorting a member of the King's Elite, the fellow's silver helm concealing much of his face. Corry paled as the soldier removed his helm and knelt.

"Lucas," she greeted, struggling to keep her voice from breaking. He was supposed to be in Yatin with Terin. What was he doing here without Terin?

"Princess, I bring…tidings from His Highness Prince Lorn," Lucas declared, removing a sealed parchment from his satchel, setting it upon the floor before him, the timber of his voice betraying his laden heart. Whatever news he brought was certainly of no good.

"Do you know the contents of this parchment?" she asked.

"I do, Highness." Lucas lowered his head, the sorrow evident in his sad eyes.

Corry's heart pounded emphatically as if to burst, her eyes shifting back and forth between Lucas and the sealed parchment on the floor.

Torg stood her right, observing the grim affair with guarded apprehension. His eye caught sight of Jonas standing on Corry's left, his face stoically indifferent, as if he expected this ill tiding.

"Clear the chamber!" she commanded.

*****

She sat the throne, the parchment slipping from her trembling fingers. Torg picked it up, quickly reading to find the source of her profound reaction, feeling the eyes of his fellow Elite upon him as he scanned the parchment.

"He's gone," Corry's haunted voice echoed dully in his ears. Lucas shifted uncomfortably at the base of the dais, and Jonas stood statue still at her left, as if resigned to whatever ill news the missive contained. Torg read the words thrice over, his heart fragmenting a little further each time, until crumbling into dust.

Terin is lost at sea and likely dead, he thought bitterly. He so regretted all the lost years, all the times he could have been part of his life but was not. His poor Valera. How would she bear such news? Terin was the child of prophecy, how could he die so meaningless a death? The mostly empty throne room felt suddenly crowded, as if the walls themselves were closing around him, as if a thousand voices rang out in a morbid cacophony, tearing at his soul.

Corry grew deathly quiet, the sounds of the vast chamber deafened by her pounding heart. She gained her feet and stepped without.

*****

She stood upon the battlements until day turned to dusk, oblivious to the winter chill billowing her cape in the wind. She gazed aimlessly to the west, seeing nothing, her cheeks stained with frozen tears. Never did she feel as alone as now, the last tendrils of happiness torn away as if they were only a mirage, a false hope for a future that could never be. She peered over the edge of the inner keep, gauging the distance to the walkway below.

Put that thought from your mind, she scolded herself. She was no coward and would not forsake her duty to her house and realm. If hope was lost to her, then she would learn to live without it. But oh, did it hurt so. No matter how hard she tried, his image danced before her, every detail of his lovely face playing cruelly in her mind. She closed her eyes, squeezing the visage from her memory, but to no avail.

Torg stood guard far behind her, keeping others away who meant only to comfort her, but no salutation or kind word could assuage her pain.

"I would speak with her," Jonas said, approaching Torg as the sun settled below the horizon.

"I believe she wishes to be alone, Jonas," Torg said, less harshly than he intended, but he couldn't know what Jonas had lost. He wondered who should be consoling who, for Corry lost her true love, Jonas his son, and he his grandson.

"I would hear his words," Corry said, overhearing them but not turning to face them, her watered eyes staring vacant to the west.

As the two men stepped near, she quickly rounded on them, a scowl contorting her face. "You knew, didn't you?" she asked, her vacant eyes suddenly afire, burning into Jonas's.

Torg regarded the crestfallen look that pained Jonas's countenance, affirming what he too long suspected.

"I did." Jonas sighed, dreading this moment when all his secrets would spill from his lips, for one part could not be explained separate from the whole. It would only lead to more questions that only the full truth could reveal.

"And you said nothing. No warning, nothing!" she accused.

"I had no choice," he said sadly.

"Speak sense, Jonas! What in the blazes are you confessing to?" Torg growled.

"He knew Terin had perished, or would perish, and yet spoke not a word of warning. You let him leave here for a fool's quest, and you said nothing," she accused.

"I did not receive the vision until after his departure, before I was to return home," he said, which explained why he lingered at Corell.

"You could have told me. There was still time to recall him before it was too late," she countered.

"I couldn't. It was his destiny."

She slapped him.

"His destiny was not to die!" she growled lowly, fighting the tightness in her throat and the tears vying to break free.

"He is not dead."

"What did you say?" Her pounding heart abated long enough for her to breathe.

"He lives," Jonas said, though his tone implied something terribly amiss.

"How do you know this?" Torg asked, a dangerous look brewing in his gray eyes.

"I have visions from time to time. They are specific in detail and never wrong. They are of things that were and things that are but never of things that will be, lest our actions alter the course of history, until now."

"Nonsense! Are you touched? What foolishness has addled your brain?" Torg growled.

"Torg, there are things about Terin and I you don't understand."

"Well, that arrow strikes the mark. I knew there was something off about you the first day we crossed swords in the training yard all those years ago."

"You said he is alive. Where is he?" Corry demanded, not caring a whit of his origin at this time.

"He was taken captive to a distant port, where he was sold," Jonas said with as little emotion as he could manage, steeling his heart to his son's fate.

"Sold?" She gripped his arms fiercely.

"Sold to whom, Jonas?" Torg growled.

"A woman with gold-speckled blue eyes and stern countenance. Her hair is ebony, with a taint of silver taking root. She is a commander of rank wearing a gold cuirass over a black tunic with shining steel vambraces and greaves. The ship docked along a stone wharf with a large palace resting upon a hill within the city, its gold minarets spiraling above a curtain wall that circled the city. Female soldiers patrolled the wharves, wearing gold cuirasses over silver tunics, with black capes and golden helms. The sigil upon their crests was a cloven black crown upon a field of white."

"Bansoch," Corry affirmed, her heart twisting in the wind, glad that he lived, but fearful of his fate. He was a slave to a powerful official in the Federation, and that portended a myriad of awful possibilities. He could be sent to the mines or galleys, ensuring a quick death. A field slave could endure for a lifetime and avoid the scrutiny of a domestic or personal slave. He was too pretty to be used in the mines, fields, or galleys, meaning the woman who bought him intended for him to serve in her household, where many were gelded, and if not, she intended him for more intimate purposes. She had to free him before any of that happened, but how? Was she already too late?

"All that you fear has not yet come to pass, though time is fleeting," Jonas's cryptic voice drawing her from her thoughts.

"Explain yourself, Jonas Caleph! The full truth! As acting regent of the realm, I call upon your oath to the Torry throne to speak it true! Every detail of your lineage, journeys, and actions!" she demanded.

Torg snorted, crossing his muscled forearms over his chest. This was a tale he long wanted to hear.

"I shared this with Terin the morning he departed, revealing my story and kinship, a tale I planned for him to share with each of you upon his return, but alas, it again falls to me. Perhaps it is for the best, for it has been my burden to bear and my sin that hangs above the realm," Jonas began, his voice a clear whisper in the winter air.

My sin piqued Torg's curiosity, wondering to what he referred, while Corry was more concerned with Terin's future than his past. As Jonas began his strange tale, she too was hopelessly drawn into the unfolding story.

"My story begins during the reign of Kal…" he began, relaying the tale. He could see the confusion at first in their eyes, wondering where he was leading them, but their confusion quickly transformed to awe, bewilderment, and understanding, until he spoke of gifting the Sword of the Sun to his father. It was then that they both suspected the awful truth and source of Jonas's shame and grief.

It all made sense, Torg thought, bereft of words. Jonas's melancholy and somber disposition, born of opposing bloodlines, tearing him in differing directions. The guilt plagued him still for gifting his father the very weapon that forged his empire, the empire that plagued the Torry Realms.

"The blood of Kal," Corry whispered. She always knew in her heart that Terin was special, but little could prepare her for the full truth. If Jonas spoke true, then he and Terin were all that remained of Kal's bloodline, heirs to a mysterious power she couldn't comprehend.

"The blood of Tyro," Torg added, now fully understanding the ghosts haunting his daughter's husband.

"The unforgivable stain," Jonas finished what he thought Torg meant to add.

"Stain? I don't judge a boy by his father's sins but by his own choices. You could have claimed your birthright but chose poverty and honor over wealth and cruelty. There's no stain upon you, Jonas, only the stain you put upon yourself. But you should have told us all of this long ago, especially Terin. You let him walk into Fera ignorant of his true birth," Torg said.

"That would have boded ill. Terin would have tried to sway my father through their kinship, but there can be no compromise." Jonas sighed.

"You are his son, the son he believes dead. Could you or Terin not appeal to his better nature? Could peace not be secured?" Corry asked. A moment before, she would never contemplate such thoughts, fully prepared to fight Tyro to the death, but Terin's heritage changed all that. Perhaps peace could be brokered with Tyro's heir fighting on behalf the Torry cause.

"There can be no peace. My mother and I fled my father's realm once he allied with gargoyles, for the blood of Kal cannot abide them. We are born to a purpose, one of the two purposes Yah ordained Kal to achieve. To unite the land under his divine rule and extinguish the gargoyles. The task was too great for one man or one bloodline, so Yah in his infinite wisdom has chosen another to unite the world under his dominion, leaving the blood of Kal the task for which we are most suited…the destruction of the gargoyles. My father will not disavow his alliance, not even for Terin or I. Had Terin asked it of him, he would have taken him captive, filling his young mind with delusions to bend him to his will."

"Terin would never bend," Corry affirmed.

"Terin is a boy. A boy who would reach out to his grandfather, seeking approval and showing him the love in his pure heart. Does he not seek your approval and acceptance?" he asked, fixing Torg with a knowing look.

"Aye. He is a good lad," Torg grunted in agreement.

"But Terin would not forsake his mother's kin for…" Corry paused.

"For his father's father," Jonas finished her sentence. "Perhaps not intentionally, but should he succumb, even slightly, he would risk the power of his blood," Jonas warned.

"The power of his blood?" Corry made a face.

"The power of his blood and mine is bestowed from Yah, given to us to counter the gargoyle curse upon Arax. Should we falter in that belief, the power will weaken and fail, for Yah would remove his blessing."

"What would happen to him?" she asked, her heart pounding again.

"The power would reverse itself. Instead of invoking fear in gargoyles and their allies, he would incur their hatred and bloodlust. They would slay him."

"What?" She gasped.

"You see, Princess, even if I chose my father over Yah's will, my traitor's blood would see the gargoyles tear me apart. That was why my mother fled the north once we learned of my father's gargoyle alliance. I was forced to amend my sin, to balance the scales for gifting the Golden Sword to my father, by aiding the last kingdom of Ancient Tarelia standing against the darkness."

"The Middle Kingdom," she answered, now understanding the burden Jonas bore.

"The Torry Realms, your realm, Corry." A wane smile passed his lips.

"You came to help us." She sighed, keeping her gaze upon him.

"Yes, and using my gift of vision, I found the lost sword of the Middle Kingdom to counter the Golden Blade. Ironic, is it not, that I gave my son the Sword of the Moon to counter the Sword of the Sun I gifted my father."

"But now Terin holds no sword," Torg snorted.

"The sword awaits him, for it is still in Lorn's keeping," Jonas said.

"If Terin has faithfully served your god, why has Yah forsaken him?" Corry challenged.

"Following Yah's will is no guarantee of triumph, but disobeying him does incur defeat," Jonas poorly explained.

"Well, what blasted good is that?" Torg growled. "Following him means naught for victory, but not following him means defeat? That seems the only advantage lies with Tyro. He is clearly not one of Yah's followers and won't suffer for turning his back on him. And if those who are unworthy of the Swords of Light end up losing them, then how does Morac retain the Golden Sword? How does a servant of darkness wield Yah's blessed weapon?"

"The Swords of Light are imbued with great power. Once one bonds with the blade, the sword will guide their hand in battle and shield them from harm. In Terin's or my hand, this power is magnified many times over mortal men, but the power is still there nonetheless. The swords were made for the blood of Kal to wield but will faithfully serve those dedicated to our quest, the destruction of the gargoyles. If wielded by any other, the bond will eventually weaken, forsaking its false master," Jonas explained.

"Tyro has owned it for many years now, and Morac as well, and the bond doesn't look weak to me." Torg shook his head.

"There is one other possibility for Tyro's bond with the sword being so strong, though this bond would not extend to Morac. The power of the swords is an extension of the power in my blood. Each are divine gifts from Yah, given for a single purpose. There is another side to the power of my blood, and Terin's as well."

"Another side?" Corry lifted a curious brow.

"Yes, for every strength, there is an equally potent weakness. The weakness in our power is reflective of Yah's benevolence. The power of our blood renders those we are meant to destroy helpless in our wake."

"Yes, we have seen the effect Terin has on our foes, but where is this weakness you speak of? I see it not," Torg asked.

"If our power makes us nearly indestructible to those we are meant to hate, the opposite is true to—"

"Those that you love," Corry finished his sentence.

Jonas gifted her a knowing smile. "Yes, Corry, love. Those we love and those who love us."

"Tyro." Her eyes drew wide. "Your love for your father strengthened his bond to the sword."

"Yes, and his love for me as well. It is this power that protects those we love from any harm by our hand and renders us helpless against them in turn. Terin loves you, Corry, and will act to protect you even in subtle ways that seem inconsequential at the time," he said as she recalled the two magantor scouts Terin saved at the outset of the siege, who in turn saved her.

"Are you saying that Tyro's love for you strengthened his bond to the sword, because you are of Kal's bloodline?" Torg asked.

"Yes, that is what he is implying," Corry said.

"Then why doesn't his blood betray him to the gargoyles as it would you?" Torg asked.

"Because he is not of Kal's bloodline, though he benefits from it through his love for me," Jonas revealed the irony that protected Tyro from the sword's betrayal by his love for his son and inadvertently the blood of Kal.

"You lost me long ago," Torg snorted, making little sense of Jonas's explanation.

"What it means is that Tyro is protected from Terin and Jonas," Corry said.

"So be it, but his minions aren't, and last I looked, it is Morac who wields the Golden Sword," Torg reasoned.

"And if we are to face him again, the Sword of the Moon must be wielded by the blood of Kal," she said, giving Jonas a knowing look.

"It is Terin's destiny, not mine," Jonas said.

"Then we must free him," she said.

"The Benotrist Navy controls the approaches to Bansoch, and a journey by magantor is a difficult trek," Torg said as she recalled her capture by the pirates in Bansoch and the long journey to Molten Isle. Escaping from the isle was one thing, but to free Terin first would require an Army, which was more than a few magantors could ferry. She could go with a small entourage and plead to Queen Letha to free Terin. Queen Letha was her father's sister and a true friend to the Torry throne. Corry wondered why Letha would allow Torry soldiers to be taken slave? Of course, a clever slaver would be keen to conceal the origin of her captives, knowing the queen's affinity.

"Queen Letha may not know that Terin is captive or where he is held," Corry said, suddenly struck by the grim realization. Diplomacy might not be enough to find and rescue him. This could be an impossible task.

"We may have to concede this battle to Terin himself, trusting him to find his way free. He must learn to fully embrace his gifts," Jonas said, knowing the others didn't share his cold acceptance of the situation.

"It is easy to disregard our responsibility freeing him, but I'll not trust my grandson's life to fate or the whim of your god, Jonas. You've been given this vision for a reason. What could be its purpose other than to impel us to act?" Torg argued.

"Perhaps to reassure us that he is well and trust that he will find his way to freedom," Jonas reasoned.

"Reassure us that he is well?" Corry's eyes hardened to narrow slits, regarding him with a murderous glare. "He is enslaved, alone, and suffering unknown hardship in a far-off land! You are his father. How can you speak of him so callously? Has your god frozen your heart?"

Jonas had learned to accept grim realities that were beyond his power to change, but it still pained him. If he allowed the imaginings of Terin's suffering to take root, he would crumble. Steeling his heart, he shook such thoughts from his mind.

"What would you risk to free him, Corry? Any mission would imperil those you send, with little hope of success. I love my son more than you know, but I wouldn't send others to their death or worse for so small a chance. I would be a poor servant of Yah if I cannot trust his will at the most critical moment of my life. I must trust Terin's life to his will and mercy."

"You sound like my brother." She sneered. The comparison hardly a compliment. "Tell me, Jonas, do all of Yah's servants use his divine will to excuse their inaction?"

"If it were only so simple." He sighed.

"Oh, but it is," she said.

"And who would you send? Who would you sacrifice to save my son? It's an impossible task."

"Difficult, not impossible," she corrected.

"Whether difficult or impossible, we need someone who can do both," Torg snorted.

"There is only one person that I know who could do it." She closed her eyes, resigning herself to the uncomfortable task, forcing her to swallow her pride and beseech the one man she hoped to never see again or owe a favor. She shook such self-pity from her mind, willing to surrender her pride, her wealth, and every worldly possession if it meant freeing Terin. It was then she realized how much she truly loved him, as everything else in life lost meaning without him to share it with.

But he is the blood of Tyro, a voice warned in her head.

He is the blood of Kal, another countered.

He is the blood of Torg, another affirmed, parroting the whisper of her heart. She didn't know Tyro or Kal, for they were only faceless names, but Torg she knew, and Terin was his grandson. If she knew only that, it would be enough. She cared not for Yah, Kal, Tyro, or the denizens of all the realms. She loved Terin the man and would surrender all for him.

"Highness?" Torg asked, seeing her working it all in her mind.

"Order Commander Nevias to prepare a magantor flax to escort me. I am leaving on the morrow. Torg, you will rule in my stead," she commanded.

"Leaving to where?" he asked, not liking this at all.

"To save the man I love."

C H A P T E R

22

Benotrist Empire, eighty leagues south of Nisan
Nivek Province, Governor's castle

Datak Culn, regional governor of Nivek, sat his place at the head of the table, joined by three visiting proctors and his regional officials, each partaking the generous feast, served by his small Army of slaves bustling about the feasting hall. A great hearth upon the near wall was ablaze, warming the spacious chamber as Governor Culn stood from his seat, raising a tankard and addressing his guests.

"To our brave soldiers fighting in the south and our emperor who sits the throne!" he stated.

"Cheer! Cheer!" His guests seconded his declaration, downing their third cup as the servants hurried to refill them.

"Let us take this night to celebrate another season of great harvest, a bountiful yield to match the bountiful victories to come," Datak Culn boasted, his eldest son and heir serving as a commander of telnic in the 11th Benotrist Legion, receiving word from him three days prior that he survived the battle of Corell and was safely garrisoned at Notsu. The fortuitus news set him at ease. He took his seat, snapping his fingers for the nearest wine bearer to fill his half-empty tankard, admiring the comely girl's lovely form amply displayed by her scandalously brief garment. Her scanty attire did little to protect her from the frigid air in the outer corridors, contrasting the thick furs and trousers of her master, who sat smugly upon his chair, running a free hand over her arm.

"Will that be all, master?" she asked, her eyes trained to the floor, awaiting his leave to step back.

"For now, Telisa." He smiled, slapping her rump as she backed away.

She took her place beside her fellow servants, standing dutifully along the sides of the chamber, each sharing similar attire and subservient posture. There were four male and seven female table servants, each bought from the western provinces of the empire.

"A fine-looking wench," Jurns Kelvar, a proctor from the western edge of Nivek Province, said, gifting the young maid an approving grin.

"Aye, a recent addition to my household, much to my wife's ire." Governor Culn snickered, his wife and children confined to their chambers for the night.

The girl Telisa burned with shame, her green eyes concealing the tempest brewing within. She stood statue still, holding the wine pitcher in her hands, feeling the guests' eyes upon her. She wore a tight woolen tunic that fell only hallway to her knees, the heat from the hearth doing little to warm her from the opposite wall.

"I am looking for another girl for my manse, but the pickings have been slim as late," Proctor Kelvar lamented, taking a healthy sip from his goblet.

"That will change come summer. The markets will be flooded with fresh stock once our legions take Corell. The rest of Torry North will falter soon after. My son claims their wenches are well bred," Governor Culn boasted, looking forward to the glorious triumph.

"I am not as certain of our victory, Governor. We've all heard the rumors of the Torry champion driving off our host time and again, spoiling our triumph. What prevents a repeat of the first battle?" Proctor Dento Faldo asked, his holdings resting perilously close to the recent bandit raids plaguing much of the Eastern Plate foothills.

"Lord Morac's injuries from Kregmarin limited him during the battle, giving the Torry whelp free reign throughout the siege. That will not happen come spring. Besides, our losses can be replaced, as we have all seen the reinforcements moving south. The Torries have no such reserves to call upon. They are a spent force, kingless and led by a girl who will soon wear Lord Morac's collar." The governor laughed.

"A glorious triumph it shall be. The emperor has decreed that all frontline soldiers will be given two slaves from the plunder. Commanders of Telnic shall be given ten, adding to your son's riches, Governor," his castellan, Hev luren, said, a humorless man nearing his fifth decade.

"Hopefully he is wise enough not to pick all female chattel. There is always a need for good field slaves, since most of our local stock are Venotrist serfs," the governor snorted.

"Serf or slave means little difference. One belongs to the land, the other a master. Buy the land, and you own the serf," Proctor Kelvar said dryly. His holdings were almost exclusively worked by Venotrist serfs, which he had collared and marked the lot.

"There's a heady difference between male slaves and serfs upon close examination," the governor said, his comment drawing a chorus of laughter, the slaves about the table not sharing their mirth. Most Menotrist slaves were gelded, where Venotrist serfs were spared the knife.

"Then our serfs would be wise to keep their noses in the dirt, instead of getting airs," Proctor Kelvar said.

"Now, now, Kelvar, there will come a time when our Venotrist subjects will aspire higher than they currently sit. Our empire is ever expanding, and we shall need to draw upon our distant kin to fuel our growth and help seed new lands. We currently stand upon the edge of Benotrist dominion. All lands to our east and north are former freeholds that joined with us to achieve a higher glory," the governor said, forking a portion of food into his mouth.

"Governor, I..." Hev Luren started to say, the castellan's vision going out of focus.

"What ails you?" Governor Culn asked, observing his castellan's swaying shoulders before his face planted in his food.

Dento Faldo quickly gained his feet, taking one step before sensing a queer feeling running north of his feet, the chamber spinning in his brain. Jurns Kelvar failed to rise at all, sliding off his chair. The half dozen others at the table started dropping in quick succession, Governor Culn staring on in alarm with the sound of clashing steel in the outer corridors.

"Guards!" he shouted, feeling suddenly out of sorts, placing his hands upon the table to steady himself. The guards posted at the entryway were already in the outer corridor, giving battle. The governor let out an abrupt scream, a dagger driven into the back of his sword hand, pinning it to the table, the slave girl Telisa pushing down upon the handle with all her might. His world went dark, the sounds of sandaled boots slapping the stone floor the last thing he remembered before losing consciousness.

*****

Governor Culn awoke, finding himself atop the battlements of his palace, a small fortress with a curtain wall the height of three men circling its outer keep. The fortress was built of gray stone, its size sufficient against slave revolts and small human armies but unsuited against gargoyles. The morning sun was just breaking the horizon, revealing the horrors committed while he slept. The garrison was put to the sword, their heads piled in the center of the courtyard below. Flames drifted above the inner keep, its entire roof ablaze, the winter wind pushing the thickening smoke beyond the palace walls. He found himself naked, his hands bound behind him, and a rope around his neck pulling him to his feet, affixed to hastily erected gallows. He was joined by his three proctors and two of his sons, each sixteen and twelve years, and flanking their father. A large crowd of peasants gathered in the courtyard below, looking upon him with heady anticipation. Some he recognized, but most he did not.

He found his wife's panicked eyes staring back at him, kneeling before the crowd, her face a bloody mess. She was similarly bound, their scullery maid gripping her hair in her hands. The woman's face was a scarred ruin, disfigured by his jealous wife three years past when she earned his favor. Since that day, she was exiled to the kitchens. His young daughters knelt beside her, each equally disfigured, their cries drowned by the chanting crowd. He stood painfully on his toes, the rope drawing him high off his heels.

How did this happen? he wondered, until noticing the winged forms standing along the outer wall and upon the roof of the outer keep, silver gray wings shielding their shoulders from the cold. They were Jenaii warriors, their silver eyes unnerving him with their intense gaze. His fear heightened as a Jenaii warrior and a small man stepped in front of him, the Jenaii wearing distinct blue mail and helm over a black half tunic, his sliver eyes appraising him with a brief gaze before looking to the others strung up beside him. It was the man that concerned him more, looking upon him with utter contempt.

"We found your keep too inviting a target, Governor," the man said, though he looked more boy than man and strangely familiar, though he couldn't place the face.

"Wh…" he struggled to speak, his throat constricted by the tightening rope.

"Spare us your pitiful pleas. Your crimes against my people condemn you," Alen said before turning to face the Army of slaves and serfs gathered below. "These men would be your masters, to steal your lives and condemn your children to torment and death. Spare them no mercy, for they shall grant none." He walked to the end of the gallows, where Proctor Dento Faldo was drawn high, forcing his feet upon an overturned bucket, his rope tied off over the top of the cross beam. Alen kicked Dento's legs free, the drop not strong enough to cleanly break his neck. The miserable wretch kicked wildly, strangling on the end of the rope. Alen moved down the line, repeating the process for the remaining proctors and the governor's sons, leaving Datak Culn awaiting his grim fate as Alen again stepped before him, carrying a bucket.

"A good governor would better defend his keep," Alen whispered, drawing the severed head of his castellan, Hev Luren, from the bucket. Taking the regional palace was far too easy, Elos and his warriors catching the garrison by surprise, sweeping over the walls just after sundown, just as the servants laced the garrison's meal with Fleacen sleeping potion. Before the food tasters felt the first effect, Elos's troops already seized the inner keep. Others landed behind the outer wall, opening the gates to Alen's ground assault. It was a daring and bold raid into the heart of Nivek Province and would send shock waves through the empire.

Elos stepped behind the frightened governor, whose toes stretched to their utmost, keeping his airway open. Elos drew the Sword of the Moon. Luminous emerald light bursting along its blade, slicing Datak Culn's legs below the knee, causing him to bleed and strangle simultaneously.

Those gathered below looked on with wonder at Elos's devastating stroke, the Jenaii warrior coming to stand beside Alen as he addressed the assemblage.

"We struck a deadly blow against Tyro's empire this night. We have suffered enough under his tyranny. From here we disperse, breaking off into separate groups. Some will go east to the Tur valley, others west to the headwaters of the Reguh. Strike the Benotrists and their allies where they are weak. Avoid them where they are strong. If they pursue you, attack where they are not. Double your strength and divide it again, spreading from region to region. Burn their crops. Slaughter their livestock. Kill them while they sleep. Poison their wells. Think not of what they shall do, but what you shall do. Spread terror from Mordicay to Pagan. Kill any slave who will not join you, denying his labor to the enemy. Victory or death!" Alen shouted, his declaration chorused by those below.

"*Victory or death!*" they chanted.

*****

"Move with haste. Keep off the roads until clear of this province. Move at night. Remember all I have taught you," Elos said, standing beside Alen beyond the palace walls. Long columns of freed slaves and serfs emptied out of the burning fortress, bringing whatever food and weapons they could carry.

"I…I am grateful for your help, Elos. I am uncertain of my success without you." Alen's earlier assertiveness addressing the rebels melted away with the prospect of losing his mentor.

They had spread their revolt throughout the foothills of the Eastern Plate, rapidly expanding their once meager force. Jenaii warriors were quickly giving way to freed slaves and serfs, breaking off into splinter groups once they grew too large. Elos's warriors were brutally efficient initiating their revolt, starting with raids on Morac's supply caravans then igniting revolt within the empire proper.

"You have learned quickly, Alen. Keep your groups small. Expand then separate, spreading far and wide," Elos repeated the sage advice.

"I would be speaking false if I said you will not be missed. I am fearful of leading without you." Alen sighed.

"This war requires each of us to walk the lonely path at times. Have faith, and Yah will guide your path. We cannot win unless each does his part. You are braver than you know. Your people hunger for hope. Give it to them. If not for the need of my presence in the south, I would remain with you. El Anthus will remain with you, with his entire unit. They will help guide you and offer sound counsel. Take heart, my friend." Elos clasped his arm before stepping away, taking flight with his small host.

"Farewell, my friend," Alen whispered as they disappeared into the late-morning sky.

C H A P T E R

23

The Southeastern Sea, Southeast of Torn.

"Ah, this is the life." Raven leaned back, resting his leg over the arm of the captain's chair, taking a sip from his cup while staring out the viewport of the bridge, calm open ocean stretching to the horizon.

"A few quiet missions are a nice change, I'll give you that," Lorken said, sitting the helm.

"Nobody trying to shoot us with arrows," Raven said.

"Or stabbing us in the back," Lorken added.

"Or drugging us with wine."

"Or hiring our former crewmate to blast us with lasers."

"Or siccing a drunken mob on us," Raven recalled his encounter in Axenville.

"I missed out on that one. Would like to have seen that." Lorken snickered.

"Yeah, it was a real barrel of laughs," Raven growled.

"Tosha did that?" Lorken made a face.

"Yep," he snorted, draining his cup.

"You know, she probably wouldn't be so hostile if you improved your bedside manner."

"If I'm gonna take advice about women, it ain't gonna be from you."

"My track record is impeccable. You could do a lot worse."

"Impeccable? What about Maria?"

"Marie," Lorken corrected him.

"Maria, Marie, whatever her name was. She nearly blasted you during maneuvers. Claimed you were making eyes at her sister if memory serves me right."

538

"That story is all hearsay. We parted on good terms."

"Good terms? She put a fist-sized laser blast in the tail of your fighter. Serves you right for dating a pilot from Red Squadron."

"That was Latesha," Lorken corrected him. "Marie was a bridge officer on the *Agincourt*."

"No. That was Olga," Raven tried to recall.

"No. Olga was a battery officer on the *Cairo.*"

"I thought that was Lucy?"

"No. Lucy was a laser tech on the *Shanghai.*"

"How many girls were you dating, half the fleet?"

"No," Lorken said indignantly. "Under a dozen."

Quarterbacks. Raven shook his head. They always received more female attention then middle linebackers. "It was more than twelve. Heck, I dated more than twelve."

"*Dated*, Raven. You never dated anyone. That requires more than one outing. Otherwise it's just a date. Singular."

"I've dated lots of girls more than once."

"Name one!"

"..."

"I thought so. It's a wonder Tosha ever married you. You should be grateful. Maybe treat her kindly since no other woman would have you."

"Treat her kindly? After all the crap she pulled?"

"Sometimes a woman has to move things along, especially with a rock head like you."

"Move things along? We went from *hello* to *I do* with nothing in between. On top of that, we sleep together one time, and now she's pregnant."

"One time is all it takes. Didn't you learn anything in sex ed?"

"I got the basics."

"Somehow I doubt it, but you'll figure it out eventually now that you're married." He snickered.

"The same as you," Raven reminded him. Lorken and Jenna exchanged vows on the *Stenox* after leaving Tro, Raven using his position as captain to oversee the ceremony. Jenna thought it an odd custom but gladly partook, joining herself to Lorken.

"What's ETA for Linkortis?" Raven asked, deciding to change the subject.

"Two days if we keep a nice, gentle pace."

"Sounds agreeable. What's the weather look like?"

"Your hand works as well as mine. Turn on your scanner," Lorken shot back.

Raven mumbled a few expletives, touching the screen attached to his armrest, displaying various data. Touching the weather icon fed a vast array of information across his screen.

"I can't make sense of this," he grumbled.

"Sense of what?"

"These numbers just fill up the screen. I don't know what any of it means."

"It's atmospheric data collection. Just press the summarize icon at the bottom of the screen."

"What icon?" Raven was rapidly losing patience.

"Oh, for crying out loud!" Lorken stormed across the bridge, tapping the icon that was clearly labelled at the bottom of the screen. "See? Right there."

"Oh. Wait, I still can't read all this mumbo jumbo," he complained as more data flooded the screen.

"Barometric pressure is there, surface temperature is there, and wind is there," Lorken began pointing out the data that was clearly labeled. "The weather is fine, that's all you need to know."

"I'll take your word for it."

"I guess you'll have to since you can't read the data for yourself. How did you ever pass flight training anyway?" How did he ever become his squadron commander was what Lorken really wanted to know.

"Fighter consoles are a lot easier to read than this primitive junk."

"Zem, Brokov and I spent two weeks building that weather program when we crashed here. It works just fine, especially without a satellite feed."

"So…clear sailing."

"Yeah, clear sailing." Lorken shook his head.

"Clear sailing, an easy mission, and a full crew. Things are looking up," Raven said.

"Speaking of our new recruits, where are they?"

"Brokov is supposed to be familiarizing them with the ship's engineering and weapon systems."

"You sure that's a good idea?" Lorken recalled Grigg and Orlom's dangerous antics at Gregok when he and Raven oversaw their pistol and rifle handling.

"They'll be fine. They both come highly recommended."

"By whom?"

"Arg says—"

"Arg says nothing good about them," Lorken said as politely as he could. The actual wording included several expletives about their mothers and their rectal passage, which he wouldn't repeat.

"That's because he doesn't like wide receivers. I told you playing defensive tackle would go to his head."

"Very funny. And I wonder where he got that idea from? Probably a dumb middle linebacker."

"Linebackers are smarter than quarterbacks. That's what Coach O'Brien always said back in the academy."

"O'Brien? The guy's a fossil. *'Run the ball, Lorky, Run the ball!'* That's all he ever said."

"That's so you wouldn't throw an interception. You have to tailor your game plan to your players strengths, or around their weaknesses in your case."

"You can steer this tub on your own if you want," Lorken warned. "Oh, that's right, you can't read the icons on the view screen."

"I've noticed you've been in a crappy mood since we left your wife behind at Gregok."

"Some of us miss our wives, Rav." It was a painful choice for Lorken to leave Jenna behind, but General Matuzak insisted. A ship was no place for a young mother and children, and there was no place safer in all of Arax for her than at Matuzak's home. It was a strange paradox where they found a planet filled with humans but were more at home with the apes instead.

The door to the outer deck quickly opened as Brokov stormed onto the bridge, visibly irate for reasons they were certain to hear about, while brandishing a bruise on his right eye.

"Which of you idiots thought it was a good idea inviting our new shipmates to join our crew?" Brokov looked from one to the other, looking for signs of the guilty party.

Raven and Lorken both pointed to each other.

"That figures." Brokov shook his head in disgust.

"Did they do something wrong?" Raven asked with his usual dumbfounded expression that Brokov knew to be an act.

"Don't play the idiot, Rav," he warned.

"He's not playing, Brokov. He really is an idiot." Lorken snickered.

"What's the matter?" Raven asked, ignoring Lorken's taunt.

"What's the matter? I'll tell you. Orlom and Grigg are what's the matter. Grigg crapped in the sink of the lave for one thing."

"Aw!" Lorken made a face. "Tell me you cleaned it up?"

"Of course I cleaned it up. But I told him repeatedly the difference between the sink and the toilet. I caught him trying to wash the evidence down the drain."

"I'm sure it was an honest mistake," Raven reasoned.

"I sent him away while I tossed the residue in the toilet and left to find something to clean the sink with, only to return to catch Orlom trying to clean it himself."

"Well, that was nice of him," Lorken said.

"With my *toothbrush*!" Brokov roared.

Of course, Raven and Lorken found that funny, which only fueled Brokov further.

"So how'd you get the black eye?" Lorken asked curiously.

"While I finished cleaning up that mess, I sent them to the rec room, ordering them to touch *nothing*! Before I finish in the lave, I hear a commotion in the hallway, where I discover Grigg playing with a pistol, aiming the barrel at the back of Argos's head."

"That's not good," Raven stated the obvious. "That still doesn't explain your eye."

"I'm getting to that. I yelled at Grigg to lower his pistol, when Argos turns about, suddenly aware of the danger he was in. Before Grigg could lower his pistol, Arg swings at him, but the slippery bastard ducks, allowing me to receive his punishment." Brokov pointed at his eye.

"That's a tough break, pal," Raven shrugged.

"That's not all!" he growled. "I disarmed Grigg and used all my ability keeping Argos from killing him. Then I asked where Orlom was, and he directs me to the stern where I had spent the morning assembling the air ski I've been working on for months. I finally tested it, running it out a quarter mile from the ship when you were at Gregok. I was going to test it again today, but Orlom had it in pieces in a matter of minutes."

"Did he break it or disassemble it?" Raven asked.

"Of course he broke it!" Brokov threw up his arms.

"Where are they now?" Raven asked.

"On the third deck, standing watch," Brokov pointed skyward.

"They should be harmless up there," Lorken said as lasers suddenly flashed across the viewport, spewing from the deck above in every direction.

*****

A few moments before

"Heh, you see this?" Grigg whispered, running his hand over the stock of his rifle.

"Careful, fatty is watching," Orlom warned, stealing a glance over his shoulder where Argos stood on the stern of the first deck below, with his powerful arms crossed over his chest, staring intently at the young gorillas standing on the third deck. He guarded the parts of Brokov's air ski spread out across the first deck around him, protecting them from the two troublemakers above. Argos voiced his displeasure over their joining the crew, but Raven and Lorken drowned out his protest by lauding their *qualifications*. What those qualifications were, were beyond him. There were thousands of apes in Matuzak's service far more qualified and mature than those two. Neither one of them could fill out their uniforms, Grigg donning a set of Lorken's clothes, and Orlom Brokov's, the Earthers' jackets swallowing their slender forms. They looked strikingly similar, though Grigg was shorter and Orlom gangly.

Argos's black nostrils flared whenever he looked at them. He shook his head before passing through the doorway, disappearing into the bowels of the first deck.

"Fatty's gone." Orlom grinned, he and Grigg lifting their rifles simultaneously, pointing their barrels in every direction.

"Oh! Oh! Oh!" Grigg hooted excitedly, a flock of soren passing overhead, before firing off several blasts.

Orlom would not be outdone and started firing as well, laser following the birds' path southward.

*****

Brokov was the first out the door, ducking a laser flashing overhead, striking the ocean's surface off the ship's starboard. Raven and Lorken paused at the doorway of the bridge, waiting for a break in the action before sticking their necks out.

"Stop shooting!" Raven yelled, keeping close to the bulkhead.

"Let me shoot them," Brokov growled, crouching as low as he could, his eye trained on the deck above.

"Aye, Captain!" Orlom acknowledged Raven, lowering his rifle.

"Aye, boss," Grigg added after Orlom slapped him upside the head, getting him to ease off the trigger, as Brokov, Raven, and Lorken stepped in the clear.

"What the hell are you guys doing?" Raven asked, staring up at them from the second deck.

"Practicing like you showed us, boss," Orlom said with a toothy grin.

"We are getting good at using these." Grigg hoisted his rifle into the air, his finger in the trigger guard.

Brokov and Lorken ducked, another blast passing overhead.

"That's enough, boys. Take your fingers out of the trigger guard," Raven ordered.

"You heard the boss, don't touch the trigger!" Orlom scolded Grigg as if he were an innocent party in the whole affair.

"I heard what he said, Dumb-Dumb. You need to listen to what he said!" Grigg shoved him in the chest.

Orlom dropped his rifle on the deck, lowering his shoulder into Grigg's stomach. Raven stepped out of the way as the two gorillas tumbled over the lip of the third deck, just missing his feet. He winced as they hit the second deck, the heavy thud sounding in his ears.

"That had to hurt." Lorken scrunched his face, he and Brokov backing to the starboard railing. Raven picked up Grigg's rifle, which dropped beside them, tossing it through the open door of the Bridge.

"Aren't you going to stop them?" Kendra shouted, suddenly appearing on the stern of the first deck, looking up at them with her fists on her hips, Argos and Zem standing to either side.

"Let them work it off." Raven crossed his arms, leaning against the back wall of the bridge, enjoying the show.

Orlom bit into Grigg's arm, as Grigg lost hold of a headlock. They thrashed about the deck, rolling into Brokov's legs, pinning him to the rail as Lorken made his escape, stepping safely to where Raven stood.

"Oww!" Brokov howled, his legs pushing painfully against the rail. Raven saw Grigg's holstered pistol sticking clear, so he stepped forth and removed it from his holster, tossing it to Lorken. He reached down, snatching Grigg by the back of his jacket, tossing him over the starboard rail, a loud splash following his descent.

"Thanks, boss!" Orlom grinned, gaining his feet, as Raven lifted his pistol as well, tossing it to Lorken before shoving Orlom into Argos's waiting arms as he cleared the ladder. Argos snatched him by the back of his trousers, tossing him over the portside rail.

"Guess we'll have to have another gun safety class." Raven sighed.

"You think?" Brokov growled, stepping gingerly on his right leg, thinking Raven should've covered that before giving them guns.

"You all right?" Raven asked.

"No, I'm not all right, but I'll manage."

"Did you get that other *thingamidigy* to work?" Raven asked.

"What *thingamidigy*? You mean the organic tissue regenerator?"

"Yeah, that's it. The one like the one that Kato took with him."

"Yes, the one we have works, and the other two are nearly ready. I'll be sure to scan my knee for damage and check on the status of our new recruits. That fall from the third deck likely broke something," Brokov snorted, jerking a thumb over the starboard rail, where Grigg was bobbing in the water.

*****

Raven and Lorken spent the rest of the day and half the next schooling Orlom and Grigg on gun safety and muzzle awareness. Their attempts at pawning off this task to their fellow crewmates was poorly met. The general consensus from Brokov, Argos, Kendra, and Zem was that if they thought it a good idea to bring those two troublemakers aboard, then they could deal with them.

"Then who is going to man the helm?" Lorken had argued.

"I'll man the helm. Zem and Arg will handle the engineering," Brokov waved off Lorken's flimsy excuse.

"I'm the captain. Somebody needs to command the ship," Raven tried to weasel his way out of it.

Brokov simply removed his jacket, placing it on the Captain's chair.

"See, my jacket can handle your complex duties."

And so it was that Raven and Lorken found themselves easily replaced, while babysitting Orlom and Grigg. By nightfall the following day, they had drilled the young apes ragged.

"Rule number one?" Lorken asked for the thousandth time as they stood on the stern of the second deck.

"Only point a gun at something you intend to destroy," Grigg and Orlom said in unison.

"Rule number two?" Raven asked, holding up the first two fingers on his right hand.

"Keep our fingers out of the trigger guard until we are ready to shoot," they said tiredly.

"Now listen, fellas," Raven reiterated. "If you want to become full members of our crew, every one of us has to agree to it. General Matuzak allowed you to join us on these next few missions, giving you a chance to prove yourselves. Take this opportunity and endear yourselves to the others."

They both stared blankly, seeming to not fully understand.

"Do you understand?" Lorken asked.

"Everyone?" Grigg asked in a small voice.

"Everyone," Lorken reiterated.

"But Fatty hates us." Orlom sighed.

"That's what we're talking about, fellas. Arg doesn't like being called Fatty. He's a little sensitive," Raven explained.

"We'll be in Linkortis in the morning. Try not to break anything in the meantime. In fact, just don't touch anything unless we tell you," Lorken said.

"And make friends," Grigg affirmed with a stupid grin.

"We can make friends. Brokov likes us. We can start with him," Orlom added, nodding excitedly.

"Yeah, start with him." Raven patted him on the back.

*****

"It's beautiful," Kendra marveled at the starlight playing off the surface of the dark sea. She stood upon the bridge, staring out the viewport with her arms crossed.

"I never grow tired of it." Brokov smiled easily, sitting the helm. The others had gone to bed, leaving the two of them pulling the evening shift.

"I have only seen the ocean from the shore and upon a small ship close to land. Out here, it is different. Endless water in each direction." She felt small before its majesty.

"It can take your breath away, especially on clear nights like tonight. Imagine the view in deep space, especially midstance between star systems. It's quite humbling," Brokov said, his voice much lower as the night wore on. She found it rather alluring.

"Is your home world like this?" she asked curiously. They often explained their origins, but she couldn't truly wrap her mind around it.

"Earth is a diverse planet. We have massive deserts, teeming jungles, and endless forests. The open steppes of Asia stretch for thousands of miles. Like Arax, 70 percent of our surface is water, much like the ocean that you sea before you."

"Which part of Earth was your home?"

"Arkhangelsk." He smiled, wondering if she could repeat it correctly.

"Arkhalsk?"

"Arkhangelsk. Or Archangel if you like."

"Arc-Angel," she managed. "What was it like?"

"Cold."

"Cold?"

"Very cold, especially in winter. It is a port city on the far northern part of my country. It straddles the Dvina River, which flows north into our Artic Ocean."

"So if you go further north, it is colder?"

"Too far north or south and you'll get cold."

"That doesn't make any sense."

"Earth is like Arax. It has polar caps at both poles and rests at similar axis, though yours is less pronounced."

"Poles?" She made a face.

He realized his mistake, having assumed she understood the physical nature of her world. "Arax and Earth are planets, and all planets are ball shaped."

"What's a ball?"

"A sphere."

"A sphere?"

"Yes. If we sailed due east"—he pointed out their port-side—"we'd end up on the western coast, near Cagan or Tenin."

"That's impossible."

"No, it's simple gravity."

"That would mean the world is round." She shook her head.

"Yeah." He shrugged as if it was obvious, but the look she gave him meant that it wasn't. "Look at the moon. It is round."

"It's not out tonight." She pointed out.

He forgot it was in its new phase and would rise with the sun. Brokov decided to start from scratch, explaining the process of planet and star formation and the principles of gravity and the spherical nature of planets and moons. He went on for some time, explaining the axis of Arax and Earth and the effect on the seasons.

"My home is near the Artic Circle, making our summer days very long and our winter days very short."

"And because we are closer to our equator..." She paused at that word, to see if she said it correctly, by gauging his reaction. "Our summer and winter days are similar in length."

"Yes, now you're getting it." He nodded encouragingly.

"It is an interesting theory." She gave him that much. She leaned back against the forward viewport, staring directly at him with a whimsical smile.

"It's not theory. It's fact."

"I am sure it is." She crossed her arms.

"You don't believe me?"

"I will give you this much, you Earthers are always entertaining."

"Entertaining?"

"Yes. There are numerous philosophers and scholars who would give a portion of their flesh to discuss such things with you. The Academy of Science in El Tova would gladly welcome your enlightened theories."

"Fair enough, so what is your explanation for the placement of the sun, moon, and Arax?"

"The moon and sun were once lovers, the moon a fearsome warrior and the sun a golden princess. Their love was forbidden by her kingly sire, so they ran away and were wed in secret, consummating their union. They dwelt in peace and love until one day her father, the king, discovered them. In his fury, he conjured powerful magic, setting them in the sky but separating them from each other for all eternity. The warrior became the moon, forced to dwell in eternal darkness, ever searching the night sky for his true love, who rested just beyond his reach. She was confined to the other sky, her golden beauty lighting the heavens, where she dwelt," Kendra finished, gazing over her shoulder to the starlit sky, before turning her brown eyes back to his blue, a mischievous smile forcing the corners of her lips. "I like that story better than yours."

"It's a nice tale, did you come up with that yourself?"

"No." She shook her head before leaning it back against the window. "My father told me that story when I was a girl." She sighed. He noted a hint of sadness at the mention of her father.

"You miss him." He recalled the details of her father's death. He was slain by Tavis Cora during the pirate wars with Tro.

"I wasn't always as you see me now," she said in a far-off voice, recalling her enchanted youth and girlish dreams of a home, children, and husband.

He regarded her for a moment, taking stock of how he saw her. She still wore her leathers and sword. Narrow steel vambraces protected each arm. Her light-auburn hair was tied off in braids. She was fairly attractive if one looked deeper, though it was concealed beneath her garb. Brokov believed most women were within a similar range of attractiveness. It was the presentation that most often caught a man's interest.

"My father was a famed man-hunter, Zarix Sarn, known from Bedo to Port West, filling contracts for regents and kings, until one day he met a beautiful merchant's daughter. They wed, and he took up a magistrate post in Caliso, foreswearing his mercenary trade."

"Sounds like the warrior and the golden princess." He smiled.

"Perhaps." She rolled her eyes, gifting him a smile before continuing. "I was born soon after, unaware of my father's past. We lived in a nice home near the sea, where we would take walks along the shore, watching the sun rise over the water. They are my fondest memories."

"So what happened?"

"My mother died birthing my brother. He died as well, strangled by his birth cord. It broke my father's heart, and he took to drink, eventually forsaking his post and returning to the life he knew. I learned at his side, tracking wanted men."

"That's a dangerous life for a child. Why did he take you from your home?"

"As I said, he was brokenhearted. Our home reminded him of what he lost." Her voice trailed, pained by the memory.

I'm sorry, he thought to say but hated that canned response.

"His heart eventually mended, though he never loved another. I was his life, and he was mine. I loved my father dearly and sought his approval and to make him proud. Then he died, murdered by a man that you later killed. I thanked Raven for that in Axenville, but I never thanked you."

"You're welcome."

They talked throughout the night, sharing their adventures, of bounty hunters, Space Fleet, and their journeys across Arax. They laughed at their similar assessment of their crewmates, especially Raven's buffoonery and Lorken's antics. Kendra mimicked Argos by puffing out her chest, grunting in anger. Zem's conceitedness was another point of agreement, both finding him insufferable at times. She reminded him that Galen was far worse. Brokov couldn't believe it but took her at her word. When morning came, it took them by surprise, wondering where the night had gone. Brokov dimmed the forward viewport, shielding the blinding sunrise off their portside bow. It was another marvel of the Earther's *magic* that filled her with wonder.

"Fifty leagues further south and we'll cut back west toward the coast. We passed the boundary of Enoructa a few miles back."

She would ask how he could tell since they were on open water. The Earthers trusted their navigational devices, and they were proven reliable.

"It was a pleasure speaking with you, Brokov." She ambled toward the door. "I think I should sleep before I fall over."

"I'll be right behind you after I wake the kids." He smiled over his shoulder.

She laughed at the reference, agreeing with the moniker describing their crewmates.

*****

551

It was late morn when the *Stenox* neared the barrier islands shielding the Linkor Delta. The sight of green swaying Frologs contrasted the aqua blue of the surrounding waters. The barrier islands of the Enoructan Coast ran in a wide arc around the Linkor Delta, with hundreds of sand bars blocking most shipping lanes. Few vessels could navigate these treacherous waters. A shallow draft was essential, but the shifting sands rendered any map older than a year nearly useless. Fortunately, the *Stenox*'s sonar easily plotted a safe passage, avoiding the deadly shallows.

"There has to be a more direct route than this," Raven complained as they zigged and zagged along the approaches to the nearest isle.

"We can always cut a path through the sandbars with our subsurface lasers. It'll kill a lot of fish, disturb their natural habitat, and waste a lot of energy, but at least it won't waste an extra ten minutes of our life," Lorken said, sitting the helm.

"Maybe we should," Raven snorted, ignoring Lorken's sarcasm as he stepped toward the door.

"Where you going?"

"Grigg's up top. Don't want him scaring the natives."

Raven stepped out, climbing the ladder to the third deck, where Kendra and Grigg stood, taking in the view. He was glad to see Grigg's pistol holstered, the young gorilla pointing excitedly to something far off.

"Look, Kendra!" Grigg's gravelly voice hooted.

Once he cleared the ladder, Raven could see over the forward wall, finding out what sparked Grigg's curiosity. Skirting the north end of the nearest isle was a large gray finned dolphin-like creature, nearly twenty feet in length, with a pale-green-skinned humanoid rider.

"That is an Enoructan scout," Kendra affirmed. She only encountered the reptilian race once before, but they were unmistakable. The beast the rider rode upon was a dorun. The Enoructans domesticated the seafaring mammals centuries before, their swift mounts able to easily traverse the treacherous waters surrounding the barrier isles and the Linkor Delta. Within moments they spotted two more doruns clearing the north end of the isle, following the first rider, all speeding toward the *Stenox*.

"They're coming!" Grigg jumped up and down, a stupid grin painting his face. Having come from a landlocked tribe, Grigg had never seen the ocean before the Ape Revolution, let alone an Enoructan.

"Just smile, wave, and whatever you do, kid, don't touch your pistol." Raven slapped Grigg on the back.

"Aye, boss." Grigg nodded happily.

Kendra shook her head, wondering if Grigg would actually listen.

"I thought you'd still be sleeping?" Raven asked, since she had been up most of the night with Brokov.

"I've never been to Linkortis or any part of Enoructa. I can sleep later," she said, taking in the scenery.

The dorun riders drew near, raising long, thin spears in their right hands, hailing the visitors. The Enoructans were slight of build, barely sixty inches, with greenish scaly skin and large, bulbous dark eyes. They circled the *Stenox*, raising their spears higher into the air before drawing up beside the vessel.

Raven leaned over the side of the *Stenox*, giving them a salute, the strange custom surprisingly known by the Enoructans from the Earthers' previous visit. The dorun riders touched their spears to their naked chests, returning the salute with one of their own. They followed alongside the *Stenox* as the ship cleared the north end of the isle, dozens of other dorun riders coming into view, some lightly clad like their escorts, wearing little more than brief kilts made of versk skins. Others rode blue-finned doruns, wearing boiled leather breast plates, girdles, and vambraces, light and flexible, the official garb of the royal cavalry. Kendra marveled as the dorun cavalry raced alongside the *Stenox*, the mammals' cone-shaped noses riding the calm surface, water spraying their riders' stoic faces. The inner waterway separating the barrier islands from the Linkor Delta was nearly two leagues wide, with pristine light-blue water. Behind this beautiful waterway were more than two thousand isles of the Linkor Delta, some as small as three feet to as large as several leagues. Hundreds of canoe-sized crafts traversed the shallower waterways, driven by poles men experienced with the more stable routes of the Linkor. Kendra noticed the riders running their hands affectionately along their doruns' necks. It was a sign of the bond between rider and mount. A red-skinned female rider stood up in her saddle, waving as they passed. Kendra waved back, warmed by the friendly gesture. The natives were of three prominent colorings, green, red, and aqua blue, though most of the females were distinctly reddish in hue.

Hearty cheers greeted Argos and Orlom once they stepped onto the stern of the first deck. The two gorillas pounded their chests, responding to their hosts' respectful greeting.

"Why do they cheer us so loudly?" Kendra asked.

"Not us. Arg." Raven jerked a thumb over his shoulder toward the big guy below.

"Why?" she asked as Grigg just snorted.

"He's Matuzak's champion, and they respect strength. Throw in the close friendship between the ape tribes and the Enoructan peoples, and there you have it," Raven explained.

"Do their warm feelings extend to us?"

"I guess so." Raven shrugged.

"That's not very reassuring," she quipped.

"Does it really matter, Kendra? It's not like they're going to beat us up or something."

"They did in Axenville," she reminded him.

That remark caught Grigg's attention. "Is that true, boss?" He looked sadly to Raven.

"Well, it was just me against the whole town, kid. And my gun got stolen."

"How many did it take to bring you down?" Grigg wondered.

"Several hundred, if I remember correctly."

"Three dozen," Kendra corrected, rolling her eyes.

"That's a lot." Grigg sighed with relief. Raven was his hero, and anything less than an Army taking him down would be disappointing.

"You bet it was a lot, kid. I took a few lives with me too." He made a couple of shadow punches, mimicking the fight.

"Why did they fight you?" Grigg asked. Raven was terribly fearsome and the largest human he ever met.

"For the bounty," Kendra answered dryly, weary of the tale.

"Who put a bounty on you?"

"My wife and her father," Raven growled.

"Wow! She must be quite a woman." Grigg smiled, feeling better about Raven's run-in with the mob at Axenville. To him, it was obviously a mating ritual of sorts. It was obvious that she was merely testing his strength, seeing how many men it took to subdue him, measuring his worthiness.

"Yeah, she's quite a woman." Raven scratched his head.

The farther they went into the delta, the larger and higher the islands grew. Some sported cone-shaped stone dwellings built on higher rocky elevations, wherever they could be found. Smaller thatched huts dotted the lower elevations, more suited to the aqueous soil so prevalent throughout the delta. They spotted a small redoubt some distance off their starboard bow, with warriors clad in iron helms and mail manning its upper ramparts.

"We're getting close," Raven said, pointing out the small fortress, one of several watchtowers guarding the approaches to Linkortis.

Kendra gasped as the way ahead opened significantly into a massive lagoon, with several large islands resting on its far side. Thousands of faces greeted them, most traversing the lagoon atop pontoon boats, doruns, or canoes. The sprawling metropolis rested upon the far islands with hundreds of large domed structures peeking above earthen walls. Each of the isles was connected by wide stone bridges, their prominent arches large enough for ships to pass underneath.

"Linkortis, I presume?" Kendra asked.

"Yep," Raven said, resting his forearms on the forward wall of the third deck.

Scores of dorun cavalry joined their escort, guiding them into the heart of the port city, passing between two of the larger isles before drawing up beside a large stone wharf, where hundreds of onlookers gathered about.

"We have company," Kendra said, indicating the gathering crowd as the *Stenox*'s starboard eased up alongside the stone lip of the wharf, before stopping with a sudden jolt that nearly took them from their feet.

"Hey, ease up on the old girl, it's the only ship we got!" Raven barked into his comm.

"Quit your bitchin'. The hull's made of pure trundusium. It doesn't scratch!" Lorken growled back through the comm.

"Well, we aren't. We almost did a Peter Pan off the third deck," Raven answered back.

"Maybe if Peter Pan was a baby elephant." Lorken snickered, imagining Raven in a pair of green tights splashing in the water.

"Jerk," Raven mumbled.

"Who's Peter Pan?" Kendra asked.

"Ah, a stupid fairy tale about a flying boy, or something like that. I don't know, I never read it." Raven shrugged.

By then, the crowd had grown exponentially, the good citizens spilling out into the streets to see their guests. Up close, Kendra was able to get a better look at their hosts. The Enoructans were of a similar size and shape, none seeming any taller than sixty inches, with scaly skin in hues of green, red, and blue. Their noses were narrow up top before flattening out with wide flaring nostrils above thin lips. Their small round ears seemed pinned to their oval-shaped skulls. Most of those gathered upon the wharf wore brightly colored robes that draped their sandaled two-toed feet. The Enoructans recognized Argos, despite his Earth garb, cheering as he stepped onto the lip of the wharf. Their cheers were deafening, nearly drowning Kendra's voice, the sound of their collective voices akin to rushing waters.

"Who are they?" she asked Raven, the crowd parting for two Enoructans dressed in shimmering scarlet robes and large golden headdresses.

"Two of their tribal leaders," Raven said as Argos stepped forth to greet them, the crowd quieting as they exchanged friendly greetings. After the brief exchange, Argos returned to the *Stenox*, meeting Raven and the others on the first deck, as Brokov, Zem, and Lorken stepped without to meet them.

"They invite us to meet the full council tonight in the grand hall," Argos said.

"They agree to discuss Matuzak's terms?" Brokov asked.

"I didn't get that far. They only asked me to come on behalf of the Ape Republic and bring Zem on behalf of the Earthers. We will deliver the general's plans there, I guess," Argos explained, scratching his head.

"Why Zem?" Kendra asked.

"Why Fatty?" Orlom mumbled low enough for Argos not to hear, gaining a snicker from Grigg.

"The chieftains hold a deep respect for the Earthers and recognize Zem as the greatest of them," Argos explained.

"The Enoructans are obviously very perceptive. I accept their invitation," Zem said, rather pleased with himself.

Kendra laughed, as Lorken and Brokov rolled their eyes, and Raven shook his head.

"Don't let it go to your head, Lieutenant," Raven reminded him of his junior rank, which was a bitter point of contention for the big android, who was promised a rapid promotion had they not been stranded on Arax.

"I'll remember you said that, Raven, when I'm a general one day, and you're still a squadron commander," Zem said dismissively.

"You won't even make captain if we never get off this rock." Raven shook his head.

"Space Fleet knows our last known trajectory and will map out all possible paths we might've taken. It is only a matter of time before they find me," Zem said.

"Find you? What about us?" Lorken pointed out.

"I'm certain they will be pleased to recover you as well, but it is I that will hasten their urgency. I am the first independent artificial life-form ever created. My contributions to the advancement of our civilization far outweigh what any of you hope to achieve," Zem said dismissively.

"At least we have families to go home to," Brokov said, reminding Zem that he was truly all alone.

"As do I," Zem said, shooting Raven a lopsided grin. He straightened his pistol belt and smoothed out his thick jacket. "Come, Argos, let us treat with our esteemed host," Zem said, stepping onto the wharf.

"What was that all about?" Kendra asked, as Argos and Zem followed the chieftains, disappearing into the crowd.

"That's just Zem getting under my skin." Raven shook his head.

"I don't—" Kendra started to ask, when Brokov touched a hand to her shoulder.

"Zem was created by Raven's brother. Their personality and familial bonds are interlinked. He brought Zem to Raven's home after he was first created, and he got along swimmingly with Raven's family, especially his father."

"He refers to Zem as his favorite son." Lorken snickered.

"And Zem calls him Dad." Brokov smiled.

"Yeah, very funny." Raven growled, stepping back inside as the others broke into laughter.

*****

The evening found Argos and Zem seated in the great hall, an impressive domed structure in the center of Linkortis. Fourteen chieftains managed to gather there on short notice from the nearest lands. They sat in a circle upon large stone chairs that barely fit Zem and Argos. The chieftains were clad in versk skin shirts, trousers, and helms, with wicker breast plates, the garb of their warrior class. Zem counted twenty empty chairs, those assigned to regional chieftains too far away to be summoned in a day.

"You honor us with your presence." Chief Lutis raised a goblet to Zem and Argos.

"Mighty Zem!" Chief Ulos seconded.

"Mighty Argos!" Chief Ilen heralded.

The remaining chieftains raised their goblets, honoring their guests.

"It is we who are honored," Zem's metallic voice boomed proudly, his luminous blue eyes sweeping the gathered chieftains seated within the circle. "I have traveled the many star systems that dot your night sky, many beyond your imagining. I have visited hundreds of great civilizations. None exceed your stoic wisdom and keen powers of observation. Despite the primitive technological stagnation that afflicts your world, you possess a rare understanding of the nature of the universe. I commend you!" Zem lifted his goblet, pouring the wine into his metallic mouth, the taste analyzer in the back of his throat processing the texture and signaling his pleasure sensors if it tasted good or not.

"Thanks," Argos managed to say, forgetting his prepared speech as he raised his goblet. Somehow things always sounded better before he tried to say them. The Enoructans regarded him with deep respect, never thinking to mock Argos's simple nature. As a people, they respected honor and strength, two qualities they found in their ape brothers to the north. As Matuzak's champion, Argos exemplified those qualities, and the chieftains understood this well.

"Each of you represents the greatest of your peoples," Lutis continued. "Zem is the most powerful and intelligent of the Earthers, and Argos the champion of the Ape Empire. We accept you within our circle." Lutis downed his goblet, the others following in kind.

Zem nodded in agreement, happy that at least one civilization on this stupid planet recognized his true worth, two if he counted the apes. Argos gave the council a toothy grin, finishing his goblet before the others.

"Has the present council reviewed General Matuzak's proposal?" Zem asked, cutting to the point of their visit.

"We have," Chief Noldan said.

"General Matuzak is an honorable ape," Chief Louven added. "We are heartened by his words of friendship and brotherhood."

"He speaks many truths," Chief Ulos said. "Our two peoples share a rich history, dwelling in peace since the times of ancient past. Never have we warred or coveted each other's lands or wealth. We dwell side by side, where the Creator placed us."

"We have considered Matuzak's proposal and will share it with the full council once they answer our summons. You speak honestly, mighty Zem, and we shall speak honestly in return," Chief Lutis explained, extending his open hands to his fellow chieftains, sweeping them around the circle. "General Matuzak offers to join our peoples within one republic, establishing guarantees of individual liberties and a balanced representation of tribal size and individuality. It is a fair and sincere proposal, but speaking on behalf of the council members present herein, we must decline. Joining a young republic is bold, and we are a cautious people. Revolutions are precarious creatures, often imploding upon themselves. The heroes of one day are cast as villains the next. In good faith, we will forward his proposal to the full council, but I doubt it will be better received than from the chieftains gathered here."

"General Matuzak did not think you would accept but is happy to call you his brothers," Argos conceded.

"Mighty Argos!" Chief Noldan said, his dark bulbous eyes blinking rapidly as he spoke. "Though we hold deep reservations on a political union of our two peoples, we are receptive of the general's proposed military alliance."

"It was Matuzak that drove the Casian League from our shores, liberating our coastal waters of their imperial aims. He warns of the war spreading across Central Arax, rightly fearing it will reach our lands. Should warring powers think to assail the new Ape Republic, then they would certainly extend their ambitions to Enoructa," Chief Lutis explained.

"Those of us gathered here agree to Matuzak's proposed military alliance and will forward its approval when the full council is assembled," Chief Noldan stated.

"We are most curious, however, of your role with this alliance, mighty Zem?" Chief Lutis asked, the eyes of his fellow chieftains staring intently at their powerful guest.

"General Matuzak and the ape tribal elders offer sanctuary. We Earthers do not abide emperors or kings, but a republic..." Zem's deep metallic voice strangely softened. "A republic is an entity we embrace. Matuzak is our friend, and we accept his invitation. In times of peace, we will make the Ape Republic our home. But in times of *war*...we will make their enemies our own!" Zem's voice echoed strongly, his uncharacteristic passion not lost on the assembled chieftains.

"What of your fellow Earthers? Do they share your commitment to the Ape Republic?" Chief Noldan asked. If the Earthers were formally aligned with the Ape Republic, then that would extend to them as well.

"We are in complete agreement. We are now citizens of the Ape Republic," Zem declared, lifting his right palm to Argos, who slapped it with his own, the odd behavior obviously a strange Earth custom of some sort.

"We are also receptive of his trade proposal, which we assume is linked to the military alliance. We hold little love for the merchant leagues that shackled our trading lanes in recent times. The ape revolution freed Enoructa of their insidious influence. An alliance with our ape brothers strengthens our hand in dealing with them," Chief Lutis said. He knew that a separate trade zone extending from Linkortis to Torn would effectively cut Tro from the Casian League and all points west, thus cutting the Casian's lifeblood. Such a threat would either force war upon the Casians or bring them to negotiate a fair-trading alliance between all four powers. The power of the *Stenox* firmly on Matuzak's side removed war as an option for the Casian League. To further solidify their leverage over the Casian League, Matuzak intended to bring Tro within the fold before negotiating with the Casians. With war now on Tro's doorstep, they were hopelessly exposed to Tyro's adventurism. Tro was the largest port in Arax, and its ruling families were able to avoid entangling alliances that would likely favor some trading partners while offending others. With no major powers nearby to threaten their autonomy, this strategy proved both wise and successful. But the rise of the Benotrist Empire changed all that by extending their borders to Lake Veneba and now seizing the crossroads of Bacel and Notsu. Tyro need only sneeze, and Tro would fall. They were desperate, and desperate men were more agreeable negotiating deals that they would not otherwise consider. Only the Ape Republic could guarantee their independence, protecting them from Tyro, and Matuzak would offer that protection for Tro's joining his new trade consortium. After that was achieved, they would force the Casian League into favorable trading terms, opening the east to Casia and the west to their consortium.

"General Matuzak will be pleased with your partnering in trade and defense, if not outright political unification," Zem said.

"Two out of three should count for a successful meeting, though the full council of chieftains must agree to the terms," Chief Lutis said.

"We will await your decision," Zem replied.

"And then you shall approach Tro with similar terms, we assume," Chief Noldan said.

"An ape delegation is already en route," Zem explained.

"Hmnn," Chief Lutis pondered, rubbing his scaly chin in thought. "I thought Matuzak would send you after treating with us." What he meant was that presenting the Earthers as part of the defense alliance would be difficult to turn down.

"That would have been a good idea until my friend angered the Troans. We won't be welcome there for a long time," Zem shook his head, recalling Lorken's actions during their last visit.

*****

The Earthers remained in Linkortis for ten days before the full council could be summoned and vote on Matuzak's proposals. As expected, political union was declined, but the military and trade alliances were approved. During the ten-day wait, their hosts invited the *Stenox* crew to feasts every night, sharing in wine, merriment, and good food. Brokov and Kendra took the *Spectre* offshore for a fishing expedition, bringing back ample helpings of short nosed volle, similar to mahi back on Earth, that Brokov favored. The Enoructans enjoyed the Earthers' stories and music, as did their ape friends. As much as they liked Zem, the Enoructans did not agree with his choice of music in "Anchors Aweigh," the martial tune failing to match the quality of the other selections Brokov and Lorken recommended. Grigg and Orlom found their acceptance a welcome respite from their poor start aboard the *Stenox*. They found being members of the

Earthers' crew made them quite popular with the Enoructans, which further inflated their egos.

Seeing the apes well represented on the *Stenox's* crew, the Enoructans asked if one of their own could join them. Their request was well received, and they offered up their finest warrior, Ular, son of Chief Ulos, to represent them. Ular was a green-scaled warrior, standing of a height of sixty-two inches, wearing versk skin trousers and vest, with bladed weapons strapped to either thigh, shin, forearm, and upper arm. He could swim underwater for twenty minutes without air, dive to incredible depths, and see underwater and at night. He further impressed Raven by doing backflips with relative ease, backflips while throwing knives at stationary targets and finally at moving targets.

Once the Enoructan chieftains approved the military and trade alliances, the *Stenox* was underway, back to Torn Harbor with their newest crew member, Ular.

*****

"To increase speed, push this lever forward. Pull it back to reduce it," Lorken explained the helm function to Ular, who listened attentively. It was a welcome change to Orlom and Grigg's reckless antics and inability following simple directions.

"The wheel device turns the ship, left to port, right to starboard, yes?" Ular looked over his shoulder to Lorken for confirmation.

"Yep, as simple as that." Lorken patted him on the back as he sat the helm, the gesture causing the Enoructan to stiffen, unaccustomed to being touched in such a way. They were one day out of Linkortis, and he was still getting used to his new crewmates' extraverted manners. Ular found them a strange lot, from the reckless Orlom and Grigg to the swaggering Captain Raven, they all had distinct personality quirks. Argos spoke little, other than grunting his displeasure, unless it was time to eat, then a childlike glee overtook him. Kendra seemed to roll her eyes with everything the others did. Brokov and Lorken were both irreverent, belittling their crewmates, especially the captain, but both were good instructors, and Ular listened to every word they said. Though the chieftains favored Zem, Ular found all the Earthers quite impressive, if not eccentric.

"That screen is the subsurface sonar." Lorken pointed out the view screen to his left.

"That identifies any objects below the waterline?" Ular asked, his dark bulbous eyes blinking.

"Yes, good job, Ular. You're getting the hang of it." Lorken hit him on the back again, which nearly shook his brain. "You can expand or contract the view by touching the screen like this," Lorken said, demonstrating how to do it.

"And this other screen is above surface sonar?" He regarded the screen above it.

"Radar. Sonar is below the surface, radar above it. I'll show the advanced instruments like weather and ship diagnostics later. Go ahead and give it a spin."

"A spin?" Ular asked, his voice sounding like running water, something the others were getting used to.

"It means go ahead and drive the ship."

Ular nodded, easing the accelerator forward, the *Stenox* taking off in a smooth transition. Lorken was impressed, expecting the Enoructan to slam it forward, jerking the ship like Orlom did when he instructed him. He looked over his shoulder to Raven and Brokov, who stood behind him, and shrugged, surprised by Ular's deft touch, as if to convey, "not bad."

"I think we found a job for you," Raven said. "Sure as hell can't trust Orlom and Grigg at the helm."

"It will be a shorter list if you name what they can do rather than what they can't," Brokov mumbled under his breath.

"It would be the same list we use for Raven," Lorken quipped, drawing a scowl from their captain.

"Why don't you put it on autopilot and show him something else," Raven said.

"Come on, Ular, let's do some target practice." Lorken switched on the autopilot after double-checking the coordinates before stepping without.

"Well, what do you think?" Raven asked, the door closing behind them as Ular followed Lorken outside.

"He's too good to be true. Do they have any more like him?"

"I didn't think to ask."

"He sure as hell beats the last two recruits you and Lorken picked up in Gregok, but that bar was set pretty low." Brokov shook his head.

"Ah, they'll come around. It takes some folks longer than others," Raven dismissed his concerns over Orlom and Grigg.

"Let's hope they come around before blowing up the ship or shooting one of us by mistake."

"They're just a little rambunctious. I mean, they are apes, after all," Raven pointed out, as if that should explain everything.

"Yes, to go along with the one ape we already had."

"Arg isn't like them."

"I know, Rav, I know, but we've doubled the size of our crew, and it's making me a little nervous."

"Arg has proven himself, and we've fought side by side with him during their revolution."

"Yes, and Kendra seems more than capable," Brokov pointed out, recalling the shift where she stayed up with him, talking the whole night through.

"Grigg and Orlom need a little seasoning, and that leaves Ular, which brings us back to my first question. What do you think of him, besides being too good to be true?"

"He seems competent enough, but can we trust him? That's the question."

"He is quiet, but the Enoructans named him their champion, and Matuzak swears they are honorable friends."

"Then we'll see how he works out. Hell, why not, we already have as diverse a crew as we can imagine. I guess we'll pick up a bird-man and a gargoyle next to complete the collection."

"Forget the gargoyles, that's just asking for trouble, and those birdmen seem a little stuck up if you ask me."

"How would you know? I don't recall meeting any of them."

"Yeah, we did. Remember when we stopped over in Port West last year? There was a whole ship of them, two piers down from us."

"I didn't notice. I was probably busy working below while you were goofing off," Brokov figured.

"Yeah, goofing off! Who was it that journeyed to Fera and spent a few months traipsing through the Benotrist countryside, trying to get to Tro, while the rest of you hung out on the ship, eating warm food and getting a fresh shower every day? Oh, that's right, that was me." Raven jerked a thumb toward his chest.

"If you hadn't broken most of the equipment we sent with you, you wouldn't have had to go so far out of your way. Boy, you're a klutz sometimes." Brokov shook his head.

"That was all Cronus's fault for getting captured in the first place."

"Yeah, what was he thinking? I mean, there was only ten thousand gargoyles against his one-hundred-man unit. That was very thoughtless of him getting captured and making you go get him." Brokov rolled his eyes.

"Very funny. The thoughtless part was not joining our crew and going back to Corell. At least here he and Leanna would be safe."

"You judge a man for fighting for his country, Rav? He's doing what he knows to be right. Didn't we do the same? Weren't you the one to lead the defense of Solar System Prime when the Aurelians slipped an armada past our outer defenses?" he reminded him. Raven flew his fighter through the superstructure of an Aurelian command ship, destroying it from the inside. The bold tactic turned certain defeat into an improbable victory. The maneuver made Raven Earth's greatest hero, his name known from Brussels to Tokyo, from Cape Town to Oslo. It also granted him immediate promotion to captain and command of his own squadron, before being reassigned to deep space exploration and the fated voyage that brought them to Arax.

"I know." Raven scratched his head. "I wonder how they're doing. Haven't heard a word since Kato decided to go aid Corell." They hadn't received word of the victory at Corell, the battles in Yatin, or Kato's death.

"I'm worried about them too, Rav. News travels slow unless someone sends a magantor to deliver it, and the Ape Republic is not high on their messenger list."

"Once Kato comes back, we'll be in pretty good shape. Wish we could talk Ben into coming back, but that doesn't seem likely. The look in his eyes at Fera was joyless. It was like he was dead inside." Raven's voice was almost a whisper.

"He probably needs time, Rav. Jenny's death…well…he just needs time." Brokov couldn't put those thoughts to words.

"I don't know. I've known him for years, Brokov. He is my best friend, my brother by marriage, and the one I know better than any other. That man is gone."

"Maybe not," Brokov said hopefully. "He loved her, Rav. That kind of love is stronger than the hate or indifference he uses as a shield against the pain. He'll come around."

Raven wasn't so sure. His father once said a person could sometimes love someone too much. Should such a love ever be severed, it could take their soul with them.

"Cheer up, Rav. We'll get Kato back while we wait for Ben to come around. Meanwhile we can train our new crew, return to Gregok, and enjoy a quiet life for a while."

"Can't enjoy it for long. We have other stops to make after we deliver the Enoructans' answers to Matuzak. Hopefully we'll have our new shipmates trained up to acceptable standards, like not killing themselves or us, or sinking the *Stenox*. Well, maybe just Grigg and Orlom since that's who I'm worried about. What a crew. They're a colorful bunch."

"Yep, me, an android, three gorillas, a lizard man, a female bounty hunter, and two idiots. What a bunch." Brokov snickered, as Raven punched his arm, leaving a fist-sized bruise on his shoulder.

Tyro stood upon the dais, listening as the woman's silken voice took him to a far-off place. He learned over the years to steel his heart, denying himself, lest his yearnings draw him back to memories, memories of her. She was his first love, his true love, his life. If he closed his eyes, he could hear her now, her voice as lovely as the maiden gracing his great hall, singing their son to sleep. He oft stood in the doorway of his room, listening as her soothing voice put the child at ease, filling his virgin mind with peaceful thoughts before drifting off to sleep. What he wouldn't give to go back to those peaceful days, leaving the burdens of this life behind. His life was a balance in those days between love and vengeance, and he was unable to let go of the latter. Eventually the former was removed, torn away by evil men, leaving only the one path for him to follow.

He lost his family to his Menotrist foes, and so he hunted them down, exacting from them his righteous judgement for their many sins. Never again would the Menotrists brutalize his people, subjecting them to the cruelest inclinations of their depraved minds. And where were the Venotrists, Yatins, and self-righteous Torries when the Menotrists were committing such crimes against his people? They were silent at best and complicit at worst.

Tyro released a heated breath, becalming his restless spirit. His anger always simmered, like the tumult raging in his heart, yearning to break free. Even constrained, his wrath transformed to a cold fury, cerebral and controlled, directed upon his foes with calculated cunning. He knew what the people of other lands called him—*gargoyle lover, betrayer of mankind, evil*—but who were they to judge him? Where were they when the Menotrists murdered, tortured, and enslaved his people? The gargoyles never submitted his people to such abuse. They suffered in kind, chased from their nesting grounds by the Menotrist overlords who ruled much of the old Northern Kingdom. Why shouldn't he have made common cause with the gargoyles? They helped him conquer the Menotrists, granting him justice for their wretched crimes. Was it not right to do so?

The more his thoughts lingered upon the mountains of slights and offenses of the Menotrists, the angrier he became, filling him with unquenchable rage. No matter what he inflicted upon them, it could not sate his vengeful thirst. The anger was a constant companion, his fellow traveler on life's tortured journey. So few things brought him joy because of it. Only his daughter vied with his anger for dominion of his thoughts. Tosha was the salve blunting what he lost with his first wife and son, giving him respite from his festering rage. He thought of Letha, his beloved second wife, who now despised him for attempting to bring her realm within his own. Could she not see it was the only way he could protect her? Now she hated him for it.

Such was his life until his eyes fell upon the neckless Morac had taken from the Torry scribe, whose name haunted his waking thoughts—Terin Caleph.

Tosha claimed Terin was given the charm by his father, Jonas Caleph, who carved the visage of the third woman on the necklace. The others were carved by his own hand, before giving it to his son, his precious Joriah. Could he and Jonas be one and the same? And Caleph, where did that name originate? Joriah's maternal grandfather was named Cal and grandmother Ephena. Did he use both their names to form a surname? The Kalinians never used surnames since those who dwelt in the secluded valley intermixed over the centuries into one distinct bloodline.

Tyro recalled that fateful day when he returned to them, finding everyone in the vale dead, slain by Menotrists. He never found Cordela or Joriah's bodies, however, holding out hope that they survived, but after years of searching, he found nothing. Did they survive by fleeing south? Why didn't they return to him once he was victorious? His wife would've been his empress and his son a prince. Why did they not return to him? These questions plagued him. He needed to find the boy, but Terin would be difficult to capture. And to think he was here under his very nose. If only he knew. When he learned of Morac's defeat at Corell, he was wroth, but the reports detailing the heroics of a Torry champion who repulsed attack after attack, turning gargoyles into cowardly wretches, sparked his interest.

The Torries chanted their hero's name over the battlefield time and again—Caleph! There were too many different accounts of his fell deeds, removing doubt of who it was. Adding to this was Thorton's testimony of facing the boy at Telfer, confirming what Terin was capable of.

The Kalinian blood, he mused. The boy was his grandson; he was sure of it. But what of Joriah? Did he yet live? He needed to find him and bring him home, something his most trusted agents were working on for many years but now had a name and a place to narrow their search. Terin was another matter. The boy could single-handedly foil his carefully laid plans. The thought of his own blood destroying his empire further fueled his anger at the Torry Realms. If the boy was his grandson, then he belonged to him, not the Torry throne.

As the woman began her next song, he caught sight of Ben Thorton standing alongside the near wall, staring at the woman with his characteristic stoic indifference. The great hall was filled with imperial courtesans, commanders, and members of his Elite, each partaking in a revery of wine, food, and song. Everyone save Thorton. The man was a mystery. He did not drink or engage in foolish banter. His disposition was always grimly serious but not prone to anger. He was singularly focused on the *greater good,* as he repeatedly claimed, which brought him to his side. Tyro was grateful for his help, learning much of his home world, but knew nothing of the man himself. Ironically, it was Tosha that revealed much of what he knew about the man's personal history, which she gleaned from her time with Raven. That him and Raven were once as close as brothers was not surprising, if not concerning. Would the two ever renew their friendship? Such a thing would be disastrous for his cause.

No, Tyro reflected, that was not possible with Thorton's slaying of the Earther Kato.

Tosha said Thorton was once as boisterous as Raven but suffered the loss of his beloved wife, which he blamed on Raven, driving a wedge between them. Tyro understood how the love of a woman could divide two men who once loved each other like brothers, but Thorton didn't hate Raven. He simply felt nothing. As Tyro thought about it, apathy was the opposite of love, not hate. Tyro couldn't understand apathy, for his own heart was fueled by love and rage. Despite this, whenever Tyro saw Ben Thorton, he saw himself.

Thorton noticed the emperor approach him as he watched Ella perform. She moved gracefully across the hall, torchlight shimmering off the rich folds of her emerald gown. He almost wondered if this was the same girl who spent all that time in the field with him. She was always beautiful, especially when he first saw her perform at Tenin, but now she surpassed even that. Her black hair was bound atop her head, emphasizing her delicate neck. Her smile was genuine, touching her eyes with feminine warmth. Her charms were not missed by the other men in the chamber, but none dare approach her, believing she belonged to him. He caught her stealing a glance, gifting him a subtle smile.

"Your slave is quite fetching," Tyro said, stepping near. They stood off to the side, apart from the revelry.

"She's not a slave," Ben said dryly.

"She came willingly?"

"No."

That made no sense, but Tyro persisted. "You favor her, I see." He hadn't seen Thorton show any lustful interest before.

"I favor her voice. As far as her heart, she is free to do with it as she pleases."

"You protect her but make no claim upon her. Interesting," Tyro mused.

"If I have to force a woman to my bed, I wouldn't want her."

"Then why did you take her in the first place?"

"Her voice." He left unsaid that if he hadn't taken her, another would have, knowing the fate of beautiful women in captured cities.

Her voice? Tyro thought on that, realizing there was only one reason for such an obsession. "Your first wife," he said.

"Yes," Thorton grunted, the subject a sore point for the Earther.

"My first wife was the same. If I close my eyes, I can hear her now through the voice of your companion," Tyro said, regarding Ella.

No one could replace Jennifer, but Tyro's observation was true. "Aye" was all he could manage to say.

Of all the men on Arax, Thorton was the only one Tyro spoke with so informally. Others flocked to his cause, prostrating themselves to win his favor. Thorton did no such thing, simply offering his help. Though he was second among Tyro's Elite, their association was more of an alliance than emperor and subject.

"I never speak of my first wife, wishing to not think of what I lost. The only salve for that bitter wound is the blood of those responsible. During the early days of our revolution, I returned home to discover my wife's kin slain, everyone in their vale murdered by Menotrists. I never found her body or my son's. I searched for many years, to no avail, believing them dead, until Morac came upon the necklace torn from Terin's throat."

"Necklace?" Thorton made a face, wondering where Tyro was going with this.

"It is the necklace I gifted my son, and Terin claims his own father gifted to him."

"His father might've found it or stole it," Ben said.

"Perhaps, but I know the power of my son's blood. Tell me, Thorton, what did you observe at Telfer and Mosar?"

"As I said earlier, Terin leading the defense of Telfer, driving off every attack upon the castle. Once he departed, the castle was doomed."

"Anything else?"

"He slew my magantor and many others, forcing my detachment to use ocran for much of the campaign. And…" Ben paused, unable to fathom the most improbable thing the boy did at Telfer.

"And?" Tyro asked impatiently.

"He deflected my laser, sending it back to me." He shook his head at the impossibility of it all.

"Truly?" Tyro lifted a surprised brow.

"Yes. The blast killed my magantor at Telfer. He deflected my shots at Mosar as well, before flying to the north wall of the city, slaying General Yonig with thousands of gargoyles surrounding him, standing around like statues waiting to be pushed over. His feats are impossible unless you believe in magic…or God," Ben said dryly.

"The boy did all that?" Tyro was dumbstruck.

"Yep. Like I said, it's impossible unless…"

"The swords have a magical property to them, able to guide the hands of those who wield them, as I can attest. Where this magic comes from, I can only guess, but once it is coupled with the magic of Terin's blood, it is a sight to behold. Regardless, the boy must be taken alive." Tyro sighed.

"Easier said than done. Let's say we do capture him, what do you do with him then? I've seen the effect he has on the gargoyles. His mere presence might fracture the empire."

"Let them fear him. It is a power any emperor would embrace, and if he refuses to accept this mantle, he will be wed to a Benotrist noble woman of my choosing and locked away for his own safekeeping, until he sees reason. If he is not agreeable to my terms, then his offspring shall be, offspring that he will not poison against me."

"If that's what you want, I'll do my best, but I've seen the boy in battle," Ben left unsaid that Terin wasn't likely to fall into their hands by force of arms.

"There are other ways to leverage behavior, my friend," Tyro said cryptically. "Leave Terin to me. I have other pressing matters for you to attend."

"You want me to return to Yatin and resolve the crisis there?" Ben asked.

"No, I believe both sides have settled into strong defensive positions. Our legions there are severely reduced and, without Yonig, are pressed to hold Tenin and Telfer. The Yatins are too weak to take them without Torry support. The Torries will need to withdraw to counter Macon and Morac's spring campaign upon Corell."

"True, and we can't advance on Mosar without adding fresh legions."

"Which I refuse to do. Morac's new campaign will further strain our reserve forces, which will fuel the slave revolts springing up in the east," Tyro said.

"Revolts?" Ben asked.

"Yes. It seems the Jenaii have instigated a slave revolt in the greater Nisin Region, even being so bold as to pillage the governor's palace of Nivek Province. The entire garrison was put to the sword, Governor Culn found hanging from gallows atop the battlements."

Thorton was not surprised. Brutal regimes are often beset by uprisings, especially during war.

"With Yatin settling into a defensive posture, I have need of you in the east."

"To put down this revolt?"

"Primarily yes, but another matter requires your particular insight first. I've received word from my agent in Tro, a member of my chosen Elite, one Hossen Grell, that the Ape Republic is forging an alliance with Tro. This alliance is a dagger to our throat. Morac's overtures to Tro have been met with arrogance and insult. They demand exuberant docking fees for any of our vessels landing supplies for our legions at Notsu."

"What do you wish me to do about it?"

"I will discuss our options tomorrow with fewer ears about," Tyro said.

"Then I'll use tonight to rest before my next adventure." Ben shrugged.

Tyro shook his head, wondering if Thorton ever enjoyed himself. "If I were you, Ben, I'd take that beautiful woman and make her my own."

"I had a wife. Don't care much for another," Ben said, though Tyro didn't believe him.

"What of your legacy? You have invested much in the future of our world. For what purpose is your efforts if not to further your bloodline?"

"I have a son."

"A son who is lost to you across the expanse of space, if what you say about the nature of the universe is true."

"I am glad he is there rather than suffer this brutal world."

"You denounce the cruelty of my empire yet support it at the same time. You have a strange sense of honor, Ben Thorton," Tyro said.

"As cruel as you are, your contemporaries are no better. Your people have committed atrocities against each other for thousands of years. What difference will a few more make? But I warn you, once you establish dominion over Arax, the barbarity *must* end. That means eventual abolition of torture and slavery," Ben warned.

"Slavery is the engine of our world, Ben. That will be a difficult task."

"The important ones always are." Ben thought of Lincoln tolerating slavery in the border states during the Civil War in order to end the foul practice for good after achieving victory. He was no fool. He knew these people wouldn't change overnight. Change will come, its speed dependent on many factors. He could hasten the reforms if he could convince them of a greater threat.

"As I've said before, Tyro, you need to do what I suggest *before* my people find your world," Ben reiterated.

"If they are as powerful as you claim, what prevents them from taking what they want?" Tyro asked, always captivated by his conversations with Ben Thorton. Thorton was the only one to speak with him by name.

"Earth is a complex world. We have more than 123 nations, but they pool their resources for their collective security. This loose federation of sorts is good at military operations and terra forming lifeless worlds, but as I've explained before, Arax will be a game changer for our people. Your fate will be decided by 123 different heads of state, none of which will want to see another establish dominion of your world. The only option will be for them to treat with each nation state of Arax on equal footing to them individually. This would be good in theory, the voices of each realm on Arax equal to any nation of Earth. The problem is the nations of Earth aren't the only voices who have a say in how things will run. The Earth Directorate, the entity that oversees the defense of Earth and its colonies, employs a vast bureaucracy. Now, these *bloodsuckers* are the vilest scum to ever breathe air," Ben growled.

Tyro was taken aback by his hostility to these *bureaucrats* he speaks of. Thorton was the most logical, emotionless human Tyro had ever known, yet the topic of Earth bureaucrats made him quite animated.

"They will find any hole in your defenses and exploit it, without any vote or debate back on Earth. Your continent has numerous areas that are unclaimed, or untamed. The Bureaucratic Corps will sweep in, establishing zones of interest in these areas. They will lavish the people who live there with everything their hearts could want, winning them to their cause. Those people will be the acknowledged rulers of their lands and sign over mineral rights and writs of alliance. Then they will move on to your weaker nations and city-states. Tro, Sawyer, the Nayborians will all quickly join. Before you know it, you, the Torries, and maybe the Jenaii will be the last ones standing and have to take whatever deal they offer or be isolated, surrounded by lands once inferior but enhanced with technologies that you can never compete. Eventually, some of your own people will cross over, fracturing your states from within."

Ben's dark vision of their likely future made Tyro's blood run cold. Ben picked up on this, with a positive message, his selling point that explained his motivation in helping Tyro to begin with.

"Much of this can be prevented *if...*" He paused, emphasizing the next point. "If all of Arax is unified under one authority. When the Earther expeditionary forces arrive, you will greet them as if expecting them and present your terms of integration. You will offer a formal alliance, with equal seating on the Earth Directorate. Each of the peoples of Arax must be represented, gargoyles, humans, apes, Jenaii, and Enoructans. By this time, slavery must be abolished, as well as torture. If not, individuals from Earth will take it upon themselves to intercede in your affairs, even if the Directorate does not. Imagine armies of Earthers coming here, implementing justice on their terms."

Tyro could ill imagine. He understood the power one Earther wielded, let alone thousands setting down across his lands, each one capable of killing thousands of his soldiers. Tyro stewed, torn between his need for vengeance on all the nations opposing him and the need to prevent what Ben warned about.

"There is always the possibility they will never find us, but it is your responsibility to plan for either contingency," Ben said.

"If they do arrive in the near future, your presence will go far in bringing our peoples to a favorable agreement," Tyro pointed out.

"I'm afraid I won't be of much use. Once they arrive, I will turn myself over to a military tribunal for killing Kato. Though it was self-defense, they might see it differently. If all goes well, I will speak on your behalf. I would also resign my commission and stand beside you during negotiations, though in my world I am only a low-ranking pilot. I would like nothing more than for your people and mine to one day be one."

"You are an idealist, Ben. If our people become friends, we can lend our strength to each other."

"I'm no idealist, just a pragmatist. I base my decisions on logic, guided by experience. If I leaned to an idealist bent, I would be weeping for my friend." Ben sighed, thinking of Kato.

"Do you regret killing him?"

"Regret means changing past decisions if you were able, but if I were back again in that village, I would still do the same thing. So no, I don't regret my shooting him, but I do regret that the blast killed him. Such is war," Ben said.

"I have never regretted killing any Menotrist. My only regrets are in not killing more," Tyro said.

"I envy you." Ben sighed.

"Envy me, how so?"

"You had revenge to mend the loss of your wife."

"And you did not? I cannot imagine you not killing the man responsible for your loss."

"It is not that simple. The men who you thought killed your wife wanted to hurt you and took pleasure in your suffering. The man responsible for my wife's death didn't kill her. He simply let her die to save another, sacrificing her life for one unworthy, though I begged of him to not do it," Ben said in a deathly whisper, a faraway look in his eyes.

"Raven is the man you speak of," Tyro surmised, which explained the animosity. But if he was guilty of such, why didn't Ben kill him? Why didn't Ben hate him, as Tyro hated his Menotrist kin?

"He is."

"And who did he save in place of your dear wife? Who did he save in place of his own sister?"

Ben didn't answer for a long time, a painful silence passing between them.

"Therein lies the problem, for the man he saved was...*me*."

Tyro paled, the unspoken anguish of the man pouring off him in waves of self-hatred and grief. What could one say? How could he ever gain justice or revenge for his loss when the ones responsible were his dearest friend and himself?

Another painful silence passed between them. Tyro finally understood what drove the man and why he and Raven were forever separated by a woman they both loved but in different ways.

"Onto our next priority. If I'm going east, I'll need Zelo to come with me," Ben said, looking across the room where the gargoyle stood among several members of the Elite, showing them his new weapon.

Tyro's gaze followed where Ben was looking, observing Zelo wearing Kato's pistol and holster. "Is he proficient with it?"

"He's getting better. With a little work, he'll be as good as any first-year cadet at Space Fleet Academy," Ben explained.

"He is yours," Tyro conceded. Ben had struck up an odd friendship with the gargoyle, Zelo reciprocating the fondness.

"Thank you. He is a good soldier. Professional and competent. So was Neon, but such is war," Ben said, regarding his slain comrade who died at Kato's hand.

"I have another that might prove useful on your mission." Tyro pointed out an emaciated man standing among the revelers, his malnourished form drowning in his thick robes.

"He doesn't look so good," Ben said, looking at the gaunt face and sunken eyes of a broken man.

"He is fresh from the dungeon, but I've decided to gift him a chance at redemption and...revenge." Tyro smiled knowingly.

"Revenge? Who is he?"

"Come, I will introduce you," Tyro said, leading him to the pirate lord Monsoon.

Torn Harbor

Torn Harbor rested at the mouth of the Torn River, the deep, navigable waterway that bisected the Ape Republic. As the key stopover point between Tro Harbor and the southern ports of the Casian League, Torn dominated the trade routes of Eastern Arax. The east bank of the Torn River cut sharply east as the west bank ran directly north to the sea, with most of the harbor resting upon the extreme end of the west bank. A series of dangerous shallows ran under the eastern approaches, with jagged rock formations that tore the hulls of approaching ships, thus earning the port its name. Three leagues north of the harbor rested a light beacon upon a small rocky isle. The beacon was constantly alit, guiding ships around its northern face before sailing safely into the harbor.

Most of the ships were docked along the west bank, where a series of natural stone lips ran for several leagues, forming natural piers. A large inlet jutted in along the west bank farther upstream, allowing additional moorings, where much of the 1ˢᵗ Ape Fleet was berthed.

Much of the city was built along the causeway connecting the inlet to the stone piers at the mouth of the harbor, a collage of stone warehouses and wooden dwellings built of timber from the forests upstream.

The late morn found Raven and Admiral Zorgon on the third deck of the *Stenox*, overlooking the mouth of the harbor, watching with interest as an ape galley traversed Torn's tranquil waters. Her crew tested their catapults, their fire munitions falling short of the small target craft alongside her portside bow.

"Bah! My cross-eyed aunt Becta can aim better than this miserable lot," Admiral Zorgon snorted, disgusted with the crew's performance. Zorgon was admiral of the 1st Ape Fleet, with most of his sixty galleys based in Torn Harbor. Many of his ships were recently commissioned, with newly conscripted crews.

"Well, that's why they need training, Admiral. You can't build the roof before the walls," Raven pointed out.

"Roof? This sorry bunch is like a rotten foundation on shifting sand. They look like they have the shakes. Just look at them!" Zorgon growled, pointing a furry finger as the forward catapult crew mishandled loading a munition, fire spreading across the foredeck.

"Maybe you should give Aunt Becta a try after all." Raven shrugged.

"Maybe I will," Zorgon growled before signaling his aides gathered on the pier below, to recall the warship. "Hopefully they can manage to put the fire out before the ship burns up. Farmers." Zorgon shook his head. "I asked for apes with sea legs, and all I get are country lads. Most haven't seen the ocean, let alone a ship. How can I make a Navy out of this sorry lot?"

"In all fairness, Admiral, there weren't that many ape sailors before the revolution. You've recruited nearly every merchant sailor to fill out two-thirds of your ships. If you want my advice, thin out those with experience to all sixty of your ships, and fill in the rest with the green boys. The others will train them to standard soon enough."

"I would, but our new president wants me ready to sail to Tro in two days. I'd rather go with forty competent crews than sixty that aren't worth a spit in the wind."

"It's a long journey from Torn to Tro, Admiral. Plenty of time to train up your crews. Brokov said the weather looks good for the entire eastern seaboard for the next twenty days. Good weather and calm seas make a perfect environment for training your recruits."

"Twenty days, huh?" Zorgon scratched his chin with a furry digit.

"Twenty days," Raven affirmed.

"Perhaps I'll chance it. I wish you were going with us."

"I would, but we're not welcome in Tro at the moment, and I have a little matter to attend back west."

"Yes, your princess. Every ape in the republic is talking about it. I hear tell she hunted you from Fera to Tro, that she set a drunken mob to attack you, and tricked you into wedding her. Are these tales true?" Zorgon asked curiously.

"Unfortunately." Raven shook his head.

"What a woman! You must be proud to boast such a lass?" Zorgon grinned, slapping Raven on the back.

What a woman? Raven wondered if Zorgon was nuts. Were these traits to be extolled? Of course, the apes looked at things differently than others. Aggressive mating practices were the norm for both male and females of all the ape tribes.

"She's quite the treasure," Raven snorted, deciding to go along with it.

"Certainly. Any lass that draws your eye is one I'd like to meet." Zorgon grinned.

"Maybe you will," Raven said, if he could talk her into coming back with him, that is.

"I remember when I wed my Letta. She was a fiery lass. I was half drunk when she bashed me over the head with a cooking pan. The next thing I knew, we were wed. To this day I don't remember the ceremony or even our first night." Zorgon grinned, trying to recall any of it.

"She sounds like a fine wife, Admiral." Raven went along with it, realizing his ape friends were a bit odd. It reminded him of something his father used to say, *"Everyone around here is nuts but you and me, and you're a little bit off."*

"Aye, a fine wife. She's borne me three sons and four daughters. My eldest, Gorgank, can drink Matuzak under the table," Zorgon proudly boasted.

"*No!*" they heard Brokov shout.

There, on the wharf behind the *Stenox*, Brokov was hunched over his newest creation, with Ular beside him and a guilty-looking Grigg standing nearby, shrugging his shoulders and lifting his hands, pleading his innocence.

"You're not the only one with crew problems," Raven said just as Orlom came running along the wharf, chasing after a spherical metal part rolling away from the others.

"Orlom!" Brokov's voice broke with panicked desperation as the young gorilla chased after the rolling part along the wharf, the object coming to a stop short of the stone lip, before Orlom stumbled into it.

Raven winced as Orlom followed the part off the end of the pier. A loud splash followed, Brokov putting his hands to his head in disbelief.

"Maybe we should give Aunt Becta a try too." Raven shook his head.

*****

"You finished?" Raven asked as Brokov entered the bridge. Raven sat the captain's chair, pretending to be busy, fiddling with the view screen.

Brokov didn't dignify that question with an answer, having spent the entire day repairing the air ski that Grigg and Orlom managed to break.

"Orlom and Grigg will be bunking in your cabin from now on," Brokov said before calling Ular onto the bridge, sending him to fetch his things from the third crew cabin.

"Where's Ular going?" Raven asked, lifting his head from the screen, watching the back of Ular's scaly green head disappear through the cabin doorway.

"To fetch his things. He'll be bunking in my cabin. Grigg and Orlom will be with you." Brokov gave Raven an evil glare.

"Ular is bridge crew. He belongs up here with me and Lorken," Raven pointed out.

Brokov painted a fake smile on his face as Ular stepped out of the third crew cabin with his bundle of belongings. "Just put your things in my cabin below, where I showed you," he said as Ular exited the bridge, his smile turning into a snarl once the door closed. "Don't pretend you've been busy, Rav. You've probably spent half the afternoon playing Star Blasters on your game console, while the rest of us were working."

"I spent the morning meeting with the admiral discussing upcoming deployments," Raven said defensively. "And I haven't played Star Blasters in months." He was actually playing Planet Smasher all afternoon but saw no reason to point that out.

"Deployments? Who do you think helped train and outfit half their Navy while you and Lorken were in Gregok? Me, that's who." Brokov jerked a thumb toward his own chest.

"And a fine job you did by the looks of it." Raven snickered.

"Don't even start. None of those idiots you observed today were trained by me. I worked up twenty crews to proficient standards. They will have to train the rest on their own for a while, while we take you to see your girlfriend."

"My wife, actually," Raven pointed out, still seated while leaning comfortably back in his chair.

"Wife." He shook his head. "I still don't how you pulled that one off."

"She didn't actually ask me. All she did—"

"Was offer you a cup, I know. Perhaps if you researched the locals' customs, you might've known the significance when a woman's father offers you both a drink from the same cup. Oh, that's right, you don't read." Brokov rolled his eyes.

"Are you finished?" Raven sighed.

"I'm just getting started! Not only did I spend the entire day fixing Orlom and Grigg's mistakes, I also had to babysit the two of them while you chatted with the admiral. Now it's your turn to spend some quality time with them. It will be good practice for your upcoming fatherhood.

"You think my kids will be anything like those two?" Raven jerked a thumb over his shoulder, knowing they were somewhere outside.

"Your kids will be half you and half Tosha. What do you think they'll be like?" Brokov threw his hands up in the air.

"*Oh…*shit." Raven hadn't thought of that.

"Exactly. And those two idiots are the warm-up act before the big show. In any case, they get to bunk with you now. Just guard your toothbrush before one of them cleans the toilet with it."

"They didn't do that on purpose," Raven pointed out.

"No. They did it because they're *morons*. Now you and Lorken get to bunk with them. I'll take Ular since he is quiet, respectful, and doesn't smell."

"Smell? What's wrong with Orlom and Grigg's smell?"

"Oh, you'll find out." He grinned evilly, shaking a finger at him. "Especially after they eat fish for dinner."

"Fish? Does it give them bad breath?"

Brokov shook his head. "Wrong end of the body. And it only happens when they're sound asleep."

"Wonderful." Raven shook his head. "What about Arg? Is he coming too?"

"He's staying with me. He is at his wits' end with tweedle dee and tweedle dumb, I'll tell you that. When Lorken gets back, you can tell him about his new bunk mates. All four of you deserve each other." Brokov stormed off.

"Where are you going?"

"To lock away my air ski in the lower hold before those knuckleheads break it again," Brokov said before passing through the door.

Raven shrugged, switching his view screen back to Planet Smasher once the door closed.

*****

The next morning found Raven on the bridge, sitting at the captain's chair while stifling a yawn. It was a long night between Grigg's foul gas and Orlom's snoring. He could well imagine Lorken's reaction to the new sleeping arrangements upon his return from Gregok. He'd been gone two weeks now, visiting the ape capital and settling his family in before they journeyed to Bansoch. The *Stenox* was not an ideal place for infants, and Matuzak insisted Jenna and the children remain in his household.

Raven wondered if he could talk Tosha in bringing their child here. The Ape Republic was the Earthers' home now and was probably the safest place in all of Arax, being both isolated and powerful.

"Grigg and Orlom keep you up all night?" Kendra asked, standing off his right while holding the tissue regenerator. She ran her dagger along her left arm, raising a line of blood before testing the device, the tissue mending as she ran it over the sundered flesh.

"They weren't a problem at all," he lied, not giving Brokov the satisfaction of being right.

"Liar," she said dryly, inspecting her arm for any lingering effects. Brokov had improved upon the first iteration of the device, reducing it to one single tube, with an attached optic. It was much easier to handle, lasting longer between charges.

"You know, Kendra, I wouldn't recommend practicing with that thing by cutting yourself. You never know when one of Brokov, Kato, or Lorken's toys will break on you."

"According to Brokov, they shouldn't break unless you, Grigg, or Orlom get your hands on them." She smirked.

"Things break when you're getting shot at or having piles of rubble raining down on your head." He recalled the events at Fera.

"He said you'd use that excuse."

"He did, huh? What else did your boyfriend say?"

"Boyfriend?" She stopped what she was doing, giving him a dark look.

"You and Brokov have been spending a lot of time together." He couldn't help needling her. He could tell he cut close to the mark by the blush reddening her deep olive skin.

"You are such a child." She rolled her eyes.

"Hah, I knew it." He grinned, her response confirming his suspicion. It didn't escape his notice the time they spent together volunteering to take the same night shifts and their sharing of duties.

"I'm not going to be lectured on love by the likes of a man whose wife locked him in a cage, just like I found you." She crossed her arms, regarding him with a raised brow, tapping her foot.

"All couples go through some rough patches, Kendra. It's not my fault Tosha was a bit hormonal at the time."

That comment got him nowhere as she shook her head.

"You're impossible. How are you ever going to survive the royal court at Bansoch?"

"Survive Bansoch? What are they gonna do, beat me up?" He dismissed the danger.

"That's what happened in Axenville."

"I was unarmed, by myself, and facing the entire village," he pointed out.

"Whereas you'll be armed, with us, but facing an entire kingdom." Her last word proving the idiocy of his logic.

"Look, Tosha isn't going to start something with our child in the middle. It will be a nice, quiet visit with my wife and mother-in-law. The only argument we'll have is picking out baby names. If it's a boy, she'll want to pick something stupid, like Tyro or Brokov."

Before she could react to that, Grigg came rushing through the door.

"Hey, boss, come outside. Magantors!" the young gorilla shouted excitedly.

Raven and Kendra exchanged a look before hurrying outside. Magantors were rarely sighted in the Ape Republic, and none were in service to any of the ape tribes. Exiting the bridge, their gaze was drawn skyward, where a dozen of the giant avian circled overhead, looking for a place to land. Raven could see human riders wearing Torry uniforms, save for one individual dressed in the same black trousers and jacket he wore.

"Lorken?" Raven made a face, spotting his friend sitting behind one of the riders, pointing out the *Stenox*. Raven made a cursory scan of the other mounts for any sign of Kato but finding no trace of him. They circled overhead before setting down upon the wharf near the *Stenox*, an armed contingent of ape soldiers greeting them with swords drawn, before Lorken set them at ease, dismounting from the first warbird to set down, waving them to put away their weapons. The rest set down in good order, their commander approaching the ranking commander of the ape guard, offering him a scrolled parchment detailing their authority to treat with the *Stenox* by order of General Matuzak.

Lorken quickly broke off from the group, accompanied by two of the riders, walking briskly toward the *Stenox*.

"You're back early," Raven commented as his friend drew near. By now, all the crew except Zem was on the stern of the first deck, observing the new arrivals.

"Who are your friends?" Brokov asked as Lorken climbed aboard, the others following him onto the ship before removing their helms, revealing a thickly built fellow wearing the blue tunic and silver armor of the Torry Elite and an exceptionally attractive woman dressed in a tan tunic with silver breastplate and greaves.

"Corry," Brokov greeted, taken aback as the Torry princess regarded him.

"Brokov," she greeted politely, her eyes recognizing Argos standing beside him but not the others gathered on the first deck, until stopping at Raven. She took a deep breath, bracing herself for the interaction she never wanted to revisit.

"Let's talk inside, Rav. Everyone will need to hear this," Lorken said, stepping between them.

"Is it Kato? Is he all right?" Raven was having none of it, needing that question answered before he took one step.

"Kato was doing well last I saw him, Captain Raven," the stout-built soldier accompanying her said.

"Who are you?" Raven asked.

"Lucas."

"Lucas," Raven snorted, giving the Torry Elite a cold look, taking his measure.

"Kato is in Yatin with the Torry 4th Army. He is fine as far as they know," Lorken said.

"Yatin? That's a little far off his range. What happened to coming back after Corell? In fact, what happened at Corell?"

"We'll discuss everything inside, Rav. There's no point in having the entire harbor hearing our conversation," Brokov interjected. Sometimes Raven was too muleheaded to reason with.

Corry had deep misgivings in treating with Raven, regarding the large Earther with a guarded heart. He was the most difficult man she ever encountered, rude, irreverent, and extremely dangerous. Despite all this, he was fiercely loyal to his friends, as his concern for Kato could attest. Terin often spoke of said loyalty, recounting their rescue of Cronus and all they endured to make it so. Would he feel the same loyalty to Terin?

"Then why are you all here?" Raven asked, looking first at Lorken, then Lucas, and finally at Corry. Lorken was several days early and was at Gregok, which meant the Torries went there first. Was the urgency of their mission so great that the princess of the Torry Realm felt the need to traverse halfway across Arax to find them? It had to be important to Lorken also, for him to cut his visit with Jenna short. Was it Cronus? Did something happen to him? He doubted Corry would come herself if that was the case.

"Terin always speaks highly of you, Raven, defending your honor when others dare speak against it. I hope your affections for him are equally loyal," Corry said.

"Terin is your friend, is he not?" Kendra asked, wondering if that was the same Terin they often spoke of.

"Come inside," Raven said.

*****

Lorken sat at the table, recalling the last time the dining cabin was this crowded. It had to be the planning of Corry's rescue from Molten Isle. No, he corrected himself. This was the largest gathering, with Kendra, Ular, Grigg, Orlom, Lucas, and Corry joining them, gathering around the table with himself, Raven, Brokov, Argos, and Zem's broad frame filling the doorway. The cabin was never built for so many at once, but everyone wanted to hear what was to be said.

"All right, spit it out," Raven said. The last news they had of Terin was what Kato sent in his missive upon reaching Notsu, where King Lore informed them that Terin escaped Fera, successfully reaching Corell.

"Terin is being held captive," Lorken cut to the heart of it.

"By Tyro?" Raven asked.

"No." Corry shook her head sadly.

"Then who?"

"He was lost at sea at the Battle of Carapis and taken by slavers, who sold him at Bansoch." Corry lifted her chin, steeling her heart lest her voice break with emotion.

"Slavers?" Brokov rose up in his seat, his dark eyes narrowing severely at the mention of that word.

"Carapis? Where the hell is Carapis?" Raven made a face.

"The Yatin Coast," Lucas answered, standing behind Corry, who sat at the table opposite Raven.

"Back up a minute." Raven scratched his head. "Why don't you start with what happened at Corell. The last thing any of us heard was that your father and Arsenc fell at Kregmarin, and Kato was staying with the Torry Cavalry to lend aid. Now, start from there."

And so Corry began, retelling the siege of Corell and its aftermath, struggling to keep her emotions in check. Any mention of her father might make her crumble, and that was the last thing she wanted to do in front of Raven. She continued on, telling of the events at Sawyer, where Cronus likely was, and the Yatin Campaign. She spoke of the Battle of Carapis to the extent that she knew, finishing with her journey to Gregok.

"How do you know he was captured and not lost at sea?" Brokov asked, her story missing some important facts.

"If your people saw him loaded on a slave ship, why didn't they stop them?" Kendra asked, standing along the opposite wall beside Ular, with her arms crossed.

Corry gave her an annoyed look before releasing a sigh, looking down at her hands folded on the table. "Our people were not there at the time," she said.

"Then how do you know he was captured and not drowned?" Raven asked.

"Tell him!" Lorken said. "He'll believe you."

"Believe what?" Raven asked.

"Terin's father has many unique abilities, much like his son," she said.

Raven agreed, if half the things she said about Terin at Corell were true.

"When I received word of Terin, it was only that he was lost at sea. Jonas knew otherwise. He said that Terin lived, was taken captive to Bansoch, and sold to a powerful house. I risk your mockery for revealing this truth, a truth no reasonable person would believe. Some would say I should lie, offering you another explanation for confirming Terin's fate. I can offer nothing more than Jonas's word for what I believe. If Terin is captive, there is only one group of men that can free him. What I need to know, Raven, is if you will help me, and how much you demand in recompense?" she asked, raising her chin, steeling herself for whatever he would say.

"Keep your gold, Corry" was all he said before standing up, ordering Zem to the engine room and Brokov to the bridge, the rest of the crew following them out the door.

"Come on, Grigg, we have work to do," Lorken said.

"All right, boss." Grigg gave a toothy grin, following Lorken, leaving Lucas and Corry exchanging confused looks, as Raven started for the door, leaving them the last ones to remain.

"Raven?" she asked, wondering what his answer was, her voice causing him to stop.

"Better get off the ship unless you're coming along."

"You're leaving?" she asked, wondering if he even heard her question about rescuing Terin.

"Terin's not going to rescue himself," he said.

"Are…are you going to help me?" She made a face, frustrated with his half answers.

"If Terin's on that island, we'll find him. We lift anchor within the hour."

EPILOGUE

Torry North
Caleph home

Valera drew the skirt of her gown above her knees, washing her cooking pot in the stream behind their home. She finished, stepping onto the low grass of the bank, stretching her sore back. The late winter air felt refreshing as she gazed skyward, watching the clouds drift lazily above. She wondered where her boys were, her husband and son. The news of their victory at Corell swept through the area like a driving wind, neighbors near and far coming to share in the victory with her. The legend of Terin and Jonas spread like fire on dry leaves. She received each visitor with patient kindness, thanking them for their friendship. Their neighbor, Devlin Jorgen, stopped by every other day with some of his brood, helping her with whatever task she struggled with. Their help was most appreciated, considering her delicate condition. After two decades of trying for a second child, she found herself quickening with Jonas's seed, which he was yet unaware. She longed to share with him this joyous news, running her free hand over the small bump now emerging.

What will Terin think having a little brother or sister? she thought happily, lost in her musings. *What will Jonas think?* She smiled at the thought. He would be so proud, as much as she was proud of him for his fell deeds at Corell. She wondered how her father and Jonas were getting along, hoping Terin could bridge their differences and heal her family.

The snorting of ocran drew her attention, the sound of hooves striking gravel alerting her to visitors arriving at the front of their home. She quietly entered the back door of the house, setting her pot on her stove before stepping out the front door to greet her guests. Stepping without, she was greeted by a dozen riders, each heavily armed with short swords or crossbows, attired in leather riding livery. She immediately froze, uncertain of their intentions.

"Welcome, gentlemen, might I help you?" she asked politely, revealing none of her doubts.

"Yes, my good lady. We are seeking the home of Jonas Caleph, might we call on him this fine day?" the man nearest her asked, staring down at her from his gray mount. He appeared the eldest of the men, with sparkling green eyes and windswept brown hair that belied his true age.

"Jonas Caleph?" she asked in way to gauge his intent, wondering if they knew who she was.

"Yes. This is his home, we are told. Might we inquire his whereabouts, Lady Caleph?" The man looked at her knowingly.

"He is away on matters of the realm, good sir. You have caught me at a disadvantage, for you know my name, where I don't know yours." She smiled, trying to becalm her beating heart.

"My apologies, Lady Caleph, I am Hotis Vlenok. We are honored and pleased to make your acquaintance." He gave a half bow, his polite manner doing little to put her at ease.

"My husband never mentioned anyone with that name, sir. Might I ask how you know my husband?"

"Your husband does not know us, Lady Caleph. We were sent by another to fetch Jonas and his kin. As he is not here, we are charged with bringing you to our benefactor. Be assured, Lady Caleph that no harm shall befall you in our keeping," he said, ordering several of his comrades to dismount.

"You think it wise to take me hostage in the middle of my native realm?" she challenged, backing a step.

"You will come with us willingly or bound, my lady. We would prefer compliance in order to avoid any unnecessary…complications."

"Taking someone captive hardly portends good intentions, Hotis Vlenok." She lifted her chin defiantly.

"Our benefactor desires no harm to you, my Lady Caleph. In fact, he is very keen that no harm comes to you at all."

"And who is this *benefactor* you speak of?"

"Your husband's father, my lady," Hotis said, ordering his men forth.

Thus ends book three of the Chronicles of Arax: *The Battle of Yatin*.

The saga continues with book four: *The Making of a King*.

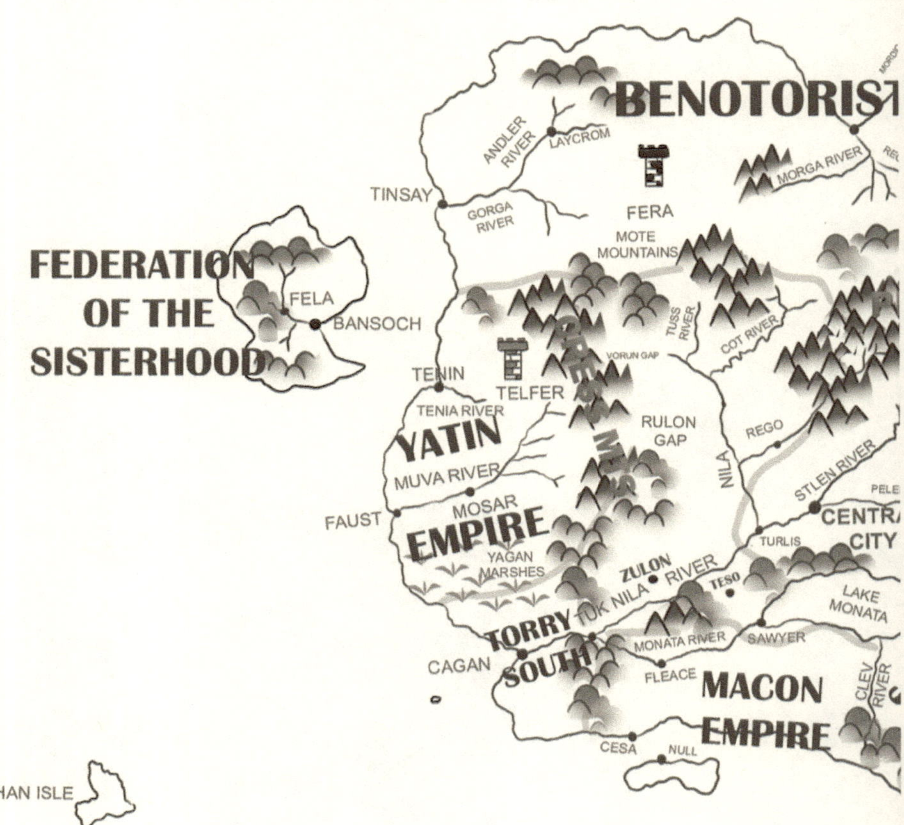

FEDERATION OF THE SISTERHOOD
BENOTORIST
FELA
BANSOCH
TINSAY
ANDLER RIVER
LAYCROM
GORGA RIVER
FERA
MOTE MOUNTAINS
MORGA RIVER
TENIN
TELFER
TENIA RIVER
YATIN
MUVA RIVER
FAUST
MOSAR
EMPIRE
YAGAN MARSHES
VORUN GAP
RULON GAP
TUSS RIVER
COT RIVER
REGO
NILA
STLEN RIVER
PELE
CENTRAL CITY
TURLIS
ZULON
TUK NILA
RIVER
TESO
LAKE MONATA
TORRY
SOUTH
CAGAN
MONATA RIVER
SAWYER
FLEACE
MACON
EMPIRE
CLEV RIVER
CESA
NULL
CHIHAN ISLE

EMPIRE
PAGAN
TUR RIVER
BEDO
CORPI
TERSE
NISIN
LAKE VENEBA
TRO
CROF
BACEL
NOTSU
ELEN RIVER
KREGARIN ISLE
BESOS
CORELL
TORRY
TALON PASS
APE
TORN
NORTH
LONE HILLS
GREGOK
EMPIRE
TORN RIVER
EL ORVA
IENAII
BARBEARIO
ELARIS RIVER
NON
PLOU
NAIBA RIVER
NAYBORIA
ENORUCTA
EL OVA
MIKUS
VARABIS
LINKORTIS
ROCKY SHORE
CASIAN SEA
MILITO
COVEN
TERIS
PORT WEST
CASIAN LEAGUE

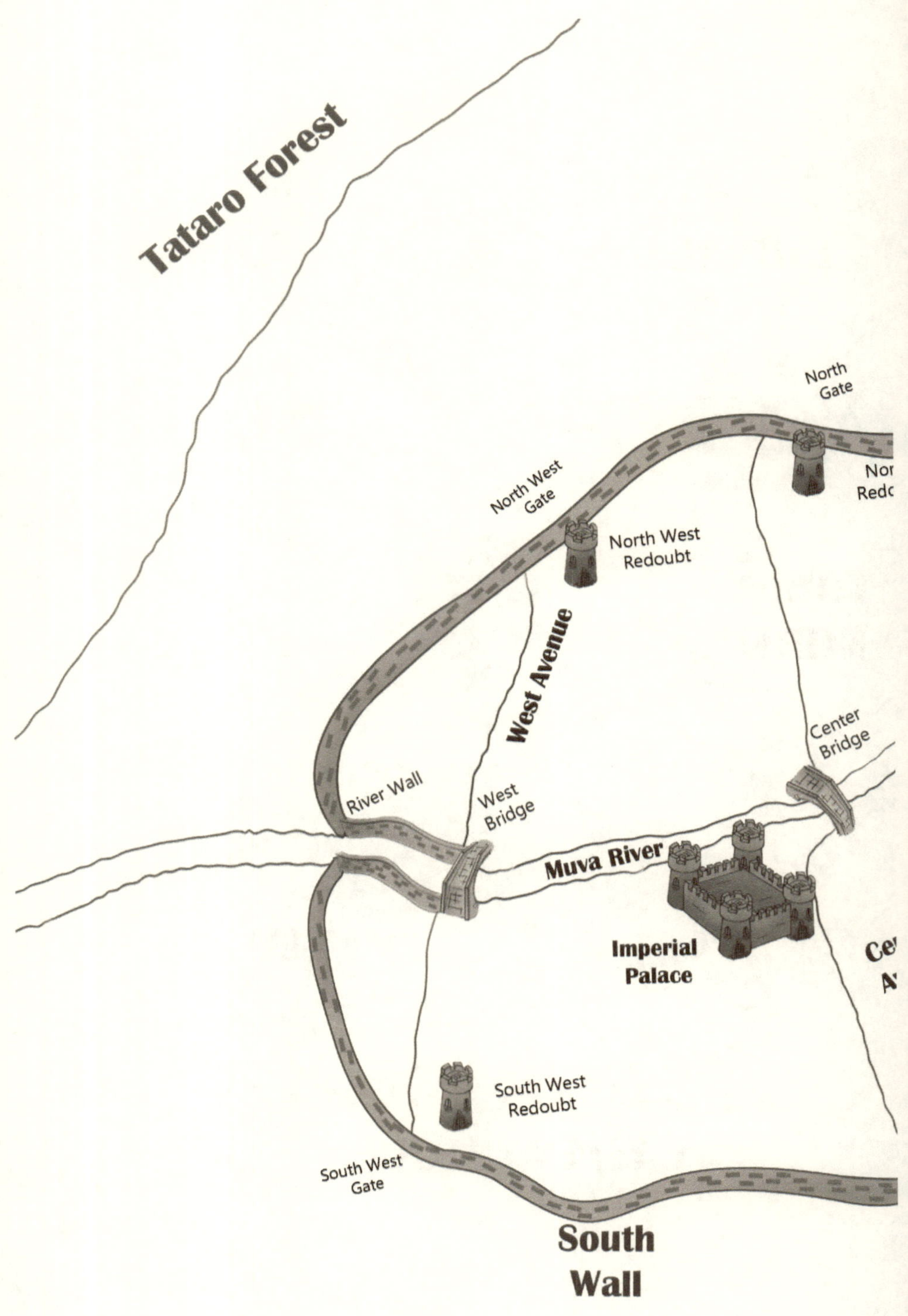

Tataro Forest
North Gate
North West Gate
North West Redoubt
Nor Redo
West Avenue
Center Bridge
River Wall
West Bridge
Muva River
Imperial Palace
Ce A
South West Redoubt
South West Gate
South Wall

MOSAR

North East
Gate
North
East
Redoubt
North
Wall
River Wall
East
Bridge
Muva River
East
Avenue
South East
Redoubt
SouthEast
Gate
nter
venue
South
Redoubt
South
Gate
th
oubt

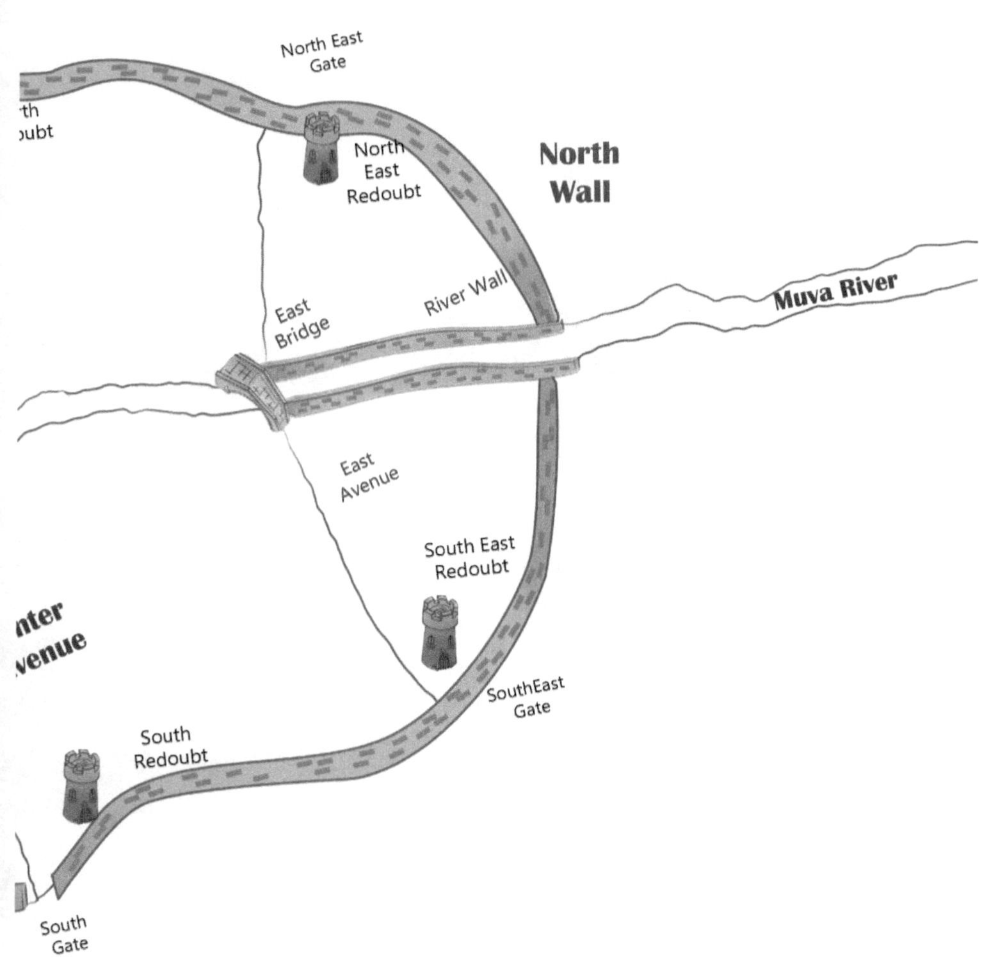

APPENDIX A

Armies of Arax

Torry Armies

Army	Location	Commander	Size
1st	Cagan	Lewins	20 Telnics
2nd	Central City	Fonis	20 Telnics
3rd	Corell	Bode	12 Telnics
4th	Yatin Border	Korath	20 Telnics
5th	(Destroyed at Kregmarin)		

Large Garrisons

	Location	Commander	Size
	Cropus	Torgus Vantel	5 Telnics
	Corell	Nevias	3 Telnics
	Central City	Torvin	5 Telnics
	Cagan	Telanus	5 Telnics

Cavalry

	Location	Commander	Size
1st	Corell	Tevlin	300 mounts
2nd	Corell	Connly	700 mounts
3rd	Western Border	Meborn	500 mounts
4th	Cagan	Avliam	500 (300 reserves)

Navy

1st	Yatin Border	Kilan (Grand Admiral)	60 Galleys
2nd	Cagan	Horikor	50 Galleys
3rd	Yatin Border	Liman	30 Galleys
4th	Cagan	Nylo	40 Galleys
5th	Cagan	Morita	20 Galleys

Benotrist/Gargoyle Armies

Legion	Location	Commander	Size
1st (Gargoyle)	Mosar	Yonig	22 Telnics
(Ten of twenty-two telnics of 1st Legion garrisoned at Telfer.)			
2nd (Gargoyle)	Tinsay	Torab	35 Telnics
3rd (Gargoyle)	Mosar	Yonig	36 Telnics
4th (Gargoyle)	East of Corell	Tuvukk	15 Telnics
5th (Gargoyle)	East of Corell	Concaka	20 Telnics
6th (Gargoyle)	Destroyed at Corell		
7th (Gargoyle)	East of Corell	Vaginak	9 Telnics
8th (Benotrist)	East of Corell	Vlesnivolk	22 Telnics
9th (Benotrist)	Mordicay	Marcinia	50 Telnics
10th (Benotrist)	Pagan	Gavis	50 Telnics
11th (Benotrist)	Notsu	Felinaius	39 Telnics
12th (Gargoyle)	Eastern Border	Krakeni	50 Telnics
13th (Benotrist)	Laycrom	Trinapolis	50 Telnics
14th (Gargoyle)	Laycrom	Trimopolak	50 Telnics
15th (Gargoyle)	Tuss River	Unknown	10–15 (Estimated) T
16th (Gargoyle)	Destroyed at Tuft's Mountain		
17th (Gargoyle)	Destroyed at Tuft's Mountain		
18th (Gargoyle)	Destroyed at Tuft's Mountain		

Garrison Forces

Fera	29 T (Benotrist)
Nisin	20 T (Benotrist)
Pagan	10 T (Benotrist)
Mordicay	10 T (Benotrist)
Tinsay	20 T (Benotrist)
Laycrom	20 T (Benotrist)
Border posts	10 T (Benotrist)
	10 T (Gargoyle)

Benotrist Navy

Fleet	Location	Admiral	Size
1st	Mordicay	Plesnivolk	50 Galleys
2nd	Tenin	Kruson	27 Galleys
3rd	Pagan	Elto (Grand Admiral)	80 Galleys
4th	Pagan	Pinota	50 Galleys
5th	Tenin	Mulsen	94 Galleys
6th	Pagan	Silniw	50 Galleys
7th	Tenin	Onab	50 Galleys
8th	Tinsay	Zelitov	50 Galleys

Yatin Armies

Army	Location	Commander	Size
1st	Mosar	Yoria	25 Telnics
	(Only sixteen of twenty-five mustered at Mosar.)		
2nd	Eastern Border	Yitia	25 Telnics
	(Twenty-one of twenty-five answered muster.)		
3rd	Southern Border	Jutol	15 Telnics
4th	Tenin	Surrendered to Torab	

Garrison Forces

	Mosar	Yakue	10 Telnics
	(Only six of ten answered muster.)		
	Telfer	Destroyed in Siege of Telfer	
	Tenin	Surrendered to Torab	

Yatin Cavalry

1st	Telfer	Destroyed in Battle of Salamin Valley	
2nd	Mosar	Cornyana	800

Yatin Navy

Fleet	Location	Admiral	Size
1st	Tenin	Sunk in Battle of Cull's Arc	
2nd	Tenin	Sunk in Battle of Cull's Arc	
3rd	Faust	Horician	40

Jenaii Armies

Battle Group	Location	Commander	Size
1st	Corell	El Tuvo	10–12 Telnics
2nd	El Orva	Ev Evorn	20 Telnics
	(Casualties suffered at Corell replaced with soldiers of the 1st Battle Group.)		
3rd	El Tova	En Elon	20 Telnics

Garrison Forces

	El Orva	El Orta	15 Telnics
	El Tova	En Vor	5 Telnics

Jenaii Navy

Fleet	Location	Admiral	Size
1st	El Tova	En Atar	20 Galleys
2nd	El Tova	En Ovir	20 Galleys
3rd	El Tova	En Toshin	20 Galleys

Naybin Armies

Army	Location	Commander	Size
1st	Northern Border	Duloc	3 Telnics
	(Seven detached to expeditionary force, destroyed at siege of Corell.)		
2nd	Plou	Rorin	10 Telnics
3rd	Non	Corivan	10 Telnics
4th	Western Border	Cuss	10 Telnics

Garrison Forces

	Plou	Cestes	5 Telnics
	Non	Rasin	7 Telnics
	Naiba	Tesra	3 Telnics
	Border Posts		5 Telnics

Naybin Navy

Fleet	Location	Admiral	Size
1st	Naiba	Gustub	10 Galleys
2nd	Naiba	Galton	10 Galleys

Macon Empire Armies

Army	Location	Commander	Size
1st	Fleace	Noivi	10 Telnics
	(Five telnics sent to siege of Sawyer, five remaining with General Noivi.)		
2nd	Sawyer	Vecious	15 Telnics
3rd	Western Border	Ciyon	10 Telnics
4th	Null	Farin	8 Telnics

Garrison Forces

	Fleace	Novin	5 Telnics
	Cesa	Clyvo	5 Telnics

Macon Navy

Fleet	Location	Admiral	Size
1st	Cesa	Goren	20 Galleys
2nd	Null	Vulet	20 Galleys
3rd	Eastern Coast	Talmet	20 Galleys
4th	Western Coast	Gara	20 Galleys

Ape Empire Armies

Army	Location	Commander	Size
1st	Gregok	Cragok	20 Telnics
2nd	Torn	Mocvoran	20 Telnics
3rd	Talon Pass	Vorklit	10 Telnics
4th	Northern Coast	Matuzon	10 Telnics
5th	Southern Coast	Vonzin	10 Telnics

Garrison Forces

	Location		Size
	Gregok		10 Telnics
	Torn		10 Telnics
	Talon Pass		10 Telnics

Ape Navy

Fleet	Location	Admiral	Size
1st	Torn	Zorgon	60 Galleys
2nd	Torn	Vornam	40 Galleys

Casian Federation Armies

Army	Location	Commander	Size
1st	Coven	Gidvia	12 Telnics
2nd	Milito	Motchi	12 Telnics
3rd	Teris	Elke	7 Telnics

Garrison Forces

	Milito		3 Telnics
	Coven		4 Telnics
	Port West		3 Telnics
	Teris		3 Telnics

Casian Navy

Fleet	Location	Admiral	Size
1st	Coven	Voelin	100
2nd	Milito	Gylan	80
3rd	Port West	Gydar	60
4th	Teris	Eltar	60

Federation of the Sisterhood Armies

Army	Location	Commander	Size
1st	Bansoch	Na	20 Telnics
2nd	Fela	Vola	20 Telnics
3rd	Southern Border	Mial	20 Telnics

Garrison Forces

	Bansoch		10 Telnics
	Fela		10 Telnics

Sisterhood Navy

Fleet	Location	Admiral	Size
1st	Bansoch	Nyla	120 Galleys
2nd	Bansoch	Carel	80 Galleys
3rd	Southern Coast	Daila	50 Galleys

Teso Armies

	Location		Size
1st Army	Southeastern border	Hovel	4 Telnics
2nd Army	Central Teso	Velen	2 Telnics

Zulon Armies

| 1st Army | Northern Border | Zarento | 2 Telnics |
| 2nd Army | Western Border | Zubarro | 3 Telnics |

City-State Armies

| Sawyer | 5 Telnics | 100 Cavalry | |
| Rego | 3 Telnics | 100 Cavalry | |

(Rego garrison size fluctuates with new conscription.)

| Notsu | 3 Telnics | 200 Cavalry | |

(Of Notsu's three surviving Telnics, two are joined with Torry forces, along with their cavalry.)

Bacel	Destroyed at Kregmarin and siege of Bacel		
Barbeario	8 Telnics		
Bedo	10 T0elnics	100 Cavalry	40 Galleys
Tro Harbor	10 Telnics	50 Cavalry	50 Galleys
Varabis	5 Telnics		30 Galleys

ABOUT THE AUTHOR

Ben Sanford grew up in Western New York. He spent almost twenty years as an air marshal, traveling across the United States and many parts of the world, meeting people from a broad range of cultures and backgrounds. It was from these thousands of interactions that he drew inspiration for the characters in his books. He currently resides in Maryland with his family.

9 798988 862494 3